THE RUSSIAN DOLL

A Raymond Mackey Mystery

Book Two

Owen Thomas

Author Website: http://owenthomasliterary.com

OTF Literary, Anchorage, Alaska.

ISBN: 979-8-9871677-6-2
Library of Congress Control Number: 2022919188

ONE

The bedside clock is a branding iron. My retinas take the news about like you'd expect. I close my eyes again, but that turns out to be pointless. I can still see the numbers floating in the dark: *3:00 AM.*

I pull back the covers and get myself upright. I get dressed in yesterday's clothes and go downstairs, Phil at my heels meowing for attention. My head is still sloshing from the Old Forester. Coffee would be nice but there's no time for that now, so I wake up the Camels and shake one free, patting my pockets for a light as I step outside on the stoop and close the door. I have to stop to set the flame, cupping the tip of the cigarette against the hot wind in my face. I drop the lighter back in my pocket and look around.

She's already waiting at the curb.

"You're late," she says. I close the door and lean my head against the back of the seat.

"Stop talking nonsense," I say. "It's way too early for me to be late."

She watches me with the lie on her face that we're in no kind of hurry. Like we have all the time in the world.

"Those things'll kill you, Mack."

I let out the smoke and bend forward, feeling around under the seat.

"What, the Camels?" I ask as my fingers finally find the Sig Saur. "Maybe." I sit up and nose the gun into my shoulder harness where it belongs. "But they'll have to get in line and wait their turn. I'm betting they never make it."

She pulls away and we ride without talking. I want to sleep. I close my eyes and the time once again glows red in the dark, throbbing with my pulse: *3:00 AM.* I try to ignore it, feeling for the black space between the numbers, looking for anywhere my bourbon-soaked brain can curl up for a nap. Her car is plush and quiet. The city moves beneath me in soft thumps and rumbles. She smells like forest beneath fresh snow.

"Want to tell me where we're going?" I ask.

"You'll know when you know," she says. "Maybe try being a big boy detective and figure it out for yourself."

We ride in silence. I can't keep my eyes open. Beneath me, Chicago is a city of muted vibration, mumbling up through my bones in rhythms of villainy and hope. All the buildings have eyes, and they watch us pass. Hard not to feel the conspiracies of malice, burning cold florescent inside. I don't need to see the proof. I know it's there. Just like I don't need my eyes open to feel the moon up in its pocket of muffled light, begging to be untied and set free.

The Camel smolders between my lips. The Sig burns next to my heart. I don't want to be here, sitting upright in a car next to a beautiful woman, packing a loaded gun under my arm. I want to be home. Lying down next to a beautiful woman and uncorking a loaded bottle. Forget the gun.

And then, finally and all of a sudden, we are still.

"Let's go," she says, opening her door. I lean forward in the seat, peering through the windshield. The headlights wash the end of a building on the far side of a hundred feet of gloom.

"Where is this?" I ask. "What is this?"

"You'll know when you know," she says. She reaches down and pulls the thing that pops the trunk. "Get to it."

I push open my door and step out into a warm wind blowing in my face. I drop the Camel and walk around to the back of the car. I close my eyes. This part is never easy. I have to prepare myself. I lift open the trunk with a finger.

It helps that she is so tightly wrapped. Her body is easier to lift. Easier to manage in my arms. Easier to bend over my shoulder like a long sack of flour.

It's a tough walk around to the front of the building. The snow is black without the headlights. Like I'm plowing through ash. The hot night air in my face is relentless. I look back to see if she's still by the car, but then I can hear her in the dark up ahead of me.

"Getting old, Mack," she says with a smile I can't see. "Back in the day you could carry one of her on each shoulder."

When I finally reach her, she's leaning up against the front of the building. My shoulders and knees are starting to feel the weight.

"Here?" I ask, looking. The door is metal and black. The next door down is red. And the one after that too. They keep going off into the gloom.

The number on the front isn't a number. It's a word I can't read. I look a little closer.

"What is this place?"

"You'll know when you know, Mack. How many times do you want me to say it? I'd unwrap her face before you knock. Don't make them do it."

I prop the body up against the door, glad to have her off my shoulders. I yank the sheet down off her head and we both look at her for a few seconds in silence. I want to arrange her hair and clean up her face. Smith & Wesson did her make up like they were in a hurry.

"She'd have hated looking like this," I say. "She was tough, but Suri cared how she looked."

"Then maybe you shouldn't have pulled the trigger," says Marlo. She's right and we both know it. My heart weighs more than all three of us put together. "You're out of time, Ray. They know we're here. Knock already."

But I don't have a chance to knock. The door starts to open on its own, and Suri starts to fall away with it. I let her go, wanting to protect Marlo from what's coming, but Marlo is gone now. All over again she is gone. I pull Sig from the holster. No time to aim. I stiff-arm the thing into an opening darkness that is like a sideways jaw, a fetid maw looking to swallow me whole, and I start shooting, firing blind, the muzzle flashing a burnt orange into the void.

The noise is deafening and sets my ears to ringing.

It sounds like a telephone.

TWO

Fear. That's always the first reaction.

Look at him jolt. Like he's been shot. Eyes popping open with that shock of adrenaline. Muscles tensing in that first instant. His nervous system electrifies as his brain scrambles to catch up.

Look at how quickly one hand grapples at his chest as the other grabs the steering wheel. Like he's having a heart attack. Maybe he is.

It sounds like an old-timey telephone, a ringtone so loud it rips through the quiet car like a chain saw through metal.

Not always, of course. The ring volume is strangely random, ranging from silent to piercing depending on God-knows-what. He'd change the volume if he could, but he can't. He's stopped trying. The phone won't do the things normal cellphones are supposed to do. And it does plenty of other things normal cellphones are not supposed to do.

Like, just maybe, channeling the afterlife.

He should scrap the phone altogether, but he won't. He has his reasons. This phone is with him for as long as it takes a charge.

So, he keeps carrying the thing around like a pocket-sized cattle prod with a random trigger. Scares the crap out of him every time it rings at full volume. It's a natural enough reaction for any normal person.

Of course, Ray Mackey's not exactly normal. Crazy, in fact, if you ask some people.

Stubborn, too. Tell Ray he needs to get a better phone and that's at the top of his list of things not to do, even as his heart is rabbiting for cover. He's so stubborn his normal reaction to fear is to dig in his heels. He resents being pushed around by the adrenaline that wants to save his life. That'll get him killed one of these days.

The second ring is as loud as the first.

No question that Ray's days are numbered. It won't be some carnivorous cancer or a falling piano or a hidden assassin's bullet that gets him. It won't be because his instincts suddenly fail. He'll see the train coming and, out of pure pigheadedness, he'll refuse to get off the tracks. When the rock and the hard place finally start to come together and begin to squeeze the daylight out of the world, Ray will resent his lack of options. He'll demand a different reality. He'll look at a crappy deal and try by sheer force-of-will to turn a pair of threes into a royal flush.

Just like now. Look at him clutching at the phone in his pocket. Right behind the jolt of alarm is a rush of stubborn hope. Even as the dream is fading and he knows what the sound is, he's still refusing to acknowledge it isn't Marlo on the other end of that sound. He's working to smudge the difference between a heart rabbiting from fear and a heart rabbiting for love. He's a sap, this guy. He's determined that this call be from a dead woman.

Marlo, he thinks. *Maybe it's Marlo.*

But even as the dream slurps away down the drain and hope flickers anew in his eyes, some part of him knows better. It's not Marlo. Hasn't been Marlo for months now. Not since last summer in the Chicago railyards, right before nearly catching a bullet in the head. Smitty had caught a bullet instead, but only because Ray's phone had known precisely when to ring.

And that was the last time. Marlo had stopped calling altogether.

Maybe it had never been Marlo in the first place. We find a way to believe what we want to believe. In his quieter moments, when the Old Forester has softened him up and it's just Ray on the couch with Phil in his lap, listening to Ella or Carmen or Billie shaping the lamplit smoke, Ray starts to wonder whether it was ever Marlo calling at all. He starts to wonder whether his particular brand of crazy has expanded into the neighborhood of schizophrenia. He wonders, more and more these days, about the inescapable certainty of Marlo's death and the discomfiting notion of him working overtime to hallucinate a better option: Marlo dropping dimes from up in the big dream.

Doesn't help matters that I'm always here, watching Ray like he's a bug under glass. Even now as he yanks the phone from his shirt pocket in a panic, he can feel me up here, like I'm hovering three feet over the hood, looking at him through the windshield. He doesn't like that I am reading his every expression with the benefit of every thought in his head. Assessing. Judging. And then sending it all back to him like his brain has been spliced into a closed-circuit surveillance feed.

I say *his brain*. It's my brain too. It's the same brain. Ray doesn't just feel me out here looking in. He sees what I see. He sees himself through my eyes, and he doesn't usually like what he sees. The shrinks call it Depersonalization-Derealization Disorder. The big 3-D. To Ray… to me… it means never being alone.

Ray doesn't let the phone ring a third time. He looks at the screen, hoping to see Marlo's calling card: *Unknown Caller. Number Blocked.*

But it is not her. All over again, it is not her.

He closes his laptop and leans his head back against the seat, rubbing his eyes. He adjusts the heat vent to get the hot air out of his face. He drapes an arm over the steering wheel.

Then he answers the phone.

THREE

"Lieutenant." My throat is dry and my voice is weak. I have to say it twice. "Lieutenant."

"Officer Mackey," says Twill. "What's your twenty?"

Twill's tone, like his personality, always leans formal, even when he's making an effort to be casual or good humored. It's not an act. And it goes too deep to be something he picked up at the police academy. That kind of thing has to do with how a guy was raised. It goes back to the parents. The good money is on Orland Twill having been raised by people who inspected his bed every morning as he was polishing his shoes before school.

Kids who mostly raise themselves —kids whose parents inspect the inside of empty bottles every morning —tend to turn out differently. Less formal, for one thing. Alcoholic for another.

But I'm starting to get the hang of Twill now. It has taken a few months for me to find the vein of good-natured humor in Twill's otherwise by-the-book style.

Not that I completely trust the guy. That may never happen. I don't really trust anyone other than Phil. But I know enough that calling me *Officer Mackey* is just Twill's way of acknowledging that I am now, once again, a sworn member of the Chandler Police Department. Pigs ought to start flying any day now.

"I'm in my car parked outside the courthouse," I tell him. I put Twill on speaker and set the phone down on top of the laptop, looking out across the parking lot. "Joliet took care of a bunch of evidentiary housekeeping then recessed for an hour. Didn't make sense for me to come back to the station. They should be ready to start up again in another fifteen or so. Unless you're like me and think this is all a complete waste of time."

Twill is silent for a moment. A drawer closes in the background.

"You think Dunn will testify today?" he asks.

"Hard to say. Far as I know, Arty's up early in the batting order but they still need to finish the opening statements and then get through the basic forensic testimony. Joliet made it pretty clear she wants to keep things moving."

Twill gives me his best scolding tone.

"Her name is Jolie, Ray. Judge *Jolie*, not Joliet. Let's have a little respect for our judiciary."

Outside, a couple walks arm-in-arm across the lot. They make their way slowly, moving as if through a field of sleeping snakes, trying to not slip on the ice, gleaming with morning sun. The wind is a ghost yanking angrily at the woman's scarf. She hunkers further down into her coat. Her companion glances back at me as if he can feel me looking. I can relate.

"No disrespect intended, LT," I say. "It's actually more of a compliment. Judge Joliet."

"I'm well-aware. Nevertheless."

"You're the boss. What do you want me to do?"

The boss. That's a trip and a half. Policing is not something I thought I'd ever want again. Not after having been kicked out. And working for IAD? Come on.

Internal Affairs is not my idea of policing. Thirty years working shoulder-to-shoulder with the rank and file gets you a firm belief that IAD is all problem and no solution. At best, a political cosmetic. At worst, IAD amounted to anti-policing.

But now, here I am, working the other side of the line. Which makes me an idiot, because three decades working homicides is likely to make IAD a disappointing experience.

But it's work. And it beats a part-time gig detaining pimply-faced shoplifters at the mall.

"Have you seen our complainant yet?" he asks. "What's his name again? Pleasant?"

"Pleasants, with an S," I say. "First name Daniel, aka Scooter, according to his sheet. He was in the courtroom first thing this morning but then he left when Joliet... sorry... *Judge Jolie* excluded all potential witnesses. If Scooter testifies it won't be for a while. The defense case is at least ten days out."

"Was he with anyone? A lawyer?"

"No. He was alone, looking exactly like you'd imagine an almost-convicted sex offender who owns three adult bookstores."

"Almost convicted?" Twill asks.

"The kid was fifteen, but they couldn't make the case stick. Turned out she hated daddy more than she hated Scooter. They locked Scooter up not for that but for assaulting the arresting officer with a dart."

"A dart?"

"Lucky shot. Scooter hit the bullseye. The officer in question is now drawing a pension and wearing a patch. Scooter served seven out of ten and has been out for about five, scratching his itch in the smut trade."

"How'd he look in court?"

"Unconvincing. Wearing something around his neck that was supposed to be a tie. Might have been a black stocking. Honestly, LT, this is all a waste of time. We've got more important concerns."

"All of which are currently off limits to you, Mack. The task force leak. The dry cleaner. The mayor. Even finding Suri. All of it. If it relates in any way to José Beggamon or that organization, then you keep your hands off." Twill pauses. We're both listening to the silence. "I want to hear you say that you understand these words."

I sigh so he can hear it. But I don't mean it to come out so loud.

"Mack."

"I understand. I told you before. I do. It's just… It's not… I mean for fuck's sake, LT."

The couple outside nearly makes it to the sidewalk before getting knee-capped by the wind and going down. She goes first, pulling him down on top of her. The guy stands them both up again with the help of a nearby bumper. The woman reemerges without a hat.

"Listen," says Twill. His voice has a new edge. "I was lucky to get you in the front door. Keep your head down and your nose clean, and I'll keep working on getting you included. In the meantime, stay in your lane, Ray. Scooter Pleasants is in your lane. The dry cleaner, the mayor, José Beggamon and Suri are not in your lane. Got that?"

"Yeah. I got that."

"If you get yourself fired, I'm going to think that's too bad. If you get me fired because I stuck my neck out to get you the job, then I'll make sure you never work again."

Of that I have no doubt. That's the other thing about Twill; no bullshit. He means what he says.

"I got it. I got it. I just can't believe we're dancing to Scooter's tune. You should read his file, LT."

"I don't need to read his file, Ray. It's old and irrelevant. This is the job, okay? This is what IAD is all about. You're not homicide anymore. You're policing the police. Get used to it or go back to following shoplifters at the mall. Pleasants may be a sleaze, but not to you. To you he's a citizen with a complaint about an officer of the law."

"He's a child-molester."

"Not according to the State of Illinois. You said they got him for assault."

"Yeah, and they got Capone on tax evasion."

"I'm not kidding, Ray. Pleasants has done his time. He's entitled to the same protection and treatment from the Chandler Police Department as any other citizen."

"Okay, already." It takes some effort to keep the irritation out of my voice. Odds are spectacular that I'll be on Twill's shit list sooner or later, but later would be better. "I've heard this lecture. What am I doing?"

"Well." Twill's indecision tips. "I think you're there for the day. The IAD complaint is too new for you to be on Arty Dunn's radar yet, so keep a low profile. Don't make any contact. You're just an interested spectator who couldn't resist the pretrial publicity in the Root case. It may turn out to be a waste of time, but as long as the defense has Scooter on the witness list, I think it would be good for you to watch them both testify. And if there is any kind of interaction between the two of them…"

The couple has safely crossed the street. They pass the courthouse and turn the corner. The windblown scarf, yellow wool grabbing at the gray stone, is the last to disappear.

"LT."

"What."

"Who's got the dry cleaner detail? You've got Santiago on the dry cleaner, don't you?"

"Santiago's on a two-week leave."

"Right. You've got him on the dry cleaner. Shit."

"I mean it, Ray. You keep clear of that."

"Yeah, yeah. Shit. See you later, LT."

I end the call and drop the phone back into my shirt pocket. I reopen the laptop up against the steering wheel. The screen glows to life and I stare, wincing into the square of light, trying to pick up the thread from where I'd left off before falling asleep.

I close my eyes and lean back against the headrest, trying to find the story again. Trying to load it all back into my fingertips.

I don't want to be here, sitting upright in a car, outside the county courthouse with a phone in my pocket and a computer in my lap. I want to be home in a recliner, with a bottle on the table and Phil in my lap. Dreaming about Marlo.

FOUR

I open my eyes.

The screen in front of me is like a frying pan to the face. Too much light blasting out from between too few letters, which seem to me like scratches on the surface of the sun.

The hangover doesn't help. I've had five years of mornings and early afternoons to sleep off the Old Forester from the night before. The new routine of reporting bright and early for work feels about as normal to me as shaving with a butcher knife and brushing my teeth with battery acid.

Just the same, the laptop has never been my style. I miss the sheet of paper inching up out of my old Smith Corona. It's an antique. A dirty turquoise Corsair. Bulky and heavy as the *Queen Mary*'s anchor. Not all the letters leave the mark they used to. But it works. I like the gunshot feel of those keys. I like the sense of power in my fingertips.

Makes me feel like a writer.

But the Corsair can't get the job done. Not in the digital age. So, I only use it to get me going. To inspire whatever is inside my head to come out and be sociable. Once the story gets some momentum of its own, I make the switch to the laptop. But not happily.

Now that I'm fully employed again, I bring the laptop with me so I can write a sentence or two at lunch or, like today, in the little gaps of downtime between the things I do to earn a paycheck from the City of Chandler. Can't do that with an antique Smith Corona.

I reread the last paragraph for the hundredth time. It's not that I don't know what comes next. I know exactly what comes next. I lived it. What comes next is the security guard, driving his Kia around the corner of the Chinatown Target.

It's an alarming and highly inconvenient development. Detective McMannis, his face badly beaten, is trying to wipe a dead man's car clean of fingerprints. He's only just discovered the pocket camera stuffed between the front seats. It's three in the morning and his informant is running for her life from the mob and the cops. McMannis doesn't have time for the security guard.

So, yeah, I know what comes next. But finding the right words? Rousting them and convincing them to show up for work, in the right order, and to do their job? That's the problem at nine in the morning when all I want to do is go back to bed.

Not that it really matters. This book will meet the same fate as every other book I've written. It will pass from agent to agent on its way to the morgue where the literary coroner on duty will scribble the title onto a toe tag –"Message in a Bullet" –and close the drawer with an uncaring bump of the hip.

A hard gust from out of the north shoulders up against the Impala, rocking the car. I close the lid to the laptop and toss it onto the passenger seat. Across the street, people make their way to the courthouse, huddling against the wind in small, darkly bundled groups, like so many musk oxen defending against wolves.

I recognize Mickey Shaw and the defense team pulling their rolling brief cases full of exhibits, marching into battle to defend Wrigley Menard against charges of murdering Curtis Root. Mickey's a foot taller than the rest of his team. His ponytail loves this wind.

Arty Dunn is coming from the other direction. He's a tree stump, this guy. Arty's one of those cops who always has to have his badge handy in case he has to prove he's a cop. He just doesn't look the part.

Arty makes it to the door first. He holds it open for Mickey Shaw and keeps holding it until the last of the defense team and all the rolling baggage are safely inside. Arty looks my direction as he waits. Maybe he can feel me out here watching. Anti-policing. Making sure that a scum like Scooter Pleasants gets just a little more respect from a cop like Arty. Twill wants me to keep a low profile. I can't imagine a lower profile than staying in my car.

Yes I can. Going home and crawling back into bed would be a lower profile. A lot lower.

I turn the heat up a notch and bury my hands down into the pockets of my coat. One hand finds a lighter and the other finds the cigarettes. I knock out a Camel and fire it up, cracking the window so the heater and the wind can fight over who gets the smoke.

It's too goddamned cold. The wind has been blowing a deep freeze off the lakes for weeks. The world is covered in ice. A foot of snow would feel like a blanket. But it's too cold for snow. The Chandler skyline is choked with smoking buildings that shiver in the rising sun. They all seem so fragile, ready to crack and calve off into the streets like urban glaciers.

The people too. Like little splinters of ice wrapped in useless insulation.

Dante says the ninth circle is frozen. I always suspected the devil lives in Chicago.

FIVE

Ray steps through double wooden doors and into the back of the courtroom. Heads turn in unison, like he's interrupted a congregation of owls. The eyes betray a collective hope he might be someone special. Like they think the judge might just surprise everyone and enter through the back of the room this time. Or like some Chicago celeb might be dropping by to see what all the fuss has been about.

Oprah, killing time. Michael Jordan. Barak.

It's just nervous energy. They're all feeding off each other as they wait.

Ray grimaces. The room is packed. He should have resisted the nicotine and come in earlier. He takes off his coat and folds it over his arm. He looks for a space between the shoulders.

Celestyn Fila is in her usual spot up front, facing the room, a step below the judge's bench. Celeste has been an in-court clerk for as long as Ray can remember. Pushing sixty, she still has the hair and the heart of a teenager. The hair is brassy-blond wrapped up in a beehive. The heart is well-insulated, wrapped in the same dark, almost-too-small polka-dotted prairie blouse she always seems to be wearing. Celeste has her father's Polish nose and her mother's large, dewy blue eyes. When the courtroom is quiet and no one but the witness is supposed to be talking, Celeste uses those same dewy blues to flirt with men she finds attractive or wants to make uncomfortable. Ray has never figured out which one of those he is. Maybe both.

Celeste smiles and tilts her head ever-so-slowly toward the front of the courtroom on Ray's left, behind the defense table. It's the only open seat in the room. Ray nods his appreciation and begins to move that direction.

People return to shifting uncomfortably in their seats, clearing their throats and sniffling. There's a cough in the back of the room that's going to get old in a hurry. All of them seem to have already lost interest in Ray Mackey, the nobody newcomer. Or, at least, all of them except Celeste and one other person who keeps his eyes on Ray all the way up the aisle. Hard to miss, this guy. Center of the room. His baldhead is like a large white bucket on top of a mountain of bricks. The people behind him won't be able to see a thing.

They catch eyes once. Ray lingers for just a second. Buckethead doesn't blink. Ray looks away and keeps moving.

Mickey Shaw is at the defense table, bent over a yellow notepad. He taps it with a pen for the benefit of his accused client, Wrigley Menard, a greasy noodle of a kid who looks about as comfortable at the table in his borrowed suit and tie as an eel at a sushi bar. His longish black hair won't stay tucked behind his ears, which are a little small for the job.

Ray sizes up the defendant in a couple of blinks. He's guessing Wrigley's father was not the only Chicagoan to name his boy after the storied stadium, no doubt hoping the kid would one day grow up to run those bases. Wrigley, disappointingly, must not have run anywhere except into a blind alley of petty crime. His is a life, Ray guesses, named not for the field of dreams but for the colonies of gum stuck to the underside of the stadium bleachers. Wrong Wrigley. Probably explains why he goes by Jake.

Wrigley is hunched forward over the table, nodding soberly at whatever Mickey is explaining. Tucking that hair.

Mickey pauses and looks up as Ray makes his way carefully along the narrow space between the gallery seating and the waist-high bar that separates the spectators from the trial participants.

"Raymond Mackey," says Mickey, dropping the pen and swinging out a hand. "As I live and breathe. I heard you were back in the game. Working for the good guys now, are you?"

Their informal repartee has always been old-school-chum cordial, sharply at odds with Mickey's aggressive cross-examinations of Ray over the years, accusing him of all manner of cheating for the sake of a conviction. Perjury. Hiding evidence. Rigging line-ups. The works. Whatever Mickey has to say to create reasonable doubt in the mind of a jury. *Is there anything you won't do, Detective Mackey, to score a win for the blue team?* Mickey had asked once, flailing his arms in righteous anger as the prosecutor had bolted up from his seat, objecting.

Mickey is famous for switching gears on the jury without any warning, affable charm, and good-natured golly-shucks-self-deprecation one minute and boiling rage the next. The strategy was always to capture the jury's attention as early as possible in the trial and never give it back. It works more often than it should.

"Counselor," says Ray, shaking hands. "I see you're still keeping the same company."

"Salt of the earth," says Mickey, bracing Wrigley on the shoulder. Wrigley keeps his head down like he's been told. Nothing about that face is going to win him any friends. No way he's testifying in his own defense. Also, no way he can afford Mickey Shaw to pull him out of the fire.

"Well." Ray nods. "May truth and justice prevail."

He keeps moving toward the only open spot on the long wooden bench. He positions himself between a young woman who seems associated with Mickey's defense team, and a mostly bald, bespectacled man whose open laptop suggests he is employed by someone who buys their ink by the barrel. The *Tribune* maybe. Or the *Chandler Times*.

He takes a casual glance over his shoulder before sitting. Some people are joined at the shoulders, talking in hushed tones. Others are tending to their phones. Buckethead Mountain still only has eyes for Ray.

Ray turns and lowers himself to the bench. Celeste is still painting him with her eyes. She stands like she is ready to declare her feelings, straightening her blouse over the flare of hips.

"All rise."

SIX

I do as I'm told and stand back up. I can feel the entire room behind me do the same. Celeste looks directly at me as she speaks. Like she's introducing me to her parents.

"The Circuit Court of the Twelfth Judicial District is now in session, the Honorable Camilla Esperanza Jolie presiding."

Judge Jolie strides in carrying a black binder. The robe makes her look like she's floating. She sets the binder on the desk in front of the large black chair and remains standing for a prolonged second or two, surveying the room. She nods and pulls back her chair.

Jolie's on the bench ten, twelve years now. She broke some Will County records when she took the oath. First Hispanic. First woman. First judge under the age of thirty-five. She has a lean seriousness to her face. Straight black hair, curling slightly at the jaw line. Dark, clear eyes. Hardest eyes I've ever seen on the bench. She never uses the gavel. Not that I've seen. Doesn't need it. All she has to do is look at you and your head feels gaveled enough.

She has a reputation for being a prosecutor's judge. Understandable, since she cut her teeth in the Cook County prosecutor's office. Then, right out of the gate, she presided over a string of high-profile state racketeering convictions and sent a bus load of criminal ambition to Stateville Correctional with maximum sentences. Then came the fraud conviction of the state senator. Mark Milford. Off he goes. After that was the get-away driver for the savings and loan robbery gone bad. Felony murder. Life in lock-up. Joliet Prison had been mothballed for the better part of a decade by then. That didn't matter. Judge Jolie had herself a nickname.

"Please be seated." She says the words almost before Celeste is done speaking, like the non-evidentiary ceremony of the courtroom is well past irritating. She sits and opens her binder. "Counsel, are we ready to continue with opening statements? Mr. Shaw?"

Mickey stands, fingertips on the shoulder of his client.

"We are ready, Your Honor."

"Ms. Cavelle, are you ready to begin?"

I don't know Jaclyn Cavelle except through the media storm of attention the Root case has inflicted on Illinois news consumers. In person, she looks much too young for a trial of this magnitude.

Jaclyn whispers something to a lawyer next to her at the table and then stands. She's a dead ringer for a young Dinah Washington if Dinah had been a foot taller and spent less time singing and more time training for the summer Olympics. Javelin maybe. Pole vault.

"The State of Illinois is ready, Judge," she says.

"Very well." Judge Jolie pivots to Celeste. "Madam Clerk, will you please bring in the jury."

Jaclyn Cavelle sits and swivels in her chair, leaning over the railing to whisper something to an attractive, tastefully dressed woman. Expensive, but not too expensive. Late forties. Not a lawyer, judging by the uncertain way she leans toward Jaclyn. She is the only person in the first row who's not a whiter shade of pale. I'm guessing she's Curtis Root's widow. She nods and leans back in her seat. I can't see her without staring rudely at the woman sitting to my immediate right. The notepad in her lap is blank except for an underlined heading: Shaw Openings –Defense.

To my left, the reporter next to me is clicking away on the keys.

I lean back and adjust the coat in my lap, trying to mind my own business. Not an easy thing for me.

Mickey Shaw stands, gathering his notepad. He's wearing his trademark boots. Black, made of alligator or snake or something else low to the ground. He gives Wrigley Menard a buck-up swat on the shoulder. Wrigley looks up and Mickey gives him a wink. He heads for the podium to wait as the jurors file in and take their seats.

Some people don't register a heartbeat until they've got a slug of caffeine in their system. They need a cup of coffee to turn the lights on in their eyes. Mickey Shaw is not himself unless he's drinking in the drama of a high-stakes criminal trial in a packed courtroom. His easy-going charm is pressure-activated. Without the tension to keep him awake and relaxed, Mickey's just another mob lawyer laundering four hundred bucks an hour.

SEVEN

"My client is a drug dealer."

Shaw lets the sentence hang. The jury shifts uncomfortably in the box. He has one hand in a pocket as the other swings his notepad idly against his leg. His ponytail quivers a little, like it's measuring fluctuations of the energy in the air.

"*Was* a drug dealer, I guess I should say. Was. He's completely out of the business now."

Shaw points, bouncing his finger in the air.

"Because my client, Wrigley Menard –his friends call him Jake, by the way – Jake Menard sold marijuana. Not the hard stuff. I'm not talking about heroin or cocaine. He sold pot. Mr. Menard made a business of selling illegally what the State of Illinois has now decided is legal to sell. Like when Prohibition ended. On Monday people go to jail for selling a bottle of beer and then on Tuesday all the bars are opening up. It's like that now with pot. Nowadays people can just get in the car and go the store for some weed. The wacky tobacky."

Someone in the back of the room sniffs out a laugh. The reporter next to Ray is nodding as he types.

"Now. You may think that's a great thing. Or you may think that's a terrible thing. Maybe something in between. Doesn't matter. Doesn't matter and I don't care what you think about marijuana."

Shaw walks back to the defense table. He takes his hand out of his pocket and places it on Wrigley's shoulder. Wrigley keeps his eyes down. The hair slips out from behind his ears.

"Because history is history. It's just a fact. It used to be that people went to prison for selling beer in a dark alley. It used to be that people needed to call someone like Jake here to get them a little baggie of pot. People would call Jake up and arrange for him to come out to wherever they felt it was safe to meet so they wouldn't get caught. And Jake would pack up a supply of pot and get in his little, white, beat-up Honda and then head out. That's how it was done in the long-ago, olden days of last year."

A soft laugh rolls over the spectators and into the jury box. Shaw lets it come like a wave sliding up onto a beach and then seeping away.

"That's how it was done. And the prosecution yesterday afternoon tossed-out that phrase... *convicted drug dealer*... so that you'd take it home with you overnight and think about it and come back today with all kinds of ideas about what that means."

Shaw wags a finger in the prosecutor's direction.

"Ms. Cavelle didn't give you any context, did she? She didn't explain that by calling my client a convicted drug dealer what she meant was that he'd been caught selling grass."

Shaw spreads both arms wide, inviting inspection.

"But did I object? Did I leap up from my table over there with my finger in the air? No, I did not. No. Because Ms. Cavelle is right. She's right. Marijuana is a drug. Jake Menard sold that drug for money against the law. And Jake was convicted for selling that drug. He was convicted several times. Went to jail once. So, stay tuned for that. I suspect Ms. Cavelle will be spending all kinds of time on that rap sheet. Just in case you forget."

Shaw paces the room slowly. He drops his notepad on the podium and crosses his arms. He waits long enough for people to wonder if he's going to continue.

"Trials are about the truth, ladies and gentlemen. I'm here to tell you the truth. I'm not here to pull the wool over your eyes. I'm not here," he gestures toward Jaclyn Cavelle, "to starve you of context so that you run off with the wrong impression. Truth. All of this is about the truth. Okay?"

Two of the jurors actually give slight nods.

"So the truth is that Jake Menard sold pot to people who wanted to buy it from him. And the truth –the *truth* –is that Curtis Root was one of those people."

"Your Honor," Jaclyn Cavelle is on her feet. Everyone looks. She speaks politely. "The State objects on the grounds previously explained."

Judge Jolie's face is a study in restrained irritation. "Ms. Cavelle. This is an opening statement. I think I have been very clear. Your objection is noted and overruled. Please be seated."

Cavelle lowers herself to her seat as the judge pivots toward the jury box.

"Ladies and gentlemen of the jury, I will remind you of what I advised yesterday during the prosecution's opening statement. Opening statements are not evidence. The purpose of opening statements is to provide the lawyers for each party an opportunity to tell you what they *think* the evidence will show. In the next few weeks, you will need to evaluate that evidence for yourselves and reach your own conclusion. Mr. Shaw, please proceed."

Shaw has made sure he is standing in front of the prosecutor's table.

"Thank you, Your Honor," he says, looking at Cavelle. Then he turns to face the jury. "I want to make something perfectly clear. Curtis Root's death is nothing short of tragic."

He points to the large photograph leaning up against the prosecutor's table. Curtis Root had an open face. Light brown skin and hazel eyes. Big smile. He's forty-something in the photo but he had a collegiate look to him. The photo they are using is of Curtis up on a ladder propped against an unfinished house, hammer in his hand. In the background is a blurry sign, but most of the word *Habitat* is clear enough.

"Tragic," repeats Shaw. He nods to the woman sitting in the audience behind Cavelle. "His wife has lost a husband; a good one, by all accounts. Curtis Root's son has lost a father. Again, a good father, by all accounts.

"And we all know that he was a successful businessman in this state. Even if you haven't been inside one of the *Tap Root Kegs*, or *TRKegs* I guess they're called now, seven of them, scattered around Illinois, I know you've seen them. The business continues on, but the founder is gone. Tragically gone. This is a tragedy, full stop. It doesn't matter that Curtis Root routinely purchased marijuana, which was every bit the illegal act as selling it, by the way."

Judge Jolie, interlacing her fingers on the notebook, glances directly at the Jaclyn Cavelle, waiting for her to repeat the mistake of objecting. Cavelle takes the warning and looks down at her notepad with a silent sigh.

"Doesn't matter," says Shaw. "Liking drugs, buying drugs, violating state law, does not make Curtis Root's death any less tragic. And, if the question is whether or not his death was tragic, then it also does not matter one little bit who Curtis Root chose to conduct business with. Or where he got his money. Or what he did with that money."

Cavelle is suddenly on her feet, ripping away the jury's attention. Her face is hard with anger.

Judge Jolie cannot keep Cavelle's mouth from opening to speak, but she can prevent her words from making it out into the courtroom.

"Overruled," she says before Cavelle can utter a sound. The word is like a spear. "Ms. Cavelle, you will sit down, and you will remain seated. Ladies and gentlemen, I will remind you again that the opening statements of the parties are not evidence. Mr. Shaw, please continue."

Shaw nods to the jury. He speaks in a soft, casual tone. Just between friends.

"That's okay," he says, tipping his head sideways toward the prosecution. "I told you this trial would be about the truth. And the truth is hard to hear sometimes. Lawyers are people too. Believe it or not."

The jury smiles at this. A couple of them chuckle and shake their heads. *Lawyers are people. Come on.*

Shaw gives the levity a little room to breathe. Cavelle fumes in her seat.

"So maybe we can have opinions about Mr. Root's drug use and even about the kind of people that he chose to do business with... specifically, to borrow money from... and while that may be relevant to figuring out what happened to Mr. Root, it does not, I repeat it does not, take away from the fact that his life was cut tragically short."

He points again at the photo of the smiling man up on a ladder.

"Someone took that life with a bullet to his head. Just like the prosecution told you yesterday. Someone executed Curtis Root with a point-blank shot from a .38 caliber handgun to the back of the head, in his bedroom, at approximately nine o'clock on the night of Tuesday, February 5 of last year. Cold-blooded murder. And someone must pay for that horrific crime. If we care at all about Curtis Root and his family, then by God someone must pay for this heinous crime."

Shaw wanders. Hands in his pockets. Head down, like he's watching his boots. When he reaches the defense table he turns back to the jury and looks up.

"Are we okay if the someone who pays is just... *anyone?* As long as someone pays the price?"

He waits, as if for an answer. Then he gestures an open hand back toward counsel table, to Wrigley Menard.

"Will *anyone* do? Is it okay if we just pick someone convenient? Maybe a convicted drug dealer that no one cares about. Would that be okay?"

Another pause that might never end. Shaw answers his own question.

"Of course not. We all know better. Of course it's not okay. It has to be the person responsible, doesn't it? It has to be the person who *actually* fired that bullet. *That's* who must pay for the heinous, tragic murder of Curtis Root."

Shaw points sternly at Jaclyn Cavelle.

"And the law, ladies and gentlemen, the *law* says that it is the sacred responsibility of the prosecution –it is the prosecution's responsibility –to prove they've got the right guy. And the prosecution has got to do it with evidence so compelling, so unassailable, that it leaves absolutely no room in your mind for any, and I mean not *any*… reasonable… doubt."

Shaw strides to the podium. He flips a page of notes, reading. Then another. The room waits. A man in the back stifles several coughs.

"Oh, go on and let it out," says Shaw. "Good as time as any. Coughing's no crime. We're all human."

The man clears his throat just as a woman, middle-left, muffles a sneeze into the flesh of her arm.

"Hold on now," says Shaw, turning. "Pretty sure that was a sneeze."

The spectators laugh. The jury laughs. Shaw does not laugh. But he smiles. First at the sneezing woman, then at the room. Then at the jury. He is a teacher. They are his students. Learning is fun.

"Now," says Shaw, pointing at the prosecutor. "You have already seen with your own eyes just how good Ms. Cavelle is at her job. That was something yesterday, wasn't it? Smooth as silk. She makes this case sound easy. Nothing to it."

Shaw flips through the pages of his notepad, now as if he is looking for something in particular.

"Here it is," he says, finally. "Let me just hit the highlights. I know you've been thinking about it all night but let's just take a second to revisit the case the prosecution is trying to sell.

"It's a burglary gone bad, right? That's the theory. You've got the convicted drug dealer defendant. We just talked about that.

"You've got the neighbor, Mrs. Marsh, who sees my client lurking, that was the word, lurking around the property of Curtis Root on the night of the murder. Jeans. Dark coat. And Mrs. Marsh also sees a little white Honda parked up the street from the Root home. An unusual car for that neighborhood. Beat up and dirty and scratched. Easy thing to notice and remember.

"Around the back of the house, you've got boot prints in old snow, leading up to a broken basement window. You've got the same boot prints on the carpeting in different rooms of the Root home, including up in the bedroom where Curtis Root was found shot to death."

Shaw points to Wrigley.

"You've got a pair of boots in Jake Menard's closet with a sole pattern and size that match the boot prints found outside and inside the Root home.

"You've got an open safe, in the bedroom closet, missing a few hundred dollars in emergency money.

"You've got security camera footage from the outside back of the Root home, near the broken window, that shows… well, that shows Jake Menard, according to Ms. Cavelle. Jake Menard in a dark coat with a hood.

Shaw spreads his arms again.

"And there you have it. That *is* easy, isn't it? Maybe we should just all go home."

He extends his left arm and crooks his right forefinger into his sleeve, as if to pull it open.

"Ever go see a magic act?"

He does the same to the opposite sleeve.

"You sit there, and you watch the stage, and your head is spinning, and you ask yourself did that really just happen? Did he really just saw that lady in half? Yes, say your eyes. He really did. Did he really pour a glass of water into an empty top hat and then pull out a live rabbit? Yes, say your eyes. We were there. We saw it happen.

"But by the time we get home from the show our brains are back in charge, right? We know we've been tricked, we just don't know precisely how. We haven't seen the truth. We've seen an *illusion* of truth. We realize, when we stop and think about it, that we looked everywhere the magician told us to look. The magician points a finger, and that's where we look. We look away from whatever else might be interesting."

Shaw holds up a hand, fingers splayed.

"Like fingerprints. Did you notice that the prosecution didn't say anything to you about fingerprints? You think that's because there weren't any? Really? But of course there were. They were all over the place. They just didn't belong to Jake Menard.

"I know. You're thinking gloves. What burglar-turned-killer doesn't wear gloves? Well, remember that security video? It's not going to show you much, but it will show you a hand that was not wearing a glove."

Shaw looks at his own hand, then shows it again to the jury.

"Now, I'm not saying they couldn't find Jake's prints anywhere. They just couldn't find them in the house. They did find some of his prints. They did. Jake has been arrested. His prints are in the system. Those are definitely his fingerprints at the scene of the crime.

"But then why didn't Ms. Cavelle tell you about those prints? You'd think that might help her case, putting Jake at the scene.

"She didn't tell you they'd found his fingerprints because they found them in only three places. On the doorbell. On the dashboard of Curtis Root's car. And on the passenger door handle of that car. The prosecution didn't mention those fingerprints because they don't fit the story they want to tell you."

Shaw points suddenly to the ceiling. Everyone looks.

"See how that works? The magician is pointing in a different direction. You're not supposed to be looking at Curtis Root's car. That car, a spotless black 2018 Mercedes Benz, was in the driveway, locked. No sign of forced entry. The keys were inside Curtis Root's right front pocket.

"So." Shaw puts his hands on his hips and screws up his face. "Why are my client's fingerprints all over that dashboard? How'd he get inside that car? The evidence will show he didn't break in. So then how?"

Shaw waits a couple of beats. Then he raises a finger and widens his eyes, like an idea is dawning.

"Maybe he used the keys. Fished them out of the pocket of the man he'd just shot in cold blood, went out to the car, took off the gloves he must have been wearing when he was inside the house, unlocked the car, climbed in the passenger seat, placed his fingers all over the dashboard. Then he must have gotten out of the car, locked it up again, put on his gloves, went back inside the house, and returned the keys to Curtis Root's front pocket. All just for the fun of it." Shaw lifts his voice and raises his hands as if embracing some great truth. "Because we all know that a burglar would have no interest in stealing a 2018 black Mercedes."

Shaw shakes his head, acknowledging the ridiculousness of that proposition.

"The boot prints. Let's talk about those. The evidence will show that the boot prints are from a pair of size-ten Timberland Pro work boots. Among the best-selling boots in this country including northern Illinois. I've got a pair of those boots. Maybe you do too. I know I haven't killed anyone. Have you?

"The security footage. There's just under two seconds of it. You heard that correctly. Less than two seconds. You're going to see a Caucasian person, from behind, in a black coat and a black hood. Part of an ungloved hand is in the frame. Okay? Those are the only facts revealed in that footage." Shaw holds up a new finger with every fact. "A white person —wasn't a goat or a pig —it was a person, wearing a black coat with a hood, and not wearing gloves. That's all you get from that video.

"Now. Ms. Cavelle is going to have to bring in experts to confirm the gender of the person and to estimate the height and weight of the person in the video because none of that is clear from the footage itself. And it will shock you to learn that these experts imagine a person who is male and about my client's height and weight. What are the odds that the experts the prosecution has chosen to put in front of you would come to that conclusion?"

Shaw dramatically pulls open his sleeves again. First the left, then the right.

"What are the odds of that? But wait. Wait." Shaw swings a pointing hand behind him toward Wrigley. What about my client's face?"

Wrigley looks up with an expression of mild surprise. *What about my face?*

"Didn't the prosecution tell you yesterday that they've got his face on that one-point-seven-second video clip? Yes. She did say that. But, as you'll see, the security camera angle is from behind." Shaw brings the edge of one hand to the back of his head like it's a hatchet. "From behind. So then how do they supposedly have his face?" He looks slowly from juror to juror, brow furrowed. "That's about as impossible as pulling a rabbit out of an empty hat. Right?"

Shaw takes a couple of steps back. His expression is no longer confused.

"Here's how this one works. You ever look at the patterns in tree bark and think you see the face of someone you know? Maybe your father? Maybe Jesus? The prosecution is going to show you an enlarged still photo taken from dark-of-night, poor-resolution security footage, that shows part of a downstairs window. With a serious expression, Ms. Cavelle is going to point to what she will represent to you is the reflection of the left side of my client's face. And guess what. She's found a couple of well-compensated experts who will testify that they just happen to see the very same thing. The left half of my client's face. Imagine that. She wants you to convict a man for murder based on a bank shot off the window.

"Now. Because you take the task before you seriously, I know you're not going to just take the word of the prosecutor or her hired experts. You're going to hold that photo in your hands and give that whitish smudge in the little bit of window a good look. Is that Jake Menard? Is it your father? Is it Jesus?"

Shaw saunters to the podium for a brief look at his notepad. He nods to himself and drifts back out into the middle of the room.

"And then there's that coat," he says. "Mrs. Marsh will testify she saw my client lurking in a dark coat. She doesn't know if it had a hood. Remember how Ms. Cavelle dramatically revealed that the police had found a pair of size-ten Timberland Pro's in Jake Menard's closet? *Hoo-wee!* That one was right out of *Law and Order.* Well done. I could almost hear the theme music in my head. Could you?"

Laughter.

"The boots!"

Laughter. Louder this time. Not everyone. Not the judge. Not Jaclyn Cavelle. Not the Widow Root.

"Funny, though." Shaw's smile fades. "I don't recall Ms. Cavelle saying anything about finding a coat. She didn't, did she? Where's the coat? The black coat with the hood we can see in the security footage. If those are the Timberland boots in his closet... then where's the coat?"

The jurors are all taking notes. *Where's the coat?* He waits for them to finish.

"There is no evidence, ladies and gentlemen, that my client has ever owned or worn such a coat. They found the dark green coat Jake wore when he went to deliver Curtis Root's pot. But that's not the coat in the video. It's green, not black, and it doesn't have a hood. So what's a determined prosecutor to do?"

Shaw shrugs his shoulders dramatically.

"Well, she's going to do what every good magician does. She's going to point. She's going to tell you to look at something else. She's going to show you a photo taken five years ago." Shaw holds up his right hand, fingers spread. "Five years. After Jake was arrested for —you guessed it —possession of marijuana with intent to distribute. In this photo, you'll see Jake coming out of liquor store in a black coat with a hood. It's him. It's Jake."

Shaw pauses, letting the new confusion build a little.

"There are two reasons Ms. Cavelle wants to show you this photo. First, it's a surveillance photo, and just in case you have forgotten, she wants you to remember that Jake is a —say it with me —a convicted drug dealer. Second, she wants to suggest that Jake is wearing the same coat that you will see in the security camera footage taken outside the Root home the night of the murder. She wants you to come away with that impression."

Shaw walks to the prosecution table and looks down at Cavelle. She crosses her arms and leans back in her chair. She tries a look of amusement but misses the mark. Shaw keeps looking as he speaks.

"Now. Is she going to bring out yet more experts to *prove* these are the same coat?"

He turns back to the jury for the answer.

"No, she is not. She can't. Because if you look very carefully you will see that they are not the same coat. She's suggesting something that is not actually true. She's selling an illusion.

"Smoke and mirrors. That's a phrase borrowed from the world of magicians. Smoke. And mirrors. The prosecution in this case wants to point you away from the truth. Look that way. Look over there. A convicted dope dealer breaks into Curtis Root's house after he is conveniently spotted by the neighbor and triggers the security camera. He leaves boot prints everywhere and fingerprints nowhere. He is surprised in mid-burgle when Curtis Root comes home from a party. He forces Curtis to open the safe at gun point, then shoots him and leaves him for dead, taking a few hundred bucks with him. It's so easy, says the prosecution. It's so easy.

"Come on." Shaw swings his hand through the air in a big sweeping motion. "It's *too* easy. You give the evidence a good, honest look. You'll see.

"So, you ask, if not Jake, then who? You want to know what I think happened. I get it. But it doesn't matter what I think happened. The prosecution has to prove its case and it cannot do that. The prosecution must prove that Jake Menard did this terrible thing. And yet it cannot do that. Not to the satisfaction of people who are paying close attention to the evidence. Not by a mile.

"So, it doesn't matter what I think." Shaw smiles a little. "But I'm going to tell you anyway. As long as you are testing Ms. Cavelle's theory against the evidence, you may as well test my theory.

"Curtis Root wanted dope. His wife was out of town visiting their son in school. Curtis was going to a party after work, and he was planning to bring enough marijuana to share with his friends. He was that kind of guy."

Shaw points to Wrigley.

"So, he calls his go-to dealer, Jake Menard. He tells Jake to meet him at the house. Jake pulls together the pot, puts it in a baggie and makes the trip to Curtis Root's house. He knew how to get there. Because Jake had done this before. Several times. It's what he did back then in the ancient, long-ago time of last year when pot was illegal. It's how Jake made his living.

"So, Jake parks his white Honda up the street, just to be discrete, and walks up to the house. No car in the driveway. He walks up to the front door and deposits his thumbprint on the doorbell button. No one answers the door. Curtis is not home. So Jake sits on the steps and waits. The neighbor, Mrs. Marsh, sees him waiting as she drives by, and then she passes by the Honda. She makes a mental note.

"Eventually, Curtis pulls his black Mercedes into the driveway. Jake opens the passenger door, leaving his fingerprints, and climbs in. Curtis hands over some cash, and Jake hands over a bag of fifteen pre-rolled joints. Enough for everyone at the party and some extra. Curtis lights one up and they talk, mostly about the news that Illinois might finally be making pot legal. Curtis is interested in what Jake plans to do if that happens. First the official dispensaries, but maybe someday the state would allow a pot delivery service. Jake leaves some prints on the dashboard as they talk."

Shaw shrugs his shoulders, spreading out his hands.

"And then that's that. They each get out of the car. Curtis goes inside the house to get ready for the party. Jake heads to his own car and drives away to deliver a different baggie of pot to a different person in a different place. Because that's what he did. That's how he made his money. He drove off and never came back. End of story."

Shaw crosses his arms and looks down at his boots. He kicks at something invisible. He shakes his head, as if disagreeing with himself.

"Well. No. It isn't the end of the story, is it? It's the end of the story as far as Jake is concerned. But Curtis…"

A new heaviness settles over the courtroom. Shaw issues a remorseful-sounding sigh.

"Curtis goes to his party. Some of the people there will tell you that he was not there five minutes when he got a call. He tells his friends that he needs to run an errand. His words. 'I need to run an errand.' He promises to come right back.

"He drives back home. Why? Because he needs money." Shaw's words are sharper, suddenly. Faster and more forceful, like he's shifting into a different gear. "A lot of money. Not a little. A lot. Fifty thousand dollars. Maybe more. Why?"

Jaclyn Cavelle's hands are each flat against the table. Her legs are tensing as she leans forward in her seat. She's ready to stand. Shaw does not continue. He points to Cavelle and looks back at Judge Jolie.

"Your Honor," he says. "I think Ms. Cavelle might have something she wants to say."

The judge purses her lips, looking from Shaw to Cavelle, who slowly stands, and back again.

"Counsel will please approach," says the judge.

The lawyers make their way to the judge's bench as she flicks a switch that sends a hiss of white noise through the courtroom speakers. Judge Jolie hunches forward to receive them. Jaclyn Cavelle whispers in anger, jabbing her pen in Shaw's direction. Shaw is calmer. He shakes his head and shrugs his shoulders a lot, seeming to suggest that the prosecutor's anger is unfounded.

Beneath the rain-like hiss, the room remains quiet but restless. People fidget in their seats, repositioning the coats and purses in their laps like pets. The man in the back with a cough decides that now is a good time to relieve the pressure. A woman behind the widow Root places a hand on her shoulder with a squeeze.

And look at Ray. The old lump. He uncrosses and re-crosses his legs. He can't sit for as long as he once could. Age has given him more padding, but it's somehow less cushion than he needs. The bones from the waist down start to ache if he doesn't get up every so often and move around.

Unless he's in a Barcalounger with Phil on his lap.

Or on a bar stool. Then he has as much stamina as ever. Stonehenge stamina.

Look at those restless eyes. He wants a cigarette. He's managed to stop drinking until sundown or until he's off work, whichever is later. I'll give him that much. But that doesn't mean he's not counting the hours until that first pour.

Ray refolds his coat. He's trying to keep his eyes away from Celeste, who sits calmly facing the room, waiting for him to look up at her. And he does. He looks. Of course he does. He can't help himself. Celeste catches the look and beams back at him.

Ray smiles and nods and turns away, looking at the room behind him. The bald behemoth is still back there, towering over his neighbors. His eyes are heavy and sullen, but not unintelligent. They know things.

Ray faces forward and leans back against the bench. He pulls in his chin, allowing his glance to slip sideways so that he can read the screen of the laptop next to him. The reporter's fingers are flying silently over the keys. It's the number that leaps out.

$50,000.

The flying fingers pause, hovering, as the reporter turns his head. Ray looks away.

"Ladies and gentlemen of the jury," Judge Jolie's voice fills the courtroom as the electronic hissing stops. Cavelle crosses the room back to her table. Her face reveals nothing. Mickey Shaw smiles patiently. "I will remind you once again, that an opening statement is not evidence. The defense, like the prosecution, is entitled to explain its theory of the case, but it is your job to weigh the actual evidence as it is presented. Mr. Shaw, please continue."

"Thank you, Your Honor," says Shaw. He takes a beat or two to find the eyes of each juror. "Fifty thousand dollars. Ms. Cavelle is concerned that I'm just pulling that number out of you know where. Out of thin air. Well, I'm not. You'll hear the evidence. I'm going to put a man named Raimey Liston on the stand. And Mr. Liston is going to tell you that Curtis Root was holding fifty thousand dollars, in cash, at his home. Roughly fifty. Forty-seven. Forty-nine. Fifty-one. In the ballpark of fifty thousand.

"And who is Mr. Liston to know such a thing? Good question. Mr. Liston is a former employee of Curtis Root. Mr. Liston was an accountant for the *Tap Root* business before he and Mr. Root had a falling out some years ago. Mr. Liston will testify to a conversation he once had with Curtis. This was after the business had opened its third restaurant and was drawing up plans for the microbrewery. The conversation was about some cash —roughly fifty thousand dollars —stored in a safe at the original *Tap Root Kegs*. Mr. Liston was more than just a little curious about the money because none of that cash had been accounted for by the business. After all, that's what accountants do. They account for money."

The man in the back coughs. One leads to two and then a spasm. Shaw waits until it is quiet again.

"So. What was the explanation? Curtis Root's explanation to Mr. Liston was that he'd been skimming from his own business. A little here. A little there.

Because he wanted a tax-free cushion in case he ever needed it again. The experience of nearly going under and losing the business was an experience Curtis never wanted to have again. He had expenses, including a son to put through college in the not-too-distant future.

"It was a heated conversation. Mr. Liston will tell you all about it. But the upshot was that Curtis Root ultimately removed the cash from the restaurant and took it home.

"Now I told you this trial is about the truth. Is that the truth? That Curtis Root was skimming cash from his own business to avoid paying Uncle Sam?"

Shaw's face is contorted with incredulity. Then it relaxes.

"No, it is not the truth. No, it is not. The truth, ladies and gentlemen, is that the money did not belong to Curtis Root. The truth is that the money did not come from Curtis Root's business. The truth is that the money belonged to… well, let's use the term that Mr. Root eventually used with Mr. Liston. Co-investors. Business partners. Silent partners. That's who it belonged to."

A low murmur moves through the gallery like a stench. Several jurors are writing. Cavelle is writing too, shaking her head. Shaw lets the discomfort build.

"It worked like this. These business partners brought Curtis cash. Curtis kept it secure at home. Convenient as it might have been, he just can't keep stacks of cash at work. At least, not after his conversation with Raimey Liston. So he kept the cash at home.

"And what does he do with this cash? Well, every day he takes a little of it in to work with him and slips it into the *Tap Root Kegs* income stream. Then he makes sure the business pays his silent partners in exchange for some service that they perform, or pretend to perform, at exorbitant rates. Mr. Liston will tell you that those services included several things, like marketing consultation, snow removal and also a restaurant cleaning service. Then these co-investors, these silent business partners, would bring Curtis some more cash to replenish the supply. And maybe, I'm just guessing here, maybe they'd add a little extra on top for Curtis. For his trouble and risk. And then the cycle would repeat itself. Money in, money out, money in."

Shaw crosses his arms. He makes a slow tour the length of the jury box from one end to the other and halfway back again.

"Curtis Root was not skimming from his business to avoid paying taxes. That is not the truth. The truth is that Curtis Root was laundering money for the mob."

"Objection!" Cavelle's tone is a healthy blend of emotion. She is exasperated and indignant. She knew it was coming, but she makes a good show of being shocked. She stays in her seat. She knows the answer. Behind her, Mrs. Root wipes away tears with the backs of her thumbs.

"Overruled," says the judge. "This is an opening statement, Ms. Cavell. I won't warn you again."

Judge Jolie is barely done speaking before Shaw continues.

"Why?" he asks. "Why was he doing this? Because back in the day, *Tap Root Kegs* was only one small bar out in Bolingbrook, teetering on the edge of bankruptcy. Curtis needed money and these guys had the money to give. They kept him from going under. Then they backstopped the business finances and helped him grow. And look at it now. Seven bar-restaurants. The *Tap Root* microbrewery. A line of *TRK* products. Business is booming. Okay? It was a mutually beneficial relationship.

"So, let's get back to Tuesday, the fifth of February. Why is Curtis leaving the party and going home for cash? Because he's giving it all back. He's had it with these guys. These silent partners of his. He wants out of the relationship, and he wants them out of the business. He doesn't need them anymore. He doesn't want the risk. He's done. He's returning the money and kicking them to the curb.

"Tuesday. February five. That's the night Curtis' silent partners decided they were ready to settle accounts. They didn't care that Curtis was at a party. He was the one who wanted out. And now was the time. They wanted to meet. They wanted Curtis to bring them their money."

Mickey Shaw finds his way back to the podium. He flips through three more pages on his notepad.

"What happened next?" he asks, looking up again. "Hard to know. Pretty clear they —whoever they are, this group of criminals —didn't wait for the meeting. They knew where Curtis kept their money. So they sent someone directly to the house. Who? I don't know who. I wish I did. I promised you the truth and, folks, the truth is that I don't know who was in that house waiting for Curtis to show up."

Shaw manages a look of remorse. Like he has let everyone down.

"I don't know. But whoever it was, he was wearing Timberland Pros. He was wearing a black coat with a hood. He broke in through the basement window and waited for Curtis to come home and get the money. Waited for him to open up that safe. Then he shot Curtis to death in the bedroom. Point blank. One bullet. He took the cash and disappeared.

"Okay, but why? Why kill Curtis if Curtis is ready to return the money? Again, I don't know. Not for certain. I can imagine that these silent partners of his didn't like being kicked out of a good deal. Maybe they didn't like that Curtis knew their names and faces. Or maybe things just went bad that night in the house. Maybe Curtis started to fight back. I don't know. We may never know."

Shaw moves to the prosecution table and takes another long look at Jaclyn Cavelle. He shakes his head to himself, like he is trying to manage some rising tide of disgust.

"But the question you should be asking yourselves, as jurors charged with finding the truth, is why the prosecution is not planning to share any of what I just told you. How many times has Ms. Cavelle tried to stop the words from coming out of my mouth in this opening statement?"

"Objection." Jaclyn Cavelle is calm, preparing to stand.

Shaw lifts his eyebrows to the jury with a gesture toward the prosecutor. *See what I mean?*

"Sustained. Mr. Shaw, you are to refrain from that kind of commentary."

"Understood, Your Honor," says Shaw in a way that borders on dismissive. "The question you should be asking, ladies and gentlemen, is why the prosecution is trying to pin the murder of Curtis Root on a two-bit pot dealer like Wrigley Menard over there."

Shaw points to his client without turning away. Wrigley looks up pitifully. He tucks a strand of unctuous black hair back behind his ear. Shaw knocks his knuckles against the prosecution table and turns to face the jury.

"Here's a theory for you to think about as you sift through the evidence in this case. Ms. Cavelle is just doing her job. She's ably representing the State of Illinois on the basis of the information she has available to her. She's trying to score a win with a conviction and any conviction will do. But all the *evidence*," Shaw scratches quotation marks in the air with his fingers, "that Ms. Cavelle is going to show you in this case, has come from the Chandler Police Department."

Shaw turns his back on the jury and moves to the center of the room. He slowly, casually pans the gallery of people, as if to make sure everyone is listening. His head stops turning. He could be looking at the reporter who stops typing and looks back, as if concerned the softly clicking keys of his laptop has finally become intolerable.

But Shaw is not looking at the reporter. He's looking directly at Ray.

Ray's body stiffens and he uncrosses his legs. He sits up a little straighter in his seat. His eyes sharpen their attention. Whatever is going on, he knows, suddenly, that he is more than just a spectator. Judging from her expression, Celeste can see it too. Shaw raises his voice.

"And the Chandler Police Department, ladies and gentlemen, is infamous –I tell you it is *infamous* –for its ties to organized crime."

An explosion of motion and sound from the prosecution table as Jaclyn Cavelle rockets to her feet and her notepad spins off the edge and down to the floor.

"Objection! Your Honor, I object to this!"

"Sustained! Mr. Shaw, you will..."

But Mickey Shaw is not stopping. He breaks away from Ray and continues, much louder now, as he turns to face the jury. He points to the photo of the victim.

"The Chandler Police Department is hip-deep in the muck. They are protecting the people who murdered Curtis Root."

"Objection!"

"Sustained! Mr. Shaw!"

Mickey Shaw is shouting.

"The police have manipulated the Illinois Department of Justice..."

"Mr. Shaw!"

"... into railroading my client..."

"Objection!"

"Mr. Shaw!"

"... so that the mob can murder with impunity!"

EIGHT

I'm worried about the reporter. His mouth hangs open like a door with a busted hinge. He stares down at his keyboard like he's watching ten finger-sized seizures.

The room behind me is a turmoil of agitated murmurs. People are loitering. Standing but not yet leaving, like there might be more to see. Jolie has excused the jury and recessed for the day. Two Illinois Troopers have retaken custody of Wrigley Menard, spiriting him away through a side door in the courtroom. He's out of the suit and back into his orange onesie. It's over for the day. But the people are hanging around anyway. Just in case.

Associates for Mickey Shaw and Jaclyn Cavelle are at their respective tables, putting papers into folders and folders into stacks and stacks into boxes and rolling luggage. The lawyers are gone. They accepted the judge's invitation for a discussion in her chambers. I'm guessing Jacklyn has tied Mickey to a chair so the judge can beat him with a rubber mallet. Maybe they're taking turns.

Up front, Celeste has her head down, working busily on something I can't see. That makes this a good time to leave. I start to stand.

"Why was he looking at you?"

I look down at the stringer. He hasn't changed. Mouth open. Fingers flying.

"What?"

"Mickey Shaw. He was looking right at you before he pulled the pin on that grenade. You connected to this case somehow?"

"How do you do that?" I ask.

"What?"

"Type and talk at the same time. How do you do that? I couldn't do that if my life depended on it."

The fingers stop. He looks at me. He's older than I thought. The nimble fingers threw me.

"Lots of practice," he says. "My life does depend on it. Well, my livelihood anyway. What's your name?"

"My friends call me no comment," I say. I finish standing and put on my coat. I make the mistake of looking around. Celeste is suddenly all eyes. She waves. I nod back with something like a smile.

"Do you know Mr. Shaw?" he asks. "Are you with law enforcement? You've kind of got the vibe."

"The vibe?"

"Yeah. I call it the Miranda vibe. Were you involved in Wrigley Menard's arrest?"

"I have the right to remain silent," I say. "Anything I say can and will be used against me."

The man laughs. He pulls a card from his shirt pocket and hands it up to me.

Theodore B. Myerson works for *The Hawk*. It's a scrappy on-line rag based out of some west Chandler basement. The paper is named after the north wind that blows in off Lake Michigan and slices through the streets of Chicago like a flying razor blade. *The Hawk* has a loyal-enough following, particularly in Chandler. It publishes things that other publications —with all their award-winning integrity and pesky journalistic standards —can't or won't print. *The Hawk* traffics in conspiracy culture and public personalities brought low by scandal. It owes no small amount of its subscriber base to a particularly snarky sex column. The personals in the back help keep the freaks from getting lonely.

I look at the card. *Hunting the Story Behind the Story.* That's the motto tucked between Ted's name and that of his employer. Better than *We'll Print Almost Anything,* but not as accurate.

I pocket the card just to be polite. Ted here is making a living just like anyone else. They say the human race owes its existence to parasites. Who am I to judge?

The Camels in my pocket suddenly want some air. "Have a good one," I say, and I start to turn away.

"Okay, look." Ted holds all ten of his spastic fingers up in the air. They quiver in surrender. "It's off the record. It's all just background."

He looks up at me like he's just cleaned my windshield with his sleeve. This is the part where I'm supposed to feel grateful and reach for my wallet. He thinks I'm teetering. He gives me another push.

"I'm just curious." He thrusts out a hand for a shake.

I shake his hand and give him the same nod I gave Celeste.

"Nice to meet you, just curious. I'm just leaving."

I exit the courtroom into a hallway choked with people. They look up at me in knots of twos and threes as I approach and then look away again as I pass, realizing that I'm no one worth paying any attention to. I'm not Mickey Shaw or Jackie Cavelle or a member of a trial team. There is no reason to try to read my face for clues about what any of what just happened in that court room actually means.

Down the hall near the restrooms one of Jaclyn Cavelle's helpers is talking to Arty Dunn. Arty looks to be in his early fifties. Coarse, stick-straight chestnut hair and a wide goatee. I don't know why all the cops in the property crimes division like leaving the middle third of their face unshaved. Arty is looking up from his bench, nodding as he listens to the young, professionally dressed woman.

I know that conversation. I've lived it a hundred times. As a witness you aren't allowed to watch the testimony, so you cool your heels outside the courtroom for an hour, sometimes more, alternately sitting and pacing, because you'd rather be early than late, and then someone who wears a suit much better than you ever will comes out and tells you that things went a little long and that you've wasted your day waiting to be called. So you come back the next day and do it all over again. Easy money, sure. But waiting around at the mercy of a process that I can't see, hear or control makes me feel old.

I can't imagine that it's really so different for anyone else. In the end we're all just waiting around. At some point, this second or the next, today or tomorrow or the next day, it will be our turn. *The morning went a little long; so probably after lunch. Today went a little long. Come back tomorrow. Sit here and wait. Be patient. Distract yourself. Keep yourself entertained while you wait. Bring a book. Make a list of things you need to do.* But then, inevitably, at some point, time will stop. The waiting will end. The big double doors will open and the long finger will emerge from the black folds of the robe. And then it's over for good. Our turn to walk through those doors.

Arty Dunn does not look my direction. Even if he did, he arrived at Chandler PD after I was booted so he doesn't know me from Adam. Soon enough he'll hate me. Soon enough I'll be the enemy.

I keep walking, mindful of Twill's instruction to stay off Arty's radar for the time being.

I make it to the elevator and knuckle the button, looking back at the gabbing throng. They're all of average height. Everyone has hair. The mountain of bricks with a bucket on top is nowhere to be seen.

The elevator doors open and I turn to see Daniel Pleasants inside. He has changed out of the cheap suit and the thing that might have been a tie he was wearing earlier this morning. Now he's in paint-stained jeans and a camouflage hunting coat. We stare at each other inside an elongating second. I go first.

"Mr. Pleasants," I say, wondering at the odds that, had I said nothing, he might have stepped out of the elevator and not recognized me. I should have given those odds a chance to breathe.

"Hey," he says, pointing. "You're… you're… I forgot your name."

"Mackey." I step in, hoping Scooter will go on his way and we can end things here. The man gives me the willies. "Ray Mackey. Chandler Police. IAD."

Scooter stays where he is. I push a button to hold the doors open.

"Mackey!" he exclaims, pointing. "That's right. Officer Mackey. I'm so bad with names and faces." I want to tell him that I bet he remembers the names and faces of teenage girls just fine. But I don't. That would just prolong things. Scooter gestures at my wishful thinking in holding the doors open. "Oh, let 'em close. I'll ride along and come back up. You here for the Menard trial?"

I release the button and the doors slide closed. My eyelids do the same.

"Yeah," I say, feigning coincidence. "You?"

"Yeah, man." He pokes himself in the chest with his thumb. "Witness for the defense. I was here this morning but the judge kicked out all witnesses. I just wanted to, like, sit in. You know?" He gestures. An indecipherable tattoo covers the back of his hand. It starts at the first knuckle of each finger and disappears up into the sleeve of his coat. "Like, just, you know, to get a feel for things."

Once upon a time, Scooter was probably a decent looking guy. Maybe if you saw him from the widow of a moving car, out on some field throwing a football, you'd think, yeah, pretty good-looking kid. Sturdy frame. Blond hair. You'd be willing to bet some money that Daniel Pleasants was in good with the girls. But you'd think differently today. Scooter's frame has turned saggy, and the blond hair has turned white. The eyes, which you never could have seen from that moving car when you placed your bet, are small and dark and too intense beneath their hoarfrost brows. They're too close together, those eyes, hiding in deep sockets like a couple of black eels. Had you been able to see Scooter's eyes from your speeding car all those years ago, you'd have put your money back in your pocket and kept your betting mouth shut.

Because Scooter's always had those eyes. He's always looked a little crazy. He's never been in good with the girls, except in the way that got him arrested and that should have sent him to prison. His teeth are yellow from neglect. One of them on the side is gone entirely. I'm betting that's where he holds his cigarette.

"Nope," I say, like I share his disappointment. "Can't watch the show if you're a witness."

Scooter shakes his head.

"Dumb ass rule if you ask me."

"Why are you here?" I ask. "Defense case is not for another couple weeks at least."

"Thought I'd catch Mickey Shaw on a break. I've got some questions."

"Good luck," I say. The elevator doors slide open. "I suspect Mickey's a little pre-occupied about now."

I step out, hoping we're done. I almost say good-bye. Scooter steps out with me.

"Hold up," he says. He's prepared to follow me out the door to the car. Like we're old friends. I don't want a new old friend. I always seem to lose those. So I stop. He screws up his face into a question mark. "What's the deal with my case, man?"

"What do you mean?"

"What's happening? What's the shitbag got to say for himself?"

Scooter's eyes seem suddenly smaller. Closer together. His voice is too loud. I keep my voice low and calm. Rule number one when dealing with crazy.

"These things take time, Mr. Pleasants. IAD took your complaint three days ago. We'll be following up with Officer Dunn, and with you, in due course. You're going to have to be patient with our process."

"No, no." Scooter says this like I've proposed that he drink from the toilet. "Sorry, man. I'm like fresh out of fucking patience. Understand? That guy is running a game on me, man. He's a fucking shakedown artist with a badge. I'm tired of putting up with his shit. Okay? I'm trying to run a business in this town."

I bite my tongue. It's all I can do to keep from offering my assessment of the three porn shacks that comprise the *Pleasant Palace Adult Books and Video* empire.

Biting my tongue is not enough. I have to look away. Because I'm still facing the elevators, I can see what Scooter cannot. Arty Dunn, stepping off the elevator and headed straight for us. It's happening too fast for me to do anything about it except hope that he keeps moving and minds his business. Fat chance.

"Hey, Mack!" Arty flashes me a big smile and claps me on the shoulder. He slows but doesn't stop. I can feel Scooter next to me turning his attention. Recognizing. Reacting. Arty points at me good-naturedly as he passes. He's walking backward now. "How you been, buddy? Looking forward to talking soon. Maybe we can take care of business over a beer."

"You piece of shit," Scooter shouts at him. "I'm going to fucking bury you, man!"

People are looking. Two of the security officers at the metal detectors give us their full attention.

"Hey there, Mr. Pleasants," calls Arty with a genial wave. "Didn't see you there. Nice camouflage! Almost didn't see you! Take care, pal."

Arty rotates forward just in time to push open the main doors, one with each hand, and step out into the blast of cold sunlight. Before the doors close again Scooter is on me, savage and close. I can smell the sausage he had for breakfast.

"What the fuck, man? Is that how this is going to go? Investigating your best friend over a beer? That's some corrupt bullshit, man!"

I'm not a beer guy. Not anymore. But I'd rather be having a beer with Arty Dunn any day of the week than having this conversation. One of the security officers has decided he needs to leave his post.

"Lower your voice," I tell Scooter. "Calm down. I've never met the man. He's just spinning you up."

"Not what it looked like to me, Ray. You're all a bunch of fucking snakes."

"Gentlemen." The guard is pointing at the front doors before he reaches us. He's got his serious expression on, but I know better. Inside he's giddy at the break in conveyor belt monotony. "Time to take whatever this is outside."

I slip my badge out of my pocket and let it hang between my fingers. First time I've been able to do that in a long, long time. It feels good. Some guys my age can flash photos of their grandkids. Cute, but not as effective. The guard pulls up short, dropping the finger and the attitude.

"Need a hand?" he asks, almost hopeful.

"I'm good," I tell him.

The guard turns on his heels. Scooter keeps at it, pointing at the guy's back.

"Oh, and who's that? Your fucking cousin? Your brother? Another best friend?"

I take a step closer. A basketball wouldn't fit between my face and his.

"I'll say it one more time, Mr. Pleasants. You need to calm down. I don't know Officer Dunn. I've never met the man. And even if I had, it would not make a bit of difference in our investigation."

Scooter inhales to speak but I hold up a hand and keep it there, mostly because of his breath.

"No," I say. "We're done here. We have your complaint. We will investigate in a timely and professional manner, and we'll be in touch as necessary." I jerk my head in the direction of the elevator. "You have yourself a good day."

I turn and start walking. Scooter's words hit me in the back as I am almost to the front doors of the courthouse.

"This is a big hairy cover-up, man! You all protect each other! There is no fucking justice!"

I push through the door and step out into the wind and sun. The world feels like an ice bath on the deck of a clipper ship. I pull up my collar and aim for the parking lot across the street. I have to wait at the curb as a black F-150 roars past. Behind the wheel is a mountain of bricks.

NINE

He's not ready. Look at him. Window open so he can smoke. Blasting the heat. Driving in circles. Going anywhere but where he's supposed to go. He's not ready for the chair.

The chair is behind a desk with his name on it. The desk is under a stack of files inside a room with weak coffee and strong fluorescents and windows that don't open without the help of something big and heavy. All of which is tolerable except that the room is up on the fifth floor of a building chock full of cops. Ray is glad for the badge. Surprisingly so. But the badge comes with that building. And the building comes with all those other people carrying all those other badges.

A lot of those people don't know Ray. They hate him anyway. Not for who he is so much as for what he does in that building, which is to help advance the mission of the Internal Affairs Division of the Chandler Police Department. Which is to investigate cops. Police the police.

The people who actually do know Ray not only hate him for what he's doing now, they also hate him for what he did five years ago. Or, at least, what they think he did, which was to leak vital task force information to José Beggamon, the guy at the top of the single largest, fastest-growing crime syndicate in the midwestern United States. Drugs. Guns. Prostitution. Human trafficking. Beggamon's got his hands into all of it.

Not that those hands come with any fingerprints. All the good guys really have on José Beggamon is a name, which is as real as a seven-dollar bill, and his reputation, which propagates like a series of ghost stories from one police water cooler to the next.

The street calls him Big Man. But he has a thousand names. A thousand faces.

Politicians. Judges. Police. People you'd least expect. Ray used to be one of those least-expected people. Now, for a lot of cops in that building, he's the opposite.

Not fair, certainly. But, like Marlo used to say, the world is a lot flatter than it is fair.

Once Ray makes it up to the fifth floor and is inside the Internal Affairs office, then he can relax. Then it's just the IAD team: Twill and Santiago and Sandra Booth and the staff. But getting up there is awful. The parking lot, hallways and elevators of the Chandler Police Department are nothing but gauntlets of averted eyes and awkward silences. A walk of shame. Every day.

So, no. He's not ready. The poor hump. Driving around like he's looking for a lost dog. Look at him. He should be sitting at his desk hunched over a file. The Root trial recessed early, a gift from the gods of productivity. Ray should be working his backlog, sifting and sorting complaints about everything from sexual harassment to excessive force, to the use of language unbecoming. Twill had said he needed Ray's help. He wasn't kidding. Ray hadn't expected such a mountain of malfeasance, most of it petty. He had expected, instead, mountainous malfeasance. He had expected the worst of the worst.

He had counted on it.

At the very least, Ray had expected to be helping Twill in more meaningful ways: combing the city for signs of whether Suri was still alive. Or surveilling a Chicago dry cleaner for clues as to how Suri had been able to pull the mayor's dry-cleaning ticket from the pocket of a very dirty and now very dead cop on the Big Man payroll named Anthony Rickens. Or even just continuing the mission of ferreting out other Big Man moles from the ranks of the CPD. That was how he wanted to help. That was why he had accepted Twill's offer.

But Twill couldn't do everything at once. The lieutenant had worked the minor miracle of getting Ray reinstated. He'd been the one to put the badge back in Ray's pocket, which had straightened Ray's spine just a little. Ray needs to accept that the reinstatement has come with conditions. He is confined, for the time being, to working the normal fare of IAD cases. However routine. However petty.

He should be working those cases.

Instead, he's sucking down Camels and letting the Impala go wherever it wants to go. He's all the way out in East Chandler. Seventy-Third Street. Seventy-Fourth. The bars are all closed. They drift away behind him, marking lifeless spaces like tombstones in the sun. The liquor stores are open, draped garishly in neon like hookers out turning an early dollar.

He takes a right on Warner.

Bucks is the place with dollar bills on the ceiling and Ray's tab under the counter. It comes and goes, locked tight for another five hours. There have been days when Doris opened up *Bucks* and his foot was in the front door before she could turn on the lights. Not today. Not for a while now.

But look at the fingers drumming the steering wheel. He wants a drink. One shot of Old Forester would work wonders.

Not today. Driving past *Bucks* is about as close to that kind of relief as he can get. He promised himself. Not a drop until sundown. Not a drop while he is working. If nothing else, that's what it meant to be back on the job.

Ray cranks the wheel until he's pointing west again, toward downtown Chandler and the building full of cops who hate him.

In his chest he aches for Marlo. Still. Now more than ever.

He pushes the accelerator.

TEN

Lieutenant Twill is partial to blue pinstripes. They make him look even taller and leaner than God intended. His fingernails are always well-manicured. I think he polishes his head.

He's on me before I can get my coat off. He wants a debrief. I bypass my desk and follow him to his office. It's like following a well-dressed Q-Tip. Twill closes the door behind us as I'm pulling my arms out of my sleeves.

"What's the word?" he asks.

"Cold," I say. "I've got a lot more words to go with that one, but I need to thaw them out first."

I sit as Twill moves behind his desk. He's not amused. I hit the highlights of my morning in Judge Jolie's courtroom. When I get to the end, he stares at me in disbelief.

"The Chandler Police Department is protecting the people who murdered Curtis Root," says Twill.

"That's what he said."

"The CPD is running interference for the mob."

"That's the theory."

"Because the department is lousy with corruption."

"Yeah. *Hip-deep in the muck* I think were his words."

I decide to leave out the long and knowing stare that Mickey Shaw had given me before he dropped that particular bomb. It was probably nothing but my over-active imagination. My hypersensitivity at being known by so many as a corrupt cop. I don't want Twill to regret bringing me on board. That will come soon enough.

"Jesus," says Twill.

"His name didn't come up, but it's still early in the case. Maybe Jesus was the wheel man."

The phone rings. Twill picks up the receiver and listens.

"I'll tell him," he says. "Okay. That's fine. It will be a few minutes. Thank you." Twill hangs up and looks at me. "You've got a visitor," he says.

"Me? Who?"

Scooter Pleasants is suddenly in my head, answering my own question. I feel a pang of worry over what he might have eaten for lunch.

"No idea," says Twill. "Sandra put whoever it is in the small meeting room. Let's finish up and you can go find out. How was Jacklyn Cavelle with all of this?"

"Jackie turned herself into a rocket and never came back down to earth. Jolie had been shutting her down all morning over Root buying weed and laundering money. The prosecution wanted a clean, upstanding victim, but Mickey had other plans and the judge was clearing a path for him to make his case."

"Unusual for her."

"Surprised me a little too. But then Mickey dropped this police corruption thing on the table like a rotting fish. Jolie wasn't happy. I'll be looking for bruises tomorrow."

"Mickey does love the chaos."

"Yeah, and gavels to the skull. And briefcases full of money."

Twill tuts out the civics lesson I should have seen coming.

"Everybody's entitled to a defense."

"Sure. Why not. Launder the mob's money as legal fees while you accuse the victim of money laundering and you accuse the police of collaborating with the mob, hoping to acquit the client that the mob is paying you to defend."

Twill laughs as he reads a blue message slip and then wads it up. He drops it in the trash. "You don't know any of that, Mack."

"You're right," I say. "I don't."

He gives me a dubious look.

"You're saving that one for your next book maybe."

"Maybe. It's eerie how well you know me, LT."

"Right. Anything between Arty Dunn and his accuser today?"

"Funny you should ask," I say.

I bring Twill up to speed on my encounter with Arty Dunn in the courthouse lobby. The story makes his head itch.

"Thought you haven't met him."

"I haven't. Arty was ringing Scooter's bell. It worked too. Scooter is now convinced the fix is in." I jerk my thumb over my shoulder. "I'm guessing that Scooter's the one waiting for me so he can yell at me some more."

"Comes with the territory," says Twill. "Every cop we open up a file on thinks we're biased as a matter of principle. We hate the badge. We're the enemy within. And every complainant thinks we're out to protect our brothers and sisters in blue. There's no winning that part of the game, Mack. You just have to work the case. Hunt down the facts. Write the report. Move on. That's the job."

"Hey, at least the job's not about figuring out whether the Mayor of Chicago is in bed with Big Man. Or hunting moles right here in our own department. Or finding Suri, who could already be dead. Because any of that would be, you know, awful."

Twill just looks at me. He's given me the speech already today. He's not going to give it again. I don't want to hear it anyway. I let him off the hook.

"Yeah, I know," I say. "You want me to be patient. I'm ten years older than you are, LT. The younger can't lecture the older about being patient. It's supposed to work the other way around. My father tried to teach me patience."

"Didn't take?" Twill asks. I shake my head.

"Guess I was a hopeless case. He left when I was four. Ran off in the middle of the night with a half-naked woman. She was painted on a bottle of rum."

Twill sniffs a laugh.

"I'm hoping your mother was a more patient parent."

"Less. She took a powder when I was two. Met a man who drove a taxi. He was doing about sixty through a red light in Chinatown."

"Jesus, Mack."

"Yeah, him I met at the orphanage. Jesus and I never got along much. The nuns always took his side. Look, LT, I know I've got to keep my head down. I said I will, and I will. What do you want to do about Arty Dunn?"

Twill shrugs.

"Well, at this point, there's no reason not to get him in a room. He obviously knows about the complaint. Go ahead and set up an interview. Copy the union."

"Hang on." I cross my arms. "Shouldn't that be a little concerning?"

"What?"

"That Arty Dunn knows we've got a complaint against him, before we've notified him about that complaint."

Twill is quiet, pursing his lips. He takes an interest in a paperclip.

"Good question," he says.

"I mean does the whole goddamned building leak?"

"Maybe Scooter shot his mouth off. Maybe he threatened Arty with a complaint. Maybe Arty sees IAD talking to Scooter in the courthouse lobby and just puts two and two together."

"Pretty quick math," I say, trying my best to sound dubious. "Arty's eyes lit up in the split-second he stepped off that elevator. And how does he know I'm IAD?"

Twill looks at me like I'm crazy. I am crazy. But the look doesn't mean to imply anything diagnosable. He knows about my disorder. He doesn't seem to care and he's managed to convince the higher-ups that my kind of crazy is all part of same frame up that got me kicked out of the department in the first place. I think he believes the same thing. So the look doesn't mean crazy-crazy. Just stupid-crazy.

"Come on, Mack," he says. "You're a minor celebrity in this building, and not the glamorous kind. Word gets around. You're thinking about leaks, but I'll bet Arty knew all about you before Scooter Pleasants darkened our door."

"You think?"

"It's not impossible," says Twill.

I stand, knocking his desk once with a knuckle.

"Lots of things aren't impossible, LT."

ELEVEN

Ray leaves Twill for his own desk, made of black metal and tucked inside a gray fabric cubicle. The walls of the cubicle are just high enough to encourage a false sense of privacy but not so high as to encourage absenteeism. You have to crouch down in these things to be alone.

There are five of these cubicles in the IAD office. They each come with a shelf for light-weight essentials. Ray's shelf is completely empty except for a small photo of Marlo. Which means the shelf is completely full. The shelf should buckle and collapse from the weight of her memory.

It's the photo he took of her camping, two Septembers after they were married. In the foreground is the campfire. Behind her is the amber sunset-glow of the pond at the McCully Heritage Project, autumn rioting from every direction. She is in the blue flannel shirt he still has in the back of his closet, sitting on a log, arms folded over her knees. She'd worn her hair longer back then. Brown tendrils levitate in the breeze.

For someone so expert at photographic surveillance, Marlo was never fond of being photographed. That tended to make for portraits of consent and resignation. Like this one. An imminently practical woman indulging an act of sentimentality. She never mugged or flashed her infectious smile. She did not primp her hair or pop her soulful brown eyes. Nor did she play games of evasion. She simply looked and waited for the click.

The result was something hauntingly honest. Eternal. Heartbreaking.

Once the camera was down, she'd usually burst out laughing.

Ray hangs his coat over the back of his chair. His screen-saver cycles randomly through a series of stern reminders and tired aphorisms in red script lettering.

Age is nothing to joke about.

Touching is tricky.

See something, say something.

The computer is a spare sent up from Human Resources on the first floor. Whoever had it last was on PowerPoint duty. Ray's a closet luddite, which means he has no idea how to make the messages stop, but he's too embarrassed to ask for help.

Report your relationships.

Each command swells, filling the screen before fading away. It feels like a kind of computerized telepathy. Like he's tapping into someone else's thought bubbles.

Look before you leap.

He sorts through the stack of green files until he finds the one that has Scooter Pleasants' complaint inside. He grabs a pen and a notepad and heads for the smaller of the two meeting rooms that IAD uses for interviews.

On the way he passes by Santiago's empty cubicle. He shakes his head, averting his eyes. He's trying not to think of Santiago, sitting in a car outside the same Chicago dry cleaner that puts the starch in Mayor Royce's monogrammed shirts. Keeping track of who comes and goes. Taking pictures of people and license plates.

Look at him pull his shoulders back. He's trying not to feel sorry for himself. He's thinking that it should be him out there in the car with a camera. It should be him looking for an explanation for why one of Big Man's brutes had the mayor's dry-cleaning ticket in his pocket.

Of course, it's not like Ray can begrudge Santiago anything. Ray's head would be all over the side of a rusty railcar were it not for Santiago.

But still. I can see it in his eyes. He thinks it should be him out there.

TWELVE

I can feel my mood starting to tilt downhill. It's the thought of Santiago out on the street doing real work while I'm taking dictation from a convicted pedophile… well, a pedophile who has been convicted of something else … indulging his persecution complex by listening to how he's been done wrong by the Chandler Police Department. It's enough to bring up my breakfast. I haven't had any breakfast. I'm starving.

I push open the door to the smaller meeting room ready with a warning for Scooter Pleasants: he gets tossed out into the hallway the first time he calls me a name, raises his voice, or breathes on my face.

The warning never makes it out. The person at the table is not Scooter Pleasants. The person at the table is the opposite of Scooter Pleasants. In every way.

The woman stands and smiles, a bit nervously it seems. The young girl next to her looks up at me in the doorway and sets down a blue marker next to a collection of others. Then she stands up too. I feel like the president.

"Mr. Mackey?"

I'm guessing mid-to-late thirties. Older than she looks if this is her kid. Pure, pale, wrinkleless skin, tightly wrapping a round, Slavic face. Full, ruddy cheeks beneath watery, gray-blue eyes, dramatically dark brows, and a healthy head of mahogany hair that brushes her shoulders. Her genes are tinkering with the odometer. When she's eighty she'll look fifty. Fraudulent, sure, but no one in her life is ever going to complain. Her lips are red and plump with confidence. They make the introduction like a couple of pros.

"I'm Nadia King," she says. "This is my daughter, Danika. I'm so sorry for the intrusion."

"Quite all right," I say, closing the door. "How can I help you?"

"I was planning to just make an appointment. The woman…" she points a finger at the office behind me, "I don't know her name… she just told us to wait in here. I can come back another time if this is inconvenient."

I keep my face in check. No sense broadcasting that I don't care why she's here. Compared to what I thought I was in for when I opened the door, I'm ready to clear my schedule for the rest of the day. It will suffice to tell her there is no need to make an appointment. I never get the chance.

"I'm coloring a blue dragon," says Danika. She's got the bright, thin voice of a talking doll on a bedroom shelf. She still has her coat on. A pair of wool mittens and a red wool hat are on the table. Her blond hair is gathered into a ponytail.

I scratch my head and squint down a look of confusion.

"Don't know if I believe in blue dragons. Pretty sure dragons are purple."

Her expression is suddenly scolding. Then she follows up.

"No. Dragons are green. But mine is blue because blue is magic." She holds up the coloring book laying open in front of her. The dragon is upside down. "And the fire is green. And his eyes are yellow diamonds."

"He looks only half-blue," I say, like I'm trying to make up my mind.

"I just started, mister," scolds Danika. Nadia suppresses a laugh.

I set down Scooter's folder and my pad and pen on the table. I pull out a chair and sit. Nadia, too, lowers herself back down into her chair. Danika remains standing. She's waiting for me to concede. I do.

"That," I point at the drawing, "is the most ferocious upside-down half-blue magic dragon with yellow-diamond eyes I've ever seen in my life. It's my new favorite of all the dragons."

It's all she needs. Danika drops back down into her chair, seizing the marker. Her head is bowed and the pink tip of tongue squeezes itself through the corner of her tiny mouth like it wants to supervise.

"So." I move my attention from daughter to mother. I click my pen and date the top sheet on my notepad. I make a silent wager that Nadia's been on the receiving end of some vulgarity from a jackass cop who thinks his badge gives him license to harass. Some rookie wrote her a speeding ticket and offered to tear it up for the price of a date. She doesn't want the cop to lose his job over it, but she thinks someone should know about it just the same. "How can I be of assistance?"

"I got your name from Jack Kline," she says. I shrug, not connecting with the name. "He said you call him Jimmy. He doesn't like that name by the way."

"Jimmy?" I say, surprised. So much for keeping control over my face.

"He's Jack to me. I know the two of you are not…" I watch her dress up a grimace as a smile as she chooses her words. "Not especially close. He thought you might be able to help."

"Okay. And how do you know… Jack?"

"I'm in real estate and Jack's a lighting supply contractor. We crossed paths every so often and one thing led to another. We kind of saw each other for a while. Didn't really take." She shrugs, almost apologetically. "I can be a pill."

Maybe. I don't know this woman, however much I might want to. But I know Jimmy. My impulse is to let her off the hook.

"It would take a lot of pills to put up with the Jimmy I know."

"He's not so bad," she says. "A lot better than my ex, anyway. Jack just wasn't quite ready for a family, I think." Nadia silently tips her head down toward Danika, who is now laser-focused on one of sixteen dragon talons. "And she always comes first. I haven't seen Jack for months."

"It's been years for me," I tell her. "I figured he was in Florida. Jimmy always rambled on about the Keys. Wanted to pet a marlin."

Nadia laughs at this. It's the kind of sound you want to go on for a lot longer than it does. I've always known my brother-in-law as an idiot. Nadia's laugh proves it all over again. Kid or no kid, who lets that laugh go?

"He let you call him Jimmy?" she asks.

"Didn't have much choice," I say. "His big sister called him Jimmy. I just followed her lead."

Nadia's expression melts into something pleading. Her hand extends, flattening against the table.

"Jack told me about Marlo," she says softly. "I'm so sorry about your wife, Mr. Mackey."

I'm sorry too. She doesn't know how sorry. No sense in giving her a tour of the abyss. I give her some mock reproach instead.

"First, Nadia, call me Mack unless you're trying to make me feel old, in which case, mission accomplished. Second, thank you for the condolence. It has been some years since she died."

"But it feels like yesterday," she says. "Doesn't it?"

"Yes," I say, feeling the edge of the world somewhere nearby. "You're right about that. I hope you're still too young to have lost anyone you love."

Nadia swallows and looks down at the table. I can see I've stepped in it. She's not too young after all.

"I'm sorry," I say. I shouldn't have assumed. Nadia shrugs without looking.

"My big brother," she says with a sigh. "Jovah. He was killed ten years ago in May. He's… he's kind of why I'm here, Mr…..." She looks up at me. God, those eyes. "He's kind of why I'm here, Mack."

"Okay." I lean back in my chair. "Well then this is the part where I stop running my mouth and listen."

I watch her pull into herself, like she's thinking about where to begin. Her expression darkens from daylight to dusk.

"My brother… Jovah was a police officer for the Chicago Police Department. He…"

"Hold on," I say, breaking my four-second vow of silence. "Sorry. Joe? Your brother was Joe Novak?"

She nods. The sad smile is back.

"He is Jovah to me," she says. "My family is Belarusian."

"I know that case," I say. "I didn't know your brother, but I know the Wayne Bishop case. Everybody does."

Truth is, I don't know if everybody really does know about Wayne Bishop. I'm amazed these days at what people don't know. Not knowing things is our new national pastime. But everybody who was reading a Chicago newspaper ten years ago knows. Every cop in Illinois knows about the murder of Joe Novak.

Nadia is nodding.

"I thought you might be familiar," she says. "Jack said you would."

"That must have been an ordeal for your mother," I say. "To go through all of that. What a mess."

"Terrible."

"She attended the trial? What there was of it anyway?"

"No, no. She was too fragile. Alex and I had to work shifts staying with her at home."

"Alex?"

"Alexi. My younger brother. For a while we thought we feared that after losing Jovah we would lose her too. The trauma was too much for her, on top of the grief. Nightmares that Wayne Bishop would be set free and would come back to kill her in her sleep. It pushed her over the edge, I think. She kept deteriorating, even after the case was over and Bishop was killed. She's in assisted living now."

"I'm very sorry to hear that, Nadia," I say. Danika holds up the dragon.

"I'm making red nose holes," she declares. "Because there's fire in his nose, not just in his mouth."

"Thought you said the fire has to be green," I tell her. "I'm confused."

I can see the question stumps her. She pulls the book back, assessing her work, frowning in concentration. Then she shakes her head.

"It comes out green, but the *inside* fire is red because that's the hottest. Inside is the hottest."

"You're the expert," I say with a deferential nod. Danika dives back in and I look to Nadia. "You've got an artist on your hands."

Nadia smiles and strokes the back of Danika's head. She looks back at me.

"I don't want to waste your time. Let me tell you why I'm here. My mother is trying to recover something taken from her home the night of Jovah's murder. Something Wayne Bishop took, I suppose so he could sell it. It ended up as evidence, but we never got it back."

"What is it?"

She starts to shape the air with her hands, holding something invisible over the table.

"It's a hand-painted, wooden… Do you know what a *matryoshka* doll is? Babushka dolls. Nesting…"

"Yeah, yeah." Now I'm making my own invisible snowman. "Little… like one inside the other, smaller and smaller. Russian women and girls."

"Yes. Exactly. She had one of those on a shelf. In her living room. It's very old. Given to her by her mother who had received it as a gift from her mother, my great grandmother, Verochka Volkova. I have no idea what it's worth. Probably nothing. But it's of tremendous sentimental value to my mother."

"Hmm." I scratch my head. "Well, they'd certainly want to keep all the evidence in case of any appeal. That's standard. But Bishop plead guilty. There was no appeal. And once he met his maker in prison… that's it. No need to hold on to the evidence after that."

"That's my understanding too. And they've returned all the other things Bishop stole."

"Ah. They have."

"Yes. All the things my mother does not really care about."

"But not the doll," I confirm.

"No. We've tried."

"What specifically have you tried?"

"We've called the police. We have written and called the district attorney."

"Barbara Bannon?"

"Yes, but also the other one. Her predecessor. Mr. Kimball. He's moved away."

"Roger Kimball's long gone," I confirm. "What does Bannon tell you?"

"She insists it was returned with the other evidence. But it wasn't."

"You're sure."

"Positive. We were waiting for it. We never got it. I think maybe someone over there just kept it. They just liked it and kept it. The doll is beautiful if you like that sort of thing. I don't know what else to do but hire a lawyer. Jack suggested that maybe you could ask some questions before we took that step. I'm not really interested in hiring someone to sue the city for a wooden doll."

I turn the problem over in my head. She doesn't like the silence.

"Jack knows you don't like him much," she says. "I don't know the details. But he said you've got a good reputation. He thought maybe you'd be able to get to the bottom of things."

A good reputation. The words are an obscene punchline to a mean joke.

It hits me that Jimmy has been living under a rock. He's got no idea I was booted. No idea my new reputation is as a suspected criminal collaborator. A double agent whispering secrets to Big Man. No idea I've spent the last few years writing pulp fiction inside a bottle of bourbon. All Jimmy ever seems to know is what he needs from other people.

A month after Marlo's funeral Jimmy poked my house in the doorbell, asking to borrow ten thousand dollars. It was money he knew Marlo would have given him. We'd have fought about it and maybe ruined a dinner or two, but Marlo would have won. Marlo always won. But at that time Marlo was suddenly gone forever and I was still reeling. Jimmy played my grief like a pro. He watched from my dining room table as I silently argued with myself as Marlo's stand-in. Marlo won again. I'd forked over a check and Jimmy promised to pay it back as soon as his latest venture —a roof gutter repair company —bore some fruit.

I am many things, most of them not so flattering. It so happens that idiot is not on that list. I knew I'd never see the money again. Just like I knew Jimmy's business start-up story was a ruse. Jimmy's extensive experience with gutters has never required any ladders. I figured he was off to Florida to put my ten grand on some greyhound chasing a metal rabbit. Jimmy wouldn't have fooled Marlo either. No one ever fooled Marlo. But Marlo would have given Jimmy the money anyway.

So, I gave Jimmy what he came for. Then I made him help me move some heavy furniture around the house. We muscled a big oak desk out of the garage and up two flights of stairs into Marlo's old sewing room just so I could have a place to write my mysteries with a view of the neighborhood. We caught our breath over a beer and an awkward silence and then I was glad to see him go. Wherever Jimmy has been since, and whatever he has been doing with himself and my money, he has not been keeping up with current events.

"How'd you find me?" I ask.

"Jack said you were a homicide detective. This was months ago, before, you know, we called it quits. I called and asked for you, but no one got back to me. I finally just decided to come by. They sent me up here." She shakes her head in a kind of soft bewilderment, her eyes searching mine for encouragement. "Do you have any ideas?"

Ideas. Yes. I do have ideas. All of my best ideas all involve taking Nadia and little Danika and her dragon out for pizza and ice cream, just so I don't have to open the Scooter Pleasants file in front of me. But I know that's not what she's asking.

"Chicago and Chandler are different police departments," I say. "I don't know how much help I can really be. I appreciate Jimmy's confidence, but I'd hate to get your hopes up."

"I have no expectations," she says. "Only that it might be worth having someone on the inside ask the questions. Maybe you'd get some meaningful follow-up. I can pay you for the help. I can…"

"Stop." My hands are up. "You're not paying me anything. Civilians don't pay cops. Pay your taxes. And I'm not sure I can do anything. I'll make some calls. I'll try to get some answers. How can I reach you?"

She recites her phone number and I write it down on my pad.

"I can't tell you how much my family appreciates the help, Mr. Mackey. My mother especially."

"Mack," I correct, holding out my hand. She leans in and takes it between both of hers. The soft envelopment is a bodily sensation. I wonder how I have lasted so long without that feeling. Nadia smiles.

"Thanks, Mack."

THIRTEEN

He's at the window. Notepad in one hand, mug of weak coffee in the other.

Five floors down sits the police-only parking lot, frozen and wind-blasted to a bright shine and dusted with sand to keep the City of Chandler from slipping on lawsuits. The striped wooden arm of the security gate is stuck at a forty-five-degree angle like a minute hand stuck on the number two. Maybe it's the cold. That's the explanation for most problems recently.

A man in coveralls is banging the thing with a wrench, trying to take the gate off its bolt.

Ray doesn't care about the gate. Or the man with the wrench. He's watching a young woman and a younger girl cross the street to the public parking lot. They're holding hands. The girl wants to hop her way across. Her hat bounces on her head like a red frog, egging her on.

"Scooter Pleasants sure knows how to clean himself up," says Twill from behind. I can tell Ray is surprised to have been caught watching her. Embarrassed even. No one else would ever see that. But I do. Ray doesn't let on.

"Drinking bleach wouldn't clean up Scooter," says Ray. "I might recommend it to him anyway."

"What's her deal?" asks Twill, stepping up to the window.

"Friend of my brother-in-law. Just needs a favor."

"Oh?"

"Couple of phone calls. Lunch hour, off-the-clock stuff."

Moonlighting is strictly forbidden. Ray can tell Twill has other questions lined up in the silence, hands waving in the air. Twill sends them all away.

"I need the body cam analysis on Hernandez. Report is due in two weeks. And don't forget to notice up a meeting with Arty and the IFOP."

Ray lifts the cup and drinks.

Nadia is packing Danika into the back seat of a small, blue car. She straightens and closes the door, hair in the wind. Ray turns his back on the window.

"That's next, LT," he says. "Can't wait."

FOURTEEN

I spend some quality time in my cubicle, poking at my keyboard.

It's the muscle memory in my fingers that makes me think of the half-finished novel waiting on my laptop now locked in the truck of my car. Detective McMannis is about to be discovered outside a Chinatown *Target*, wiping down a dead man's Pontiac. My fingers want to help McMannis out of his predicament. My eyes want to find Phil up on the big oak desk at the window, curled up next to a bottle of Old Forester. My ears are listening for Ella. Billie. Dinah.

An office phone trills all my senses into a sulk of disappointment. My coffee cries out for a spike of something from a flask I refuse to carry. I can't drink what I don't have. It's either moderation now or the wagon later. I don't want to be that guy.

I put together a standard pink sheet for Arty Dunn and the Illinois Fraternal Order of Police: "Notice of Investigation pertaining to a complaint of alleged misconduct in the performance of official duties." I request a meeting in the IAD offices late tomorrow afternoon, knowing that Arty will be waiting to take the stand in the Root trial earlier in the day.

Not that it matters. This is a choreographed dance. First, I send out the notice. Then the IFOP will call to reschedule for a later date, far too many calendar pages into the future. Then we'll get on the phone and negotiate something in the middle that nobody likes. It's a civil bureaucratic game of *How Much Do I Hate You* that IAD and the IFOP like to play with each other before all the knives come out into the open.

I print out the pink sheets and sign them and put them in the box for hand delivery. Then I send out the emails just to make all the color-coded paper a waste of time, trees and dye.

That done, I try my best to focus on the other files on my desk. On top of the stack is a complaint of excessive force used in removing an intoxicated vandal from a squad car.

Under that file is a race complaint by the mother of a teenager, hauled out of her history class by two officers on an apparently baseless tip that the girl has been making teenage dreams come true out behind the gymnasium.

The worst of them is the complaint about a white motorist named Edith Adams shot and killed in a crossfire between four cops and a Honduran cab driver named Jaime Hernandez. Jaime was wanted for violation of his parole. A tip that he had a firearm in his car turned out legit. IAD's question is whether turning the crowded *Food Mart* parking lot into the OK Corral was a good idea. Edith Adams' family —one husband and three kids —doesn't think so.

I pull out the Hernandez file. I'm not the lead. All the ink spilled to date makes it too high profile for me to carry. So, the case belongs to Twill. My job is to write up an analysis of all the witness statements and to re-summarize the initial summaries of four body camera recordings.

Good desk work, in other words. Keeps me out of trouble and away from shady drycleaners.

I give it my best. Twenty minutes and I can't get through the first witness statement, Agatha Cullion, a retired insurance agent who had dropped her eggs and orange juice to crawl under a nearby pickup truck as the bullets starting flying. My attention drifts, leaving Agatha to listen to panicked screams and to watch the orange juice gurgle past, floating yolks out across the dirty ice in front of her. The only thing in my head is my conversation with Nadia King.

I can't tell you how much my family appreciates the help, Mr. Mackey. My mother especially.

I close the Hernandez file and open up the Chicago police force directory. Barbara Bannon's name is in the B's right where it's supposed to be, minding its p's and q's. I don't expect a District Attorney to answer her own phone, but that doesn't stop her.

"You mean *the* Raymond Mackey?" Barbara asks.

"No," I say. "The other one. The one no one wants to turn into a hood ornament."

"I don't want to run you over, Ray. I want to shake your hand."

"You do?"

"Yes. I read all the Chicago IAD reports on what went down last year in the railyard. And Bloomington too. And Dekalb. I didn't know Smith, but I knew Tony Rickens. Not well. I put him on the stand a couple of times. But I knew he was bad news. Guess I didn't know just how bad. You're lucky to be alive."

"True," I say. "That sound you don't hear are champagne corks all over town not popping."

Barbara laughs a little.

"Not surprised," she says. "It's going to be a long road back, Raymond. Especially with the rank and file. They don't read the reports I do. Twill's in your corner. Keep your head down and do good work. Climb out of it. What can I do for you?"

What she can do for me is purchase space in the *Tribune* and share her opinion with the entire world. She can subpoena a meeting with every person who has ever heard my name and spread the gospel of my innocence. But I'm concerned that's asking too much on the first phone call.

"I'm trying to help out a woman named Nadia King," I say.

"Ahh," Barbara says. "The missing doll."

"Yeah. She said you've spoken."

"Several times. She's tenacious, I'll give her that. But there's no *there*, there, Ray. We've looked. The doll was checked into evidence when they arrested Wayne Bishop and tossed his apartment. It was returned to Ivah Novak with a box of her other things a month or so after Bishop took his last shower."

My computer gets bored from the lack of attention and nods off. It dreams like an electronic fortune cookie.

Mind the clock! Don't steal time!

"You think someone in the system could have pinched it?" I ask.

Barbara laughs a little at that.

"You mean risk getting fired and going to jail over a wooden doll? Come on."

"Have you run that theory to ground? I'm just asking the question, Barbara. I don't know anything."

"I've got better things to do, Ray. We've all got better things to do. No, I have not run that one to ground. The paperwork shows the doll was returned. That's good enough for me. Have you looked into Ivah Novak? I understand she's gone around the bend. Odds are it's behind a couch cushion, don't you think?"

"Yeah," I say. "Most of my life and half of my money is somewhere in my couch cushions. That would be my bet too. I haven't talked to Mrs. Novak. You're my first call. How many rules are we breaking if you email me the evidence file?"

"Fine by me," she says. "Cases don't get any deader. The whole thing is archived at this point. As long as it's not coming from my office. Attorney-client and all that. I'll need to talk to someone with a badge. What's your address?"

I give Barbara Bannon my email and thank her for the help.

"Good luck being back in the mix, Ray," she says. "It's going to be rough for a while. Watch yourself."

"Thanks," I say. "Always do."

FIFTEEN

Five o'clock and a handful of seconds. Ray zips up his coat and steps out into the icy talons of the hawk. He holds the door for a long-limbed man coming up the concrete steps. He takes them two at a time like he's running uphill hurdles, pressing the flats of his palms against his ears to keep them out of the wind.

The man looks up and gasps out a thank you before they can recognize each other.

Stretch Martin has worked CPD Homicide for donkey's years. He and Ray go way back. Stretch knew Marlo even before Ray did. He choked up in the middle of his toast at the wedding. Sweet guy, Stretch. Like a brother.

"Should've left those ears at home," says Ray.

"Fuck you, Mack."

Home. That's exactly where he wants to take his own ears and every other part of him. He wants to go into his kitchen, rip open a box, slide a brick out onto a plate and put the plate into the microwave. Light a fire. Put on some music. Pour out a splash of Forester and tell Phil about his day until she's stretched out and purring up a soft storm. Open up his laptop and write Detective McMannis out of his jam.

But he can't go home. Not just yet. He owes Doris a visit.

He descends the stairs as fast as he can manage without breaking his neck. He's near frozen by the time he reaches the Impala and seals himself inside. He starts it up and turns the blower to full even though he knows that anything warm is still five minutes away. He fires up a Camel to keep his lungs from shivering. He opens a gap at the top of the window.

Ray puts the Impala in reverse, maneuvering the wheel with two fingers, keeping the other hand stuffed into his coat pocket. Outside, the lampposts are swaying and the wind is blowing away the last of the daylight. The long wooden arm on the security gate is completely gone now, probably reclining on a shelf in some dimly lit, well-heated warehouse.

He finds the road and squeezes the gas. He aims for East Chandler.

Marlo never cared two hoots for any holiday on the calendar. The more patriotic or religious the holiday, the less she cared. The quickest way to irritate Marlo was to tell her how to think about a particular day of the week. But she was always big on birthdays.

Anniversaries are personal, Ray. And birthdays are the most personal of all anniversaries. Another trip around the sun should get you a hug and a kiss at the finish line from anyone who's glad you're still alive. Those are your friends.

The last five of his birthdays have come and gone without Marlo waiting for him at the finish line. Old Forester had always been there, trying to pick up the slack. Old Forester and Phil and Doris.

Those are your friends.

SIXTEEN

Seventy-Fourth and Warner is coming to life. *Prancers*, where desperation gets naked and climbs a fire pole every night from five until two, is thudding its usual bump-and-grind on the corner. A tall man in a short coat is looking to get warm in all the wrong ways. He hunches in the wind, pulling open a door to a red light that throbs around the black silhouette of a two-hundred-eighty-pound man on a stool. Tiny Tyke is all about birthdays. More than almost anything, Tiny cares about when you were born.

I keep rolling up the block. On the opposite side of the street is *The Bar*. I've been inside twice, years ago, both times to flash a badge and ask a lot of personal questions. The owner of *The Bar* has devoted the same attention to ambiance that he put into coming up with the name. It draws a rough crowd; bikers and bangers and three-time losers looking to connect with old cellmates. The stereo is missing a volume knob.

A few doors down is *The Wicked Squid*. Used to be a barbershop in another life, back when the whole neighborhood could hold its head up a little higher. Now the old barbershop belongs to a Korean tattoo artist, JoJo Lee. JoJo's in his early thirties with a disarming smile and a design fetish for motorcycles and dragons. He makes his money off the intoxication and sexual frustration that drifts his way from up the street. JoJo is South Chandler's answer to the sea anemone, plucking easy food out of the current.

I cross Seventy-Third, pull into the corner lot and park. I can't bring myself to stop the chugging of warm air out of the vents. I kill the lights, keep the motor running and stare out the window at *The Bodega* across the street. I can see Rocky Esposito inside holding court with his customers. He's moving his arms in wild circles to tell a story for which, if I know Rocky, there is no ending in sight. At some point the icy wind will be a preferable fate and the customers will take their change and receipts and their bags of snacks and smokes and make a move for the exit. Rocky will keep at it until the door is all-the-way closed again. Then he'll wait for the next one.

A pair of headlights wash my rearview as someone parks. It's my cue to stop avoiding the cold and get a move on. I cut the engine and pop the trunk, stepping out into the weather. I walk around back to get the thing I'm here to deliver. I grab the bag and close the trunk. Ten spaces away a truck idles, droning into a howl of wind that devours white smoke from the tailpipe like something savage.

I'm obviously not the only one delaying the inevitable.

I turn up my collar and push into the gust, out of the parking lot, across the street and up the block until I'm standing just outside *Bucks*. There's a tall pile of dirty black rags in the doorway. It's got a hairy white face on top.

"Spare a dollar?" asks the man. His voice is deep and grainy and tired. "Trying to get out of this wind."

I put the bag under my arm and fish my hand into my back pocket.

"There's a hostel three blocks north," I say, opening my wallet. "Smells something awful, but it's cheap and its warm." I pull out a five. A dirty hand emerges from the bundle and takes it. "Unless maybe you're planning on buying honest Abe here a drink."

"Night's young," he says, disappearing the bill into his folds. The man's eyes are wind-boiled and veined red with cold. They slip away and reappear in a slow blink. "Thanks, brother."

I pull open the door to *Bucks* and step inside.

It's cozy and womblike with low-wattage amber lighting and the smell of roasted nuts. The quiet applause is not for me. It's forty-five years old and was intended for Carmen McCrae as she leans into "A Song for You" at Sugar Hill in San Francisco.

The entire ceiling is covered in thumb-tacked dollar bills. Hence the name. A couple thousand George Washingtons ripple in the sudden breeze like an upside-down lawn. All those bills are autographed. I'm guessing half of the signatures are mine.

Kyle Aubrey looks up from behind the bar as the door closes. Not just Kyle. Everybody. Maybe fifteen people, singles and doubles, shift and turn and size me up. I'm a temporary diversion, soon forgotten.

"Look what the weather blew in," says Kyle. He's got a clean collegiate look to him, but I'm guessing that's only because he showers every day before class. "Haven't seen you since yesterday this time."

"Smartass," I say, loosening my coat and bathing gloriously in warm air. "Do that thing you do, kid."

"Coming up, Mack," he says reaching for the bottle.

"Where's the birthday girl?" I ask, looking around.

Kyle puts a tumbler on the bar and pours out three fingers.

"In the back getting on her coat. Five minutes later and you'd have missed her."

I put the bag on the bar and take a stool. Kyle and I shoot the breeze as I nurse the bourbon like I don't care much; like I haven't been imagining this moment all day. I'm just starting to think about the next one when Doris shows, hugging me from behind. I talk to her in the mirror behind the bar.

"I'm supposed to do the hugging, Doris," I say. "Let me look at you."

She lets go and I stand and turn. I hold her face in my hands and peck her on the lips.

"Happy Birthday, Doris," I say. "You don't look but a day older than yesterday."

She beams back at me. Her hair has got some extra above-shoulder curl to go with all the below-shoulder curve that somehow passes for normal. For a dirty blonde, Doris always knows how to clean up. Buck was famous for openly admiring the way his wife entered a room. Back when Buck and Marlo were still in the world, the four of us went out to dinner a lot. Sometimes we'd pile into one of the back booths right here and empty a few bottles for no good reason. Marlo once accused Doris of faking a small bladder just so she could leave and come back again. Buck told his wife not to mind the mean lady. He refilled her water glass to the rim and then kept pouring. We all laughed a riot.

Tonight her dress is black and clings like it's afraid of being left behind. Doris is my age and shorter, but tonight she looks younger and taller. I gesture at the heels.

"You're moving up in the world," I say.

She pulls open her coat and fakes a curtsy. "Doris has a date."

"So that's why you're leaving so early," I say. She acts offended.

"You expect me to work the wee hours on my birthday?"

"I expect you to save yourself for me."

"Tired of waiting for that, Mack," she says. "A girl has got to mind her options before she runs out of time."

"Trust me, Doris, your options are timeless. What's his name? I'll get a jump on the arrest paperwork."

"I'm not telling you anything, Mack. You're too protective."

"So, he's the one, is he?"

"He's the one tonight. He's very sweet. We'll see about tomorrow."

"Got time for a toast and a present?" I ask.

"As a matter of fact, I do." Doris turns so I can help her out of her coat. "He just called. He's running late."

I throw the coat over my arm and grab the bag off the bar. Doris reassures her dress with the palms of her hands.

"Bad sign, Doris," I say, heading for a booth. "He already doesn't deserve you."

SEVENTEEN

Look at him. It's as close to a date as Ray will ever have for the rest of his days and he knows it. Doris brings out his confidence. He feels like a man who might be worth having. But it's only because she's safe. He's playing Russian roulette with a plastic gun, pretending at the odds and laughing them away. If Doris were ever to get serious, Ray would turn to stone.

But Doris knows better than to get serious. Marlo saved him. Then she ruined him.

Kyle brings a fresh round, and they toast another year. Ray pushes the paper bag across the table.

"I can't even begin to guess," she says suspiciously.

"It's a puppy," says Ray, taking a drink. "It pees on other men."

Doris sets down the glass and reaches inside. She pulls out the frame and holds it in both hands.

"Oh, Mack." Her eyes well up until a tear threatens to jump. The back of her finger comes to the rescue. "Oh, Mack. I love this."

She brushes her thumb over Buck's face, black and handsome in his own rugged way. Marlo is riding piggyback. Her arms around Buck's massive shoulders. Her laughing face pressed next to his.

"I was going through some boxes," says Ray. "I made a copy for each of us. She was hard to capture. They both were. But I think this does it."

"Up at the lake." Doris says it like she is talking to herself. "Devil's Kitchen."

Ray lays his hand over hers to keep her from floating away. The tears are back. She sniffs.

"Damnit, Mack."

"Sorry," he says. "Had I known you had a date I'd have made the photo bigger."

Doris laughs and blots her eyes.

"You're an ass. I love you for this. Thank you." She kisses the photo and slips Buck back into the bag with a quick deep breath. "We have to talk about something boring, Mack. Seriously. I can't go out like this. Now I just want to go home."

"Mission accomplished," he says. "I'll take you. Better yet, let's go to my place and watch cat food commercials with Phil." Doris smirks. "Fine. Bring your date. He can make dinner and empty the litterbox."

"Tell me about the job," she says. "How is it back in that building? Are they being nice to you, Mack?"

It's an opportunity to share his feelings. To let it all out. The anger and the hurt and the rest of it. Maybe it's his turn to cry. But Ray isn't built that way. He's never been that guy. He keeps it all bottled up so that he can pretend he's still in control of himself. Ray hasn't been in control of anything since Marlo. The pressurized grief in his chest feels normal now. That feeling is how he knows he's alive. When the heart attack finally comes it's going to move all the seismic needles within a hundred miles. It will finish him off for good.

So he deflects the question. He talks instead about Nadia King and the missing Russian doll.

"Why'd they keep the doll in the first place?" she asks. "Wasn't like they were prosecuting for theft."

"Because the things Bishop stole put him at the scene of the murder."

Doris checks the door. It's the third time in as many minutes.

"I barely remember the headlines," she says. "I was in over my head trying to learn how to run this damn bar on my own. Buck kept it all in his head."

Ray takes her back in time, hitting the highlights. Joe Novak, rising star in the Chicago Major Crimes Unit, gunned down in his mother's home by Wayne Bishop, a doughy, drug-addicted miscreant with too much hair. Bishop was like a wad of discarded gum on the floor of a barbershop. The shaggy black mane, the beard, the eyebrows, the backs of his hands. A *Tribune* writer covering the trial called Bishop a hirsute Cheshire Cat for the way he liked to turn and grin at the gallery. It was a high-wattage spectacle for such a petty, smash-and-grab grunt. Cop killers always get the headlines.

"Bishop had a sheet a mile long and an inch deep," says Ray. "Small stuff. Lots of breaking and entering. Plenty of possession busts. Third degree assault.

Stealing cars. And then one pull of the trigger and bingo, he promoted himself to the big leagues."

Doris shakes her head.

"He broke in with a gun, Mack. Sounds to me like he was ready for the big leagues."

"Not by a mile. Bishop wasn't looking for a fight. The house was dark and quiet. He thought it was empty. Turned out the widow Novak was upstairs sleeping."

"Elderly?"

"Seventies. Dinner at lunchtime and counting sheep early. Ivah woke up to a full bladder and a noise downstairs. She assumed it was just her oldest boy Joe, coming to check on her after his shift, just like always. So she comes downstairs in a bathrobe to find a runty adult bear rooting around in her hall closet with a flashlight."

"That poor woman," says Doris. "I'd have had a heart attack right there."

"Tough old bird, Ivah. Belarusian according to Nadia. She fought him. Scratched him all up."

"Good lord."

"Yeah. But then Bishop put a .38 in Ivah's face and marched her into the kitchen. He put a rag in her mouth, put a garbage bag over her head, taped her to a chair and went off to pilfer his way through the house. Before he could finish, Joe dropped by to check in on his mom."

"It's coming back to me. The garbage bag and being taped up. Did Joe even get a shot off?"

"Never saw anyone to shoot. Bishop put a bullet through the back of Joe's head as he was standing in the den, probably trying to figure out all the broken glass on the carpet under the window. So down goes Joe. Bishop is rattled. This is a whole new caliber of trouble for him. He aborts the mission. Grabs up his bag of goodies and takes off."

"And he took the stupid doll with him? Who does that?"

Ray shrugs and finishes his drink.

"First I've heard about the doll," says Ray. He points, still holding the glass. "But I'll tell you this: a more seasoned psychopath would have hung around long enough to spend an extra bullet. Better to get rid of the witness and improve your odds."

"Mack." Doris' face is disapproving.

"I'm just saying Bishop was out of his league. This was not a killer. This was a petty thug who panicked and left a living witness."

"A single bullet to the back of the head sounds like a killer to me," she says. "Sounds like an execution."

Whatever Ray wants to say next has to wait in line. His gaze leaves Doris for the table. He's thinking.

"What is it?" she asks. "Mack?"

"Nothing," he says, his eyes coming back to her. Then he says it again, just to convince himself. "Nothing. I'm just saying Bishop acted like an amateur. He screwed the pooch. Left Ivah in the kitchen taped to a chair, screaming for Joe. Trying to, anyway."

Doris is no longer weepy over sentimental photos. She hasn't checked the front door in minutes. She's caught up in the sordid ugliness. It's the stuff that cops and crime writers find irresistible, no matter how they try to rationalize their obsession for the details. But it fascinates everybody, not just the professional ghouls like Ray. We can't help it. We imagine the people we love. We imagine ourselves. Bloodless faces, lit in the burst of a camera flash, washed in the red and blue lights, drowned in the indignity of violence. The more random and inexplicable the violence, the greater our horror. The greater our need to imagine ourselves right into the ugly middle of it.

All of us. Doris too. She closes her eyes.

"I'd die," she says. "If it was Buck in the next room and I was in the kitchen? Or if I had a son who'd come to check on me? I'd die."

"Well, she didn't. Wayne Bishop did the dying."

"Good riddance. I hope it hurt." Doris empties her glass.

"There's very little question about that," says Ray. "Everything takes a long time in prison. Even bleeding."

"This is not a birthday conversation, Mack."

Ray grimaces.

"You're right. Sorry. I was just trying to get you back into a dating vibe."

Across the bar the front door opens and a man blows in. Long wool coat and leather gloves. Earmuffs. He closes the door behind him as he pulls off the gloves and stares up at the ceiling through steaming glasses. You can always tell the first timers at *Bucks*.

Doris looks around at the door, then quickly slides out of the booth and stands, gathering up her coat and the paper bag with Buck and Marlo inside.

"This is him?" asks Ray, looking up at her. "Honey, you can't date a guy in earmuffs. You just can't."

She ignores him and holds up the bag.

"I love you for this, Mack," she says. "I'm not kissing you goodbye, even though I want to."

"Have it your way, Doris," he says. "You won't have another chance. Not until tomorrow."

Ray watches her go. The man with the furry warm ears receives Doris with gleaming white teeth and a hug just cautious enough to make Ray wonder how many times they've done that. The man helps each of Doris' arms find a sleeve and then pulls the coat over the back of her shoulders. She's a little taller than he is. She needs to get out of those heels. Ray's wondering if that's on the menu for later.

Doris turns and nods coyly to the booth. Ray lifts his empty glass. A last word to Kyle behind the bar and the couple heads for the door.

It seems to open by itself. As Doris and her date slip out into the wind, another man comes in out of the weather to take their place. He's big enough for both of them. And then some.

EIGHTEEN

I watch the guy take a seat at the far end of the bar and I wonder if the stool can take the weight.

Kyle fixes him up with something gold and foamy. I focus past him, on the mirrored wall behind all the bottles. I'd be able to make out his face were it not for two bottles of Campari. Doesn't matter. I already know the face more than I care to.

He looks up at the ceiling, to the left all the way to the door and then to the right all the way to the restrooms, mesmerized by all those bills. He's another *Bucks* virgin. I can feel his urge to verify that the ceiling behind him is also covered with autographed money. He wants to swivel on that stool.

But he doesn't. He can't. He knows I'm back here.

I grab my coat and put it on, then walk my empty glass up to the bar. I take a seat on the next stool.

"I see you finally decided to get out of your truck," I say. I can feel him turn and look down at me. "Why waste gas waiting for me to come outside when you can come in, have a drink and wait for me to leave."

He stands and I look up into a pair of big, black eyes drilled into an enormous white granite face. It's like the Mount Rushmore gang has made an ugly new friend. His mouth is nothing but a thick, straight gouge beneath the toppled pyramid of a nose that has clearly been broken more than once in a violent life spanning maybe fifty years. For all the stone of his face, his ears have a rubbery, batwing quality, hanging out a little from his bald head.

I wait, but he says nothing.

"Sorry," I say. "This is a new experience for me. I've never been followed by a building before."

He grabs his beer and walks to an empty table. Kyle is on his way down to see if I want a refill. I wave him off, sliding my empty his way. Then I get up and follow. At the table, I pull out a chair and sit again.

"You're too big to be in the business of following people," I say. "You're terrible at it. Leave that kind of thing to the moon."

He takes a thoughtful drink but keeps the thought to himself. I give him another push.

"But you might think about going into the shade business. Rent out your arms to the birds. Or maybe you should just tell me what's on your mind and stop pretending that I can't see you."

The man rotates his head. His eyes fix.

"I'm not pretending, Mr. Mackey." The sound of his voice is heavy enough to move the needle on a scale. But it's not a dumb sound he makes. It's a voice of confidence. It knows things. "I'm just looking for a good opportunity to talk."

"Okay," I say. "Let's talk. Let's start with a name."

"Public," he says. "John, Q."

He holds out a massive paw and I take it.

"Okay, Johnny Q. You're shy. I get it. Why are we talking?"

It takes him too long to let go of my hand. But he gets around to it eventually.

"We have a mutual friend," he says.

"A friend. Let me guess. Arty Dunn got my pink sheet today. He sent you out into the cold as a character reference."

The man pours in a mouthful of beer and swallows. It's the sound ocean liners make when they sink.

"Arty's a good man," he says. "Wrongly accused by a bad man. Very bad."

"Let's say I buy that. And maybe I really do. Where do you come in? Not through the front door I'm guessing."

"Just passing along some information I thought you might find… persuasive."

"I'm all ears."

But he's not interested in my ears. It's my eyes he cares about. He fishes a white envelope out of an inside pocket of his coat and drops it on the table.

"What's this?" I ask. "A letter? You breaking up with me already?"

He doesn't answer. He finishes his beer in one swallow and stands, rising like an elevator in the Sears Tower. I open the envelope with two fingers and peek inside. It does look like a letter, several pages long. I look up.

"There's more if you need it," he says. "Maybe a lot more. Doing the right thing should be easy."

It sounds like he's done, but he isn't. I can tell there's a little more. So I wait for it as he looks down at me with as much of a smile as a gouge in a slate of granite can deliver. He lays his drinking hand on my shoulder. It feels like a piano.

"And painless," he adds.

Three steps and he's halfway to the door. Another three steps and the cold wind is suddenly rushing in to stab the customers and harass the canopy of money. Then he's gone. I open the envelope.

It's not a typical letter, full of alphabet strings and punctuation. Three pages, consisting of only three inkjet-printed photographs. Each photograph is worth a thousand ugly words, give or take.

Scooter Pleasants in a tan and blue SUV. The blurry building in the background is home to the Northrop High Eagles. The person in the passenger seat has long black hair, a yellow coat and no voter card.

Next. Scooter from beneath a dirty shade pulled over a dirty window. He looks like a hairless cat without his clothes. He's standing between a table and a high-backed wooden chair. The chair is wearing a yellow coat.

Next. A tan and blue SUV parked in a narrow, icy-gray driveway that leads to a small, bruise-colored house crouching beneath a single, leafless oak. White shades have been pulled behind two of the windows. Slumped in the passenger seat is a girl. Long black hair. Yellow coat. One hand, chipped red nails, held over her eyes. No one else. Just her.

I refold the pages and try to put them back where they came from. But the envelope isn't done.

Ten more. Smaller. Portraits. All of Ben Franklin.

And something else. A black plastic poker chip. It's broken. Like a clock for people who don't care for the time between midnight and three. A pizza two slices shy of a full pie. In the center of the chip are three embossed capital letters: KFC. I turn the chip over and over, thinking about the future.

Suddenly I'm hungry. I put the chip in my pocket, hoping to trade it for a Camel. No such luck.

Dinah Washington is in the air, asking for someone to cry her a river. She doesn't sound picky; maybe anyone will do as long as they're real tears. No one in the room seems to care much.

I'd do it. For Dinah. For Marlo. For Ivah Novak. For whoever this kid in the yellow coat is. I'd shed those tears. But I'm afraid I'd never be able to stop.

I fold up all the ugliness and stuff it back in the envelope and put the envelope in my pocket. I stand up and nod goodbye to Kyle behind the bar.

"Streets are icy, Mack," he says, pointing at me with a bottle of something I want. "Watch yourself."

Outside, the tower of rags with a face is still there. He's found a way to make his desperation look like patience. That should be worth something. Tonight it's worth a portrait of Ben Franklin.

NINETEEN

He seems at peace.

That's what it looks like from up here against the ceiling. Like he's finally found the sweet spot of the day at three minutes to midnight. Eyes closed. His back sagging into the mossy-green couch like a lost hiker succumbing to Earth's spongy invitation.

Phil, curled up in a soft, white ball and purring against his chest.

Ella, breathing out Duke Ellington like a lullaby on a breeze.

Look at him. Like he's drifted off to sleep on a cloud of contentment.

Not true, of course. Ray's as wide awake as I am. He's closed his eyes only to help manage the relentless barrage of new questions now competing with old worries.

His goal, initially, had simply been to finish a chapter. He had wanted to write Detective McMannis out of trouble in that *Target* parking lot. He wanted to write McMannis another step toward protecting his old informant from everyone who wants to kill her. The cops and the mob. But that modest literary effort had turned out to be the beginning of tonight's undoing.

Ray's idea of pulp fiction is to reheat the leftovers of his own experience. It's just another installment in a serial pulp autobiography, complete with made up names and a marquee title intended to evoke something in the vein of vintage detective noir. *Message in a Bullet.* Who wouldn't read that? Except maybe everybody. Not literary agents. Not if history is any guide. Not even if Humphrey Bogart came back to write the query letter and offered to do live readings.

Working on the book had been neither productive nor relaxing. It had only made him wonder about Suri, his *actual* former informant. The woman who was *actually* on the run from all the people who *actually* want to kill her, maybe including the mayor of Chicago and his drycleaner. Ray figures it's a good bet Suri is back to not trusting him, particularly after the bloodbath in Bloomington. She'd be reconsidering the rumors about him that she had once tried to deny. She'd decide the rumors were true after all, and that Ray really had hitched his wagon to Big Man's dark star.

The thought had been enough to make Ray close his laptop and forget about the book. If Suri is still alive, then she probably hates him all over again. She probably believes he put her up in that Bloomington no-tell hotel just to isolate her; just to keep her contained so Big Man's boys could step out of the dark and rub her out of existence. Now she's running scared with no one to trust. She's running from Ray as much as she's running from Big Man. She thinks there's no difference.

And that thought kills him. He hates that idea like poison.

But Suri, as a worry, as a vector of Ray's stress, is not resolvable. There is nothing he can do to find her or help her. His impotence is as demoralizing as it is maddening.

So Ray had broken his two-drink moratorium and enlisted the aid of another tumbler of Old Forester. That third drink had led in short order to a fourth, which he poured over three cubes of ice and took to the couch where he reclined on the cold rocks of brand-new concerns:

Mickey Shaw, staring at him across that courtroom, tossing the police corruption grenade as Judge Jolie ramped up into anger.

Nadia King, at her wits' end over a missing doll that Barbara Bannon and the office of the District Attorney insists has been returned.

Arty Dunn, pretending to be his buddy, somehow aware of the IAD investigation before any official notice.

Scooter Pleasants, a low-life pedophile playing the victim of a police shakedown.

Giant John Q. Public, tailing him around the city with an envelope.

A teenage girl, crying alone in her yellow coat.

The late Wayne Bishop, standing over the fallen Jovah Novak, somehow both a petty criminal out of his depth and a single-shot executioner with ice water in his veins.

Doris, dating a man with earmuffs.

Little Danika, defending the incongruity of a blue dragon breathing green fire.

Marlo. Marlo. Marlo. Always Marlo.

Ray's eyes open. He looks right through me up at the ceiling light.

Not enough bourbon in the world to fix these kinds of problems. No sleep tonight. Not for him. The poor, old hump. Look at him. Like he's died with his eyes open.

Here lies Ray Mackey, a man at rest, but not at peace.

TWENTY

Celestyn Fila was born with bat radar. She looks up as I slip in. Some of the jurors notice the brassy-blonde beehive change positions. Now they're looking too. I do my best to keep the colossal wooden door from thumping to a close. My best isn't good enough. More heads turn. One of them belongs to fast-fingers Ted Myerson, reporter for *The Hawk*, just where I left him yesterday. Another belongs to Mickey Shaw.

Judge Jolie is oblivious to my existence. She keeps her head down, making notes like she's taking a test. Her face is still and serious and her sleek dark hair quivers in a curl at her jaw line like a black breaker on a light brown beach. Every so often, her eyes flick up from whatever note she is making and then sideways to the witness stand where a police uniform is wrapped around a fat guy with a thin mustache. He's a forensics cop, busy playing a game of question-and-answer catch with Jaclyn Cavelle. They take turns pointing to a drawing on an easel that shows two stick figures, one slightly taller than the other. The shorter figure is pointing a gun at the taller one. It's one of those stick-figure guns that shoots colored arrows and dotted lines and numbers.

The room is only half-full. My guess is that two hours earlier the place was packed, people hoping the fireworks that ended the opening statements yesterday might continue. Everyone thought they'd found a new favorite TV show. But then the new day started with the State of Illinois putting on its forensics case, which is like watching someone build a replica of the courthouse with toothpicks. That's when some of them remembered they have lives to live. One-by-one they had quietly bundled up their coats and purses and slipped out, getting back to their original programming. Changing the channel with their car keys. So now the gallery is peppered with empty gaps where people used to be.

I pan the heads and shoulders. If giant John Q. Public was here before, he's not here now.

The seating gaps are all singles and doubles. Five empty spaces together would be ideal. One for me and four for the angry hangover. The best I can do are two spaces on the back bench, one for me and the other for my coat. Celeste keeps a serious expression on her face but finds a way to widen her blue eyes into a full-body tackle. I nod and keep moving.

Jaclyn Cavelle wants permission to put a poster-sized photo up on the easel. Judge Jolie looks down at Mickey Shaw. Mickey nods.

"No objection," he says.

"Exhibit 4 is admitted," says the judge. Cavelle points at the easel.

"Officer Bates, I'm showing you State's Exhibit 4. Do you recognize this?"

"I do."

"Can you tell the jury what this is?"

"This is a photo of the crime scene taken by the CPD forensics team."

"And what does it show?"

"It shows the upstairs master bedroom in the victim's home."

"Curtis Root's bedroom."

"Yes."

Jacklyn uses a laser pointer to draw a sloppy circle with a beam of red light.

"And what is this?"

"That's the bed."

"No, I mean what are these shapes? Here. And here. And up here."

"Those are blood spatters."

"And this?"

"That's brain matter. And bits of skull."

The jury squirms. Just what Cavelle wants. She keeps drawing little red circles of light.

"And up here? By the pillow?"

"Again, that would be brain tissue."

"And in the course of your investigation did you scientifically and definitively establish the source of the blood and brain tissue and skull fragments?"

"Yes we did. It's the victim's. Curtis Root."

"Your Honor, I'd like to introduce State's Exhibit 5-A."

Judge Jolie flips a page in a large black binder and then looks out at the defense table. She doesn't need to ask the question.

"No objection," says Mickey. He leans sideways in his chair and shows his client a piece of paper, presumably a copy of the exhibit in question. Wrigley Menard stops fidgeting with the tie he is still not used to wearing and looks. He's not sleeping well in lock-up. The skin beneath his eyes is getting baggy and sallow, like dirty wall paint bubbling out from a slow leak. He tucks a dark strand of oily hair behind his ear and nods.

Jacklyn places a computerized rendering of the Root's bedroom on the easel, making it share space with the enlarged photo. She walks Bates through the tedium of authenticating the drawing as one prepared by the CPD forensics team and then gets him to point out the highlights. The door. The windows. The bed. The walk-in closet.

Red dots –large, medium and small –cover the floor, the depiction of the bed, the headboard, the bedside lampshade, and the back wall. That's the blood. It looks like a satellite map of Illinois lake country. The largest lake, the Lake Michigan of the Roots' bedroom, is at the foot of the bed where they found Curtis Root's body, face down in the carpet. The red lakes get smaller and farther apart as they move up the bed toward the headboard.

"Okay, and then what are the black dots?"

"Those depict the gray matter. The brain tissue. And bits of skull."

I lean forward and look around for Curtis Root's widow. Someone has wisely suggested she skip the forensics testimony, although I'm betting Cavelle would not have minded a fainting widow in the front row.

"And why is it important to separately depict the brain tissue and skull fragments?"

"They're solids. Larger and heavier than liquid drops of blood. They have a slightly different trajectory and distribution. Sometimes that can provide an extra layer of information. So we try to make note of it. Just part of the normal forensic process."

"Officer Bates, is it possible in looking at the distribution pattern of blood and brain tissue and skull fragments to form an opinion as to the trajectory of the bullet from the gun into the skull?"

"Yes."

"And from that, the height of the gun when it was discharged?"

"Yes."

"And from that, the height of the person who fired the gun?"

"An approximation. Yes. Using the boot print patterns in the carpet to measure distance from the body, yes."

"And have you, as a part of your forensic investigation, conducted that kind of analysis?"

"I have."

"I'd like you to walk us through that analysis."

He does. It's a story no one really needs to hear because everyone already knows how it ends.

I'm not at all sure why I'm here in the first place. Initially, the idea had made a certain sense. Arty and Scooter are both named witnesses. So why not watch them both from the shadows before the investigation officially begins? I get that. But Arty Dunn obviously knows who I am and what I'm investigating. The pink sheet is out. There are no shadows anymore. Maybe there never were any shadows. So why am I sitting here with my hands in my lap like an out-of-work hump trying to stay awake at a matinee?

The room is warm. The woman on the other side of my folded coat yawns in a silent, agonizing scream. I close my eyes. Just for a second. Maybe two.

The lights are too bright. That's why it's so warm. Someone catches on and brings them down to a soft glow. Bates has disappeared into shadow, but Cavelle keeps asking questions anyway. A talking cigarette shows up through a side door, thinking it has all the answers. The words come out in puffs of smoke. It's a Camel, between five foot eight inches and five foot ten inches tall. Approximately.

My eyes open and my head jerks up. The woman sitting next to my coat has an irritated expression on her face. The expression wants away from me. It pulls the woman's head the other direction, like a mother pulling her child away from a homeless, gin-soaked heap of rags on the street corner asking for a buck or two. My upper body is curling sideways in her direction, like it wants to whisper a secret.

I sit up and check my mouth. It's wet. Mickey Shaw is just rising, brushing the sleeves of his suit.

"Thank you, Your Honor. Officer Bates, what about the fingerprints?"

"I'm sorry?"

"You identified yourself as the Forensics Lead, correct?"

"Yes."

"So then you were responsible for coordinating the CPD's collection of all the forensic evidence found at the crime scene, including fingerprint evidence, correct?"

"Yes."

"Why didn't you testify about fingerprints?"

"I wasn't asked a question about fingerprints."

"Oh. That's right." Mickey turns in a slow circle, pausing briefly as he faces the prosecution. "You weren't. Well, then let me ask you a couple. Did you find any fingerprints?"

"Yes."

"Did any of those prints belong to any one of the ten fingers attached to the hands of my client," Shaw points back at his table, "Mr. Menard?"

"Yes."

"And where were those prints found?"

"A thumb print on the doorbell. Various fingerprints on the passenger door, door handle, and on the dashboard of Curtis Root's car."

"How about inside the house?"

"No sir."

"None?"

"No sir."

Shaw lets that bit settle for a second, nodding.

"Officer Bates, are you saying that there were no fingerprints at all inside that house?"

"No. That is not my testimony. There were lots of prints inside the house. None that matched Mr. Menard's prints."

"Not in the bedroom?"

"No."

"Not on the floor safe in the master closet?"

"No."

"What about downstairs near the broken window?"

"No."

"And what does that tell you?"

"What does it tell me?"

"Yes sir. What does it tell you?"

"It tells me nothing except that the defendant's prints were not found on any bondable surface. Doesn't mean he wasn't inside."

"But we could say that about anybody, couldn't we?"

"I don't understand the question."

"Were your prints found on a… a bondable surface, Officer Bates?"

"Mine?"

"Yes. Yours."

"No."

"But that doesn't mean you weren't there the night of the murder, now does it?"

"Objection." I can't see Jaclyn Cavelle's face, but my ears know irritation when they hear it.

"Sustained." Judge Jolie gives Mickey a hard look. Mickey catches it with a sideways nod.

"Officer Bates, can you explain to me why a burglar rings a doorbell of a house he intends to rob?"

"No. Maybe to see if someone is home."

"I see. Just to make sure that whoever might be home can see him and identify him in advance."

"I didn't say it would be smart."

"Was Curtis Root's car locked or unlocked when CPD arrived on the scene?"

"Locked."

"Any broken window or sign of forced entry?"

"No."

"How did CPD gain access to the inside of the car?"

"We used the keys."

"Where were the keys?"

"In the victim's pocket."

"Which pocket?"

"Front right."

"And you testified earlier that Mr. Root was found face down, correct?"

"Yes sir."

"And did the blood pattern on the bedroom carpet where you found Mr. Root suggest to you that someone had made the effort to roll him over in order to get the keys out of his pocket, then later put the keys back into his pocket, and then return the body to the original position?"

"That's not something we would necessarily be able to tell from the blood patterns."

"So then the answer to my question is that the blood patterns did not suggest any such course of events."

Bates sighs like he's no longer having fun.

"Correct."

"Did you find any evidence at all to suggest that course of events?"

"No."

"Officer Bates, was there any sign of my client's fingerprints anywhere but on the passenger side of that car?"

"No sir."

"And the prints that you found in the house… you said you found a lot of fingerprints?"

"Yes. That's to be expected."

"Whose prints did you find?"

"Mostly those of Mr. and Mrs. Root. Their son, Stephen. But there were others."

"And did you check those other prints against your database to try and identify the owners?"

"Most of them, yes."

"Most of them?"

"We focused on the bedroom. A lot of those prints were partial and not reliable enough to run."

"I see. Did you make the effort to compare the partial prints to my client's fingerprint pattern?"

"Yes."

"And you did that because the readable part of the print could conceivably have matched up with the corresponding part of Mr. Menard's finger."

"Correct."

"Would not have been definitive, but," Shaw shrugs amiably, "it might have been useful information."

"Correct."

"But not even the partial prints matched up with Mr. Menard's fingers."

"Correct."

"Did you compare the partial prints against the prints you have in your database belonging to known violent criminals or people known to be associated with organized crime."

"Well… no. That would be…"

"And who instructed you not to conduct that analysis?"

Bates is confused. He looks up to Judge Jolie, like he wants her to intervene.

"What? No one. I mean…"

"So then it was your decision? Officer Bates? *You* personally decided not to take the extra step of matching the partial prints found at the crime scene with even a subset of the prints in your bad guy database?"

"That's not… that's not possible."

"Not possible?" Shaw turns to face the jury. "We all just watched you use a collection of skull fragments to guess my client's height. But you're saying now that examining fingerprint fragments is a bridge too far for criminal forensic science."

Cavelle is sitting rigidly at attention. Both hands are flat on her table, fingers tightly together. In my business, most people lose their humanity to a collection of tells. This is one of hers.

"It would not be admissible," says Bates.

"I didn't ask you about admissibility."

"It's not feasible for us to do that."

"Seemed feasible enough when you were looking to see if those partial prints matched my client's fingertips. My question, Officer Bates, is whether it was your decision to not try to match those partials to anyone else."

"It was not, like, an actual decision. We can't feasibly test every print and partial print, no matter how old or degraded, on every surface in the entire house. To be useful a print has to be…"

"And if someone within the chain of command of the Chandler Police Department had specifically instructed that you *not* test the partial prints at the crime scene against prints for any subset of people working, say, in organized crime circles, criminals known to have previously resided in this very county, would you have obeyed such an order?"

"I don't… I don't…"

"Was your job ever threatened?"

Cavelle is a Jaclyn-in-the-box.

"Objection. Your Honor, this is highly improper. Counsel is assuming facts for which there is absolutely no evidence."

"Sustained. The jury is instructed to ignore those last two questions and the witness is instructed not to answer. Mr. Shaw…"

Judge Jolie doesn't finish. She doesn't need to. She just holds her pen up. Mickey Shaw raises both hands just a little, surrendering like she's Babe Ruth rolling War Club through the air in slow menacing circles.

"Officer Bates," says Mickey, "you testified earlier that the person who shot Curtis Root was between five foot eight and five foot ten inches tall."

"Correct."

"The highest end of the range topping out at five-ten."

"Correct."

"How tall is my client?"

"Five-nine and a half."

Mickey makes his face into a pretend grimace.

"No, no. I'm sorry. I should have been more clear. My apologies. Five-nine and a half is his actual height. How tall is Mr. Menard wearing a pair of Timberland Pros?"

Bates is quiet. He knows better than to look at the prosecutor. He does it anyway. Cavelle leans back in her chair.

"I… I have not made that calculation."

"Oh," says Mickey, pretending disappointment. "You haven't. But he'd be taller than five-nine and a half, right?"

"Yes."

"By about an inch and a quarter?"

"I don't know."

"You don't know. Do you know how tall you are?"

"Me? Five foot seven."

"Five-seven. Plus an inch and a quarter puts you right at about five-eight-and-a-quarter."

"I guess."

"Okay. So then where were you on the fifth night of February last year?"

TWENTY-ONE

It's a chance for Ray to stretch his legs. Whatever madness is behind Mickey Shaw's method, it pays dividends in the form of improved circulation.

Ray stands along with everyone else, stretching his arms and rolling his head around on his neck. It looks like courtroom yoga. He makes it seem like it's all about stiff muscles. Maybe that fools some people. I can tell he's just trying to avoid eye contact with Celeste during the recess.

Jolie never had much choice. Another recess was the only way to calm everyone down, probably including her. Jaclyn Cavelle was running out of new, non-obscene words and was starting to sputter. They tried a bench conference, but the electronic white noise was not up to the task. Various jurors had started to connect at the shoulders and whisper questions to each other during the commotion. So, Jolie had sent them away to their room. Then she'd let Mickey have it between the eyes.

"You will not turn this trial into a circus of unfounded innuendo, Mr. Shaw."

Mickey had done his best to fend her off. Officer Bates, he asserted, had not murdered Curtis Root and the defense was not suggesting otherwise. His point, rather, had to do with what Mickey claimed was the overly generic quality of the State's evidence and a forensic process that failed to exclude other potential suspects.

Jolie was not impressed enough with the argument to even give Jaclyn Cavelle a crack at a response. Instead, she'd demanded that Mickey Shaw empty his pockets.

"You want to keep dropping those kinds of hints, Mr. Shaw, then I want you to disclose to the prosecution whatever evidence you may have to support a cover-up by the Chandler Police Department. And I want you to do it by the end of the day with a copy of everything to me. I will recess until tomorrow morning so that you can take care of that. Am I clear?"

Mickey had nodded from the podium, cool as an ice cream cone in a silk suit.

"Your Honor is rarely lacking in clarity. But the court's request is beyond the scope of mandatory discovery set forth in Rule 413. I will be filing a motion to prevent the discovery so that we can resolve those concerns first. And that probably means an interlocutory appeal before we can resume."

If Cavelle had tried to contain herself, she failed.

"Your Honor, what you just heard is a ploy to derail this entire trial. This cannot…"

"I have ears, Ms. Cavelle," Jolie had said, looking without moving her head. "Who is your next witness after Officer Bates?"

"Arthur Dunn, Your Honor," said Cavelle.

"A police witness employed by CPD?"

"Yes."

Judge Jolie had refocused on Mickey, leaning forward on her elbows, tightly clasping her interlaced fingers.

"Mr. Shaw. As an officer of this court, can you represent to me that you are currently in possession of evidence reasonably tending to suggest that the Chandler Police Department was in any way complicit in the murder of Curtis Root or the wrongful accusation of your client for that crime? I suggest you answer this question carefully, sir, because I intend to hold you to it."

"My case is rapidly evolving, Your Honor. I think we can all agree it is not in my client's interests for me to be making promises to the jury that I cannot keep. The Chandler Police Department is perfectly capable of explaining what it did, and what it did not do, in its investigation of this crime."

Judge Jolie had stared down at her hands for a long time, like maybe she expected them to say something.

"That, Mr. Shaw, is not an answer to my question."

"No, Your Honor. No, it isn't."

TWENTY-TWO

It takes Cavelle another half-hour with Bates on redirect to clean up Mickey's mess. She's competent, all right. More than competent. I know her type. She's an inexhaustible force. She gets up every morning hungry for the fight. She lives to win, this kid. The ring on her finger is no surprise. She's a catch. She's going places. But she'll have a collection of those rings before she retires. She'll keep them all in a juice glass on the windowsill above the sink, among the little pots of barren twigs and scorched-out, burnt-paper petals. Because Jackie Cavelle's not a plant-watering, relationship-nurturing person. She's a war machine. She's either fighting or she's dying.

But her teeth are still too white. She's too young to appreciate that the lightest touch is often the most effective. Too young to have full control of her anger, which seeps out with every question as a top note of sarcasm. Mockery. Sure, she cleans up Mickey's mess well enough. She gets Bates to confirm that no one ordered him to fix an investigation. She gets him to say that he's not covering for some nameless, mob-connected triggerman. Bates follows Cavelle's lead perfectly. His answers come out boastfully proud and offended and they strut around the room a couple of times. But Cavelle puts too much muscle into the whole production. They're both having so much fun at being offended, they've forgotten that they owe it all to Mickey Shaw. They never stop to ask why.

One look at Mickey and I can tell he's pleased. I can't see his face, but I don't need to. His ponytail is giggling. His posture in that chair is smiling like a kid on Christmas. Denials of corruption are exactly what he wants. This jury doesn't live in Mayberry. These are cynical times. A denial of corruption is how we measure the corruption. Its depth. Its sincerity. It's always the corrupt ones that deny corruption the loudest. Any time an officer of the law declares that there is nothing to see here, there is almost always something to see here.

Mickey Shaw is hardly the first defense attorney to try to play a song with bells that can't be un-rung. Judges with Jolie's experience see that every day. But Mickey is not playing a song. He's conducting a requiem for the truth. Makes a guy wonder whether Beethoven has come back with a law degree and patrons in the cement business.

I probably should have left after the recess. The lack of caffeine and nicotine in my system has given my hangover the run of my head. All my hangovers like to bowl and this one is no different. I've got half a mind to leave and take a nap in my car before going to the station. But the other half of my mind wants to hear Arty Dunn testify. As usual, gravity is the tiebreaker. So I stay put. I sit on the hard maple bench and I watch the show and I wait.

"Your Honor, the State calls Officer Arthur Dunn."

Arty Dunn makes his way up the aisle to the witness stand like he's about to tell a couple of fun stories about the bride and groom. He's not in his dress blues. He's wearing a white shirt and a black tie inside a nubby gray sport coat. His dark slacks have a little flair to them at the hem. A little swish. Like they know people are watching. I can't tell if he knows I'm here. He does not look my way as he passes. He sits and raises his right hand and calls himself Arthur and pledges a heartfelt devotion to the truth.

Cavelle walks Arty through the bare bones of his career and his current role as a detective working in the Property Crimes division of the Chandler Police Department. Cavelle's pace through the questions suggests that Arty's importance to the case is limited. She just wants a couple of facts out of him. It's a smooth back-and-forth. I can tell they've been through it all before in somebody's office or conference room. She's not leaving anything to chance.

"Detective Dunn, did you have occasion to interact with Curtis Root prior to his murder?"

Arty is one of those that looks at the person asking the question until he hears the question mark. Then he turns his head and gives his answer to the jury.

"Yes."

He looks back at Cavelle.

"When was the last time you spoke with Mr. Root?"

Arty scratches his goatee, like he has to think about it. It's a silly pretense. He knows all of this cold.

"Last year. Mid-January."

"Can you explain the circumstances of that discussion please."

"Sure. I went out to Mr. Root's house in response to concerns he had the previous night."

"What concerns?"

"He'd heard someone out behind his house. He felt like someone was looking to break in or was casing the place. He called me and I drove out there to meet him."

"And you investigated those concerns."

"I did."

"What evidence, if any, did you find to suggest an attempted break-in?"

"Nothing. Clean windows. No pry marks."

"Did you find any evidence to suggest someone had been evaluating the house for a future burglary?"

"Yes. I found a set of boot prints along both sides and the back of the house. We'd had maybe a quarter inch of snow earlier that week, so they were pretty clear. They went one way around the house and then the other way. Clockwise, then counterclockwise, stopping at all the bottom floor windows."

"Did you draw any conclusions from the prints?"

"It supported Mr. Root's concern that someone had been looking for entry points."

"So nearly a month before Mr. Root was shot to death in his home, you found evidence that someone was casing the house for a future burglary, looking for entry points."

"Objection, leading," says Mickey. "I don't believe footprints have motives."

Judge Jolie nods. "Sustained."

"Detective, you saw evidence that someone had been casing the house for some purpose."

"Correct."

"And do you know whether there had been recent burglaries in the Chandler Heights neighborhood?"

"I did look into that after the fact. There had been three burglaries within the past six months occurring within about a four-mile radius of the Root home."

"Any arrests or convictions as to any of those burglaries?"

"No. Not yet."

"Do you have any leads into those other burglaries?"

"Those investigations are still on-going."

"Have those investigations generated any suspects?"

"Those investigations are still on-going. I'm not able to say more at this time."

"I understand. Have there been any burglaries in the Chandler Heights neighborhood since the date of the defendant's arrest?

"Not to my knowledge. No."

"Did you further investigate the boot prints and who might have made them?"

"No. There was not much to do at that point. I took a bunch of photos for the file. Mr. Root and I discussed enhancing his video surveillance system to better cover the back of the house."

"And do you know if he followed through with that recommendation?"

"He never followed up with me personally about that. But I do know that another camera had been installed since my visit out to the house in January."

"And you know that from the evidence in this case? After Mr. Root's murder?"

"Yes."

Cavelle turns her back to Arty and heads for her table, speaking as she goes.

"Your Honor, I'd like to introduce State's Exhibit 7."

Judge Jolie checks her book.

"Mr. Shaw?" she asks without looking.

Mickey flips the pages of his binder. Everyone waits.

"No objection, Judge," he says finally. Cavelle hands Dunn several sheets of paper clipped together.

"Officer Dunn, do you recognize the photographs that comprise Exhibit 7 and, if so, can you tell us what they are?"

"Yes. These are the photographs that I took of the prints I found outside the Root home that day."

"And since the time of Mr. Root's murder, have you had occasion to determine the type and size of boot that made these prints?"

"Yes."

"And what did you find?"

"Wasn't too difficult. Timberland Pros. Size ten."

"You're sure about that."

"Very sure."

"Thank you, Detective. No further questions."

Judge Jolie swings her attention to Mickey, who is already standing, one hand squeezing Wrigley's shoulder.

"Mr. Shaw," she says.

"Thank you, Judge. I'm confused, Detective Dunn. How is it that Curtis Root knew to call you directly about his concern?"

Arty listens, then turns to the jury.

"I'd known Mr. Root for several years. I think he trusted me with these kinds of issues and my name came to mind."

"So you had been friends with Mr. Root prior to this visit."

"No. Not really friends. Our contact was always in a professional capacity."

"And how did this long-standing, professional relationship start?"

Arty rotates back to the jury like it's story time.

"The first *Tap Root Kegs* establishment was partly destroyed in a fire. I was assigned to work with the Fire Inspector in the investigation. I first met Mr. Root interviewing him in that case. After that we had occasional contact on some vandalism issues. Security questions."

Mickey nods, interested, like this is all new information.

"And that is the only context in which you have encountered or interacted with or observed Curtis Root: him as a business owner or residential property owner and you as a police officer responding to his property-related concerns."

Arty pauses at this, like he wants to play the question back in his head before answering.

"Yes. That's correct. A couple of years ago, out at the *TRK* restaurant on Wimbley Road, a gentleman plowed his pickup into the side of the building. I got that call too."

Mickey nods and then gives a dramatic shrug.

"Sometimes a man just prefers drive-through dining."

The room comes together for a big laugh. The jury. The gallery. Arty Dunn. Wrigley Menard. Even Judge Jolie lets a smile slip. I can't see Jaclyn Cavelle's face, but I'm guessing it's showing some strain. Mickey stares down at his boots, shrugging it all off like he's bored with his own wit. He doesn't wait for the laughter to stop.

"Who set that first fire, Detective?"

Arty's expression is frozen in mid-chuckle. The hole in his goatee closes so he can swallow. Then it opens again.

"Excuse me?"

"I think you heard me, but I'll ask it again. Who tried to burn down the original *TRK* establishment on October 4, 2005?"

"It was not… that fire was not determined to be an arson."

"Officially. But you know otherwise, don't you?"

Cavelle is on her feet, pointing and saying her favorite word. Jolie sustains, but Arty can't help repeating himself. He forgets to look at the jury this time.

"No sir. No sir. That fire was not determined to be an arson."

"Detective, are you familiar with the term protection racket?"

"Objection!" Cavelle spits it out like it's three separate words.

"Sustained. Mr. Shaw…"

"Withdrawn, Your Honor. I'll move on. Detective Dunn, please explain to the jury who Daniel Pleasants is and why he has filed a complaint against you."

TWENTY-THREE

Ray's not fooling anyone. Certainly not Orland Twill.

Just look at him. The way he fills that stiff chair like yesterday's laundry. Eyes like the last two coals glowing out of a pile of ash. He should have taken that nap when he had the chance. Now the day is on the move and Ray's an old dog on a short leash. It's all he can do to keep from being dragged.

"You look like hell." Twill's expression offers about as much comfort as the chair.

"Thanks, LT. You don't need to shout."

"Maybe you should give the bottle a rest, Mack. Get some help. I don't want to…"

"Then don't."

It comes out too sharp. I can tell Ray regrets it. But he doesn't take it back. Twill makes him wait for a response. All Ray can do is wince in the silence.

"Okay," Twill says eventually. "Let's pretend your drinking is none of my business. But if you don't get your shit together, this is going be a mighty short ride for you. That's a promise."

"A short ride to a bottle of aspirin and a pillow sounds great to me. I'm fine. Couldn't sleep last night, that's all. And I just spent all morning on a hard bench watching Mickey Shaw sodomize the justice system." Ray starts patting his pockets. "I don't suppose they've changed the no-smoking policy in this place."

"No."

"I'll give you nine hundred dollars if you look the other way."

"Is that a bribe? You haven't read IAD's mission statement, have you?"

"It's on my list."

Ray pulls out the envelope he has been carrying in his pocket since his drink with Giant John. He hands it across the desk.

"What's this?"

"Nine hundred dollars. Like I said."

Twill pulls the cash halfway out, fanning the bills. Then he returns it all to the envelope. He pulls out the pages with the photographs of Scooter Pleasants and the girl in the yellow coat and the chipped red nails. He unfolds them and lays them out on the desk.

"Talk."

Ray gives him the whole story. Mostly. He leaves out the part about the extra Ben Franklin he gave to the raggedy man outside in the cold.

"Do you know this guy? The one who gave you this?"

"I had Sandra run the plates on the F150. They came back to a Bruce Lubeck."

"What do you know about him?"

"Lives up near Tinley Park. Used to drive an F150 until someone took it for a drive and never came back."

"Great. Any leads on that?"

"No, but I'm guessing whoever took it uses pine trees for toothpicks and keeps a blue ox chained up in his backyard."

"So," says Twill, scratching his chin, "whoever he is, he wants to buy a light touch on Arty Dunn."

"Yeah. And he wants Scooter to make old home week up in Stateville. I don't know about you, but that works for me. I bet they throw Scooter a prison party he'll never forget. You know how they love molesters out there." Ray leans in and points to the girl crying in Scooter's truck. "I'm headed out to Northrop High School this afternoon to see if I can find this kid."

Twill looks up sharply from the photos.

"Negative. We'll refer this to Special Investigations and Juvenile Support. Where it belongs. Scooter's crimes, whatever they are, are outside our lane. We keep our focus on Arty Dunn. And by we, I mean you. That's what IAD does in the world, Mack."

"LT, Scooter needs to go back in the hole." Ray leans over the desk and taps one of the pages. "There's a girl out there in serious trouble. Seventeen at best and she's already stuck on the bottom of the barrel. I can't spend my time chasing down Scooter's bullshit complaints without also working the other side of it. I'm not asking to run the whole case. I'm just talking about a little…"

"No."

"Twill. Lieutenant. Listen."

Twill slaps the desk with the flat of his hand.

"That's it. And I'm serious. I know this doesn't feel like real policework to you. Homicide has ruined you for anything else. I get it. But don't compare this to working homicide. Compare this to working the shopping mall. This is the job, Mack. I don't want you working non-IAD files. And if I find out that you are…"

He doesn't finish. Orland Twill is not a man who does unnecessary things.

Ray sits upright in the chair. This is the most awake he's been all day. Nothing like a little anger to clear away the cobwebs. Problem is, the thing he says next may be the last thing he ever says as a cop. I know Ray better than anybody. Enough to know that he has no idea what he's going to say next. Neither of us do.

"This is not…"

"No," says Twill. "This is the part where you tell me that you understand completely."

A knock on the door swings everyone's attention. Rafael Santiago pushes his head through the opening.

"Hey, LT," he says. "Hey Mack. Sorry to interrupt. Thought I'd drop by for a debrief. I'll be at my desk."

"No, come on in," says Twill. His eyes find Ray again. "I think we're done here. Right, Mack?"

Ray and Twill look at each other for a rubber second. Ray finally nods and stands as Santiago steps into the office and pulls back a chair.

Raffi's got a lean, athletic body that plays with gravity, like his bones are hollow and filled with helium. Back in his prime, Ray had been a marvel of muscle and bone. He could play the part of a brick wall whenever he needed to. But Santiago is one of those guys made to climb and clear brick walls like they were nothing but cracks in the sidewalk.

"What's the word, Raffi?" Ray extends a hand, and they shake. "Enjoying your leave time? Soaking up the sun and sucking down margaritas on dry-cleaner island?"

Santiago shrugs.

Not much of a talker, Santiago. He holds his cards close. Ray likes that in any man. Even better, Santiago can make a .38 caliber bullet drill George Washington's eye out of a quarter while hanging upside-down from an open railway car in the middle of a rainstorm. From thirty feet away. In the dark. Ray likes that in a man too.

"All of my vacation photos are of license plates," he says, sticking a piece of gum in his mouth. "A front row seat at the Wrigley Menard trial isn't exactly hard labor, Mack."

"The Chinese can bore a hole through a man's skull with little drops of water," says Ray. "Where can I find that?"

"Slow going?"

Ray nods sideways toward Twill.

"I was just telling the boss here that Mickey Shaw's strategy seems to be to force a recess every other question."

"Prosecution getting any traction?" Raffi asks.

"Hard to say. Cavelle's going for the interrupted-burglary-turns-deadly angle. This morning she used Arty Dunn to insinuate that Wrigley Menard is behind a spate of Chandler Heights burglaries over the past six months."

"Is he a suspect in those cases?"

"I'm guessing no. They're hoping it's enough to say the cases are still being actively investigated and to then make eyes at Wrigley. Maybe the jury makes the leap. If he was really a suspect, they'd find a way to get that out there."

"Against policy," says Twill. "They can't do that. Even if they could Judge Jolie would never let it in."

"Maybe," says Ray. "I still think it's a bunch of smoke. Meanwhile, Mickey's having the time of his life."

"I read the paper," says Santiago. "Looney Tunes, man. He's telling ghost stories."

"Maybe," says Ray. Raffi scoffs.

"Come on. You think he's actually going to put on corruption evidence?"

Ray looks from Santiago to Twill and back again.

"What I think is that this department will have to defend itself on that score until the end of time. Do I think CPD is serving up Wrigley Menard to take the fall for some connected triggerman? No. But do I think Curtis Root was washing dirty money? I think that's possible. And, if so, then it means he was rubbing shoulders with the wrong kind of people when he took that bullet. Makes a guy wonder whether the State's burglary-gone-bad story holds any water. And somewhere out that direction is reasonable doubt."

"But has there been any evidence?" asks Santiago.

"On the first day of the State's case?" Ray laughs a little. "Mickey's keeping his power dry for when it's his turn. Meantime, he's saying a lot of things the jury can't unhear."

Twill is folding up the pages of photographs and putting them into an evidence envelope with the cash. Santiago watches. It's not his style to ask. Twill makes a note on the envelope and looks up.

"Mack here says Mickey's trying to make Arty Dunn into a shakedown artist."

"Huh?" Santiago looks to Ray for more. Ray gives him some.

"Mickey's hinting that Root first climbed into bed with the mob when someone set fire to his restaurant. Arty caught that case fifteen years ago. Mickey wants us to believe that was no accident. Root got to stay in business and out of bankruptcy as long as he washed mob money. No testimony on that yet, but that's where Mickey's going. He's hinting that Root was locked into a protection racket and that Arty was there from the beginning. Arty lost the power of speech when Mickey asked him to account for Scooter Pleasants' complaint."

"Who is Scooter Pleasants?"

"I can't answer that without getting fired," says Ray. Twill's smirk covers his irritation like a suit that's three sizes too small.

"Scooter's an IAD blue file Mack is working. He's out the back end of a seven-year stretch for assaulting an arresting officer. He may be on his way back where he belongs. In the meantime, he's a citizen and a businessman accusing Arty of shaking him down for money to keep his sex shops from burning down."

"Ah," says Santiago. "Suddenly Mickey Shaw is not so crazy."

"Mickey's anything but crazy," says Ray.

"What's Arty's side of it?"

Ray shrugs.

"Haven't interviewed him yet. That's set for this afternoon but I'm waiting for IFOP to tell me where I can stick the appointment."

"What did Arty say in court?"

"Jolie wasn't having it. She instructed him not to answer and then she set Mickey's head on fire with her eyes. Or maybe it was my head she set on fire. I need an aspirin." Ray takes a step for the door.

"Feeling okay, Mack?" asks Santiago.

"Fine. Need a good night's sleep is all. I'll get out of your hair…" Ray shoots an unnecessary look at Twill's baldness. "Well, Raffi's hair… so you guys can get to some real police work. Enjoy your leave, Raffi."

Santiago and Twill trade glances over the desk. Ray turns and pulls open the door. Now all three of us have eyes on his back. We know a situation headed south when we see one. All of us. Even Ray.

TWENTY-FOUR

I spend some quality time at my desk. For me, that's like a fish spending quality time on the beach. The screen saver on my monitor is feeling poetic about productivity. *Stealing Time is but a Crime.*

I try to be productive while I wait for the IFOP rep to tell me they need to reschedule Arty Dunn's interview. I check my email. Nothing yet, but that just means that the complaint against Arty has the union wrapped around the axle. They'll wait until they're ten minutes late to let me know they aren't coming.

But there is an email from a Sergeant Burt Medford of the Chicago Violent Crimes division. Sergeant Medford doesn't like words, apparently, or he'd use more of them. More likely it's me and my reputation and my new IAD address he doesn't like.

Off. Mackey: Per D.A. Barbara Bannon, Wayne Bishop files attached. Sgt. Burt Medford.

The message includes dozens of attachments. The file names are all so truncated and riddled with acronyms it would take a Pentagon cryptographer to make any sense of them. I click on one file at random. Wayne Bishop is suddenly staring out at me through his mangey nest of black hair. His eyes are dirty fried eggs with small black yokes. His beard reveals a mouth that is slightly open, like he's trying to smile or say something to the guy taking his mug shot. The tips of his upper teeth are yellow.

This is not how I should be spending my time. I'd told Twill that helping Nadia King was strictly an off-the-clock favor for the friend of my brother-in-law. A couple of phone calls, tops. I've got other, much more important work to do. For one thing, the body camera footage of Jaime Hernandez and the Chandler police playing cops and robbers in the *Food Mart* parking lot is not going to re-summarize itself. Chasing down a Russian doll is not something the taxpayers of Will County are paying me to do.

I lean back in my chair for a discrete look around. Twill's door is still closed, which I'm guessing means Santiago actually has something to report about who else is using Mayor Royce's drycleaners.

That shouldn't make me care any less about my duty to the taxpayers. It really shouldn't.

The open file on my screen is forty-one pages long. Arrest, crime scene, evidence, and interrogation narratives by various Chicago police officers with a role to play. I spot read here and there. The interview records. Forensic reports. Photos of Joe Novak's body in his mother's den, bent grotesquely backwards up against the spattered wall beneath the broken den window, like his spine was close to snapping. The photo of the empty chair in the kitchen from where Ivah Novak had listened to her son die.

I'm amazed how easily it all comes back. Like it was one of my own cases. I had nothing to do with the case, but most of it is still in my head. How Ivah Novak had picked Wayne Bishop out of an especially short and hairy photo line-up. How the Chicago PD had snatched him up outside a South Side chop shop. He'd already unloaded most of the things he had stolen, but some of Ivah's possessions were still in Bishop's apartment. Those things, along with Ivah's eye-witness identification, was enough to make the case against him.

Or, at least, it should have been enough. Cop killers are good for more than splashy headlines. They also tend to inspire Chicago law enforcement toward an overabundance of enthusiasm. They didn't need Bishop's confession. But they beat one out of him anyway. Not literally. They wore him down in an all-night three-on-one session after whispering the part about having a right to a court-appointed lawyer.

Maybe I remember the bit about the confession because confessions have always interested me. The confessions that come easily. The confessions that come out with teeth. The confessions that come too late to do any good. I'm intimately familiar with that kind. Just ask my late wife.

It's not like Wayne Bishop was ignorant of his legal rights. He'd been busted so many times he had to have known the Miranda warning like words to a nursery rhyme. I'm guessing he knew what a court-appointed lawyer was; probably the only kind of lawyer he'd ever known. And time after time each of those lawyers had watched Bishop get convicted of the offenses charged. By the time he was arrested for killing Joe Novak, Bishop must have valued a free lawyer like a drowning man values free bricks.

So, locked in a room with three homicide detectives who were all souped up over the murder of one of their own, Bishop had not demanded a court-appointed lawyer.

And he eventually confessed. Not to the murder itself, but to tying up Ivah Novak and burglarizing her home on the night and approximate time of the murder. And that was okay by the cops. That worked. It put Bishop at the scene committing a felony or two at the time Joe lost his head. That was close enough.

But Bishop had made them work him over for almost fourteen hours before signing that piece of paper. He was so exhausted by then that he asked if he could go to sleep, just a short nap, before reading and signing. Just so he could think it all over. He may as well have asked them if he could go to Disneyland. The boys in blue all but held his eyes open and moved the pen for him.

That's when Bishop had said he just didn't understand why he was not entitled to a lawyer. He told his interrogators that it didn't make sense to him that the rules for murder were different. He'd always had a lawyer on other kinds of charges. He'd never been charged with murder before. Why were the rules about free lawyers different when it came to murder? The cops had explained again what they had explained before. Louder this time. Bishop had asked if he could make a phone call.

Twenty minutes later, Bishop's free lawyer was out front demanding to see his client; pointy boots, ponytail and all. Funny thing about that; Mickey Shaw never works for free.

I look at my watch. Ten minutes until the meeting with Arty Dunn and twenty minutes until that same meeting is postponed. I close the file and click on ten other links until I find what I'm looking for. It's an Affidavit of Return of Property consisting of three paragraphs of ass-covering legal boilerplate followed by an itemized list of Ivah Novak's property. Little things, mostly. The things Bishop had not yet managed to sell. Some raw gemstone jewelry from the bedroom. A gold-plated cross. A statuette of somebody's somber saint. A worn, fabric purse that I'm guessing came with a wallet and other things when he snatched it. There are eight items on the list. Number seven is the only one I care about: *one painted wooden doll, 3" x 7".*

I keep scrolling. The affidavit attaches a photo of each item of property. The doll is painted to resemble a Russian woman, bundled against the cold. Her cherub-cheeked face peers from inside a red head covering. Her arms and hands are painted along the sides of a jollily rotund body wrapped tightly in a yellow and blue sarafan. Across her belly is painted a bouquet of purple, yellow and red tulips. It is hard to tell the woman's age, but she's older than she looks. It's the cold breath of Mother Russia and the hard labor that puts the glow in her cheeks. She seems dusty. Her paint has faded and lost its gloss. Aside from a minor scratch and a tiny chip in the paint, she seems in good condition. There's a straight horizontal crack across her midsection. Good money that's where she opens up to reveal a younger version of herself waiting inside and probably five more ever-smaller versions after that. She's got an odd smile on her lips. She got it from the same place the Mona Lisa got her smile. Who knows what it means, but probably not happiness.

I scroll back up to the signature line on the affidavit. Casey Randolph Sweet. That's the name of the guy swearing that Ivah Novak got all her things back. That's who I want to talk to. I make a note and close the file and then poke around in our database until it coughs up a number for Chicago Evidence Control. A woman answers the phone like it's hers. She tells me that Randy Sweet no longer works for the Chicago Police Department. I ask her how long he's been gone but she says I have to talk to Human Resources for that kind of information. She connects me but I hang up before anyone can answer. No sense in letting this guy know I'm coming. So I search for him like I'm a regular cop and he's a regular citizen. I poke his name into an official records search. Five minutes gets me a bucket load of Sweets in the greater Chicago area. Three of those are named Casey. Only one gets to call himself Randy.

I write down the address and stuff it in my pocket just as Sandra Booth grips the side of my cubicle.

Sandra's the only hold-over on Twill's IAD team. Just as everyone else was swept out onto the street, Sandra kept her job by being indispensably integral to the IAD records system. That and Twill needed someone who could help shoulder the caseload while he was rebuilding the department. Getting rid of Sandra would have been like getting rid of the shelving and the ink and the coffee.

Fortunately, her low-key demeanor, her no-nonsense work ethic, and her investigative competence make for an easy officemate.

She peers around the edge of the cubicle to look down at me. She's a fine-boned librarian with a badge. Thin voice. Straight, mousy-brown hair losing the battle to gray. She tucks a sheet of it behind her ear.

"Finish up the solitaire, Mack. Your Two O'clock is here. I put them in the big room."

TWENTY-FIVE

Ray may be losing everything else, but he's still got his game face. Essential for game-haters. Essential for supposedly neutral investigators.

He'd love to see Scooter Pleasants disappear over the side of a cliff. He has to use Scooter's other name –not Daniel, the *other*-other name, *Complainant* –just to keep the bile out of his throat and the disgust out of his tone.

"Again," says Ray. "I haven't prejudged anything the complainant has alleged. It's still an investigation at this point."

He sets his pen carefully back on the notepad, looking slowly from Arty Dunn to Ian Garrety and back again. Arty crosses his arms and waits. Long day for Arty. He's still in the same sport coat and tie that he was wearing on the witness stand.

Ian Garrety is a bulldog, hunched low over the conference table waiting for a bone or a bowl of slop. His face is a blistered salmon color and he's missing half of his left eyebrow, which maybe fell off in the tanning booth. His black hair won't commit to full coverage, so Ian has retaliated by going full jarhead. He does his best to look bored and angry and amused. He's new at IFOP, still too green to have all his best conference room expressions under control.

Ray's guessing Ian is one of those who wanted to drive a cruiser like his father or brother but either couldn't hack the academy or got bounced after too many write-ups for excessive force. Now he's got a desk at the union riding shotgun for the real cops who just happen to be facing IAD investigations and disciplinary actions. Thanksgiving dinners must be hell on Ian's ego. His pulse throbs the veins in his neck, his hypertension counting backwards like it's New Year's Eve.

"Bullshit you haven't prejudged," says Ian. "You think Officer Dunn here is an arsonist. He's been wearing a badge in this state for eighteen years and you want to lock him up as a fire bug."

"No."

"Yes. You're essentially accusing him of arson. First shithead's truck and then the porn shop." He points sideways. "Does this look like someone who goes around lighting people's tailpipes? No way he's getting a fair shake in this… what'd you call it? An investigation? It's another IAD hit job."

Ray ignores Ian and keeps his focus on Arty.

"I'll lay it out once more. The complainant has not alleged that you set fire to anything. The complainant alleges that, during the course of your investigation into the fire that damaged the *Pleasant Palace Adult Books and Video* store on West Malcomb, you told him that his odds of him staying in business would improve if he paid for some extra security protection."

Arty spreads his arms out over the table, looking sideways at Ian and back again. Below the surface, it's not so hard to see Arty's back-slapping affability. His is the Superbowl party everyone wants to crash. He's got more than a couple shirt-off-his-back stories to his name.

But you never really know anyone. Not until they're in a corner.

"Yeah. I did say that." Arty's face is a question mark with a goatee. "So what? It's true. I'd tell that to any business owner dealing with vandals and arsonists. Even businesses like Scooter's. Is it going to hurt my feelings any if any of his places burn to the ground? Not one little bit. He's scum, okay? The world would be a better place. But I offered the guy a tip that he might want to look into some security options. So what?"

"The complainant alleges that you were recommending *yourself* as that security option."

"Bullshit," says Arty. "I never said that. I never implied it. What, he thinks I was offering to spend my time camped out in his parking lot? Looking for … for taggers and firebugs among the degenerates he calls customers? Searching people for cans of spray paint and gasoline?"

Ray smiles. It's a lie, this look. It says he has nothing better to do. Nothing he'd enjoy more than sit in a conference room explaining the obvious.

"No, Detective. I think the concern is that unless the complainant, Mr. Pleasants, greased your palm on a regular basis bad things would happen to his bookstores."

"Bookstores." Arty laughs. He's sincere enough that it makes you want to like the guy. But then that passes. He jabs the top of the table with his forefinger.

"Cut the shit. You want me to take this seriously? Then let's be honest here, Mack."

"Officer Mackey."

"Fine. Let's be honest here, Officer Mackey. Scooter doesn't own any bookstores. Okay? He owns three disgusting smut shacks. Got that? A child molester turning a buck dealing that sewage. He shouldn't be anywhere near those kinds of places let alone own them."

"Mr. Pleasants has never been convicted of child molestation or any other sex crime."

What an act. There is nothing Ray says or does to betray just how much he hates making an argument out of those words. But I can tell anyway. I can see the blush spreading over the back of his neck. I can see the slight pulse in the hinge of his jaw. He wants to start throwing chairs around.

"Oh, give me a break," spits Arty. "This guy is a textbook pedophile."

"Any actual evidence of that?" asks Ray, as if this is a spontaneous question. As if he had not just handed over such evidence to his own lieutenant.

"You mean other than the case that got him arrested for sexually assaulting a minor?"

"Yeah," says Ray. "Because that case never got a conviction, did it?"

"No, but I don't need any more evidence," says Arty. "Just look at the guy."

"Who cares if he was convicted?" Ian almost shouts it, leaning into the table. The veins in his neck are straining against his collar, trying to loosen the tie. "We know what he is. We know because…"

"Mr. Garrety." Ray levels his gaze. "I will say this again and for the last time. IFOP has a right to observe this interrogation. You have a right to take notes. You have a right to participate only as absolutely necessary to protect Officer Dunn's interests. You do not have a right to interfere with my examination. Am I clear about that?"

Ian Garrety's face finds a deeper shade of red. His features squeeze together like he's trying to push something too big through his nose.

"The only thing I'm not clear on, Officer Mackey, is how a traitor like you got his badge back. I hear you're about as dirty as they come. Guess it's fitting you found your way into the IAD cesspool. Defending maggots like Scooter Pleasants. Your kind of people."

Ray smiles again. Less convincing this time.

"No. My kind of people are the ones who know the difference between doing their job and taking up space. I'm not defending anyone in this game, Mr. Garrety. That's not my job."

Ray looks at Arty, nodding his head in Ian's direction.

"You really sure this is how you want this interview to go, Arty? I'm trying to figure out your side of things here. This is your chance. But I'm not big on wasting time. When I sit for too long my ass starts to hurt and my mind starts to wander. If your side of things is that I'm a traitor and that I shouldn't have a badge and that IAD is a cesspool, well then, I'm ready to make a note of all that and move on to other witnesses. I'm happy to let Ian here have your last word. In fact," Ray pushes back the chair, and stands. He's angry enough to turn the table on top of both of them. "In fact, that sounds good to me. Let's go with that. Your answer to all of this is that I'm in the wrong job. Thanks for coming in."

Arty looks up at him, not moving.

"What other witnesses?" he asks.

"Oh, are we still in the mood for a conversation?"

Ray looks from one to the other. Ian keeps his face to his notepad, scribbling.

Arty sighs and gestures to Ray's empty chair.

"What witnesses?" he asks again.

"You tell me, Arty." Ray sits. "Was anyone present when you had your conversations with Mr. Pleasants?"

"No."

"Where did you interview him?"

"On site. The place on West Malcomb. We were looking at the scorch marks. That's where I asked my questions."

"Arson."

"Hardly. Mischief. But, yeah, that was the finding. Not much damage to the place. Too bad."

"Suspects?"

"None."

"How hard are you looking?"

"Please."

"How hard are you looking?"

"It's not at the top of my list, okay?"

"Did you make any recording of your conversation with Mr. Pleasants?"

"No." Arty nods at the green file folder on the table next to Ray. "I wrote it up after."

"And no one else was nearby? Maybe some employee who could have overheard what you actually told him? A customer?"

"Just me and Scooter."

"Anything you can offer me that makes this more than just a swearing contest between you and him?"

Arty snorts and shrugs. Ian Garrety shakes his head in a kind of disappointed amusement.

"I'm not afraid of a swearing contest with that piece of garbage," says Arty. "Bring that on any time. If and when this goes to court, Scooter's not going to play so well to a jury."

"A jury? I'm just starting this investigation and you're talking about a jury? I didn't make you for such a pessimist, Arty."

Arty shrugs. "Look. This goes however it goes. Okay? Touch me or my pension and I'll sue the department and the city blind. And you too if I can. If Scooter's credibility is the best you've got, then you've got less than nothing. He's not going to play well is all I'm saying."

"How well do you think you played this morning in the Wrigley Menard case?"

Ray is trying to keep him off balance. It works. Arty smiles to himself. It gives his face something to do as his brain tries to figure things out.

"Yeah, I saw you sitting back there," he says at last. "Your life must be some kind of boring, Mack."

"You have no idea. This seems to be your day for answering questions about shakedown protection rackets."

"Maybe you didn't notice. Judge Joliet said I didn't have to answer any of those questions."

"It's Judge *Jolie*. Show some respect. And I'd be very surprised if Mickey Shaw was done with you just yet."

"Sounds like you're pulling for Wrigley. Why am I not surprised? Wrigley and Scooter. Water finds its own level, I guess."

"Mr. Pleasants claims you gave him your cellphone number. That true?"

"I told him to call me if he had questions. Or if he came up with any information on who might have started the fire."

"IAD gives us business cards. Homicide too. We always had business cards. Budget problems in Property Crimes?"

"I was out of cards."

"Why the personal cell number?"

"Wasn't thinking. Moving too fast. Just wrote down the wrong number."

"Did he ever call?"

"No."

"Did you ever contact him again after that interview?"

"No."

"He says different."

"He's lying."

"You know we'll be checking your cellphone records."

Arty leans in. "Knock yourself out. You said there were other witnesses. I'm asking you again, Officer Mackey, what other witnesses?"

"Sorry," says Ray. "That's not for you to know at this point."

"What?" Ian Garrety is back to a shout. "That *is* for him to know. That absolutely is for him to know."

Ray shakes his head.

"Not until the investigation is complete, written up, approved and we can all get together again for the closing conference."

"This is bullshit," says Arty, now a long way from affable. He points his finger. "This is dirty. You're dirty, Mack. *You* are." It's his turn to push back his chair.

"Am I?" asks Ray. "You want to tell me why you're trying to bribe your way through this investigation?"

Arty's head snaps up. His eyes are fixed and hard.

"What the fuck are you talking about?"

"I'm talking about the man who approached me yesterday. He put a bunch of money in my hand and then asked me to look the other way in this case. Seemed to think you were a great guy and that Scooter was a terrible guy. You two seem to think a lot alike."

"You're just lying," says Ian. "You're just..."

"Stop jerking me around, Mack," says Arty.

"I'm not jerking anybody around. My lieutenant logged the cash into evidence this morning."

"What man?" asks Arty. "Who?"

"How much cash?" asks Ian.

"You guys don't seem to get it. This is the part where I ask the questions. One of them is still on the table waiting for an answer." Ray looks at Arty. "How about it, Detective?"

Arty's face is red with rage. His voice is suddenly a heavy, feral animal crawling over the table.

"I'm not bribing anyone. I have no idea what you're talking about. There's your fucking answer. Go stick it up your ass. I don't know why you're out to bury me, and I don't really care. It's enough for me to know it."

Ray nods like he's just been told the time. Then he slips two fingers into his shirt pocket.

TWENTY-SIX

I place the broken poker-chip on the table and push it to the center with a finger.

I've watched too many people die. Usually gunshot wounds. Too many times I was the one who made it happen. Out on a sidewalk. On staircases. Behind the wheel of a car. Once on a ratty couch as the cushion underneath began to seep like a wet sponge. There's a kind of relaxed horror that takes possession of a man's face when he realizes that he's bleeding out. When he feels his own traitorous heart pumping the life out of his body in thick, velvet gushes. All the struggling stops. The muscles start to relax. The muscles that give a man's cheeks some shape and character start to soften. His skin starts to sag a little with the coming pallor. The eyes let go of their hope like little helium balloons. Then the part of him that used to hope is bumping along the ceiling looking down at the carnage and the silent horror of himself. Take it from me. I get that view from the ceiling twenty-four-seven. It's impossible to turn away.

Arty Dunn is headed for shades of zombie white. His mouth opens, but it's Ian who does the talking.

"What the hell is that?" he asks.

"Looks like maybe Arty knows what this is," I say without looking away. I have no idea what's going on, but I know better than to let anyone know. "How about sharing with the class, Detective?"

But Arty can't take his eyes off the chip.

"Arty?"

He flickers back to life like a fluorescent bulb in a morgue and looks at me.

"I… what, you want to play poker now, Mack?"

He wants it to be a joke. He's trying. But no one is laughing. Especially not Arty.

"So, then your answer is that you don't know what this chip is or what it means. You really want to play dumb on this, Arty? Now's your chance."

Arty pulls the chip toward him. He picks it up and holds it in front of his face. It's like he's picked up a black hole and seen his own face looking back out.

I hold out my hand. It takes a second, but then Arty looks up at me. Like it's just the two of us in the room. I've been working the streets long enough to recognize fear when I see it. Bullshit bravado aside, Arty is terrified. He drops the chip in my palm.

"No idea," he says. "Are we done?"

I keep thinking about the look on Arty's face all the way out to Northrop High School. It's a long enough drive as it is, even without the traffic so afraid of the ice. Green doesn't mean *go*. Not today. Today green means sit behind the wheel and ponder the meaning of colored lights in the sky. Only honking means *go* and *go* means either crawl or spin the tires in place, which amounts to the same thing. Only two cars make it across the intersection before yellow starts swinging its elbows for red.

I tell myself I don't mind. It gives me and the Camels plenty of time to think about Arty's face.

Fear and hate are the ugly, ill-mannered twins everyone mixes up at the family picnic. You have to pay close attention to tell them apart. Arty Dunn hating me is easy enough to understand, especially if he's innocent of shaking down Scooter. I haven't met anyone who can shrug off being unjustly accused. Certainly not me.

But that wasn't hate. Not there at the end, handing me back that poker chip. That was fear. Deep fear. That was a man bleeding out on a dirty sofa. The question is why.

I blow some smoke out the window, but the frozen air isn't taking it. The wind shoulders itself hard against the Impala and stuffs the smoke back in through the crack. The heater vents don't want it either. I pull the poker chip out of my shirt pocket and turn it over and over for another good look. I rub my thumb across the embossed letters. *KFC*.

I'm not dumb enough to think Colonel Sanders has anything to do with Arty or Scooter or the bald brick mountain who gave me this broken black chip. But I'm smart enough to know that poker chips are just pieces of plastic unless you give them a meaning. A message. I pocket the chip and fish out my phone.

"Sandra. It's Mack."

"Mack. LT was just asking for you."

"What's he want?"

"To find out how your meeting went."

"Went great. Arty apologized and ran off to buy Scooter some flowers."

"Right. He's also looking for those Hernandez body-cam summaries. What do you want me to tell him?"

"Tell him I'm at the dentist."

"That true?"

"Okay, tell him I told you I'm the dentist."

"Right. When will you be back?"

"Someday. Sooner if they change the rules about smoking and drinking. I need a favor."

"Of course you do. Because I don't have my own cases."

"Take it easy. I just need to borrow your memory."

"Okay."

"In the olden days, back before Chandler IAD, you worked the Chicago arson squad, right?"

"For about ten minutes. Central Investigations kept yanking me around. But, yeah, for a little while."

"Remember the *Kings Flush Casino* case?"

"Oh yeah. That was a biggie. I was officially CPD by that time though. Mike Perry was the Fire Inspector. Begged me not to go over to the dark side. I wanted to chase bad guys and he said you can't chase them if you're working with them. Not a fan of police. I think Mike got lonely picking through the char."

"And all these years later you're in IAD, chasing bad cops. Imagine that."

"Funny thing is I kind of miss the fire cases. Different kind of paper trail. Forensics are everything. *Kings Flush Casino* was a rat fuck, though. Don't miss that one."

"Who was working the homicide lead on that case for Chicago PD?"

The phone goes silent as she thinks. Another violent gust rocks the car as I veer north into the east Chandler sprawl of lower middleclass neighborhoods, small brick boxes huddled beneath giant red oaks and sycamores. The trees are mostly skeletons. They've already given up everyone they know but the wind doesn't seem to care, rattling them for all they're worth. So now the trees are just making up the names. Implicating everybody. Anything to make it stop.

The guy in the green GTO ahead of me wants two lanes to himself so he has some more room to make love to his phone.

"Come on, you idiot."

"Excuse me?" says Sandra. She's ready to be offended.

"Sorry. I'm talking to the guy in front of me but he's busy. What do you remember?"

"I remember *Kings Flush* was nearly twenty years ago, Mack. I don't know. I'd have to look."

"Think you can pull some strings with Chicago PD to kick loose the file?"

"You mean like all four thousand pages?"

"No. Just the final report."

"Arson or homicide?"

"Both. And Sandra?"

"Yeah?"

"Maybe no one else needs to know I'm asking."

"I can keep a secret. But what's this got to do with Arty Dunn?"

"I don't remember saying it had anything at all to do with Arty Dunn."

Northrop High School is a low, squat brick building with a few excited flags out front and a great big sleepy box in the back where they keep the basketball hoops. Off to the side of the building is a parking lot and beyond that is a bunch of chain link fencing that someone put up to make sure the oval track and goal posts don't escape. There is a large mosaic bald eagle on the front of the building. Its talons are open and extended toward three sets of double doors, like it's swooping down to pluck some kid off the sidewalk as he makes a run for the busses.

I slip the Impala into a space across the street beneath a no-parking sign and let it idle in the wind. What I want to do is march inside and start asking questions about girls with long black hair and bright yellow coats and signs of emotional scarring. But I can't do that and also keep my job. So I settle for the next best thing, which is to risk looking like a parent or a pervert and wait at the curb for a few minutes, hoping I get lucky. I figure if she happens to make an appearance, I can at least tail her to where she lives and use the address to get a name and a family background.

It's more than a long shot. In fact, this makes a long shot look like a sure thing. But, like Marlo always used to say, every brilliant idea in the history of humankind grew out of some ugly, ridiculous notion. Life itself has always been a one-in-a-trillion proposition.

Twenty minutes get me a knock on the window by a security guard who doesn't like the way I look. I flash my badge and send him packing. Teenagers, fat and skinny, sullen and silly, come out the front doors mostly in groups of three or more. I figure I'm looking for a single. Someone in yellow walking the blues, head down in a shroud of black hair. A color isn't much to go on, but the kids of east Chandler aren't the kind that have lots of options. They've each got one winter coat hanging on a peg by the front door for when the temperature drops, and they wear it every single day until the lawn mowers come out of hibernation.

I give the game another twenty before packing it in. I'm too late. School is already out. I pull away from the curb thinking I should head back to work and put Twill at ease. But then I have another idea and I like that one better. I stop at the corner so I can fish around in my front pocket without killing anyone. I find my note with the address of Casey Randolph Sweet.

No one ever goes back to the office after an afternoon at the dentist.

Wouldn't want anyone to think I made that up.

TWENTY-SEVEN

At least his headache is gone. It's the best he's been all day. He looks like someone chasing the glimmer of a purpose before it drops out of sight beneath the horizon of another day gone. Because once it drops, then comes the dark and all its perfect memory and amber-colored addictions.

Ray picks his way out of east Chandler to the interstate and points the Impala north. Once he has his lane, he opens up his phone and dials.

"Yellow Cab. Raj Malik."

"Yeah, I need a cab that purrs like a kitten and smells like a Camel. You got one of those?"

"Hey, Mack!"

"What's the haps, Raj?"

"Makin' a living man. You know. What's up with you? You're not out at the railyards, I hope."

"I don't like trains anymore. Can't take the headache."

"How's the new-old job?"

"I like it almost as much as I like trains. Say, I'm looking to lose some money for a favor. You in?"

Raj laughs. Hard not to imagine the white teeth glowing out of that young, brown face.

"Anything, man. Long as it doesn't get me killed. Never can tell with you."

"Killed? Raj, those Camels of yours will stomp your lungs into dust before I can even mess up your hair."

"Look who's talking."

"Besides, in this relationship I'm the one who does all of the almost-dying and you're the one who likes to play cavalry."

"Fair enough. What can I do for you, Mack?"

Ray explains the job. It's not complicated and it's not dangerous. Raj is game just like Ray knew he would be. Raj makes it sound like he's in it for the money. But Raj Malik is as good as they come. He'd do it for free. Even if the job was complicated. Even if it was dangerous. And Ray will pay out double what he owes. Just because. He'll pay out like a man with no friends.

TWENTY-EIGHT

Randy Sweet's place is two stories of peeling gray paint and cracked siding. The house seems a little nervous. The windows are steamy and streaked on the inside and the rooftiles are flapping. It looks like it's getting a high-colonic when I pull up so maybe that explains it.

The front door is wide open. Emerging from within are two large, dirty-white tubes that stretch across the frozen yard and connect to something loud and heavy inside a black van that belongs to Dan's Restoration Services. The driver's side door is open and a leg is sticking out. I park on the street and get out.

"You Dan?" I shout to the owner of the leg. He's got a scratchy red beard and dirty hands and a clipboard with a workorder on it. He keeps scribbling as he answers.

"No. I'm Walt. Who are you?"

"I'm a guy looking for the owner of this house, Casey Sweet." I jerk my head toward the house. "He inside?"

It's a stupid question that gets me a funny look and a headshake.

"You know where I can find him?" I ask.

The man seems confused until my badge clears things up. He points.

"He's got a girlfriend three blocks that way on Wood Haven. Little blue house. Can't miss it."

"You two friends or something?"

Walt thinks this is funny.

"No, his friends call him Mouth. I don't call him that."

"Mouth? Odd thing to call a person."

"Yeah, well, he's an odd guy."

"What do you call him?"

"Asshole. Maybe you're off to arrest him."

"Oh yeah? If I was to arrest Mouth for something, what would you want that something to be?"

"Dating my sister."

Walt is right about not missing the house on Wood Haven. It's so cute it looks plastic. Too cute for the neighborhood; robin's-egg blue with trim white shutters and a little brick chimney. It belongs in a make-believe town next to a model train track. It sits in the back of a snow-covered, postage stamp lot empty of trees. Five or six wind-whipped bushes crowd up beneath the windows like they're scared of the sidewalk. There's a black Sentra holding down a straight, narrow driveway. The strip of pavement stops in the middle of the yard like it's looking for a garage that walked off in the night. Or maybe someone took it.

I pull up at the curb and then get out and head for the front door. The wind doesn't like this idea much, but I didn't make the drive just to be a kite stuck in a tree. I make it to the stoop and give the house a stiff poke in the doorbell.

A petite, birdlike woman answers the door in a green apron. She's got her brother's face without the square jaw and the beard. Long, fine strawberry-blonde hair. Sharp green eyes. Her nose is thin and pointed. She could pick a lock with that nose. She cocks her head at me from across the threshold.

"Yes?"

She has a long wooden spoon in her hand. Her perfume smells like soup. Something dark and Hungarian.

"Hi," I say with a half-wave. "Sorry to bother you. I'm looking for Casey Sweet. He around?"

She smiles like I've said something sad.

"Oh. No. I'm so sorry. You just missed him. Can I give him a name and a way to reach you?"

"Sure," I say. "Let me give you a card."

I work my wallet out of my back pocket. The wind curls around my head, reaching inside the little blue house to ladle out another whiff of whatever it is she's cooking. I hand her one of my new IAD cards. I try to take a good look around over her shoulder as she reads. A gigantic television sits across from two matching recliners. On the television, a large, bejeweled woman holding a wooden spoon is frozen over a cauldron on a stove. Her eyes are wide and her mouth is open, like she accidentally dropped a diamond ring in the stew.

"Officer Mackey," she reads. Then she looks up, petite avian features pinched in concern. "What is this about? Is Randy in some sort of trouble?"

"Oh, not at all," I say. "I'm working a case for a friend. Not even official business really. I just needed to chat with Casey... or Randy, I guess... about his old job for Chicago PD."

"How did you know to look for him here?"

I nod sideways, into the wind.

"A contractor down at his place said I might try your house."

The little bird woman rolls her green eyes and nods like the world suddenly makes all kinds of sense.

"I'll give Randy the message when he gets back from the store," she says.

I thank her and point over her shoulder at the television.

"Whatever show you're watching sure smells good," I say.

She turns around. Now we're both looking at the woman still frozen in suspension over the pot. The television is framed on two sides by white wooden shelving. Not a big reader, this one. Miles of bookshelves and not a single book. Instead, there is a lot of negative space, like she collects it and arranges it just so, pushing it together and separating it with other things she likes to collect, like family photographs in gold frames and ceramic figurines too small and far away for me to make out what they are. But the collection of Russian dolls is as plain as day.

TWENTY-NINE

He's going to run out of gas. If he sits here idling much longer, the thing will start to sputter and then stop.

Not that the walk wouldn't do him some good. He needs the exercise. But the cold wind would kill him within five or ten blocks. They'd find him along the side of the 355 on-ramp, an old man bent in the shape of an Impala driver's seat, broken cigarette mashed between his frozen blue lips.

He used to be a specimen, this guy. He used to chase people. Through South Side alleys into wind so cold it could turn a man's lungs to ice. Up and down fire escapes. Over rooftops. Before that, gangs of people would chase him across the gridiron, converging in a mad rush on his heels and then just give up the effort and fall to their knees, crying like you do when you realize there was never any real hope in the first place and wishing you'd never tried. The Northwestern offensive coach used to regularly knock the quarterback in the helmet with his clipboard: *just get the goddamned ball to Mackey!*

He was something once. Mackey the Magnificent. Now look at him. Jesus.

Ray adjusts the heat vent and lights up another Camel.

He's got each of the front windows cracked so the wind can blow in and keep on moving, taking the smoke to wherever it has abducted the clouds. In the west, the sun is slipping off the edge of the icy winter sky. White wisps of vapor begin to gray. Blue slowly inks its way down into indigo.

He pulls out his phone and dials, keeping an eye on the little blue house. It's exactly the same as he'd left it twenty minutes ago, only now it's a half-a-block smaller and cuter.

"Ms. King? Hi. This is Ray Mackey, from Chandler PD. Is this inconvenient? You sure? Oh, as good as can be expected, I guess. Be nice if this wind would give it a rest. How are you?"

If he's fooling her, he's not fooling me. This isn't business. He doesn't have to make this call. He knows what he's going to do, and he doesn't need Nadia King's permission or more information. He just wants to talk to her. He wants the sound of her voice in his head, refreshing the memory of her face. He tells himself he's not in love and he should listen. Because he's right about that. This has nothing to do with love. This is an old man who's been in the dark for too long. He just wants to crack the door a little. Let a little sliver of light into the room. Pathetic, but true.

"I'm guessing little Danika says that blue dragons love the wind, the colder the better. Am I right?"

He laughs, working it, less for her benefit than his own. Like the sound itself might keep him warm. Of all the things Marlo has left him without, physical intimacy might be the least of it. Laughing in the company of a beautiful woman is way up there.

Well. Laughing, full stop.

"Yeah, well that imagination is taking her places," he says. "You wait and see. Is she into dolls yet? With the frilly dresses and the hats? Ah. Well she will be soon enough, trust me. Best dragon food ever."

Her laugh lowers his lids. He takes another hit on the Camel. Come on, Ray. Get to it, man.

"Speaking of dolls, I'm calling because I think I found your mother's doll. No, I don't have it yet. I can fill you in on the details when I hand it over. Right now, I just need to ask you something. Is there anything about the doll that makes it easily distinguishable from other Russian dolls? I've got a photo, but... what's that? Yeah, I got it from the evidence file Bannon sent me, but I left it on my desk and my memory isn't what it used to be."

A dirty, white pickup passes and slows to a crawl as it approaches the little blue house. It rolls up the driveway and stops behind the black Sentra, disgorging a stubby, stogie of a man in a long brown coat to his knees and a dark wool beanie pulled down over his ears. He looks like a three-quarter-smoked cigar that has figured out how to drive. The cigar is smoking a cigarette. The cigarette gets one last drag before the wind carries it across the yard.

"How many dolls are inside the main doll? So, four total? Is there a chip in the paint or something? A signature? Different colored eyes? Anything unique?"

The man pulls a paper grocery bag out of the truck and closes the door with his hip. He crosses the tiny patch of snow to the front door and disappears inside.

"That's it," says Ray. "Perfect."

The front door closes and the light above comes on. The bushes beneath the front windows move in angry fits, trying to scrub the paint off the house.

"Got it. Yeah. Okay, Nadia. Thanks for your time. Hard to say. Tonight, if I'm lucky. I'll call and let you know. If things go my way, how can I get it to you? You want to drop by the station tomorrow? Oh. Sure. No that works too. Italian is fine by me. Italian's great. Danika too. Absolutely. Dragons love Italian."

THIRTY

It's past time to be home. I can feel Phil getting hungry. Her can-opening skills need work but she's more than mastered the cat telepathy.

It's not just Phil calling me home. There's a frozen brick of food to nuke and a dry tumbler in need of an ice bath. Not to mention the drama inside my laptop. Detective McMannis' time is rapidly evaporating up into a hot Chicago night. He's not just going to save himself.

I'd planned to wait another thirty minutes. My body hurts from all the sitting. Reclining is what I need. Hydrated reclining. But talking with Nadia King has given me the incentive to dig around for a little more stamina. No Russian doll, no pizza. No pizza, no Nadia. One slice will get me a nice case of indigestion, but I've suffered a lot more for a lot less. I'll make that trade any day. I turn off the engine to keep some gas in the tank.

I'm nothing but a Camel nose glowing in the dark by the time my phone finally rings. It's as loud as Gideon's trumpet, shrieking through the quiet car like an air raid siren. My brain seizes in its momentary alarm, so my hand takes charge, thrusting itself inside my coat, reaching either for the .38 in the shoulder holster that isn't actually there or for my panicked heart. It finds the phone instead.

Just one ring. Then silence, long and dark and empty like a mountain mine shaft with no bottom. I flip open the cover and read the tiny screen like it's a message in a fortune cookie.

Unknown Caller. Number Blocked.

Marlo.

The name —the idea of her —starts as a solid answer in my brain that quickly degrades into an aerosol wish, like a vivid dream diffusing away in daylight.

I'm still clawing at the sense of her in my head, trying to keep her from dissipating, when the phone rings again. It's quieter this time. I don't recognize the number on the screen. I don't need to. I give it another couple of rings to get my wits back in line. Then I answer like I haven't been waiting. Randy Sweet sounds perplexed.

"You wanted to talk to me about something?"

"Yeah, Randy. I'm sorry to bother you, especially at home. I appreciate you calling back. I called your department line, but they wanted me to talk to HR. I decided that I'd rather drink paint."

"I hear that," he says. "Bunch of smiling robot psychos."

"Showed you the door, did they?"

"Shit-canned me a year ago. Long story. What's this about, man?"

"I'm with Chandler IAD. I'm working a case for a friend. Not an official investigation. It involves the old Wayne Bishop case. I'm assuming that rings a bell?"

"Yeah. I guess. I mean, I didn't have anything to do with that case. I know more about it from the news than anything else."

"Well, you did have a very small role to play. My research says that you were the guy who certified the return of evidence to Ivah Novak."

"Oh, yeah, that could be. But I did that like, all the time, man. That was just part of the job. I didn't have anything to do with the case."

"I get that. Thing is that Mrs. Novak seems to think not everything in the evidence locker found its way back to her. I'm trying to track it down."

"Yeah, look, Officer Mackey, here's the deal." I can feel him backing away, right on schedule. I keep quiet and let him take some rope. "I'm not going to be much help here. It was just, like, a check-the-box process. I get the order for evidence return. I pull up the item list in the system. I take the list to evidence control. I verify the items on the list. I bag them up. I seal the bag. I sign the seal. I reach out and make contact with whoever. Ivah Novak or whoever. They show up. I sign a verification. They sign a verification. I hand the stuff over and then I'm done. I literally have no other involvement. If she's accusing me..."

"She's not accusing you of anything. She doesn't know you exist. She's just a nice old lady who can't find something on that list of yours."

"Not my list, man. That's what I'm saying. I don't know anything about anything. I couldn't even begin to tell you what was on that list. How long ago was that return?"

"Three years and change."

"Ancient history. There's nothing in my head about that, man."

"Okay," I say. I give him my best frustrated sigh. "I hear you. I can't remember past yesterday myself. Worth a shot, I guess. I appreciate the time."

Silence fills up the phone. It's one of those pauses that doesn't know what to think of itself. A smart man would hang up and go toss the evidence into the neighbor's yard. Casey Randall Sweet is not that guy. He's not going to sleep tonight without knowing a little more about just how close he came to getting caught. I hold my tongue and wait for the question to poke its head out and look around.

"What's she missing?" he asks at last.

"What? Oh. It's a little, oh, what do you call it, like a fake-diamond brooch in the shape of a frog."

"Hmm. No. There was nothing like that. I'd remember something like that."

"Okay, well that's helpful right there," I say, optimism rising. "All I really need is something certain I can take back to her. That sounds pretty certain to me. You're saying it wasn't there to be returned."

"Yeah. A thing in the shape of a frog? A brooch or whatever? I'd remember that. Was that even on the item list?"

"No. That's just it. She says it should have been."

"Yeah well, again, I don't have anything to do with what's on the list. I just make sure it all gets returned. There was no frog thing. There was like a purse and a little religious saint statuette thing and a painted wooden doll. Some other things. No frog jewelry. In fact, no jewelry, period."

"Got it. Thanks. Why'd you take the wooden doll?"

"What?"

"You heard me. Or does your hearing come and go like your memory?"

"What is this? You said…"

"I said *Ivah* wasn't accusing you. I didn't say anything about me. I'm accusing you of felony stupidity."

"Hey, fuck you, man."

"Here's the thing, Mouth. Ivah's Russian doll is sitting on the shelf about eighteen inches to the right of your girlfriend's monster television. There are three or four others there too; a whole gaggle. But you know the one I'm talking about. I'm guessing it's the one you're looking at right now as your pulse starts to rabbit."

"Look…"

"No, Mouth. I've done enough looking. Time for listening now. I know what it's like to want to please someone you love. She's a collector, your gal. She loves things like this. Little ethnic dolls and doodads. You want to make her happy. She can cook a pot of soup that'll make you cry out for your mother. She's the kind of woman who won't think twice about putting you up for a few weeks when the weather turns cold and the pipes in your walls start to leak and the whole place turns to mush. She's the kind who goes to the well for you and asks her brother for a favor even though you always run him down behind his back and even though he's not so fond of you either. She'll do that for you every time. So, who wouldn't want to please a woman like that? I get it. I really do. So you see this Russian doll in the evidence locker, and you can't help but think of the smile on your gal's face when she unwraps it. You could go out and shop for a doll of your own, but you're too cheap for that. Just like with the plumbing. Why pay for something you can get for free? Am I right, Mouth?"

"No," he says, but the sound comes out soft and packed in cotton. "You're not right. I'm hanging up."

"No, you're not. Because you're worried about what happens next. You know that stealing evidence out of lock-up is a sure ticket to your own lock-up. So you're going to hear me out, Mouth. The thing in your favor is that this is not the kind of thing I do for Chandler PD. This is strictly a side-line for a friend. My LT wants my ass in a chair working on his cases. Chandler PD has its own HR goons and he's got them on speed dial. He won't think twice about feeding me to the wolves unless I get his work done. So, my LT knows nothing about this errand for a friend. Now, District Attorney Bannon knows I'm sniffing around. She gave me the information that got me to this phone call. But she doesn't know anything about you, and I don't think she really gives a rat's ass."

I wait for a second. Silence.

"Still with me, Mouth?"

A pot clangs in the background.

"Now. One call from me and all of that changes. We get a warrant and the boys and I are coming over for soup and then we're all going to go visit your old friends at Chicago PD."

"I don't have… *the thing* you're talking about."

"Sure you do. Otherwise, you wouldn't mind saying the word into the phone while your girlfriend's right there stirring that pot. I know you're thinking that maybe it makes sense to just get rid of the doll before we drop by to read you your rights. Makes sense, I guess. But the photo I took over your girl's shoulder while you were out getting groceries is going to make that a real bad choice."

It's harder to snarl in a whisper, but Mouth gives it his all anyway.

"What is it you want from me?"

"I want the doll," I say, lightening my tone. "I want to close this sideshow and get back to chasing the real bad guys. In the scheme of things, you haven't killed anybody. At least, not to my knowledge. You just wanted another bowl of hot soup. I get that. I don't want to make a mountain of paperwork out of a molehill. I just want a sweet, old widow whose son was gunned down, to get back a keepsake that means something to her. Okay? Randy?"

"I'm here."

"Good. Now. Here's the important part. Helping me do that maybe makes you a decent guy. A decent guy with poor impulse control and epically bad judgment when it comes to pretty women. But preventing me from returning this doll makes you a heartless prick who needs to learn a tough lesson in a small cell with neighbors who really don't like cops. So, Mouth, I've got to ask: who's the real you?"

There's an extra-long pause this time. In the background a woman's voice is adamant about the dangers of over-seasoning. The voice grows farther away. Then it disappears.

"Assuming you're right about all of this," says Randy, "and you're not, this would confirm possession. What's to stop you from…"

Randy doesn't finish. I finish for him.

"What's to stop me from arresting you? Nothing except my low tolerance for wasting time on bullshit. And, not for nothing, Mouth, I already have you in possession of this doll. A picture's worth a thousand words."

"At best, you have my girlfriend in possession."

"Think that one through, Mouth. I'll wait. If you want me to put your girlfriend in handcuffs let me know, but that'll put a quick end to the soup. You're the one with access to the evidence room, not her."

"How do I know you're real police? This could be anyone's card."

"You think there's some cabal of wooden doll thieves pretending to be cops?"

"So maybe you tell your friend, and your friend makes a phone call. How am I better off?"

"You? I don't care about you, Randy. What makes you think I give a shit about you? You should be asking yourself how *I'm* better off. Because I don't want that road. That just makes me a witness in an investigation that I'd prefer not to have anything to do with. Then I get raked over the coals for not making an arrest when I should have? I don't think so. I'd rather just return the item to where it belongs. No names or addresses. Everybody wins. But listen, listen. This is not my decision to make. Okay? You tell me how you want to play it and let's just do that. You want me to do this all by the book?"

Randy sighs into the phone. I can tell he's thinking about how he's going to explain things to the chef.

"When?" he asks.

"Right now. Go for a walk. I'm half a block north. Look for the headlights."

"Fuck."

"What. You think I went home? Understand that I know what I'm looking for, so don't bring the wrong one. Russian inscription on the bottom with two large letter V's and the date 1847. Three smaller dolls inside. If I have to come back out here, Mouth, I'm not coming alone."

THIRTY-ONE

Ray waits, windows up, blowing into his hands to keep them warm.

He has to clear his breath from the windshield above the steering wheel. He wants to keep an eye on the house. Its colorful cuteness has slipped away in the dark. The rest of the street unspools in a straight line of shadowy boxes. The glow from all the windows is broken and skittish on the snowy ground, like leaves of light raked by the shadows of angry bare branches. Halfway up the block, a round rubber garbage can makes a break for a better neighborhood.

It takes Randy fifteen minutes to make up his excuse. It must involve a need to go back to the store because he walks no farther than the pickup. He climbs in and starts it up and backs out of the drive. Ray turns on the headlights. The truck moves slowly up the street.

The windows line up and roll down in unison. Randy Sweet's got a puss made for radio. His skin is as smooth as a golf ball. His eyes are strangely small and too far apart, like they can't stand the nose between them, which juts off his face like an old boxing glove, inviting the next punch. But it's Randy's mouth that really takes the cake; all of it, in one bite, along with the candles and the plate. It's a long, fleshy rectangle stretched over a set of teeth that don't want to stay inside. The smile must be frightening.

Fortunately for Ray, Mouth is not in the smiling mood. He holds a paper bag out into the wind.

Ray takes it. He reaches inside and pulls out the painted doll. He turns it upside down and snaps on the interior light. He squints and nods, then he opens up the doll by carefully separating the top from the bottom. There's a smaller version inside. He pulls that one out into the light. He repeats the process until he can count to four then he combines them all back into one. He sets the doll on the dash. Then he looks back at Randy.

"You know, there's a place on Cottage Grove that sells these things. Just south of Seventy-Ninth. I forget the name. They're not expensive."

"You're going to keep your end of this bargain," says Randy. It's not a question. His tone is top heavy with barely controlled rage. His eyes are surprisingly powerful for being so small. They were made for boring.

"Never really know," says Ray. "I'd keep looking over my shoulder if I was you. Meantime, enjoy the soup."

"Maybe that's good advice for everybody. Even you." Mouth's maw does not fully close behind the words. There's one more word inside. It wants out into the wind with the others. "Mack."

Randy's body jerks as he rams his foot down into the gas pedal. The tires spin on the icy street until the truck eventually finds purchase and lurches forward, fishtailing back and forth over the edge of control.

Ray watches the truck get smaller in the rearview mirror. Even long after the truck is gone, he keeps looking, playing the sound of his own name over and over in his head. *Mack.* Cold air pours into the window like the North Sea into a ruptured hull. He tries to translate the feeling in his gut into something that makes sense.

Ray starts the car and blasts the heat. He rolls up the window.

The Russian doll looks at him from the dashboard, a complicated smile painted on her face.

There's another complicated smile inside that one.

And another.

And another.

THIRTY-TWO

My paranoia and my gut talk behind my back all the way home. It's a nervous, whispering kind of chatter. Something is wrong, they say. Something is off. I try to interrupt, telling them it's just hunger. Fatigue. I'm not used to such long days of deprivation. I miss the sound of ice cubes.

The doll on the dash seems like she's smirking. I put her in back in the bag and put the bag in the passenger seat. It doesn't help any. I can still feel her next to me. She knows something I don't. That's my least favorite thing in a doll.

I drive with my attention split ahead and behind. I used to have a reliable radar for when I'm being followed. Just a little buzz in the back of my brain. That buzz has given me the edge over the other guy more times than I can count and has saved my life at least twice. But now, feeling followed is par for the course with me. That's what it means to have a Triple-D disorder. I'm always followed and following at the same time, like a dog chasing its own tail.

So the little buzz is constant now. The signal is muddy. All the headlights behind me look the same.

I take the long way into my neighborhood. I can't say why. Call it senseless precaution in an uncertain world. It allows me to approach my house from the north, around a long bend, so that I can see the place I live in from a distance. I click off the lights and slow to a crawl before the road straightens out.

The house is right where I left it this morning, only darker and colder now and brimming with neglected feline energy. That, and there's a car at the curb across the street, a champagne-colored Chevy Malibu with a missing mirror on the passenger side. The streetlight puts a silhouette behind the wheel. Could be someone waiting for my neighbors to come home from cruising the Aegean. But that makes for a long two-weeks.

I ease the Impala to the curb, three houses from my own, and cut the engine. I reach over and unlock the glove box. I open it up. The Sig Sauer 9mm comes out and the doll in the paper bag goes in. I slip the gun into my coat pocket and step out into the wind for a walk I don't want.

He'd see me in the mirror if he was paying half-attention. His cellphone offers something more interesting. I can't see what that might be, pocket porn or cat videos, but whatever it is lights up the front seat like a handheld supernova. I stop when I get enough of a side view of the guy's face to know I didn't need the gun after all. I stand in his blind spot, staring at him, baffled at what he's doing here.

Then it starts to make a little sense. Not much. But maybe just a little.

And then I'm too tired to care. I turn around and head back to the car, a frozen, paranoid fool. The Sig Sauer in my pocket keeps banging against my hip, just to rub it in.

I start the engine and surge forward, lights ablaze, pulling into my driveway. I watch the car behind me at the curb as the garage door takes its time letting me in. The Malibu is dark now, cellphone off. I expect him to get out and cross the street before the garage door closes behind me. He doesn't.

THIRTY-THREE

If Ray could open a can of tuna with one hand and a new bottle of Old Forester with the other, he'd do it. I'll give him credit for the right priorities.

Phil supervises from the countertop as Ray makes his apologies. He tries to explain about looking for a girl in a yellow coat and about having to play games with Casey –Randy "Mouth" –Sweet. Phil meows her lack of forgiveness, then leaps down to the mat on the floor where the bowl will go. She sits precisely, white tail dusting the floor behind her. She does not look up.

Ray sets the bowl in place and pitches the empty can into the trash.

Then he takes care of the empty tumbler. He skips the rocks. Turns out it wasn't the sound of ice cubes he missed after all.

He closes his eyes as he sips. From up here, it looks like a silent prayer. Like he's asking for some measure of forgiveness for having feared that this moment in the day might never come.

He opens his eyes and looks at the freezer, the frozen white box full of other frozen boxes. He wants to eat. Something. Anything. But he knows better. Dinner will have to wait. He doesn't like others watching him while he eats. Not even me.

Ray finishes the drink and pours another. He leaves the kitchen for the living room. He sits in the recliner and sips, waiting. It takes longer than he imagines. Long enough to make him wonder if he was wrong about the coming intrusion.

But then the door makes its sound.

THIRTY-FOUR

I make him knock a few more times. That way we can both pretend we haven't been waiting.

"Hello, Mack," he says, as much with his sister's smiling brown eyes as with his mouth.

"Hello, Jimmy."

I try my best to look pleasantly surprised. I surprise myself more than anyone. I have a hard time caring what Jimmy thinks about anything, including me. I spent a lifetime caring about Jimmy while Marlo was still around. A kid brother of hers is a kid brother of mine, no matter what kind of trouble he's into. But Marlo's gone now. She doesn't have a kid brother anymore. Neither do I.

I hold the door open, letting in all the cold air as he stamps his shoes on the stoop. He's trying to hard-sell me on his respect for me and my home. Last man to do that on my stoop was holding a Bible, demonstrating his faith that I was going to let him inside. In a just world, Jimmy here should meet the same fate. What kind of man shuts the door on God but holds it open for Jimmy Kline? Maybe a man who wants what he deserves.

Phil is suddenly up on the back of the couch. She meows just once. Cats don't have wallets, but she's thinking the same thing I am anyway.

I show Jimmy in and fix him a drink. I refresh my own and add some ice. He follows me around about five paces behind, one hand in his pocket, leaning against doorframes and bookcases and countertops. Phil keeps a watchful distance, waiting for a lap to make an appearance.

Jimmy has had more than his fair share of mulligans in his forty-eight years of walking around, stepping on rakes. Never his fault, of course. Always a one-off that no one could have ever seen coming. He's always falling ass over teakettle, half an inch short of some new promised land with rivers of honey and women aplenty, his for the price of a song and a parking ticket at some casino.

Locked up or dead have always been better guesses than Jimmy standing on the stoop with his hand out, palm up. So Marlo was always relieved to see him. She liked to celebrate by emptying her wallet into one of Jimmy's pockets. Then she'd empty mine into the other pocket. Generally speaking, Marlo was a sucker for no man. There were only ever two exceptions to that rule. One was her kid brother, and the other was her husband. She always saw Jimmy's lies for what they were. She knew what he was about from the very beginning. She didn't figure me out until the very end.

Jimmy owes most of his good fortune in life to a caring sister and good hair. He's still got the hair, silky and dark, flopping and swooping in all the right ways. That and whatever black magic makes those lips of his move. Jimmy could talk a nun into a bad habit. The women love him. Go figure that one. He's trim and well-proportioned and knows how to clean up, but I'm amazed no one can see the sign on his forehead that says *You're going to regret this*. Maybe the swoop of hair gets in the way.

He hasn't changed much since the last time we saw each other, hauling my desk out of the garage up to Marlo's old sewing room. I can't say he looks five years older. Probably because I look ten years older. Seems about right that Jimmy somehow convinced the gods to make me pay that debt too. He gets to be Dorian Gray and I get to be the old painting hanging around waiting for him to come back for another look. I guess someone had to weather Marlo's death looking no worse for wear, so it may as well be Jimmy. The ten thousand out of my checking account had hurt like hell at the time. But I wasn't myself. The ink on the check to the funeral home was still wet and Marlo was still floating around in the air. So I said okay and wrote him out a one with four zeros. I'd figured Marlo would have wanted me to do it. I'd figured I'd never see him again. I was wrong.

We speak with a casual intensity about meaningless things, whacking away the weeds that are choking the pathway to Jimmy's true purpose. I ask what he's been doing. *This and that* seems to be about as detailed as he really wants to get. But he sees me lift an eyebrow so then he lets out a little more. He tells me that most recently he has dusted off his electrician's license and has been working as a lighting contractor. I could tell him that I already knew this. But I could tell him lots of things.

We score our points with feather dusters. He asks how my writing career is going. I ask if he ever cornered the roof gutter repair market. If he knows anything about me getting kicked out of CPD Homicide as a suspected criminal conspirator and then getting rehired with IAD, he does a good job keeping it to himself. A crack about me chasing down murderers makes me think he's behind the times. Then again, maybe that's what he wants me to think.

Jimmy sits in my recliner and nurses his drink. Phil keeps Jimmy's legs warm as I start a fire.

"Why are you here, Jimmy?" I ask the question with my back turned, jabbing an iron poker at a log.

"Just in the neighborhood, Mack. Thought I'd drop by and see how you're making out. I know Marlo was a blow. And I know I kind of disappeared on you. I feel bad about that."

I return the poker to its holder and turn around, waving away the fake apology like a bad smell.

"Why are you here?"

Jimmy smiles. We both do.

"Right," he says. "Well. In addition to that, there is another thing."

"Ah."

"Not money." He holds one hand up, half surrendering or swearing allegiance to his drink. "I'm not here looking for a loan."

"Don't be silly, Jimmy. You've never been here looking for a loan."

"I'm not here for money, Mack, is what I'm saying. I'm trying to help a woman I care about. My fiancé. She needs my help, and I need yours. A couple of phone calls is all I'm asking. I think maybe you can unlock some doors that I can't."

I sit on the couch for the story. It's one I've heard before, but I don't let on. It's got a twist or two I'm not expecting, and I like that in a story. So I keep quiet until he's done.

"Never thought of you as the marrying kind," I say. "I figured you'd play the field until you fell into a hole and they covered you with dirt."

"Me too," he says. He gives me a sheepish laugh. "Love changes a man. Don't need to tell you, Mack."

"So let me make sure I understand. You're in love with the sister of poor, dead Joe Novak. What's her name again?"

"Nadia."

"Nadia."

"Nadia King. She kept her ex's name. Don't ask me why."

"And Nadia's mother…"

"Ivah."

"Ivah. Nadia's mother, Ivah, thinks the Chicago Police Department still has her Russian doll."

"Right."

"And Ivah is in what kind of shape? Mentally, I mean. Is this a credible concern you think?"

The fire pops. Jimmy sips and winces.

"Well, Ivah's getting up there. Eighty-something. She's in a home now and a little soft between the ears. Frankly, Mack, between you and me, I don't care about this thing, this doll, one way or the other except that Nadia really cares. I care because she cares. You know?"

"Sure, sure," I say. "I get that. True love. And Nadia cares because Ivah cares, and Ivah cares, why again? Is this thing valuable or something?"

Jimmy gives me a scowl and shakes his head.

"Sentimental value only. Handed down from mother to daughter going back to the beginning of time."

"And Nadia is certain her mother's doll was never returned. You're both certain this isn't a snipe hunt."

"She seems pretty certain," says Jimmy, "yeah. But Nadia's not exactly…" He has to search for the right words. He seems to think they might be up on the ceiling. "Nadia's not the most discerning person you'll ever meet. Very shy. Very sweet. Very trusting. Too trusting. She's likely to believe Ivah's side of things no matter what. She's made a couple of calls about the doll and gotten the run around. She doesn't know what else to do. She's basically given up. I thought I'd see if you had any good ideas or if maybe you'd be willing to make a call or two. People are more likely to take you seriously."

"What's Nadia think of this plan?" I ask. "Bringing me in to help."

Jimmy sighs and pokes a floating ice cube with his finger.

"Haven't told her," he says. "I don't want to get her hopes up. If you come up empty, it's probably better she never knows. If you find the thing and bring it back, I get to be a hero." He looks up. "Nothing wrong with that, right?"

His smile is just between us guys. A tongue of hair swoops over one eye. He tucks it back into place.

"I'm not sure I can be of much help," I say. "I don't work at Chicago PD. It's like another country over there. They don't owe me anything."

"Yeah, I know. But you speak the language, Mack. You can have a cop-to-cop conversation. I can't. Nadia can't. You can make them understand that this is about more than just a stupid doll. Marlo always said you have a way of getting people to pay attention. That's all I'm asking for."

It's a cheap ploy for the only thing left in my heart. I want to stand up and grab the fire poker and swing it at him just to show off my skill at getting people to pay attention. I'm worried I'd hit Phil, so I leave the poker alone and take another drink.

"I'll give it my best shot," I say. "But I can't make any promises, Jimmy."

"Good, because I'm not accepting any promises, Mack. Do only what you can do."

I nod, thinking about the doll tucked away in my glove compartment.

"That's what I'm best at," I tell him. "How do I reach you?"

Jimmy lifts Phil off his lap and sets her on the floor. He stands, digging into his pocket. He reaches down and hands me his card. Kline Electrical Contracting.

"Thanks for the drink, Mack." He waits for the card to go in my pocket, then hands me the empty glass as his face counterfeits some more sincerity. "It was good to catch up. I'll get out of your hair."

"Getting out of my hair is easy, Jimmy. Your hair I worry about. Does Nadia know what she's in for, what with all the shampoo and conditioner that comes with you as a husband?"

"I promised to cut it," he says.

"Well, there's commitment for you," I say. We shuffle for the door like we're not in a hurry to end things. "When's the big date?"

"Haven't set it yet," he says. "Not until summer. But this year for sure. Ivah's not getting any younger."

"No one's getting any younger, Jimmy. Except you maybe. Is Ivah looking for grandkids?"

Jimmy smiles like I've asked if he has plans to raise wild badgers.

"I've never been much for kids," he says. "Can you imagine me as a dad?"

"No, and I only mean that in the worst possible way. What about Nadia?"

"No interest in kids, thank God. We want to travel. Live life. We're too irresponsible for children."

We shake hands like a couple of life-long chums.

"And here I thought true love changes a person."

Jimmy laughs and gives me a backward wave and steps out into the wind. His Malibu with the missing mirror is in the driveway now, like it had never been waiting across the street at the curb for untold hours. It gleams darkly in the house lights. The color may be champagne, but it's not the bubbly kind you pop on New Year's Eve in that last hour when everyone is forgiven and everything is possible. Jimmy's champagne is the kind you unscrew and drink out of a paper bag. It's warm and flat and tastes like the opposite of hope, dying on the palate like a bad joke for suckers desperate for a laugh.

I toss another log on the fire and reclaim the recliner. Phil takes her place and licks a drop of Old Forester from the tip of my finger. I close my eyes. I wonder how a man can know so much less about the world after a full day of walking around with his eyes open.

The only thing I know for certain is the shape of the bottle on the kitchen counter.

Just like a lighthouse, that thing.

THIRTY-FIVE

We all wonder about the end. Whether it will be loud or quiet. Violent or gentle. Whether we will know it is coming or be taken by surprise. We wonder who will be the first to find us. We worry about our dignity in that one moment. We wonder, maybe above everything else, what is to be interrupted. What last experience is to be cut short? Our last thought. The last glimmer in our mind's eye. We can't help it. Our species is darkly sentimental that way.

Ray is no exception. Just look at him, sitting up in bed, eyes wide and panting, gripping the sheets. He has rocketed out of some nightmarish violence and landed here, back in his own bedroom, as drunk as he was when his head first hit the pillow. Even as the hellscape in his mind is fading, all those same questions are now taking shape in the gloom along with the bedroom furniture.

How will it all end? Is this it?

He looks up in my direction, here where the wall meets the ceiling, as if I have an answer. As if I have been paying attention as he slept. He wants to know if this is the end. He wants to know if the sound in his head is something stolen from the dream, or if it belongs in this world. Is it just the Old Forester playing games, or is it the sound he has been waiting for? The sound of the end.

He can't hear anything over the panting. So he stops breathing and listens. We both do.

THIRTY-SIX

When I was seven, living at St. Evangeline's, I was bullied by a trio of twelve-year-old thugs-in-training. In their hunt for entertainment, they discovered that provoking expressions of fear was a laugh riot. That made an orphanage full of abused and abandoned kids a ready-made carnival.

Droopy McCallister was the worst of them. I don't think I ever knew his real first name. Kevin. Arthur, maybe. Whatever it was could never have done justice to the meaty eyelids that never seemed to open all the way. Behind those lids were two disturbingly small and dull eyeballs, with pupils like ragged black holes, access points chewed by tunneling, flesh-eating bugs. Popular kid, Droopy. He made friends less by force of personality than by force of logic, given that it was always better to be Droopy's friend than Droopy's enemy. There was no middle ground. His favorite game was to get an audience of two or three other kids to crowd around my cot while I was sleeping so he could drop my own Bible on my face. Rocketing awake, the first thing I'd see was the lower half of Droopy's tiny mean eyes. He liked to snap his fingers as he whispered.

"Could have killed you like *that*, Ray-Ray. In your sleep. Just. Like. *That.*"

I half-expect to see those same eyes again, right now, as if Droopy McCallister is in my bedroom dropping Bibles and snapping his fingers and breathing in my face.

But there is only darkness in front of me. And the memory of a sound in my head. A snap.

I'm woozy, sure. But I'm used to woozy. I take to woozy like a sealion takes to water. I can do all kinds of things drunk, like cheat on my wife and write bad crime fiction and pour myself a drink.

And hear things I shouldn't be hearing.

The sound comes again. *Snap.* This time there is no confusing it with a dream.

I get out of bed and reach for the nightstand. My balance is not as good as my hearing. I hit the floor like a sealion still very much on the beach.

I open the drawer and grab the Barretta. It's my gun of choice for the nightstand ever since Marlo passed. Compact, but easy to grab in a hurry. I keep it handy just to satisfy my paranoia that it's safe to go to sleep.

It's not like Marlo being in the bed could have ever protected me from violence. I outweighed her by double. But in that first year, her being gone and the bed being suddenly empty was a kind of nightly violence all its own. It's enough to make you wonder what's going to happen next; whether the darkness that took the love out of your life so quietly is now coming for the rest of you. You wonder. You worry. You worry about the shape of your reckoning stepping out of the dark with a bag full of pain slung over its shoulder. You worry because you know that pain is what you deserve. You wonder if you're going to make it through the night without a reckoning coming to close the loop of your existence. You cling to silly hopes for solace. You abandon the master bedroom and start sleeping in the guest room thinking maybe the reckoning might not know where to find you. You think maybe the reckoning will send an agent to do the dirty work, someone of flesh and bone to teach you the lesson, maybe someone inexperienced and who flinches at loud noises. So you get the old Barretta out of the gun safe and tuck it into the bottom drawer of the nightstand. You keep the drawer cracked. Just a little. Just enough so that you can ram your hand down in there if you need to.

Enough Old Forester in your system and you start to believe you've done something meaningful to protect yourself against what you deserve.

Snap.

I get into a bathrobe and make my way through the dark. I pause every few feet to listen and wish I'd gotten dressed. Terrycloth was made for comfort, not credibility. Not dignity. Who will be the first to find me at the end?

The house is freezing, colder and colder with every step. Two more *snaps.* By then I'm at the top of the staircase. I stop and listen to the air molecules rubbing shoulders.

Phil's softness is suddenly rubbing up against my bare shins. I push her away, back in the direction of the bedroom. She meows her objection and takes a position in the middle of the hall, a pale, white Sphinx in the dark.

Snap.

And then something else. Something heavy in motion. I've been around humans since I was born. I know one when I hear one.

I take the stairs slowly, avoiding the ones that complain and trying not to fall. Adrenaline has packed the wooziness back into the bottle for the time being, but the cork is loose and working its way back out with every step.

The first thing I notice at the bottom is that the back door is wide open. A winter breeze is blowing up the hall in cold gushes, pushing the wooden blind away from the adjacent window and then letting it swing back against the wall. Turns out I'd missed the sound by a letter.

Slap.

Slap.

My hearing may be off, but the Old Forster has not diminished the olfactory. I smell cigarette smoke on the breeze. Not my brand. Something acrid and oily. It's enough to make a camel give up smoking for good. There's a sound from out in the backyard, through the open door. I move slowly, making the Barretta lead the way. That's when the lights go out.

It feels like a heavy pillowcase. Whoever is behind me is as big as he is quiet. The bag has a drawstring that tightens like a noose around my neck so I can barely breathe. Whoever he is pulls my head hard to the left until the wall has other ideas, then he yanks the other direction just to even up the concussions. My ears are ringing. I feel light-headed. All I really care about is oxygen and my left hand is frantic to loosen the noose around my neck. My right hand has a mind of its own. It pulls the Barretta up and back and squeezes the trigger in a spasm, sending two rounds in directions I can't begin to guess.

The grip from behind does not let up. The only thing that changes in my life is that suddenly there are two of them, the guy behind me and now someone ripping the Barretta out of my hand. I'm glad to let it go. Now all ten fingers are at my neck trying to let in some air. The stars start to twinkle in the darkness.

The guy behind me starts to walk, dragging me backwards by the neck, away from the open door and into the house. I hear the back door close and from that direction, two words not intended for me:

"Tick-tock."

The dragging proceeds around the corner into my living room. Then it stops. My body falls hard. The side of my head recognizes the edge of my coffee table on the way down. My cheekbone feels like a golf ball leaving the first tee. I taste blood.

Not much I can do but gasp, so I do that with abandon. I keep at it even as I hear the duct tape coming off the roll. It goes around my neck to keep the bag on. It smells like old grease and cigarettes inside. They roll me over on my stomach. One of them wants to push my face through the floor with his boot while the other one zip-ties my hands behind my back. I don't care about any of it. All I care about is the air.

"You want to live?"

The voice belongs to whoever had closed the back door. The guy with the zip-ties. Not the guy standing on my face. The guy in charge.

I cough and gasp. It's all I can do.

"I'll take that as a yes. Where's the doll? Get off his head. I want him to hear what I'm asking. Where's the doll?"

It takes a while, but I get it out.

"What... what... doll?"

My answer wins me a hard kick in the cheek. I can feel it open up the gash that the corner of my table had already started. I get another hard kick in the side just to make sure I'm clear on who is in charge. I try to curl up in a ball but the big guy with the blood on his boot steps on my lower back.

"No," says the other one. "We're not playing this game, Officer Mackey. Hold him."

I hear the guy who isn't stepping on me walk away. It's a slow, plodding, clomping sound he makes as he goes, like he's carrying something heavy with one hand so that one foot lands harder against the floor than the other. The front door unlocks, open and closes. A full minute passes before the door opens and closes again. I can hear him approach. I can feel him standing next to me.

"Here," he says. I can hear something pass from one to the other above my body. "I'm going to ask again, Officer Mackey. Tell me the truth or you're going to wish you had. Where is the doll?"

"I don't... I don't..."

"You don't what?"

"I don't... play... with dolls."

It's a two-bit ploy for extra time. A couple of bullets in my own ceiling means maybe someone in the neighborhood woke up and called the police. But these boys are working a deadline. *Tick-tock,* he had said. I brace myself for another kick to the gut.

"Fine," says the talker. "Take off his legs."

There are a lot of sentences in this world to get a man's attention; that one is somewhere near the top of the list. The other guy takes his boot off my back, and I can feel him moving. They both are. They guy with a voice kneels on my back, pinning me to the floor.

Panic starts to take over. Blind fear at what I don't know. I start pulling, trying to separate my wrists, but the zip-tie is secure. I try to wriggle free. The guy on my back is easily the lighter of the two, but he's heavy enough to get the job done and keep me where I am. He yanks my chin up off the floor, pulling my head backward like he wants to snap my neck in half. Then he rolls the duct tape several times around my head where he guesses my mouth is. His guess is perfect.

A new smell. Motor grease. Gasoline. He mashes my face down into a cushion from my couch. Breathing is tough all over again.

I feel my entire body give itself over to adrenal dilation, flooding every pore with alcohol sweat.

I try to tell them I'll play ball. I try to tell them I'm done stalling. I try to tell them I don't care about a Russian doll. I try to tell them the damn thing is out in the car where I left it.

But neither of them can hear me. Not with the duct tape and my face in the cushion. They can't hear anything.

Not once the chainsaw starts up.

THIRTY-SEVEN

So then. Answers. At last.

The end will be loud. Violent. A surprise. Ray didn't see this coming. Neither did I.

It will end in his living room. It will come as he is face down in his bathrobe. A bag over his head. No legs attached. And no dignity. The dignity took a powder as soon as Ray pissed himself and started screaming against the sound. No surprise there. Ask any cop like Ray who has been finding bodies for thirty-plus years. There is no such thing as a dignified death by violence.

That's the other question he can answer now. It will be an officer working the graveyard shift, responding to a report of shots fired. That's who will be the first to find him. And that poor person will never be the same. Ray will be immortalized in nightmare and psychiatric billing invoices and stories not meant for grandchildren.

But at least he has some answers about the end of things.

I know everything that's happening inside that screaming, stinking bag. Behind all that terror, he's reaching for Marlo. He's trying to climb his way up into the big dream where all of this will stop forever. But he can't find her. All he finds is more terror.

And another question.

THIRTY-EIGHT

Who cuts off a man's legs for information? That's what fingers are for. These boys are rank amateurs at torturing out answers.

Or maybe they're experts. Who wants to worry about cleaning up after a chainsaw when the sound alone will get the results you want?

I listen for the saw to change pitch. Hard to do over my own muffled screaming. But I then hear the sound deepen as it chews in. Two quick cuts. Half of my couch –either the front or the back or the left or the right, I can't tell which –thumps heavily to the floor as the saw sputters to a stop.

Legs, he'd said.

I smell urine. Someone is crying. I don't think it's either of them.

The guy with the voice unwraps the tape from around the bag over my head. He's not gentle about it.

"Where's the doll?" he asks.

"Down… Downtown." I have to stop to allow a violent fit of coughing and spitting inside the bag. They're polite enough to wait. "At the station. It's at the station. Jesus Christ. It's in my desk. Bottom right drawer."

I can't defend my lie. I can't even own the words as something I want to tell them. Most of me wants to tell them where it is. Most of me wants to draw them a map to my garage. But I got my fill of being bullied at St. Evangeline's. It makes me irrational. People who know me would say there's a more general personality defect at work here. I don't like being told what to do in my own home. Marlo used to tell me that one day my stubbornness would get me killed. I never knew Marlo to be wrong about anything.

There is a long, ugly pause. I can feel them looking at each other. I'm waiting for the sound of that saw. The man with the voice is suddenly down on his hands and knees, pushing his head up next to mine like a jackal at the throat of some dying beast.

"Your life depends on you understanding what I am about to tell you," he says. The whisper is its own kind of chainsaw. "Someone will be by tomorrow. Let's say sometime after midnight. I want to see the doll in your mailbox. Not in a box. Not in a bag. Just the doll. If the doll is not in your mailbox, we'll be back at a time of our choosing. If we so much as sense a police presence in the vicinity, we will be back one last time. And you'll never see us coming. Okay? Understand? We're going to set fire to your house, Ray, and we'll use your actual legs for kindling. Can I get an amen?"

"Amen," I breathe back at him. It comes out with a cough of bloody drool that soaks into the bag around my mouth. It's the truest thing I've ever said to the man.

Response time for the Chandler PD is slower than any man under attack in his own home should want. I wish it had been slower.

My hope was to clean myself up and change out of my head-bag before I have to start in with the explanations, but I don't even come close. I'm still on the floor when the knocking comes, propped up against my couch, hands behind my back, bleeding into the bag over my head. At least I've got my voice back. I shout at them to come in.

When the bag finally comes off, I'm looking at two cops, young with clipped, square heads and confident eyes. I've never seen either of them before. But they sure know me. They read my face like it's the box score on a bad bet. But they treat me like a citizen, and I act like one. They free my hands and stand me up, something I don't take for granted. My slanting couch can't say the same. I look at the two front dismembered legs and think of what might have been.

Phil is on the shelf next to the television, wide-eyed and watching the commotion. I wonder how much of the ugliness she witnessed. I know the saw must have sent her flying back upstairs, but she didn't stay under the bed for hours like she does when the lawn mower comes out. She came back down to help or say goodbye or count the pieces. Something about that melts me a little.

One of the cops sits me in the chair where Jimmy Kline had downed a glass of bourbon and told me a pack of lies only a few hours earlier. The other cop brings some damp towels from the kitchen for my head and mouth. He disappears again to poke around my home and look at the holes in my ceiling. His partner asks me for the story while we wait for the EMT's. I put pressure on the open head wound and dab at my mouth and give him just enough of the truth to do the job. It's a version of the interrupted burglary motif from the two dramas that keep circling my brain: Curtis Root walking in on Wrigley Menard and Ivah Novak walking in on Wayne Bishop.

"What were they after?" he asks.

"Beats me. Money, maybe. Gold bullion. They should have done some research first. All I know is that they were pissed off at the interruption. They wanted to scare some manners into me." I point to a pack and a lighter on the coffee table that nearly broke my skull open. "I need a cigarette."

"Not a good choice, Mr. Mackey," he says. "You might have a concussion."

"Just the thing to accessorize the lung cancer. What's not a good choice is you standing between me and those Camels."

We look at each other as he thinks for a second. Then his eyebrows do their version of a shoulder shrug, and he reaches for the pack. I knock one out and light it up. It's as much to cover up the smell of urine as anything else, but the nicotine is like a warm bath for my nerves. I close my eyes. It feels like the Old Forester is finally coming out of hiding. I'd like to curl up and go to sleep, but maybe that's just the concussion singing lullabies.

"How about a description," he says. "Anything at all?"

"Two males. One of them was big and good with his hands. He knows how to work a sack and a chainsaw. The other likes to kick and give orders. He was the one in charge. The other one was just a bag of muscle."

"Who brings a chainsaw to a burglary?" he asks.

"I think they brought a truck to the burglary and the saw was inside."

"Why do you say it was a truck?"

"I could hear the saw go back in the bed when they left. Metal on metal."

"We'll get someone out to dust for prints," he says.

"Knock yourself out," I say. "You won't find anything. They were gloved up."

"How do you know?"

"Zip-tie man. I know latex when I feel it."

"What did they say to you?"

"Not much. Take his legs off. I remember that part. Who called you by the way?"

The kid jerks his head sideways.

"Neighbor. A Mrs. Kravitz? She's worried about your cat."

"Judith always has her priorities right."

The EMT's interrupt, coming through the door in a burst of radio static, gloved-up and carrying red plastic tackleboxes. They take away the cigarette without asking. I get a flashlight in the eyes, and they poke blue fingers at the gash in my face. They want to give me a ride to the hospital for some stitches. I tell them I know how to drive, and they remind me that I'm a walking concussion that smells like the alley behind a distillery. We play that game for a while until I give up just to stop the talking.

One of the EMT's follows me upstairs and waits in the hall as I step into the bathroom. The man in the mirror thinks it's Halloween. I clean myself up and change into some real clothes. The EMT follows me downstairs, one hand on my shoulder just in case I get wobbly.

At the bottom, I look down the hallway at the back door, just like I had before, only this time with all the lights on. The door is just closing behind the radio squawk of one of the cops joining his partner in the backyard to take pictures. The window blinds are still. No broken glass on the floor. No splintered jamb.

Phil is at my ankles, meowing up a storm. I pick her up and carry her to the kitchen, scratching the top of her head. I give her some extra food. She's not hungry.

THIRTY-NINE

"Mr. Malik."

"Mack?"

"Yeah. You taking fares?"

"You mean, like, right now?"

"You think people don't need transportation at six in the morning? Your generation gets too much sleep."

"Where?"

"Holy Cross. Emergency entrance."

"You okay, Mack?"

"Sure, sure. Let's go to breakfast. I'll buy you something to eat and teach you all about birds and worms."

They go to *Sonny's*, the twenty-four-hour diner on Seventh and Prine. It's the one with a *Specials* sign up on a pole out front that never seems to have all the letters it needs. That makes it a sign of the times. He tends to drop in whenever he's confused and finds himself a few letters shy of making any sense.

Ray looks like something Raj Malik scraped off the side of the road. He has a pinkish-white square stuck to his face that covers real estate from his lower left temple to below his cheekbone. The patch is large enough to make him think about selling advertising space. Beneath the bandage is a Frankenstein merit badge: a swollen red slit sewn together with three sutures. Around his neck is an angry ligature mark in shades of pink and blue and gray. His right orbital bone sports an ugly, purpling bruise beneath a strip of medical tape.

That, and he seems a little hung-over and low on sleep.

The server is a beautifully statuesque, twenty-eight-year-old Egyptian named

Cleopatra. Her parents could be egomaniacal monsters, but the name fits her like a glove that's a little too small. So Ray calls her Isis. She's too busy taking in the carnage of Ray's face to get the first word.

"Isis, this is my friend, Raj Malik. He eats for free whenever he wants. I'm good for it. Eventually."

Raj looks up at Isis and shakes his head. Isis smirks and rolls her chocolate brown eyes. She sets two waters on the table.

"What in the hell, Mack?" she asks. It comes out like a scold. "You look terrible."

"Thanks, Isis. I devoted a little extra time this morning."

"How's the other guy?"

"Guys. And they're fine. Their hands and feet are little sore, but they'll recover in no time. Tell us about the special. Sign out front says we can get it without vowels."

He always asks about the special but never orders it. Instead, he orders his usual black coffee, two over-easy eggs with bacon, and a buckwheat pancake on the side. Raj orders oatmeal and orange juice. Isis takes it all down and disappears into the greasy hiss coming from the kitchen.

"I used to eat oatmeal," says Ray. "Then my teeth came in and Mom thought I should be a big boy and try solid food."

Raj lets the bait sit there.

"What were they after, Mack?" he asks, continuing the conversation from the car. He's got stars in his eyes. Raj loves this stuff. And Ray knows it.

"A Russian doll. Made of painted wood. About yea high. Three other dolls inside."

"No, Mack. Seriously."

"I'm as serious as a heart attack, Raj. Friend of a friend asks me to track this thing down for her mother. It's a personal heirloom seized as evidence in an old murder case. She thought maybe it had been lost in the system. Turns out someone in the system liked the thing so much he pinched it for his girlfriend. So I'm supposed to go find it and I do, in record time. Now it seems like my friend's friend's mother isn't the only one interested."

"Is it, like, valuable or something?"

"I'm betting on the *or something*. I just don't know what that is yet."

"Are you going to try to get it back?"

"No need," Ray says. "I still have it. The couch killers promised to come back for it. Either that or they finish the job on me and burn my house down. My choice."

Raj has forgotten how to blink. Isis drops off the coffee and the OJ and disappears again.

"Jesus, Mack," says Raj.

"I figured you for a Muslim."

"The Koran lets us say Jesus if we want to. Burn your house down? For a doll?"

"Yeah. Criminals these days, right?" Ray takes a sip. "Thing I can't figure is how they got into my house without breaking in."

"Do you hide a key someplace outside?"

"No. Judith next door has a key so she can take care of Phil. I could follow up on that, but it's unlikely anyone pinched her key. Judith sleeps with one eye open. Which reminds me. Now that I've been warned, maybe it's a good time for Phil to take a vacation."

"Does that mean you're not giving them the doll?"

Ray doesn't answer. He stares into space like he's trying to solve a puzzle.

"What's wrong?"

"Nothing," says Ray.

"Need any help?"

"Yeah. Know where I can find a steel couch?"

"Seriously."

"You're already helping, Raj."

"The yellow coat?" he asks. "That's connected to this?"

Ray takes another swallow and shakes his head.

"No. Different deal. How's that coming?"

Raj shrugs. "I've been staking out the school every chance I get. No luck. You sure she even goes to that school?"

"I'm not sure of anything. You should be asking me if the girl owns a different coat."

"Does she?"

"No idea. Give it a couple more school days and then bag it. And keep track of your time and mileage, Raj. This is not a favor." Ray points with his cup. "Got it?"

"Sure Mack," says Raj. "What's her story? Is she like a witness or a victim or…"

"Both. She's a one-way ticket back to prison for a guy pretending to be human. And I want to be the guy to take him there. But finding the girl would sure help. Give it another couple days. Three. Four if you're bored. Maybe it's time for me to pay the man a surprise visit. If the girl is with him that makes it all the easier."

"Need a ride?" Raj asks.

"No. Thanks though."

"You can't drive, Mack. Remember. Doctor's orders."

The kitchen door swings open. Isis appears like a vision in the Egyptian desert bearing hope for the destitute and hungry. Ray smiles enough to make the bandage wrinkle.

"You know, Raj, sometimes it's like you don't know me at all."

FORTY

I impose on Raj to take me to the pharmacy and then home. He's clingy. He wants to be involved. I send him on his way disappointed and with his wallet a little thicker than it was when he woke up.

Phil is waiting on a couch cushion when I come in. The cushion is on the floor, having rolled from what is now essentially a spongy green ramp in my living room. We both head to the kitchen for a Percocet and a can of sardines. I throw back a pill with a glass of water and sit on the floor to feed Phil by hand. She keeps one paw on my leg to keep me from leaving. Everybody's clingy today.

"Who brings a chainsaw to a burglary?" I ask. Phil doesn't know either. She takes another sardine.

I empty the rest into her bowl and struggle back to my feet. I tour my entire home, room-by-room. As best as I can tell, nothing has been touched. They dismembered my couch and used my head to put dents in a couple of my walls. But that's it. Could be I surprised them before they ever got started looking. That could be.

I inspect both doors, front and back. I check all the ground floor windows. No signs of forced entry. No scratches in the paint. Any lock can be jimmied. But some locks are harder to jimmy than others. Those are the kind I have. These guys were either very talented or they had a key. That idea makes my head hurt more than it does already. It's the kind of hurt big pharma can't touch.

The garage door is unlocked. I always lock the garage door at night. And I always double-check it before I go upstairs to bed. It's one of those routines so ingrained it's impossible to avoid without really trying. Like brushing your teeth or refilling an empty glass. So who unlocked it? Best guess is the cops. Would have been standard in responding to a crime like this for them to open every door and look around. I'm ready to accept that answer until I open the door and take a look at the Impala. It's sitting in there in the dark, just like I left it. Except that the interior light is on.

My garage suffers from the residential equivalent of atherosclerosis. Over the years, the walls have attracted all manner of clutter. Sets of suitcases and bicycles and boxes of things I don't need but can't bring myself to throw away. Marlo was a neatnik. She loved throwing things away. I can't seem to do that, mostly because everything reminds me of her. The upshot is the Impala's driver's side door only opens about halfway, just enough to let me in and out if I'm watching my weight, but not enough to automatically turn on the ceiling light. If the car is in the garage and I need an interior light, I have to do that manually.

So then who climbed in and turned on the light? What reason would the cops have to search my car?

I make as much of a beeline for the Impala as my garage will allow. I climb in and reach over to the glovebox. I know even before I can see inside that there is no possible outcome —doll or no doll —that will make any sense. If they already had the doll in the bag, why torture the furniture in my living room?

But they don't have the doll. I do. She's right where I left her. Smiling quizzically from the shadows.

And that doesn't make any sense.

FORTY-ONE

Ray's phone conversations with Judith Kravitz are always awkward. The timing is off. They can't get a rhythm, always talking over each other, stopping and starting, like rush-hour traffic trying to take turns through a broken stoplight. It doesn't help that Judith is paranoid and tends to examine every word for evidence of some undeclared agenda. Today is worse than usual, but only because Ray has an undeclared agenda.

He thanks her for calling the police, giving her a G-rated, nothing-to-worry-about version of the previous night. A couple of punks on a lark, now learning a hard lesson. He's credible enough, maybe because Judith can't see the bandages and bruises move as he tells the story through the other end of the phone.

She says two gunshots woke her up. She had no idea what direction the shots had come from, but they sounded close, so she called the police. She could not see anything from her bedroom window, so she just sat in the dark and listened. She says that Roger Hemmecks, the neighbor she loves to hate, the one with a power tool fetish and the kids who can't keep the ball on their side of the fence, had picked that ridiculous hour to cut some firewood with a chainsaw.

"I told them to go arrest Roger for disturbing the peace as long as they were in the neighborhood. That kind of racket at two in the morning? I said to take his terrible children while they're at it. They're going to prison eventually anyway. May as well give them a preview of coming attractions. But I don't think the police were interested."

"Well," says Ray, picking up the severed couch legs and setting them on the coffee table. "Cops have a thing for gunshots. How'd they figure out to come knocking at my place?"

"I told them I heard a clanking in your driveway and doors closing and then someone driving off. Guess it turned out to be right."

"You did good, Judith."

"So then you're okay?" She asks this with an uncharacteristic hesitation and concern. "I mean, they didn't…"

"I'm fine," he says. "Say, Judith, I'm going to be out of town for a couple of days. Are you available to keep Phil? I'd like to keep her out of the house while I'm gone. I think last night rattled her a little."

"Poor dear," says Judith in a tone so unlike the one that had just called for the premature incarceration of the neighbor's children. "I'll come get her as soon as I'm dressed."

"No hurry," Ray says. "I'm headed out now, so I'll be gone. But you still have my key. Right?"

"Yes. I think so. I don't know why I wouldn't have it."

"Maybe you should go look and make sure, Judith. Just so I know you have it before I leave."

The line goes quiet. The quiet lasts too long for it to be an awkward pause, so he knows she's looking. The silence elongates. A little longer means she can't find the key. Which might explain some things.

A little longer comes and goes. Ray starts to wonder not only how they were able to snatch Judith's key, but how they even knew that Judith had a key to snatch. Then he hears her pick up the phone.

"Got it," she says. "Right where it's supposed to be."

"That's happening a lot this morning," says Ray, almost disappointed. "Glad to hear it. I just fed Phil. She'll be good for a while. Don't let her boss you around, Judith."

Phil is at his feet. She looks up at him and meows and twitches her tail. She sits and lowers her head and seems to survey the room in series of quick, fleeting glances. Then she looks in my direction, up near the ceiling light. She wants to know whether she'll ever see this place again. She wants to know if Judith next door will be the one feeding her for the rest of her life when Ray just doesn't come home again.

I wish I could tell her I knew.

FORTY-TWO

The ER doc is in my head, poking me in the concussion and telling me not to drive. Lucky for me I don't have a concussion in my foot. It still works the gas just fine. I try to drive slowly but the honking from behind hurts my head.

The sun doesn't help. It comes through my windshield like someone has greased the fingerholes in Apollo's bowling ball. Amazing something so painfully bright can be so ineffective at warming up the air. Eight degrees outside, struggling to a high of eleven.

Much as I love the land of Lincoln, the snowbirds have the right idea. I should be on a houseboat six months a year, floating the Keys with a hold full of Camels and hooch for ballast. Pulling fish out of the drink for dinner and drinking like a fish for breakfast. Spending my days asleep and my nights writing bad pulp fiction about washed-up retired gumshoes getting into deep trouble with shallow women. I'm too old to be assaulted by the elements. It's all I can do to fend off the people.

I stop at a light and watch three people cross the street in front of me. They don't talk because they don't actually know each other. They huddle together anyway, like a small herd of muskox forging a cold Russian river. Each face is a red, pinched study in pain.

I aim for the station, figuring I should brief Twill on my night. Before the day is done, he will learn the news from someone else. Someone who has seen my name on the shots-fired report, or someone plugged into the gossip mill. Better Twill hears it all from me. But that will require coming clean about my work for Nadia King and explaining why what should have been a couple of quick, off-the-clock phone calls has turned into grindhouse cinema.

But, as the station looms into view, the idea of playing the closed-door question-and-answer game makes everything hurt just a little more. I make a last-minute turn and point the Impala for the courthouse. I'd like to see Arty Dunn finish his testimony. I'd like to sit still in a warm building and watch other people play the question-and-answer game. If I can stay awake.

There's a woman standing in front of the doors to the courtroom. Her back is to me as I exit the elevator onto the third floor. If I was on my game, I'd have recognized Celestyn Fila's beehive and detoured into the men's room. But I'm not, so I don't. I just keep walking until I'm looking over her shoulder at the notice that she's posting on the courtroom door. It doesn't mince words.

Trial in the case of State of Illinois v. Wrigley Menard is cancelled for the day.

Celeste must have a sixth sense about being crowded from behind. She turns abruptly.

"Officer Mackey." Her smile comes quickly to life, a heat lamp melting away the irritation. But then her face gets a good look at my face and rearranges itself all over again. "My heavens! What happened?"

"Morning, Celeste. Oh, it's nothing. Fell down the stairs trying to put my best face forward. What's going on here?"

Celeste doesn't want to let it go. Her dark brow furrows over her eyes like weather gathering over a couple of blue Polish lakes. She lifts a hand in the direction of my bandage. The hand still has a tape dispenser in it. I take a step back.

"No, thanks. I've got enough tape on my face for two men."

Celeste laughs a little and blushes, lowering the dispenser. She's got a girlish quality when she's embarrassed that makes me seem like the cool upperclassman I never was.

"What's happening here with the circus?" I ask, letting her off the hook. She whispers so as not to be caught talking out of school.

"The prosecution called yesterday afternoon. They've lost contact with a witness and wanted to reschedule his testimony for later in the trial. The defense objected. Then a juror called in sick this morning with the flu. So, Judge Jolie just cancelled the trial until tomorrow."

"Which witness?" I ask, pushing my luck. Celeste gives me a comic scold and pushes me gently in the chest with the tips of her fingers.

"Trying to get me fired, Officer?"

"Call me Mack. And no, I'm not trying to get anyone fired. Sorry, Celeste. Never tell a man what he wants to hear. It only encourages him to keep coming back for more. Good talking to you. Stay warm."

I give her a wink and turn to go. I'm a real ass when I need to be. Ask anybody.

"Mack."

I turn back in time to watch her lips make the shape of Arty Dunn's name.

I sit in the parking lot with the car running, blasting the heat and watching people, steam trailing from their heads as they chug between buildings and cars like so many Gore-Tex locomotives. I think about Arty Dunn suddenly missing in action, conveniently in the middle of an examination by Mickey Shaw that was just starting to get interesting. Then I think about that face he made. Not his courtroom face; his broken poker chip face. The face without any blood in it. In the unlikely event IAD were to substantiate Scooter's shakedown claims against Arty, that would automatically lead to a criminal inquiry and Arty's career would be in the crosshairs. But that's not what has Arty spooked. And now Jaclyn Cavelle can't find her own witness. Maybe Arty had a bad night. Maybe worse than mine.

Twill sees me before I see him. I'm still unzipping my coat when I look up and spot him in his doorway. I can tell he already has the news, even from across the room. He steps out of sight inside his office, leaving the door open. His invitations don't get any clearer. I drop my coat over the back of my chair and head that way. Sandra Booth looks up as I pass her desk. My face is an eyeball magnet.

"Start from the beginning," Twill says when I close the door.

His long legs slope up from his chair and finally come to a stop inside a pair of polished, black shoes resting against the edge of his desk. He's leaning back in his chair with a notepad in his lap. He makes a sharp, clean scribble with a double underline.

I can see he's ready for a long story, but I decide to give him the short version, the one that leaves out most things truthful and interesting. It's not that I want to lie to my own lieutenant. Not any more than he wants to listen to me waste his time. But he has already made it clear my job is to investigate complaints of misconduct, not crime. He's already taken the girl in the yellow coat off my desk and Nadia King's Russian doll is sure to follow. It's better for both of us that he gets the short version. That's what I tell myself as I come to my anti-climactic, shoulder-shrugging conclusion. Twill takes his shoes off the desk and sits up straight.

"So you've got no idea what this is all about," he asks skeptically.

"No idea."

"How'd they get in?" I figure he's already seen the report, or he will eventually, so there's no getting around this part.

"No forced entry," I say. "I must have left the door unlocked when I went to bed."

"Interesting," he says. "And a little too convenient. Maybe they had a key."

"Maybe," I say. "Not sure how that happens though. I accounted for the only extra key. Unless…"

That last word sneaks out while my lips are still moving. Twill picks it up and adds a question mark.

"Unless?"

"Nothing. I was just thinking about last summer. All those cops in my house."

"Oh. You mean when you beat a Bolivian half to death and tied him up in your basement with duct tape and a bicycle lock?"

"The way you say it makes it sound like it was my fault. But, yeah, that's the time. They used my neighbor's key to get in. Maybe…"

"Maybe some cop made an impression of your key and tucked it away?" Twill crosses his arms. "Have any theories for why a police officer might want to do something like that, Mack?"

He's good. Thirty seconds and we've drifted away from no idea to some idea. He's working me.

"Beats me, boss."

"You want me to believe that you've got no idea who these guys were or what they were after."

"Maybe they wanted money. Maybe they're out to steal my doll collection. Maybe the Jehovah's Witnesses are changing up their strategy. Maybe…"

"Maybe that's enough," he says. "I get it. You're completely in the dark. I don't buy it, Mack. Whatever this is, you want to run it down yourself and you don't want me to tell you not to. I get it. So, let's continue this conversation when, inevitably, I have more information. In the meantime, you look like death on a cracker. How do you feel?"

"That's about right," I say. Twill sets the pen carefully on the tablet and pushes them both away.

"Why are you here?" he asks.

"I thought I could sit through the rest of Arty's testimony."

"And?"

"Judge Jolie cancelled the trial until tomorrow. Seems Jaclyn Cavelle has lost contact with Arty and she wanted to shake up the witness order. Mickey Shaw has other ideas, like finishing his cross-examination. Then a sick juror called in to give the judge reason to pull the plug."

"Okay. And where does all of that leave you?"

"With a concussion and a pocket full of Percocet."

"Is this the part where you show me a doctor's note and I tell you to go home and then you go out and play detective instead?"

"You act like this is a movie you've seen before."

"I have."

"How's it end?"

"With my shoe up your ass and your badge in my drawer. That's how it ends. So, let's get that started."

We look at each other across the desk for a few seconds disguised as minutes. We both know that this is my last chance to tell him what's going on. I nod and stand up and open the door.

"Watch yourself, Mack," says Twill.

"No problems there, LT. Always do."

FORTY-THREE

Ray is no stranger to having the chain of command wrapped around his neck. More than three decades of following orders would make that hard for any cop to avoid now and then. It's impossible to avoid if the name on your badge happens to be Raymond Mackey. Every one of his lieutenants can tell the same story. They've all written that story down a few times.

Ray tells himself he is who he is. Not much of an excuse. He knows that without rigorous obedience to the orders of a publicly accountable command structure, police departments are just a different kind of mob. But he tells himself anyway. He is who he is.

Marlo is in his head, slinging memories around.

She had once objected to Ray's decision to investigate a gangland murder on his own time, side-stepping an order to stand down. The order had come from a lieutenant who, in Ray's opinion, was more concerned about avoiding a high-profile case he couldn't clear than he was in trying to bring some measure of justice to two orphaned kids who had lost a mother to a stray bullet through a thin wall.

"Nosek's looking for a reason, Ray," Marlo had said. "You going to give him one?"

"Not if he doesn't find out."

"Let him give the case to Chicago PD. They want it. They'll solve it."

"I want it. I'll solve it."

"Or you could just choose to follow the rules for once."

"That's something coming from you," he'd said, anger rising in his face. "Every rule you've ever met looks like a suggestion. We are remembered for the rules we break, Marlo."

"Oh, that's a gem. Who said that?"

"Douglas McArthur."

"Who is he again?"

He'd finished his drink, kerosine for the fire. Marlo had kept at it.

"Look, I work for an insurance company, Ray, not a police department. I carry a camera, not a gun. Sure, I go my own way and I always think I know better than the people who give me a paycheck and one day I might get fired for it. But nobody's going to shoot me in the head because I've charged out into battle without backup. You want to piss off the President, be my guest. Far as I know, Douglas McArthur always had plenty of backup. And, just so we're clear, cautionary tales are just as hard to forget."

Ray heads back to his desk and puts on the coat. The folder on his chair catches his attention. He picks it up for a look. Inside are two stapled sheafs. They each come with a small yellow note stuck to the front, right beneath the logo for the Chicago Police Department.

One says *KFC Fire*. The other says *KFC Homicide*.

Ray looks across the room at Sandra Booth. She's already looking his way, waiting. He nods. She nods back. Then she turns and resumes her work.

Ray tucks the folder under his arm and pushes in his chair. The jolt brings the screensaver on his monitor to life. The words float like fallen leaves drifting on a black current, changing color from orange to red as they hit the edge of the screen and float in the opposite direction.

Workplace Safety is Priority #1.

FORTY-FOUR

Ten o'clock in the morning and the *Pleasant Palace Adult Books and Video* on West Malcomb is dark and quiet on an empty square of broken, icy concrete.

It's alone in the world, this building. Unless you count the big green dumpster hunched in the back. Its nearest neighbor to the south is a substation that feeds the thirty square blocks north of Jasping Road and all the way up to Chester. Across West Malcomb is a *Double Value Liquor* store. It squats next to a pot start-up called *High Heaven.* On the other side is a discount tire store called *Rolling Rubbers*, which is trying its best to work the double-entendre from inside an old, decommissioned *Chevron* station. It's a sorry line-up of business. But I'm guessing they all feel a little better about themselves looking at what Scooter Pleasants has going on across the street.

Pleasant Palace is a low, windowless building, made of wood and painted entirely black, except for the dirty-red front door and the silver-gray flashing along the flat roofline. Skewering the middle of the empty lot like a toothpick in a square pancake is a scuffed, black iron pole. The pole holds up a white rectangle that used to spell out the name of the place. Most of the letters have long since disappeared, but five have stayed loyal to the end. They're all Scooter needs to get the job done: ADULT.

One car sits in front, an orange Kia Soul, motor running and pushing a white stream of exhaust out into the morning air. I pull up alongside and take a look. A thin red straw is stuck firmly into the hole of a fat white face. The man looks up as I put the Impala in park. He's wearing a Bulls cap pulled so low his eyes are obscured and he has to tip his head back to see me.

He lets the straw go. A thick wrinkle in the dough stretches itself into a sheepish smile. He lifts a hand to offer a pretend toast with whatever Burger King has given him to drink as he waits for his morning smut. I can see him wonder if maybe I'm here to open things up and turn on the lights.

Odd thing, waiting for smut. The internet should mean never having to wait. You'd think all these places had gone the way of *Blockbuster Video*.

But he's a people-person, this guy. The merchandise is just a consolation prize. He's here to make friends and I can tell by the smile he thinks today might already be shaping up nicely. I give a curt nod and a two-finger salute. He'll take it as encouragement, but his type takes everything as encouragement except maybe the one-finger salute and it's still too early for that kind of thing.

We don't have to wait long. At ten-fifteen a tan and blue rig pulls into the lot, Scooter Pleasants at the wheel. He drives past us without a look, steering the SUV out of sight around back. Three minutes later the red door of the building pops open and a disembodied arm waves around in the cold air then slips back inside.

The guy next to me unburdens his Soul, making it rise an extra five inches off the parking lot. He beeps the Kia with his key fob then trudges a straight line between my bumper and the building on his way to Scooter's front door. I'm guessing this is the fastest he'll move all day.

I watch the man push open the door and step inside, then I cut my engine and climb out. I head around back to have a look in the windows of Scooter's SUV. The cold air fights for a chance to come in and warm up so I keep my mouth closed and zip up my coat and hunch my body into the sun.

Appearances to the contrary notwithstanding, I have a stubborn optimism that never really goes away even in the worst of times. It likes to play the lottery and vote for politicians and think silly things like *maybe just one drink*. That part of me hopes to see a girl with long, black hair and a yellow coat sitting in the passenger seat of Scooter's rig, crying as she waits for him to come out. Just like the picture. That part of me is used to being disappointed.

Instead of a girl in the passenger seat, I find lots of trash. Empty beer cans and a paper bucket half-full of chicken bones and gristle and oily napkins. On the floor is an old edition of *The Tribune* beneath a pair of boots, an open box of Milk Duds, and a cracked headlight. The front page shows Samuel Trenton Royce inside of a smart blue pinstripe, one hand on a podium. I can't see the mayor's mouth because of the Milk Duds, but I'm guessing it's open.

I walk back around to the front of the *Pleasant Palace* and step inside. The light is so old and tired that it almost doesn't reach the floor, seeming to hang in dirty tatters from two dusty ceiling fixtures at opposite ends of the room. The air is warm and rank with a sourness that clings to the back of my throat like the smell of rotting wood or reams of soggy paper drying after a flood. The walls are lined with wooden shelving faced with propped up magazines and DVD cases, each a snarling carnage of lost and soulless youth. Three more rows of double-sided shelving stretch from one end of the store to the other. They come to a stop a few feet short of a glass display case that pulls double duty containing a stubby forest of neon sex toys and holding up a small cash register.

The fat man from the Kia is in the back corner, gawking at the back of a plastic-wrapped magazine. He looks up when I close the door and gives me another nod just like before. This one I plan to ignore entirely. Daniel Pleasants makes that easy.

"Well, look here what the cat drug in," Scooter says, coming through a hole in the wall from behind the display case. He's in an open-flannel shirt over a black tee that features a smiling skull with a hand-grenade in its teeth. His stringy, white hair is a bird's nest and he hasn't shaved since I saw him last.

"My cat wouldn't be caught dead in this place," I say.

He smiles enough to show the gap in his teeth. The gap slowly disappears as he gets a look at my face.

"What the hell happened to you?"

"Got in a fight with myself about needing to come inside to see you, Scooter. I lost."

"Scooter? My name is Mr. Pleasants. You're lacking formality today, Officer Mackey."

In the mirror above the register I can see the man in the back-corner scuttle behind a row of shelving like a roach at the click of a light switch. I'm guessing he's allergic to badges.

"That name is only for courtrooms and police departments," I say. "In this…" I have to look around for the right words, "… palace of human debasement, the best name you get is Scooter."

"Ah, come on, Mackey," he says laughing, his little eyes glinting darkly in their wide-set holes. "Debasement?"

"Well, it sure ain't the penthouse, Scooter."

"Why are you here? You gonna tell me that your pal Arty Dunn resigned and said he's sorry?"

"No."

"Maybe you're bringing me a check. Coming to compensate me for my emotional distress caused by the thuggery of the Chandler Police Department."

"No."

Scooter flattens both hands against the top of the glass display case so firmly it wobbles on its uneven legs. Two purple dildos topple over onto the fuzzy handcuffs. The hand-tattoo that I could not discern at the courthouse turns out to be a black snake, tail wrapped around one finger, coiling over the back of his hand and disappearing up his sleeve.

"I figured not," he says, no longer smiling. "Then why are you in my face? Here to shake me down just like your friend?"

"Told you once, Scooter," I say, "Arty's not my friend. He's also MIA. Don't suppose you'd know where he is."

"No idea. Why would I know and why would I care?"

I fish the poker chip out of my pocket and set it down on the counter, keeping my eyes on his.

"What's this?" I ask.

Scooter leans forward and cocks his head. Then he looks back at me, screwing up his face.

"It's a poker chip, shithead. We only take real money here. Why are you asking?"

"A man gave that to me to give to Arty."

"Yeah? What do I care? What man?"

"One of your enemies. I'm sure that list fills a phone book."

It gets his attention. Suddenly Scooter wants information.

"Enemy? Who?"

"Don't know his name."

"How do you know he's my enemy?"

"Because he's trying to send you to prison."

"Prison?" Scooter inflates in no time. His face starts to change color. "Fuck you, man. Prison. I haven't done anything. This is just more intimidation. You just want me to lay off Arty. This is just…"

"Settle down. I don't want you to lay off Arty." I give it an extra beat or two. I put the chip back in my pocket. "But the guy who gave me this sure does."

"Who? Who the fuck, man?"

"Never seen him before."

"Motherfucker have a face?"

"Yeah. It's big and square and made of granite. And it's a long way above the ground. One shoulder in Michigan, the other in Iowa. Bald as the moon."

A short, sharp glimmer of understanding flickers over Scooter's face. I seize on it like I'm catching a firefly in a jar.

"Thought so," I say. "Hard to forget a man that big, isn't it?"

"I have no idea, who…"

"Come on, Scoot. The mountain man is bad news, and you know why. Not the kind of enemy I'd ever want to have. That man wants to bury you in an orange onesie."

Stillness crawls over Scooter's body like a shadow. I keep my mouth shut for a minute so he can start to think about just how deep the hole is behind his heels. When I figure he's had enough time to think about things, I give him a push.

"Anything you want to tell me before I interview the girl?"

He has to swallow before he can utter the inevitable.

"What girl?"

"You just don't know anybody today, do you? Don't play this game, Scooter. The high school girl in the yellow coat. The shy, sad one in all the pictures."

"What pictures? I don't have any idea what…"

"Save it. Your public defender is going to want that part to sound fresh and unrehearsed. Better I get the story straight from her anyway. "You know, she really doesn't seem to like you very much."

Scooter's eyes grow wild and excited, searching my face for answers. But my face isn't giving out any answers so all he can do is listen.

"Lucky for you there's a bunch of extra hoops to jump through before we can interview minors," I say. "Have to get the parents and counselors involved. Everybody's got a schedule. Now's your time to get ahead of this."

"This is a setup," he shouts, paranoid rage finally riding to the rescue. "This here is fucking entrapment is what it is. This is all about Arty Dunn trying to shut me down. You're either in on it or he's got you so… so…" He's so worked up he's sputtering. "Goddamnit! The little whore said she was nineteen."

I know better than to lose my cool at that sort of statement. Experience teaches you to take a breath and count to ten. My hands don't make it to three. They reach across the display case and grab Scooter by his tee-shirt, one on the neck hole and the other by the skull eating the hand-grenade.

"She's sixteen if she's a day," I growl. "And a man like you sees that from a thousand yards away."

"I didn't know. I didn't know. I swear to God."

"God's not taking your calls, Scooter."

I pull him toward me, against the counter, just hard enough to bring down the whole damn thing in a crash of cash register and dildos and broken glass. In the mirror above I can see my would-be smut-buddy slip out the door behind me. I was wrong about how fast he can move.

I step over the wreckage of glass and pliable neon plastics and try to pull Scooter to his feet. He plays heavy, flopping in the direction of the toppled display case. He's trying to cover up a snub-nosed .38 with his arm, but he comes up a couple inches short. I step on his wrist like I'm trying to flatten the tattooed snake. I use a nearby pen on the floor and stick it through the fingerguard of the .38. I lift it up into the air above Scooter's face.

"Reaching for this?" I ask.

"It's for my own protection," he shouts in an aggrieved whine.

"A convicted felon with a loaded gun. Imagine that."

"I have a right to protect myself."

"I'll be sure to make that argument to your parole officer." I open my coat pocket and let the gun drop inside. I stand Scooter up, one hand on each shoulder. "Or maybe you want to tell me what happened. Let's start with how you met her."

"I want a lawyer," he says. "Motherfucker."

"Absolutely. You need a phone?" I pat him down. It's in his back pocket. I hand it to him. "Here it is. Let's all meet at the station and get this thing rolling. I'll call lockup and make a reservation."

I pull my own phone out of my pocket and open it up.

"Wait," he says, both hands floating up. "Hang on. I… I just… I was just giving her a ride. She, like, came on to me, man."

"Because you're so irresistible to women. How do you fend all of them off?"

"Seriously. I swear. I swear. She was, like, all over me, man. I open the door and she gets in and I ask if she wanted to go to my place and she was like all in favor, man. Yeah, okay, I get that I'm an ugly piece of shit. Ha, ha, ha. Think I don't know that? How often you think I don't have to pay for it? She said she was fucking nineteen."

"If she'd told you she was Wonder Woman, would you have believed that too? How'd you come to give her a ride?"

"She was hitching," he says. "Thought she needed help."

"Hitching where?"

"Out on McKenzie Road. Bad area of town for…"

He doesn't finish.

"You mean for a girl," I say. "A bad area of town for a girl."

"For a young woman."

"Right. You need to think about your lies before they make it out of your mouth, Scooter. She says you picked her up outside Northrop High School. Lie to me again and I'll arrest you right now."

"You're the one lying, man," spits Scooter. "Little bitch isn't talking to you or anyone else."

"Yeah? Why's that?"

"She can't. She don't talk. She's like a mute or whatever."

"Thought she told you she was nineteen, Scooter."

Scooter's entire face powers down for a second as he thinks, then it flickers back to life.

"I asked and she nodded," he says. "I asked several times."

As much as it pains me, I keep my eyes on Scooter's face. I keep my mouth shut. I let the silence build until he starts to squirm.

"What, man? I'm telling you the truth."

"Well, if you're telling me the truth then she played you for a fool, Scooter, because she's sure talking up a storm now. So now the truth train is leaving the station. Last chance for you to get any credit for cooperating. I want to know how it is you met her at that school."

Scooter closes his eyes and contracts all the muscles in his face, squeezing it like a fist.

"Okay, okay. Fuck!" The magazines lining the walls snuff out the shout like wet fingers over a match. "He said she'd be at the corner. I didn't even know about the school. He never said she was a student. And I even fucking asked her, man! I, like, pointed to the school and asked her and she shook her head. I asked her if she was nineteen and she nodded. She fucking nodded!"

"Hold on," I say. "I'm confused. Lot of undefined pronouns there, Scooter. Who were you supposed to meet at the corner?"

"Emily. Who do you think?"

"Emily who?"

"I don't know her fucking last name, man. Wait..." Scooter's eyes narrow into slits of suspicion. "You mean *you* don't know her last name?"

"Slipped my mind," I say. "I can't remember things like I used to. Especially names. Who suggested you should haul your stale cookies out to Northrop High?"

Scooter lowers his chin to his chest, looking at the overturned display case. He's got that ugly feeling that any man gets in the gut when he feels like he's being played. He's thinking that maybe I don't really know anything at all and here he is singing for his supper. I try to rattle him again before he clams up for good.

"You know what," I say. I turn him around by the shoulders and hold his wrists together behind his back. "Save it. You're not in the answering mood. I get it. Where are your keys? I'll lock up. And you'll need to have someone come down and get your car. It'll be good and stripped before you make bail."

"Wait..."

"You have the right to remain..."

"Wait, goddamnit." He spins around to face me. The front door opens and a tallish guy steps in. He's a wiry black man wrapped in a checkered coat four sizes too large, and a pink skullcap pulled low over his ears.

"We're closed," shouts Scooter. The man stops in his tracks as the cold air surges in from behind him like sea water over the gunnels of a trawler. The man looks at us standing over the toppled counter and the floor strewn with broken glass and sex toys. Then he raises his left arm to look at his watch. The coat sleeves are so long he has to work at it. Scooter shouts at him before he can confirm the time.

"Get the fuck out!"

The man gives me a look of disappointment. I jerk my head. He backs out and closes the door. I start to turn Scooter around again but he's not having it.

"Wait. Okay. Just... I'm having a snort down at *Last Call* with a buddy of mine, just, like a week ago."

"What buddy?"

"Doesn't matter wh..."

I harden my eyes.

"What. Buddy."

"Jesus. Name is Billy Wise. I know him from Stateville lockup. He was coming out as I was going in. He did a full nickel. He got caught flushing product down the shitter. He was in too much of a hurry to take the blow out of the bags."

"Billy's not so wise, maybe. He still in the game?"

"I don't know, man'" Scooter snaps. But I give him a look. "Maybe, yeah. Probably. You ever heard that story go any other way?"

"No. But that's not your scene, is it, Scooter?"

"You want to hear this or not?"

"I'm listening."

"We're having a drink and shooting the shit and the biggest piece of meat I have ever seen sits down and slaps Billy on the back."

"Name."

"I don't know his name. Hell, I think."

"His name is Hell?"

"I said I don't know, man. Billy said 'Hell is back' when the man sat down. Kept calling him Hell. Said they have the same PO and that Hell spent fifteen birthdays in Pontiac on a sex trafficking rap."

"And?"

"And the conversation might have turned that direction. Okay? Billy and I might have started bitching about how the local talent is getting older and scarier and more expensive by the night. Hell said he could hook us up with a free sample that would make us lose our minds. Said this gal Emily was just the thing. Gave us the when and where. He said he'd set it up."

"And Northrop High School didn't tip you off that maybe this wasn't a good idea?"

"He just gave us the cross streets. He said she'd be waiting."

"Ahh," I say. "Yellow coat."

"Yeah, man. Yellow fucking coat. Shit. I was gonna keep rolling when I saw the school but then there she was. Yellow coat. You know? Coming for me. I opened the door and she hopped right in, man. I thought she was nineteen. I asked her."

"Yeah. You keep telling me that. Why you? Why not Billy?"

"I paid for the beer," says Scooter. "I paid for Hell's beer too. He threw back sixteen ounces like it was in a Dixie cup."

"I've seen that trick. Where can I find Billy Wise?"

Scooter's neck goes limp.

"Aw, leave Billy out of this, man."

"We're way past that, Scooter. Stop whining. I'll tell him you didn't make it easy."

Scooter lets out a sigh that weighs more than he does. He rubs his eyes.

"Fuck. Fine. He's a fish chopper for a place called *Windy Wharf Seafoods*. Okay?"

"Chandler?"

"Aurora. How does this shit play out, man?"

"How does it play out? I sit down with Emily, and we talk about the day she was born and why she's taking her coat off for greasy old men like you. That's how this plays out." I take a step closer, putting our faces nose-to-nose. Glass crunches beneath my shoe. "In the meantime, Scooter, your entire world just shrunk to two addresses: the one where you live and this shithole. If I can't find you in one of those places at any time of the day or night, if you don't answer your phone when I call, then you can start counting the minutes until you're back in the system."

He gestures to my coat pocket.

"Can I have my piece back?"

"Boy. You're not so smart, are you? Slip up once, and you're going away for everything, parole violation too. Lie to me once. Disappear on me once. Get in my way once. And that includes spooking Billy Wise."

"And if I play ball?"

"I won't tell Hell you ratted him out."

"Gee, thanks. What about my beef with asshole Arty?"

"No change. My job is to find out what happened between you two. If Arty's dirty, I'll bring him down." I get out of his face and step back over the toppled counter. I turn back to see him staring at me with a mixture of hate and agonizing worry. "If you're right about Arty, maybe you guys can be cell mates. That'd be fun. I'd buy a ticket to see that."

FORTY-FIVE

Look at him. Head back against the seat. Eyes closed.

He's telling himself he needs to think things through. He needs to sit quietly and sift information. Connect dots. But that's not what it looks like. From up here he looks like an old man taking a nap in the *Pleasant Palace* parking lot. Disturbingly close to the truth. Anyone driving up for their morning cup of porn would think so.

Sure, he's running on empty. No food. No sleep. Everything hurts in places too deep for the drugs to touch. Every shift in position comes with a wince and a groan. Sure. Okay.

But this? This is not a good look on any self-respecting cop. This is embarrassing. He needs to go home if he's going to do this.

Come on, Ray. Stop acting your age.

Of course, home is where all the pain started in the first place. Just ask the couch. He's betting that going home only gets him more of the same. He's not crazy for thinking the Impala is the safest place to close his eyes. Not crazy, but wrong.

Nothing like a bullet or two to clear things up.

FORTY-SIX

Three shots. The pops hit my brain so fast that they register as a single sound, one segmented detonation amid a showering of glass.

I throw myself sideways, pulling for the Sig in its shoulder holster as I flatten myself as much as I can against the passenger seat. It's the best possible move if the next shot is coming through the driver's headrest. It's the worst possible move if the shooter is running in for a closer shot.

I take a breath and reach for the passenger door handle. I pull it and inch open the door, wriggling myself forward, gun first, toward the opening. I wrench my head sideways so that I can see who might be coming to deliver the last few seconds of my life.

All I can see through the crack is half of the *Rolling Rubbers* sign across the street.

It's unusual for the Triple-D to kick in when my adrenalin is up. And yet, there it is, broadcasting in my head like a memory loop: me scrunched up in the front seat, my legs still mostly beneath the steering wheel as I slowly widen the passenger door. The only man I see is me. I'm used to that.

Triple-D is the kind of crazy that's tailor-made for the want-to-be novelist. My brain is thinking in the third person. But it usually waits for times when the bullets aren't flying. I want to shout at him, this guy, this over-the-hill lump huddling in the front seat. I want to show him how vulnerable he is to a bullet to the back of the head.

I wrench myself sideways enough for the Sig to cover the driver's window. I remember Scooter's snub-nose .38 in my coat pocket. My best evidence of his parole violation and I'm about to ruin all those fingerprints. I pull it out anyway. One gun in each hand. I'm a decent shot with my right hand. My left hand could aim at the air and miss.

I free enough of my left leg to push against the closed door and wriggle slowly out of the passenger side. The .38 leads the way as Sig keeps an eye on the driver window. I push the door open enough to reveal the rest of the *Rolling Rubber* sign across the street and most of the *Double Value Liquor* building.

A delivery truck rattles into view from right to left, then disappears as it trundles away up West Malcomb. A Checker Cab does the same, and then a city bus. They keep moving at a slow but steady pace like there's nothing to see. An Indian-looking woman on the bus is just starting to look but then is gone, disappearing behind a rust-colored garbage truck growling its way west in the near lane. I give myself a firm, steady push, trying to keep Sig aimed at the driver's window. The cold air claws at my face, collecting my breath in fluffy-white armloads like goose down for pillows.

I wish I could stop seeing myself as clearly as I do. It's not pretty. The Impala extrudes my body out onto the icy parking lot like the last of the toothpaste. I do my best to get a line of sight beneath the car, looking for legs that might be attached to someone with a gun that's missing three bullets.

I don't see any legs.

But I do hear footsteps, coming from behind just like always.

I roll a full one-eighty onto my other shoulder faster than should be possible for me, pointing both guns in the air, ready to blow a pair of holes into I don't know who.

"Jesus!" Scooter throws his hands out in front of him toward the guns like maybe he doesn't get what catching a bullet actually means.

FORTY-SEVEN

"What the fuck, man?!"

Ray has to think about it for a second. It's a good question. He doesn't have an answer. But his trigger fingers eventually relax.

It's the paperwork as much as anything else that keeps him from unloading on Scooter Pleasants. That and Ray thinks maybe it's not a good look for IAD to be shooting its complainants in the face. Lieutenant Twill might have something to say about that.

Ray pulls himself up and gets Scooter down onto the parking lot, trading places just so everyone knows their proper roles. He examines the street in both directions, but it doesn't have any answers. He puts a few tough questions to Scooter, but that turns out to be pointless. The only thing Scooter knows is what gunfire sounds like. Ray already knows that.

Turns out the Impala is the only one with any information worth a damn. Ray puts the guns away and uses a pen knife to dig two 9mm slugs out of the passenger-side dashboard. The third slug is in the trunk. He sends Scooter back inside and slips the pen knife and the slugs into his pocket. Then he heads across the street to find out who saw what.

He knows the answer. But he goes anyway.

FORTY-EIGHT

Nobody listens to good music anymore. You can't walk into a store and hear the voice of someone who knows how to carry a tune coming through the speakers. Someone who knows how to bend a note around her finger as a bass and a piano hang out in some dark corner sharing a smoke and a drink and talking about the neighborhood. Ella or Carmen or Billie or Dinah.

Not these days. The kids selling tires inside *Rolling Rubbers* are all in for the hip-hop beat. Mr. Ponytail in the *Double Value Liquor* thinks booze sells better with a head-banging vibe. Too bad. Ella may have had perfect pitch, but she'd never have been able to cover up three gunshots.

I talk to all the employees and even a couple of customers. Everybody knows how to shrug their shoulders to the beat. It's the dance of the know-nothings, more popular than the twist or the mashed potato.

I head back across the street to the Impala, narrowing the universe to two possibilities. The first possibility lacks a certain ambition, rambling on about random violence outside porn shops in bad neighborhoods. The second possibility has more personal appeal and is simple to grasp: it's all about me.

No one knew I'd be dropping in on Scooter; not even me. That means I've been driving around dragging a heavy shadow. Whoever it was must have parked nearby and waited for me to finish up with the porn king of East Chandler and come back out to the car. I'm guessing he looked for a lull in traffic, rolled forward on West Malcomb until he had the line he wanted, squeezed off three rounds easy as you please and rolled away while I played hide-and-seek.

The question is why.

The answer has something to do with the little wooden doll in my glovebox but I'm not smart enough to figure out the rest. Someone is bent out of shape that I have the thing. Angry enough to ruin my couch and end my life outside Scooter's little shop of horrors. But if me taking possession of the doll is such a problem, someone is doing a piss-poor job of taking it back. Why not take it off my hands when they had the chance?

I open up the Impala and brush bits of back window out of the seat. I climb in and close the door. I return some semblance of order to the *Kings Flush Casino* reports, which are now on the floor of the passenger seat, bent and coming out of their folder. I start the engine and blast the heat, trying to warm my hands. The two bullet holes in the dash are like a pair of eyes. Like the doll is in there looking back out at me. I open up the glove compartment.

She's still there, unharmed. I'm starting to hate that smile. I take her out and hold her in my hands, face up.

"What gives, doll?" I turn her over and over like a wooden gourd.

If she knows, she's not saying. Back in she goes. I slap the little door closed with authority and head off to find a hardware store.

It's another hour and three rolls of duct tape before I've jerry-rigged a Visqueen back window and I'm rolling west for Randy Sweet's place. After talking with Scooter, my plan had been to head over to Aurora and drop in on Billy Wise; watch him cut up fish and bend his ear about the mountain man and the yellow-coated girl. But the holes in my dash and the guy in the mirror with the ligature welts around his throat have managed to reshuffle the deck. Randy was not happy about me taking his girlfriend's doll. The way he spit my name before speeding off into the night makes me think maybe he's heard the name before. I'd like to know where.

Maybe it's nothing, but he's as good a place to start as any.

The little blue house is right on the corner where I left it, only sunlit and all the cuter for the little mail truck out front. I pull up to the curb a couple of houses away just to watch things for a minute. The mail truck scuttles off across the street sending a stream of exhaust up into the leafless branches of an oak, a white-gray tail looking for the ghost of a kite.

It's a quiet street this time of day. Deserted quiet. Everyone is in school, at work or checking in with their parole officers. Three houses up the road the mailman walks a package to the front door. He knocks and the door opens like magic. Two arms extend from inside to claim the box. The door closes again and the mailman heads back to the truck.

So at least someone is home in the neighborhood. House arrest maybe.

The little blue house I care about acts like it's empty. No cars in the driveway. No lights in the windows. No one coming out to get the mail.

I unclip Sig in the shoulder holster, just so he's ready. Two guns strikes me as heavy for this kind of visit. I take Scooter's .38 out of my coat pocket and tuck it under the seat. I climb out and look both directions for any idling cars. The wake-up call at the *Pleasant Palace* has left me spooked. Somewhere out there is a quiet car with a loud gun inside that likes to play follow the leader. I kept a close look out on the drive over, playing all the tricks that thirty years in this business teaches you about busting tails. Last-second turns. Looping. Running reds. Quick parks. I know how to watch my back better than most, just ask the guy up on the ceiling. But it's harder to do when your back window is plastic.

So I take a good look around just to be sure.

I walk up the street and across the yard like I'm invited. I give the door two knuckles and wait.

Houses have a feel to them when they're empty. This is one of those, four walls around a bunch of air that holds not so much as a whiff of soup. I try again and then the doorbell just to be safe. Nothing. I decide to walk in a circle with the house in the middle.

Mouth's girl keeps a tidy yard. There's a prefabricated shed in the back with a stack of four tires on the side secured with a red, locking cable. I keep moving. The house has plenty of windows and just as many shades. There's a coffee can by the back door full of sand and snow. It looks like a battlefield in a war fought and lost by Winston-Salem, littered with crumpled, forgotten soldiers. I don't make the girlfriend as a smoker. I'm betting she doesn't want the smell inside. She makes Mouth take his habit out back. He gets his fix out in the cold, leaning up against the door and looking across the yard at the tires stacked up by the shed. Soup like that? It's the least he can do.

I put my ear to the back door. Nothing. I keep moving.

The east side of the house comes with a trim little cabinet, just the size for a couple of garbage cans. I open it up and look inside. The cans are plastic, one black and the other green. The green one is for recycling. It's half-full of glass and tin and bad journalism. Martini & Rossi vermouth and Del Monte stewed tomatoes and an old copy of *The Tribune*. Mickey Shaw and Wrigley Menard sit together at the counsel table, smeared with pasta sauce and flecks of olive.

The black can is for the trash. I lift the lid. Rotten timing. Never go snooping after the garbage truck has been by. It's empty. Almost empty. There's a white paper stuck to the bottom of the can. I look around to make sure I'm alone, then reach inside and pull it free with two fingers.

It's a piece of butcher paper about one-foot square, the kind that usually comes wrapped around a couple of steaks that get handed over a glass counter in exchange for a small fortune. I give it a sniff. I don't have the best nose, but it doesn't smell like meat. It smells like garbage. It smells like something I want to drop back in the can and leave behind. But under that sour stink, it smells like fish.

I turn the paper over. There's a curling, foil sticker half peeled off. *Windy Wharf Seafoods, Aurora Illinois.* I don't need to sniff the sticker. I can smell unlikely coincidences a mile away.

FORTY-NINE

I check the mailbox before I go. It's good for a name, but not much else. Ainsley Harper gives money to the Democrats and likes to catalogue shop for shoes and kitchen gadgetry. She may or may not care that the apocalypse is nigh and that there is a church on Clarendon and 125th Street that seems to have all the answers.

Back at St. Evangeline's I lost count of the number of times I was threatened with eternal damnation. Talk of hellfire tends to get an orphan kid's attention. But the nuns overplayed their hand. They predicted the future so many times that eventually I just started to expect it. Once a thing becomes inevitable and beyond my control, I tend to stop worrying about it.

Take death. Inevitable. Everybody dies. I don't worry about death. It's getting killed that concerns me.

I drive around the block and up the street to the house that Casey Randolph Sweet called home before his pipes burst and turned the place into a swimming pool. I pull into the empty driveway and climb out without thinking. It's all one sheet of ice. I go down hard on my elbows and can feel last night's boot in the gut all over again. Inside my coat, Sig slips out of his holster, clattering out onto the ice. I have to scrabble for it to keep it from sliding under the car. I put the gun back where it belongs and get back on my feet, carefully negotiating my way across the yard.

I ring the bell twice and wait as the heatless sun bakes my cold shadow against the door. No one answers. I consider taking a tour around back like I did at Ansley's place. Later, I think. I'll bring some ice skates.

I make it back to the Impala without breaking my tailbone. I start it up and back out into the street, looking hard both ways for cars that aren't empty and cold. I don't see anything, but I sit there anyway, cutting the street in half, waiting for something to change. Anything. Because he's out there somewhere. I can feel him. Whoever it is. The mountain man, the guy Scooter knows as Hell? Maybe. Casey Sweet? Maybe. The guy who stinks of oily tobacco and keeps a chainsaw handy? Maybe. Or, more likely, someone entirely different. Someone with my name and address on the back of a photo of me coming out of some building.

But it's someone.

I knock out the last Camel and light it up. One last look for trouble, then I crank the wheel and put the thing in gear.

Aurora is a long drive for a cut of fish. Makes me wonder who's making that drive, Ansley or Mouth. I work my way north to pick up Interstate 88, figuring it's time to drop in on Billy Wise and see what he knows. But then that idea gets an idea of its own.

I pull out my phone and call the number I remember seeing on the side of a van. 1-800-RESTORE. The woman answering phones at *Dan's Restoration* is in too much of a hurry to be friendly. I tell her I need to talk to Walt Harper. She wants to know who I am and why I'm calling so I give her my name and tell her it's about the gusher Walt mopped up for Casey Sweet on Sylvan Road. The line goes quiet for a minute. Walt picks up just as I'm merging onto I-88.

"Yeah."

"Walt. Officer Mackey, Chandler PD. We spoke yesterday in a driveway."

"Okay."

"I'm still trying to connect with Casey Sweet. I was wondering if you know where he works."

"Anywhere and everywhere, man. He's one of those what do you call it, home network computer fix-it guys. Helps all your gadgets talk to each other."

"A techy troubleshooter."

"That's it."

"Only way I know to fix electronics is with a chainsaw. I don't suppose he hauls one of those around?"

"I think he knows what he's doing. He used to work at Chicago PD until he got himself fired."

"What happened there?"

"Don't know and don't care. He's squirrelly about it and we don't have that kind of relationship. We've had maybe three beers together. Which is about two and a half too many."

"Who signs his paychecks?"

There's a commotion in the soundscape. Walt says something to someone else. Then he's back.

"Sorry. Mouth's his own boss. *Sweet Solutions*."

"Sounds like he bakes cupcakes."

I expect something like a laugh. I get the opposite.

"Look, man," says Walt, "I'm on my way out for job, so…"

"Got it. I'll get out of your ear. But listen Walt, you ever seen Mouth in the company of a very large man, bald head, square face, looks like someone chiseled him out of the Grand Canyon?"

"Hmm." I can hear him thinking, burrowing those dirty fingers around in the red beard. "Doesn't ring any bells. I think I'd remember that. But look, like I said, Mouth and I don't really hang."

"Any mutual friends?"

"Nah."

"Any of his old cop friends ever come around?"

That's the question that gets me a laugh, only not the funny kind.

"You do know that I don't live with my sister, right? I don't, like, ride along with them on their dates. I've got my own life and family."

"I get that. Just thought she might have said something. Maybe everybody gets together for Thanksgiving. Christmas. Ball games."

"Nah. It's not like that, man. And Ansley's only known this guy for, like, six months. He'll be history by Thanksgiving."

That one clanks in my brain like someone dropped a wrench. I'm too close to the black Escalade next to me. He wants in my lane and lets me know it. I ease off the gas and let him merge.

"Six months? I figured they'd been at it longer than that. How'd they meet?"

"Tech support. Her printer wasn't talking to her electric toothbrush or whatever. Look, man…"

"Yeah. Okay, Walt. Thanks for your time."

"Hey," he says.

"Yeah."

"Is she borrowing trouble with this guy? I mean should I be telling her something?"

I tell him I don't know, which just happens to be the truth. I don't know anything and the pile of what I don't know is getting deeper by the second.

Why, for instance, does a man working in the Chicago PD evidence control unit steal a wooden doll for a woman he hasn't met yet?

FIFTY

The *Windy Wharf Seafoods* sticker has an address on it that doesn't exist. That, or he's lost. One is easier for him to conclude than the other and driving around Aurora in circles isn't helping.

The light on the dash tells him the Impala is dry. He guesses they could both use a drink.

He pulls into a *Chevron* and gasses up. Then he heads inside for a bottle of water and directions.

The gal behind the counter looks the worse for wear. Milky eyes pushed deep into a wrinkled, sallow face that hasn't chewed food with a full set of teeth in a long time. She's got a smoker's mouth and the yellowing fingernails to match. He's guessing three or four packs a day. The hair is long and thin, dusty black and not as supple as it used to be. But it's hanging in there. It won't quit, this hair. She won't let it quit. It reminds her of the days when everything seemed to be going right. Back when her eyes were bright and her skin was taught over her frame and her teeth gleamed in the sun and the boys came in swarms like libidinous insects humming in the summer heat. Back then, when the smile was a kind of quiet laugh and the eyes were an open invitation, the hair had been thick and silky and cape-like, taking to the slightest breeze like a kind of dance mermaids do in the moonlight.

Long time ago, that hair. Now it's rolled up in a bun and wedged inside the jaws of a brown plastic clamp. Like an old dinosaur nearly had her for lunch and lost his dentures.

Ray puts the water on the counter and holds out a piece of plastic. She stops what she's doing and looks up at him, taking the card. She flinches a little. He sees pity in those milky-blue eyes. Pity. She's taking in the bandage and the bruises and the welt around Ray's neck and wondering how they got there.

But he feels like the look goes deeper than that. It feels like she's looking at him —the head, the chest, the hands —and wondering what he must have looked like forty years ago. She's trying to fathom the man he used to be and connect that to who he is now.

But that's not possible. He's tried. He tries every day. It's like looking for an address that doesn't exist.

She takes the water and rings it up. He asks her for a pack of Camels.

FIFTY-ONE

She puts the pack on the counter and I ask if she knows where I can find *Windy Wharf Seafoods*.

She turns and points through the window like it might be right across the street. It isn't. Her directions go on for a bit and her finger keeps bobbing in the air as she talks, like she's dinging a bell only dogs and angels can hear. Turns out there are two Devonshires, a road and a street, and I've been circling the wrong one.

"Take a right when you get to the Dairy Queen." She finally retracts the arm and turns back to me. "If you pass the castle, you've gone too far."

"A castle in Aurora," I say. "Who knew."

She smiles a little, not enough to show the missing teeth, but just enough to reveal the ghost inside.

"Doesn't look like a castle, silly," she says. "Looks like an old, run-down motel."

Her directions are spot on. I do go too far and it's the dingy little *Castel Motel* that swings me back around in the right direction. *Windy Wharf Seafoods* looks like a boxy white turtle; a flat, square building in front connected to a larger warehouse-sized building behind. There are half a dozen cars in the lot and two refrigerated, moving-van-sized trucks, each sporting a logo that features oversized *W*'s looking windblown and covered in spume.

I park and head inside. Something smells fishy, but I expected that. The guy behind the counter looks like he lives in a Mrs. Paul's commercial. He's big and brawny, stuffed inside a black cable sweater and wrapped in a bright, plastic apron the color of lemons. Way up on top, waves of curly brown hair escape from beneath a knit wool cap, foaming down the sides of his face into the froth of a full beard. He looks up and nods, then finishes wrapping something in butcher paper and fixes it with a foil seal I've seen before.

The line he's working is three deep, so I wander the room bending down over rows of freezers with my hands behind my back. A kid, early twenties, lean and not so big but hung with muscle, comes through a swinging door with a tray of fish steaks. He's in an apron too, only it's white and smeared with gray and red. He tries to slide open the freezer next to me, but it keeps closing on him as he manages the tray. On the third try I grab the door and hold it open.

He nods sharply and makes a sound of gratitude. The sound is a word, guttural and dense. My tongue couldn't lift that word if my life depended on it.

I only speak one language and sometimes not even that one so well. I can pick my way through the romance languages enough to get by. Most African and East-Asian languages are a complete mystery to my ears. I couldn't even tell you what language I'm not understanding from those parts of the world.

But Russian is different. I know when I'm not understanding Russian every time.

"You pulling all of this meat out of Lake Michigan?" I ask the kid.

He looks at me uncertainly and gives another sharp nod like before. He finishes stacking the product and closes the freezer door.

"Don't suppose you've got any chicken," I say. "A guy I know says it tastes like shark."

Nothing.

"You happen to know what time it is?"

Another quick nod and a sheepish smile. He pushes past me for the swinging door. Turns out the score is even on not understanding languages. Difference is I'm on the home team. I don't have to speak Russian in order to get a job and understand what my supervisor wants me to do so that I can keep it.

He kicks the door open with his foot like he's done it a billion times before and then he's gone. As the door is swinging closed, I get a fleeting glimpse of long tables. Men in rubber boots. Black hoses hanging from above. A man laughs as he pushes a rolling black crate.

"Help you?"

It's the big guy from behind the counter. He's gotten bigger since I saw him last but that's because he's left the counter and decided to come over for a closer look. He must think I'm the fishiest thing in the room because there are still two people at the counter waiting to check out. He sounds friendly enough, but I liked him better when he was way over there.

"I'm looking for Billy Wise," I say.

The man crosses his arms and furrows his brow. Behind that beard someplace is a frown. So much for friendly.

"Billy's on the job right now," he says. "He expecting you?"

"I doubt that very much," I say.

"Then maybe you can wait until he's off shift. I can get him a message."

"Sure," I say. "That'd be great. The message is that I drove all the way out here and I'm not leaving until I talk to him."

"Sir," he says. He must think he's standing too far away. "You *will* leave… if I ask you to leave."

"But it's a two-part message," I tell him, pulling out my badge. "And this is the important part."

We share a long second or two of staring. Even the waiting customers get in on the act.

"Wait here," he says eventually, heading for the swinging doors. Then he turns back. "What's the name?"

"Officer Mackey."

"Wait here."

Anytime someone says *wait here* to me twice it makes me want to do the opposite. But I don't. I nod at the customers and smile and act like a cop without a warrant who just a few hours ago told his LT he was going home for the day. The woman nods back, turning away as she shifts her basket to the other hand. The Asian man in a long, wool topcoat over a suit and tie looks at his watch. I shrug an apology and he looks away with a sigh.

I stroll the room pretending some interest in the fish. They stare up at me from their little white trays, each eye a pale citrus, glassy and frozen in terrible surprise. I've spent too much time in too many morgues. Working homicide changes a person in ways you'd never expect. I don't like looking at food that looks back.

In one corner of the room is a wire display rack loaded with spice rubs and sauces, fish knives, thermometers, a stack of *Windy Wharf* calendars and a series of small paperback cookbooks. It gets me a nice angle on the swinging doors so I pick up the calendar and pretend to be interested, waiting to see if I can get another glance inside the warehouse.

There's an attractive blonde on the cover holding up a large Chinook Salmon on the end of a hook. The fish is fat and silver and heavy enough to bring the tendons out in the woman's neck. She's bracing herself against the gunnel of a trawler, one red boot up on a white, overturned bucket and nothing but gray waves and a blue sky in the background. The smile on her face might be bigger than the salmon. I flip the calendar over. Turns out the gal on the front is Miss March. The eleven other women are each in different poses: some sitting on a barrel, others standing. Some are wearing hats and a couple go for black earmuffs.

But the smiles are all the same. So is the white bucket and the red boots and the boat and the water and the sky.

Same hooked fish too. Twelve pretty fisherwomen and one hooked fish. That hardly seems fair.

"This way."

The voice comes from the front of the store. Either the clerk has gone out the back of the warehouse and walked around the building to the front door, or he's got an identical twin. He's propping the door open with one leg, I guess just in case I've forgotten how the hinges work.

"He's this way," he says, then turns apologetically to the two people in line. "I'll be right back."

I follow the man outside and around the warehouse. He doesn't speak except when we round the last corner. He points to another white refrigerated van backed up to a loading door. A short man in a puffy black coat and a white baseball cap is moving a large rolling crate out of the van and down a ramp.

"That's Billy," he says. "Billy is busy. Shorter would be better."

"I don't know," I say. "He looks plenty short to me. But I'll pass that along."

He looks at me through a cloud of steam that clings to his beard like it wants to stay warm. Then he turns and walks off the way we came. I continue around back and stop next to the truck.

"Mr. Wise?"

"Heavy on the mister," he says without looking up. "Call me Billy. And watch your feet."

He squats at the base of the large rolling crate and opens two latches. One side of the bottom third of the crate swings open to reveal a solid wall. Billy puts a finger inside a loop of nylon and pulls upward so that a panel slides up into the upper two-thirds of the crate. A stream of fish water and ice spills out into the parking lot, draining out from around three large white plastic bags. I take a step back behind the growing puddle.

"I'm Officer Mackey, Chandler Police. Sorry to bother you. I'd like to ask you a couple of questions."

"Chandler?" asks Billy. "What kind of questions?"

He looks up at me briefly as he rotates the crate. He's one of those guys who was probably cute as a bug when he was a kid but then he grew up and got stepped on. An accident of some kind has left him with scarring and an asymmetrical face. He might be the only person alive that can look at the wreckage of my face and not see anything remarkable. The left side is lower than the right. The nose can't make a straight line and the mouth, abnormally small for the rest of the face, seems twisted into a perpetual pucker. But his eyes are quick and sharp under the dirty white brim of the cap, like a couple of finches darting for cover. I can see him looking at my face, taking inventory of the abuse. Neither of us will sell any magazines.

Billy opens the compartment on the opposite side of the crate. He slides up the interior panel just like before and there is another rush of water and ice.

"The kind that need answers," I say.

"Mind if I keep at it?" he asks, pulling one of the large white bags out into the slop with a grunt. "Kinda cold out for wet hands."

"Go right ahead," I say. "I'm looking for a guy, a small giant; goes by the name of Hell. I'm told you might know where I can find him."

Billy heaves the bag up onto his shoulder with another grunt like it's a big bag of flour or potatoes. *Perma-Freeze Artificial Ice*, it says, red letters bending over his back.

"Goes by what, you say?"

"Goes by the name Hell."

"Hell. That's a name all right. I don't know anybody by that name. Glad I don't." Billy heaves his shoulder and dumps the bag into the back of the van. "Who told you I did?"

"That doesn't matter, does it?"

"Depends. Maybe whoever gave you my name just wants to fuck me over."

"Got enemies, do you?"

Billy makes a noise that might be a laugh.

"Pope's got enemies, man."

"Sure. But the Pope never did a nickel in the joint for intent. You've got to take the drugs out of the baggie before you flush, Billy."

Billy looks up at me, eyes hot.

"Fuck you, man. No offense. This is from Scooter, ain't it?"

"Scooter who? You know a guy named Scooter who knows a guy named Hell?"

"I don't know anybody who knows anybody, man. Scooter knows that story about me is all I'm saying."

Billy pulls out another bag and heaves it up into the truck. I point to the cart.

"So where in the hell are the fish?"

Billy slaps each of the upper two sections of the cart. He unclasps a latch at the top and props open the lid with one hand. He's not tall enough to do it comfortably. On his toes, he jams his hand down inside and feels around, then pulls a frozen fish out by the tail in a shower of ice and thrusts it my direction.

I don't know my fish, but even upside down this one looks like maybe he knows me. Knew me. Something about my face makes Billy laugh.

"What, never seen a walleye before?"

"Sure. You ever seen a barstool at a place named *Last Call*?"

Billy's smile, if you can call it that, fades. He jams the walleye back into the ice and latches the lid. His hands are red and raw with cold. He wipes them on his pants and then pulls a pair of thick neon-orange gloves out of his coat, cursing the cold.

"Maybe next time try putting those on first," I say.

"Can't work the latches with these things."

"Tell me about the bar."

"Where again?"

"*Last Call*. It's in Chandler on West Filcher. Cute little place if you like rat holes."

"Never been there."

"Not what I hear, Billy. I hear your elbow prints are all over that bar."

"Then you should get your hearing checked, man."

Billy gets back to work. He pulls out the third bag of Perma-Freeze and gets it up into the truck. He rotates the crate around to start on the other side.

"Ever have sex with a girl named Emily?"

In my business they call that kind of question a *slap*. Breaks up the rhythm. Reminds people like Billy that they aren't in control. Gets their attention.

Billy straightens himself again and puts his neon hands on his hips. The slap has left him dizzy.

"What?"

"Pretty sure you heard me. Emily. Long black hair, yellow coat, sad face. Looks exactly like someone you shouldn't be having sex with."

"I don't know what you're talking about."

"Sure you do, Billy. But tell me where I can find Hell and maybe I don't care who you've had sex with."

"For the last time, man, I don't know anyone named Hell or anyone named Emily. Anyone else in this guessing game or are we about done? I'm on the clock here."

"Yeah. Casey Sweet. Some people call him Randy. People like you call him Mouth." I nod at the tall, rolling crate. "He could be a cousin to that walleye in there."

"Yeah," he says carefully. "I know Mouth. He the one who sent you? Fucking Mouth is behind this? Prick. What's he saying?"

"He says five years wasn't enough to teach you anything, Billy. Says you went right back into the game and never skipped a beat. Says you're sloppy and reckless and that you'll be back in a onesie in no time. Says you keep company with some bad people. People that don't have your best interests as a priority."

"Yeah, like maybe him." It comes out as almost a shout. "Like maybe fucking Mouth. Maybe you should be asking Mouth about…"

"About what? About Hell?"

A horrified laugh sneaks out into the cold, hiding inside a cloud of steam.

"You think I'm stupid, man?"

"Stupid?" I curl my thumb and forefinger into a circle and hold it in front of his face. "Billy, the pipe that connects the toilet to the plumbing is about this big around. You have to take the drugs out of the baggie before you flush."

"Fuck you, man. I don't know any guy named Hell, okay? But if I did, I'd probably step in front of a moving bus before talking about him to the fuckos in blue. A name like that? I'm just saying. And if I was you, I'd probably want to spend my time asking assholes like Mouth about all of *his* best friends. And maybe I'd be talking to Scooter about *his* sex life. So fuck you, officer. No disrespect but fuck you. Because none of this shit is about me, okay? Are you arresting me for something?"

"Arresting you? No. I'm talking to you. Would you like to be arrested?"

"I've got work to do."

Billy closes up the bottom of the cart and begins pushing it toward the warehouse.

"Hey, wise guy," I say. Billy Wise pauses and drops his head, then turns around to look. "Next time you talk to Hell, you tell him I'm looking for him."

FIFTY-TWO

Winter sleeps in his bones. It makes him feel his age. Ray Mackey's been putting the old in cold for a while now. The liquid sunshine doesn't goose that internal thermometer quite like it used to, and he hasn't felt the comfort of a warm body since Marlo passed.

Florida, he thinks again. Baja. Someplace warm.

He idles in the *Windy Wharf* parking lot, rubbing his hands over the blower. The Impala doesn't heat up quite like it should. Something about plastic for a back window is less effective at keeping February outside. The guy from *Mrs. Paul's* pokes his beard out the front door twice to check on him, craning his neck all directions, blowing steam and pretending he's looking around for the sun.

But the sun is right where it's supposed to be, a bright ball of onion bobbing in its endless periwinkle-blue cocktail. The man pretends he doesn't see the idling Impala. He closes the door again.

"Yeah, I'm still here," Ray mutters. "You hairy creep."

He pulls the little plastic bottle out of his coat pocket and looks at it. The pain hates the cold even more than the rest of him does. He rattles the Percocet around. They're full of promises. They all want to help. But he'd trade them all for a few shots of Forester, just enough to dull the throbbing in his face. He doesn't need another monkey on his back. It's all he can do to manage the alcohol and nicotine.

He pockets the pills, trading them for the new pack of Camels. He knocks one free and lights it up. He takes a deep drag, closing his eyes like he wants to keep the smoke inside. His hand drapes itself over the gear shift, waiting for his brain to give the order.

The drive back to Chandler gives him time to think. Time to smoke and solve problems. Time to answer riddles about unfindable girls and chainsaw soirees, poker chip bribes and protection rackets and hit job homicides made to look like burglaries gone bad. Dismembered couches and perforated dashboards and back seats strewn with glass. Painted dolls within painted dolls.

But Ray doesn't use the drive time wisely. He tries. He tries to pry open the *Windy Wharf* warehouse like it's some kind of clam; some kind of oyster with a pearl inside that might shine some of its moonlight and help him figure out the lay of the land in this nightmarish dreamscape. But he's too distracted to shuck shellfish for answers. Look at the lower jaw, moving back and forth, rolling that Camel. Look at the forefinger tapping the back of the passenger seat. He's got pizza on the brain.

Not pizza itself so much as pizza with Nadia King. The date with Nadia –it is not a date, it is anything but a date, he refuses to think of it as a date, he is almost angry when his thoughts drift in the direction of it being a date, but it keeps happening anyway –the date has been on the horizon of this day from the moment she had first made the proposal. Nadia, he had thought –foolishly, shamefully, pathetically –would be waiting for him at the end of this day, removing triangles from a flat circle of dough and cheese.

That thought, as much as anything else, has been keeping him warm.

FIFTY-THREE

I pull into *Pizza Maria* forty minutes early.

But that's just me. The late model Buick playing games with my sideview mirror ever since Aurora is right on time. There is no such thing as early or late when you tail someone. This guy, whoever he is, is precisely where he needs to be at precisely the right time. For him it's all one long, rolling moment of Zen.

Makes me wonder how long he's been at it. Did I pick him up at the *Windy Wharf* or has he been with me all day? Is this the guy who squeezed off three rounds outside the *Pleasant Palace* or do I have a new friend? I don't want any new friends. It's getting hard to keep track.

I pull into the lot and park close to the front of the building. A young couple holding hands pass into my headlights on their way to the door. She is unsteady, heels on ice, clinging to his arm, six inches of red skirt extending out from beneath her black down jacket, blonde corkscrew curls sweeping her shoulders. He's not big or brawny, this guy; her date. If she goes down on the ice, she's taking him with her. But right now, he looks like King of the World. He could slay entire armies.

That's how he feels anyway. King of the World. I remember that.

I keep my lights on so they can see, turning them off only once this guy has pulled the door open for her and she steps safely inside.

Dusk is just pulling the sheet up over the day. The dark is starting to rise like a lake of shadow up around the tires of every car, filling the icy potholes and slopping up against the side of the building. I keep my eyes on my side mirror. I don't have to wait but a few seconds. The Buick passes behind me and circles around to the back of the lot. It parks. The headlights go out.

We sit in the gathering dark and stare at each other for a while, him forward and me backward. I pull out my not-so-smart phone and mash some buttons.

"Raj. It's Mack."

"Hey, Mack."

"Can you talk?"

"Since I was two," he says. "I can sing too."

"Too bad you're not funny, you'd be dangerous. You up for some extra scratch?"

"The girl in the yellow coat?"

"Forget her, she can't be found. This is something else."

"Yeah, Mack. Anything."

He's like a puppy, this kid. So eager to help. He has romanticized this awful business. Hollywood has glamorized the grit and Raj is all in. I can't help thinking of Suri, aka Ginger Turner, aka Courtney Briggs, the opposite of Raj Malik. Suri had the street in her blood. She knew what she was doing. Starting as a teenager, every day of her life was a bump and grind with death. But she could handle herself. A survivor. Then I came along with a shiny badge and a lot of questions about a lot of bad people. We used each other for years. She got some money and a meal, and I got an education: names, locations, and who was working for whom. Suri could get into a bad man's pocket in ways no one else ever could and our relationship made me one effective detective. But it also relocated Suri's daily dance with death up onto the edge of a razorblade. Now she's somewhere out on the streets, hiding in shadows, waiting for Big Man's people, including any number of cops and maybe even the Mayor of Chicago, to find her and cut her up into little pieces. All partly because of me.

And now here I am tapping Raj for a favor, dangling a junior G-man badge from across a busy street.

Asking him to look around for a girl in a yellow coat is one thing. But this? This? With a legless couch waiting at home, a sheet of plastic for a back window, bullet holes in my dash and an extra set of eyes at my back?

What are you doing, Mack?

It's Marlo, deep inside my head. Or it sounds like her. I try to defend myself.

It's not a date. It's not a date. A bad dodge and I know it. *Raj will be fine. He'll stay in his cab.*

"Still there?" Raj asks. "Mack?"

"Yeah. Yeah, I'm here."

"Well? What's the job?"

"There's a seafood store. It's out in Aurora. *Windy Wharf Seafoods*. It's on Devonshire. I'll save you an hour and tell you that it's Devonshire Road, not Devonshire Street."

"Okay. What am I doing?"

"You're looking for a real big guy. Looks like the Chrysler building with a couple of ears. Bald. Drives a black F-150. Goes by the name Hell."

"Hell?"

"That's right. But listen, Raj. Keep your distance. You won't need to get close to him; you should be able to see this lug from two blocks away. Stay in your cab. This guy could snap you like a Pakistani toothpick."

"That sounds vaguely racist."

"Dead is dead, kid. And I'm fine with all the races. All of them except the human race, which is starting to bother me more and more. He could snap you like a human toothpick. That better?"

"Better."

"You hear what I'm telling you?"

"I hear you, Mack. What do I do if I find him?"

"Get the plate number if you can. Let me know where he goes. And keep track of your time, including there and back."

"So, just to be clear," Raj says. I can hear him lighting up a cigarette. "Hell riding a black F-150 and no citizen's arrest."

I can feel him smiling on the other end of the phone. It feels less like a smile than a hot coal in my gut.

We end it there. I look at my watch and call Judith Kravitz to check in on Phil and see if anyone is roasting marshmallows over the smoldering husk of my house. She picks up after the second ring. Phil is fine, napping off and on in her front window. Judith thinks Phil likes watching for birds. I don't tell her that Phil is actually watching for me, wondering where the hell I am and why I've turned her over to the neighbor.

What are you doing, Mack?

It's not a date. It's not a… Phil will be fine. I might lose the house and a couple of legs, but the cat will make it okay.

Judith is still worked up from a noontime confrontation she started with Roger Hemmecks. Seems Roger had the cheek to deny taking a chainsaw to some logs in the middle of the night. Their discussion segued into what Judith thinks about Roger's kids. Roger took exception. Judith predicted that, come summer, they're never getting the next ball back.

I thank her for watching Phil and tell her I will resume possession in a couple of days.

Behind me, the parking lot is filling up. I can't see the Buick anymore, but I know it's still back there. I look at my watch. Still twenty minutes early. I open the glove compartment and take out the Russian doll so I can hand it over to Nadia just like I promised. Makes me wonder how to explain that the doll comes with some people who want to take it away again. Maybe enough to cut off her fingers.

What are you doing, Mack?

And then there's the other thing I don't want to think about. Jimmy Kline.

Nadia calls him Jack, a mistake, a dalliance that never panned out. Sure, except that Jimmy calls her a fiancé and knows her ring size.

Nadia has a daughter. Okay, but Jimmy thinks it's kismet that Nadia doesn't want anything to do with children.

Jimmy wants me to find the doll, hand it over, and make him a hero in time for the nuptials. Nadia knows I already have the doll and wants me to take it out for pizza.

Jimmy lies like he breathes. Nadia, meanwhile, breaks the sincerity meter. Little Danika and her dragon are just piling on.

This contest should be as clear cut as it ever gets. That's what worries me.

The doll in my hand has an opinion, maybe several, one inside the other. But she's not sharing. She'd rather smile at me in the dark.

Marlo is in my head, like it was yesterday, opining on one of my homicides. I was at a dead end, time ticking away. We were in bed, staring at the ceiling.

Stop looking for the liar, Mack. Everyone is lying. That's the only truth worth a damn in this business. So start there. Everyone is lying. Make the bastards prove otherwise and maybe you'll find the truth before it bleeds out.

I put the doll back in the box, slapping the door closed and locking it.

I climb out of the car and head inside for a beer and a slice of indigestion. I am easily more nervous about dinner with Nadia than I am about the guy back there in the Buick, sitting in the dark watching me open the front door of *Pizza Maria*.

I remind myself again that this is not a date. This is just business, now more than ever. Business.

But I'm only proving Marlo's point. Everyone is lying.

FIFTY-FOUR

There is a short line at the hostess station.

Ray looks around, just to make sure he hasn't missed her. Tables of two, mostly. Lots of white teeth and healthy hair and savage eyes glinting in candlelight. He wants to ask for a booth. Something in the shadows. He wants to avoid a room full of people speculating about the relationship. Half will make him as Nadia's father and Danika's granddad. The other half will decide he's a cradle-robbing creep.

Ray palms the back of his neck, his go-to self-conscious tell. Not that anyone else would ever know. But I'd love to play a hand of high-stakes poker with this guy.

He keeps the angst to himself and lets the teenager at the hostess station make the decision. He follows her to a square, checkered table in the dead center of the main room. She places a wine list on the table and leaves him standing, holding two menus and looking around for easy alternatives to center stage. There aren't any. He takes off his coat and sits down and makes polite with the water girl. She's small and sleek, somebody's muskrat daughter earning money for a prom dress. A sprig of ponytail quivers when she moves. Her face shows the impatience of youth tightly wrapped in an expression of over-practiced hospitality. She wants to know how many people.

"Two and a half," says Ray. "And probably a dragon."

She stops pouring.

"Okay. I don't know what that means, so…"

"Three glasses of water, please."

He used to be a restaurant guy. If Marlo could cook, she never let on. They had that in common. Dining out was part entertainment, part romance, and part laziness. They had their favorites. Places that saw them coming and got the right drinks ready. *Henry's Attic* on South Lark. *Fortuna Grill* across from the theater. *Luigi's*, with the whole tableside-flambé production and the homemade ice cream.

Not anymore. Those places are as dead as she is. Dead to him anyway. She took them with her.

He's strictly a diner-man now, at least when he's not cooking spaghetti or nuking a frozen brick of something in the microwave. He's into twenty-four-hour joints. Truckstop pancake houses. Places to eat before the bars are open and after they're closed. Where the lights are always on and the air smells like coffee and butter and bacon grease. Places that pour the kind of high-test brew you can take to-go if you need to strip some paint or degrease a carburetor. They've got a loyal, low-brow clientele, these joints; sad sack, high-and-dry loners looking for comfort in the greasy cloud of steam hissing out of the kitchen and plates piled high with the culinary violence of food battered and smothered and rolled up in carpets of sugar and fat. Places where the uniforms have nametags, and the menus have pictures. Where the waitstaff see you coming and don't do anything particularly special except maybe point a chipped nail at an orange vinyl booth by the window and grab a silver pitcher. Maybe they ask you about the bruises. Maybe they banter for a minute or two in an off-color way that gives you something to remember on the drive home. The always-open diners expect you to be alone. They salt everything except the wound.

FIFTY-FIVE

Nadia King shows up on the money, a kid by the hand and enough smiles for everybody.

I stand so she can see me. The couple next door stops chewing and looks up, like maybe I'm about to sing a song or make a toast. I don't do either. Nadia gives a small wave and points Danika my direction, letting go of her hand. But the smile fades when she gets to the table. She covers her mouth in shock and I realize I've forgotten about the battlefield between my ears. She looks like I need a drink, the kind a beer and wine license won't cover.

"Officer Mackey…"

"Mack."

"Mack, what happened?" she asks just above a horrified whisper.

"It's nothing. I should have warned you. I'm fine."

"And your neck." She sends a tentative hand my way but then she pulls it back in. "Who did this?"

"Part of the job," I tell her. "It happens sometimes."

"Not… not the job you were doing for me … I hope …"

"No, no. Nothing like that. I've got a job on the side catching pianos for a little extra dough."

She looks away, hiding her discomfort by getting Danika out of her coat and seated.

"Have you been here long?" she asks, not looking.

"Just sat down." I edge around the table to pull out her chair. It is a kind of muscle memory that moves me. I am only partly in control of myself. Nadia smiles tentatively.

"Thank you," she says. I help her slip out of her own coat and she sits. The cold air is trapped in her hair. She smells like a winter forest.

"No one pulls out your chair," observes Danika.

"That's only for the beautiful, the brilliant and the bold," I say. "I'm none. Which are you?"

She has to think, which requires a momentary wrinkling of her face.

"All three," she says eventually with a shrug. Next to her Nadia smirks behind the menu.

"Good answer, kid," I tell her. "You're going places."

"I just got here," she protests.

"Eventually, eventually. Dinner first."

Danika turns to her mother.

"Which one are you? Are you all three like me?"

Nadia opens her eyes to me as if for the first time. The look lingers for a breath, taking another inventory of my face. I want to answer for her. I want to ask her to stand up so I can scoot her chair in all over again. That soft declaration of affection. That dance of small gestures. Holding a coat. Holding a chair. Holding a door. I remember that.

I can't help but think of Doris, eyes damp, clutching the photograph of Buck, walking across the bar toward the man in glasses and the long wool coat and leather gloves and the earmuffs, receiving each other as people do when they don't know what's going to happen next, but they've got the courage to find out.

Nadia finally looks down at Danika.

"None," she says. "I'm just tired and hungry."

"I'm all three," says Danika.

"Where's your dragon?" I ask.

"At home," she says. "I have three." She consults her fingers and holds several of them up for me to see. "I mean I have four. They're at home."

"What? Cooling their heels back at the castle? Aren't they hungry?"

"Not the castle. At my *house*. And they only eat people, not pizza."

"Take a good look around," I say, squinting and pointing discretely in all directions. "Nothing but people with lots of sauce and cheese. Just saying… dragons might like this place."

She giggles and we talk nonsense for a while, a dizzying mix of this world and the fantasy in Danika's head. The kid is in control and she knows it, testing me with one outlandish invention after another, each of which leads to a disbelieving interrogation from me and then some illogical vindication that leaves me speechless in defeat. All of it makes Nadia laugh. Her eyes close and her chin inclines, like the sound is a kind of song she sends out over the restaurant. She catches me watching.

"You'll never win," she says, gripping my forearm for only a moment.

"I can see that," I say. "I know some hardened criminals that are easier to crack. She could send a prosecutor or two to the funny farm."

Nadia lifts her eyebrows. The smile hangs around, but it's no longer the laughing kind. It's the waiting kind of smile, encouraging the segue we've both been expecting.

"Speaking of prosecutors," she says.

"Right. The doll."

A lanky fellow with a fat tie and an unfortunate mustache stops by to give us his name in exchange for a drink order. Nadia orders a glass of wine. I double check the liquor license and order a beer. Danika also orders a beer. Nadia has to add the part that goes at the beginning.

"Root beer *is* beer," Danika insists like she's ready to go to the mat. Nadia opens her purse and extracts a small book. The cover shows a rutabaga in a hat holding a garden hoe. The title splashed across the front is in cartoon Cyrillic.

"Look at your book so I can talk to Officer Mackey," she says. Danika takes the book and Nadia refocuses on me. "You were saying."

"Yeah. So I pled your case to DA Bannon. She told me the same thing she told you: everything was returned, you're wasting your time. But I got her to send me the evidence file. That file coughed out the name of the guy who was responsible for making sure Ivah got her things back."

"What's his name?"

I grimace at her.

"I'm going to leave the names out of this, Nadia. At least for now. I have my reasons. I think it's better for everybody."

"Okay," she says. "If you say so."

"Good. So I track the guy down. Turns out he pinched the doll to give it to his girlfriend. She seems nice enough and twice as clueless about her boyfriend."

Nadia's perfect skin wrinkles perfectly between her eyes.

"But that's... that has to be a serious crime."

"It is. If he had shoplifted the doll, it'd be nothing more than sticky-finger petty theft. But stealing from an evidence lock up? That sends the boyfriend up the river. I told him I'd let it all drop if he turned it over. So that makes him as gullible as he is guilty."

The smile is back. She squeezes my arm as she squints a little, like her eyes are applying the pressure.

"That's why you won't tell me his name, isn't it?"

I pat her on the hand.

"Boy, nothing gets past you, does it? I figured you'd want me to go after him."

"You were right. That's stealing, Mack. He needs to pay a price."

"No argument here, Nadia. He'll get his. But for now, better that he thinks he's in the clear. My mission, your mission, was to get the doll back as quickly and easily as possible. I wanted to put it in your hands without making it evidence all over again."

"I see," she says. "I suppose that makes sense. So where is it?"

The server interrupts to deliver the drinks and take the order. Mother and daughter tussle over the merits of spumoni as an entrée. It's my last chance to think how I want this to play, so I take a quick inventory. Outside is a doll inside a doll inside a doll inside a glove compartment inside a car inside a city that always seems to like things the hard way. The car's got a perforated dashboard and extra air-conditioning in the back seat and a guy in a late-model Buick out there keeping watch, making sure no one breaks in to steal the thing, except maybe him assuming he knows the doll is there and is brave enough to smash and grab right at the front entrance. The doll in question belongs to the mother of this woman with a face I don't want to disappoint. But I can't turn over the doll without knowing why people want to kill me for it. If there is something extra special about this doll, and there must be, then I have to wonder why Nadia sent me out to get it back for her in the first place.

And then there's Jimmy.

Out in the dark I can feel the doll smiling. She's having more fun than anybody else.

Everyone is lying. That's the only truth worth a damn in this business. So start there.

"She'll have a small cheese pizza, no sauce," says Nadia. "And I'd like a small…" She stops and looks at me, hand lightly on my forearm again. "You want to split something?"

"Sure," I say. "Fire away. I'm not picky."

She orders a salad and a medium Chef's Mistake. The chef doesn't know the half of it. This will be a mistake for a week. The server disappears. I rip off the Band Aid.

"I don't have the doll with me," I say. I watch the lie land and inflate her eyes a little. "It's safe. It's locked up. My lieutenant wouldn't want me to release it to anyone except the actual owner, which is Ivah. He'd be afraid that if the doll doesn't find its way home, we'll get a complaint from Ivah, or maybe even your brother, accusing my department and the City of Chandler of losing it all over again."

Her expression dims and she leans back in her chair, like she needs to see me from farther away. The extra distance leaves me cold.

"Nadia, it's not personal," I say. "He doesn't know you like I do."

"And you don't know me at all. Is that about right?"

We look at each other. Her face is flush with anger or hurt or embarrassment. Maybe all three. I nod.

"Right," I say. "I don't."

"So then it is personal."

"Okay, maybe it is. Here's the thing, Nadia. I had a visit from Jimmy last night. You call him Jack, but the guy I know couldn't wear that name any better than he could wear Paul Bunyan's suit. He'll always be Jimmy to me. He asked me to find the doll and give it to him so he could give it to you. He seems to think you've stopped trying to find it. He's also under the impression, by the way, that you two are getting married this summer. He's looking forward to a lot of carefree, nuptial bliss; the traveling kind, without the burden of parental responsibility."

Her eyes go a little vacant and I have to wait a few seconds for the light to come back.

"I see," she says, glancing briefly at Danika. "So you think I've been lying to you."

"Somebody sure is," I say. "And I'm inclined to think it's Jimmy only because that's what Jimmy does best. But it does make me wonder, Nadia… if what you say is true and Jimmy gave up on you months ago because, as you said, you can be a pill, then why does he want the doll? He wants it bad enough to ask me for help and Jimmy doesn't darken my door unless there's something in it for him. Usually money."

"Jack is not a truthful person."

"And water is wet. Tell me more."

She closes her eyes and slumps a little in her chair. She said she was tired and hungry, but it looks like humiliation has joined the party. The eyes open slowly.

"I have lied to you," she says. "Not because… I mean… I just didn't think it was important. Jack and I didn't split up because I'm a pill. I didn't want to run him down. I was asking this huge favor and…"

"And you were afraid maybe I secretly liked him like a little brother."

"Yes."

"And now you're wondering what you ever saw in the guy."

"Yes."

"Well, let me remind you. You liked the hair and the smile and the laid-back charm. That little thing he does with his mouth before he tells you a story about one of his exploits. That's a prelude to a lie, just for future reference. You thought maybe Jimmy was going places. Then you found out the charm comes off on your thumb like cheap shoe polish and that if Jimmy's going places, then it's only as far as you can carry him on your back."

"Yes," she says, her eyes pleading. "He just… I honestly think he was after money."

"Can't say I'm surprised. But then that must be some real estate business you've got."

"No. You're right. I don't have any money. I mean, I have just enough. Nothing extra."

"That sounds familiar."

"But the doll… it's valuable."

"How valuable?"

"Close to a hundred thousand dollars, I think. I don't know exactly. Ivah had it appraised years ago. It's an original Meknikov."

"That's an expensive-sounding name the way you say it. Then again, I think you maybe you can make anything sound expensive."

Her eyes take the compliment and glimmer back a smile.

"Shashenka Meknikov," she says. "A Russian artist. He died a century ago. The doll is in good condition. Or, at least, it was in good condition when Wayne Bishop stole it. We haven't seen it since then."

"It's still in good condition," I say, "as far as I can tell."

"That's a relief."

"So, you happened to mention the doll to Jack and that turned him into Jimmy."

She gives me a contrite nod.

"Before we started dating, I told him about trying to get the doll back from the police. He asked about it. I did mention it was valuable."

"You more than mentioned it," I say. "Jimmy asked for an estimate, and you gave him one."

"Yes."

"And the relationship suddenly started to sound permanent."

"Yes."

"But Jimmy was just biding his time until he could leave you for the little painted lady."

"It would seem so. Eventually, it was all he talked about. He thought I wasn't trying hard enough to get it back. He suggested I get you involved. Eventually, we had a big fight. Not about the doll; just normal relationship stuff. He was too controlling. He treated me like a child. I cut off contact. And now... well now it sounds like he's trying to get the doll back himself."

She leans in, bringing herself close again. Smelling like she does means never having to say you're sorry. She does it anyway.

"I'm so sorry I lied, Mack. I'm sorry I didn't tell you everything. I didn't think any of... of... *that* mattered."

"You originally told me you had no idea what the doll is worth. Probably worth nothing, you said."

"I didn't think that was relevant to getting it back." She hesitates. "And I didn't... I didn't..."

She can't seem to finish, so I finish for her.

"You didn't know me from Adam."

She gives me her sad, beautiful best.

"No. I didn't. I'm so sorry. It wasn't personal."

"You thought maybe if I knew the doll was worth something you'd never get it back."

"Yes."

"So, it was personal, actually."

The smile gets a little sadder.

"Yes. Money complicates everything."

"Doesn't it though. Smart lie if you ask me. I'd have done the same."

"Really?"

"Sure. For all you knew Jimmy and I were working together. Forget about it."

"I really don't care anything about the dollar value of the doll. Its value is sentimental. It belongs to Ivah. It was a gift to her from her grandmother."

"Verochka Volkova."

"Yes. You remember."

"Not a name that likes to be forgotten. So the initials on the bottom of the doll are hers. Your great-grandmother's."

"Yes. Shashenka Meknikov made it for her. They were… involved."

"Ah. This doll seems to be the thing to give women you want to impress. Is Ivah going to give it to you when she goes?"

"Yes." She looks over at Danika, bent into her book. The hat-wearing rutabaga and a carrot are riding a motorcycle through Red Square. "And I will eventually give it to her. It is not for selling."

"And how does all of that sit with your brother?"

Nadia scoffs.

"Alexi knows it comes to me. He doesn't care. He doesn't need the money."

"I see. What does Alexi do in the world?"

Nadia's face arranges itself into something as bored as it is beautiful.

"These days he's an advisor to Mayor Royce."

FIFTY-SIX

Hard thing to keep your cool when the sky opens up and something like that drops in your lap. Ray's a better poker player than I like to admit. Not a twitch. Like she'd asked him to pass the parmesan.

But behind those calm eyes Ray's brain is all over this coincidence, giving it the full interrogation with the hot lights and the rubber hose.

He's thinking about Suri, angry and bruised and bleeding, pocket-fishing in Tony Rickens' pants and coming out with the mayor's phone number on a dry-cleaning ticket. He's thinking of Rickens pulling Suri out of the trunk of his car by the hair, ready to bury her in a landfill before she managed to turn the tables with a rusty nail to the eye and six bullets from Rickens' own gun just to make the point.

He's thinking of Suri barely escaping a bloodbath in a Springfield hotel as men with badges tried to put her down.

He's thinking of Santiago on assignment taking pictures outside of a Chicago dry cleaner.

And he's thinking about Big Man. José Beggemon. The boogie man who seems to turn up everywhere, under every rock, behind every stench, and now, just maybe, inside a Russian doll.

"The mayor," says Ray, acting impressed. "Heady stuff."

"Boring stuff," Nadia says with an exquisite eye roll. "Labor stuff… like some kind of liaison stuff I don't understand. And I don't want to!"

She laughs, throwing her head back. Ray's laugh chases hers. Maybe he's fooling her. He's not fooling me.

"You can keep me clear of politics too," says Ray. "I don't have time for the extra shower and delousing. What put Alexi up into that circle?"

"Alex," she corrects with a comedic flourish. "He goes by Alex for the *important* people. Only Ivah and I call him Alexi." Her face gathers a sudden shadow of sadness. She looks down at the table. "And Jovah. Jovah called him Alexi. Jovah refused to call him Alex. And Alexi refused to called Jovah Joe. It was a big joke between them."

"Surprised Alex didn't go for the badge like his big brother."

Nadia shakes her head. Then she taps it.

"Alexi was always the smart one. Joe was fast and strong. Alexi had the brains. And the determination. Never say *'you can't'* to Alexi."

"You saying cops can't be smart and determined?" He says it as a joke. She's not laughing.

"They were close. Alexi still misses his big brother. He took it hard. We all did."

I can see him counting seconds in his head, just enough of them to be polite to the memory of Jovah Novak before he can keep digging. Danika has other plans.

"I'm tired of reading when I'm so hungry," she says, dropping the book on the table. Nadia smiles.

"It's coming soon."

"No, it isn't. It's never coming until after I'm dead of starving to death from being hungry."

Ray picks up the book and flips through the pages.

"Can you read all of this squiggly nonsense?" he asks.

"Yes, but I like reading the pictures best," she says.

"Is this your favorite book? Maybe you and your dragons read the pictures together."

"I told you my dragons are at home. And they don't know how to read."

The server shows up with two pizzas. Nadia returns the book to her purse as Mack makes room on the table.

"Mine is the cheesiest one," says Danika, bouncing in her chair.

Nadia gets to work pulling free a stringy triangle of cheese and dough. She places it on Danika's plate, talking to Ray sideways, without looking.

"So, Mack. About the doll. Tell me what I need to do."

FIFTY-SEVEN

I limit myself to two slices, which is three slices too many. The chef's mistake was in not selling an angioplasty for dessert. He could make a killing without anyone dying.

Nadia agrees to meet me in the morning at Ivah's nursing home so I can hand over the doll to its rightful owner. I offer to make the visit tonight, but she says Ivah has been lights out for hours. It seems her mother's head hits the pillow at four o'clock these days. That sounds good to me. I could use a blanket and a bottle. I can count the number of hours I've slept since yesterday on two fingers. People like to say cute things like *I'll sleep when I'm dead.* I feel like I'm getting close.

Then again, a good night's sleep is not as good as people think. Since trouble always seems to work the night shift that seems like a curious time to be unconscious. Maybe the real problem is not the sleeping part but getting out of bed before it's time. Had I just stayed under the covers last night I'd probably have a functional couch and fewer bandages in my life. Had Ivah not come down to surprise Wayne Bishop digging through her closet all those years ago, she'd have skipped being bagged and trussed up in her kitchen. Maybe if she'd have stayed in bed, the night would have played out differently. Maybe her boy Jovah would still be alive.

I want to ask Nadia more about Alexi, but Danika has other plans for the conversation that don't involve planet Earth. Nadia, too, seems disinclined to be interrogated over dinner. So I let the subject go, figuring maybe it's better that I back off for now and see what tomorrow brings. I concentrate on the pain throbbing in my face and the indigestion building in my gut.

When the time comes, I palm the server with my card, and he slips off before Nadia can object.

"That's not fair," she says. "You barely ate anything."

"I ate some pills at the hospital."

She cringes.

"That's terrible. You should at least take the rest home."

"I'm taking more than enough home already. It was my pleasure, Nadia."

"Then I'll pick up the next one," she says, squaring her shoulders and sitting up straight. She holds out her hand. "Deal?"

I take her hand in mine. It's smooth and soft and attached to the rest of her, something I expected but it still makes an impression on my blood pressure. We shake.

"Okay," I say.

"Good. Just us. I'll arrange a sitter. Maybe we can go someplace where you'll actually eat something."

"It's a date," I say, not meaning to say those words. Or to mean them.

When the bill comes, I do the math and sign where I'm supposed to, and we all stand. I help Nadia on with her coat.

"Thank you," she says. "Tomorrow then? *Golden View* lobby?"

"Eleven sharp. I'll bring a date. You'll like her. She smiles too much but I think she's a doll."

I say my goodbyes and tell them I need to visit the restroom, so we part company at the hostess stand. It's impossible to lie about something that's always true, but I come about as close as you can get. I do need to visit the restroom, urgently, but I also don't want to walk out the front door. Instead, I take care of business and then head out the back exit into the employees-only lot behind *Pizza Maria*.

The wind has picked up its razor blades again. The cold is savage and sharp and knows where to find the pain in my face like a finger to a bullet hole. I remember last summer when it was so relentlessly hot the soles of your shoes melted on the sidewalk, mixing with all the frying eggs. I silently take back all the complaining I did about the heat. I'd welcome it back with open arms and frozen flowers.

I want to die someplace warm. The Bahamas maybe. Baja. Someplace the air doesn't bite.

Dante has Satan frozen in ice up to his chest, beating his wings to create a wind that keeps everything in his circle frozen. I'm guessing he winters in Chicago.

I hunker down into my coat and walk up the block a ways before crossing the street and doubling back on the other side. Once I'm well past the restaurant, I cross the street again and head back, approaching the front lot from behind. Turns out the Impala is right where I left it. So is the Buick, three rows back and smoking a tailpipe, blowing gray exhaust out into the breeze.

I move slowly, using a couple different parked cars to block the line of sight just in case this goon is awake and using his mirrors. I make a note of the license plate for future reference and ease Sig out of his holster. I close the last twenty feet quickly, pressing the barrel against the window with a sharp tap. The man behind the wheel recoils sideways. I try the door, but it's locked. I give him a second or two to collect his wits and assess what's new in his life. Then Sig gives the window another tap. The man jolts at the sound and throws his hands up in the air. He's ready to surrender everything right here and now.

Well. Everything except maybe his rights under the First Amendment to make a hash of the news.

"Unlock the goddamned door, Teddy. It's cold out here."

FIFTY-EIGHT

His hand spasms at the button and everything clicks. I climb into the back seat and close the door.

"Turn off the car and hand me the keys," I say. I don't have to ask him twice. Theodore Myerson, ace reporter for *The Hawk*, does as he's told. His aspiring baldness is nestled inside a wool hunter's cap. He doesn't look any less like a thumb, but he looks warm. "Any weapons in the car, Teddy?"

"No."

"You wouldn't lie to me, would you?"

"No, sir."

"Both hands on the wheel, ten and two, where I can see them."

He does what I ask. I remember those long, white fingers, dancing on his keyboard. They're just as long and white gripping the wheel, but not as graceful. I find his face in the rearview mirror. He's still rattled but getting better every second that I don't put a hole in his back.

"Maybe you want to tell me why you've been following me across the Land of Lincoln in a Buick."

"No, sir."

"No, sir, what?"

"No, sir, I don't want to tell you."

"And why is that? Does it rhyme with First Amendment?"

"Yes, sir."

"You think you've got a constitutional right to be my shadow?"

"No, sir."

"Cut the yes sir, no sir crap, Ted. That's not helping you any here. So, you're chasing me because you're chasing a story. And I'm a character in that story.

We've established that much. And it doesn't take a genius to conclude that it has something to do with the Wrigley Menard trial since, as far as I know, that's the only thing you and I have in common. How am I doing so far? Don't answer if I'm right on the money."

Theodore's eyes leave the mirror, but his mouth stays quiet.

"Right," I say. "So then the question is what makes you think Jake Menard killing Curtis Root has anything to do with me. Is that a question the founding fathers will let you answer?"

"No, sir. I mean, no."

"I'm shocked. Then let's not talk about the story you're writing, Ted. Let's talk about how long you've been following a police officer."

I can see he has to think about that for a second. The apple in his throat moves like a nervous yo-yo.

"Just today," says Myerson.

"Starting when?"

"This morning."

"Starting at the Chandler police station?"

"Yes, sir. I mean, yes."

"And you've been on me all day."

"Yes."

"So then you were a witness to an attempted homicide outside *Pleasant Palace*."

It takes him so long to answer this one I have to lean over the front seat so I can look at him face-to-face. He nods. I push myself even closer.

"You the person taking shots at me, Theo? Did you try to kill me this morning?"

His eyes get all excited. He tries to turn and face me. He has to pull back against the window to keep our noses from knocking.

"No, no, no. Not me. I…"

"Hands on the wheel."

"I didn't have… I mean… I have no idea…"

I lean back a little, giving him some space.

"From where I'm sitting, Ted, you might need to lawyer up. We're going to have to take a hard look at this. I can't rule you out from the back seat of your car."

"Rule me out? For what?"

"Depends. Attempted murder. Conspiracy to commit murder. Aiding and abetting."

"No, no… seriously. I was just… I was just following…"

"Yeah. I know. Following me for reasons you won't share as someone, maybe you, maybe some goon riding shotgun in this very car, tries to paint the inside of my windshield. And you want me to just shrug that off? I'm supposed to be okay with all of that and just let you go on your way? You really think that's how this is all going to play out?"

"That's not…"

"You really think you're sleeping in your own bed tonight, Teddy?"

"That's not what happened. I swear."

"Oh, you swear. Well. As long as you swear. Fuck you, Ted. Let's go find you a cell to swear in."

I fumble at the door handle.

"No, no. Please."

I put the fumbling on pause and get back in his face.

"Then start talking. Who sent you?"

"Nobody."

"Okay." I open up the back door. "Let's go."

"No, no, no. Nobody sent me. It was my idea. I'm a reporter, man. I'm just chasing the story."

I close the door again. "What story?"

"I got word this morning that the trial was postponed. I called… my source."

He's waiting for me to insist on a name so that he and Alexander Hamilton can refuse to tell me. I keep quiet and wait.

"My source said that no one could find Arty Dunn. He was supposed to continue his testimony but he's, like, gone."

"I'm listening."

"My source does not seem to have any idea where Arty is but claims you threatened Arty at a meeting."

"Threatened how?"

"I don't know. Only that you rattled him somehow and now he's gone. My source told me some… stories… that might be relevant."

"About Arty?"

His Adam's apple is bobbing again.

"About you."

"Ah." I laugh a little like this part is amusing. It isn't. "Stories about how I was kicked off the force for leaking tactical intel to the mob?"

Myerson swallows and nods.

"Something like that. Yeah."

"You believe those stories, Ted?"

"I don't know," he says, speaking to his bony white knuckles. "Should I?"

He's feeling less like a potential gunshot victim and more like a reporter. He's turning this into his interview, working me for information. That suggests the newspaperman motive he's selling is probably legit. That doesn't make me want to hit him any less.

"I guess you'd better hope those stories are false. Right, Ted? You're a lot better off in this situation if I've always been a good cop."

He doesn't know what to say. The Adam's apple does a couple of push-ups.

"Believe what you want, Ted. Doesn't make any difference to me. What I want to know is how any of it connects to Arty Dunn."

"According to my source…" He breaks off and sighs, looking out the window. "The speculation seems to be that organized crime is trying to keep Arty from testifying. And … and …"

"Spit it out, Ted."

He looks at me.

"And that you've been sitting in the courtroom to deliver that message."

"Keep him from testifying about what?"

"I was hoping you could tell me."

He pivots another couple of degrees my direction. His face has pulled on an old school chum sincerity. Just a couple of guys talking in the dark. He's no good to me that way so I get back into his face and rattle the cage a little.

"This is not your interview, Ted. Why did you try to kill me? Who are you working for?"

"I … I … No…"

"Newspapering not paying the bills? Or maybe that's always been the cover for you. What's your editor's name over there at *The Hawk*. Time to get him involved. What's his name?"

"He's not… there's no reason…"

"What's his fucking name?"

Something about me shouting makes him want to face straight again.

"Frank. Franklin Corey."

"Did Franklin Corey sign off on your day today, Ted? Is he a part of this game?"

"No. Just me. My source thinks… you've got something to hide."

"So, you thought you'd follow me around. Maybe I've got Arty Dunn tied to the top of my car like a deer. Maybe I pull him out of my trunk. Is that it? Maybe you catch me in a séance with the ghost of John Gotti."

Myerson starts to whine. Not a nice sound coming from a grown man.

"I didn't know, man. Maybe it was all bullshit. Trial was cancelled, I had a free day. I thought I'd just… see if I'd learn anything new."

"So you learned that I like porn for breakfast, seafood for lunch and pizza for dinner. You feel edified, Ted? You learn a little something about me?"

"I learned someone wants to kill you."

"Right. What else?"

"You spent a long time at *Windy Wharf Seafoods*, talking to some guy unloading fish."

"What else?"

"Nothing. You've either got a daughter or you're seriously punching above your weight."

Time for me to lean forward again.

"Took a peak inside, did you? Want to talk about *your* personal life?"

"No."

"Want to talk more about punching?"

"No."

"That's no sir to you, Ted."

"No, sir."

"You tend to say stupid things when you're nervous?"

"Yes, sir."

"I'd work on that if you really want to keep your genes in the pool. Let's go back to the part about me almost getting killed. What did you see?"

"I was parked half a block past the porn shop, using my mirror. You were in there a long time. I wasn't looking when I heard the shots. I didn't realize they were for you. I thought they were coming from the other side of the street." He points next to him. "I, like, dropped down here in the front seat, waiting for more. But there were only three shots. I didn't see the shooter. It was only when I saw you in the parking lot that I realized the shots were probably for you."

"What about vehicles leaving the scene?"

"No screeching tires or anything like that. I figured the shooter must have been on foot. There was a truck that drove past me and turned, but he was moving slow."

"Truck. What kind of truck?"

"I… don't know. A pickup. Small. White."

"Plates?"

"Come on."

"What, too much detail for *The Hawk*?"

"No, I…"

"Who was driving the truck?"

"I don't know. I didn't think it was anything to pay attention to."

"What kind of reporter are you, Ted? Who drives slowly after gunfire? Was it a man or woman?"

Myerson shakes his head.

"I don't know."

"And so, realizing that you had just witnessed the attempted murder of a police officer, that's when you came running over to report what you'd seen."

"I didn't see anything."

"Yeah, you keep saying that and I keep not believing you."

"I didn't… I didn't want…"

"Stop sputtering, Ted. You saw me almost die and thought you were onto something. A mobster cop with mobster enemies. You were busy writing headlines under your dashboard. You didn't want to give up our little game of follow the leader. You thought I'd lead you to Arty."

"I was chasing the story. It's what I do."

"No, what you do is annoy me. Here's a headline: Theodore Myerson caught following Raymond Mackey a second time. You think about how that story ends. See you in court, Teddy."

I open the door and climb out into the wind. I close it again and nose Sig back into his holster. I can hear Ted through the glass. Something about his keys.

I walk across the lot and back into *Pizza Maria* where I hand Ted's keys over the hostess and tell her I found them in the parking lot. Back outside, I hold up both empty hands in the direction of the Buick.

The Impala is a block of ice. I turn the engine over and knock out a Camel. I cup a flame to the tip and pull in some heat, closing my eyes to the nicotine reunion in my head.

I check my mirrors. Ted's waiting for me to leave so he can go get his keys. I don't disappoint him.

FIFTY-NINE

He drives for home. He wants his old life back. The one with a hot fireplace in the wall and a cold drink in his hand and an old cat in his lap. The life that features a blank sheet of paper curling out of an antique Corona Corsair upstairs on a large, battle-scarred desk beneath a window that looks out over the quiet suburban smile of Maltese Road and the neighborhood beyond.

Not that he's using the Corsair these days. Detective McMannis, suspended in the act of wiping the fingerprints from a dead man's Pontiac, is trapped in the laptop now, along with the rest of *Message in a Bullet*. Ray wants to get back to that. He wants to deliver McMannis and the start the next book. He likes the idea of sitting by the fire, nursing a drink, as the Corsair waits patiently upstairs for his return. He misses that long-ago life. Yesterday, technically, but only when you count the hours. To him it feels like a decade ago.

He slows as he approaches the house, but he doesn't stop. He keeps driving, satisfied at the absence of smoldering ash and firetrucks. No sign, either, of any violence to the mailbox in which a certain doll is to be waiting.

He keeps rolling to the stop sign and then around the corner, out of sight for anyone on Maltese who might be paying attention. He pulls to the curb, sitting and smoking and thinking. He wants to sleep in his own bed. He wants the comforts of home. He's not even asking for all the comforts. Phil is safe next door with Judith. He'd keep the house dark and hold off on lighting a fire. Just a drink or two in the dark, listening to Sarah Vaughan stir the pot at Chicago's own *Mister Kelly's*, circa 1957, or maybe a little Abbey Lincoln singing about how happiness is *a thing called Joe* so he could whisper-sing along and swap in the word *Forester* at just the right time. He wants to listen to the ice cubes clink in their bath until he falls asleep.

But that's another life.

He pulls the rearview so he can see his face. He's not looking at the bandage or the red mark around his throat. He's looking into his own eyes. He sees the same fear I do. Raymond Mackey is afraid. And that's what scares him. Because he's not used to being afraid. Thick in the head, stubborn, forgetful, lazy, drunk. Sure. All those things. But rarely afraid. Something about being unable to breathe in the darkness of a burlap sack pulled over his head, waiting for the sensation of a dull chainsaw taking off his legs has got him spooked. Knowing that they, whoever they were, were just trying to scare him, that they never intended to cut off his legs, doesn't help. He was a believer at the time. That's the feeling he can't shake. The sensory recall is too intense. It comes with the taste of blood and the smell of urine.

They may not come to the house tonight. Probably won't. But sleep won't either.

Another gust rocks the car.

He angles slowly away from the curb. He's going to drive for a while, pulling the wheel this way and that like he doesn't know where he's going. But we both know otherwise. He'll drive a few miles south, past the old depot made into a railroad museum with a vintage restored locomotive engine out front, gleaming slick black beneath a sheen of moonlight; past the Chandler Library with its front steps made to look like famous book spines; and then up the hill where Freytag Way bends along the perimeter of cemetery fencing and the sprawl of Will County glitters in the dark like a phosphorescent tide. He'll follow the road until it T-bones with East Haybale Road and he is forced to choose between some dairy farms and a fertilizer plant to the east or, to the west, the hive of humanity so densely packed with villainy and virtue you can't tell one from the other until the dance is over and you're feeling around for your wallet and a pulse. But that's no more of a choice for Ray than the color of his own eyes.

He takes a long drag and blows out a memory of Marlo, pouring herself a drink and finishing up an argument over Ray's bullheadedness.

"A man gets to decide who he is anytime he wants, Ray. As long as he decides correctly. Try to decide you're someone you're not, try that just once, and the world will laugh in your face until you figure out the truth."

"You're saying I can't change. Is that it?"

"Sure you can, honey. But only if that's the kind of man you are. Guess we'll see."

No mysteries here. Ray is Ray. When he gets to the T-bone at Freytag Way and East Haybale, he's going to pull that wheel to the west, rolling back down the hill and across the concrete flatlands where the air flashes red and blue and the buildings like to get together to make alleys where they can show off their dumpsters and their dead. He'll play minotaur in the maze for a while, but eventually he'll zero in, circling the general vicinity of Seventy-Fourth and Warner until he hits the bullseye.

He'll sit in the car for a bit, flipping through the *Kings Flush Casino* files, still in the seat next to him. Something to do as he finishes up the cigarette. Once the Camel gives up its last glow, Ray will decide he may as well finish reading someplace where he doesn't have to burn gas to stay warm. So he'll haul himself out into the cold and head for the place he was aiming for all along.

Quiet place. Money all over the ceiling.

He turns on the radio. Billie Holiday is just working her way into "Ill Wind." She seems to think it's blowing in a bunch of nothing good.

SIXTY

The heap of rags with a face is in the doorway again. I can only see his tired, bloodshot eyes. If it is possible to have a bloodshot voice, he's got one of those too.

"Hey, brother," he says. "I remember you."

"I'll bet you do," I say.

"Spare a hundred?"

"Your prices have gone up."

"Your charity raised my expectations."

"Prepare for an adjustment." I fish out a ten. A dirty hand emerges to take it but I don't let go just yet. "You need to take it up the street. No offense, but you're not so great for business. Go sit someplace warm. Get a tattoo or something."

"Got enough of those already."

"Oh yeah?"

I let go of the bill and Alexander Hamilton disappears into the pile.

"Had to prove myself," he says.

"I don't figure you for a gang banger so I'm guessing that means either military or prison."

"Bit of both," he says.

"And did you? Prove yourself?"

"Yeah." The rags push away and step out on to the sidewalk. "To everyone but me. Thanks, brother."

Bucks is only a quarter full. Kyle is at the bar telling a story that involves a fish, a football and six rabbis. The two couples in front of him are laughing, eating it up with fists full of peanuts and pretzels. He catches me in his peripheral vision and grabs a glass from under the bar without breaking his stride. He pours in twice as much Old Forester as he should, which is roughly half of what I need. He puts the glass on a napkin, gives me a wave and a wink and keeps going, doing his best to impersonate a rabbi going long for a flying fish.

I don't break my stride either. I nod to Kyle, grab the glass and follow Billie Holiday to the back of the room where there's a booth that's just my size and too shy for much light. I drop the KFC files on the table, shed the coat and wedge myself into the corner. It feels good to sit again. I haven't sat down since the car. I close my eyes and sip.

There might be words to describe how that feels but I don't know what they are.

I open the KFC arson file, picking up where I'd left off when the Camel had called it quits. I'm two-thirds of the way through the summary report, written by a Chicago Fire Department arson investigator named Michael Perry. Nearly half of the east wing of the *Kings Flush Casino* went up in smoke that night. Most of the gambling space was spared but the administrative offices were destroyed.

The fire crew found one person dead, a Nathanial Marciewicz, according to the dental records in the coroner's report, a detail that Investigator Perry tucks away into a footnote along with other information not specifically relevant to the origins of the fire. Mr. Marciewicz had worked as KFC's Executive Operations Manager for six years. He was fifty-eight when he caught fire. Turns out it wasn't the fire that killed him; not unless the fire beat him to death with a pipe before it started scorching the walls and carpets.

According to Investigator Perry, the fire started simultaneously in three places: a bottom drawer of Mr. Marciewicz's desk, across the hall in the paper-rich environs of the KFC Human Resources Department, and down the hall in the paper-poor confines of a computer server room.

Another sip, another page. Investigator Perry devotes a second footnote to evidence developed in the concurrent homicide investigation: access to the administrative offices at three o'clock on a Sunday morning had been through a rear utility door normally reserved for large, rolling machines like the kind that can make photocopies or that can turn three cherries into a pile of silver. The fire inspector's footnote does not explain how, exactly, Chicago Homicide determined that Nathanial Marciewicz's killers got in through that service entrance. Nor does it shed any light on what Marciewicz was doing in his office at that hour.

What I remember about the case is sketchy at best. Two guys did the deed. Former employees swinging a shank of iron. According to the press, these boys really put the grunt in disgruntled. *The Tribune* made them as cavemen clerks with a score to settle with the boss. That's where my memory throws in the towel, except for the very end of the story. The ex-employees each caught one of the last lethal cocktails before the State of Illinois retired the death penalty. The last call of last calls. Back in the day, appeals and all, it took on average fifteen years to ride the train from conviction to convulsion. These boys hopped an express and got there in ten.

Investigator Perry can't help but drop another footnote before he signs his name. This one lands heavier than the rest.

"The undersigned notes for the record that while the conclusions in this report regarding the character, origins and propagation of the fire have been confirmed and independently verified by available evidence, those conclusions have been reached notwithstanding a regrettable lack of coordination with the concurrent investigative efforts of the Chicago Police Department Violent Crimes Unit. The undersigned expressly disclaims any and all responsibility for conclusions reached by the CPD VCU which, while nominally incorporating many of the findings of this investigation, have not been confirmed by this office. This note is not meant to imply any dereliction of duty by the CPD VCU Investigative Liaison Officer Hill."

Wouldn't be the first investigative turf war between the fire freaks and the homicide humps. But to warrant a footnote in an official report means it got ugly.

I look up to see that Doris is behind the bar holding an open ledger. Kyle is bent over her shoulder. He points, she points. Something is not adding up. Probably my tab. The widow-widower telepathy kicks in and Doris glances up my direction. I lift my glass. She waves and gets back to business. In the air above me, Betty Carter and Ray Charles go on about how cold it is outside. Like I don't know. I take a drink and trade arson for murder.

The VCU murder investigation report lays out a plot by two KFC employees, Donald Bratton and Derrek Pine, to kill their former boss, Executive Operations Manager Marciewicz, after having been terminated for insubordination just over a month earlier. The report cites the coroner for a cause of death of blunt force trauma to the skull. The murder weapon was four-foot section of pipe found in a dumpster two blocks away. Forensics had lifted partial prints of each employee from the pipe and found bits of Mr. Marciewicz in the threads.

So Bratton and Pine had taken turns. They'd swung until they each felt better. They'd swung until Mr. Marciewicz had climbed up out of his body and into the big dream where he'd have a better view of what was going to happen next. That's when they had set the place ablaze with three high-intensity, likely military-grade, incendiary devices, one in the boss' desk, one buried in HR, and the third in the server room. Bratton and Pine had saved the pipe from the heat and ditched it safely in a dumpster just to make sure everyone was clear that the police should be looking for rank idiots. I'm guessing it took less than a week to get the mug shots.

According to the report, Bratton and Pine had gained access to the building through a rear utility door secured by an electronic lock. The question was how. Good thing the casino had closed-circuit security cameras on every exterior door to show who was opening what for whom. Unfortunately, the computer server on which such information is preserved was destroyed in the fire. I don't need a bookie to tell me the odds that that's just an unfortunate coincidence.

If memory serves, the press coverage of the trial told a story of simple revenge: a couple of angry, out-of-work morons who missed their paychecks so much they killed the guy who used to sign them. Bratton and Pine then burned the place down thinking that would cover up the murder. Turned out to be two short trials. The forensics and the testimony by someone connected with the supply of the incendiary devices sealed the deal for the prosecution. Juries were out maybe thirty seconds each.

But the actual VCU investigation report has kind of a different smell to it. Revenge, sure, but a different kind of revenge, one that might not have much to do with two lug-heads missing out on a Christmas bonus. The VCU investigator spends a whole page scratching his head about Marciewicz. He wonders if maybe Marciewicz had arranged to meet Bratton and Pine and had let them in through the rear service door. The VCU investigator tells the story in a way to suggest that maybe the victim was dirty. Casinos at three o'clock Sunday morning is where water finds its own level. That's the smell of this thing. Sewage.

I empty the glass. I have an urge to close my eyes just to think things through;

just to see if I can connect any dots between the KFC arson-homicide and a broken poker chip in an envelope full of cash. It's the same broken poker chip, literally from Hell, that ended up pulling the rug out from under Arty Dunn's blood pressure. For the life of me, I can't find a connection, which means the odds are spectacular there isn't one. Odds are the poker chip means something special between Hell and Arty that has nothing to do with *Kings Flush Casino*. The chip was a message, and Hell made me the messenger. Someone is trying to control Arty Dunn. Or maybe *was* trying, past tense. Maybe Arty has recently been controlled down into a trunk for a ride out of town. Maybe he's been controlled down into a shallow grave. Could be. Which means maybe it all really does have to do with Arty testifying in Wrigley Menard's murder trial. Or maybe Arty was mixed up in something completely different that doesn't have anything to do with Wrigley Menard and Curtis Root. Maybe.

I'm drowning in an ocean of maybes. I had hoped the casino fire might provide me something to work from; a bit of solid ground to stand on. But now I'm getting the queasy feeling that the sordid history of the *Kings Flush Casino* is just another swell in the fetid sea of Chicago crime.

But I don't want to give up. Not yet. I want to keep thinking. So I do. It's the kind of thinking that requires some quiet, closed-lid concentration.

SIXTY-ONE

This makes twice in three days. First in Judge Jolie's courtroom and now in *Bucks*. Who needs a bed when you can get your forty winks sitting up?

Not a good look on Ray, sleeping in public. Makes him seem old. They say you're only as old as you feel. If that's true, then he should be dropping dead any time now.

But he doesn't drop dead.

He straightens his head against the back of the booth and flutters his eyes open.

Doris is sitting across from him. Her hair is pulled back with something he can't see, but wisps reemerge over her shoulders. Behind her face, inside looking out, is the younger version of herself; the knock-out blonde with the soft blue eyes married to big, black Buck. He is remembering her as she was then, sitting across from him in this very booth, looking at him like she is now as Marlo and Buck laughed about something silly. He's watching the years melt away, taking with them the sun damage and the extra flesh beneath her jaw, polishing up her teeth and sheening her hair. And inside that younger face is yet another, younger still. The stringy, hipless, toe-headed schoolgirl from Springfield running barefoot in the park after her older brother, long before Ray ever knew her. But still, there she is. And inside that face, yet another. And another. It goes on forever. She's like a bottomless Russian doll connected, one to the next, by the same pair of soft blue eyes.

Ray yawns and glances down at the table. The empty tumbler has made friends with a mug of coffee.

"You look like hell," she says.

"No." He rubs his eyes. "Trust me, I've met Hell. If I looked like Hell no one would ever touch me again. At least not in a way that requires stitches."

"What?"

"If I looked like Hell, maybe I'd know where to find him. For as big as he is, he can play hide and seek like nobody's business."

"Ray, you're not making sense."

He takes a sip of coffee and winces.

"Probably the concussion."

"A concussion?" She reaches, lifting his chin with a finger. "Ray, who did this to you?"

"Couple of lumberjacks I found in my living room. They thought I was a tree."

"Are you all right? I mean…"

"I'm fine, Doris. Stop worrying." He shoos away her hand. "How was your date?"

"What?"

"You know. Your date. Tallish guy with furry ears. Can't miss him unless you're at the zoo."

Doris leans back against the booth and laughs to herself, shaking her head.

"Okay, I guess," she says. "Still early."

"Did you let him get to first?"

"You want me to give you a matching bandage for the other side of your face?"

"Sorry. What are the chances of getting some bourbon in this coffee?"

"None."

"He doesn't deserve you, Doris."

"Yeah? Who does, Mack? You?"

"No. Not even close. But I'm used to not deserving the women in my life. That's natural for me. That's the way I like things. Let's get married so I can get to work not deserving you properly."

"Say it like you mean it, Ray," she says. She means to get his attention and I can tell from the silence that it works. But then Ray drowns the empty beat between them in his coffee. He winces again.

"Don't play truth or dare with the concussed, Doris. We can't tell one from the other."

"If you have a concussion maybe you shouldn't be at a bar drinking and sleeping."

"It was drinking and sleeping that got me the concussion in the first place. They go together like bourbon and coffee."

He looks at her hopefully.

"Still no," she says.

"You're a tough one, Doris, you know that? Maybe Buck had all the muscle, but you had all the iron."

"You know, Mack, maybe if you started dating your life would turn around. Maybe you wouldn't almost die in some Chicago railyard or show up here looking like an old punching bag."

There's a comeback for that. Ten of them; five about dating and another five about punching bags. But I can tell all the dating talk has now got him thinking about Nadia King. Taking off her coat. Pulling out her chair. The laugh in her eyes and the way she smells. Sure, he knows less and less about her with every passing day. But the less he knows the more he likes. Now she's living rent free inside his head. Even the indigestion from the pizza only makes him think of her. Inappropriate, sure. Probably impossible too. But at his age, inappropriate and impossible describe roughly ninety percent of his existence.

"Dating takes courage I don't have, Doris."

"Let me make sure I understand. You're not afraid to die but you're afraid to date."

"I'm afraid of dying on the date. That's not going to do anybody any good."

Doris leans in so she can look him in the eyes.

"Marlo would want you to be happy, Ray. She'd want you to get out there. I'm out there. I'm trying."

"Yeah. Well. If I looked like you, I'd be out there too. Hell, Doris, if I looked like you, I'd date myself and stay in. Maybe Marlo would like a lot of things. Maybe she wants me to stop with the sauce and retire the Camels and take up ballroom dancing. But Marlo's not here. If she really wanted all those things, then maybe she shouldn't have left in the first place."

Ray wrenches his eyes away, pretending to want another drink of coffee. Doris can only watch.

"Ballroom dancing," she says at last.

"Yeah. Well."

Doris lets it go. She pokes at the papers in front of him.

"So, are we pretending that this booth is your bedroom or your office?"

"Sleepworking," he says. He puts down the coffee and picks up the VCU report, flipping through the pages. "I'm at my best when I'm unconscious. Let me ask you something."

"Okay."

"What's so scary about a poker chip?"

"A poker chip? Like a gambling thing?"

"Yeah. You know, a poker chip. I show it to you and all the blood in your face heads south. You almost pass out you're so scared."

"Maybe it reminds me of something. Something horrible."

"Okay. Like what?"

"I don't know. It reminds me of the worst hand of poker I ever played. I got drunk and bet the farm and lost it all. My husband is so upset he clutches his heart and dies on the spot. People in suits show up and take everything. The house. The car. Clothes. Jewelry. Everything. I spend years living in misery, sleeping on the street wrapped in rags and begging for money. Drug addiction. Sexual depravity. The works. I almost die twice every single day. Then I get a lucky break. I start clawing my way back. I sober up. I get some money. I get some friends. I get a place to live. I meet a nice man. I start to feel happy. I'm ready to kick the past to the curb. The guy proposes and I say yes. I come over and buy you a drink and tell you the good news. And then you put a poker chip on the table."

"Jesus," says Ray. He pats her hand. "Doris, I've got a novel that needs finishing. You want to take a crack at that?"

"Well, you asked. Can I take it that all this paperwork here involves a poker chip?"

"Something like that."

"And did I solve the mystery?"

"No. But don't feel bad, honey. This is a mystery that doesn't want to be solved. Not by me anyway."

"Then you need some help. Time to stop trying to do everything yourself for a change. You've got a whole department behind you, Ray. Maybe you should use it."

"The whole department would like to see my whole body on a spike, Doris."

"That's old news. You've got a lieutenant… Twizzle…"

"Twill."

"Twill. He believes in you, or he wouldn't have hired you back. Get him involved."

"I would but he's out shopping for a good spike."

"I see. So, you're out there on your own. Again." Doris stretches across the table and cups her hands beneath his jaw. "People beating on you and not a friend in the world."

She kisses him on the forehead, then wipes off the lipstick with her thumb.

"I've got a friend," he says.

"Yeah?"

"Yeah. She's a blue-eyed peach with a heart of gold and a thing for helping the hopeless. One problem with her though."

Doris scoots out of the booth and stands, hands on her hips, ready for anything.

"What's that, Mack?"

"She can't make a good cup of coffee to save her life."

Ray watches Doris make her way back toward the bar. Kyle looks up in time to see her point to the back room. Kyle nods and resumes ragging down a glass as Doris disappears through the opening in the wall. Ray takes a drink of coffee then pushes the cup across the table. Above him, Shirley Horn is in the heart of "Once I Loved." He picks up the VCU report again and flips through the pages he has already read. Then he gets to the one he hasn't.

He stops. Folds it over. The creases between his eyebrows deepen and he brings the whole thing closer to his face. He makes a small sound. A gasp pretending to be a laugh. He sets the report on the table and leans his head back against the booth. The dollar bills on the ceiling are laughing in the forced-air heat.

"All of that money," he says to himself. "Little green suits, drying out on the line." Then he smiles.

SIXTY-TWO

Twenty minutes, listening to the buzzing in my head. The buzz is complicated. It's two buzzes together; a bumblebee playing the kazoo. One buzz comes from the Old Forester. The other comes from the first solid lead I've had since before my couch turned into a leftist. The puzzle in my jumble of a head just got a corner piece.

Everybody at the table agrees I need sleep and lots of it, but nobody thinks that's going to happen without another drink or three. I gather up the reports, put on my coat and head for the front door. Doris intercepts me. I pass her sobriety test with flying colors and give her a kiss.

"See," she says, "coffee did your mood some good."

"Doris, if I ever disparage your coffee again, you have my permission to cut me off and only serve me booze. Sure, go ahead and laugh, but I'm serious. Kyle's my witness."

I give Kyle a wink and shoulder my way through the door, out into the sobering cold which has been sharpening its blade under a moon of frozen ingot. The Impala takes the key but not happily, like someone has glued the locks. The engine turns over like a body in the snow. I have to give it some gas and profanity to bring it back to life, but it's roaring soon enough. I blast the heat, wake up one of the Camels and then put the car in gear. Rocky Esposito is just pulling the bars down over *The Bodega* across the street, steam leaving his face like he's a tea kettle in a porkpie hat. I give him a honk and a wave and then put on some speed.

I make a beeline for 125th Street and Chelsey, the closest place I can get both a stiff drink and good night's sleep without a chainsaw wake-up call. *The Bakersfield* is a luxury hotel exclusively for optimists without much to spend. I know I only fit half of that bill, but I show my mug at the front desk anyway.

The clerk keeps his opinions about my face to himself and hands over a key card.

I head to the bar for a nightcap and a reread of the VCU investigation report. Some people live to work, others work to live. Then there are the people who work to die at the office. Nathaniel Marciewicz is one of those. He clawed his way up the corporate food chain to become Executive Operations Manager of the *Kings Flush Casino* only to become a piñata. I'm guessing his business card was too small to fit the part about also being a presidential drycleaner. If there is one truism carved in Chicago cement, it's that once you agree to launder money for the mob, there is no such thing as changing your mind.

It's still just a guess, sure. But most good police work is just guesswork with a badge and extra-low expectations of other humans. It's the little buzz in the back of the brain that tells you that you're on to something. The buzz tells you to keep going in some direction or another until you get close enough that your sense of smell can pick up the rot and take over.

The buzz in my head tells me two things. It tells me I shouldn't have skipped dinner. My head has found a one-drink-gets-you-two, do-it-yourself happy hour. Easy enough. But it also tells me that Nathaniel Marciewicz made fifty-eight trips around the sun only to be beaten and burned for saying no. He wanted out in a world with no exits. Bratton and Pine were not insubordinate. Marciewicz was the one who was insubordinate. Bratton and Pine were not working for Marciewicz. Marciewicz was working for Bratton and Pine.

And they were all working for Big Man. Maybe everyone is.

I finish the drink and take my buzzing up to bed. I keep the lights off, dropping my coat in a chair and squeezing out of my shoes. The mattress catches me like a pop fly hit from another planet. The clock on the nightstand wants me to believe it is exactly midnight, lying to me over and over.

But for the bourbon, I'd be afraid to sleep. Sleep is the only way last night can happen all over again. Those boys have the address to dreamland. They'll show up with their duct tape and their sacks and their chainsaws and this time they'll really do some damage. What's not to avoid? I'd find a way to stay awake. Drive the streets. Go to the all-night grocery on East Markum and 128th Street and wander the aisles reading the labels of all the things I used to be able to eat. But having friends like Old Forester means never having to be afraid of sleep. I give myself over to gravity.

Marlo doesn't like it when I fall asleep on the couch and then decide to make a night of it. She's afraid it will do something permanent to my posture. She doesn't want to be married to a hunchback. She calls for me to come upstairs to bed. I try to get up, but I'm so thoroughly covered in burlap bags I can't stand. They're damp and smell like mold and stale cigarettes. I manage to get them off me and stand and stuff them into the fireplace. I call up to Marlo that I'm coming, and she calls back down for me to answer the door. So I do. Marlo is at the door, winter raging in flapping cold, white sheets behind her. She steps in and thanks me and turns so I can take the coat off her shoulders. Her hair is longer and darker than I remember. She smells like forest. I hang the coat in the closet. When I return, she is standing at a square table in the living room. I pull out her chair and she lowers herself, sitting as if on a cushion of air, never touching the wood. Marlo calls me again from upstairs and I call back that I'm on my way. Nadia King looks up at me and smiles. "Let's order the mistake," she says. Only she doesn't say it. She thinks it. I try to think back my answer, pushing it at her through my eyes. But it won't come. It's like trying to push an elephant through a keyhole. Marlo calls down for me to come up. My answer wants out. Nadia reaches for my face. She wants to help. She wants to let the answer out from behind the bandage underneath my eye. Then the answer finally comes free. It sounds like an old-timey telephone.

I open my eyes. The clock on the nightstand is sticking to its story, but the phone in my coat on the floor keeps calling out the lie, over and over again, until finally it stops. But not for long. It's an ugly, adult-language game of hide and seek before I can stop the sound and put the thing to my ear. Whatever time it is, Lieutenant Orland Twill sounds about as happy to be awake as I am.

It takes a long, cold shower to dry out my wits and wake myself up. The kid behind the counter in the lobby is surprised to see me again so soon. All five clocks on the wall behind him say it's too early for any questions. He asks one anyway.

"Was anything wrong with the room?"

"The room was perfect, kid. It's the city that's the problem. Coffee."

He points to an alcove in a corner of the lobby. I tip him with a used-once card key and head for the tower of paper to-go cups and the silver vat of caffeine. The coffee bar is fresh out of bourbon, so I take it black with two lumps and a

Percocet. I point myself at the revolving brass door that sits idly across a sea of beige tile, waiting to spin me back out into the cold. If there's ever an award for best architectural metaphor, I'm nominating the revolving door at the *Bakersfield Hotel.*

The very sight of *Pleasant Palace Books* makes me want to take another shower. The red and blue lights give the place a swollen, throbbing presence in the dark; a hammered thumb feeling, that my head seems to understand. Three black-and-whites, an ambulance, and two unmarked cars with dash lights and blinkers. Everything but the roller skates and a disco ball. I park along the side of the building. I kill the engine, drown the Camel in a puddle of coffee and climb out. The cold at my face is so bracing it hurts; like a hard slap by a hand loaded up with rings. But I strangely welcome that feeling now. The cold might just be the one thing holding me together. I can feel all the lights starting to come back on.

A uniform at the front door holds up a hand until I flash him a badge. He stands aside and lets me through. Inside it's warm and crowded with cold shoulders. I should have suspected a Ray-haters convention. I'm the last person any of these humps want to see. A couple of them are busy dusting Scooter's magazine merchandise for prints and taking their time about it. Another couple are clustered up front where I'm guessing all eyes are on what used to be Scooter Pleasants. The room flares white with camera flash followed by a burst of radio static, the crime scene version of a thunder and lightning storm.

I pick out Stretch Martin like the Eiffel Tower in Kansas. He sees me too and elbows Donovan Howe, standing next to him. Donny looks at me and then back up at Stretch. There's another camera flash from somewhere in front of them and Donny turns back around.

But not Stretch. He keeps looking. Then he points.

"Out, Mack. Homicide and CSI only. IAD waits outside. You're going to contaminate my scene. Like everything else you do."

The whole room is looking at me now. Except Scooter. From what I can tell, Scooter is looking at the floor. Not that he's seeing anything. He's face down inside the same shattered glass display case that I had knocked over about seventeen hours ago. His arms are unnaturally at his sides. Nothing broke his fall except jagged shards of sheet glass. Another flash turns all the red to a nauseating pink. I try to be accommodating.

"I'll come back with matching booties and gloves. Maybe a hat."

Stretch shakes his head.

"You'll wait outside, Mack. Better yet, go back to your hole."

SIXTY-THREE

Poor Ray. Smoking out in the cold, too stubborn to wait in the car like a child. It's reminding him of the indignities of working security at the mall. Waiting on the periphery as the real cops take care of business, dismissing him like his thirty years working dead bodies hadn't earned him some respect.

He'd told himself he was done with this feeling. Sure, he knew this part would be rough. He knew IAD was a universe away from Homicide, but he'd figured that when it came down to the actual work, IAD was still part of the family. He'd figured at some point everyone would have to stop hating each other long enough to say grace and carve the turkey and pass the stuffing. He's rethinking that one now.

They used to be like a family. Stretch. Donovan. Deke. Grizz. Bumper. The whole crew. Used to be that every one of them would put it all on the line for Ray. And he them. Ray might be back on the force, but he's still out of the family. He always will be.

Now they see him as just another of Big Man's many faces. A part of the ghost story. Already dead.

Smitty had also been in the CPD Homicide family. But he's dead now too. Not metaphorically dead. Actually dead. Two bullets through the chest dead. Ray hadn't pulled the trigger. Santiago had done that. Upside-down from the top of a train car in the middle of a downpour, Santiago had ended Smitty, and thank God. But that didn't matter. Just like it didn't matter that Smitty, and not Ray, had been Big Man's boy on the inside of the task force, leaking like a rusty elbow joint under the sink. Ray had a Big Man-shaped stain on his reputation. That kind of stain is worse than blood. It doesn't come out easily. Maybe not ever.

Smitty, meanwhile, had taken two to the chest at a time when his reputation among the crew was still solidly intact. Guilty as sin, no doubt about it. Ray had nearly died in a Chicago railyard proving that point. But death had come for Smitty before anyone on the CPD Homicide crew had had a chance to change their minds about him. Smitty hadn't been disgraced and driven off the force. He was just, suddenly, gone, dead in a shootout with IAD as Ray watched, leaving behind a collection of good family memories. *Remember that time Smitty showed up wearing… Remember when Smitty said… Remember that time we were playing poker and Smitty…*

The last memory anybody has of Ray is him turning in his badge and leaving the force in disgrace, lucky to avoid prison, for leaking task force intel to thugs like Cecil "Cosmo" Green. Never mind that Ray had never leaked anything to anyone. Never mind that Smitty had framed Ray to deflect attention from himself. Never mind that Smitty had, from the beginning, been playing every cop in the building for chumps. Smitty even had a street name. "The Russian." After his favorite drink.

But never mind all of that. Because it's Ray Mackey, who everyone remembers as the dirty cop.

He should go back to the *Bakersfield* and give the front door another spin; give the night clerk something to laugh about. No sense in losing sleep just to stand out in the cold.

But he won't. Not Ray. He'll freeze to death first. He'll almost die outside Scooter's porn shop for the second time in twenty-four hours before letting them have the satisfaction.

SIXTY-FOUR

The EMT's carry Scooter's body on a gurney out over the parking lot and stuff him into the back of the ambulance. Stretch watches him go from the doorway. He knows I'm still here, but he doesn't look. Then he does. He pulls off his gloves and powder-blue booties and hands them to the cop at the door. Then he heads my way.

"You look like shit, Mack," he says with a chuckle. "I heard you got worked over last night. Can't say I was too disappointed."

He's got the same long, narrow face to go with the body. A couple more legs and people would be petting his nose and feeding him oats.

"Good to see you too, Stretch."

"Did you at least get in a good punch or two?"

"His boots will never be the same."

"If you find these guys let us know. We'll all pitch in for a medal."

I take a long drag and let it out again.

"I'll keep that in mind," I say.

Stretch's face hardens. He doesn't like me not playing along. He waits a few seconds, but then he can't take it anymore. He's bigger than I am, so that means there's more for the cold to squeeze.

"Well Jesus Christ, Mack. You going to tell me why the fuck you're here?"

"You were having such a good time being an asshole I didn't want to interrupt and ruin all the fun."

"Fine. Let's get out of the cold where we can talk without freezing to death. Your car or mine?"

"I'm comfortable." I take another drag. "Feeling chilly?"

Stretch sighs and looks around, stuffing his hooves in his pockets. The ambulance beeps as it maneuvers backwards around the corner of the building. Stretch levels an impatient look like a loaded gun.

"I'm listening," he says.

"My LT picked up the news about Scooter. He told me to come down."

"What's Twill care about a dead scumbag like Daniel Pleasants?"

"He's an IAD complainant. Was."

Stretch laughs. Part surprise, part disgust.

"A complainant. You're still keeping top-notch company, aren't you, Mack? So then you know all about doorstop Daniel back there. IAD is taking complaints from child molesters. That's great."

"Alleged child molester."

Stretch makes a face.

"Right. Who's the complaint against?"

"Can't say. Confidential."

"Bullshit it's confidential."

"IAD has rules, Stretch. They're not mine to waive."

"Fuck IAD's rules. And since when did you care anything about rules?"

"Since always."

"No, you can't play the boy scout, Mack. Not anymore. This is a murder investigation. Pleasants makes a complaint to IAD and then ends up dead and you expect me to ignore that because IAD likes its secrets?"

"Not saying that, Stretch."

"Then let's have it."

"You're not listening. It's not my information to give. You'll have to go over my head. That shouldn't be hard with those legs. I can't talk about it."

The ambulance rolls past. The driver gives Stretch a wave to ignore.

"Then why are you here?"

"Look things over. See how Scooter bowed out. And to tell you that IAD wants to be dialed in."

Stretch stops blinking, like maybe the cold is close to winning the battle over his face.

"Fuck you," he says.

"Look, IAD has its own interest here. I'm sure Twill will open our file to you, but Homicide needs to do the same."

"Here's a counterproposal. You give Homicide everything we need and stay the fuck out of my way. How's that for a plan?"

"Above my paygrade," I tell him. I drop the stub and step on it. "You'll have to take that up with your LT. I'm guessing Wexler already has an email from Twill in his in-box."

Stretch takes his hands out of his pockets and moves a step closer. He bends over me like a limber smokestack, billowing steam. Stretch could do some damage if he ever decided that's the way things should go. I don't move a muscle that might suggest I harbor any such concerns. But I keep my weight on my left foot, just in case my right knee needs to find Stretch's nuts.

"Let's get this straight, Mack. I couldn't give a single fuck about your LT or my LT. Okay? I'm not giving you information about anything. You used to be a good cop. One of the best. No joke. We all thought Ray Mackey hung the fucking moon. But it turned out you have a thing for passing information on to shit-bird criminals. Then good cops end up dead."

He's not expecting a laugh. Neither am I.

"Come on, Stretch. You're too tall to be so short-sighted."

"Yeah, well. There it is anyway."

"There what is? You know Smitty was dirty. He even looked like a mole."

"Smitty being dirty doesn't mean shit about you."

"How is it you think I got hired back?"

"Don't sell me that garbage. I don't waste time trying to figure out how or why IAD does what it does, including who it hires. This is real simple, Mack. Don't expect any information from me. Not on this case or any other."

I know better than to keep trying. I show him my palms.

"I don't expect any information from you. Not right away. Not until I'm off suspension. But my LT will want to see it in the meantime."

"You're suspended?"

"Not yet. Give me a couple hours after sunrise."

"What'd you do this time?"

"Rejoined the force. I'll be back in business as soon as you rule me out."

"Rule you out?"

"Yeah. Suspect-wise."

"What are you saying to me, Mack?"

"I'm saying your boys in there are going to find my prints on some of that glass. I don't want that to come as a surprise. There's also a witness out there someplace. I'm guessing he's a regular. A fat guy who drives an orange Kia that's two sizes too small. He likes to look for company in the magazine aisle. Find him and he'll tell you Scooter and I exchanged some words this morning. Yesterday morning."

It all gets Stretch's attention. He wants me to spell everything out. I give him the whole alphabet except the letters that come between A and Z. He doesn't seem any happier.

"Again. Mack. What was the subject of your discussion with the victim?"

"Again. Stretch. I was here to follow up on information pertaining to the victim's complaint with IAD."

"His complaint against who?"

"I can't tell you that. You must really like this song."

"Why did it get rough?"

"It didn't get rough. It got testy. Scooter turned bratty and I grabbed him by the collar. The piece-of-shit display case fell over. Everyone played nice after that."

"Funny way to treat a complainant."

"That was the only way to treat Scooter. But your concern for the alleged molester is duly noted."

"Did he have a solid case against… fuck… against whoever?"

"Still working on that. Could go either way."

"So, you got the information you came for, knocked over the counter and then what?"

"I left. I was in and out in maybe twenty minutes."

Stretch looks past me at the Impala and its sagging plastic window.

"Your car is starting to look like you, Mack. What the hell happened?"

My stomach flips. Could be hunger. Or maybe I'm still a little soft from the booze. But I don't think so. The point of no return always announces itself to me as a certain queasiness in my gut, like the world is shifting a little on its axis, maybe just enough to tip that first domino. My choice is always either to let the domino fall or to shove it hard in another direction.

Never lie in a murder investigation. That's always a good rule of thumb, one I have passed along to more than a few who needed the advice. No reason the advice doesn't apply to me. On the other hand, the last thing I want is Stretch sticking his nose into the gunfire that put two slugs in my dashboard and a third in the trunk. He'll impound my car as a crime scene just for the fun of it. And he'd be right. Shots fired outside the *Pleasant Palace* maybe fifteen hours before it turns into a murder scene? I'd think that smelled rotten too. My car and everything inside of it will turn into evidence, including the doll in the glove compartment, which will go right back into custody.

Not to mention Scooter's gun under the seat; the one Scooter begged me to let him keep for protection. Maybe if I had let him keep it someone else would have ended up on the floor. Maybe Arty would be getting the ambulance ride and Stretch would be stuffing Scooter into the back of a squad car. But that's not the way things played out. I beat Arty to the store and took Scooter's gun away and left my prints behind just to make the frame up easier. Scooter got to defend himself with a rolled-up magazine. A good man might lose some sleep over that. Fortunately, I'm not such a good man. And you have to find sleep before you can lose any of it.

It's not my conscience I'm worried about. It's the case. Cases. Stretch and the boys will put me under the hot lights for as long as it takes to learn every lead I've been chasing for the past two days and then every last one of those leads will be crushed like so many delicate wildflowers beneath careless boots. They'll get to Nadia. Jimmy. Mouth. Billy Wise. Sandra Booth will have to tell them I've been digging into the KFC murder. Stretch will find it more than just a little suspicious that I did not report the shooting that happened a hundred feet from where I'm now standing. That'll put the smell of blood in that long nose of his. He'll do everything he can to make me a suspect. He'll keep me up on the board for as long as he can for everyone to see. The trail will inevitably bring them to the doorstep of Theodore Myerson who will have a lead story for *The Hawk* half-written before they stop asking him questions. He'll be sure to include his "well-sourced" suspicions that I'm trying to intimidate Arty Dunn from testifying in the Wrigley Menard murder trial; the same Arty Dunn who is now most inconveniently missing in action. The resulting public attention will be the uncomfortable kind, convincing Twill and everyone he reports to that it had been a mistake to hire me back. Convincing them that I really am playing for the wrong team.

And the entirety of that headache starts with me explaining why I have a plastic window.

Another queasy spasm in my gut. I put my shoulder to the teetering domino and push it back upright.

"Oh, that," I say. "The guys that did my face also do windows. Two for one special."

"Does… *that*… have anything to do with *this*?" Stretch jerks a thumb over his shoulder. "With doorstop Dan? Don't you lie to me, Mack."

"I have no reason to think they're connected. Maybe now you can tell me how Scooter went. I'm guessing gunshot. Robbery-murder."

Stretch looks at me. He's thinking, and not just about whether he should tell me what happened. He shakes his head.

"Plenty of cash in the till. No gunshot wounds. No sign of shots fired."

"Okay. No guns. So?"

"Someone broke him like a stick. Both arms and his neck."

"You mean like with a bat?"

"Too early to know. Plenty of blood. But…"

Stretch pauses, still thinking. This is the part where he misses being able to use me as a sounding board. We used to do that all the time, back when everybody would die for each other. I wait to see if he can get out of his own way.

"But all from his nose. No bruising. And when someone starts swinging a bat, it's almost impossible not to go for the head. It's like being in t-ball all over again. They always go for the melon."

"They do," I confirm, thinking about Bratton and Pine going after Nathanial Marciewicz. "Always. But not with Scooter?"

Stretch talks to the ground.

"Every greasy hair on that head is fine. Just the arms. And the neck. Like someone thought he was a screw-top soda."

"Not easy to do," I say. "Scooter wasn't exactly a child."

"You'd have to be big," Stretch says. "Strong."

I tuck that one away for later, keeping the focus on more immediate concerns.

"Take a long look at me," I say. He does, blowing steam out into the wind. I spread my arms. "Take your time. You think I could pull off that kind of stunt these days? Even sober and after a good breakfast? Maybe you should go ahead and rule me out now and we can just jump ahead to the cooperation part."

"Maybe there were two of you," he says. "Or more. Maybe you supervised. Held a gun on him while the others broke him into kindling."

"Well, which is it, Stretch? Do I coddle child molesters by investigating their claims against police or do I supervise their torture? I'm confused."

Stretch doesn't give me an answer. I don't expect one. Still too many other questions in his head.

"Last chance, Mack. What's the name of the cop you're investigating? Who was Scooter accusing? I'll settle for a first name and the department. You want a killer with a badge out on the street? You want that on your conscience? You want me to clear you? Then give me a name."

"I'll give you the name Scooter had for him, but only if you didn't get it from me."

Stretch looks at me and nods.

"It's a start."

"Officer," I say. I kick at the dead Camel in the dirty snow. "That's what Scooter called him."

"Fuck you, Mack."

"Back at you, Stretch. Happy hunting."

SIXTY-FIVE

He stands in the IAD doorway, slowly unzipping his coat.

Four in the morning and the place is lifeless except for Ray and me. Hard to decide whether I count as life, hovering here against the ceiling panels. As merely a dysfunctional perspective on himself, an extrapolation of Ray's own fractured psyche, I suppose I have no business being counted. And yet, in the moments when he is most alone, Ray turns to me for the solace of companionship. There is measurable comfort in knowing that I am here, offering my two cents.

He steps in and closes the door, keeping the lights off. Monitors across the room glow like bits of a fractured moon as a kind of starlight winks on every phone. It reminds him of those first months after Marlo passed, so afraid to be home alone with the rabid, frothing savagery of his grief that he worked around the clock instead, sleeping on the couch of the Homicide breakroom whenever his eyes refused to stay open.

Stretch Martin had come in one night for something he had forgotten. Ray had sat up and rubbed his face and confessed that he didn't know how he was going to make it through another day. Stretch had disappeared for a minute and come back with a bottle of Dewar's and taken a seat at the break table and poured out two glasses. He'd offered up a toast to Marlo and they'd sat in the dark for a few minutes, saying nothing. Then Stretch told Ray the story of how he and his ex-wife had lost their son at the ripe old age of three and a half. Ray doesn't remember the name of the disease. The boy's organs had turned toxic. Stretch blamed his own genes. So did his ex.

"How'd you live past something like that?" Ray had asked.

"I didn't," Stretch had said to the empty glass. "I didn't survive. I grew up Catholic. I married a Catholic. That was always supposed to be the answer. That's what my parents taught me. That's what I believed. The way you put yourself together and found the strength to survive until the next day was to lean on Christ as a personal savior. Well, I guess I took it personally."

Stretch had shaken his head with a pathetic laugh. I'd kept my mouth shut.

"I lost my boy and my faith on the same day. Connie left me a year later. It all came crumbling down on top of me. Took shelter in a bottle for a while. Eventually, I tried to put all the pieces back together. Sobered up. Found a cute woman looking at me in a bookstore one day and I bought her a ring. Frances is another devout Catholic, of course. It's like I was looking for someone to bring back the faith."

"Did it work?"

"Hell no. I go through the motions every Sunday for Frannie's sake. I'm a closet atheist now. Everything dead has stayed dead and I'm still only part of a person, Mack. Thirty-two years and I'm still a broken piece of a person. And now you are too. I'm not going to lie to you. The sooner you accept it, the better."

"What keeps you going?"

"Frannie," he said, looking up. "I'd be lost without her. But also the job. Walking through the ruins of other people's lives. Taking my rage out on bad people. Working shoulder to shoulder with good people like you and Deke and Donovan and Smitty. I'm here for you, Mack. I want you to know that. I want you to count on it. It's a good thing we do together. We're all here for you, man."

Less than a year later, no one had been there for Ray. Except Smitty, the one who had set him up in the first place. Smitty had wanted front row seats for the big fall.

Stretch had left the bottle in the breakroom and let him cry in peace.

Unlike Homicide, IAD doesn't have its own breakroom. It doesn't have a big refrigerator to hum him to sleep. Doesn't matter. That's not why he's here. He walks through the dark to his desk, hangs his coat over the back of his chair and sits hard, like someone has turned up the gravity.

The screensaver glows to life, no less quick with motherly wisdom for the early hour.

Safety Is No Accident. Stay Alert —Don't Get Hurt.

SIXTY-SIX

My badge is waiting on Twill's desk when he walks into his office and turns on the lights. Next to the badge are the body cam and witness-statement summaries in the Hernandez case. Better late than never. I look up out of my cubicle in time to see Twill standing in his open doorway. He jerks his head. I push back my chair.

He's sitting behind the desk when I close the door.

"I'm having trouble deciding which surprises me most," he says, "the Hernandez casework, your badge on my desk, or you walking around before daylight."

"You told me to be here to debrief on Scooter," I say with a shrug. "I'm here."

"Since how long?"

"Four o'clock and some change. I wanted to get Hernandez off my back. Sorry that took so long."

Twill picks up the badge.

"And this?"

"Thought I'd make it easy," I say.

"Leaving us so soon?"

"Yeah. Since you get paid the big money, you get to decide for how long."

"Speak."

I tell him about my visit with Scooter yesterday morning and watch Twill's face start to change color. By the time I get to the part about my prints on the glass counter and telling Stretch that he needs to clear me as a suspect, Twill's eyes are closed.

"You think you might have told me that when I asked you to go out there?"

"I wasn't thinking. You pulled me out of a dream I'd like to get back to. Besides, it was all the more important that I tell Stretch ahead of time what he's going to find."

"He going to keep us in the loop?"

"He didn't like that idea much. I told him the decision had already been made. If you haven't squared things yet with Homicide, you might want to put that at the top of your list."

"What time did you visit Scooter yesterday?"

"I was there when he opened up. Tenish."

Twill juts his jaw out a little.

"You told me you were going home with a concussion," he says.

"I did."

"You lied to me."

I'm not so smart in the morning, so I squint a little at that and shake my head.

"I never actually said I was going home. I said I had a concussion and a headache. You told me to go home. I decided I needed some air instead. I brought the concussion and the Percocet brothers along for the ride."

"You were specifically ordered, Officer Mackey, to let Special Investigations and Juvenile Support worry about the girl in the pictures. Specifically. Ordered."

"I know. That part is straight-up insubordination. I couldn't let go. And I don't expect you to let go."

Twill turns the badge over and over in his hand. All I can do is wait.

"Any leads come from this grossly insubordinate investigation?" he asks at last.

"Yeah," I say. "Some. Scooter described a drink he had with a fellow ex-con named Billy Wise. Billy served a nickel in Stateville for slinging. There's a toilet story I should tell you when you're in a better frame of mind. Let's just say Billy Wise is chronically short on wisdom."

"If they were smart, they wouldn't be criminals."

"Tell that to Big Man and roughly half of Congress."

"What's Billy doing now?"

"Still slinging. Only now in addition to the drugs, he's slinging fish for a seafood joint in Aurora. Scooter tells me that he and his buddy Billy were knocking one back at *Last Call* out in East Chandler. They met up with a guy who sounds a whole lot like the giant who handed me the photos of Scooter and the girl. They call him Hell."

"Hell?"

"Probably an endearment from his mother. The way Scooter tells it, Hell is into flesh trafficking. He was the one who arranged Scooter's hook-up with the girl in yellow."

I have to wait for Twill to catch up. It doesn't take him long.

"And then Hell took Scooter's picture and gave it to you? He sets up Scooter to sink him? To take him out of the game and torpedo his IAD case against Arty Dunn?"

"Looks that way to me," I say. "Question is who the hell is Hell to Arty?"

"One hell of a friend."

"Maybe," I say, not convinced.

"Maybe? The pictures put Scooter away and the IAD case against Arty disappears. What's the…"

I look down at my hands. "You don't have the whole picture, LT."

Twill gives me back a slow, sour smile.

"I wonder why that is, Mack."

I reach into my pocket and pull out the poker chip. I hand it over the desk.

"What's this?" he asks.

"It was in the envelope along with the photos and cash."

"Why didn't you show me this before?"

"Afraid I'd never see it again. I wanted to show it to Arty before it disappeared."

"Did you?" asks Twill, anger refreshed.

"I did."

"And?"

"Like I'd put a rattlesnake on the table."

"Afraid."

"Yes. Hell, if that's his name, was sending Arty a message. A warning. He knew I'd deliver it."

"A warning about what?"

"I'm guessing it's about the Wrigley Menard trial. Hell was there to watch opening statements. That's no coincidence, LT."

Twill holds up the chip.

"And you think this is to keep Arty from testifying."

"Or to make sure he testifies in the right way."

"And which way is that, exactly?"

I give him a shrug.

"Beats me. Like I told you before, Mickey Shaw is trying to make Arty into a player, using his badge to shake down people like Scooter and Curtis Root to keep their businesses from catching fire. Shaw is hinting that Wrigley Menard is just a fall-guy for some mob triggerman who put an end to Root for wanting out of a beautiful relationship."

"Money laundering," says Twill.

"Right."

Twill drops the badge and focuses on the poker chip, rolling it contemplatively between his thumb and forefinger.

"Okay. So let's pretend all of that is true, Mack. If I'm the mob, I send this guy… Hell… I send Hell out to deliver a scary poker-chip kind of message to Arty. And that message is what? Get Wrigley Menard convicted?"

I nod.

"Yeah. Do your part to get him convicted. Keep your mouth shut about the truth. Maybe that means he has to deliver fabricated evidence. Some careful perjury. Frame Wrigley but good. We'll protect your credibility in the courtroom by taking Scooter off the board, you help convict Wrigley."

"Or else," says Twill.

"Right. Or else."

Twill stops eyeing the chip. Now he's eyeing me.

"Why don't you seem convinced?"

"Because I'm not," I say.

"Why?"

"Don't know. Maybe because it all makes too much sense. Maybe because Arty has suddenly taken a powder."

"So?"

"So the mob tells you to testify or else, right? And you take that threat seriously. You don't want to be broken like that poker chip. So why do you not show up for court and do what you're supposed to do?"

Twill scratches the cue ball above his eyes.

"You said Mickey was cocked and ready to hurt Arty's credibility with evidence about Scooter's complaint."

I nod.

"Jolie shut him down, but Mickey is still Mickey. He's not giving up. Although now I guess he has to take Scooter off his witness list."

"So," Twill tosses the chip on the desk, "maybe Arty was sent out to pull Scooter's plug. Take away the threat that Scooter will testify."

"That was my first thought when you called last night with the news," I say. "The poker chip was an instruction to Arty to take care of the Scooter problem. Don't go back to court until there is no Scooter problem."

"Works for me," says Twill. But now my head is shaking. The more I think about it the more that piece doesn't quite fit.

"I don't think Arty did the deed, LT."

"Why?"

"Stretch Martin says Scooter died because someone broke him like a toothpick and then half-unscrewed his head from his shoulders. Someone big who didn't need a gun."

"You mean like this Hell guy?"

I shrug. "Could be. But not Arty."

"Maybe it was Arty that put Hell in play."

"No. Arty isn't telling Hell what to do. Besides, killing Scooter just makes Arty look worse. It's bad enough that Scooter has filed a shakedown complaint against Arty. What kind of fantastic day does Mickey have in the courtroom if Scooter suddenly turns up dead and Arty is a person of interest in a homicide investigation?"

"Hmm. Well, maybe whoever is pulling Arty's strings isn't thinking things through."

"The mob isn't stupid. Not Big Man's crew anyway."

Twill leans forward.

"Do not tell me, Mack, do not tell me, that you think José Beggemon is behind this. I don't even want to hear you say the name."

Shaking my head so much is starting to hurt, but I do it again anyway.

"No worries, LT. That's all José Beggemon is: just a name. And that name is about as real as moon cheese."

"Good."

"Big Man, however, is as real as it gets." Twill closes his eyes. "And I'm starting to think Big Man is behind just about everything. I'm starting to think Big Man invented the original wheel and then waited around just so he could have a getaway car once banks and liquor stores were invented."

"Damnit, Mack. I'm asking for evidence. Do you have any actual evidence?"

We look at each other for too long. He can see me wrestling. If I give it up like I'm supposed to, like a good cop should, does he take it away? Does he drop my badge in that drawer and pick up the phone and give it all to someone else? I owe the man my life. That's not worth so much. But maybe it should buy him the truth.

"Yes," I say. "I do."

The knock on the door seems to take them both by surprise. Twill looks up and Ray rotates in his chair. The door opens enough for Sandra Booth to stick her head through.

"Sorry, LT," she says. "I just wanted to let you know I'm off. I'll keep you updated. The preliminaries for Ralston and Michaels are in processing. You should get copies tomorrow. Still waiting on Edmonds. Nothing more I can do there until the IFOP pulls its head out and deals with it. Unless you want to get involved. Your voice carries a little farther over there."

"It will wait until you're back," says Twill. "Good luck, Sandra. Hope it all works out."

"Thanks, boss," she says, then gives Ray a quick glance as she retreats.

"Hey, Mack." She closes the door on the last of his name.

"What's with her?" Ray asks, turning back around.

"Headed to Connecticut. Her mother landed in the ICU last night."

"What happened?"

"Pneumonia. She thinks this is it."

"Are they close?"

"I didn't pry."

"Mmm," says Ray. "Something's not right there, LT."

"The woman is eighty-nine, Mack. At that age nothing is right."

"Not talking about the mother," says Ray.

Twill scowls.

"Then what on earth are you talking about?"

Ray points to the broken black poker chip on the desk.

"I'm talking about Sandra."

SIXTY-EIGHT

I give Twill the condensed version of history. He remembers the *Kings Flush Casino* drama with about as much clarity as I had, so I fill in the blanks from the reports Sandra had given me.

"What am I missing?" he asks.

"Bratton and Pine weren't disgruntled employees looking to get even. They were Big Man goons working as employees only so they could oversee a massive money laundering operation. Marciewicz had the rotten judgment to want out. I'm guessing he hired them and then decided it was all over. Turns out he was right about that."

"That's in the report?"

"No. Nothing close to that is in the report."

"Evidence?"

"None."

"Then where is this coming from?"

"Little bumble bee in my head," I say.

Twill closes his eyes and takes a deeper than normal breath.

"Jesus."

"Well, he's not involved as far as I know, but everybody else seems to be."

Twill looks up.

"Like?"

"Like Sandra Booth, for one."

The idea upsets him. His face doesn't try to keep it a secret.

"Come on. Involved how?"

"Back then Sandra Booth was Sandra Hill. One of her jobs was working as the Chicago PD liaison officer. She was supposed to make sure that Chicago Fire

273

and Chicago Homicide got everything they needed from each other and that they played nice in the same crime scene sandbox."

"Okay," he says uncertainly.

"Both reports make it pretty clear that wasn't an easy job. The fire investigator was a guy named Michael Perry. His report claims that Chicago Homicide was being stingy with their evidence, especially as to how Bratton and Pine got in through an electronically locked utility door in the wee hours of an otherwise quiet Sunday morning. The homicide report also fails to produce any theory as to why Marciewicz was in his office at that time."

"Well, the casino was a twenty-four-seven operation, right?"

"Yeah, but so is the Chandler Police Department. When was the last time you showed up for work at three o'clock Sunday morning? The casino was open, but the admin offices keep normal business hours."

"Okay. I hope you're getting to the part about why you're working decades-old homicide cases, Mack. That one is dead and buried."

"You're half right, LT. It is buried, but it's still got a pulse."

"What do we know now that we didn't then?"

"We know that Sandra Hill had the least desirable job in the Chicago Police Department. Chicago Fire in one ear and Chicago Homicide in the other ear, yelling at each other through her head. It was so bad that both reports singled Sandra out for trying her best to do her job despite the sniping."

"You've succeeded in making me feel sorry for her, Mack. Is that what you want?"

"I asked Sandra who was working the homicide end of things for Chicago PD. She told me she doesn't remember."

Twill's eyebrows lift and he opens his hands over the desk, bafflement taking possession of his face.

"Mack… It was twenty years ago. Do you even remember what you had for breakfast?"

"Percocet, over hard with a side of nausea."

He looks at me like I've finally gone around the bend. The crack about my concussion isn't far off. I don't give him the chance.

"Look, LT, you ever known Sandra to forget anything?"

Twill sighs and shakes his head.

"No. Not much."

"Right. I don't know the woman well, but she strikes me as a walking filing cabinet. She remembered Fire Inspector Michael Perry like he was her own father. You don't think it's odd that she wouldn't have a better memory of who was yelling into her other ear on that case? Probably the biggest case —hell, maybe the *first* case —she worked on at CPD."

"So?"

"So why lie? Why hedge?"

"Any number of reasons, Mack, none of which have anything to do with Big Man."

"And if I tell you that the name of the man Sandra couldn't seem to remember was Anthony Rickens?"

The name lands like a javelin between the eyes.

"What?"

"Yeah. That's the other thing we know now that we didn't know back then. Tony Rickens was running the *Kings Flush* homicide investigation for Chicago PD."

Twill picks up the poker chip again and turns it over a couple of times. Then he looks at me.

"You're sure?"

"It's his signature on the report."

"And you think that puts Big Man in the picture? You really do think Big Man is everywhere, don't you?"

The question brings me to an instant boil. In my head, Tony Rickens is pulling Suri out of the trunk of his Pontiac by her hair, bleeding, battered and bruised but not quite ready to die. Rickens may be dead for underestimating Suri's will to survive, but Suri is still somewhere out there running from the two organizations Rickens served and that set me up as a criminal conspirator: the mob and the police. That's a lot of extra syllables when it only takes two: Big Man.

I can tell Twill is sorry he asked the question, but I'm too angry at the suggestion of paranoia to let it go. Never accuse the mentally ill of having a mental illness they don't actually have. I'll cop to a dissociative disorder all day long, but don't accuse me of paranoia. I lay it on thick.

"Are you serious? Was Big Man in the picture? Come on, Orland. You wrote a report not six months ago…"

"I know, I know. Look…" He's got his hands out, trying to calm me down like I'm a spooked horse, but I'm not ready.

"That report got me hired back because it turned out Smitty and Tony Rickens were running the show for Big Man and that I was not a mole. I was never a mole. You know goddamned well that Tony Rickens puts Big Man in the picture. Big Man is, in fact, fucking everywhere. And that's why I'm here, LT. Not to summarize your bullshit body-cam reports and wait for Raffi Santiago to come back with… with fucking license plate photos."

Twill's face is suddenly as hard as mine is hot. His words hit the desk like rocks.

"I do not have a hearing problem, Officer Mackey. You will dial it back. You've already got one foot over the edge of the cliff, and I suggest you stop hopping up and down like a lunatic. Am I clear?"

We stare at each other for a second or two. I can hear my own breathing. I'm the first to blink but too slow to speak.

"Am I clear?" he repeats.

"Yes, sir," I say, swallowing. I try to muscle my heart back into its cage. My head feels like a bad day in Falluja. "I apologize. I'm sorry. I'm still a little raw, I guess."

"You guess? Well, you can stop guessing."

"Sorry. I'm low on sleep. I'm a little low on everything. Sorry."

"I was only asking if you thought Rickens was carrying mob water as early as the *Kings Flush Casino* case."

I rub my face with my hands, remembering the part beneath the bandage a little too late. The shock of pain brings back some common sense. I take a calming breath.

"Yes," I say. "I think Big Man was using the casino as a dry cleaner."

"Okay."

"Nathaniel Marciewicz was the manager with his tit in the ringer. I have no idea what they had on him, maybe just his own greed. Maybe something else. With so much money coming in and out, Bratton and Pine got hired on to make sure everything went smoothly. I'm guessing those two had a lot of early Sunday meetings with Marciewicz. But then at some point the relationship went south. Marciewicz wanted out or maybe Big Man just stopped trusting him. Whatever the reason, Big Man orders Bratton and Pine to make the hit. He's likely got someone else on the inside to clean up the evidence and to plant the incendiary devices in a way that takes out the server room."

"Why not Bratton and Pine? They're already there."

"Maybe. But it takes an extra level of stupid to drop a dirty murder weapon in a nearby dumpster. That looks to me more like a knife in the back. Which means someone else was involved. Someone who could put those incendiary devices in all the right places. Take out the server room so that either the door camera data was destroyed or to keep anyone from figuring out that the door cameras had been turned off when Bratton and Pine showed up with their pipe. Today, all that data would be up in the cloud. But back then…"

"It was in the on-site servers," says Twill. "So they destroyed the servers."

"Right. That takes someone on the inside. I'm guessing that same guy had instructions to drop the pipe in the dumpster. Forensic gold, just so Bratton and Pine could go down for murder."

"And Big Man burns his own people because?"

"Maybe because he knows that the big truth is on their lips the first time they get jammed up. Better to take them out while you still control the board."

"Why not just kill them?"

"Because that's just duplicating the same risk. What, get two more guys to kill the two guys you don't want around talking about killing? Why kill the witnesses yourself when you can have the State of Illinois do it for you?"

"You're not making any sense. Don't they just blab the truth and name names? Turn State's evidence just to avoid the death penalty?"

"Blab the truth to who? The police? Tony Rickens was the police."

"Their lawyers then."

"I wondered about that too until I did some poking around on the computer this morning while I was waiting for you. There was only one lawyer. Singular. They both hired the same guy. Want to guess who?"`

Twill's face goes slack as he thinks. But he's no dummy. He gets there soon enough.

"Christ," he says.

"You're way off, LT. Jesus was a carpenter. The answer is Mickey Shaw. Big Man bought Bratton and Pine an expensive lawyer to push them right into the needle. A killer-kabob made to order."

"My head hurts."

"Mine too."

"What makes you think Sandra is on Big Man's payroll?"

"I never said I thought Sandra was on Big Man's payroll. I said something isn't right. Do I need to slow down?"

Twill's face turns sour.

"I like you better when you're apologizing and afraid for your job. Let's go back to that."

"Remember when I told you that Arty came up to me in the courthouse after the first day of the Wrigley Menard trial?"

"Yes."

"Slapped me on the back just to cause problems with me and Scooter?"

"Yeah."

"And I told you that somehow he must have known about Scooter's complaint before we had actually issued the notice?"

Twills' face recoils.

"Sandra? You're reaching, Mack. Could have been all kinds of things. I've known Sandra longer than you have. She didn't leak the notice of complaint."

"Hold on. There were two notices, remember? The first one was wrong, and we had to redraft it."

"And?"

"The first notice stated that someone had set fire to Scooter's truck and then the porn shop. A closer look at Scooter's complaint showed that his truck never caught fire. It just happened to be parked next to the corner of the building where the fire started. I misunderstood Scooter's complaint. So, then we corrected the notice."

"Yeah. I remember all of that. Why do I care?"

"You care because we never issued that first notice. You care because Arty's IFOP representative came to the meeting under the firm impression that Scooter was complaining about a burned-up truck."

I let the information sit. His eyes drift away, like they're looking for some privacy to think things through. I'm not ready to let them go.

"The only way IFOP gets hold of that completely incorrect information is from IAD. From *this* office. That's a very small handful of people, boss. Even smaller when you take you and me out the equation. Makes me start to think all over again about why Sandra is brushing dust over the memory of Tony Rickens.

I'm guessing she knows my history and, for whatever reason, doesn't want to help me make the connection."

"Why would Sandra care? About any of it? Why would she care if you did connect Big Man to the casino case? So what? And why would she care about Scooter's likely worthless complaint against Arty Dunn?"

"Maybe she doesn't. Maybe Big Man cares and Sandra cares about Big Man."

"You're suggesting, once again, that Sandra is on the take."

"No. Could be fear. Maybe he has something on her."

"Okay, but why would Big Man care about Scooter and Arty?" I start to answer but Twill's not done. "And if Mickey Shaw is also working for Big Man, as you suggest, then why is Mickey trying to paint Arty as a dirty cop working for the mob? You'd think Big Man would not want Mickey to be blowing the whistle on police corruption."

"Because Mickey's not just a lawyer, LT. He's a fixer. I think it's Bratton and Pine all over again."

"A fixer. And the problem to be fixed is what? Who? Arty Dunn?"

"Maybe. Yes. Question is why."

Twill hears me, but I can tell he's trying to keep the words from reaching his brain. He keeps talking like I haven't said anything.

"And not for nothing, Mack, but other than Mickey Shaw slinging his shit around the courtroom and Scooter spouting off his nonsense, do you have any reason to think that Arty Dunn is not actually a good cop coming up on twenty years of law enforcement service? I mean, hell's bells, the man could be innocent. That's something I'd think you would be able to relate to."

"I do relate, LT. I do. I'm not out to smear Arty. You might recall my lack of enthusiasm for investigating Scooter's complaint. Maybe Arty is clean as a whistle. But I'd like him to clear some things up."

"Like?"

"Like where he's been, for starters. Like why he decided to no-show the continuation of his testimony under cross-examination on subjects like why he is being accused of running a protection racket. I'd also like to know how he first got into policing."

"Why would that matter?"

It's the question I've been waiting for. I trade it for one of my own.

"You know what Arty was before he joined the force?"

"No, but I think I'm about to."

"According to Rickens' report, Arty was Assistant Security Director for the *Kings Flush Casino*."

I could go out for breakfast and come back again and Twill would still be staring into space.

"The inside man," he says, only he says it to himself. I pound the nail a little harder.

"Two years after the fire and Arty is through the academy and working for Chicago PD. Homicide. Under Tony Rickens."

Thirty seconds. Forty-five. I start to get sleepy watching Twill think and listening to him breathe. But I manage to keep my eyes open and my mouth shut. Finally, his eyes find mine. He picks up the poker chip and slips it in his shirt pocket. Then he picks up my badge and flips it across the desk into my lap.

"Let Stretch do his job. Stay out of his face until he wants an interview and let me know when that happens. Stay away from Sandra. Stay away from Santiago and the dry cleaner. The mayor. Suri. All of that. Those are hard boundaries, Mack. For now, at least. I'm not going to ask you what happened to your back windshield because I'm already full up on half-truths and lies. I'm not going to tell you to go home and sleep because I'm full up on insubordination and the day hasn't even started. But understand this, Officer Mackey: jerk me around again and I will drive you back to the shopping mall myself."

SIXTY-NINE

Ray keeps a hand on the big wooden door until it closes quietly behind him.

Celeste Fila is a vision in lavender, great swaths of it, as if the brassy-blonde beehive has been plopped down upon some purple hill in Provence. Her drugstore eyelashes butterfly out a greeting. It gets her a subtle nod and a sideways smile in return.

He can sit anywhere. The gallery is empty except for a front-row smattering of paralegals behind the prosecution, and ace reporter Teddy Myerson, in his usual place, hunched over his laptop behind the defense. The jury box is like a sad, empty rowboat left at the dock.

Jaclyn Cavelle is alone at her table, standing at attention. On the other side of the podium, Mickey Shaw and Wrigley "Jake" Menard sit shoulder-to-shoulder at the defense table. Up on high, Judge Jolie pauses in mid-sentence as Ray makes his way to the back row. She is leaning forward against her desk, looking down on the others in a way to emphasize her authority. It's a perspective that easily lends itself to judgments and opinions. I can relate. The difference is that Jolie can issue her judgments and opinions and make everyone below step to. I have an audience of one and no power of enforcement. I hold Ray in contempt eight days a week, but I can't lock him up to save himself.

Jolie glances at Ray, appearing to wonder momentarily whether he is here to play some particular part in the proceedings. But then she moves on.

"But the prosecution needs to acknowledge the merits of the defendant's concern. Officer Dunn is a witness for the State of Illinois."

Ray sits too heavily, dropping his coat on the bench, zipper first. The clunk is enough to get everyone's attention. One by one, they each make a casual half-turn to see who has come in. They all think it just might be Arty Dunn and come away disappointed. The looks from Ted Myerson and Mickey Shaw linger longer than the others. Judge Jolie keeps it coming.

"He's your witness, Ms. Cavelle. You've had your opportunity to use him for your purposes. Mr. Shaw has a right to cross-examine and he, quite understandably, has a strong preference to do so in the context of Officer Dunn's testimony on direct. I understand that you would like to just move on and pick up that thread later. And we may have to do exactly that if your witness doesn't show up. But before your umbrage gets the better of you, let's just pause for a second and acknowledge that Arthur Dunn is your responsibility. You called him. And you've lost him. You don't know where he is. And now, with the jury having heard only your side of Officer Dunn's testimony, you are asking… no, you are demanding… that the defense pay the price for that. Does that strike you as particularly fair?"

Jaclyn clears her throat, underlining or crossing something out on the pad in front of her.

"No, Your Honor. The State's request stands, but I do apologize to the court and counsel for my tone. My candle has a flame burning on each end these days. I did not intend any offense."

"Thank you, counsel. Now." Jolie pivots in her seat. "Mr. Shaw. While I can appreciate that you would like to continue your cross-examination of Officer Dunn, he cannot be found. Not good, I agree. But that is the hand we have been dealt."

Mickey Shaw rises, his deep-blue suitcoat unbunching, falling so that it hangs perfectly over his shoulders, just as each pant legs slides fully over its boot. He gives each shirt cuff a slight tug and clasps his hands behind his back, as if to mimic the hair he has gathered in a black elastic band at his nape.

"Your Honor, I appreciate the court's perspective. Nevertheless, it remains true that Arthur Dunn is, as you say, the prosecution's responsibility. Ms. Cavelle cannot put the man on the stand, use him to insinuate that my client is a serial burglar with an itchy trigger finger, and then keep me from cleaning all of that up. Every day that implication goes unchecked is a day it solidifies as fact in the collective mind of the jury. Not to mention my growing concern that Officer Dunn's relationship with the victim is not as he testified."

The judge clears her throat.

"Are you suggesting that Arthur Dunn was somehow complicit in the murder of Curtis Root? Before you answer, counsel, I am mindful that we have at least one member of the media in the courtroom. We can all adjourn to my chambers if necessary."

"No need, Your Honor," says Mickey. "Without intending to cast any premature aspersions as to Officer Dunn, it is by now no secret that the defense believes there are those, inside and outside of the Chandler Police Department, who are working mightily, and knowingly, to convict an innocent man."

Judge Jolie slowly closes her eyes and lets out a sigh.

"And you think Office Dunn might be in a position to help you in that regard, is that it?"

"Well, Judge, it would be mighty helpful if the prosecution would allow me to examine him so that we could all find out."

"Well, you are certainly free to call him in your case, counsel. He is on your list."

"He is. But the moment of cross-examination is now, and I cannot examine a piece of paper. I'm not trying to be cute, here, Your Honor…"

"I'm relieved to hear that, counsel."

"My point is that Officer Dunn has become a critical witness and I'm quite certain Ms. Cavelle knows this. He's not someone who can just wait until later, whenever she decides to bring him back."

"I object to that," says Cavelle. "Your Honor, we have nothing to…"

Jolie points at Cavelle without looking.

"We have heard from you, counsel. Your objection is noted. Please be seated. Mr. Shaw, the witness may be the prosecution's responsibility, but I have not heard anything to suggest that his absence is anyone's fault or that the prosecution is playing those sorts of games. At some point I think we should all be concerned about what has happened to Officer Dunn. I am assuming that concerted efforts are underway to locate him. But, in the meantime, this trial must move forward. I have jurors with jobs and lives of their own to consider and a long line of cases backed up after this one."

"But, Your Honor, with all due…"

Jolie shakes her head. Her precise Hispanic features are closed for the business of persuasion.

"You've been a lawyer a long time, Mr. Shaw. You well know that changes in the witness order happen in virtually every trial. Not ideal. But that's the way it is. I will consider a curative instruction to the jury if you want to take a crack at a draft. In the meantime, I am granting the Prosecution's request that, in the event Officer Dunn is still absent when we resume, we proceed with the next witness and pick up with your cross-examination later in the trial."

"I renew my objection for the record, Your Honor," says Shaw.

"Duly noted. As it happens, and as we have already discussed, we still have a problem with the flu. Juror number ten, and now, as of this morning, juror number six, are indisposed. Am I correct to understand that you both agree we should rely on our alternates and resume tomorrow even if jurors ten and six remain too ill to attend?"

"Yes, Your Honor," says Mickey.

"Yes, Judge," says Jaclyn, rising halfway. "The State agrees."

"Okay. Again, not ideal. But…" Jolie doesn't finish, making a note of something with her pen and hands a sheet down to Celeste. "Thank you both. We will adjourn until tomorrow morning."

Jolie stands and exits to a shuffling of papers and opening of briefcases. Jaclyn Cavelle caucuses over the bar with her paralegals. Mickey Shaw has a few words of encouragement and a swat on the shoulder for Wrigley who stands and holds out his hands for two uniformed Troopers. They snap on the bracelets and take him away through a side door as Ted Myerson stands and hunches over the bar toward Shaw.

Ray stands and grabs his coat and heads for the big doors. Then he stops. He knows he can't let it go. We both do. He turns and heads the other direction. At the front of the courtroom, he walks up the first row and takes a seat next to *The Hawk*'s answer to Edward R. Murrow.

Myerson and Shaw stop talking and look at him.

"Raymond Mackey," announces Mickey, genially, leaning back in his chair. "What brings Chandler IAD to our little corner of the sandbox?"

"Best show in town," says Ray.

"Not today, I'm afraid. You must be bored to tears."

"Don't be so modest. You're never boring, Mickey."

Mickey gestures at Ray's face.

"Looks like you've seen better days."

"I've seen a lot of better days, but they always belong to someone else." Ray looks up at Myerson. "How you doing, Teddy? You don't look so good either.

We're not like Mickey, you and me. Mickey always looks like a tall stack of money."

Myerson nods an uncomfortable greeting. He shifts his weight and adjusts the laptop in his hands. Ray turns back to Shaw.

"Teddy and I had a little date last night. I think he wanted pizza but was too shy to come inside. So we sat out in his car and had a nice talk. Didn't we, Ted?"

Ted's too busy tasting something sour to answer. Mickey gives an apologetic smile.

"I'm afraid we're kind of in a private conversation here, Ray."

"You're not afraid, Mickey. That's just you being polite. You're not afraid of anything or anyone."

"I'm not sure I understand."

"Come on. It's true. Ted and I cast teeny, tiny shadows compared to you. Then again, we tend to keep company with humans our own size. Your shadow is looking more and more like Faye Ray's."

"Interesting," says Mickey.

"Isn't it though? And since when is talking to a newspaperman a private conversation?" Ray tips his head toward Ted. "These guys don't keep secrets, Mickey. Ted told me last night you're his source for all things related to me. I didn't even have to work him that hard. We both marveled at all the things you told him."

"That's a lie," says Ted, turning to Mickey. "I never told him any..."

Mickey holds up a hand, shaking his head, smile on his face.

"Stop, Ted," he says, pushing the hand a little closer. "Just..." He looks at Ray. "Officer Mackey, how can I help you?"

"I'd like to know why you want the genteel readers of *The Hawk* to think that I've been driving Arty Dunn around in the trunk of my car giving him pointers on how to testify."

"I never said that," says Ted to Mickey. Mickey ignores him.

"You're making something out of nothing, Ray. Ted was curious about you. He asked me some questions. It's no secret that CPD showed you the door because of..." Mickey looks to the ceiling for the right words. "Your unsavory connections. I assumed Ted was already up to speed on all that history. It sounds like maybe his imagination took him for quite a spin when he had nothing else to do."

"Sounds to me like you've already debriefed," says Ray.

"Oh yeah," says Mickey with a laugh. "You got him all worked up with the bullets and the porn. I know it all. But I try not to judge other people's lives, Ray. How you jump-start your mornings is none of my business."

"Well, Ted here seems to think it's his business. And he claims he got that idea from you."

Myerson snaps his laptop closed in his long-fingered hands.

"Mickey, seriously, I never said anything about…"

Mickey slaps the counsel table. It's loud enough to shut Ted up. Mickey glances backward. Twenty feet away, Jaclyn Cavelle is still sitting at her table, pretending not to listen. When next Mickey speaks, his voice is low and calm.

"Look. Officer Mackey. Raymond. If you know where to find Arty, I think everyone, most especially Judge Jolie, would appreciate being let in on the secret. If you don't know, well, then we welcome you to the club of the clueless. Either way, friend, no one bears you any ill will. Certainly not me."

"And what makes you think I know anything?"

Mickey shrugs.

"My sources tell me that you and Arty had a not-so-friendly chat right before he turned invisible."

"Just doing my job," says Ray.

"Oh, I have no doubt. The question is what that job was."

"My job as an IAD investigator. What else?"

"Don't know, Ray. You tell me. Sometimes there's a job within a job within a job. The only job that really matters is the one inside at the very center."

You've got to hand it to Ray. That face doesn't register anything. Not a wrinkle out of place. Not so much as an extra blink. No one could possibly tell that somewhere in that slightly soggy brain, his instinct kicked in, translating the word "job" into "doll."

No one can feel the universe break open. No one except Ray. And me.

"My only job is to investigate complaints," says Ray with a shrug. "That's what I do now."

"Yeah, but very interesting investigations," says Mickey. "Anyone putting the boys-in-blue through their paces is doing my kind of work. From what I hear, Donald Pleasants has got Arty cold on working a protection racket." Mickey gives him a wolfish smile. "Care to comment?"

Ted Myerson looks surprised at hearing a question that sounds like it should have been his to ask.

"Sure," says Ray. "Maybe we can also talk about who is paying you to represent Wrigley Menard. You go first."

"I suppose I could subpoena you," says Mickey, ignoring the question. "Put you on the stand."

"And ask me about an on-going internal investigation of dubious relevance to the murder of Mr. Root? You really think the judge likes you that much?" Ray makes a face. "Come on, Mickey. You're a lot of things, but dumb isn't on the list. Besides, I could just as easily haul you in for a lot of questions about the interesting company you're keeping these days. Not sure you have time for that right now."

Mickey laughs.

"We need to play poker sometime, Ray. Bring all of your money."

"That'll be the shortest game of poker in history, Mickey. I'm about to spend all I have on a new back windshield."

"Oh yeah? That sounds like a story."

"Careless me. I backed into a couple of bullets. Like you don't know."

Mickey pretends offense, clutching pearls he's not wearing.

"Me?"

"Try again," says Ray. "That poker game is looking better and better. You want to tell me who you sent out to put on that little shoot-'em-up show for Teddy here or do I have to work for it?"

Mickey laughs and shakes his head. He looks at Myerson, then back to Ray.

"I have no idea what…"

"Of course you do. And so does whoever is paying your fee. I'm still behind, I know. I'm slow but I'll get there eventually. Maybe it's as simple as you trying to stage a little pretend drama between me and Arty. I'm looking into things for Scooter Pleasants and someone pumps my car full of bullets? And outside Scooter's porn shop no less? Any cop worth his salt files a report, demands an investigation and puts Arty Dunn at the top of the list of people to talk to. Mighty convenient to have a reporter on the scene for that show. Not that Teddy actually saw anything from under his car seat, but he got the picture. Maybe enough for a paragraph that the jury can read. Or maybe a question or two for the Chandler Police, just to make sure they feel the attention and Arty gets suspended pending investigation."

"Is there a point here someplace, Ray?"

"Sure. The point is that Arty's looking worse by the day which for you means he's looking better and better. No wonder you're so anxious to finish your cross-examination. Fortunately, there's no need to kill me for any of that. A broken windshield will do just fine."

Myerson's eyes widen a little like maybe he suspects the world is not as it once seemed.

"I hear you write fiction, Ray," says Mickey. "That true?"

"Off the mark, am I?"

"Off your meds." Mickey's eyes are hard. He points a finger toward the big double doors. "Go write a book."

Ray nods. Then he stands. He swats Myerson in the arm.

"It's enough to make you wonder if your source is actually a sewage pipe. See you in the funny papers, Teddy."

Ray grabs his coat and heads up the aisle for the exit. Then he stops and doubles back. Mickey Shaw and Ted Myerson are all eyes as he steps through the little swinging door in the bar and leans in next to Jaclyn Cavelle.

"Hi," he says in a whisper, extending a hand. "Raymond Mackey. Chandler Police."

Jaclyn flips her pad over so he can't see and shakes his hand uncertainly.

"Officer," she says.

"When you find Arty Dunn, tell him I'm looking for him."

"You and everyone else," says Cavelle. "Why are you saying this to me?"

"Because I needed to say something and this is the only thing that came to mind on short notice."

"I don't understand."

"Neither does Mickey Shaw. Difference is that Mickey's kind of not understanding will make him worry that I'm over here giving you the goods on his mob connection. Goods I don't have, but I'm just going to keep whispering anyway. Might help if you flipped over that pad and took some notes."

It takes a couple of beats, but then Jaclyn does as he says. Her pen makes curlicues and triangles.

"Is that something you actually believe?" she asks. The question gets her a disbelieving smile.

"Come on, Ms. Cavelle. You expect me to believe that you don't already believe it? Mickey's as dirty as mud. It's the thing everybody believes without actually knowing. I don't know if you've got the right guy in Wrigley Menard. Maybe, maybe not. Your burglary case feels thin to me, but that's just me knowing not much of anything. What I do know is that if Mickey Shaw wants to set Wrigley free, and if mob money is paying him for that effort, then acquittal is the exact opposite of what needs to happen here. Okay?"

"You actually want me to agree that I'm doing the right thing?" she asks.

"Hard to tell these days what the right thing actually is. The wrong things are always easier for me to spot. And right now the wrong thing is sporting cowboy boots and a ponytail. That's probably enough fake conversation to throw Mickey off his game. I'm guessing that Mickey's coming over for a friendly chat as soon as I'm out the door. Hold your cards close and maybe he'll lose some sleep about what you know. Good luck tomorrow."

"Uh… thanks, I guess," says Jaclyn, clearly confused. They shake again. I can tell she doesn't want to let Ray go. "Hey. Do you want to grab some coffee, or…"

"Thanks, no," he says. "Got to go see an old lady about a doll."

SEVENTY

The Golden View Senior Community is nestled into a back pocket of southeastern Will County. You could hit Indiana with a rock if you needed to. Not that you ever really need a reason.

I'm old enough to remember when the view out this way was less golden than it was tall, green and leafy. It all seems a lot shorter and grayer now. I had a foster family that lived in this area when I first broke into the double digits. The Krugers. Just the two of them. Carl and Edith. I remember a big billboard a mile or two south of the place they lived. A big pair of red lips kissing a cool spire of soft, white ice cream. In the heat of summer, three seconds looking at that sign as the Krugers' blue station wagon whizzed past was enough to drop the temperature by a degree. *Softies Drive-Thru.* Edith always wanted to make the detour on the way back from church. Carl was tight with a nickel and didn't want to encourage his wife's sweet tooth, so he was full of excuses.

Not that Carl was completely against ice cream. He was always good for a jumbo chocolate Softie after he hit me. Something cool and creamy to take the edge off his anger and make everything okay again. Edith came to his defense in the end. She told St. Evangeline's I was asking for it.

No dummy, Edith.

The place Ivah Novak calls home is a pale, concrete, two-story building in the shape of a pair of captain's wings. The facility is backed up against an arc of hardwoods just wide enough to create the illusion of forested living and to obscure any view of the nearby grove of two-bedroom apartments. There is also a peekaboo view of a mini-mall and a doc-in-the-box emergency clinic. I'm guessing the golden view part happens when the sun is setting and the molten red light of late afternoon picks up the dust in the air. That or it has something to do with the cost of elder care.

Nadia is in the lobby as promised. Her head is down, watching her thumbs work her phone. She looks up as I approach.

"Good morning," she says in a way I almost believe.

She's one of those people. She's got one of those smiles and a pair of those eyes and one of those relentlessly cheery tones that she knows how to use. One greeting can sweep the dead bodies and ugly conversations out of your day and make it feel like it actually is a good morning.

"Morning, Nadia," I say. "Where's kiddo?"

"School."

"Guess those dragons won't train themselves," I say. She laughs. I want that to be my new mission. Making Nadia King laugh. Instead, I hold up the wooden doll. She takes it in one hand and beams. It's like they're smiling at each other.

"She's beautiful," says Nadia. "She's so cold."

"She likes it that way," I say. "She's Russian. I took her out for coffee and she ordered an iced vodka."

Another laugh. It is a good morning. Scooter who? Mickey who? Nadia tries to hand back the doll.

"No," I say. "You're the one who never gave up, Nadia. You should be the one to hand her over."

Nadia smiles sweetly.

"Thanks, Mack."

A white-haired woman in an electric wheelchair glides into the lobby, one Chicago Bears pennant taped to each handle. She's in a nightgown and a sweatshirt, large orange socks on her feet. She coasts to a stop at the frost-rimmed windows that look out at the parking lot and leans forward, craning her face one way, then the other.

"Not until tomorrow, Alice," says a voice from behind. Nadia and I both turn.

Not far away is a fortress-like reception area. An apparently humorless gray man in a green cardigan is sitting in a chair too low for the high counter. I can only see from the top of his head to the bottom of his arm pits. He's got short, thinning white hair and one of those sitting-behind-a-counter faces, full of boredom and authority. Probably why they hired him.

In front of him, hanging from the desk, is a large hand-tooled wooden sign – *Golden View Welcomes You!* –with each letter painted its own cheery color.

Hanging on the wall behind him, above an array of black office equipment, is a large television monitor that cycles through photographs of residents enjoying themselves. Each photo lasts about five seconds before dramatically atomizing to reveal the next.

"Alice," the man says again.

"What?" The woman does not look.

"Not until tomorrow."

"Not until tomorrow?"

"Not until tomorrow."

"You said that yesterday."

"No I didn't."

"Okay," says Alice. "Tomorrow, then."

She reverses her chair away from the windows then speeds off up the wide, floral-themed hallway from which she emerged, like a bee back into a garden.

"Can I help you two?" asks the man. I'm guessing from the nametag he answers to Frank.

"Yes," says Nadia, leaving me for the main desk. "We're here to see my mother."

"And she is?"

"Ivah Novak in 2113."

As I step up next to her, the man is placing a pair of large, black glasses on his beak and pecking at a keyboard. It takes some painful expressions, but he finds what he's looking for.

"Okay," he says. "One moment."

He picks up a phone and dials.

"And what are your names?" he asks. His eyes seem a little glassy and unfocused. Could be the readers distorting them, magnifying the reddish glaze of advancing years. But I know better. I can spot a drinker trying to numb himself through the morning like I'm looking in the mirror. I'm guessing the rectangle shape pushing out from inside the cardigan is one of the silver, sloshy kind.

"I'm her daughter, Nadia King, and this is Officer Mackey of the Chandler Police Department."

"I'll need to see identification," he says, then points to a computer keypad at the other end of the desk. "And you'll need to sign into the kiosk with your name and phone… Mrs. Novak? Ivah? Yes, this is Frank at the front desk. Yes, good

morning. I have some visitors down here for you. Well, it's your daughter, and…
yes, your daughter, Nadia, and also an Officer Mackey. Yes. And they've come to
see you. Would you like to come down or should I send them up? Okay. Yes.
Thank you, Mrs. Novak." He replaces the receiver and looks at us again over his
glasses. "Identification. And then you need to sign in. She said you can go on up."

I reach for my wallet and hand over my license. Frank makes notes on a
clipboard. Nadia has to set her phone and the doll on the counter so she can dig
her wallet out of her purse and then her license out of her wallet. Her phone
glows to life like maybe it objects to being set down.

I don't like to think of myself as a nosey man. But something glows at me and
I pay attention. The text is short, from someone she knows as Ivan H.

Замок.

I glance at the doll on the counter. She's smiling at me in that way she does.
She sees it too.

Замок.

The screen is dark again by the time Nadia is handing her license over to
Frank. I don't know about the doll, but three o'clock in the morning is never
okay with me. Nothing good ever happens then. That's when Bratton and Pine
dropped in on Nathanial Marciewicz twenty years ago. Case in point.

Frank hands our ID's back and we take turns typing our names and phone
numbers into the kiosk. When I'm done, Nadia heads up the hall where Alice
had gone. Frank has other ideas and starts pointing.

"Lot shorter this way," he says. "East hall to the elevator. Second floor and
then left all the way to the end."

The door to 2113 is ajar when we get there. Nadia eases it open, calling out.

"Mama?" I step in behind and close the door. It's a tidy suite of three narrow
rooms: a living room, a bedroom I can't see, plus a small kitchen. The south wall
of the living room has large windows looking out at the trees. Nadia has to call out
again before she gets a thin, muffled response from the direction of the bedroom.

"Mama?"

"Vannaya!"

Nadia gives me an apologetic smirk and mouths the word bathroom.

"I like a woman with priorities," I say, and we shuffle further in.

There's just enough space for the furniture, like every other room I've ever seen in my life. A well-worn couch is backed up against the wall in front of a low, glass table cluttered with pill bottles, remote controls, readers, magazines, a pack of Parliaments, and half-empty bottles of water. The couch cushions are loam-colored with throw pillows of ochre and rust, huddled in groups of three at each end. There's an oak credenza beneath the main window squeezed between an artificial Ficus and a navy-blue swivel chair stacked with celebrity-gossip rags on one end, and an identical blue chair, this one empty, on the other. On the wall opposite the couch is an etagere made from the same oak as the credenza. Tchotchkes caucus in crowded neighborhoods. Painted miniature teacups. Small woven baskets full of shells, beads and lavender. A forest of crucifixes. A town of framed photographs. The shelves are calculated to look random in length and vertical spacing, but they all seem to agree on the importance of saving a big open rectangle in the middle for the flat screen television.

"Are your parents still alive," Nadia asks, sitting in the empty blue chair.

"No," I say. "Not for a long time."

"Siblings?"

"Just me. Probably good I got to skip the elder care part. I'm not sure I'd be such a dutiful child. You must be up here every week."

"Just about," she says. "I don't always make it. Work and Danika keep me running."

"That's a lot to fit in. I'm sure you're ready for bed."

Her eyes flash back at me the awkwardness of my own words.

"At the end of the day," I add, stuffing my hands in my pockets and rocking on my heels.

The couch looks low and soft and a little too inviting. Sitting might mean never getting back up again. Ivah's been through enough in her life without having to feed and water the strange detective who sat down once and never left. I point to the cigarettes. "They let her smoke inside?"

"No," says Nadia. "They've got places outside."

"In this weather? That just makes smoking dangerous. But maybe it's safer than a flaming couch. You a smoker?"

"Once. I turned green and lost my lunch. Never again."

"Good for you. The trick is to skip lunch and have nothing to lose."

"No thanks. You may as well have a seat, Mack. Sometimes it takes her a while."

I wave her off and turn, drifting to the etagere.

"I'm fine. No need for me to get too comfortable. This shouldn't take long, and I can be out of everybody's hair."

Jovah Novak is hard to miss. His official department photo towers over the others. He's in his dress blues. Black tie. The hat with its white and blue checkerboard band pulled firmly over his broad forehead. His square face is arranged in a stern, protect-and-serve expression. It all fits nicely in the gilt frame.

Next to Joe is a younger, leaner man with similar features. Alexi, I'm guessing. He's at a white table in a black tux, flashing a mouth full of teeth. He's got his brother's eyes, the same mineral blue but missing the seriousness.

Partly behind Alexi is a photo of the brothers as boys, maybe eight and five. They're both in pajamas at the base of a Christmas tree brandishing toy guns. Joe has a plastic Winchester, Alexi some other kind of rifle. Hard to say who drew first but from the looks of things they both died laughing. In the background, coming around the back of the tree, is part of a dress wrapped around part of a person. I'm guessing Ivah a good thirty-something years ago.

"Where were you?" I ask, lifting the photo.

"Probably in a crib," says Nadia. "Too young for toy guns. And probably camera shy even then."

"Camera shy?" I put the photo back.

"Always have been. Still am. Cameras feel like guns. Unless I'm in groups. Then I'm better."

"Seems a terrible waste," I say. "Face like yours."

"You're sweet. Just don't point a camera at me."

On the next highest shelf is a collection of older photos, mostly small, sepia images in oval frames. A small house. A wiry man in work pants with suspenders, muscular hands at the ends of long arms, flat against his sides, waiting for something that his expression fears might never come. The dirty, white oval between his black beard and his hat is just wide enough for a couple of large, dark eyes on either side of a prominent ridge of nose. The neighboring photo is of a matronly woman on a buckboard, black rump of a horse in the foreground. Her face is hard and dour, betraying no patience for photography.

"Your grandparents?"

"Great grandparents," says Nadia. "In Novogrudok. Well. Between Novogrudok and Minsk."

"Belarus."

"Yes," she says. "You see the photo of the children?"

There is only one. Black and white, but not as faded. Thirteen girls all in a line from shortest to tallest. Behind them is a white stone church. Dark skirts, white blouses, dark kerchiefs tied in loose knots. Not a smile to save your life. Except one. Her hair is braided. One arm thrown around the shoulder of the girl next to her, the other arm up in the air and waving.

"Third from the left," I say.

Nadia laughs and lifts her hands in a soundless, congratulatory clap.

"Very good," she says.

"I'd know that smile anywhere. You don't seem so shy to me."

"Safety in numbers," says Nadia.

"Your friend here looks like you stole her lunch money."

"Belka. Always a grouch."

"In fact, you're the only kid here with a smile."

"I was a pretty happy girl, I guess. Poor but happy."

"She was good girl." The new voice comes from behind, low and old.

I turn to find Ivah Novak in the doorway. She is short and stooped with straight gray hair. Her eyes are small, sunken craters. Her high cheekbones have stopped doing the cheeks any favors, creating a concave, sloughing-sand look to the sides of her face. Half of a white cotton collar has escaped the neck of a sweater that is too large. The collar stretches up along her neck, waving for help as she is devoured whole by a cranberry cashmere python. Ivah's mouth, wrinkled from age and smoking, is proportionally small and open.

"Mama!" Nadia stands and steps gingerly between me and the table, embracing the woman around the shoulders in a brief flurry of Russian. Ivah pats her on the back like she's trying to put out a fire.

"Mama," says Nadia when they have separated. "This is…"

"Is beautiful daughter, eh?" Ivah's crooked finger is pointing at me and her dark, thin eyebrows are arched in humorous anticipation. She's only accepting one answer. Luckily, it happens to be the truth.

"Yes, ma'am," I nod. "She is."

"Mama…" Nadia scolds gently.

"You will be to marry?"

Ivah makes her eyes wide which only seem to deepen the craters. I smile and shake my head. "Your daughter is much too smart for that, I'm afraid."

Next to me, Nadia makes a sound of embarrassed exasperation.

"Mama, ty smushchayesh' menya."

But Ivah is not listening.

"She needs man," Ivah says, matter-of-factly.

"Mama, stoy!" says Nadia. *"Eto ne sposob vesti sebya! Mozhem li my prosto sdelat' eto?"*

Nadia looks at me apologetically, then turns back to Ivah with a sigh. "This is Officer Raymond Mackey. He is with the Chandler Police Department. He…"

"My boy was police department," Ivah says to me. "Jovah."

I step closer, extending my hand. Ivah takes it and squeezes in a two-handed grip that, beneath the paper-soft skin, is bony and surprisingly firm.

"Yes, I know of your son. I am very sorry about what happened to Jovah, Mrs. Novak. But it is very good to meet you."

"Was good boy, Jovah. Always want good thing."

"Yes, I'm sure that's true," I say. She extracts a hand and wags a finger at me. Her face is stern and accusing.

"Bad thing cannot be good thing. Bad thing is always bad thing."

"Mama…"

"You're right, Mrs. Novak," I say. "You're right about that."

"He was still good boy, Jovah.

"Officer Mackey has been helping me, Mama."

Ivah's eyes narrow as she releases my hand. She points at my neck like she might touch it.

"You choke?" she asks, then turning to Nadia. *"Oni yego dushili?"*

"Mama." Nadia's tone is scolding and spilling a kind of alarm.

Ivah's eyes are now on my bandage.

"You fight?"

"No," I lie to her. "I'm fine. I'm clumsy."

She points to her own neck.

"I am put in bag and tie to chair."

"Mama."

She holds out both wrists to me as if to show me the ligature marks that are no longer there. She points again to my neck. She wants to show me that we are the same in this way. Marks of violence.

"They make tight," she says. "Too tight."

"Yes," I agree, but it is the only word that makes it out before Nadia takes stern control.

"Mama. That's enough of all of that. *Khvatit etogo. Dovol'no.*" Nadia turns for the chair, bringing back her purse and a smile for the record books. "We have something for you that will make you happy," she says.

Ivah is slow to turn away from me and refocus. Nadia removes the doll from her purse and holds it out. Ivah remains motionless for long seconds, then reaches both hands out for the doll and takes it gently in her hands like a tiny baby.

"*Ona vernulas',*" Ivah says in a whisper. "*Ona vernulas' ko mne.*"

"Yes, Mama," says Nadia. "She has come back to you."

Ivah walks slowly to the couch, stroking the doll's face with her thumbs. She sits, turning the doll upside-down and stroking the inscribed initials and date. She looks up at me and smiles.

"Verochka Volkova," she says, touching her chest gently with her fingertips. "*Babushka.* Is grandmother."

I smile and nod. "Yes, ma'am."

Ivah takes the top half off the doll in an unscrewing motion and sets it on the table. She removes the likeness inside. She gently repeats the process twice more until the table is littered with the shells of half-dolls and she holds in her hand a small, solid wooden doll painted to look almost exactly like the others.

Ivah looks at me and points to a small, rectangular woven basket on the side table. I step forward and hand it to her. She pulls off the top and jabs a finger inside, rooting through a collection of pens and paperclips until she finally extracts a small pair of fingernail scissors.

"Mama…" says Nadia, sounding confused.

Ivah turns the doll upside down and jabs the point of the scissors into a small slot in the wood. She turns it like a screwdriver. The wooden plug comes free.

SEVENTY-ONE

So, baby doll is not so solid after all.

Ray glances over at Nadia and back again. He puts his hands on his hips. They both look like they're watching some kind of street-side magic trick.

Ivah sets the plug on the table, then uses the point of one scissor blade to dig out a small roll of paper. She sets down the doll and the scissors next to her on the couch and carefully unrolls the scrap to its full length. She grabs a pair of large, black readers from the table and puts them on. She doesn't need them. She doesn't have to read anything. She knows this thing by heart. But she pretends anyway.

"*Moy tsvetok. YA derzhu tebya v samoy glubine sebya. S.M. 10 yanvarya 1847.*"

Ivah looks up at Ray. "Is from Shashenka Meknikov to babushka," she says, beaming. "Was great artist."

Ray looks over at Nadia. She's got one hand loosely over her mouth. She looks at him in a kind of wonder.

"I'm guessing that ups the value a bit," says Ray.

"I had no idea," says Nadia, reaching for the paper. Ivah hands it to her. Ray watches Nadia mouth the words to herself in silence.

"That's so romantic," she whispers.

"Care to translate for the lazy monolinguists in the room?"

Nadia looks up at him briefly, as if remembering she is not alone, then back down at the paper between her fingers.

"My flower. I hold you in the deepest part of me. S.M. January 10, 1847."

Ivah holds out her hand. Nadia returns the script.

"Secret," says Ivah with a satisfied nod. "They are hiding. No one is knowing. Am happy is back safe."

"We would never have gotten the doll back without Officer Mackey's help, Mama," says Nadia.

Ray stoops a little.

"I'm so happy we could return it to you, Mrs. Novak. I'm sorry it was lost for so long."

She looks up from the old message, sizing Ray up.

"You are good boy," she says. "Like my Jovah. Like Alexi. Is good boy, too, Alexi."

Nadia and Ray trade a smile and a sideways glance as Ivah rolls up the message and then retrieves the tiny doll. There is a rattle. Ivah gives it a shake.

The thing that falls out through the hole in the bottom is a black plastic rectangle with a small, silver prong. It lands soundlessly on the couch, soaking in the attention.

Ivah looks at the thing like maybe she's never seen a flash drive before.

SEVENTY-TWO

"What is that?" asks Nadia.

Ivah picks it up and holds it up to her face, squinting. She hands it up to me before I can ask. So I ask her something different instead.

"You ever seen this before, Mrs. Novak?"

She shakes her head and shrugs.

"*Nyet.*" Then she turns to Nadia. "*Eto to, o chem vse eto?*"

Nadia ignores the question and stands close, leaning over my shoulder for a better look.

"Mrs. Novak, I'd like to ask you something. When was the last time you looked inside that doll?"

She looks up at me in confusion, the readers on her nose distorting her dark eyes.

"Am looking just now," she says, jutting the doll my direction. "You saw."

"Mama." Nadia bends to look Ivah in the eyes. "He wants to know about before today. *On khochet znat' o toy nochi, kogda byl ubit Dzhova.*"

Whatever she said, it's only good for another shoulder shrug and head shake.

"Long time," says Ivah. "Is long time."

"Mrs. Novak, I want you to think back over the time since your son died. Both when you were living at the old house and since you have moved into this place. Has anyone come around asking for this doll?"

Ivah looks down at the little doll in her hand, saying nothing. Nadia attempts a translation, but Ivah bats the sound away with the tips of her withered fingers. Then she looks up at me.

"*Nyet.*"

"What about before the night Jovah died. Did anyone show a special interest in the doll?"

"Jovah," she says.

"No, Mama," says Nadia. "He means before the night Jovah died."

"*Da.* Jovah. He is always liking doll. Always he is taking apart."

"You mean as a boy?" I ask.

"*Da.* As boy. As man."

"What about Alex? Alexi. Did he like the doll too?"

Ivah makes a face like I've asked her if Alexi ever picks his nose. She shakes her head.

"*Nyet.* Alexi never. Is good boy. *Nyet.*"

"What about your daughter?"

Ivah's eyes slot sideways to look at Nadia, but they are back on me in less than a second.

"*Nyet.*"

I take my leave with the flash drive in my pocket. I ask permission, but they both seem to know better than to object. All Ivah seems to care about is the doll and the note inside. Nadia thanks me twice, once in a way everyone can hear, and once with her eyes. We agree to meet up later to talk about whatever it is I learn.

I step off the elevator and can see Frank at the front desk. I watch him watching me get bigger as I make my way up the long hall. When I stop growing, I put my badge on the counter so he has something else to look at.

"I'd like to take a look at the visitor log for room 2113."

"That sounds like a search warrant kind of request," he says.

"Might be," I say, nodding. "Might be. Depends."

"On what?"

"On your blood alcohol level."

We look at each other for a few seconds. I wait patiently as Frank thinks things through. He finally looks down and pokes at his keyboard. He turns the monitor around and tilts it up so I can see it. I have to tell him to advance to the next screen four times. Then we go backward.

"Okay," I say. "Thanks for the help."

"Is this anything I should know about?" he asks, repositioning the monitor.

"That depends, Frank."

All of the computers in my life are in places I don't want to be. I settle for the Chandler *FedEx* on Donner and 68th Street. The place is hopping. Lines at both registers and most of the computers are in use. But there's an empty workstation in the corner with my name on it. I don't bother taking off my coat. I sit and swipe my credit card in the reader. Then I insert the flash drive and take a look at the directory. It doesn't take much looking because there's only one file: *roster.xls*.

I double click the file and a spreadsheet opens up to fill the screen. The spreadsheet consists of a single page with thirty-two numbered rows that begin with number 301 and end with number 332. The rows are divided into five columns. Left to right, the columns are labeled: NAME, ROUT, ACCT, DATE and PYMT. Under each numbered row are between one and three non-numbered rows in which there is no data except in the DATE and PYMT columns. Lots of numbers. Numbers everywhere. But it's the letters I care about most and all of those are in the first column. I don't recognize all the names, or even most of them. But the names I do recognize –number 303, 305, 307, 311 through 315, 317 and 325 –each take turns leaping off the screen and slapping me around.

I stare until all the numbers and letters start to look alike and then blur into indecipherable shapes. I hit the print button and close my eyes. The printer next to me starts to whir to life and I can hear the rubber rollers pull in a sheet of paper. I try to decide what all of this means. My brain is fresh out of opinions. But my stomach has a few.

SEVENTY-THREE

Cleopatra pours without speaking, sizing him up with the big, brown, translucent almonds she uses for eyes. Her sleek hair is tucked behind her ears. Glitzy pyramids dangle from her lobes. *Sonny's* is humming with the lunch crowd. Ray sits in silence, hands on the table, waiting.

"When's the funeral?" she asks.

"Whose?"

"Yours. You look worse than you did the last time I saw you and I didn't think that was possible."

"Thanks, Isis," he says. "I've always been an overachiever at looking awful. What's the special?"

"Why do you even ask, Mack? You want black coffee, which you now have, two eggs over-easy with bacon, and a buckwheat pancake on the side."

"Says you. What's the special?"

"Okay," she says. "I'll play. We're doing a huevos rancheros and the sandwich today is a Reuben."

"What?" Ray sits up a little straighter in the booth. "*Sonny's* does a Reuben? I didn't know that. I love Reubens."

"Great. Change is good, Mack. Be a brave boy." Isis sets down the carafe and pulls a pad out of her pocket. She starts feeling around for a pen. "So. One Reuben."

Ray takes a sip of the coffee then sets down the cup and smiles.

"No. I'll have two over-easy eggs with bacon, and a buckwheat pancake on the side."

Isis drops the pad back into her pocket and reclaims the coffee. "I'm shocked. Where's your friend?"

"What friend? I don't have any of those."

"Sure you do. The two of you came in together. He was the cute, normal one."

"Oh, you mean Raj Malik?"

"Yeah, him."

"You interested?"

"Maybe. Is he attached?"

"Oh, sure. Arms, legs, couple of feet. He's got all kinds of attachments. Any attachment in particular that you want me to ask him about?"

Ray gets the laugh from her he's after. I can tell he's going to tuck it away as a victory, a memory that he can stir into his drink later tonight. Knocking Isis off balance enough to make her laugh might be the only thing Ray actually accomplishes today.

"No," she says, pointing. "I don't want you asking him anything about anything. But if you wanted to recommend our specials…"

She doesn't finish. She doesn't have to. She leaves Ray with a smile that belongs up on a movie poster. It's a time-travel tear-jerker, this movie, starring a cast of impossibly attractive and energetic twenty-somethings who remind us that we can never go back. Not a movie recommended for guys Ray's age.

He pats down his pockets for a cigarette. He knows he can't smoke inside, but that doesn't stop the search. It's not about the smoking. It's about the thinking. It's about the puzzle in his head. The cigarette is just a torch in that darkness; it helps him see the shapes of the pieces. Even unlit.

The search produces a Percocet, which he takes with a swallow of water. He deputizes the thin, red stirring straw in his coffee as a stand-in cigarette and fishes the spreadsheet out of his shirt pocket, smoothing it against the table.

He stares. He chews the straw and stares. The Rockettes could come in for lunch, high kicking their way across *Sonny's Diner* and pouring free shots of Old Forester; Ray wouldn't twitch a single muscle except maybe those that are helping him mash that straw between his teeth. He's lost in the puzzle now. Nothing else matters. Not the ache in his head or the void in his stomach. Not the coffee going cold in its cup. Not the slow parade of people coming and going through front door of the diner, zipping and unzipping their coats, doffing and donning their gloves and hats. None of that reaches him. Ray is deep in the well now, pondering the collision of two universes that, only less than an hour ago, he believed had nothing to do with each other.

It takes Isis to finally break the spell. She sets the plate of food on the table. It's probably the aroma that makes him blink more than the clunk of ceramic against Formica.

"What's wrong with the coffee?" she asks.

"What?" Ray looks up. "Oh. Nothing. It's cold."

"Well, you have to actually drink it, Mack. See, that's the real important part about coffee."

"I'll try again," he says, already looking back at the spreadsheet. "I'll do better, Mom."

"Uh, uh," says Cleopatra, shaking her head and grabbing the cup. "Don't put that on me, Mack. I am *not* your mom."

Ray looks up at her, suddenly and directly. She thinks she finally has his full attention. Anyone would.

Not me. I know better. Ray can't even see her. In this moment, nothing about Isis exists except the sound of the words she has just spoken. Words that now he can't stop hearing. He takes the straw out of his mouth and blinks, looking at her as if for the first time.

"No," he says. "You aren't, are you."

SEVENTY-FOUR

I eat with one hand and scroll through the contact numbers in my phone with the other. My contact list is about as organized as a tickertape parade in a hurricane. For some reason Santiago's number is not under S's where it's supposed to be. It's one level up fraternizing with the R's. I take a drink of coffee and hit the button. He picks up on the first ring.

"Raffi. Mack."

"Hey, Mack."

"You alone?"

"Just me and my camera. What's doin', man?"

"We need to meet."

Silence. Then a sigh.

"Not a good idea, Mack. I know you're itching, but LT was pretty clear. I'm not..."

"No, no, no," I say. I laugh a little like the idea of me meeting up with him to talk about things he is not supposed to talk about is a ridiculous notion that I would never consider. "Not you and me, Raffi. You and me and Twill. I think we need to caucus. Something has come up. You guys need to be dialed in."

"Hold on." I can hear the burst of camera clicks in the background. "If Twill wants me to come in and meet, I'll be there. It's got to come from him. You're working the wrong end of the food chain, man."

"LT's my next call," I say. "I just wanted to give you a heads up."

"Sounds good."

"But, hey, as long as I have you on the phone..."

"There it is," says Santiago. Now he's the one laughing under his breath. "Mack, what is it you would like to know and that I cannot tell you?"

"Have your list of license plates handy?"

"What do you think?" he asks.

"White Toyota pickup. Illinois plate tango tango bravo seven lima nine."

I wait. There's a horn honk from his end. Then another. I can hear Santiago turn a page.

"Affirmative," he says, eventually. "White male. Orange laundry bag going in. Shirts on hangers in plastic on the return."

"Let me guess. About five-seven, brown wool beanie and a long brown coat. Looks like a turd with legs. Ugly as sin with a mouth that belongs on a whale shark."

"I don't know, Mack. You know how many photos I've taken in the past couple of days?"

"Come on, Raffi. How many big-mouth whale shark walking turds do you actually see in a week?"

"Okay, so maybe that rings a bell. You have a name?"

"Casey Randall Sweet. Used to be a Chicago PD grunt once upon a time. His girlfriend calls him Randy. Everyone we care about calls him Mouth."

"And who is it we care about again?"

"Big Man. And the Mayor of Chicago."

"Jesus, Mack."

"Yeah, him too."

SEVENTY-FIVE

Someone has been feeding my caseload. The stack of files in the corner of my cubicle is growing like a teenager. It's got the sullen, stooped posture of neglect. A week from now it'll be bumming cigarettes and wanting to use the car.

I lean back in my chair for another look across the office. Twill's door is still closed. Sticking my head in had been good for an unambiguous invitation to do the opposite. Whoever was on the other end of the phone had Twill's full attention and wasn't interested in sharing.

So I left, detouring past Sandra's desk on the way to my own, resisting the urge to rifle through all the drawers for clues about who she likes to call when no one is listening. Maybe she's keeping visitor hours in a Connecticut ICU and maybe not. Could be she never really left town. Maybe she's got a desk over at the IFOP where she types up her secret reports. Or worse; maybe the ninety-four-year-old mother with a tube in her nose actually looks a lot like a fat, middle-aged ex-con with a cigar in his mouth, hungry for details about what goes on in the Chandler PD. But I knew tossing Sandra's desk would probably get me fired for nothing. She's too careful. Too clean. So, I'd kept on walking.

Santiago shows up one and half seconds before two o-clock, just like I'd expect. He looks at me as he walks in. I point to Twill's office and shrug. Rafael nods. He unslings his camera and takes a seat at his own desk, picking up his phone.

I reconsider the slouching pile. I could tend to other work as I wait. The excessive force complaint. Or the race complaint. Those are just the files on the top of the stack. I could at least make a show of it.

But I don't. My head is a Tokyo subway car at rush hour. There's just no room.

I take off my coat and pull out the spreadsheet. This is the only thing my brain has room for now. This is enough. I flatten it out against the desk. My monitor glows to life. Random, floating dots coalesce into a pithy caption beneath a smiley face.

Happy Employees = Productive Employees.

Well, then. That explains it.

On the shelf above me, Marlo has her opinions. She's keeping them to herself, just like always. The same strands of her hair are still suspended in the same frozen, eternal gust. Her eyes, the same. Indulgent. Anticipating. Waiting for me to push the shutter button. That's the thing about asking someone to look at a camera. You immortalize an act of waiting. I can feel the impatience accumulating behind those eyes. She wants me to know what to do. And then she wants me to do it.

The list in front of me is upside down to her, but Marlo knows the bigger picture that I still can't see. Just like always.

I lean back in my chair again and look up at her, crossing my arms. The ache is deep in my chest, ageless, right where I left it. Marlo is perched as if on the far lip of a moonscape crater, putting me at ground zero. That's where I live, still marking the point of impact.

What am I missing? My eyes ask hers.

Everything, she replies.

Twill's door opens. I look over in time to see the last of him disappearing back into his office. Santiago and I glance at each other and stand.

I close the door behind me and take the chair next to Rafael who leans forward, elbows to knees, and unwraps a piece of gum. Twill is behind the desk, long legs crossed with his hands in his lap, fingers interlaced. I don't need a telegram; the posture says it all. He wants me to know that he doesn't have time for this conversation but that he has made time anyway. He has pulled the emergency brake on a train already behind schedule. Just for me. He has pulled Rafael in from the field. Just for me. Twill's eyes are calm, but laser-steady, burning a message into my forehead. *This had better be good.*

"Thanks for making the time," I say. It gets a nod from Raffi.

"What's this about, Ray?" asks Twill.

I don't really know how to answer that question, so I just start talking. I keep to the essentials, trying not to wear out the welcome I never really had in the first place. I begin with my first visit from Nadia King and her request that I find her mother's doll. I keep Jimmy out of the mix. I give them a refresher on Ivah and the whole Jovah Novak story. I explain how the information provided by DA Barbara Bannon led me to Casey Sweet.

"The guy called Mouth," says Raffi.

"Right."

"Mouth?" asks Twill.

"You should see the maw on this guy, LT."

Twill waves his hand, moving me along.

"Never mind," he says. "So he stole the doll for his girlfriend, and you got it back. Can I assume you have advised Chicago PD and that... that... *Mr. Mouth* has been processed?"

"No."

"No?" Twill closes his eyes for longer than a blink. "The man stole State's evidence, Ray. Don't you think..."

"It's bigger than that, LT. That's not a trigger we want to pull right now. I didn't know it at the time. I just wanted to return the doll to Ivah Novak without it being confiscated all over again. I planned to deal with Mouth later. But then things got weird."

Twill leans forward for a pen and makes a note on a nearby pad. He puts the pen down and crosses his arms again.

"Imagine my surprise," he says. "I'm listening."

"You remember what I told you about the girl in the photos with Scooter?"

Twill nods.

"What girl?" asks Raffi.

I look at Twill with the question in my eyes. He nods his assent.

"Let me back up and bring you up to speed," I say to Raffi.

I cover the old territory for Santiago's benefit, but I can tell that Twill is making good use of the refresher. I start with the money from Hell meant to grease my palm for Arty Dunn's benefit along with photos likely to send his accuser, Scooter Pleasants, back to state housing. The girl in yellow has got a name now. So I use it.

"Emily," says Twill. "How long have you had her name?"

"Scooter coughed it up. He thought I already had the girl in hand and that she was dropping his name left and right. That shocked Scooter because, according to him, Emily doesn't actually have the power of speech."

"She can't talk?"

"That's what the man said. But Scooter died thinking she could sing."

"Because you helped him think that," says Twill.

I nod.

"So should I add this to the growing list of things you've chosen not to tell me?"

I nod again. "Yes, sir."

Now Twill's nodding too, but the way he does it doesn't seem so agreeable.

"Continue."

I pick up the thread, explaining to Santiago about the broken poker chip that had turned Arty into a piece of chalk. I take them through the basics of the *Kings Flush Casino* case, including my theory of a money-laundering operation gone bad. By the time I get to the part about Rickens being the homicide lead and Arty Dunn as the *KFC* Assistant Security Director, I can tell Santiago's head is spinning.

"So, wait." Raffi's got his eyes closed, trying to assemble the pieces. "Hold on. These guys… Bratton and Pine… they put an end to Marciewicz. Extra vicious, just to send a message to anyone else who may be thinking about getting out of the business."

"Right."

"Arty Dunn is on the inside and helps make all of that happen."

"Right."

"Lets them in. Torches the surveillance server."

"Right."

"Then he makes sure Bratton and Pine go down for the murder by dropping evidence in the dumpster."

"Right again."

"Tony Rickens comes in swinging his badge and makes sure the evidence shows Bratton and Pine as just a couple of disgruntled employees. They both lawyer up for free and Mickey Shaw throws the fight, making sure they get the needle."

I nod. "You got it."

"But why? Why burn your own people?"

Raffi looks at Twill for the answer. Twill shrugs.

"You're asking the wrong guy," Twill says. Then he looks at me.

"Because if you're Big Man, people are fungible to you. There's an inexhaustible supply of Brattons and Pines. Once they do your dirty work, they become a risk not worth having. You're better off without them." I turn from Raffi to Twill. "I think he's trying to do the same with Arty Dunn."

It's new information for Twill and I can tell it gets his attention.

"What does that mean?" he asks. "You going to tell me you've found Arty?"

"No, nothing like that. Could be the guy who finds Arty will be some poor schmuck cleaning out the cement mixer."

"Then what are you saying?"

"I'm saying that Big Man is using the *Kings Flush* murder as leverage to make Arty hang himself on the witness stand in the Wrigley Menard trial. That's what the poker chip means: testify like we want you to, or else."

"Or else?" asks Raffi

"Take your pick. Or else we release the evidence that you helped Bratton and Pine play Marciewicz like a piñata. Or else you go up for murder. Or else we just skip all of that you end up like Marciewicz. Big Man knows how to make a credible threat. He got Hell to deliver the message to me because he knew I'd pass it along to Arty without even knowing what I was doing."

"Feeling used, are we?" Raffi asks it with a wry smile.

"Little bit. Yeah."

"Okay," Twill draws out the vowel sound, stretching the word over three full seconds. "And the plan is to make Arty hang himself at Wrigley's trial how, exactly?"

"That's the question. I've been thinking a lot about Scooter since he checked out."

"I'll bet," says Twill.

"Checked out dead?" asks Raffi.

"Oh," I say. "Yeah. Scooter's in the morgue."

"Since when?"

I look at my watch.

"Twelve, thirteen hours ago. Someone tried to twist his head off. I'm betting on Hell, but we'll see. Stretch Martin and the boys are digging in."

"Man, am I out of the loop."

"You've only got eyes for dry-cleaners, Raffi. We like that about you. Anyway, I've been thinking a lot about Scooter. He accused Arty of shaking him down. Cash for protection from whoever set fire to Scooter's palace of depravity."

"So?" asks Twill.

"I first opened that file thinking the odds were huge that Scooter was full of it. He had a beef with Arty and wanted to jam him up. But what if Scooter was telling the truth? What if Arty really was shaking him down? What if Arty set the fire or had it set? And what if Scooter wasn't the only one? What if that was Arty's thing?"

"I'm drowning in what-if's, Mack," says Twill. "Any evidence?"

"None."

"So you're wasting our time with rank speculation."

I can feel him slipping away, the press of other business scratching at the door to his attention like a dog that wants in from the cold. I lean forward in my seat.

"No, LT. I don't think so. Mickey Shaw is a man who knows where all the bodies are buried. That makes me care a lot about what questions he chooses to ask a guy like Arty Dunn. It took Mickey half a second to establish that Arty was the investigator on the first *Tap Root Kegs* fire, implying that the fire was arson despite the official findings. Mickey all but accused Arty of being involved. That's when Judge Jolie shut him down."

Twill frowns and scratches his head.

"You think Arty was shaking down Curtis Root from the beginning."

"The story Mickey is trying to sell the jury is that Arty was… let's say *involved*… Arty was involved in convincing Curtis Root to invite the mob into his business. The upside for Root is that he goes from the edge of bankruptcy to a growing *TRK* empire without any intervening fires. All he has to do is agree to launder the dead presidents and never say no to his new overlords. He forgot that last part and it got him killed. Big Man sent out a pro to do the job and poor pot-dealing Wrigley Menard got snatched up as the patsy to take the fall."

"Okay, but come on, Mack," says Twill, almost irritated. "That's Mickey Shaw saying whatever he needs to say to get his client off."

"Sure. But if the truth can get that done, then so much the better. I think Mickey knows that Arty has been carrying water for Big Man ever since Marciewicz hit the floor. Arty's next step on the ladder of success was to leave the casino for the police academy. Then, as if by some miracle of coincidence, he ends up working for Chicago PD under Tony Rickens. I'm guessing Rickens taught Arty everything he knew about small business development."

I take a breath and assess my audience. No one is interrupting. I dive back in.

"So, follow me on this. Arty's a good soldier for years. He helps Big Man pull in Curtis Root, which turns out to be a real feather in his cap when the *TRK* business really catches fire. Not *fire*-fire; *money*-fire. Arty gets a lot of Big Man atta-boys for that one. Arty gets confident. He thinks he's a rising star. By the time he transfers to Chandler PD, he starts thinking about having his own little racket. Why not? What's it to Big Man if he dabbles as long as he keeps it small?"

"Scooter," says Santiago.

"Yeah. Scooter. But I'm guessing the Scooter shakedown was the last straw. I'll bet there were other protection-racket notches in Arty's belt before Scooter. Big Man decided he wasn't interested in the budding competition. Big Man takes a long look at Arty and sees someone he can't trust and who knows way too much for his own good. Maybe Tony Rickens had always played Arty's protector. Then Arty transfers over here to Chandler. And then Suri turns Rickens into Swiss cheese at the landfill..."

"So Arty's suddenly on his own," says Raffi.

"Right. Then Scooter starts shouting from the mountaintops about Arty doing things he shouldn't. Big Man decides enough is enough."

Twill makes a face.

"Says you. There's no evidence of any of this, Mack. You're saying Arty is dead?"

"Could be. No one seems to know where he is. Or maybe he's off someplace getting coached on his testimony."

Twill is still resisting.

"This is the part I understand the least, and that's saying something. Just what, exactly, do you think they want him to say at this trial?"

"You want me to guess?"

"Have you done anything else since you sat down?"

"My guess is that Mickey puts Arty in the chair and, for starters, gets him to admit that he perjured himself."

"How?"

"So far, Arty has been the perfect prosecution witness. He follows Jackie Cavelle around the courtroom like a puppy. Predictable stuff. Curtis Root was concerned about someone casing his place. Root calls Arty out to look around because over the years Arty had been Root's go-to cop on security-related concerns. Arty testifies to a spate of break-ins in Root's neighborhood. Right? It all generally supports the idea that Wrigley is a punk who broke into Root's house on a treasure hunt and started shooting when Root came home and surprised him. With me?"

Twill nods.

"Mickey knows that's all bullshit because," I put my finger in the air, "because Mickey gets the inside scoop from Big Man. Mickey knows the real score. Mickey knows that Curtis Root was up to his eyeballs in mob money and that Arty Dunn, for years, helped make all of that happen."

"You want me to believe that… wait…" Twill closes his eyes and pinches his temples like he's fighting an ice cream headache. "You want me to believe that Mickey Shaw… is being paid by the mob… to represent an innocent man… and that his legal strategy is to use Detective Arty Dunn… to establish that the mob… the source of his legal fees… is responsible for Curtis Root's murder."

I open my mouth, but Twill isn't done.

"And… as Mickey Shaw exonerates his client… Arty Dunn essentially indicts himself on the public record as being a dirty cop."

Twill and I look at each other.

"Well, the way you say it makes it sound crazy."

"It *is* crazy, Mack. Why does Arty do such a thing?"

"Maybe because it beats a lead pipe to the skull. Or maybe Arty decides he can't do such a thing. Maybe he decided he doesn't like his options and so he just disappears in the middle of the night before Mickey gets another crack at him."

"Come on," scoffs Twill.

"Then where is he?"

"I don't know where he is, Mack, but…"

"I think Mickey was loaded for bear, LT. His next questions were going to be all about Scooter's shakedown claims. Starts to look like maybe Arty is working for the wrong team. Then Mickey lets it slip that Scooter is recently and conveniently dead. Not good. From there I figure Mickey starts tossing out one incriminating connection after another. The idea that Root got himself killed by pulling out of the money laundering business is suddenly going to start to sound plausible. And Mickey knows how to tie Arty to that first *Tap Root Kegs* fire, the protection racket play that started it all."

"How?" asks Raffi.

"I have no earthly idea. But Mickey knows. And if they ever get him on the stand, Arty will know better than to deny those connections. Because any other way is going to hurt. Arty will be testifying for his life."

"Sounds like one of your books to me, Mack," says Twill.

"You've never read one of my books."

"There's a reason for that. What do Mickey and Big Man get out of this ridiculous… scheme?"

"Mickey gets a lot of money in fees. Wrigley Menard gets a big pile of reasonable doubt and a fuck you to the State of Illinois. Big Man gets to paint the Chandler PD as, once again, lousy with corruption. Trust me, he loves that little game. Everyone starts pointing fingers and no one has their eyes on the ball. More importantly, Big Man gets rid of Arty Dunn. Arty's testimony gets him an instant suspension. That leads to an investigation and then prosecution. Arty will have said enough under oath in open court to guarantee a reasonable threat of double digits in Stateville. Arty pleads it down to single digits and figures that will be the price he pays for freelancing under Big Man's nose. Maybe Big Man even promises to give him a job after he does his time. More likely, Big Man dramatically shortens Arty's stay with an accident out in the yard."

"Why not just put a bullet in Arty's head?" asks Santiago.

"Who's to say they haven't? He's missing. Maybe Arty bolted and Big Man knew he was never going to play ball. So he spends the bullet."

It's Twill's turn.

"But why does Big Man, if that is really who is involved here, why does he take the heat off of Wrigley Menard and put it back on himself?"

"Wrigley has already served his purpose. Jaclyn Cavelle has put all of her chips on the wrong bet. Wrigley is innocent. What does Big Man care if Wrigley goes free in a cloud of reasonable doubt?"

"Because then the focus is on Big Man for arranging Root's murder."

"Oh yeah? And who is Big Man, exactly? José Beggemon? Joe Boogieman? Come on, LT. That's nothing but a name. You can't put a name on trial. You can't put a ghost story on trial. They took care of Curtis Root because he had the gall to want out of the clean-presidents club. Just like Nathanial Marciewicz wanted out. Root had to go, no question. But why let a dead man on the carpet go to waste? Where you and I and Raffi see carnage, Big Man sees opportunity. He decides to frame Wrigley and use his murder trial to get rid of Arty Dunn."

"Lot of work for the price of a bullet, Mack," says Twill.

"Not for Big Man. Mickey's doing all the work. Big Man's enjoying himself. This is entertainment. Court TV. Worst thing that happens is that Wrigley goes down for a murder he never did. Best case is that Arty plays ball and essentially convicts himself on other felonies. Threat removed. Rickens, Marciewicz, Bratton, Pine and then, eventually, Arty Dunn, all gone. Big Man can finally close the books on the *Kings Flush Casino* liability. Meanwhile, the message to Big Man's rank and file is clear: no freelancing."

I keep my mouth shut for a few seconds. They both look a little punch drunk, trying to think things through. Raffi chews his gum at the floor. Twill keeps his eyes on the ceiling. The silence allows me to feel my own head starting to hurt. That last Percocet is burning a hole in my pocket. Santiago looks sideways.

"You said Judge Jolie was shutting Mickey down. Like she's not going to let in testimony about Scooter's complaint against Arty."

"Sure looked that way," I say. "But she hasn't ruled definitively yet. Mickey won't give up. My information is that it was all about to go Mickey's way."

Twill puts a question to the fluorescent lighting.

"What information?"

"Glad you asked."

Twill lets the ceiling go and looks at me.

"I'm not sure I am, Mack. Horoscope? Fortune cookie?"

"Close," I say. I give the boss a sideways smile. "Russian doll."

SEVENTY-SIX

Ray loves a good story. Especially when he's the one telling it. Most days he'll go around the block a dozen times to avoid human attention. But every so often he can't get enough. He's milking this one for all its worth. He's saved the best for the end. That's no accident. He lets the confusion build. Twill and Santiago glance at each other.

"What are you saying, Mack?" asks Twill.

"Those guys that got me out of bed two nights ago?"

"Yeah?"

"They weren't looking for money. They wanted the doll."

Twill clenches his jaw. Ray watches in silence. He knows better than to keep talking.

"That's not what you told me, Officer Mackey."

"No, sir."

"You lied to me. Again."

"Yes sir. I didn't think it had anything to do with anything. Except maybe my own brother-in-law."

"Your brother-in-law."

"Yes, sir. Long story. Point is, I didn't think there was any need to put any of that on your plate."

Twill stretches his torso over the desk toward Ray. Santiago leans back in his chair to let them have their moment. Ray wants to swallow. He doesn't.

"For future reference? Officer? If I ask you a question? Then the truth, all of it, belongs on my plate. Do you understand me?"

"Yes, sir. For future reference. Got it. Does that mean I have a future?"

"I wouldn't count on it." Twill slowly resumes his seat. "What makes you think they were looking for the doll?"

"My only clue was that they threatened to cut off my legs unless I told them where it was. They brought along a chainsaw to help them look under my couch."

"And did you help them find what they were looking for?"

"No."

"I see you're still walking around with both legs."

"They said they'd be back. I spent the night at *The Bakersfield*. Well. For a few hours anyway. Then you called about Scooter."

"And they weren't interested in anything other than the doll?"

"That was the only thing on their list. It made me want to go back to the beginning and start over. So I drove back out to see if Casey Sweet could shed some light on things. He was gone so I poked around in his trashcan. Guess what I find." He waits. They aren't in a guessing mood. "Some fish wrap from *Windy Wharf*."

Ray looks from Twill to Santiago and back again. I can tell he's expecting a reaction. He wants their eyes to light up and their jaws to unhinge.

"Sorry, man," says Raffi. "You lost me."

"My last conversation with Scooter turned up a connection with a dope-slinging ex-con named Billy Wise. He works for a fish monger out in Aurora. *Windy Wharf Seafoods*. According to Scooter, he and Billy met up for a drink with Hell. Hell set Scooter up with the girl in yellow."

"Emily," says Twill.

"Right. Emily. So, I'm all set to make the drive out to Aurora to have a chat with Billy Wise to see if he can point the way to Hell. I figure if I can find Hell, maybe I can find Emily. But as I'm sitting in my car outside Scooter's place, someone puts a couple of bullets through my back windshield and another in the trunk for good measure."

"Christ," says Twill, shaking his head.

"Yeah, well he's never there when I need him," says Ray.

"You're sittin' here telling the story," says Santiago. "So maybe he *is* there when you need him."

"Okay, maybe he is. Let's put a pin in that until the next time I almost die. I did a quick canvas across the street. No one saw anything, of course."

"And you didn't report it, did you?" asks Twill.

"No, sir."

"No. Of course you didn't. Because that was the one thing that was absolutely required of you as a police officer. Report the shots fired. It's going to take divine intervention, Mack, to save your job. It's going to take a miracle of grace. My day is on hold, here. Get to the goddamned point."

"Getting shot at made me think about my friends with the chainsaw. Could be a coincidence to have two attempts on my life in less than twelve hours, but I'm guessing they're connected. If I'm right, that means my broken windshield and my two-legged couch have something in common."

"The doll," says Raffi.

"Right. The doll. So I figured Billy Wise could wait for later and I headed out to shake the truth out of Casey Sweet. But, like I said, Mouth wasn't home. I went dumpster diving and found the fish wrapper from *Windy Wharf*. And that's not a coincidence either, LT. Who drives all the way out to Aurora for a walleye? I'll bet there are five dozen places between Casey's house and *The Windy Wharf* where a big-mouthed man can buy a big-mouthed fish."

Santiago looks at Twill and makes a face that goes nicely with a nod. Twill stays noncommittal.

"And?"

"And so I head out to Aurora. *Windy Wharf* is fishy. It doesn't smell right. Getting an audience with Billy Wise is like asking to see the president. I have to rattle everyone's cage. When I finally get to talk to the guy, several things are clear. One, Billy's still in the game. This is not an ex-con who has seen the light. I'd bet my couch and my back windshield he's still in the dope business. Two, he knows… knew… Scooter. And he knows Hell, just like Scooter said. Three, he's taken his turn with Emily, which goes a long way toward validating everything Scooter told me. Four, he knows Casey Randall Sweet, and not as a customer of *Windy Wharf Seafoods*. There's some bad blood there."

"Okay. So what does it mean?" asks Twill.

"What does it mean?" Ray looks from Twill to Santiago, who shrugs. "Come on, guys. I'm the one with a concussion, here. It means the people who stole Ivah Novak's doll and who keep trying to kill me to get it back are connected with the people who are looking to put Arty Dunn in the hot seat. The people who probably killed Scooter. And Nathaniel Marciewicz."

Twill lets out a long sigh through his nose. Raffi looks at his hands.

"Brother this is a tough room. These cases are all connected, guys. Look. Hell is in the courtroom on day one of Wrigley's murder trial. Day one. Hell is the one who gives me the *Kings Flush Casino* poker chip to put the fear of God into Arty. Right there —that right there —is a straight line back to Marciewicz. Hell is the one who hooks Scooter up with Emily and her yellow coat and then takes a few pictures to preserve the moment for my investigation into Arty. Hell is connected to Billy Wise; Billy, who works at *Windy Wharf* out in Aurora, lousy with Russians, by the way, judging from the chatter in the warehouse. This is the same Billy Wise, who has some kind of beef with Casey Sweet, the guy with a great big mouth who just happened to steal Ivah Novak's little Russian doll out of the Chicago PD evidence room. And not for nothing, but Casey-the-Mouth is now on Raffi's list of people using the mayor's dry cleaners."

Twill's expression sours. He looks at Santiago. Raffi nods. Twill's eyes come back to Ray.

"You know that because…"

"Because I called Raffi and asked him."

"Like you were specifically instructed not to do."

"I was inviting him to this meeting. The question slipped out. Look, LT. Lock me up later. Make it hurt if you want. We need to get to the bottom of all of this. There is something big going on here. These cases are all whispering to each other. Mickey Shaw keeps turning up like a bad penny. Here's one that will throw you for a loop. Guess who represented Wayne Bishop in the trial for the murder of Joe Novak? Don't guess. I'll tell you. It was Mickey Shaw. That makes him three for three in this little drama. You remember Wayne Bishop. He's the short, extra hairy troll who blew a hole in the back of Joe Novak's head before making off with, among other things, Ivah Novak's Russian doll."

Silence. Ray lets the room breathe. Then he lowers his voice a little.

"Wayne Bishop was a lot of years ago. *Kings Flush* is three times as old. Whatever this is, LT? It's got a hell of a long shadow. Bishop was murdered in prison. Bratton and Pine got the needle. Scooter got his head unscrewed. Arty may already be dead and, even if not, I'm still guessing he'll never need to buy another calendar. It's all connected, LT. I don't know quite why or how yet. But I can feel it. All of these people are connected."

Twill smiles. Not in a good way.

"You don't mean that these people are all connected. Do you, Mack? You mean they are the *same* people. The same… *person*, I should say. Big Man. Everything comes back to Big Man with you, doesn't it?"

Ray looks down at his lap. It's his turn to sigh. Twill keeps at it.

"People call you crazy, Ray. And I push back against that. Always. Every goddamned time. People think I'm crazy for not understanding that you're crazy. But I push back anyway. I'm six inches taller than I was when I met you because I keep sticking my neck out. You know that."

"I do, LT. I do know that."

"I don't think you're crazy. Detective Santiago here doesn't think you're crazy. But even you must understand that… *this?*" Twill gestures to the top of his desk as if all of Ray's theories have landed there in a pile. "This sounds like you're obsessive. This makes you into one of those guys who sees the devil in the wallpaper. This sounds crazy."

Ray nods and rubs his eyes.

"I'd have to be crazy, LT, not to know that this sounds crazy. Why do you think I don't tell you everything until I can tie it together?"

"You haven't tied anything together, Mack."

"I have. Some of it. I have."

"You haven't. You've given us a lot of string. I'm swimming in string here. But there are no hard knots in any of it. I don't know what's going on. Not by a long shot. But I'm a long way from a grand conspiracy under the direction of José Beggemon." Twill sits up straighter in his chair. "Now, interesting as this has been…"

Ray doesn't give him the chance. He pulls out the folded spreadsheet from his pocket and drops it on the desk. Twill looks at it wearily, clearing his throat.

"And now what's this?"

"Evidence of a grand conspiracy under the direction of José Beggemon."

SEVENTY-SEVEN

I watch him read.

"Where did you get this?" Twill asks without looking up.

"I printed it from a flash drive that fell out of the ass of a Russian doll."

Now Twill is looking at me. Raffi too.

"What?"

"It was inside Ivah's Russian doll."

Twill looks back down at the paper. I let him read. He looks up and hands it slowly across the desk to Santiago.

"I know what that looks like to me," says Twill pointing. "What does it look like to you?"

"It looks to me like one page from a register of payouts to people on Big Man's payroll. Names, routing numbers, account numbers, dates and amounts. It's Big Man. Has to be. Look at those names."

Santiago starts reading out loud.

"Number 305. Q. Young." He looks up at Twill. "Is that Quentin?"

Twill nods. I can tell that name still hurts him. Quentin the good cop. Quentin, the man Twill had claimed he would have trusted with his own life. That's why Twill had assigned Quentin to follow Suri and Carl to Bloomington and keep an eye on them. But Quentin Young had done that and a whole lot more. Quentin had made a phone call so that Big Man would know exactly where to send someone to snuff Suri out. Quentin had started the bloodbath in Bloomington and then he had drowned in it. Everyone had died except Suri. The whole affair had shaken Twill's trust in his own judgment and invigorated his shame. That kind of blood doesn't wash off easily. This kind of pain never goes away.

Santiago keeps reading. He picks out all the same names I had.

"B. Smith, that's Smitty. Rickens. And D. Porter, that's got to be Deno. Pete Phelps. J. Novak. Is that Joe Novak?"

Raffi looks up at me. I nod and he dives back in.

"Ronni Lodge. Arty Dunn. Holy shit."

Holy shit is not a name. It's a stand-in. It means Raffi's gotten to the names that are so big they won't make it out of his throat. But *holy shit* doesn't do those names justice, so I finish for him.

"C. Jolie, aka, the Honorable Judge Camilla Esperanza Jolie. And S. Royce, aka, the Honorable Mayor Samuel Trenton Royce."

Everybody is quiet. Twill's phone rings.

"I'm busy," he snaps. "I don't care. I'll deal with it later. What part of I'm busy…"

He hangs up the phone and looks at me as he extends an open hand to Santiago. Raffi hands him the paper. Twill reads it again. Behind those eyes Twill's brain is clawing back through everything I have been saying. He looks up at me because none of it is enough. He needs more.

"I'm listening," he says.

"Most of these names I don't know. We should run them all and see what comes up. Of the names I do know, most of them are dead, in prison, or awaiting trial and unquestionably Big Man associates. Smitty, Rickens, Deno, Pete, Ronni Lodge. Quentin Young. That right there is a who's-who guide to police corruption."

"I note that Andy Marx is not on the list," says Twill. "Neither are you."

"Because Harpo never took a dime from Big Man and neither did I."

"And Joe Novak did?" asks Raffi. "And the judge? The Mayor of Chicago?"

I give him a shrug. "Well, they're sure keeping some awfully rough company on that list."

"It came out of Ivah Novak's doll?" asks Twill.

"Yeah." I dig around in my pocket for the flash drive and hand it to him. "On this. It's the only file. We should have the geeks in Computer Crimes crawl through the metadata. Maybe that'll show something."

"What'd Ivah have to say?"

"Never seen it before. Far as I can tell, Ivah doesn't own a computer and wouldn't know what to do with one if she did. I pressed her about who might have shown some interest in the doll. The only name she could give me was her son, Jovah. Joe. She said he liked it. He was always taking it apart."

Raffi wads up his gum into the wrapper and arcs it perfectly into the trashcan.

"What does Joe want with a file that incriminates him?" he asks. "Why not destroy it? Why keep it?"

"No idea. Interesting, though, that Joe's not around to ask."

Twill sets down the spreadsheet. He looks at me like he's trying to read my mind.

"You don't think Joe Novak interrupted a burglary," he says. "Do you? You think it was a hit."

"I didn't say that."

"No. You didn't. But I'm starting to understand how you think, Mack. It hurts my brain."

"Trust me, it's no picknick for me either."

"So?"

"So, think about it. Joe Novak super cop buys the farm when he walks into his mother's house and surprises an armed burglar? Where have we heard that before?"

"Curtis Root," says Raffi. "With Mickey Shaw working defense in both cases."

"Right. I'm thinking Joe Novak made the wrong people mad. Or nervous. He became a problem to be solved. Like Marciewicz. Like Root. I'm thinking Wayne Bishop was every bit the patsy back then that Wrigley Menard is now. Which means Big Man was protecting the triggerman that ended Jovah, just like he's protecting the triggerman that ended Curtis Root. Wayne Bishop was crazy. He ate up the attention with two spoons. But I'm betting he was innocent."

"They'll never open that one back up, Ray," says Twill. "The *Kings Flush* case either. They're too old. Don't ask. I can't die on that hill."

I show him my palms.

"I'm not asking, LT. I know better. I just want to understand the big picture here. I need to feel the edges of this thing."

"Mayor Royce," he says.

"Don't know. But I can't say I'm shocked to see his name on the list. We're all thinking it. I mean, aren't we? Why else is Raffi spending vacation time staking out the mayor's dry cleaners? Something's hinky there. I've felt bad about Royce ever since Suri told me she pulled his laundry ticket out of Tony Rickens' pocket." I tip my head sideways toward Santiago. "At the very least I think it means that Raffi here extends his vacation. We need to run all of those plates for names and see if they turn up on this spreadsheet."

"Judge Jolie," says Twill. "You're saying she's on the take?"

"I'm not saying anything. I don't need to. It's all those numbers that have things to say. Five payments to three accounts in the past, what, thirteen months? Sixty-something thousand dollars? Doesn't look good, LT."

"Judge Jolie's reputation does not suggest someone big on cutting criminals a break."

"No," I say. "That's true. But that only makes her perfect. Who better to turn than someone no one will ever suspect working on the other side? Maybe these are all down payments on something she has yet to deliver. Check my math but that first payment to Jolie came a few days after Curtis Root took the bullet. Right about the time they put Wrigley Menard in a onesie."

Twill lets out some air and scratches his head.

"Something tells me you have a theory," he says.

"A theory is a long way off," I say. "It's always the hunches that show up first."

"I honestly can't believe I'm saying this, but I'll take whatever you have."

I take a slow breath to gather my thoughts. I've softened the ground as much as I can. They're as receptive as they will ever be.

"Arty Dunn," I say, looking at each of them in turn. "I think it's all about Arty. Judge Jolie is supposed to let in evidence about Scooter's complaint. About Arty's history with Curtis Root. Maybe more. Arty's various protection rackets. All she has to do is make a few bad decisions on evidence admissibility. It'll look like Mickey Shaw's silver tongue got the better of her. Maybe the State appeals, but so what? The damage is done. The jury can't unhear what they've heard. Wrigley gets reasonable doubt and Arty starts the next chapter of his short life as an ex-cop and a criminal defendant. Jolie is, or was, supposed to help Arty hang himself on the record."

"And then Arty disappeared," says Raffi.

"Right. So maybe Big Man had to solve the Arty problem himself and he paid the judge for nothing. That makes her smart to get the money up front. Now the trial continues, and no one knows what might have been."

"I'd be worried about Big Man wanting a refund," says Santiago. I shake my head.

"Not in a million years. Arty or no Arty, Big Man just bought himself a judge.

There is no going back. She's in his pocket now. That's forever, Raffi."

Twill frowns. His lips are tight and bloodless.

"This is hard to take in. Judge Jolie just doesn't strike me as the kind of person…"

"Yeah?" I ask him, too quickly. "Did Quentin Young strike you as the kind of person?"

It was a crappy thing to say. A finger jabbed into a bullet hole. But I can't take it back. Twill looks at me with a distant and angry sadness. The silence swells. Someone has to say something so it may as well be me.

"It was an easy mistake, LT. I'm not judging. I fell for Ronni Lodge. You fell for Quentin. We all fell for Smitty."

"I'm tired of listening to you talk, Mack," he says. "I need to think about this. I want…"

My phone rings, too loudly as usual. It gets everyone in the temple like a sonic icepick, jolting Twill's expression into an even deeper irritation. I apologize and dig around in my coat pocket. I take the call, saying as little as possible. I keep the words to five: *yes, got it, thank you.* Twill is talking again almost before I end the call.

"I want you to keep all of this to yourselves," he says. "This is so far above my pay grade I'm getting a nosebleed. I'll have to dial in the Chief."

"Yeah, but where does it go from there?" I ask. "Who can you trust, LT?"

"I've got a goddamned chain of command, Mack. What the hell do you want from me?"

"I want you to think about the consequences if someone…"

"Stop talking, Mack. Just stop. I've got a chain of command and I'm going to follow it. The Chief of fucking Police will have to decide how to move this forward. We're talking about the Mayor of Chicago here. That means Chicago PD will be all over this. We're talking about a judge of the Illinois court system. That means all of this is headed for the state Attorney General's office. We will never control this, so we are not going to try to control this. This goes up the chain. Am I clear?"

I show him my hands again. Santiago and I both nod.

"Raphael, your vacation just ended. Stay away from the mayor's dry-cleaner. Go to work on the plates you have and let me know if anything turns up."

"Roger that, boss," says Raffi.

"And you…" Twill points. "I want you at your goddamned desk doing the work the taxpayers are paying you to do. No more bullshit, Mack. Got that?"

"Yes, sir," I say with a crisp nod.

"First thing tomorrow morning, you and I are going upstairs together for an informal chat with Stretch Martin and Lieutenant Wexler so that you can explain to everyone why you should not be a suspect in the murder of Daniel Pleasants." My eyes want to roll, but I manage to keep them in place. "It took some talking, but I convinced Wexler to start with an informal, assistive chat rather than a suspect interrogation. They're not making any promises, but they agreed to an opportunity to learn what you know and then take it from there. Not an easy concession to get, given how much Homicide hates the air IAD breathes. I get to be in the room as a stand-in for your IFOP rep. So, I want you rested and ready to go first thing."

"I can't do that, LT," I say. I can't help but wince like you do before someone swings something stiff at your face.

"Would you rather be unemployed?" asks Twill.

"I'd rather be in the courtroom."

"Excuse me?"

I hold up my phone.

"That was Celeste. Judge Jolie's in-court clerk. Arty Dunn turned up with a pulse. He's set to testify. First thing."

SEVENTY-EIGHT

"Welcome back, Detective." Mickey's suit is a deep, gunmetal gray. His boots look freshly polished. The ponytail has a new luster. "I understand you have been ill. I'm sorry to hear. Maybe there's something in the air."

Arty Dunn clears his throat.

"I'm fine," he says, starting the day with an obvious lie.

Arty is anything but fine. The *something in the air* has left him looking pallid and drawn. His voice has lost its wink and smile, entering the room now without any swagger. All the fun has left his eyes which are red and skittish, like they'd rather retreat back into his face than look at anything out here. Whatever he's been doing, it hasn't involved sleeping or eating.

From up here in the rafters, I see no obvious signs of violence. But, then again, the only parts of himself that Arty Dunn is showing the rest of us are his face and his hands. That leaves a lot of secret real estate for cuts and bruises. The blazer and shirt are rumpled like they haven't seen the inside of a closet for weeks. The tie is twisted and askew, a noose without a branch.

Ray has planted himself directly behind *The Hawk*'s man on the beat. He straightens in his seat and leans forward a little so he can peer over Theodore Myerson's shoulder and get a look at the screen of his laptop. Theodore turns his head halfway Ray's direction and scowls, adjusting the computer in his lap and continuing to type sideways. Ray gives Teddy a pat on the shoulder and leans back against the bench.

"Good," says Mickey. "Glad to hear you have recovered. Detective Dunn, I'd like to pick up with where we left off. We were talking about how you had come to know the victim in this case, Curtis Root. Do you remember those questions?"

"Yes." Arty nods and mumbles to the front rail of the witness box. So much for answering every question directly to the jury.

"Sorry, Detective," says Mickey. "You're going to need to speak up so we can all hear you."

"Yes. I said yes."

"Good. And when I asked you if the only context in which you had ever encountered Curtis Root was as a police officer responding to his concerns as a business owner or as a property owner, you said yes. Do you remember that?"

"Yeah. Yes, I do."

"And is that the full and complete truth, Detective?"

"Yes. I think so."

"You think so. Well, maybe you can explain this for me."

Mickey bends to counsel table and opens a folder. He extracts several sheets of paper held together by a paperclip. He removes the paperclip and walks over to Jaclyn Cavelle, handing her one of the pages. He then crosses the room to Celeste, to whom he hands one of the pages. She, in turn, makes a mark and hands it up to Judge Jolie. Mickey turns for the witness box but doesn't make another step before Jaclyn is on her feet.

"Your Honor," she says. Judge Jolie nods without looking.

"Counsel, please approach."

The three of them huddle beneath the spray of static coming from the courtroom speakers. The jurors sit placidly for the most part. Number 10 leans toward Number 11 with a sideways whisper. Number 11 covers her mouth with both hands. She's either laughing or feeding herself oats.

Ray rotates into a slow pan of the people behind him. The courtroom is three-quarters full. He recognizes most of them from the first day. One of Jaclyn Cavelle's paralegals is leaning over the bar to place a folder in Jaclyn's chair. Next to her, Curtis Root's widow is poking away at her cellphone. I'm guessing live updates to the kids.

In front of Ray, Ted Myerson is still working the keys. Ray leans forward and whispers.

"So, Teddy, do you get credit for finding him or does the atta-boy go to someone else?"

Myerson stops typing and angles his screen down protectively. Then he returns the whisper.

"One, I don't have to tell you anything. Two, I had nothing to do with finding him and I know nothing about it. Three, would you like to comment on why your Chief of Police and the state Attorney General are meeting with the Chief Judge of the 12th Judicial Circuit?"

"What?"

"As we speak," whispers Myerson. "Top floor."

"So?" Ray tries to sell indifference with a shrug but comes up short. Look at Myerson. Those beady little eyes can see Ray's interest in this news as plainly as I can.

"So, what's that all about?" asks Ted.

"How should I know?"

"Come on now," Ted says, enjoying himself. "Thought you knew everything."

"You think the Attorney General clears his schedule with me? Or even the chief? Could be anything. Maybe they do this once a month. Paint each other's nails and braid their hair. What have you heard?"

Ted smiles.

"I've heard a free press is vital to the health of democracy."

Above them, the sonic spray of static stops. Theodore Myerson turns his back on Ray and faces front, taking the smile with him. Ray leans back slowly like nothing is wrong. But I can tell that nothing inside that cut and battered head is moving slowly, and that everything feels, suddenly, very wrong.

"The state renews its objection," says Jaclyn now back at her table. Ray blinks, attention forward.

"The State's objection is noted," says Judge Jolie. "Mr. Shaw?"

"Thank you, Judge," says Mickey. He hands the paper to Arty. "Detective, I am handing you what we will now identify as Defense Exhibit 15. Can you tell us what this is, sir?"

Arty looks but does not answer. Whatever it is doesn't do anything to put the spark of life in his eyes.

"Detective?" asks Mickey.

"This is… uh… this is a photograph."

"A photograph." Mickey musters an expression of extraordinary patience. "Yes, it is. It is a photograph. Can you describe to the jury what the photograph shows?"

"It's… it's a photo of me and Curtis Root on a bench."

"Where?"

"I don't know."

"You don't know? Would it be accurate to say that is a Ferris wheel in the background?"

"Uh…" Arty squints. "Yes."

"This photo was taken at the state fairgrounds, is that correct?"

Arty sighs and rubs his face with one hand. Then he nods.

"Yes."

"You seem younger in this photo, Detective. When was this photo taken?"

"I don't know."

"Wild guess."

"Maybe ten years ago, I guess."

"Do you remember going to the state fair with Curtis Root ten years ago?"

"No."

"But you did, didn't you? You at least met him there."

"Guess so," says Arty with a shrug.

"You guess so. Well, does this look like a police officer responding to a property concern?"

"I could have just bumped into him," says Arty.

"You were at the fair… Curtis Root was at the fair… and you see each other and sit together on a bench. Talk about the weather."

"Could be," says Arty.

"And who is the *other* gentleman on the bench? The one on the other side of Mr. Root?"

Arty squints again like he's trying to see. He's stalling. He looks like a guy peering over the edge of a cliff, trying to make out something on the ground below. Mickey gives him a push.

"Come on, Detective. You know who that is, don't you?"

"Yes," he says finally. "That's… that's Anthony Rickens."

"Okay. And who is Anthony Rickens?"

Jaclyn Cavelle is on her feet. "Your Honor, the state objects to this line of questioning as wholly…"

Judge Jolie is shaking her head.

"I've already ruled on your objection, counsel. Please be seated. The witness is instructed to answer the question."

Arty is looking up at the judge like she's the incarnation of St. Peter. The

Pearly Gate behind her is locked and she's swallowed the key. Arty looks back at Mickey, waiting patiently.

"He was a… Anthony Rickens was a police officer with the Chicago Police Department."

"So, was this photo taken back when you, too, were working for the Chicago Police Department? Before you transferred to Chandler?"

"Yes."

"You and Officer Rickens were colleagues. He was a homicide detective for Chicago PD, and you were working property crimes."

"Yes."

"And do you remember why, roughly ten years ago, you and Officer Rickens were at the state fair making a shoulder-to-shoulder Curtis-Root-sandwich on that bench?"

"Objection," says Jaclyn.

"Withdrawn. Do you remember why you and Officer Rickens were meeting with Curtis Root?"

"Tony… Officer Rickens… he had a… relationship with Mr. Root."

"What kind of relationship?"

"A protection relationship."

Mickey pivots to look at the jury, eyebrows raised.

"A protection relationship," he says. "Detective Rickens was providing some kind of protection to the victim, Curtis Root?"

"Yes. Kind of, I guess."

"Kind of you guess. Well, protection from whom, Detective? From what?"

Arty crosses and uncrosses his arms like he can't get comfortable.

"Curtis… Mr. Root was concerned for his businesses. He hired Officer Rickens to advise him."

Mickey clasps both hands behind his back. He strolls to his table slowly and then back again to the witness stand, letting the discomfort build.

"Mr. Root had hired Detective Rickens personally, you're saying?"

"I don't know."

"Well, was Officer Rickens providing Mr. Root this advice and protection in an official capacity? Was he acting on behalf of the Chicago Police Department?"

"No. It was… Tony… Anthony was freelancing."

"Was there some threat to the *TRK* business that required protecting against?"

"Mr. Root thought so, I think."

"What was the threat?"

"I don't know. You'd have to ask…"

He doesn't finish.

"Ask who, Detective? Who should I ask?"

"I don't know."

"So, is it safe to say that you are remembering now that you and Mr. Root did not just happen to bump into each other at the fair?"

"Tony… Detective Rickens wanted to meet up with him."

"About what?"

"I don't recall."

"About the protection arrangement you just mentioned?"

"Maybe. I don't recall."

"Detective, last time you were in this courtroom I asked you about that *TRK* fire in 2005. Remember that?"

"Objection," says Jaclyn Cavelle, her voice is hard and tense. Not a woman who is feeling even an ounce of control.

"Overruled," says the judge.

"You remember that?"

"Yes," says Arty.

"You told me… well, you told all of us in this room that the fire was not an arson, didn't you?"

"Yes," says Arty. "The report concluded it was not arson."

"But it was arson, wasn't it?"

Arty looks down at his hands, out of sight beneath the wall of the witness box. He looks like he wants to pry up the floorboards and start digging his way to Beijing.

"Might have been," he says. Mickey waits for more. There isn't any more.

"Did Tony Rickens set that fire?"

"Objection!"

"Overruled."

"I don't know who set it," says Arty.

"Did you set that fire, Detective, all those years ago? Did Tony Rickens ask you to?"

"Objection!"

"Overruled."

"No. I didn't… I didn't… I…"

"Let's be clear about something, Detective. You have lied to this court and this jury at least twice so far. Once…"

"Objection."

"Overruled."

"Once when you said that you had never had any encounter with the victim except as a police officer responding to property-related complaints, and then you lied again when you testified that the *TRK* fire was not arson. Why have you lied, sir?"

"I… didn't… I mean I don't… I don't know."

"And isn't it true, Detective, that the Chandler Police Department for which you work maintains a surveillance file on Mr. Root?"

"Objection," says Jacklyn with extra volume.

"Overruled," says Jolie. "Calm yourself, counsel. Please take your seat. The witness will answer."

Arty's face looks slack, eyes dazed and heavy in their sockets, a boxer who just wants it all to be over; just wanting to finally feel the canvas against his cheek.

"I… I wouldn't know," he says.

"Really? Is that true, Detective? You wouldn't know?"

Mickey heads back to the table and pulls another three pages from the file. He stands for a few seconds reading to himself. He rests a hand on the back of Wrigley's neck and gives it a reassuring squeeze. Wrigley looks up and Mickey gives him a wink. When he is done reading, Mickey drops a copy in front of Jaclyn Cavelle, hands another to Celeste, and then stands still, waiting patiently for the inevitable. Jacklyn does not disappoint. She stands, bracing herself against the table like she has some concern about the room capsizing.

"Your Honor," she says. "I… I've never seen this. This…"

"Because," Mickey interrupts, "the Chandler Police Department never produced it as it was required to do."

"Judge, this has not been authenticated. It's not…"

"I'm happy to do so, Judge," says Mickey.

Judge Jolie finishes reading, then nods.

"Proceed."

"Detective, I'm going to hand you a piece of paper and I need you to read it to yourself and just tell me whether this is a document you created on the date and time indicated in the top right-hand corner."

Arty takes the page uncertainly and reads. When he is done, he looks up.

"Yes," he says. "I did create this."

"Anything about this document suggest to you that it is not a true and accurate copy of the document you recall creating?"

"Uh… no. I guess not."

Mickey looks at Judge Jolie, the question on his face plain enough for everyone to read. Jolie looks down at Cavelle who stands again slowly as if to renew her objection and then, just as slowly, sits back down.

"The exhibit, D-7, is admitted," says the judge. "You may proceed, Mr. Shaw."

"Correct me if I am wrong, Detective, but this document would appear to me to be a summary, prepared by you, of your surveillance of Curtis Root on August 9 two years ago."

"Correct."

"Why were you surveilling Mr. Root?"

"I don't know."

"I find that hard to believe. Why were…"

"It was an assignment for the MINWIMI Task Force."

"I see. And am I correct, Detective Dunn, that by MINWIMI task force, you are referring to the regional, inter-jurisdictional law enforcement task force – Minnesota, Wisconsin, Illinois, Michigan and Indiana –that the citizens of those states all seem to hear about around election time?"

"Yes."

"And the focus of this interstate cooperative task force is to address regional organized crime issues, is that correct?"

"Yes."

"Are you or were you ever a member of that task force?"

"No."

"Okay. So why had the MINWIMI Task Force asked you to surveil Curtis Root on August 9?"

"I heard the task force was interested in the *TRK* businesses. I wanted to help."

"You followed Curtis Root around and provided the task force with a summary narrative of your surveillance because you wanted to help out."

"Yes."

"That makes it sound like it was your idea. Was it?"

Arty sighs.

"I guess. Yes."

"So then this was not actually a task force assignment then, was it?"

Arty falters.

"Not… not technically."

"Not technically. How about not at all? Isn't it true, Detective, that you were essentially auditioning to be included on the task force?"

"That's… yeah. I guess. Yes."

"So, then you have lied yet again."

"Objection," says Cavelle, keeping her seat.

"Overruled."

"I… no… I was just…"

"Maybe you should reread your own memo, Detective. According to you, the *TRK* businesses were running a money laundering operation for organized criminal interests. You thought that was your ticket onto the task force. Correct?"

Jaclyn objects, doing her best to sound disgusted. Judge Jolie isn't having it.

"Overruled. The witness will answer the question."

"I… I had a hunch, yeah."

"A hunch? Come on, Detective. You knew it was true because you were on the inside."

"No."

"No? Go back and look at that photo of you and Mr. Root and Detective Rickens at the state fair. You were in it up to your eyebrows, weren't you?"

That one gets Jaclyn back to her feet.

"Objection. Your Honor, this is completely unacceptable."

"Sustained. The witness will not answer." Jolie pivots to address the jury. "The jury will disregard that question. Mr. Shaw…"

"I'll withdraw the question, Your Honor. Detective, isn't it true that you wanted the task force to know that, in your opinion, the *TRK* business was running a money-laundering operation for one of the same kinds of criminal enterprises that the task force was assembled to defeat?"

"Yes."

"You followed Mr. Root to a suspicious meeting at a bar in downtown Chandler. You got a couple of photos. You wrote it all up in this memo and you sent it off to the task force expecting that you'd get an invitation to join. Isn't that correct, Detective?"

"That's not how the task force works. Each department independently assigns…"

"Helps to have an invitation, doesn't it detective?"

"I guess."

Mickey rattles the pages in his hand.

"And that's what this was all about. You were fishing for an invitation that you could take to your department."

Arty bends his head as if rereading the memo in his hands. Who knows if he's fooling the jury. He's not fooling me or Ray. Those eyes aren't reading anything. He doesn't answer.

"Let's make this easier, Detective. Will you read the second to last paragraph of the memo that is in your hand? Out loud, please."

"Objection, Your Honor."

"Overruled. The witness will read as requested."

Arty swallows.

"Followed Subject 1 to *Brubaker's* at 11250 Indiana Boulevard. At 9:33 PM Subject 2 entered the establishment wearing a blue Nike backpack. At 9:45 PM Subject 2 exited the establishment without the backpack and walked south along Indiana Boulevard. At 9:58, Subject 1 exited the establishment carrying a blue Nike backpack. Subject 1 returned to his vehicle. Subject 1 proceeded directly to the *TRK* restaurant located at 515 West Chatham. Subject 1 went inside the restaurant at 10:22 PM carrying a blue Nike backpack. Subject 1 returned to his vehicle at 10:36 PM without the backpack. Subject 1 drove directly to his home, arriving at 11:05 PM."

"Thank you, Detective. Who is the person you have identified in this memo as Subject 2? The person who showed up at *Brubaker's* with the blue Nike backpack?"

"Objection," says Jaclyn, the word like a bullet. "Permission to approach."

The conference is short and animated with the prosecutor having trouble controlling her arms. The words *investigation* and *Illinois* and *compromise* slip above the static. Judge Jolie jabs a finger down onto her desk, glowering angrily at Jaclyn and says something to make the prosecutor stare at the floor and seize her own hips. The judge spends the rest of the time speaking sternly to Mickey Shaw. Then she makes a flicking gesture with all ten fingers sending the lawyers back to their places. The static stops.

"Thank you, counsel," says the judge as if they had all been discussing lunch plans. "The objection is sustained, and the witness is instructed not to answer the last question. Please proceed, Mr. Shaw."

"Thank you, Your Honor," says Mickey with a nod, then readdresses his attention to Arty. "Detective Dunn. Take another look at the photograph I gave you. State's Exhibit 15. You and Detective Rickens had lots of meetings like this one, didn't you?"

"I don't know," says Arty. "I don't recall any."

"You don't recall any."

Mickey nods and turns his back, striding purposefully back to his table. He opens the file folder and extracts another sheaf of paper clipped together. He flips through the pages, one by one, first to last and then last to first, the room breathing around him. Then he turns.

"I'm going to ask that question again, Detective, and I want you to think about that oath you have already violated several times, and I want you to make sure you get this answer right. So here's that question again…"

"Objection. Asked and answered."

"Overruled."

"Isn't it true, Detective, that you had several," Mickey looks back to the pages in his hands and counts to himself, "at least nine additional meetings with Detective Rickens and Curtis Root?"

Arty closes his eyes. He looks like a man trying to remember the distant past. Or a man wishing himself into an alternate universe. Hard to tell. When his eyes open again, he looks like a man who knows the future.

"Yes sir," he says. "There were several."

"How many?"

"I don't know."

Mickey drops the pages in his hand back on the table. Wrigley picks up the packet and flips through the pages. All of them blank.

"More than ten?" asks Mickey.

"Yes."

"More than twenty?"

"I don't know."

"Why, Detective? Why these little get-togethers?"

"Tony… Detective Rickens… he collected payment in person."

"Payment in exchange for protection, I think you said. And advice."

"Yes."

"Protection from arson."

"I don't know."

"Violence."

"I don't know."

"And you were at these meetings, these protection payoffs, because you and Detective Rickens were working Curtis Root together, weren't you? You were a team."

"No, sir. I was just there."

"You set that fire, didn't you?"

"No, sir."

"You know who set it, don't you?"

"No, sir."

"Where is Detective Rickens now?"

"He died. Last year. He died."

Jaclyn is up again.

"Your Honor, I'd like to renew my objection."

"Noted and overruled," says the judge.

"Detective, is it true that Detective Rickens' body was found last year in a landfill out in Dekalb?"

"Yes."

"I believe that was reported at the time in the newspapers, correct?"

"Yes, sir."

"A homicide."

"Yes, sir."

"Do you know who killed Detective Rickens?"

"No, sir."

"Do you know if Detective Rickens had ties to organized crime?"

Arty doesn't open his mouth. He can see Jaclyn rising. Everyone can.

"Objection! Your Honor…"

"Sustained. That's far enough, Mr. Shaw. The question is stricken and the jury is instructed to ignore it."

"Thank you, Your Honor," says Mickey, as if she has complimented him on his cologne. "Detective, it is true, is it not, that you are the subject of an internal investigations complaint by a Mr. Daniel Pleasants?"

The judge's hand shoots out in Arty's direction like a piston.

"The witness will not answer that question. Counsel, I have already sustained the State's objection regarding this issue. You may not proceed."

"Your Honor, I ask for a little latitude. This line of questioning goes directly to the credibility of this witness. I think the court will see the relevance shortly."

"Mr. Shaw, you will refrain from making evidentiary arguments in open court. You will ask to approach the bench or keep it to yourself. Your request is denied. Now move on."

Mickey draws a deep breath, holds it, then lets it out with a nod.

"Detective, have you ever been accused by a member of the public of demanding money in exchange for protection?"

Jaclyn is up on her feet but does not need to speak.

"The jury will disregard that question," says Jolie. "Counsel, once more and the court will hold you in contempt. Move. On."

"Thank you, Your Honor. Detective, you have been absent and unaccounted for over the past two trial days, correct?"

"I was… yes, I was sick."

"So you said. Can you tell us where you were?"

"At home."

"Would you like to rethink that answer or should we mark that down as your third perjurious answer? Or is it your fourth? Or fifth?"

"Objection, argumentative."

"Overruled. The witness will answer."

"I was at a hotel."

"And were you staying at a hotel rather than your home because you did not want to be found?"

"Yes. I was sick. I… I…"

"Detective, where were you the day before yesterday between, say, Eleven P.M. and One A.M.?"

"Objection, Your Honor," says Jaclyn. Her face is concerned and confused. She does not seem to know why she is on her feet and objecting, only that it is necessary.

"Mr. Shaw?" asks the judge, also clearly confused.

"Your Honor, I'd like to know where the detective was during the approximate time that Daniel Pleasants was murdered."

SEVENTY-NINE

I crack the window again and exhale across the parking lot. I watch the people zigzag in the wind, kites of flesh and longing, whipped into a froth of frozen agony by forces too immense to comprehend. As if somewhere out beyond the heatless sun the gods have cracked a window and exhaled.

I keep thinking about Detective Jack McMannis. He's still stuck in a Chinatown parking lot of his own, hunched into the passenger seat of a dead man's Pontiac and staring into the glow of a dead man's camera. He'll be there until I can find time to write him out of his predicament and into something new. Something less comfortable and much closer to death.

Makes me wonder about the bigger picture. Whether we're all just a series of blips on somebody's screen, lives held in suspended resolution pending the completion of a sentence. Makes me wonder if I'm a character who, like Jack McMannis, is based on someone real. Whether my life is a close shadow to one actually lived, or merely distilled from something distilled. If there's an answer to that question, then it's at the bottom of a bottle I have yet to open. In the meantime, I miss the life that I think of as original and mine. I miss the warm weight of Phil on my chest. I miss the hum of my refrigerator. I miss the groan of the floorboards on the steps up to the bedroom. I miss not seeing my wife in all the places she used to be.

I finish up the Camel and climb out into the wind.

Three days. It feels like a year.

Twill is waiting for me in the lobby like a flagpole in a tie. As soon as he lays eyes on me, he checks his watch. I'm close enough to being on time. What's a minute or ten between friends?

"Just starting to worry," he says.

"Well don't do that, LT. Doesn't do anything but make you old faster."

"How'd Arty do in court?"

"That's a longer conversation than we have time for."

"Headline it for me."

"How's this: Detective with lots to worry about getting old faster. Here's another one: Newspaper curious about Attorney General meeting at courthouse."

Twill clenches his jaw and gives me a long blink.

"Could be anything," he says. "No story there."

"You would be right," I say. "Except that it's not just anything. It's something. And there is actually a story there. A really big one. *The Hawk* is one question away from a leak and you're one leak away from a nightmare. You know, shopping mall security never has these kinds of problems. I could put in a good word."

Maybe he's smiling on the inside, but that's unlikely.

"Keep it up," he says.

Twill turns and starts walking for the elevator. It takes him fifteen steps. I make it in thirty. He pushes the button and the door opens. We get the place to ourselves.

"You ready for this?" he asks as we start rising for the fifth floor.

"I didn't kill anyone," I say. "Not this week anyway. The sooner we do it, the sooner it's done."

"Can I ask you to not say things to piss people off?"

"Sure, LT. I can hold my breath for almost two full minutes."

"This is an accommodation. They could do this by the book. They're bending here, Mack."

"No," I say. "They're hunting. This gets them a meeting without a lawyer or an IFOP rep in the room. There's no charity here. They're lucky I don't just clam up. I'm the one taking all the risk."

"Second thoughts?"

"No thanks, I'm full."

The elevator glides to a stop and the doors open.

"I'm asking you to play nice, Mack," says Twill. "Cooperate."

I speak directly into his tie knot.

"And I hear you asking."

Stretch Martin and Lieutenant Wexler are leaning against opposite sides of the open door to one of two interrogation rooms in the homicide division. They're both busy tipping serious expressions into large mugs of coffee. I can tell they've already flipped the good cop, bad cop coin and that it came up heads for Bill Wexler. Good call if you ask me. Playing good cop is a stretch for either of these guys but it's a bigger stretch for Stretch. A little more meat on the bones and Wexler could pass for Wilfred Brimley having a bad day. He's already got the fat, white mustache and a couple of eyes looking for an opportunity to lecture. But he can find his way to friendly if he works at it.

Wexler straightens when we round the corner and puts something like a smile on his face.

"We were just starting to worry," he says, extending a hand.

"That's becoming a big club," I say.

Everybody shakes and Wexler offers coffee that Twill and I decline.

"We reserved a room," says Stretch, gesturing toward the gray metal table within. I start that way, but Twill clamps a hand on my shoulder.

"No." He shakes his head at Wexler. "We're not meeting in the box. This is an informal information-sharing."

Twill holds a steady gaze. Wexler looks at Stretch and shrugs. Stretch laughs to himself.

"Sure, LT," he says, not trying to hide the sarcasm. "Sure. Let's use the business center. Anything for Raymond Mackey."

Stretch turns and walks away up the hall. Half a dozen strides and he's around a corner.

"Off to a good start," I say. "Maybe just the three of us can meet here in the box and keep the door locked."

It's the best idea I've had all day, but neither of the LT's seem to agree.

The business center. It's a small, shabby conference room with a view of the parking garage that adjoins the *East Town Mall*. Beyond that, the *Wells Fargo* building sticks up into the sky like a middle finger. To the west, part of City Hall is visible if a guy cares to look for where Chandler stockpiles its cowardice and hypocrisy.

When I was working homicide, this is where we took suspects who did not yet know they were suspects. This is the room where we allowed them to think that they were invited to help us fill in some blanks. *We're just a bunch of clueless humps. Thanks for helping us out. We'll be in touch if we need something else.* That *something else* we ended up needing was usually a confession. The next meeting invariably took place down the hall in the box with a lawyer.

Stretch always called this room the business center because it was usually the better-dressed businesspeople who, having committed or aided and abetted some heinous crime, could receive an invitation to the police station and decide it was a good idea to try to bob and weave their way through a murder investigation. This room has seen a lot of stupidity.

The table is too small for the room, a poor substitute for something that belongs in an actual conference room. It's the shape of the last Percocet in my pocket, which is a poor substitute for the Old Forrester I can't have just yet. Stretch is already in the seat at the far end of the table writing on a legal pad. Twill and I take our seats as Wexler closes the door.

"We appreciate you coming in," says Wexler. "We're just wading into this thing, Mack, and maybe you can help point us in the right direction."

"Ground rules, first," says Twill. "He's here to provide assistance, not to be recorded or interrogated as a suspect."

"Let's just see how it goes," says Stretch, not looking up. Twill rotates and gives him the same look that always seems to get my attention.

"How it's going to go, Detective," says Twill, "is that we will stand up and leave."

"Everybody calm down," says Wexler. "I hear you, Orland. We have our deal and I'll stick to it. But I'm sure you both understand that we're not here to be lied to." Wexler pulls out a chair and sits. Then he looks at me from across the table, making his Brimley eyes big. "You lie to us at your own peril, Mack. Nothing about the informal nature of this meeting means we can't draw our own conclusions. Understand what I'm telling you?"

"I'm here to help," I say.

"Good," says Wexler. "Detective Martin?"

Stretch puts down his pen and crosses his arms.

"Daniel Pleasants," he says. "No thanks to you, Mack, we now know that he filed an IAD complaint with your office against Arty Dunn. So maybe that's motive. That puts Arty on our radar."

"What's Arty saying?" I ask.

Stretch gives me something like a laugh.

"Hell of a question from someone who made us work for that information. We haven't talked to him. He's tied up in that Wrigley Menard trial." Stretch gives me his best innocent look. "But I can promise you that when I do talk to Arty, I'll be sure to call you up right away and tell you everything I know just like you're part of the team. In the meantime, maybe you can tell me why I shouldn't throw your ass in jail for safe keeping."

"Because I'm not your guy, Stretch. Arty isn't either, by the way. But knock yourself out."

"I didn't say I thought he was our guy. I said the victim's IAD complaint gives Arty enough motive to warrant a look. Frankly, we've got nothing that puts Arty at the scene. But you? Jesus H, Mack. You're putting Arty to shame in the murder suspect department."

"Yeah? What do you have?"

"Well, let's see here. Fingerprints on the broken glass counter, for one. Then there are the two witnesses, both of whom saw you as aggressive and the victim as frightened. The fat, white guy says you were all lathered up about a girl in a yellow coat. The thin, black guy says he thought you were robbing the place. Display case all smashed up. He thought doorstop Dan looked like he was ready to shit himself. When the sun came up, we did a canvas across the street. No one knows anything because they were all closed at the time of death. But everyone sure remembers you, Mack. Said you were going door to door asking about gunshots."

Stretch makes a face and looks around the table from Wexler to Twill and back again.

"Gunshots," he continues. "Go figure. So, I go take a closer look at that parking lot. And what do you know? Safety glass all over the fucking place. Made me think right away about your plastic back windshield, Mack. You know, the same windshield you told me was broken by whoever gave you that facial. So, I come back and pull up the police report. Turns out that little bit of violence occurred at your home, twenty miles from the *Pleasants Palace* parking lot where I found all the glass. So I look for the report you are required to file when someone puts a bullet through your window outside a porn shop. But there is no report."

Stretch deals another round of astonished looks.

"Why wouldn't he file a report, I ask. Because he doesn't want anyone to know he had been there, shaking up the proprietor and smashing his dildo display case. Then I start to wonder why you would lie to the face of a homicide detective outside a crime scene. Why, I ask, would Ray Mackey lie to me? Does Ray Mackey have something to hide? And then I pull my head out of my ass and remember who I'm talking about. Of course you have something to hide. You're always hiding something. Aren't you, Mack? You can't help it. That's what you do."

We look at each other over the table, through a dark cloud of things still unsaid.

"Well," I say. "And here I am without my popcorn."

"What I can't figure, Mack, is which came first, the corruption or the crazy." Twill looks hard at Wexler.

"Bill, either you yank his chain or expect absolutely zero consideration the next time someone on your crew ends up with an IAD folder."

Wexler sighs and gives Stretch a look.

"Fine," says Stretch angrily. "Let's put a pin in just how it is you sleep at night."

"How can I help you, officer?" I ask.

"Why were you there, Mack?"

"Scooter filed a complaint against Arty. That ended up on my desk because God hates me."

"We want a copy of that file," says Wexler.

"The Chief has to sign the waiver," says Twill. "But I'll send it up."

"What's it about?" Stretch asks, still focused on me.

"Scooter said Arty was shaking him down for protection. Someone set fire to his palace of porn. No damage, but then suddenly there's Arty with his hand stuck out."

"You verified that?"

"No. I was just getting started. Could be true. Or could be Scooter had a plan to scorch his own place and file some kind of bullshit suit against the city. Anything is possible. One of them was shaking down the other, I just don't know which one is which."

"Okay," says Stretch. "So?"

"So I got a tip that Scooter was spending quality time with an underage girl. I paid him a visit to find out if it was true."

"Why? What does that have to do with anything on your desk?"

"Really?" I give him a disbelieving laugh. "How much time would you spend busting your hump over a complaint filed by someone who was actively defiling a child?"

"Okay," says Stretch, nodding. There's more coming after that but I cut him off.

"You don't think it makes sense for me to see if my complainant is feloniously engaged and needs to be processed into a cell?"

"Look…"

"You saying you wouldn't do the same?" I can feel the anger welling up in my chest. Twill is giving me the look. He can feel it too. "Just what exactly does *protect and serve* mean to you, Stretch?"

"Goddamnit, Mack." Stretch grimaces in frustration. "I said okay. Get off your horse. I get it. What's the girl's name?"

"Emily. I don't have a last name. She can't speak, according to Scooter."

"What do you mean? She a mute?"

"I guess."

"Who's the source on the first name?"

"Guy named Hell."

"Hell?"

"You heard me. H, E, double hockey sticks. About the size of the *Wells Fargo* building over there. Face like a block of iron. Don't ask me what his driver's license says or where he likes to sleep, because I don't know any of that. He gave me a photo of Scooter and the girl and didn't hang around for questions. I figured maybe Arty sent him to take some of the pressure off. I would have stopped him and taken him in for questioning, but I didn't have a tow truck and chains."

"And he tells you his name is Hell?" asks Wexler, screwing up his face.

"No. I got the name from Scooter. I showed up at the porn palace and started asking questions. Scooter tried to shine me on and things got testy. A small bird could have knocked over that rickety display case but the two of us saved the bird the trouble and did it together. If the fat guy in the corner thought I was too serious, that's only because I wanted to be taken seriously."

"And?"

"And the sound of glass did the trick. Loosened Scooter right up. He tells me about this guy named Hell who set him up with the girl. I got the *I-thought-she-was-nineteen* story, plus her first name and the man called Hell. Once he found out about the photo, Scooter felt like the girl was a set up from the start. Hell and maybe a friend of Scooter's from lock-up; a dope slinger named Billy Wise. Wise works at a fish place in Aurora called *The Windy Wharf*. I took a trip out there for a conversation. Billy didn't know anyone or anything, but he said it in a way that told me he knows everyone and everything."

"What'd you do?" asks Stretch.

"What could I do? I left him alone."

We all wait for Stretch to make some scribbles that include a couple of W's. He draws a line across the page and puts the pen back down.

"Okay," he says. "Windshield."

"When I'm done talking to Scooter, someone puts three nine-millimeter slugs in my car; with me in it. Yes, I'll send you the slugs. No, I did not see the shooter. No, I did not see a vehicle. I did a canvas, as you know, and came up empty."

"You didn't file a report?"

"I went about my day."

"Because?"

"Because? Take your pick. Because I had a concussion and the idea of paperwork made me want to be unconscious. Because I knew the investigation would be a pain in the ass and it would come to nothing. Because I figured the shots had nothing to do with Scooter and everything to do with me, personally. Because I knew the odds were spectacular that the boys who tuned me up at my house had taken their act on the road and were following me around."

Stretch and Wexler look at each other, sharing a moment of bafflement.

"And you don't want to get to the bottom of what that is all about?" Stretch asks.

"Sure I do."

"Then why keep it under wraps? Why lie to me about it when I asked you directly?"

"There's a long list of people that want to see me dead, Stretch. Half of them are cops. Maybe you're on that list. I'm the Baby Ruth in the swimming pool. Think I don't get that? If you're in my shoes, how eager would you be to keep the police informed about what you knew and what you didn't?" I tip my head sideways. "My LT is in the loop. Him I trust. You suddenly concerned about my well-being? I'm touched. You want to bust my balls for not filing a report? Be my guest. File a claim with IAD. We'll get right on that. In the meantime, maybe you can focus on figuring out who put an end to Scooter."

Stretch breathes at me through that massive horse nose for a few beats. Then he looks at Wexler, who passes the look along to Twill.

"Has he, Orland?" Wexler asks Twill.

"Has he what?"

"Kept you in the loop? About all of this?" Twill does not hesitate.

"Every step of the way."

I remember what Twill told me yesterday about feeling taller for sticking his neck out so many times. Now he's going to have to stoop to make it out of the room. I make a mental note to go quietly when he fires me. He's earned that.

"Where were you between eleven and two night before last?" asks Stretch.

"At *The Bakersfield* trying to get a good night sleep without getting my head kicked in."

"Witnesses?"

"Kid behind the desk. He'll remember me."

"Why?"

"Because I look like I look. Because I closed down the bar. And because I checked out three hours later. His face seemed to think that was odd."

"Why the hurry?"

"Because LT wanted me to come see you and find how Scooter ended things."

"Broken is how he ended things," says Stretch.

I spread my arms.

"Take a good look at me, Stretch."

"We've had this conversation," he says.

"Yes, we have."

"I take it you think we should be looking for Hell instead."

I drop my arms and lean in a little closer, locking eyes with my old partner.

"It's Hell you're looking for. You're going sooner or later, Stretch. May as well get started."

EIGHTY

Just the three of us in the elevator. Only those two get counted as non-imaginary.

A stranger would think them strangers, Ray and Lieutenant Twill. They don't say a word to each other as they drop two floors then walk the long hall to IAD. Ray follows Twill to his office and closes the door behind him.

"Thanks for that up there, LT," says Ray. "You didn't have to."

Twill slips out of his suit jacket and fits it over the back of his chair.

"You going down in a fireball of lies doesn't help me, Mack. You get that, right?"

"Yeah," says Ray. "I do."

"You go down, I go down."

"I get it," says Ray. "And I didn't lie."

"Yeah? How many times did you mention the Russian doll? Or that flash drive? Or Casey Sweet? Or Tony Rickens? Or *Kings Flush Casino*? Or…"

"I also didn't say anything about my prostate or my acid reflux. Yeah, so I made some judgment calls on the fly. I gave them what they needed to rule me out and advance their investigation. They've got a real suspect now. But I didn't lie. Everything I told them was true."

"You sure as hell took a lot of credit for keeping me informed. Jesus, Mack." Twill shakes his head to himself with something like disgust. "You're really something else, you know that?"

"I've tried to be something all my life, LT. I'm used to being something else. Tell me what's next."

The request gets Ray a rueful laugh and a gesture of exasperation.

"Hell if I know, Mack. You're already in this thing up to your ass and I know better than to think you're going to stop working the case… cases, even if I tell you to stand down. And yet I'm now officially dialed in and I can't have you wandering around in what is now a state corruption investigation. And I can't look the other way and then cover for you later. I can't do that. I won't do that."

"I'm not asking you to," says Ray. "Suspend me. Send me home to think about things."

Twill laughs again.

"Seriously, LT. Do yourself a favor. IAD can't turn a person of interest in a murder investigation out on the street with a badge. It's standard policy and Scooter's given you the perfect reason."

"Who needs Scooter?" Twill asks. "You've given me all the reason I need."

"See there? That's the spirit." Ray pulls out his badge. "Ask me for it, LT."

Twill looks at the badge. His hand comes off his hip to take it but then Twill's desk phone does what it does best. Twill takes the call standing, contributing a couple *yes sirs* and a *thank you* with a lot of silence in the middle. Near the end comes Ray's last name. *Mackey?* Twill speaks it as a question. No surprise there. The question of Raymond Mackey is one for the ages. It's stumped every boss he has ever had. The nuns had never been able to answer that question either. His parents had never tried. I've got an answer or two. I know a lot more about Ray than he does, but that's not saying much. He's as much a mystery to himself as he is to anyone else. There's Marlo, of course. She seemed to get the answer to Raymond Mackey in record time. But she checked out without passing it along.

Twill nods as he listens before he speaks his final *yes sir*. When he hangs up, Twill continues to stare at the phone like maybe the next bit is telepathic.

"That was either the Chief of Police or your father," says Ray.

"My father has been dead nine years."

"Have you seen the Chief lately? He's not looking so good either."

"The Attorney General has been fully apprised of the information you found in the doll. The Chief Judge of the 12th Judicial Circuit has been briefed insofar as it concerns Judge Jolie. A meeting with her is imminent if not already underway. Depending on how she responds, every effort will be made to conduct an investigation discretely, without disrupting her caseload."

"How does that make any sense if she's on the take?" asks Ray. Twill smiles.

"Any idea what kind of shit hits the fan when you bench a sitting trial judge pending a corruption inquiry? I don't make these decisions, Mack."

"What about the mayor?"

"A much bigger deal. Messier. Partisan. They're not reading me in on that one, and I don't want them to. They're going to chase their tails for a while before anybody does anything. Meantime the OAG is looking to subpoena financial records for a subset of the names on that spreadsheet."

"The safe ones, you mean. The people who are dead."

"Dead, in jail or headed for trial."

"But not the judge."

"I seriously doubt it. They might ask her to cooperate. She'll lawyer up and make them do everything the hard way. Then they'll feel better about going for a subpoena." Twill's eyes take over the conversation for a second. "And as for you…"

"Let me guess." Ray puts his badge away. "Chief doesn't like the optics of disciplining the guy once suspected of being a Big Man mole. Not right now. Two plus two equals another department corruption problem."

"Something like that," says Twill.

"Sure, I'm up to my ass but so are both of you for bringing me back on board. The Chief doesn't like the Scooter situation any more than you do, but he knows that even a non-disciplinary suspension is going to create some waves beneath a boatload of *I told you so's*. So, he wants to keep things quiet. Two investigations done on the QT. How long you think that's going to last? Meanwhile, you're supposed to keep me close. Within eyesight if possible."

Ray stops talking and waits. Twill stares down at his desk, hands on his hips. Then he looks up.

"He needs you to do your job, Mack. So do I. You're riding a desk until further notice."

I know what he's thinking.

Ray wants to tell him that riding a desk was all the job ever was in the first place. He wants to lecture Twill on the difference between working IAD files and working homicides. He keeps it to himself. Maybe he's getting smarter.

EIGHTY-ONE

Twill switches gears, pumping me for information about Arty Dunn's return to the spotlight. I give him the short version, just enough to make him wonder if Nostradamus is somewhere in my family tree.

"So let me get this straight," he says. "Arty essentially outs himself as in league with Tony Rickens to squeeze Curtis Root and the *TRK* business. He then owns up to surveilling Root and outing *TRK* as a money laundering operation, all in a bid to get a seat on the task force. Tell me you didn't know that was coming too."

"News to me."

"The guy with the Nike backpack?"

"I'm thinking it was Tony Rickens."

"Delivering dirty money for cleaning."

"Right. My guess is that Arty was double-crossing his mentor. Think about it. Imagine that Tony gets a pair of bracelets on his way to public housing and that opens up a new protection market for Arty. Maybe he sells himself to Big Man as the new Tony, with a coveted spot on the task force no less. Wouldn't surprise me if it was Big Man that put the whole play in motion."

"Sacrificing the *TRK* operation?" Twill asks.

"Come on. He finds another one. One drycleaner goes out of business, another one opens up. Big Man knows how to walk away, LT. Just look at *Kings Flush Casino*. Burn everything and everyone and walk away. Maybe it was worth trading *TRK* and Tony Rickens for a mole on the task force."

"Okay, but then something went wrong," says Twill. "Arty doesn't get the task force gig. Tony doesn't get nabbed. *TRK* keeps cleaning cash."

"Right. A big nothing-burger. But not because Arty didn't give it his all. So, he still thinks of himself as an up-and-comer. He's gotten Big Man's nod of approval. He starts getting bold. Starts shaking down lowlifes like Scooter, only when Arty does it he doesn't pay anything forward. It's all off the books. Big Man catches wind of that and decides Arty has to go. Just so happens that Curtis Root decides he wants off the bus at around the same time. So Big Man offs Curtis Root, sets up Wrigley Menard as a patsy for the murder and sends out Hell with a poker chip-reminder of Arty's past. Then he pays a fat retainer to Mickey Shaw to make it all happen, plus a little something-something to the judge, and he sits back to watch the fun."

"And now it's all but done," marvels Twill. "Root is dead, and Arty has cooked himself. That's… that's…" Ten minutes ago he wanted to fire me. Now he thinks I'm Sherlock and can't finish his sentences.

"Diabolical? I'd say so, yeah. Arty finished the morning as a serial perjurer with, let's call them likely ties to organized crime, suspicions of involvement in the *TRK* arson, investigation interference, extortion, money laundering, the works. He's done. Some locked-up Big Man soldier is already sharpening a shiv with Arty's name on it. Meantime, Arty's IAD file just got a whole lot more complicated. And we're not the only division coming for him. This will be a feeding frenzy. I'm surprised the Chief didn't say anything."

"He hinted," says Twill. "He's holding those cards pretty close for now." He shakes his head in something like amazement. "It played just like you predicted. And the judge let it all in?"

"She made it easy, LT. Arty is kaput and, not that Big Man cares two figs about Wrigley Menard, but Wrigley's now floating on a cloud of reasonable doubt."

"All bought and paid for. A god-damned judge. What's the world coming to?"

That last bit isn't for me. Those are words a man mutters to himself as his idelism starts choking for air. But I respond anyway.

"I'll tell you what the world's coming to, LT. The world is coming to Big Man on bended knee. Arty played his part out of fear. That much is clear. He just wants to keep breathing in and out. He tried to turn invisible, but that didn't work out so well. Whatever he's been through in the past forty-eight hours convinced him there was only one way to keep his heart beating. As for the judge, hard not to marry up her evidence rulings this morning with that spreadsheet."

"Guess we found that spreadsheet too late," he says.

"Why? Because we might have been able to save Arty's career? Keep him in the shadows a little longer? Or because now an innocent man is probably going to get off? Why isn't this justice, LT? Why aren't we a couple of ghouls for thinking it's not justice? Just because Big Man is pulling the strings?"

"You're forgetting that Curtis Root is dead," he says, "and whoever did it is still out walking around. You're forgetting we have a judge on the take."

"So it would seem," I say.

Twill squints, hands on his hips. He's twice as perceptive as I give him credit for.

"But?" he asks.

"I don't know. Probably nothing."

"But?"

"It's just… She still didn't let anything in about Scooter. Mickey kept trying and she kept slamming the door. In the end Mickey had to kick that door open and dump Scooter's body on the record all by himself. Jolie excused the jury, held him in contempt and fined him a thousand dollars on the spot. She all but invited Jackie Cavelle to move for a mistrial."

Twill shrugs. He needs more so I give it to him.

"Well, if you're getting paid to help Arty Dunn hang himself, then why not let the jury hear that Scooter was murdered after accusing Arty of extortion? She let Mickey run the ball to the five-yard line and then tried to shut him down. Doesn't make sense."

Twill frowns.

"Maybe she was putting up a show of restraint," he says. "Something to blunt any criticism. The job on Arty was essentially done so she pulls back."

"Maybe. Still seems a little off to me." My head hurts trying to hold everything together so that it makes some kinds of sense. It all wants to come undone. "And the money seems…"

"What."

"I don't know. Jolie has to be making something north of a hundred thousand tax dollars a year. Why risk everything for the number on that spreadsheet?"

"Because maybe she's in debt. Or because maybe that's just the tip of the iceberg. That spreadsheet page was just one of hundreds we haven't seen, Mack." Somehow, when I wasn't paying attention, Twill tore up his skeptic card and became a true believer in judicial corruption. Now he's the one working overtime to keep me on board. "Hell, what if that number was a *monthly* figure?"

I don't answer that one. I keep at it like he's not here.

"And another thing... if you go through the trouble of setting up Wrigley Menard as a patsy to keep your real triggerman out of trouble, don't you want Wrigley actually convicted for the crime? But how do you go about hanging Arty for being a secret gangster without at the same time suggesting that Curtis Root was killed by the mob and not by some two-bit pot dealer? Getting Arty means losing the patsy and risking that the real shooter will eventually get picked up."

Now I'm the one mumbling to himself. Twill is silent. We play the staring game for a few seconds.

"What are you saying, Mack?"

"I'm saying maybe I don't know anything anymore, LT."

My head has gone soft. Nothing that a stiff drink in a dark room won't cure, but Twill is low on sympathy. He gets irritated all over again and sends me to my florescent-lit cubicle instead. He tells me that spending an afternoon on other work is the answer. Could be, but if so then I never really understood the question.

I sit at my desk and stare at the stack of files propped up against the wall of the cubicle. Inside each of those folders is a separate nest of alleged malfeasance by a member of the Chandler Police Force, most of it internal, petty and likely rooted in some kind of misunderstanding. The files that involve allegations of criminal misconduct –the IAD blue files –are fewer and all bunched near the top, enjoying the lofty view that comes with their priority over the others.

I try to imagine lifting my hand, pulling a file off the top, opening it up. I don't come close. Instead, I conjure little Danika King telling me in all seriousness that she prefers to keep all her dragons in a castle rather than at home.

Thinking of her makes me wonder when it is that we stop living in the world that we imagine for ourselves. Makes me wonder what, or who, manages to convince us that's a good idea. José Beggamon, maybe. Why not? He's everywhere else, why not in our pre-adolescent imagination, letting the air out of our wonderment? Whispering the end of every story we have yet to read. Explaining every magic trick we have yet to see. Clipping the wings of dragons. Why not? Let's put that on Big Man too. Slitting the throats of Santa and the Tooth Fairy. It's all José Beggamon. Joe Boogieman.

Across the office, Raffi is working his phone and his computer at the same time. His elbow holds open a file that wants to close. Here's a guy who can walk and chew gum. I remember him hanging upside-down from that boxcar in the rain, one hand gripping the slick, red rail at the top of the open door while the other sent two bullets into Smitty's chest. That was after Raffi had dropped both Deno and Pete in the split-second before Deno twitched his trigger finger to put a bullet in my brain.

So, thanks to Raffi, my brain is still with me, poisoning my lungs and my liver with addiction, fracturing my consciousness, and torturing my heart by playing endless memory loops of my wife. I'm still here. And I have a hard time believing that's because the god in which I don't believe wants me pushing paper around this little cubicle. What was all of that for? Why am I still here if not to keep Big Man from getting bigger one cop, politician and judge at a time?

Marlo bores through me from the shelf above. I am the darkened tunnel to her train, her eyes seeing in me everything I cannot.

What's it all about? I think up to her. *You could solve this riddle in half a drink.*

She doesn't answer. The wisps of her hair hang in their perpetual breeze. Her lips could show Mona Lisa a thing or two about secrets. That knowing-non-smile makes me nostalgic for the Russian doll that used to sleep in my glove compartment. All of the women in my life seem to know the answers before I even know the questions.

The monitor in front of me glows to life. Letters tumble in space, dropping one-by-one into fortune cookie wisdom.

Garbage in, garbage out. Good decisions require good information.

My desk phone rings and I snap up the receiver. Theodore Myerson sounds like a cat with a canary in its mouth.

"Hard man to find," he says, chewing.

"From the guy who likes to follow me all over town? You're a hard man to avoid, Teddy."

"Switchboard sent me to homicide. Then HR. This is my third try."

"And you found me anyway. Is there no end to your investigative brilliance?"

"I'm calling for a comment," he says.

"I have several. You're not going to like any of them."

"*The Hawk* is posting a story this afternoon. I'd like to read you a couple of paragraphs."

"I'd like to do a lot of things, Ted. That doesn't mean any of them are a good idea. Do I have to pay attention?"

"Sources within the Chandler Police Department and the Illinois Office of Attorney General confirm the discovery of new information directly implicating a sitting Will County Circuit Court Judge with possible financial ties to a criminal enterprise. Speaking on condition of anonymity, current and former officials in both departments have confirmed that 12th Circuit Court Judge Camilla Esperanza Jolie is currently under investigation for the alleged receipt of funds from sources believed to be associated with organized crime. The amount of the alleged payment or payments has not been disclosed. The nature of the new evidence bringing the concern to light has also not been disclosed. Sources do indicate that it was a currently serving Chandler Police Department officer who brought the concern to the attention of police and Department of Law authorities.

"Judge Jolie is currently presiding over the trial of Wrigley Menard, accused of second-degree murder in the killing of Curtis Root, owner of the wildly popular *TRK* bar and restaurant chain. As the prosecution has methodically unveiled its case in recent days, Mr. Menard's defense has repeatedly suggested that Mr. Root was involved in a criminal enterprise and that he was murdered for his involvement in that enterprise by someone other than Mr. Menard. The defense has not provided any information to suggest that it knows the identity of the person or persons who, if not Mr. Menard, might be responsible for the crime. The defense has further suggested that the prosecution of Mr. Menard has been influenced, if not orchestrated, by criminally corrupt elements within the Chandler Police Department. The Chandler and Chicago Police Departments have been rocked in recent years with as yet unsubstantiated allegations that various officers have been the source of leaks of valuable investigative information to criminal organizations, including investigative information developed by the MINWIMI Regional Criminal Task Force.

"Until recently, the Menard defense had not specifically identified any such corrupt elements within the Chandler Police Department. However, after a brief continuance due to juror illness, the trial resumed this morning with Judge Jolie presiding over the resumption of the cross-examination of Chandler Police Detective Arthur Dunn. Detective Dunn..."

"I was there, Teddy, remember? You're making me sleepy."

"You're welcome," he says.

"For what?"

"For not outing you as the source of this bombshell. Give me something about the information and where it came from, and I'll continue to keep you off the record."

"That sounds a whole lot like a threat, Ted."

"Not a threat. Just newspapering. Cooperate and I will do my best to keep you out of the spotlight. Otherwise…"

"Otherwise, you toss my name around like a filthy word. Do I have that about right?"

"How'd you learn Jolie was dirty? Does the information you found implicate anyone else?"

"Who says it was me who found it in the first place?"

"I don't reveal my sources. But let me just say, everybody that knows anything seems to know this came from you. And just in case you're not thinking ahead, Officer Mackey, thirty minutes after I post this thing, the *Trib* will be all over it."

"A real newspaper, you mean. Staffed with real reporters."

"Sticks and stones. Thirty minutes after that, the story will be everywhere. This is your last, best chance to have any kind of influence over public opinion. This thing is about to get a life of its own."

"A life of its own. Yeah, I've got one of those and I'd like to get back to it."

"Try this on for size: 'Speaking on condition of anonymity, law enforcement officials within the Chandler Police Department confirm that the new and concerning information regarding Judge Jolie was gathered in connection with an investigation into a recent home invasion, assault and attempted assassination of a Chandler police officer.'"

"Who told you that?"

"No one," says Ted. "I was hoping you could tell me that, anonymously but on the record."

"Sorry. No."

"Then maybe you'd care to explain the circumstances surrounding your early and all too temporary retirement from service."

"Which is relevant to this how?"

"Helpful historical context to the concern that Chandler PD has a problem with cops working on the wrong side of the law."

That one gets him a rueful laugh. I close my eyes and don't want to open them.

"How do I get you off the bottom of my shoe, Ted?"

"A little information and I come right off."

"I doubt that very much. I think I'll try hanging up."

And I do.

I keep my eyes closed, trying to grasp the consequence of what the world is about to learn from the fingertips of Theodore B. Myerson. Daylight might be the best antiseptic, but it also happens to be the absolute fastest way to send all the rats back into the walls and all the hypocritical gasbags to the microphones. Whenever I get around to opening up my eyes again, I need to go tell Twill about the coming shitstorm.

But opening my eyes is exactly the problem. Daylight is the very last thing they need.

EIGHTY-TWO

Darkness. Yellow firelight glows again through the shades. The windows of the house on Maltese Road, once abandoned, now flicker again with life. As anybody could see.

He is too tired now to care who sees. Caring requires energy. Ray doesn't have any more energy.

Phil is clingy. She meows and circles until he picks her up again and carries her around. So he only has one arm to work with. But he's still got both of his legs. That's a plus. Phil keeps at it.

"Come on," he says. "Judith's not so bad. She loves you. She'll spoil you rotten if you let her. She'll do anything you ask her to."

He pulls the stopper out of the Old Forrester with his teeth and pours himself a double melancholy over some ice. He sets the bottle on the kitchen counter and puts the stopper back in. He dips the tip of his finger into the glass. Phil takes the drop like mother's milk.

"Almost anything," he corrects, giving her another drop.

Ray manages the glass and bottle with his free hand and heads for the living room. Sarah Vaughan has already made herself comfortable, musing about the man she loves. Ray sets the bottle on the coffee table and nurses a little liquid gold from the tumbler as the fire warms his back. He stares at his sideways-slanted couch. I can see the muscles in his face twitch with memory. The bandage on his cheek moves like something is underneath trying to get out. His head is replaying the sound of that chainsaw. A sound that now, for the rest of his life, belongs to terror and darkness. A sound made for waiting.

He tries to reassure himself all over again. The doll was only ever about the information inside. The information is now out of the doll and Big Man knows it. Now the doll is just a doll. No need to cut off a man's legs or burn down his house for a block of painted wood. I can see him working on it. Rationalizing his decision to come home. Telling himself he's past the danger now. Telling himself it's over. Maybe he's right. Maybe. But the reassurance, no matter how many times he repeats it to himself, is only going to reach but so deep. No way he's going upstairs to sleep. Not tonight.

Ray sets the glass on the coffee table and nuzzles his face into the softness of Phil's neck. She vibrates from someplace deep. He sets her gently on the floor, then removes the Sig Sauer from its holster and sits heavily in the recliner with a long sigh.

I catch his glance across the room at the laptop on the shelf. He's thinking about Detective McMannis, still waiting in that Chinatown parking lot. He wants to write. Just a little. Just enough to feel normal.

We both know better. Writing is out of the question. So is anything normal. He's not getting out of this chair until morning. Phil quickly claims his lap, maybe just to make the point. Ray sets the gun on the floor within easy reach, then stretches for the bourbon.

He sips and thinks about Marlo up in the big dream. He wonders how often she checks in. He wonders if she's the one knocking the ice cubes against the glass.

He leans his head back. Listens to the hellish wind outside, clawing at the house. The fire pops. Sarah sings about her little home, built just for two.

EIGHTY-THREE

In the dream, I answer the telephone.

It's a big, black, old-timey thing the size of an iron sitting on the corner of an antique desk. The desk is outside where the picnic table should be, between me and the darkening lake. Marlo is behind the desk, leaning back in the chair with her feet propped up against the edge. She's wearing wingtip saddle shoes and roomy black trousers. I've never seen her in a vest before, but she knows how to wear it. The white blouse underneath is so bright it hurts to look at. She wears the hat tipped forward and a little sideways so the green of her right eye comes and goes. Wisps of her hair are suspended on the breeze that blows from behind me, past Marlo, and continues on across the lake to flap the flags of a castle. A blue dragon perches on a battlement, grooming like a pigeon.

The phone on the desk makes its sound. I could pick it up, but I don't.

Marlo's got a drink in her hand and a camera in her lap. The lens is almost as long as her legs.

The phone rings again. It vibrates like an earthquake that I can feel it in my bones.

Marlo looks at me sitting across the desk and points at the phone with her drink. All I can do is look at it. When I look back, Marlo is gone. A teenaged girl is in her place. Long black hair. Sad expression. Bright yellow coat.

Emily somehow fastens a Sig Sauer to the top of the camera like she's done it a million times before. It clicks into place, and she points the whole thing at my head like a rifle. Across the lake, the dragon hops from the battlement up to the tower, spreading its leather wings, stone powdering beneath its talons. It throws its head back and opens its jaws to make its ear-splitting screech. Instead, it makes the sound of an old-timey telephone. Emily speaks to me with Marlo's voice.

Answer it, Sweat Heart.

So I do. The handpiece is like a barbell, but I manage to get the thing to my ear. Marlo is on the other end. She's speaking Russian. I look up to Emily for an explanation. Emily is gone. It's Nadia now. She reaches over the desk and hands me her cellphone. It rings in my hand. I look at the screen.

Замок.

Marlo is still going a mile a minute through the barbell at my ear. I look up at Nadia. She smiles and opens her beautiful mouth to speak. I half-expect her to sound like a phone; everything else does so why not her? But I'm wrong about that. She sounds like a dragon.

I'm not fully awake, but I answer anyway. I sit in my lounger and stare at the empty bottle on the coffee table, trying to focus on the voice in my ear through the sloshing ache in my head. Phil stretches in my lap, splaying her paws, then re-curling. The fire is dead, and the shades are starting to blush. Outside, the wind is howling at the dawn.

"You're mumbling, Mack. Wakey, wakey, sleepyhead."

In a different frame of mind, I might have recognized her voice sooner. It didn't help that she has traded her usual chirpiness for something lower and more intimate. Almost a whisper.

"Who is this?"

"Celestyn Fila."

"What?"

"Celeste. Your favorite in-court snitch. Wake up, honey," she coos.

"Oh. Celestyn Fila." I straighten myself in the chair and rub my face. "Sorry. Thought you said West Antigua."

"Silly. Why would I say something like that?"

"Don't know," I said. "Voice like yours can make those words rub together in a way that keeps an old man warm."

"You're not so old, Mack. Say the word and I'll book us a couple of seats."

"Sweet, but I'm no chump, Celeste. Antigua's got a lot of big brown men and not nearly enough shirts. We'd make it as far as the airport bar. You'd take a powder and I'd never see you again."

"Maybe I'm not that kind of woman."

"Maybe not in Illinois."

"Think about it anyway."

"Sure. Thinking about it is easy. My problem is not thinking about it. Something tells me that's not why you called."

"I thought you might want to know something."

"Most things I'd rather not know. But go ahead and give it a shot."

"Big conference last night between Judge Jolie and counsel in the Menard case."

"Mmm. The article in *The Hawk?*"

"Yes. She's ordering a mistrial. She can't continue to preside with all of that going on."

"Her idea?"

"Don't think so. It's from on high. She spent some time with the Chief Judge yesterday. They're reassigning her entire criminal docket. Lot of unhappy black robes over here."

"What a mess," I say, trying to sound sympathetic. "How'd the lawyers take the mistrial news?"

"Mickey Shaw was sweet as pie. He said he thought it was the only sensible approach given the seriousness of the allegations against her. Then he handed over a personal check for the thousand-dollar contempt fine."

"Classy. And Jaclyn?"

"No one had to twist her arm either."

"I'll bet. Pretty messy record for the prosecution. She going to retry Wrigley?"

"She didn't have an answer for that. Too soon. Needs to talk with the DA. It would mean starting all over. Empaneling a new jury. And no time soon either. Our trial calendar is a slow-motion train wreck. Mickey is all over the speedy trial issues. He and Jaclyn struck a deal on the record."

"What kind of deal?"

"If Jaclyn wants to keep the case, Wrigley is eligible for bail."

"And Jolie signed off on that?"

"No. She can't make any rulings at all. It's going upstairs for approval."

"I'm guessing the good judge isn't so happy about any of this."

"Too angry to see straight. That's the other reason I'm calling."

"Oh?"

"She wants to see you."

That one is good for a couple of extra heartbeats. I'd switched the phone to the other ear.

"The judge wants to see me?"

"She asked me to get your number from CPD," said Celeste. "I pretended that was necessary."

"Why does she want to see me?"

Celeste laughs a little.

"You aren't a morning person, are you? You really should've taken me up on those tickets to Antigua."

"Okay," I say. "I'll come by. When does she want to see me?"

"When. Trust me, Mack. You're already late."

EIGHTY-FOUR

Judge Jolie's assistant is a wiry, young Latino with a first-day-of-school look on his face. He enjoys his job. Everything he sees seems to give him a new and special delight, every file folder, every pencil, even me, coat in hand, darkening the door to the office. My sport coat and tie have seen better days, a little shabby and fraying here and there, so they match the rest of me perfectly.

The assistant beams too many watts across the room. It's a smile that should be unlawful in traffic or before noon. I head his way and open my mouth to speak but that turns out to be unnecessary. He puts a finger in the air with one hand and picks up a telephone receiver with the other.

"Detective Mackey to see you," he says softly. He listens, nods and smiles delightedly, and then hangs up. He tips his head toward a short interior hallway. "She's expecting you," he says. "First door on the right. Can I get you something to drink?"

The question stuns me with possibility. But the kid is as smart as he is happy. He can see me thinking.

"It's not going to be that kind of meeting, Detective. Water or coffee?"

I pass on the drink and head down the hall, stopping at the big slab of oak with a smokey brass name plate. *Hon. Camilla Esperanza Jolie.*

I give it a couple of knuckles and wait until I hear something like permission. Then I twist and push.

The judge is behind a desk that looks like it came from the same tree as the door. She affects a posture of patience, hands folded in her lap. She's in a crème blouse and wearing small, turquoise hoops in her lobes. Her short, black hair leaves her face unobstructed, maybe so that her expressions will be clear and unambiguous to people paying attention.

"Mr. Mackey. Thank you for coming." For all those words, her lips don't seem to move even a little.

"Morning, Your Honor," I say. "My pleasure."

"Not for long," she says. Three little syllables that that grab my attention. They finish the job of sobering me up in a way that a sub-zero windchill couldn't quite manage.

"Oh?"

"Please have a seat."

I try to hang my coat on the pole by the door. There's an empty peg right next to the robe that gives Jolie the power to send people to prison. I miss the peg and have to pick the coat off the floor and try again. My back is to the judge so I can't see her expression. But I don't need to see it. There are only so many ways to look at a man who doesn't know how to work a coatrack, none of them good.

I make my way to the desk, taking in the room as I go. The office is a testament to compartmentalization and its knack for bringing order to chaos. There's a shelf for everything and everything has a shelf. One wall gets the Illinois and federal criminal codes. Another is devoted to black binders and case files. A small, ovular conference table is nestled in the corner of the office. I'm guessing it's for productive and collegial conversations unlike the one I'm about to have.

The wall behind the desk comes with a long, rectangular hole looking out at a sunny, cold and windblown downtown Chandler, streaked with sharply slanted pillars of steam and smoke. Beneath the window is a narrow credenza featuring clusters of family photographs. The judge is in almost all of them, acting like a happy, relatively powerless person surrounded by other criminally attractive people who know how to be in photographs.

One of the larger photos is devoted to Judge Jolie's investiture. She's younger and her hair is longer, and she hasn't yet been accused of taking bribes from the mob. Otherwise, she's exactly the same. She stands alone in her black robe. Behind her are a couple of familiar flags and the enormous seal of the State of Illinois. It's not possible for a face to show solemnity and joy at the same time. But somehow her expression manages that trick anyway. I pull out a chair and sit.

"That looks painful," she says, nodding to my face.

"It feels even worse, but only when I'm awake."

"On-the-job injury or did you get that at home?"

"Bit of both, actually. What can I do for you, Judge?"

Judge Jolie looks at me quietly for two or three eternities.

"Let me tell you some things you already know," she says at last.

"That should be easy enough."

"A local electronic… let's call it a newspaper, posted an article yesterday. That article, among other things, disclosed to the general public that I am currently under investigation by the OAG for accepting bribe money from organized crime. Turns out that's true."

"That you're accepting bribes?"

I know what she means, but two can play the attention-getting game. The question is whether that's a good idea. Her eyes sharpen just a little.

"Careful, Detective," she says. "True that I'm actually under investigation by the OAG. I learned about that yesterday too, only a few hours before the article. Yesterday was a banner day for me."

"I was sorry to hear it, Your Honor."

"Sorry, were you?" She doesn't believe me, but I didn't expect she would. I'm not sure if I believe me. "Well, let me tell you what else I learned."

"Okay."

"I learned that you work Internal Affairs for Chandler PD. And before that you were a thirty-year homicide detective."

"True."

"I learned that you were forced into early retirement under suspicion of being a mole for a criminal enterprise under active investigation by the MINWIMI Task Force."

"That's true," I say with a nod.

"True that you're a mole?" she asks.

I can't help but smile a little at the turn-about. Jolie, however, is not smiling. If it weren't for the photos behind her, I'd think maybe her face doesn't have those kinds of muscles.

"No," I say. "True that I was forced out under suspicion of being a mole. I was never a mole."

"Not what I hear," she says. "I hear the evidence was rather compelling, albeit in an inadmissible sort of way, and that you were saved by public relations cowardice."

The buzz I feel in the back of my brain is anger. I take a slow breath and let it pass.

"The evidence, if you want to call it that, was phony. What else have you heard?"

"That you're a little… what's the word…"

"Crazy?" I ask. "That one's probably true. But I find it beats sanity nine days out of ten. Plus, I find a lot of people try to steer clear of crazy, so that's a plus. Keeps the party invitations down."

She does have smiling muscles after all, they're just not strong enough to pull off sincerity when she's this angry.

"I was going to say unpopular," she says.

"Also true, especially among literary agents and book publishers."

"Unpopular within the police department, Detective. Unpopular among thirty-year professional colleagues."

"True again," I say, nodding. "Tax collectors and proctologists have more friends than I do."

"And why do you think that is?"

"Because the benefit of the doubt is expensive."

"Oh?"

"Yeah. The benefit of the doubt is always a top-shelf kind of thing. Before anyone can give you the benefit of the doubt, they've got to find it. Go looking for it. They've got to climb a ladder or stand on buckets to get to it because it's always tucked away out of sight and out of reach. And then there's all the risk. Even your friends start weighing the what-ifs."

"The what-ifs."

"Yeah. What if I lose all *my* friends as I'm trying to be fair? What if someone shoots me in the back while I'm up there on my toes feeling around for just a little benefit of the doubt that I can hand down to this poor, crazy lump that I used to call my brother? What if he's guilty and I end up looking like a rube? Turns out all of those what-ifs weigh more than the Queen Mary's anchor."

Her face is still. She wants me to finish. I do.

"But believing the lie? Believing the worst? Believing the gossip? That's easy, Judge. That's a light weight, risk-free, bottom-shelf proposition. The lies and gossip come in bulk. They taste delicious and they're almost free. Sure, I'm unpopular in the department. That's because everybody I know stocked up on the lie. They took home enough to last them a lifetime."

It's all too sharp. I was aiming for a detached wisdom born of tragedy, grandpa explaining how he lost the tip of his finger in the war, so much water under the bridge that pain has long since turned into nostalgia. I miss by a mile, managing to double the anger in the room.

"Sorry," I say. "Still too soon."

Judge Jolie considers her hands, absently twisting her wedding ring.

"You've been in my courtroom a lot recently," she says, looking back at me. "I take it the Menard trial holds some interest for you."

"Best show in town," I tell her. "Most trials are like watching a slow motion rerun of last night's news. But the Wrigley show is different. Never know what's going to happen next in that one."

"Glad you've been so entertained," she says. "Would you like to know what's going to happen next? Nothing is going to happen next. I just declared a mistrial on the record and released the jury. The Chief Judge is mulling whether to let Mr. Menard out on bail as the prosecution decides whether to make another run at him. They won't, by the way."

"Won't what? Try Wrigley again?"

"Would you? After this circus? After Officer Dunn's testimony? After that article? The stink of police corruption in the air?"

"Running scared."

"You better believe it," she says. "You don't get to be the District Attorney by running into rotor blades. For now, it's a mistrial declared by yours truly. Can't wait to see how that bit of news fans the flames of scandal."

I do my best to act surprised, not wanting to get Celeste in trouble for talking out of school.

"That's too bad," I say. "Maybe a sensible move, all things considered, but still too bad."

"Funny."

"I wasn't trying to be funny. That's usually when I get the most laughs."

"You're the only one I've encountered that thinks a mistrial in this case is a bad thing. Everyone else is either quietly delighted or relieved. The defense gets a murder prosecution derailed. Mr. Menard will likely get out of jail. The prosecution gets to put this debacle entirely on me and my convenient, show-stopping scandal, avoiding the embarrassment of a likely acquittal. The jurors get their lives back. The Chief Judge, the Illinois Bar Association and the ethics counsel all get to check a box and contain the added damage that would come with daily trial headlines, all of which would feature me as much as Wrigley Menard or Curtis Root. And the OAG gets an unobstructed crack at me while I have an open calendar and lots of spare time on my hands. Everybody's a winner."

"Except you."

"And you, apparently," she says, pointing. "You, who thinks it's too bad the case is over. I find that hard to believe."

"I've got no skin in that game, Judge."

"No? You seem pretty interested in the fate of Wrigley Menard for someone with no skin in the game. Did you have any official role in investigating the murder of Curtis Root?"

"No."

"Assisting the prosecution, in any way?"

"No."

"Any involvement in the underlying facts?"

"No."

"And yet, there you are. Every day. You seem rather friendly with Mickey Shaw and the reporter... the one who wrote the story."

"Theodore Myerson."

"You know his name."

"Lot of people know his name. He puts it in the newspaper every day and passes it around. That doesn't make him my friend. I try to call him Teddy only because he seems to hate it. Then again, all my friends hate me."

"Not all. Mr. Shaw is highly complimentary."

"Oh?" I can't help but laugh a little. "That's a good one. In what context?"

"In the context of me asking him and Jaclyn Cavelle some questions about you. He said the two of you have an adversarial history but that it has always been purely professional. He says he has always known you as an honest cop." She gestures at the air. "He stood up for you in this very room."

"Interesting. So he's okay with me being a mole for the mob?"

"He said he heard the rumors and was shocked."

I laugh again and look around the room for someone to laugh with me. There isn't anyone.

"Shocked, was he?"

"That's what he said."

"Judge, you have a reputation for having a highly-refined bullshit meter."

"That's a hard-earned reputation, Detective. And it's dead on."

"Then you know better than to trust Mickey Shaw farther than you can throw him."

"Correct. So, just to be clear, you want me to disbelieve all the nice things he said about you?"

"Look. Mickey knows his reputation in this building. His kind of dirty doesn't come off in the shower and everybody with two ounces of common sense knows the truth. He probably tries his best to care about that, but then the teller at the bank says it's his turn and he decides his life is pretty good regardless of what anybody thinks. Mickey giving me a bear hug just makes me dirty too. He knows that."

"And why would he want me to think bad things about you?"

"Beats me. But if Mickey's eyes are open it means he is playing some kind of game. What did Jaclyn say about me?"

"She pled insufficient information."

"Now that's an honest answer. She gets a medal. But Mickey? Come on. My question for you is why all the questions? Maybe that's none of my business, but since all your questions seem to include my name, you're going to have to convince me."

"I understand that you're the person offering up evidence of my corruption."

"Didn't realize that was public knowledge."

"It's not. But understand that when I ask questions, they tend to get answered. I understand I owe this entire shitstorm to you, Detective. You. A man suspected of having ties to organized crime and who has taken a clear interest in a murder trial that he has nothing to do with. A trial that, because of those shocking revelations, I have now been forced to cancel. That is why I am asking questions. And I'd like some answers. Starting with where you're getting your information, assuming you're not the one who's just making it all up. I will assume for the moment that you were only doing your job. And I will reach very high up on the shelf, Detective, and give you the benefit of the doubt that you are not the one who leaked the information to your friend Mr. Myerson. But I want a name."

I take her measure for a second or two, trying to gauge whether she's serious. She is.

"Sorry, Judge. I can't comment on that. I suppose if I were in your shoes, I'd want to beat the information out of me with your gavel. I get it. But I still can't comment, and you shouldn't want me to. In fact, this whole conversation is a bad idea."

"Is that so?"

"Yeah. I know I'm one to talk about bad ideas. Bad ideas and I are old drinking buddies. But if I were you, I'd be concerned that someone will misconstrue this little chat as you interfering with an on-going criminal investigation."

It shouldn't be possible for her to look at me any harder than she already is. She swallows and does it anyway.

"Is that a threat, Detective?"

"No. It's a helpful reminder. I'm surprised someone like you needs one."

"Someone like me? You mean a corrupt judge?"

"I don't know if you're guilty or just unlucky. It's your pay grade that gets to answer those questions, not mine. What I meant was that corrupt or not, you're a well-respected criminal judge, schooled in matters of law and ethics and the importance of propriety in all things. The very fact that you summoned me here tells me you're rattled. And for good reason. The sky is starting to crumble, and you've got OAG in your face like a bad smell. I get what's at stake here."

"Do you? That would surprise me very much."

"Yes. I do. Your career. Your good name. Not to mention your freedom if this information holds up. I know those stakes well. When that very same shitstorm hit my life, I did all the things you're doing. I got good and angry and struck out on my own, shaking everybody down for answers. That just made me look desperate. People were already teetering on the edge of believing I might actually be crazy and crooked, then I came along and gave them a good push. In the end, convincing the forces of evil to give me an early retirement rather than a prison cell took a lot of money I didn't really have for a good lawyer I didn't really like. He had to beat me over the head with his briefcase to get me to listen. Eventually I got the message."

"And I suppose you're giving me that message now."

"Due respect, Judge, but you're not thinking straight about this mess. You either haven't lawyered up yet or you haven't told your lawyer about this idea of flexing your muscle to play detective. Sure, you've got a lot of power. You can snap your fingers and yank me out of a hangover and demand some answers. You can dirty me up by talking to people like Mickey Shaw or anybody else who'd like to see tire tread marks on my face. You're right: you've got the power to get some answers. Maybe even the kind of answers you want. But in this situation, your power is not an asset. It's a liability."

I take a breath. She doesn't look any happier, but I can tell I'm making sense, so I give her a little more.

"You don't take advice from guys like me, but I'll give you some anyway. Fork over the retainer. Let your lawyer ask all the questions. I can't talk to you about this thing without an order from my department or a subpoena. Don't try to make me."

Judge Jolie gives me a polite smile.

"You make it sound like this is going to be a long haul for me. It's not. Also, I'm the best lawyer I know. I was an assistant AG before I took the robe and I unpack these kinds of investigations every month. I am not the least bit worried about the OAG getting traction. But I am determined to touch the bottom of this swamp. So, I want a name, Detective." She taps the top of her desk with a well-manicured nail. "I can be discrete. I'll keep your name out of it. But I want to know the source of this bullshit."

I give her my best look of regret and shake my head.

"Sorry, Judge. I've already given my chain of command everything I know, and I'll do the same for the OAG when it's my turn. We both just have to trust the system. Wait and let it work."

She looks at me for a second or two then rotates her chair to the credenza behind her. She grabs a photograph and rotates back. She hands it to me. A wide, white smile hangs from the face of a skinny brown girl. She's sitting in the lap of a man up on a lime-green combine. He's wearing a floppy black hat the size of an umbrella.

"That's me," she says. "I've got the cleanest fingernails in a family full of Mexican farmers. When I was a kid, my father took me back to Chihuahua every summer to see my grandparents and to drive that tractor. I grew up in Houston and stopped making those trips when I was in high school. I decided there were other ways I wanted to spend my time." She smiles a little, remembering. "My father tried every trick in the book. But I wouldn't go. Eventually he stopped trying. He'd leave me at home with my mother and make the trip alone."

She extends a hand and I give her back the photo. She lingers for a second, then places it back on the credenza.

"His last trip to see his father was his last trip anywhere. He caught a ricochet in a turf war shootout between the Guadalajara and Medellin cartels. Papa wasn't doing anything except sitting outside and having lunch with his uncle. And that was the end."

My instinct is to apologize for the loss of her father. But she doesn't want that. That's not why she's telling me this story. So I keep quiet and wait.

"Ask me how long it took the police to respond," she says.

"Okay. How…"

"They were on the scene before the first shot was fired. There were sworn police officers on both sides of that shootout, and they emptied their guns at each other. It was a cop's bullet that did the job. Hard to say for sure why we do anything in this world, but that event, more than anything else, put me on a path to law school. I wear the robe today because of that afternoon. I wanted to serve something approximating justice. I wanted to serve a system capable of protecting the innocent. To find the wolves among the flock and to put them down. A system in the great United States of America where we have a constitutional right to take every last good thing for granted, including that law enforcement will be on the right side of the fight. And I have been in that fight and giving it my all for a lot of years. A lot of years. So, when veteran officers like Arthur Dunn take the stand and lie and make a mockery of the system… when long-time cops like you, Detective, start howling with the wolves…"

"Now hang on just a second…"

Judge Jolie judge slams her hand flat against the desk with a violence that seems to come directly from her eyes.

"You will *not* interrupt me in this room."

"Permission to speak," I say too loudly.

"Denied. When long-time cops like you try to serve me up for dinner, I can't help but take that personally. The threats are one thing. I'm used to the threats by now. But when people like you, corrupt cops like you, from corrupt departments like yours, try to smear my good name, my father's good name, then you'll understand if that forms a lasting impression in my mind. When I am cleared of this… these… lies, I will retake the bench with the Chandler Police Department in my sights. You can bet that I will do everything I can to make sure the OAG turns its attention to you and that rat-infested department you call home. And you can bet I'll have the entire judiciary behind me. Let's see how you like it. And if you are ever so unfortunate as to appear in my courtroom as a criminal defendant, and I mean jaywalking, parking ticket, late library book, anything, there will be no lawyering on this earth clever enough to save you."

"Is it my turn yet?"

"It's your turn to get the hell out of my office," she says.

I've always been pretty good at taking a hint, so I nod and stand and head for the door.

"Bad day for you and the Chandler PD, Detective. A real bad day."

"Sure sounds like it, Judge," I say, taking my coat off the peg. I turn back to face her, still at her desk trying to look like she's in control of her emotions. "But it sounds like a great day for Mickey Shaw and the people who pay his fees. Makes me wonder if maybe that was the whole point."

EIGHTY-FIVE

My hangover has some intriguing ideas about the back seat of the Impala; blasting the heat and letting the engine purr me to sleep in the courthouse parking lot. Forty-five minutes would transfer some of the pain in my head to a joint in my neck, but that might be worth it. I read once that change is good.

Instead, I beat it back to the station to break the news to Twill that the Illinois judiciary is declaring war on the Chandler Police Department. Someone needs to tell the boss that he woke up today with a quaint idea of what it means to have a complicated life. May as well be me.

Two steps into IAD and I can see that Twill's door is open and the lights are off. Santiago is at his desk feeding himself a stick of gum.

"Meetings," says Raffi.

"In the building?"

Raffi shrugs.

"His coat is gone. But that's just me playing detective. What's with you?"

I give him the story. It takes longer than I think so I borrow Sandra's chair and sit down and roll it close so I can keep my voice down. Santiago listens without interruption. When I'm done, he purses his lips and nods.

"So," he says. "The department can look forward to the upside-down clusterfuck of an OAG investigation. And, since you work for IAD, that goes double for this department."

I nod.

"And, also, Judge Jolie and all of her judge friends hate us."

I nod.

"Nice work, Mack. That'll brighten his day. I just don't get why you don't have any friends."

"Speaking of which, I need a favor," I say.

"Sure," says Raffi. "Anything, Mack. The deeper I can get pulled into this shit-swamp the better. If I'm lucky, maybe I can get the judges to hate me too."

"It's not like that. I just need you to call up someone in Records and ask a couple of questions. Small favor. Two seconds."

"If it's so small, why can't you do it?"

"Because…" I have to pick my words carefully but that takes too long. Santiago does it for me.

"Because everyone in Records associates you with Ronni Lodge. She's one trial away from prison and you've got the plague. You couldn't get the time of day from Records."

All I can do is shrug. Raffi smiles.

"What do you need, man?"

I tell him what I need. Raffi punches in the number and rotates his shoulders away. I take the hint and roll my way back over to Sandra's desk so he can make the call without me breathing down his neck. I try to imagine who in the Records Department is going to field the call. I know all of them down there and I like most of them, but I know better than to think any of them would hold a door for me even if the zombies were at my heels.

Sandra's desk phone rings. It's not my style to answer someone else's phone, but my left hand has a mind of its own.

"Sandra Booth's desk," I say.

"That is not Sandra," says a voice from downstairs I recognize.

"Hey, Marjorie. It's Mack. I was just sitting here. Sandra's out."

"Good to know, but I can't leave a message on her phone if you pick it up."

"Sorry. I'll hang up."

"How about you tell her that her cellphone mailbox is full. Her mother can't get through. Correction: *still* can't get through. Third call from mom in the past two hours. Something about flowers for Sandra's sister. I got eight lines flashing down here and I've got to listen to this woman rattle on about her daughter's pneumonia and what kind of flowers go best with soggy lungs. I've got actual work to do down here."

"Well don't yell at me about it, Marg; I just picked up the phone. I'll pass it along."

"And while you're at it maybe you could tell her that mom needs a valium and that I'm not her answering service."

I think of correcting Marjorie; reminding her that her job is to answer the main number and to direct in-coming calls as necessary; suggesting that she is, in fact, Sandra's answering service. But I come to my senses just in time.

"Got it," I say. Marjorie hangs up. I hang up. I stare at the phone like it's a calculator, trying to add up everything wrong with that phone call. The sudden urge to rifle through Sandra's desk is overpowering so I look over at Santiago instead. He hangs up his phone.

"Who'd you get?" I ask.

"Kim. She'll get back to me. And then I'll get back to you."

"Thanks, Raffi. I owe you."

"Yes, you do. What are you going to do now?"

"Try to answer Jolie's question for myself."

"Which question?"

"She wants to know the source of my information. I have no idea. Nadia King? Ivah Novak? Casey Mouth Sweet? Shashenka Meknikov?"

"Who?"

"Verochka Volkova's wood-carving lover, *circa* 1847."

"I'm completely lost."

"Join the club, brother. Someone put damning information on a spreadsheet, put the spreadsheet on a flash drive, and put the flash drive up the skirt of a Russian doll. Who does that and why, Raffi? Ivah's best guess seems to be her son, Jovah."

"Why does he keep an incriminating spreadsheet with his own name on it?"

"Good question. But say that's true anyway. Say Joe Novak, Chicago PD super-cop, hides something in his mother's doll. One day Wayne Bishop comes along, kills Joe and steals the doll. If that's what happened…" I trail off, following the question away into the darkness. Santiago gets tired of me staring.

"Yeah? If that's what happened…"

"If that's what happened, Raffi, then that's a nefarious plot dressed up in a dime store coincidence costume."

"Well, then there you go. Joe's your source and Bishop's your hit man."

"Except that's not what happened."

"It isn't?"

"No."

"Because…"

"Because Wayne Bishop was a frame-up. He didn't kill anybody. At least not Joe Novak."

"Because you're psychic? The man was convicted, Mack."

"Yeah. But he was convicted of burglary, not murder."

"I'll take your word for it. Look, Mack…"

Santiago gestures to the open case file on his desk.

"Yeah. Sorry, Raffi. Thanks for the help."

I leave Santiago alone for my own cubicle, pulling all my questions along behind. The walk from Sandra's desk to mine takes its toll and I sit heavily. In my head Sandra Booth and her mother are in a fight with Judge Jolie. Everybody wants my attention. They all lose out to extra-hairy, crazy-eyed Wayne Bishop.

Wayne Bishop.

The blood in the veins of the police tends to run hot when it comes to cop killers. I remember from the trial coverage that Mickey Shaw made a good case that Chicago PD had planted evidence in Bishop's apartment. Someone on the team got a nervous case of the *what-ifs*. What if Bishop beat the charges? Sure, some of the things from Ivah Novak's closet were found in Bishop's apartment, but what if that wasn't enough? What if those things were too generic? A jury might believe Bishop had stolen those things from some other old lady and not the old lady with a dead son in the den. If Bishop's confession got tossed, which it did, then reasonable doubt was reasonably possible. So they, whoever it was, had sweetened the evidence pot with some not-so-generic items from Ivah's living room etagere, stashing them in a box under Bishop's bed. Whatever genius had hatched this plan had not stopped long enough to ask whether the box had already been photographed. It had.

Mickey had been prepared to shake off Ivah Novak's identification of Bishop in all the usual ways: the photo line-up was rigged; the elderly widow was confused and has bad eyesight. It was the usual playbook for Mickey. But then the heavens had opened up, and out dropped a police photo of a box of electrical cords under Bishop's bed. Nothing else, just electrical cords. Mickey had waited until after the prosecution had laid out its case and presented its evidence. That evidence had included photos of a box of electrical cords from under the bed with some of Ivah Novak's things on top. That's when Mickey had cleared his throat, adjusted his ponytail and put the Chicago Police Department on trial.

Proving beyond a reasonable doubt that Wayne Bishop had murdered a police officer in cold blood was suddenly a bridge too far. District Attorney Kimball had been forced to offer a bargain-basement plea before the jury ever got the case. Bishop, who turned out not quite as dumb as he was hairy, grinned and took the deal. Five years on a burglary conviction. Bishop ended up serving only one of those years.

Then he had taken the prison shower to end all showers.

So Bishop got the death penalty anyway, only it was the kind for suckers with no rights to appeal and no last meal.

I look up at Marlo. Her expression is the same locked vault. I know I'm kidding myself, but it seems like she thinks I'm getting closer. Wayne Bishop is the key.

My monitor glows to life. It's giving investment advice.

Positivity! Keep your workplace stock rising!

I vanish the message and hunt around for the email that DA Bannon had the Chicago PD send to me back when I was trying to figure out what had happened to Ivah's doll. It takes a few minutes but eventually I find it and look over the dozens of file attachments. Three clicks get me the evidence photos. Thirty seconds of scrolling and I come across a photo of the box of yellow electrical cords found under Wayne Bishop's bed. Fourteen photos after that is a photo of the same box, only this one shows a Russian doll on top. Bingo.

It's like seeing an old friend you didn't realize you missed. Same smile. *Guess me if you can.*

I saw an on-line poll a while back. *Who is the one person, living or dead, you most want to have lunch with?* Shocking how many people want to dine with the dead. Now I'm one of them. What I wouldn't give to take Wayne Bishop to an all-you-can-eat buffet and load his plate up with shrimp and roast beef and a couple thousand questions.

I take a flier on the next best thing, looking through the attachments for the Bureau of Prisons investigation report on Bishop's murder. No reason that should be lumped in with the prosecution case file, but a guy can dream. No luck.

I hop onto the internet and search around in the *Chicago Tribune* archives for an article I dimly recall about prison violence. I burn another half-hour before I'm ready to quit, but then there it is. *Crime and Punishment: The Problem with Prison.* A dozen or so paragraphs under the headline is a reference to Bishop's murder in the showers, not surprising given Bishop's quasi-celebrity status as an alleged cop-killer. The system locked him away for stealing things and he ended up dead. The shiv was a sharpened plastic comb that broke off inside Bishop's neck after a quick tour of his kidney and his lungs. All of that hair and Bishop gets a comb where he needs it the least.

According to the article, the BOP investigation concluded that Bishop was killed for picking the wrong gang. The *Trib* interviewed Bishop's cellmate, one August T. Pepper, a Chicago native in for a carjacking. According to Pepper, Bishop was not a violent man and was never in a gang.

"Wayne was stupid-crazy, not crazy-stupid. He knew better than to join up with the bangers. This was something different. Wayne got a raw deal."

The article moves on to a different murder in a different prison. But I'm not ready to move on. I invest another thirty minutes in the fate of August T. Pepper. That digging gets me a parole officer and the name of Pepper's employer. Turns out he's turning a wrench and running equipment for the Chicago Transit Authority. A call to CTA Human Resources puts me on the path to Maintenance. Two conversations and a lot of hold music gets me the addresses to three CTA machine shops that service the CTA Blue Line. The word is Pepper could be at any one of them. The man on the phone asks if I want phone numbers. I take them down just for the hell of it but I'm not playing that game. If I call up Pepper to let him know I'm coming, then he won't be there.

I grab my coat and head for the door. Santiago gives me a look.

"Someone's on a mission," he says.

"Going to see a man about a murder."

EIGHTY-SIX

It's like a shell game with August T. Pepper playing the part of the pea. Three machine shops to choose from, each serving a different branch of the CTA Blue Line. As a parts and equipment runner, Pepper could be under any one of those shells. Forest Park is closest, but O'Hare is likely to be the largest and employ more people. Then there's the Milwaukee-Dearborn subway which is the least convenient of the three because I'd have to wrestle with downtown traffic.

I try the hardest one first. Not because I'm a glutton for punishment but because the shell game is never about convenience. It's always about instinct. It's always about that little buzz in the back of your brain. *That one*, says the buzz. *That one*. I've learned to listen.

So I fire up a Camel and point the Impala right into the heart of Chicago proper like an arrow headed for the apple. I miss the apple and hit the construction on Monroe. I have to detour up Jackson and follow it all the way to the lake. I turn my shoulder to the Harbor and follow Lakeshore Drive south past Buckingham Fountain and Grant Park.

It's a beautiful drive in the hot sprawl of summer when the sunlit water flashes white across the blue expanse and the trees lining the parkway open their green bows like paper fans. Half a dozen park benches in this area have my name on them. All adopted names, of course. Sparks. Lizard Dick. Spunk Man. Wanda Mae. Spider. Too many times I've borrowed those names as my own for the duration of a smoke and a hoagie-with-everything from the Roosevelt Deli as I drink in the shade and look out over Lake Michigan. The lake that may as well be an ocean. It's an inviting detour for a man needing to think things through or to just turn off the static for a while. I've broken the backs of a lot of cases on those benches.

But in the white pit of winter, the invitation is different. It's not an invitation to pull over and take in the majesty of it all. It's an invitation to keep moving. It's an invitation to hit the gas and find a dark, quiet bar to do your thinking. Even on a sunny, windblown day like today, the water may be just as blue but it's a deadly, mocking blue that thickens the blood and makes the bones ache with cold. The shoreline is the grimy color of a twisted, trampled bedsheet found in the yard after the fire trucks have left. The trees are all caked with ice and the road is less a parkway than a dull, gray seam cutting through the snow. The buildings clustered just west of the Shedd Aquarium and Soldier Field, the ones poking the cumuli of the southern horizon, seem in winter more like a cluster of tall headstones marking the graves of giants.

I clear the park and swing west up East Roosevelt, back into the city. The heat from the blower is tepid and not quite up to the job. I turn it up a notch and shake another Camel free. I grab the lighter and send up a flame that sounds like a telephone.

"Mack? Raffi."

"Raffi. What's the word?"

"Well, the word is you were right, man. Records called back. Turns out Judge Jolie actually did file a threat report."

"When?"

"Ten days after they picked up Wrigley Menard and charged him."

"What kind of threat?"

"Someone wrote 'acquit or die' inside a Wrigley gum-wrapper and left it in her mailbox. Then she started finding sticks of gum everywhere she turned. Doorstep. Under her windshield wipers when she came out of the grocery store. Coat pockets."

"Coat pockets?"

"Yeah. At the store."

"So she's had a close shadow."

"Right. Then her kid calls one day from school. He's a sophomore at Northwestern. He got a wrapper under his wiper too. His said 'Doublemint Dangerous. Tell your mama.' He did. That's when she filed the formal report."

"We've got you and your family within easy reach. Let Wrigley go."

"Seems to be the message. No record of any activity since the report was filed. No record of any investigation progress."

South Michigan is bumper to bumper. I drive the length of the block between the Chicago Hilton and the Museum of Contemporary Photography without either of us saying anything. I stop at the light on East Harrison and watch a well-dressed man try to maintain some semblance of dignity crossing the icy street in this wind. He glances at me sideways, pulling his collar tight over his ears but then letting go as his hands shoot out to keep his balance. It's close, but he recovers. He straightens himself and continues like he's in full control. He's hoping I didn't see the momentary terror in his eyes.

"Let me ask you something, Raffi."

"Shoot."

"If I try to scare you into giving me something I want by threatening the lives of you and your family, and if you don't cave to that, what are the odds you're going to give me what I want if I switch up the strategy and offer to put you on the payroll?"

"Zero."

"A bribe is a business proposition. An exchange. Who does business with someone who, two seconds ago, was threatening bodily harm to you and yours? Doesn't make any sense."

"No. It doesn't."

"Are the odds any better that someone in forensics owes you a favor?"

Santiago laughs. I feel like I can hear him shake his head.

"Yeah," he says. "Those odds are considerably better."

"Be nice to know where the boys in white coats are on that flash drive."

"On it. I'll let you know."

The CTA machine shop is loud and it's dirty, but it gets points for being warm and for being the right shell at the right time. I have to follow three different index fingers through a warehouse to get to a breakroom where they think I'll find a man inside who answers to the name in my head. Turns out he's there and he's alone. My day is raining miracles.

He's in dirty blue coveralls, slouched in a folding metal chair next to a rickety round table that used to be white. He's got a brown paper bag in his lap. I'm guessing that's where the banana came from.

I can tell he used to take care of himself. Here's a guy who used to be young and cut, lean and mean with a set of shoulders that could deliver a punch. Now he's a doughy rectangle in his mid-fifties. Cauliflower ears. No neck. He's making a run at the crewcut and goatee thing, but that isn't working so well either. You have to shave the rest of your face or it looks like you're just fertilizing unevenly.

Prison can harden a man, or it can turn him into mush. I've seen plenty of both. August here has gone all in for oatmeal.

"August T. Pepper?" I flash my badge and drop my name.

"Monk," he says, looking up and extending a hand. I give it a shake.

The banana makes me wonder if maybe Monk is short for monkey. That or he's not the romantic type. I don't want to get off on the wrong foot, so I keep those guesses to myself.

"I'd have guessed Augie," I say.

"My dad was a piano player."

It takes me a second, but I get there.

"August Thelonious Pepper." August looks impressed.

"You know your jazz," he says.

"You got off easy."

"Funny, doesn't feel like I got off easy."

"He could have named you Jelly Roll. Or Liberace."

Monk chews his banana at me. I can tell light banter is not a tune he knows how to play so I get right to the point.

"I'd like to ask you a few questions about your old cellmate."

"That's a bus load of people."

"Wayne Bishop."

Monk's eyes go fuzzy for a second. He smiles a little.

"Haven't heard that name in a while. Hairy little fucker. Man was crazy. We hated each other at the end. Wouldn't shut up about anything. Like a damned firehose, twenty-four-seven. I didn't kill him."

"It's not about that," I say.

He squints up at me like the lights are too bright.

"How'd you find me?"

"Your PO."

"I don't normally work the Blue Line."

"It took some calling," I say.

"Makes you motivated, I guess," says Monk.

"Highly. None of this is about you. I'm just trying to find my way."

"Okay." Monk takes another bite of banana and chews, waiting for me to get on with it. I do.

"I'd like to know if Bishop told you anything about the murder of Joe Novak."

"Not a fan of newspapers?"

"Did Bishop's version of things read like the newspapers?"

Monk pushes out a short, sharp laugh.

"No. Wayne had his own version. His version was all about him being innocent. But then that's the same version everyone brings with them to the joint. Ain't no guilty men in prison. Guilty of being black, maybe. Guilty of being brown. Guilty of having enemies. Guilty of being a mule without any knowledge. Guilty of having the wrong lawyer. Guilty of crooked cops. Guilty of bad luck."

"I get it. What about you?"

"What about me?"

"You innocent too?"

Monk rummages around in the bag for something he doesn't find. He shakes his head.

"Nah. I did that shit. Jacking cars was my thing. I was the chop-shop king of Chicago for a while there. Didn't mean for anyone to get hurt, but there it is anyway. I own that. Only way to move on with the time you've got left is to own what you did with the time that's already gone. So I do. Always have. I pled the crime and started the meter. I try not to lie about my life. But Wayne, man, that cat was crazy. And a liar to boot. If the truth showed up with a million dollars, Wayne still didn't want shit to do with it."

"What was his story?"

"About the killing?"

"Yeah."

"I don't know. Some shit, man. He said…" He finishes the banana and drops the peel in the bag, rummaging again as he chews. He pulls out a cup of applesauce and a plastic spoon. Somewhere in the world there's a sixth grader missing his lunch. "I don't know. That was a long time ago."

"It's important. Monk."

"Lots of things are important. Officer."

Monk puts the bag on the table and the applesauce and spoon on the bag. He crosses his arms. I look around for the nearest chair and have a seat in front of him.

"I've got two twenties, a ten and a five in my wallet. I keep Honest Abe but you can have the rest if you tell me what you remember. But listen, I'm not paying by the word or for bullshit, so making up stories gets you nowhere."

Monk slots his eyes sideways to the table, like maybe the cup of applesauce and spoon get a vote. He gives me a nod. I fish out the cash and put it on the table. Monk starts to reach but I put the cup of applesauce on top of the bills.

"Save it for dessert. What do you know?"

Monk retracts his hand.

"Wayne said he had nothing to do with killing that guy. What's his name. Novak. Said he had never killed anyone in his life."

"So then he was set up?"

"I guess. If it's possible to set yourself up for something you didn't do."

"I'm confused."

"So was he. Wayne told me once that he had so much hair because all he ate as a child was raw beef liver. He also told me he and some guys spent two years tunnelling under the vault room of the Federal Reserve Bank of Chicago but didn't go the extra six feet because they lost interest. Just wanted to see if it was doable. He was a master thief bunking in the joint with a lowly jacker. Thought he had a lot he could teach me. Wanted to recruit me into his identity-theft syndicate once I was out. God he loved that word. Syndicate. He once told…"

"He lied a lot. I get it."

"I'll bet you don't get it. He lied like he breathed, man. Stupid lies too. Insulting lies."

"What do you mean he set himself up?"

"He had this long bullshit story about how he ripped off a van full of drugs from some scary people, drove to Detroit and spent a month selling it all off. Said he made millions, which you know is a lie. Said he rode high on the hog for a while, then he ran out of money and came back and did it all over again. Stole a van full of drugs. Drove to Detroit. King for a month. Then, what the hell, he went back for more. Because, you know, there's a fleet of fucking vans sitting in some parking lot, loaded with drugs, just waiting around to be stolen. Lying jackoff."

"Where'd the story go from there?"

"Third time was the charm. The way he told it, these were not people to be messed with. When he went back again, the van was full of guns."

"Guns."

"Yeah, guns, one for each guy waiting for him."

"Okay. So how is it he didn't die right then and there?"

Monk spreads his arms. The prison tats make their first appearance over the tops of his wrists.

"Right? You'd think that as much as Wayne lied, he'd actually be good at it. He sucked at lying, man. He'd just keep adding shit and adding shit, changing up the story, contradicting himself, until a Tooth-Fairy-believing-four-year-old would shake his head and walk away. Said he begged for his life. Said they roughed him up and put all kinds of guns in all kinds of places but never pulled a trigger. He said they put a sack on his head and locked him a trunk until someone in charge showed up and offered him a deal."

"A deal."

"Yeah. You want to guess?"

"He had to take the rap for a killing."

Monk gives me a look that comes with a kind of smile.

"On the money. He said they wanted him to cop to a murder. If he wanted to live, that's what he'd do. Turned out to be that Novak cop, but Wayne said he had no idea who the dead guy was."

"What about the guy in charge? Who was he?"

"Beats me, man. Wayne never said. Probably because none of this shit even happened."

"So, they wanted him to step up and take the hit."

Monk nods.

"That's it, man. Said his job was to play the part through to the end. They'd set him up with a good lawyer to get him off the hook. He'd either walk or, worst case, he'd see some bullshit time on a plea deal, but at least he'd be alive."

"And the two van-loads of drugs worth millions?"

"Clean slate."

"Come on."

Monk laughs. Seems like an okay guy for a criminal.

"That's what he said, man. All would be forgiven."

"Who's that stupid?"

"Whoever believes his bullshit story. That you?"

"What else?"

"He said they kept the sack on his head, moved him from the trunk to the back seat and took him to the body. Made him touch all this shit."

"Fibers and prints."

"That's it, man. Fibers and prints. That's what he said. Fibers and prints. It was a house, right?"

"Yeah," I say. "Old lady inside."

"That's right. Yeah, yeah. He said she was in the kitchen. Wait, was she dead?"

"You tell me."

Monk crosses his arms a little tighter and closes his eyes. I let him think.

"I think she was dead too," he says. "She was tied up or something. I'm not so sure about her. You'd think I'd remember a double homicide."

"What else?"

"Wait. Hold on." He snaps his fingers. "She was alive. He said she scratched him in the face. Or the neck. Some fuckin' place. More than once. Said he had to stand there and let her do it. In fact, that might've been when I knew for sure Wayne was full-on batshit. I mean, come on, man. What jury is going to believe that?"

"What else?"

"There was more. Knowing Wayne probably a lot more. And the story changed every time he opened his mouth. But that's all I remember. I remember he said they let him go after that. Drove someplace and kicked him out into a gutter. Cops picked him up later. A week or two, maybe. I don't know. Wayne liked to go on and on about how he played the cops for chumps. You tell me how you're playing cops for chumps by convincing them to lock you up for a crime you never committed. Turned out the stiff was a cop and Wayne got famous overnight. You could try to guess how much he loved the attention, but you'll never even come close."

"He got his lawyer as promised?"

Monk's eyes widen.

"Oh, that's right. The lawyer. Yeah. Wayne hated his ass. Said the lawyer had the cops cold on planted evidence. Talk to ten guys in prison on drug charges and all ten will tell you the drugs were planted by the cops. Wayne was singing that same stupid tune, but he'd adapted that shit for Broadway."

"How so?"

"To hear Wayne tell it, his lawyer had all the cops dead to rights. Wayne was expecting a pat on the back from the judge and a fucking tickertape parade and an apology from the Governor. Then, out of nowhere, his lawyer tells him to take five years up the ass for armed burglary, trying to sell it to him as a walk in the park and how lucky he should feel. Wayne said he was ready to fight it. Lots of bullshit about just how many ways he told his lawyer to fuck himself."

"How'd it play out?"

"He was advised he could reject the deal but that he wouldn't live for another week."

"The lawyer told him that?"

"None of this shit is true, man. This is Wayne Bishop we're talking about."

"Right, but that's what he told you."

"Yeah. Said the lawyer told him to take the deal or else. So he took it. First conversation I had with the man was about how he was on his way out. Just passing through. Like he was unsure whether it even made sense for him to make up his bunk. Lock-up was just temporary lodging until he got a new lawyer to shine a light. That never happened. Sure talked a game, though. He acted like the cavalry was coming. Like every night was his last night. And then one night it was his last night."

"Investigation found Wayne was banging," I say.

"Bullshit. No one wanted crazy on their team. They all left him alone. He was never banging."

"Then who killed him?"

"I don't know, man. And if I did know, I probably wouldn't tell you for that little stack of money under my applesauce. But look, you don't have to be gang banging to make enemies in prison. Times I felt like I might kill the man myself just to shut him the fuck up. Someone had enough."

Two men come into the breakroom laughing about a woman. She wasn't that type until she was. The man in the story gets more than he bargained for and leaves the scene without his pants. The laughter trails off as the two look over at Monk and exchange nods.

They give me a wary look on their way to a refrigerator in the corner. Something about me in the room counsels caution. I'm a stranger, sure, but I'm more than that. It's the vibe or the smell that cops give off. There's a certain type of guy who will always know. You can knock yourself out trying to cover up the vibe with a plaid shirt or a three-piece suit. The vibe is the vibe. Sometimes that's a good thing, sometimes not. This time I don't care much either way.

There's an epilogue to the story about the woman, apparently just as funny but it only comes in a whisper. My phone rings so loud it scares everybody in the room half to death and puts an end to the laughing.

"Mack? It's Jimmy. Got a minute or are you shooting at bad guys?"

"I'm busy reloading, Jimmy. Have to call you back."

"Got it. Whenever you're free."

Monk is looking at me. The guys at the refrigerator leave the room, each carrying a paper bag and a look of unsatisfied curiosity.

"My brother-in-law," I say, closing the phone. "He could have taught Wayne Bishop a thing or two about making up stories."

"I remembered something," says Monk. "Two things."

"And here I am with two ears."

"They called him a name, this guy."

"Who called what guy a name?"

"The muscle that stuffed Wayne in the trunk?"

"Yeah."

"The guy who offered Wayne a deal?"

"Yeah."

"*They*... called *him*... like, a name. Just remembered that."

"We've all got a name, Monk. You mean like a nick name?"

"Yeah. I guess. A nickname."

"What nickname?"

"Fuck if I know. I feel pretty good remembering that much. This is a reach, man. No. Wait. Almost had it." He closes his eyes. "It was like he was in the army or something." Monk snaps his fingers and his eyes flip open. "Captain! That's it. He said everybody called the guy Captain."

"Okay. Captain what? Crunch? Kangaroo? What."

"Just Captain, I think. Shit, I don't know. I'm pulling brain muscles over here."

"What else?"

"Something about his boots."

"Whose boots?"

"The Captain. Big ass boots."

"What kind of boots? Like cowboy boots?"

"I don't know. He just kept going on about the boots."

"Because they were big."

"Yeah. And weird somehow. Or maybe I have it all wrong. It was something about the boots."

"I thought Bishop was in a trunk with a hood over his head."

Monk gives me a look.

"Oh, now you want this shit to make some kind of sense? You asked me what I remember. Don't try to make sense of it, man. That's like trying to eat a Dagwood sandwich. Understand?"

"Yeah, sure I do. The applesauce isn't getting any younger and you want to get back to your lunch."

"Wayne couldn't help himself is what I'm saying. He just kept adding things. The story kept changing. It started pretty simple."

"How simple?"

"We were cellmates trading history in the dark. I had the top bunk, Wayne had the bottom. I told him about working the chop shop circuit and he tells me about stealing a fucking van. A van. So what? I've only done that a few thousand times in my life. Wayne added all the high-rolling drug bullshit later. But it started as an auto parts story. Two jackers bonding. He was going to take the van to this place on the South Side, get his cash and go. Nothing so special about that. He wanted to impress me, I guess. So that's when he started in."

"The drugs."

"Yeah, the whole thing. I could feel his little beady eyes inside all that hair, working on something better. So then suddenly the van is fully loaded with product and he's driving off to Detroit to become a millionaire. And I'm up on the top bunk in the dark rolling my eyes as he goes on and on and on, because I can see the future, man."

"The future."

"Yeah. Bunking with someone who will never shut the fuck up and never tell the truth."

"Which is what?" I ask.

"The truth?"

"Yeah."

"Wayne jacked a van. One time, not twice. He never drove to Detroit. He never became a millionaire. He dumped the cargo and turned the van into a small amount of money. There's the truth."

"And the murder?"

"Who knows. Wayne didn't strike me as the killing type. But since he said he was innocent then I'm fine with believing the opposite, because the opposite was always a pretty good bet with Wayne. And, truth is, most guys in the joint are guilty as charged." Monk raises his hand. "Yours truly included."

"What cargo?" I ask.

"What?"

"You said Bishop probably dumped the cargo before hocking the van. What cargo?"

"Oh. First time through that story he said the van was full of frozen fish. Then he gets this idea to…"

"Stop." The word hits Monk in the face better than a slap. I lean forward on my elbows. "Back up."

EIGHTY-SEVEN

It takes him two Camels to fight his way out of the city. He cracks the window every couple of blocks to change out the smoke. He can't keep it open long; it's too cold and the plastic sheet over the back window starts to pop in and out. From out here above the trunk it looks like the Impala is trying to breathe through a dry-cleaning bag. Somewhere in there is a perfectly good joke about auto-erotic asphyxiation but Ray just lets it blow away. He's not in a joking mood.

He's in the zone now. At least six different idiots new to the idea of winter driving give him reason to work the horn. But Ray doesn't take the bait. Not once. He's inside himself, much too deep now to care about what's going on around him. The cold, icy tangle of downtown Chicago is nothing compared to the ball of knotted fishing line inside the darkness of his own head.

But now at least he's found one end of that fishing line. And that makes untangling possible. Now he knows where he's going.

It's not until he hits the Lower West Side and begins angling for the I-55 that he remembers Jimmy. He parks the Camel in the crook of his mouth and pats around for the phone.

"Jimmy."

"Mack. Thanks for calling back. Is this a good time?"

"So far I'm having a ball. You?"

"Right. I'll keep it short. I was just curious to see how you were coming on finding that doll."

Ray puts the call on speaker and sets his brother-in-law on the dashboard. He takes a long drag and holds it. It's his way of counting to ten. He makes it to six.

"Just curious, are you?" he asks.

"Yeah," says Jimmy. "I don't mean to pressure, but I…"

"Want to know what makes me curious, Jimmy? I'll tell you anyway. I'm curious whether you were adopted."

"Adopted? No. I'm not. Why?"

"Because I can't figure you and your sister ever swimming in the same gene pool. Never could."

"How's that, Mack?"

"Marlo was the most ethical person to ever walk the planet. You know it and I know it. Wasn't about written rules and laws with her. She broke plenty of those in her day but only because they didn't line up with right and wrong. She knew how to treat people, Jimmy. She had a moral compass that wouldn't quit."

"So, you're saying I don't have a moral compass. Is that it?"

"No. I'm not saying that at all."

"Good."

"I'm betting you have several moral compasses, maybe a couple in each pocket. I'm guessing they're all made in China. Big problem is that you don't seem to know north from south."

"Look, Mack, if this is a bad time…"

"I mean why else does a man of average intelligence and better-than-average hair choose to devote so much energy to ripping off an octogenarian widow?"

"I'm not ripping off anyone."

"Not yet. But that's the plan, isn't it? My guess is that you've already lined up a buyer. Maybe he's a collector or maybe he's just a fence, but whoever he is, his eyes are silver dollars spinning in their sockets like a couple of tops. Because we're talking about a genuine Meknikov Matryoshka, aren't we, Jimmy?"

"A what?"

"Come on. A Meknikov Matryoshka. A year ago you'd have guessed that was a famous ballerina or maybe an automatic weapon. But you're up to speed now, aren't you? Now you know it's a Russian nesting doll. And not the kind you find in some dime store tourist trap. She's an antique. Made by a master. I'm guessing she shows up in your dreams every night stuffed with rubles."

"Mack…"

"Forget that she has been handed down from mother to daughter over generations. The sentimental value of a thing like that doesn't even register with you. You don't care what that doll means to a sweet, little old lady. You want it so, what the hell, you're just going to take it from her. End of story. You're going to swap it for a bag of cash. And why not? You sure don't have any use for a doll. No girlfriend to give it to. No fiancée. No prospective mother-in-law. You're as single and unattached and devil-may-care as ever, despite the story I got as you drank *my* liquor in front of *my* fuckin' fireplace."

"Mack," says Jimmy, trying to laugh, as if at a man out of his depth. "You don't know what you think you know."

Ray keeps on, rolling over him like a stick in the road.

"So you're going to cash out," he says. "Slip that piece-of-crap Malibu into long-term parking, and head for someplace warm. Mexico. South of France. I hear Antigua's nice. Not Florida. You'd be too easy to find in Florida, just ask any cop or bail bondsman. No, you're headed someplace where no one knows you yet. Where the daughters of the well-to-do will fall for those lips and that swoop of hair and forget about your hand working the tumblers on daddy's safe. All you need now is for your rube brother-in-law to work his police connections and bail the doll out of lockup. How am I doing… Jack?"

"You're way off."

"Am I? What's the name of Nadia King's daughter?"

"Trick question. She doesn't have one."

"Wrong answer, Jimmy. But don't feel bad. You've been played by the best."

"Played? By who?"

"Whom. And I just told you. The best."

"Do you have the doll or not, Mack?"

"Not."

"Where is it?"

"Where it belongs."

There's a long silence. It deepens like a sink hole. Jimmy's voice sounds like it's under a foot of dirt.

"Bitch."

"Now, now. Don't be sore."

"She used me. She lied to me."

Ray cracks the window and sets the smoke free.

"Lot of that going around. Using people and lying to them is all the rage these days. I see it all the time. Just the other night in my living room, for example."

"She was the one who wanted to sell it. It was her idea. You think it was my idea? I was only trying to help. She, she…"

"Stop being a baby. Face the facts, Jack. She used you to get to me. Did you think she thought you were cute? She never thought you were cute. Did you think reaching out to your police detective in-law was your idea? Guess again, Jimmy. Nothing was your idea. Well, until you had the idea to take the doll for yourself. That one was all yours. Too bad you're not a patient person. You were overeager. She saw you coming a mile away. She figured she'd be better off coming to me directly. Dropping your name in my lap. Working that smile of hers a little. She figured right."

"She came to you? She… Bitch."

"You're repeating yourself," says Ray, closing the window. "Touch her and I'll put you in jail, Jimmy. Don't think I won't. I might just do it anyway. Let's see if we can get Marlo to come back and bail you out. That's reason enough to lock you up."

"I haven't done anything."

"You haven't done anything worthwhile, maybe, but you've done just about everything else. How did you two hook up? Try telling me something I'm going to believe this time."

It's all about driving in silence for a while. The phone sits on the dash like a useless piece of plastic. Could be that something snuffed out the connection. But Ray knows better. He pulls the rearview his direction and sizes up the ugly mug looking back. His orbital is still a shade of eggplant. On the other side of his nose the white, square bandage still begs for some urban poetry. He picks at a corner of the bandage until he gets some purchase and then pulls it up a little to look underneath.

"I met her at a home design store outside Schaumburg," says Jimmy.

"Okay." One eye on the traffic, Ray keeps pulling. He doesn't like what he sees. He flattens the bandage back against his cheek.

"I was picking up some lights for a job. She needed help loading a floor lamp into her car. She thought I worked there. We hit it off. It was easy."

"Maybe a little too easy."

"I can't believe…"

"That's because you lack imagination, Jimmy. So you fell hard for a pretty face. What else?"

"She said she was in real estate. She was staging a house, getting it ready to show. She asked if I could lend some muscle. I said okay. That turned into a thing. Two, three times that week. Getting the house ready to show. I helped. It turned into…" Jimmy makes a sound. "Something about a big, empty house, Mack."

"I get the picture. You can skip all of that. Did she ever take you to *her* house?"

"No."

"But you went to *your* place plenty, didn't you?"

"Yes."

"And you didn't find that odd?"

"Not at the time. She likes the clubs. Drinking. Dancing. We put in some late nights. My place was closer."

"Funny."

"Why?"

"Because you don't have any idea where she lives, do you? You couldn't find her if you wanted to."

"No." He says the word like it belongs in an angry confession.

"What else?"

"She always had a nice supply of shit."

"What flavor?"

"Grass and coke. She said she has a friend that gives it to her. I didn't ask any questions. She just, like, gave it to me whenever we were together."

"She *gave* it to you? What, to use or sell or…"

"Sell? No. Like, in her purse. Just enough to, you know, add a little spice to the night."

"Both of you?"

"No. She liked to drink. She said adding anything to the booze makes her feel sick."

"And yet there she is with a purse full of dog treats just in case she meets a stray."

"I didn't think she was up to anything. I just…"

"You didn't think, Jimmy. Full stop. You were in clover up to your ass dimples and not asking any questions. She softened you right up. And when she thought you were ready, she started telling stories about her terrible mother's long, lost doll."

Another silence as Jimmy sizes everything up.

"Bitch."

The skin on the back of Ray's neck glows hot. I try to suggest that he take a breath but Ray's not taking my advice.

"Use that word one more time, Jimmy, and we'll finish this up in a very small room across a metal desk."

He regrets it. Coming to her defense so openly. Defending her honor. He should have taken a breath. I remind him that I was right. Now he has to contend with Jimmy.

"Hold on," he says. "Don't tell me you're into her, Mack. Don't tell me she's got you under her spell. Is it about sex or the doll or both? Let's talk about those moral compasses again."

"Settle down. She's nothing to me. I just don't like the word, that's all. We all have words that set us off and that's one of mine. I'm sure you've got your own. Arraignment, maybe. Prison. Conviction. I've always thought of you as a man without any convictions, but I might see one of those in your future."

"Again, I haven't done anything wrong."

"Conspiracy to steal an item valued in excess of five-hundred dollars. Congratulations, that's a felony in Illinois. Don't get me started on wasting police resources in furtherance of a crime."

"Oh, come on."

"What was the plan, Jimmy? I'm not messing around here. You want the cuffs? I've got a pair just for you. She made you a real estate lackey and paid you with sex and drugs. What else?"

"She hated the real estate thing. She wanted me to take her to the Keys. She wanted to start a new life. She was serious, Mack. It was a real thing. At least I think it was."

"You keep on thinking, Jimmy. That's what you do best."

"She said she could get at least a hundred thousand from a Russian collector. It would be a start."

"A pretty good start. Never mind the sentimental value to poor Ivah."

"Ivah," scoffs Jimmy. "I don't know what she told you, but she hates Ivah. Sentimentality was never a problem for Nadia. Getting the doll was the problem."

"And you just happened to know me."

"She had no idea you even exist, Mack. Reaching out to you was totally my idea, not hers."

"You know," Ray finishes the Camel and puts it to bed in the cup holder. "I finally get why women think you're cute, Jimmy. You're like a puppy that can't figure out the dog in the mirror. I was Nadia's idea from the very beginning."

"I was just trying to help."

"Yeah, you were just trying to help yourself to Ivah's doll. Nadia never bargained for your kind of lust. You shifted gears too soon and gave her a glimpse of where you were headed. So she dropped you like a hot rock and disappeared. Now where are you? You've got a phone number that no one answers and no address to chase down. You spend most nights at those clubs, but she's never there, is she? You've parked your Malibu outside the house she listed but she never shows and I'm guessing that yard sign is gone too. You've called her agency, but they've never heard of a Nadia King. Stop me if you'd rather talk about how hard it is to make up a phony business card."

"Jesus."

"Sorry, he's not taking your calls either, Jimmy."

"I've crawled all over social media. Nothing. She's a ghost. I even tried Ginny Southside."

"Who's that?"

"Someone called her that at the club once. Some friend. Huge, this guy. Biggest mook I've ever seen."

Ray laughs. He puts his head back against the seat and really lets it out. It's the sound a man makes when he gets a peek at the dark perfection of his own life. Luck has its own kind of laugh. This isn't that. This is the sound of understanding that luck, good or bad, was never invited to the party in the first place.

"What's so funny?"

"Everything's funny, Jimmy. There's nothing that isn't funny anymore. We're all going to laugh ourselves into an early grave. I'm choking on funny."

"What are you going to do? Does she have the doll? Did you give it to Nadia? Please tell me you haven't give it to that… to Nadia."

"Mind your own business, Jimmy-Jack."

"Let me come over and we can talk about it. You and me and Phil and a bottle of whatever. I have a proposition for you. Just hear me out is all I'm asking. If it doesn't play, then we just go our separate ways."

"Boy, you're a real piece of work. How about this instead. Go back to whatever hole you were in when Nadia found you. Or go back to Florida. I don't really care. Just stay away from me, Jimmy. Darken my door again and I'll set you on fire."

It's Jimmy's turn to laugh.

"Fire? Really?"

"No, you're right. I'll shoot you first so you don't run down the street in flames."

"Come on, Mack. We're family. You don't mean that."

"Goodbye, Jimmy-Jack. Phil sends her worst."

EIGHTY-EIGHT

Alice is in her wheelchair at the window, just like before. Nightgown underneath a Bears sweatshirt. I can't see the big orange socks on her feet, but I don't have to. She waves a pennant at me as I cross the icy parking lot like I'm heading for the endzone. The wind is a better linebacker for being invisible. It nearly takes me down, but I manage to stay upright. I wave back at Alice through the glass like we're old friends and pull open the door to the Golden View Senior Community.

"Afternoon, Alice," I say with a nod as I catch my breath and head for reception. Her face slackens in the slowly mounting confusion that comes from having no idea who I am or how it is I know her name. I add the only thing that matters to her. "Go Bears!"

Alice smiles again and waves the little flag. I keep walking.

Frank sees me coming. I've got his attention for the full trip through the lobby. Not much changes in Frank's world. He's wearing the same sour expression I left him with. Maybe it's all he's got or maybe he puts it on just for me. He's in the same green cardigan and I'm guessing the flask is still underneath, in the shirt pocket where it belongs, protecting Frank's heart from stray bullets.

"Frank."

"Officer," he says. "Mrs. Novak?"

I hand over my license.

"The very same."

Frank enters me into the log as he squeezes a phone receiver between his ear and his shoulder.

"Mrs.… Oh, this is Frank. Is she in? She has a visitor. Okay. Yep. I'll send him up." Frank hangs up and hands me back my license. On the big screen behind him is a man on the far side of an enormous cake. His cheeks are doing their best Louis Armstrong as he tries to blow out a forest of candles.

"She's getting her meds," he says. "You can go on up."

The door to room 2113 is ajar. I give it a firm knock anyway and wait in the hall. The voice from inside is too robust for Nadia. The words are all about swallowing.

"Honey, got to put your head back. Go on now. Point your chin, baby. Right up to the ceiling. Point and swallow. I know, I know. Tastes like an old shoe, huh? One more, Ivah. One more and I let you do your business. Then you got company coming. I don't know who. Point your chin, baby."

In another minute the door swings open. A large, pale woman in a blue smock pushes a cart out into the hall. She looks up and nods. Her eyes are large and sweet and docile, like maybe they'd feel right at home in a pasture looking over a split-rail fence. They take me in from beneath the lay-back fronds of drugstore eyelashes.

"Miss Ivah's in the baffroom," she says from the other side of the Mason-Dixon. "You can go on in."

I head for the living room. It all seems exactly the same. Every pillow. Every magazine. The little woven basket with the pens and paperclips and the pair of fingernail scissors is still open on the coffee table next to the Parliaments.

I decide that maybe it's the building. Something in the walls of this place thickens everything. The air. The reddening afternoon light sauntering in through the windows and fattening up the dust motes. Time itself is thicker here. It's all a kind of syrup, a sticky amber sap that turns everything and everyone in its path into a prehistoric mosquito paperweight or a dinosaur DNA pendant.

But there is one change. Up on the etagere, there's a new face above the television. She gives me that secret, knowing smile, like maybe she's not surprised to see me in the least. Like she's been waiting.

"Well, hello, Dolly," I whisper, taking her off the shelf. I turn her over in my hands, moving the flat of my thumb around the curvature of her plump, firm form.

I take her apart carefully, lining up the various half-pieces of her along the shelf. I notice that the smallest doll, the one that does not open into two halves, is not smiling so much as smirking. There's the smile that knows a joke is coming, and then there's the kind of smile that revels in a joke finally told. She's enjoying herself, this littlest one, and she's doing it at my expense. I turn her over and pick at the wooden plug underneath with my fingernail. It won't open without something small and sharp. I lose interest about the time I hear the toilet flush. I reassemble the inner dolls and place the old gal back up the shelf where I found her.

Nadia is waving. It's like she's trying to get my attention from one shelf below and twenty-five years behind. She's as black and white as the other girls, all in a row, but she's the only one with any color to her expression. All the others are so serious. Even the youngest, eyes like little assassins sizing up the photographer. The girl next to Nadia —Bilka or Belka or Balka —seems to slump under the weight of Nadia's arm, her face resigned and resentful at having been captured and put on a shelf, decades into the future. I turn the picture over and slide the felt stand out of the frame so I can see the back of the photo itself.

Verochka (15) 1995. St. Nicholas, Novogrudok.

I put it back and move on, bending to take a closer look at the photo of young Jovah and Alexi, shooting at each other with toy guns in front of the Christmas tree. Nothing like a little pretend yuletide mayhem to make everyone laugh. Something about the photo seemed wrong the first time I saw it and it still feels somehow wrong now. I bend a little deeper. Look a little closer. I even squint.

Then I see it, plain as day.

Marlo is suddenly in my head drinking coffee at the kitchen table, shaking her head at the newspaper. A Chicago cop had been shot in the back by his own partner.

We see what we expect to see, Ray, whether it's there or not. Too many guns in your line of work for that not to get someone killed eventually.

Somewhere inside my headache, the dominoes are starting to tip. I want to close my eyes and watch. Think things through. But Ivah Novak is not going to let that happen.

"Nadia, she is here?" Ivah asks from the bedroom doorway. I turn to see she's in a black sweater pulled over a turtleneck the color of a bloody Mary. She looks around as if Nadia might suddenly emerge from behind a chair. I shake my head.

"Just me today, Mrs. Novak," I say. "I was hoping I could ask you a couple of questions."

The hopefulness on her face clears out, making room for something more serious and suspicious.

"Is police? Is questions?"

I nod apologetically.

"Yes, ma'am. Police questions. But just a few."

She moves in slow, unsteady steps for the sofa then lowers herself. I take a seat in the chair across the low table. I can see her eyes reacquainting themselves with the signs of violence on my face and neck. Ivah leans forward just enough to reach the pack of Parliaments with the tip of a gnarled finger. She shakes one free and places it between her lips. It hangs like a thermometer. She points to the lighter on the table.

"Against the rules," I say.

Ivah nods. Then she smiles, making the cigarette point at my face.

"Always there is rules," she says.

I know the backscratching game when I see it. I reach for the lighter and she leans in for the flame.

"Spoken like a true parliamentarian."

"You smoke," she says after making the tip glow. It's not a question. She brushes her finger over the edges of her lips, then points at mine. Observant for someone supposedly getting soft.

"Camels," I say. "I'd quit, but I think they're addicted to me."

Ivah takes a drag and then extends her cigarette hand. It looks like she's sharing but then I realize it's a gesture at my face.

"You fight," she says. "You choke."

"Something like that," I say. She brings her hands up around her head.

"I am in bag and tie to chair." She returns the cigarette and holds out both hands. "They scrub. Is too hard, too hard. No listen. They tie. I am scream too tight. No listen."

"They?" I ask.

Confusion in those old eyes. They narrow, like she's trying to see through the fog in a place she did not expect to be. She takes a pull on the Parliament and nods.

"*Da.*"

"Who?"

"Is, eh, man." She gestures around her face. "With hair."

"Bishop? Wayne Bishop?"

"*Da.* Yes. Bishop."

"You said they, Mrs. Novak. *They.* Who tied you to the chair that night? Who tied you up too tight?"

"Bishop," she says. The name comes out before I make it to the question mark. Then she says it again. "Bishop."

"Just Bishop?"

"*Da.* Yes. Bishop."

"It was Wayne Bishop who scrubbed your hands too hard?"

"*Da.*"

"Why?"

Ivah smiles and extends her hand over the table as a claw.

"I scratch face," she says. "He is not want blood for police."

"Where? Where did he scrub your hands?"

"Kitchen sink. He use brush, eh, for dishes. I am scream too hard, too hard. No listen. He scrub and scrub."

"The police found you tied up in the kitchen with a garbage bag over your head."

"*Da.* Is darkness and pain."

"Who put the bag over your head?"

"Man. Bishop."

"Did he put the bag over your head before he took you to the kitchen and tied you up or after?"

Weariness climbs up Ivah's face and collapses into her eyes.

"I am saying many time. Is long time."

"I know," I say. "I understand. But this is important, Mrs. Novak. What do you remember?"

She looks at me and smokes, like maybe she's waiting for me to lose interest. I don't. Ivah sighs.

"I hear noise. I put on robe. I come downstairs. There is short, hairy man."

"Where?"

"In closet. He shows gun. He…"

"Tell me about the gun."

Ivah flattens her hand out against her chest.

"Is mine. Is my gun in my closet. He is to steal."

"Where did you get this gun?"

"Jovah gives long time. For protect." Ivah smokes and shakes her head in a private, rueful irony. "For protect."

"Okay. So, he shows you your own gun. What next?"

"He grab neck." Ivah points to my neck with her cigarette, invoking our violent kinship. "I scratch face. I am scratch two times his face. He point gun. Is my gun from closet! He is take to kitchen. He scrub with brush. I am scream. He tie hand. I am scream. He…"

"What did he use to tie your hands?"

"Eh, he use tape. You know tape?" She stretches out something invisible between her hands. "Strong tape? For box?"

"Yes. Where did he get it?"

"From drawer in kitchen. He tie hand. He tape chair. He put bag. I see nothing. Then I am hearing Jovah come. He is into den and I am hear gun. I am scream and scream. *Jovah! Jovah!*" Ivah's eyes are wide and distant. Her remembered scream comes out as a hoarse whisper. I let her sit a few seconds in silence. "He is good boy, my Jovah."

I nod and watch her smoke, thinking things through.

"You said you heard Jovah come through the front door."

"*Da.* He come after shift of police. Every night. Every night. Such good boy, Jovah."

"Why didn't you call out to him when you heard him come in the front door? How did he make it all the way to the den without knowing about Bishop?"

I know the answer. I've read the file. But I ask it anyway because you never know. It must sound like an accusation because Ivah's face takes offense. She points to her mouth.

"They put towel. They put tape. I cannot make sound."

"They taped a kitchen towel inside your mouth so you couldn't scream."

"*Da.* Yes."

I lean forward in my chair. Each of my eyes seize each of hers.

"Who is *they*, Mrs. Novak?"

She closes her eyes, sucking in the smoke.

"Bishop," she says from inside a cloud. "Only Bishop."

"You're sure about that."

"Bishop," she says, not looking.

"The police found your son's body in the den. Do you know why he would have gone to the den?"

Ivah shrugs.

"Is den."

"Yeah, but Jovah is there to check up on you after his shift. As far as he knows you're upstairs in bed, right?"

"*Da.*"

"So why is he in the den?"

Ivah waggles her cigarette.

"He like smoke."

"Ah. A smoker was he? What was Joe's brand?"

Ivah's eyebrows gesture at the pack on the table.

"Parliament," she says. "Is best kind."

I narrow my eyes suspiciously.

"Come on now, Ivah. Who's going to walk a mile for a Parliament?"

Ivah laughs and points to herself.

"Me. I am who. And family. Husband Dmitry smoke Parliament sixty year. My children, Parliament. Is best. Is best."

"Nadia too?" I ask, almost convincing myself that I don't care about the answer.

"*Da,*" she says with a brief nod.

"Then I guess I'm outnumbered," I say, holding up my hands.

"Yes. You will give up Camel."

"I'll think about it. Point is, your den was a good place to smoke."

"*Da.* Big chair. Peace and quiet. No work. No wife."

"So he wasn't just checking on you. Joe liked to come over to your place for a quiet smoke and some refuge."

Confusion.

"Refuge," I say. "A place he could escape and relax."

"*Da.* Yes. Yes."

"What about Alexi? Did he come over to your house like Jovah?"

"In daytime. Alexi is daytime and Jovah is nighttime. No every day, Alexi. Is very busy. Only sometime. They are good boys."

"Did Alexi come over that night? The night of…"

"*Nyet.* Only Jovah."

"And Bishop," I add.

"*Da.* And Bishop. Jovah and Bishop."

"Your phone records showed that you made a call to Alexi."

"Yes. I am calling Alexi when I am going to bed."

"Why?"

She makes a sound inside the smoke.

"Is long time."

"I understand. Did Alexi come over that night, Mrs. Novak? After you called him?"

Ivah takes a fresh drag and shakes her head.

"*Nyet. Nyet.*"

"How long has Alexi been working for Mr. Mayor?"

Her face registers the change-up, but not unpleasantly.

"He is work for mayor."

"Right, but for how long?"

"Long time."

"Since before Sam Royce became the mayor?"

"I am not knowing this. Long time are friends." Ivah pinches at the corner of her mouth and flicks something away. "Jovah is hating."

She starts to say something else but my phone interrupts. I leave it in my pocket.

"You answer," she says, like she is giving me permission.

"It's not important unless they call back. What did Jovah hate?"

The phone keeps at it. I jam my hand into the pocket and pull the clanging thing out into the light. I don't recognize the number. I hit the button to stop the noise and drop it back into my pocket.

"Sorry. You were talking about Jovah. Are you saying he hated Alexi being friends with the mayor?"

"*Da.* Is too much hate, Jovah. Is good boy, but…"

"Hate for who? Mayor Royce?"

"*Nyet.*"

"For Alexi?"

Hesitation. She sighs at the smoldering Parliament.

"*Da. Nenavidit* Alexi. Is good boy, Alexi. Is better boy. Is more important." Ivah taps herself in the chest with her fingertips. She starts to speak, then stops. She looks away as her eyes start to glisten. "Alexi is love family. But Jovah…" She wrinkles up her face. Fighting anger. Fighting tears. Her eyes are drowning. They are not seeing the room in front of them. I do not exist now. Those eyes are in another time and place. She shakes her head. "Jovah is police. Is all he care. Police. No one else. No his family. Only police is family." Ivah blinks. Once and then twice more. Her eyes slowly come back to the present. She wipes them with the heel of her palm. "Like you."

"I don't understand, Mrs. Novak. Why would Jovah not love his family? Did they do something against the law? Did Alexi do something wrong? Nadia?"

In the time it takes me to ask those questions, Ivah's face has regained most of its old composure. The thin, polite smile returns like a slamming door. She's as done with me as she is with that cigarette, which she stabs down onto the empty saucer in a way I can almost feel in my spine.

"Is good girl, Nadia," she says. "Sweet girl. You will marry."

I don't think she's looking for a laugh, but I toss her one anyway.

"No. Not me."

"You have wife?"

"Not anymore."

She winks.

"Nadia is liking. I can tell. *Mat' vsegda znayet.*"

"I don't…"

She smiles at my incomprehension.

"I say mother always know."

"Well, I'm much too old for Nadia."

"*Bol'shoye delo.* Old, young. She need man. Good man."

"She seems to be managing well enough," I say. I should be ready to leave it there, but I'm not. "That kid of hers is sure a handful though. Never seen such a fascination with dragons."

Ivah's face glows.

"Yes, dragon. Is such good grandson. Is gift. So sweet."

My phone sounds off again. I look around for a hammer.

"Is call back," she says. "Is important."

EIGHTY-NINE

Ray yanks the phone from his pocket and looks at the number. He doesn't recognize it any more the second time than the first. He holds a finger up to Ivah Novak and answers.

"Mack. This is Cleo."

"Who?"

"Cleopatra. From *Sonny's.*"

"Isis?"

"Yeah."

"Your instincts are great. I'm starving. But this isn't…"

"I'm with Raj. He's driving and his phone is dead. He needs to talk to you. Hold on."

Ivah is standing and beginning to shuffle away. Ray's expression tightens, half frustration at being interrupted again and half confusion. There's not enough room left on his face to show ill-defined worry, so his gut has to carry that feeling alone.

"Mack?"

"Raj. What's going on?"

"Success, Mack," says Raj. His voice is tight and excited.

"I used to know what that word means, but it's been a while."

"Hell, Mack. We found Hell. And guess who's with him."

It takes Ray a second to catch up. But he gets there.

"Yellow coat."

"Plain as day, man. They drove right past the fish place in Aurora. Black F-150. Cleo got the plate. Illinois ATB773."

Ray stands just as Ivah is rounding the corner out of sight into the bedroom.

There are a lot of ways to flee a police interview. Hers is the slowest. Raj is fumbling with phonetics.

"So that's A like apple, T like tortilla, B like banana…"

"I got it," says Ray. "Where are you?"

"On-ramp to the Eighty-eight, headed east. What do you want us to do?"

"Us? Are you on a date, Raj?"

"Kind of, yeah. What do you want us to do, Mack? He's hauling ass."

"That's what I'm afraid of. Keep your distance, Raj. No matter what happens, do not engage. This lug is as dangerous as he is big. He's a killer, Raj, and I'm betting he knows how to spot a tail. I'm headed for the car. What's with your phone?"

"I left my charging cable at home. Yesterday I bought a used dispatch system from this guy who's getting out of the cab business. Uninstalled my system and installed his. Looks impressive enough, but it turns out none of it works. I burned up my phone battery this morning trying to troubleshoot with tech support in Sarasota."

"So you're a cabbie without communication. Not a good business model, Raj."

"The King of England could fly into O'Hare needing a cab and I'd know nothing about it."

"Big tipper, the king?"

"I wouldn't know. Lucky for me I had a date with a hottie who has her own phone." I have to wait for the laughter to stop before Raj is back in my ear. "Who knew chasing hardened criminals could be so fun?"

"This isn't fun, it's serious," I say, sounding like a dad. "Call me as you change directions."

"10-4."

"And get that out of your head, kid. You're not a cop."

"Roger that."

NINETY

I rocket past Frank at the desk and across the lobby for the front doors. Alice is still at the windows. She sees me coming.

"Let's go!" she says, banging a fist against the arm of the wheelchair. Her voice is busting with hope. She wants out of her locked-up life and I'm her last, best chance. I keep running with a backward wave.

"Go Bears!" I say, like I have misunderstood. Like I'm not just another float in a parade of disappointment to poor Alice. I can feel her eyes at my back as I hazard the parking lot, losing the light of their excitement. Watching me leave.

I learned a lot at St. Evangeline's. How to be alone. How to take a beating. How to fight. How to lie. How to hide from people. I learned that the only way to beat disappointment is to expect it, to count on it, to look for it around every corner waiting to slap the grin off your face. Orphans learn from the same lesson plan as any other lock-up, like the chronically sick, or the elderly or the convict tossed into the joint for more time than he has left on earth. Lesson number one is don't trust the people and the things you think might save you. Hope is always the biggest enemy. Hope was the Big Man of my youth. Everywhere and nowhere at the same time. In everyone's eyes, hope, but about as real as a myth and as solid as a shadow. A thousand disguises. A thousand smiling faces. A thousand second chances. Always a fraud. Always a cheat. Feeding on the violence of betrayal. If God sent Jesus, then it was Satan who sent hope along to carry his bags.

But if the general experience of St. Evangeline's was deeply instructive, the formal catechism taught me almost nothing. Sister Ruth. Sister Helen. Only one thing the penguins ever seemed to care about teaching: good things are coming, unless the opposite happens. Everything is aces, unless it isn't. The Kingdom of

Heaven is yours —you'll be high-fiving Saint Peter one day —unless it isn't and you won't. Maybe that's why my parents took a powder before I was old enough to read the graffiti on the wall. Maybe they knew the truth about me. Maybe damnation is in the blood.

Awfully big on prayer, those penguins. No surprise there. They were big on prayer in the same way cops are big on guns. We all want to believe we can protect ourselves; that we have some control over what happens next. But, in the end, packing a gun is just whistling past the graveyard and a prayer is just a dirty quarter for the slot machine. Maybe that gets the job done, maybe not. You'll never know until it's too late. In the meantime, all you can do is worry that somewhere along the line you got things wrong. Said the wrong thing. Thought the wrong thing. Zigged when you should have zagged. Don't screw anything up, kid, or it's going to hurt forever. That's what I learned.

I'm not a religious man. I've prayed now and then that there's just a little more left in the bottle. I've prayed that all the cards show up in order and wearing the same suit. Other than that, I'm usually not much for prayer. Guess I owe that to the penguins. But I can worry like a pro. I worry I've misplaced a faith in myself to do the right thing by others. Not long ago I put Ginger Turner aka Suri in a trunk and asked her to trust me. Turned out I was delivering her to the wolves. She's likely dead and in pieces by now. Big Man wants you dead, that tends to be the way things go. But even if not, even if Suri has managed to survive, you can bet she hates the ground beneath my shoes. Either way it was my good intentions that made all the difference. I made the wrong play and Suri paid the price.

A few years earlier I lost my way with Ronni Lodge at a St. Patrick's Day punch bowl. She was the wrong woman at the wrong time with just the right look in her eye. I did the thing I shouldn't have done and then I did it a few more times because I like my bad decisions to have some staying power. And then, like night follows day, I lost Marlo in a puff of smoke. I know infidelity doesn't cause pancreatic cancer. I don't believe I have that kind of dark power. But someone sure does. God, Big Man, the Devil. Someone. And whoever it is, has my number. He waits for me to zig instead of zag and then he pushes some big red button with his fat, hairy thumb.

So now here I am again, slipping on the ice at the corner of *What Were You Thinking* and *This is Going to Hurt Forever*. I finally have eyes on the man called

Hell. Good for me. Problem is those eyes belong to two innocent kids who have no idea what they're doing or just how violent and depraved the world really is. They're in a beat-up taxi gunning for Hell because of me. Sure, I could call them off. Tell them to stand down. I could tell them to go fall in love chasing someone else, Cupid maybe, or the kid ripping tickets at the cineplex, someone who can't twist the heads off people like bottle caps. I could do that. Sure I could. But then again, I could do all kind of things I can't really do.

Somewhere the penguins are shaking their heads. Saint Peter too.

I'm fresh out of quarters. I used them all up at Marlo's bedside. God never took my prayers anyway. But I can worry all on my own.

NINETY-ONE

The old man can still drive. What he wouldn't give right now for a set of dash lights and a siren to clear the way. Wasn't important he'd told Twill. *I'm a desk cop now.* He'll be rethinking that one.

Ray puts the old Impala through its paces. The roads are as icy as ever, but the adrenaline takes ten years off his reflexes. Every red light between the Golden View Community and the freeway tells Ray to wait his turn, but he's not taking orders. He's not making any friends either, but as long as nobody else has dash lights and sirens he doesn't care so much about the all horns and one-finger saluting. The phone rings as the Impala finds the on-ramp and angles skyward. Isis is as keyed-up as ever.

"We're exiting the Eighty-eight at Melrose. Headed whatever way… west. Raj says west."

"Got it," says Ray. "Any sign he knows you're behind him?"

"They don't even know we exist. He's driving like a thousand miles an hour. We're keeping a car or two between us."

"Hell of a first-date, Isis. Is this what you had in mind? In my day we went to the drive-in."

"What's a drive-in?"

"Funny."

"Right on Washington. Just go, Raj. It's clear. It's clear. Go, go, go. Wait, wait. Shit. Okay, go."

"You're killing me over here, Cleo."

"Stop worrying, Mack."

It goes like this for another ten or fifteen minutes, Cleopatra narrating every turn of Raj Malik's steering wheel and Ray doing his best to recite the street names in his head so he will recognize them when he gets there.

"I think he's lost," she says eventually. "We just did a big loop. Grover to Henry to West Norton and back to Grover."

"Keep your distance," says Ray, trying not to shout. "He's looking for a tail. He could be testing you."

"He's lost," she says again. "I don't think he knows where the hell he's going."

"Keep you distance anyway, damnit. Slow down."

"Left on Franklin. He's… shit. He's pulling over, Mack."

"Where are you?"

"Corner of Grover and Franklin. He's just sitting there. Where are you?"

"Can he see you?"

"No. Least I don't think so. We're still on Grover. We're up alongside a U-Haul. Where are you, Mack?"

"Fighting rush hour on the two-ninety-four. I'm a good twenty minutes out. Maybe thirty."

"He's getting out. Jesus, he's big. That's like… holy crap. She's getting out now too. He's got her by one arm. They're headed up the driveway. That's not her coat."

"What?"

"It's a size too big. Yes it is. Totally. Look at the sleeves. Raj…"

"Isis. One person at a time. Describe the house."

"White. Two stories. Three… no, four houses from the corner. Big tree in the yard. I think it's the only big tree on the street. I don't know my trees. What is that? Sycamore. Raj says it's a sycamore. But I really don't think Raj knows either. I think he's trying to impress me with a genius-like knowledge about trees." Laughter over the phone, his and hers. "I like that in all of my Pakistani cab-jockies. Got to know their hard woods. Very sexy. He's taking my phone. He's… no! He's…"

"It's definitely a sycamore, Mack," says Raj. Ray grips the wheel and changes lanes, squeezing the Impala into a moving space that almost doesn't fit. He gets another horn and moves on to another lane. "And if you ask me Cleo here has a lot of attitude for an Egyptian hash-slinger. But she's got a smile that won't quit, and those eyes are smokin'."

"You love birds want to knock it off and tell me what the hell is happening?"

"Sorry, Mack. Hell rang the bell. They're both inside now."

"Who opened the door?"

"Don't know. Couldn't see."

"Any cars out front or in the driveway?"

"No. Just the F-150 at the curb."

"What's the number on the house?"

"Stand by one." Ray listens to the dinging inside the cab start up and fade away beneath Raj's crunching footsteps. "Four, seven, nine, two," says Raj. "Repeat. Four, seven, niner, two Franklin Street. What do you want us to do?"

Now's his chance. Ray can feel the fat, hairy thumb of judgment poised and twitching above that big, red button.

Go home, is what I want you to do. Take each other's clothes off. Laugh until you cry. Order take-out and watch bad movies. Be together and count your blessings. Trade one kindness for another until you fall asleep in each other's arms. Do as much of that as you can while you can because tomorrow is a freight train without any brakes. Be anyplace other than the corner of Grover and Franklin marking Hell from behind a U-Haul.

Now's his chance. Maybe his last.

"Mack?"

"Sit tight," he says. "Don't get any closer. Do not engage. Be ready to hit the gas and get the hell out of there if it looks like you've been made. Hopefully they'll stay put for a while. I'm coming as fast as I can."

"And if they leave?"

"Keep your distance. Let me know where they go."

"Roger that, boss."

NINETY-TWO

I call in an address look-up as I try not to kill people on the freeway. Turns out the pillows at 4792 Franklin Street bear the headprint of a guy named Garrett Hoosier. I don't get much information. Garrett is up on his taxes, and he owns the place free and clear. He hasn't left any fingerprints in a criminal database, but the address does pop up on a 2009 pre-employment background check initiated by the Illinois Department of Corrections.

So, Mr. Hoosier is in the convict business. Or he was. Or he wanted to be. Of all the things that might mean to me, a couple stand out for immediate consideration: I have yet to meet a person in the convict business that didn't love guns and hate regular police. Shameless profiling, and maybe baseless, but I add it to the list of things to worry about anyway and give the accelerator a little extra squeeze.

I once helped execute a warrant on the homes of four different state prison guards in connection with the murder of two former inmates. We were looking for the gun that did the job, a .45 caliber P-Series Ruger. We all but tore those places apart looking, but we never found that gun. What we did find was a combined eighty-one other firearms that, as far as we knew, had not killed anyone. They weren't in dusty collector gun cases either. They were all loaded and within reach from any place in any room. Those boys were ready for the zombie apocalypse. I asked one of them to explain the fetish. He went on about his home being his castle and how a man never needs a gun until he does. Then he called me a filthy name and turned into a clam.

Maybe Garrett Hoosier is the exception. Maybe he collects butterflies and stamps. More digging could get me some more information about Mr. Hoosier, but I can't dig and drive at the same time. I could ask a favor but there are only so many favors a guy with no friends can cash in on one day. I go to the bank anyway.

"Raffi. Mack."

"What's doin', man?"

"I need a favor."

"And the sun rises in the east."

"I know."

"This has got to stop, Mack."

"Yeah. I know."

"You need an intern."

"I know, I know. Look, I'm going into a situation half-blind and I need some information."

"What kind of situation?"

"The kind you don't want to know about."

"Why?"

"Because you can't un-know what you know when ranking officers start asking questions. I need this to stay off the radio."

"You ever wonder if your paranoia is getting in the way of good police work?"

"That's classified."

"Sounds about right. Try me. I'll keep it close."

"I've got a line on Hell."

"*The* Hell?"

"Unless there are two of them."

"You need back-up?"

"Maybe. I need to assess things first."

"Call it in, man. Don't put yourself out there."

"I hear you, Raffi. I need eyes on, first."

"What do you need from me?

"Two things. First priority is as much as you can tell me about a Garrett David Hoosier. Two R's, two T's, and two O's. He lives at 4792 Franklin Street."

"Got it. And?"

"Second priority is to run down a plate. Illinois alpha tango bravo 773."

"Okay. What do I get in return?"

"I'll name my first child after you."

"No." He sounds emphatic. "Don't go reproducing on my account, man. Please. I'll do this for free."

My memory isn't what it used to be. The street names Isis fed me are all in my head, but I've mixed up the order. Maybe a smarter man would invest in a smarter phone, one that can talk to satellites and show a guy where he's made a wrong turn in the world. On the other hand, if I thought a phone could do that, I'd never have consented to the shrink. He diagnosed my wrong turn in two sessions. He concluded I was secretly working for Big Man and then disassociating from myself because I couldn't stand my own company. Best part was that he did it with lots of judgment and corrupt intent. When the geniuses at Apple make a phone that can label you crazy and ruin your career, I'll take out a second mortgage and buy one.

I find my way eventually, zigging and zagging through an older, densely packed neighborhood. The houses are small and square with smaller, square windows and even smaller, square chimneys. The streets are cramped, lined with cars that haven't moved all winter. I roll down my window and shout at an old guy in a black and red hunter's hat salting his driveway from a plastic bucket like he's feeding invisible pigeons in the park. He points and I give him a nod and a wave.

The U-Haul is on the corner of Grover and Franklin, just like Isis said. So is the lone sycamore holding down Garrett Hoosier's front yard. What is not anywhere evident is Raj Malik's taxi or Hell's F-150. My best guess is that Hell and Emily and maybe Garrett Hoosier are back on the road. Which means Raj and Isis are following. If Garrett Hoosier is with them, then he failed to close the door to his garage, which now sits gaping at the top of the driveway. Two vehicles are inside, one small, black and shiny and the other big and green and showing its mileage.

I dial Raj's number. Straight to voicemail shouldn't come as a surprise. That's what phones do once the battery is dead. I curse my failing memory again and call Isis instead.

Four rings. Voicemail. I check the number and try again.

Four rings. Voicemail.

I can feel the worry warming up in my gut like oil in a skillet full of wrong. A dead phone I understand. But not answering the phone, letting it ring, that's different. All those explanations show up dressed in capital letters.

I park the Impala on Grover Street, out of sight behind the U-Haul. I close my eyes and imagine the house I can no longer see, considering my options. All of those options involve having Sig on stand-by. I pull the gun out of the holster and double-check the magazine.

NINETY-THREE

Hard to watch. This is a young-man's game. True, Ray's played the game so many times he can do it with his eyes closed, but that doesn't mean he still has what it takes to come out the winner. I may have to watch, but I'm not laying any wagers.

First things first. Before the game even starts, he's got to make it across Franklin Street. Forget the bullets, because this is the thing that's going to kill him. Icy parking lots are one thing, flat and level, most of them sanded. But the neglected, wind-polished lower-middle class neighborhood roads are another matter. The ruts and potholes take Ray's legs in separate directions just as the vicious winter Hawk shoves him hard in the back. Now it's Ray versus Gravity.

It's a prolonged fight. He manages the best he can and he doesn't give up, arms windmilling wildly, but he eventually goes down hard in the middle of the street, breaking his fall with his right shoulder, elbow and hip.

He rolls over on his back with a groan and lays there, wind blowing over his face.

It's anybody's guess at this point. Maybe he gets back up. Maybe he reaches for his phone and calls his own ambulance. Or maybe he reaches for Sig and shoots himself. Maybe it's a bullet that takes him after all.

Glad it's not me.

NINETY-FOUR

It takes me three tries to get back up, none of them particularly dignified. The only way it works is to get off my back and flip over onto all fours, then rise slowly, hands in the air like I'm surrendering. Maybe because that's exactly what I'm doing, giving up to forces of nature I cannot control.

I make it to the far side of Franklin and head for the house. All the joints on the right side of my body howl in pain but they all still seem to work so maybe I've been spared a broken kneecap and a shattered hip. I walk up the driveway for the open garage door. The car on the right is a spit-polished black Corvette convertible. Bucket seats. Spoiler. Wings. The works. The vanity plate says OORAH 01. I'm guessing Garrett only takes this baby out on cloudless summer days; a quick soaping-down and rinse on the driveway for all the neighbors to see. Then maybe he takes her out for an ice cream in the next county.

Next to the Stingray is the work horse; a moss-green, dented Ford pickup. Gun rack in the cab. Locking toolbox, shovel, and lots of old stains in the bed. The rear bumper is bent all to hell, but the Sault Saint Marie stickers are still intact, the one on the left for Michigan and the one on the right for Ontario. The boat trailer hitch has seen better days. Then again, the whole truck looks ready for the giant magnet in the sky. It's lucky to be in the garage at all.

I don't linger. I cross the driveway and head for the front door. I could ring the bell, but all my bones hurt from my fight with Franklin Street and I'm not in a polite frame of mind. I'm in a knocking mood and there's nothing quite like a fist on wood to get a man's attention. I don't know the guy, maybe he's a peach. But even if he is, this peach is keeping company with one seriously large and rotten apple, which makes me a lot less interested in giving him the benefit of the doubt.

I pull open the screen door ready to start the show but a shout from inside stops me. A man's voice. I can't make out any words. Only emotion and lots of it. Somewhere inside a door slams. I keep listening but whatever was happening has stopped.

I ease the screen door closed and head back for the driveway, then around the side and back of the house, looking for a window that might allow me a peek inside. The kitchen and dining room have windows to the backyard, which is larger than I would have guessed from the street. It comes with one of those large, build-it-yourself wooden utility sheds that always comes out looking like maybe paying a little extra money to have someone else build it might have been a good idea. I failed geometry, but I know a trapezoid when I see one. The whole thing has a warped, sinking-funhouse slant to it. The pitched metal roof has buckled away from the walls in the back and the sliding double doors aren't flush.

The shed sits in the back of the lot, separated from the house by a dirty carpet of snow. In my experience, a shed that gets used a lot in the winter comes with clear, icy path and a crappy aluminum shovel propped up at one end of that path or the other. This one comes with a just a few foot-holes punched into the snow in a line that connects the front of the shed and the back door of the house. The foot-holes are clean. Recent.

The wind whips through the backyard in a wide circle, like it's looking for me. The entire right side of my body wants to go home for a stiff drink and a hot bath. Instead, I ease up next to Garrett Hoosier's kitchen window. It looks exactly like a kitchen should if you're a single guy having a nightly affair with Mrs. Stouffer. The man likes his frozen lasagna, and lots of it judging from the open bag of trash. No crime in that unless you're washing it down with Diet Coke, which Garrett seems to buy by the case. There's a newspaper opened over the counter. I can't tell which one, but it has a sports section. The Blackhawks goalie has his stick in the air and a USMC coffee mug on his face.

I'm ready to move on to the dining room windows when the man himself wanders briefly into view and away again. He reappears twice more at regular intervals. Not happy, Garrett. He's angry and pacing, staring fixedly at his cellphone and muttering to himself.

The fourth time he comes to a stop and leans up against the kitchen counter long enough for me to get a decent look at him. He's taller than he is round, but not by much. The lasagna is clobbering the diet soda. I'm guessing he used to have a lot more muscle in those shoulders. Back in the day, Garrett could do push-ups like nobody's business. More hair too. But the hair is mostly gone now, and the muscle has melted away. That leaves Garrett here with a lot of extra weight on his bones, cheese in his arteries, a bottle of little blue pills by the bed, and a Stingray out in the garage just to wind back the time and make everything okay again.

And a gun in his hand.

It's a Glock. Nine-millimeter. Highly effective at killing people but it gets in the way when you're trying to use a phone. Garrett sets the gun on top of the Blackhawks goalie next to the mug so he can use both thumbs to text. He shakes his head angrily at the screen saying something to himself I can't make out. He starts pacing again then stops suddenly. He lowers the phone, lifts his face in a direction opposite the kitchen and shouts the first words I am able to comprehend.

"Shut the fuck up! Or I will fucking come in there and I will do it for you! Not another fucking word!"

Garrett is not alone. The hot oil in my gut starts to bubble and pop. I ease back from the window as quietly as I can, slowly retreating to the windowless side of the house.

I stand in the wind and stare at the chain link that separates Garrett Hoosier from his neighbor, weighing my options. The safe move would be to fall back and call it in, just like Santiago advised. Wait in the car for backup. Drop the word hostage into the call and they'll send out a SWAT team. The upside to that plan is I don't get plugged with Garrett Hoosier's Glock 9. Downside is I probably don't learn anything about anything from Garrett, even if he doesn't go down in a blaze of glory. He gets gobbled up by the machine and by the time I get any kind of crack at him he's done talking to everyone but his lawyer. Meanwhile, I'm spending my time off the street, in a Chicago PD interrogation room spilling my guts to people I just can't trust. Plus, there's the distinct possibility that calling in the cavalry only makes this situation worse, creating a hostage crisis that does not yet actually exist.

Marlo is in my head, pouring us both another splash over the rocks. I snub out the Camel and take the drink, defensive as usual about my filthy habit.

We've all got to die of something, Marlo. No one gets out of this thing alive.

Ray, you're going to do what you're going to do. We both know it. Rationalizing is just wasting time.

I pull Sig and disengage the safety.

Besides, the job is going to kill you long before the Camels do.

NINETY-FIVE

He goes in through the open garage, Sig in the lead, pausing between the pickup and the Stingray to take a good look in through each window. Then he presses forward.

Ray flattens his ear to the door into the house, closing his eyes to listen. If he hears anything, his face shows no reaction. He has banished every feeling from his body. Cold. Exhaustion. Pain. All gone for now. The muscle tension in his arms and legs has twisted up into a constant, quivering readiness for anything. He lifts the gun and slowly twists the doorknob.

The crack in the doorway lets a sound out into the garage. A voice. Garrett's voice, angry and threatening from somewhere deeper inside the house. Ray pushes, slowly but steadily, widening the crack until he is able to step inside and close the door behind him. He stands motionless in the small hallway, gun pointed in the direction of the sound, listening.

"The fuck you say. Who do you think you're talking to? That's the wrong fucking attitude, Hell. I'm the guy that can bury everybody. Understand, shithead?"

Ray inches forward. The flooring is hardwood, covering a landmine of hidden creaks. He tries to keep his weight as close to the wall as possible. His shoulder catches the corner of a hanging photograph, and he has to stop where he is to keep the thing from coming off the hook and crashing to the floor. He straightens it back to the way it was. It's a photo of Garrett, pre-lasagna, someplace wet and warm, sitting on a jet ski.

It's not the only one. The frames are a chintzy plastic made to look like wood, but the photos inside are an homage. Garrett in the desert holding an M27, boot on the bumper of a Humvee. Garrett in uniform on an airboat holding binoculars, boot up on the gunnel. Garrett in an autumn field holding a Remington 7600, boot on the shoulder of a five-point buck. Garrett on a trawler holding up a bloody Chinook, boot up on an overturned white bucket. Ray nods to himself and keeps moving.

"All of it, Hell. It all stinks. Don't you lie to me. Don't you… no! No, you sent her here. Don't lie to me. I know this fucking game. This is not a coincidence."

The kitchen is the first room on his right. It looks the same on this side of the window, only more so. The bag of trash and the case of Diet Coke haven't changed a bit. The coffee mug and the Glock are still reading the sports page. On the counter next to the refrigerator there's a ceramic catcher's mitt which looks to be where Garrett keeps his breath mints and his car keys.

"Because she was in my goddamned backyard. Tells me she lives down the street and that her cat is stuck in my shed. So I take care of whore number one, so she won't take off again, and I go outside like an idiot to open the shed and see what the deal is with whore number two. Next thing I know this chick is making a beeline for my back door. She fucking locks me out of my own fucking house. I gotta go all the way around in through the fucking garage. Well, don't ask me. Like you don't already fucking know. Yeah, I did, no problem there, but now she won't shut up about the fucking police. Yeah, she speaks English just fine. Too much fucking English. How the hell should I know? No. Not when I'm done, she won't."

It's three steps across the kitchen to the gun. Ray makes it in two as quietly as he can. He picks up the Glock like it's a sleeping baby and ejects the magazine. He thumbs out all fifteen rounds into the half-cup of coffee, reinserts the magazine and then almost returns the Glock to the newspaper before he stops. He's remembering an ugly lesson, the kind you don't get to learn twice. He shakes his head and pops out the bonus round in the chamber.

But he fumbles the bullet.

It misses the hard counter and hits the Blackhawks goalie in the mouth. Ray breathes a sigh of relief. He sends bullet sixteen into the drink with the others and returns the gun. In the next room Garrett never takes a breath.

"Because she looks like someone in your stable, that's why. Someone you'd send to fuck me over. You send one whore through the front door while another whore comes through the back door to take her pictures or whatever you have up your sleeve. Yeah, yeah, fuck you, Hell. That's a lie. Let me put it this way, shithead. If a cop actually does show up asking me about a disturbance? On his way to asking me about a fucking girl? Then I'm gonna know he's one of yours, bought and paid for. Understand what I'm saying? If I go in, Hell, if I so much as see the inside of a squad car, then I'm going in singing. Understand?"

Ray lowers himself to the floor, pushing back against the counter, bracing himself against the cabinets. He leans his head back against the cupboard door and listens. Ray keeps Sig pointed at the space where Garrett Hoosier is not yet standing.

"If the man has some problem with me, after all I have fucking done for him, then he needs to act like a man and tell me himself. Tell him I don't need these fucking games. Pin this shit on me? On me? Fuck you. After all I've done? In fact, tell him I'm done. Yes. Done with a capital fucking D, okay? What repossess? Bullshit, repossess. I earned that car. There's a bullet for anyone who touches the car, okay? Let's just get that straight. And as… no, I'm still fucking talking here… as for you, you can turn your ass around and come get these skanks out of my fucking house. Both of them."

The silence is sharp and sudden, exactly the kind that focuses your attention and makes you squeeze your grip. Ray levels the Sig Saur with both hands and waits. Where there was once an angry voice, there is now disgusted muttering.

And new movement. Standing. Pacing.

"I can hear them in the backyard, you know." The voice belongs to Isis, shouting from a small room. A bathroom or a closet. "The house is already surrounded. It'll be better for you if you just let us go now. It's going to be a lot worse if they find us like this."

"Goddamnit!" shouts Garrett. "I told you to shut the fuck…"

He doesn't finish. There is a heavy stomping through the house for the kitchen. Ray stiff-arms Sig toward the hallway at the entrance to the kitchen. Garrett's profile is suddenly there —a beefy shoulder, a hip, the back of his head —and then gone again as he snatches the Glock off the counter and storms off the other direction. Ray gets to his feet and peers over the kitchen counter in time to see Garrett disappear from the adjoining dining room.

Somewhere a door opens violently.

"I told you to shut…"

"Mack! Mack!" Isis screams his name, her voice desperate and reckless, punching through the walls in search of him. "Mack! We're in the bathroom!"

Ray rockets to his feet and makes one step for the hallway. Then he stops. His body maybe old, but that brain still works. He lunges back across the kitchen for the ceramic catcher's mitt.

"Mack! Mack!"

Only one key fob comes with a remote. Ray squeezes the panic button. It's a shrill, piercing whistle that drills through every eardrum within an eighth of a mile. Ray pockets the keys, then crouches back up against the kitchen cupboards.

Tough position for a man his age. But he doesn't have to wait long.

Garrett Hoosier thunders back through his house for the garage where his Stingray is busy waking the dead. Ray closes his eyes, like he's silently counting the steps.

The eyes open again.

There he is. Ray's looking right at me. This is the man I used to know.

He holds Sig at the ready. Then he juts his leg out into the hall.

NINETY-SIX

A flying Hoosier sounds like a freak show circus act to me. Maybe a kind of bat. Maybe in Indiana they'll start in about some basketball superhero.

Not in Chicago. On Franklin Street, a flying Hoosier is an angry lasagna addict who leaves planet Earth for short distances only to land on his face and break his nose on the hardwood flooring.

Got to hand it to him though, he holds onto that Glock. Garrett skids to a stop near the garage. I stand up as he is rolling onto his back, just getting the taste of his own blood, trying to get his bearings. Trying to figure out what's brand new in the world. Behind him, out in the garage, the Stingray is screaming for help. The blood's all over the lower half of his face, like I've interrupted a hyena in the middle of breakfast. He grabs at his nose with his left hand and aims the Glock at my head with the right.

Should have left the nose alone. He howls out his pain, taking his hand away. Then he remembers the stranger in his house and repositions the gun. He sprays as he speaks, sounding like he has a bad cold.

"I will fucking…" he starts.

"I know," I say. I give him a sincere nod so he knows I'm listening.

"I will blow you away, man." He may be yelling at me, but his eyes are on Sig. This is a man wondering if he should be counting his last seconds. I figure there are only a few of those left before he pulls the trigger as his last best option. That's coming eventually, but I'd like to delay it as long as possible, so I try to lower the temperature a little. I slip my hand in my pocket and squeeze the panic button again. The shrieking whistle stops, and a new silence washes in like a gentle wave.

"I know," I repeat. "But before you blow me away, Garrett, maybe we should have us a little talk. And before we have our talk, maybe you should clean up. You're a mess. Let's get some ice on that nose. At least a washcloth. Paper towel. Something." I step into the kitchen. "Where should I be looking?"

"Who the fuck are you?" he shouts.

Isis yells again for all she's worth from the other end of the house.

"We're in the bathroom! Help us! We're in the bathroom! What's happening?"

The sound of her sends Garrett back over the edge.

"Shut! Up! Shut…"

"Oh, let her scream," I say, opening up drawers around the sink. "She'll be okay. There's time for her later. Am I right, Garrett? Ah. Washcloth. This'll do."

Garrett spits. I can hear him moving.

"I'm going to ask you again. Who the fuck are you? And what are you… Ow! Fuck!… What are you doing in my fucking house?"

I can hear the hysteria starting to seep out of his tone. He thinks he might live after all. The Glock tells him everything is in hand except the nose. The nose is telling him the hand isn't helping and to keep it on the Glock.

I wet down the rag and walk back out into the hall. Garrett has propped himself up against the wall. Now both hands and the Glock are sticky-red. I can see he has wiped the sweat out of his eyes with his hand, so now they're red and sticky too. My back is turned for ten seconds and he's gone from hyena to psycho clown. I'm careful to keep Sig pointed at the floor. I drop the wet cloth into his lap.

"Name's Mack," I say. "If you don't want strangers in your house, Garrett, maybe you should keep your garage door closed."

Garrett grabs the cloth and holds it as carefully as he can against his nose.

"Ow! Fuck!"

"Broke my nose once," I say. "I was thirteen, playing catcher in the cheap-penguin leagues. The nuns dumped all the money into Bibles, which left nothing for a catcher's mask. The pitch came in fast and low and the batter –rubbery kid we called Noodle –Noodle took a step backwards before he swung. Nearly took the nose clean off my face. Some kind of pain."

"Do I look like I want a fucking story? What the fuck do you want? Mack. Hell sent you, didn't he?"

I think about that for a second. Then I nod.

"You're no dummy, are you, Mr. Hoosier? I am here because of Hell."

"Motherfucker," he says, mostly to himself. "I knew it. After all I've fuckin' done for those…" He grips the handle of the Glock like he's squeezing a lemon and points it directly up at my head. "Don't you even fucking think about…"

"Look. Garrett. Calm down. If I was here to kill you, you'd be dead already. How about I put my gun away and you put your gun away and we talk like, well, we talk like a couple of reasonable guys. Like a couple of neighbors over the back fence. Mid-July. I've got a rack of ribs cooking on my grill and you've got a T-bone on yours." I nod to the photo of him and the five-point buck. "Or maybe some venison. All that delicious smoke in the air. Someone's got a radio on. You like Sam Cooke? He's good for grilling."

I slip Sig back in his holster and shrug. Garrett stares up at me, blood bubbling out of his nostrils and slicking a fresh path over his lips and down his chin. His eyes are trying to figure me out, but the pain keeps getting in the way.

"You want a Diet Coke?" I ask. "I'll get you a drink."

"I don't want a fucking drink," he says, spitting again, painting the floor and wall with his own blood. He looks at me warily, setting the Glock in his lap, careful to keep the grip in position just in case he needs it in a hurry. He uses both hands to gently brush the cloth over his face. "What I want is for you to just deliver the fucking message and then get the fuck out. And take the girls with you. Leave me the fuck alone. All of you. I'm out of this shit show. Forever."

"You sound bitter, Garrett," I say, leaning against the wall, crossing my arms. "That's not healthy."

"Fuck healthy," he mumbles angrily into the cloth. He looks at me. "Since when does the man care about healthy? I put my ass out there for him. For years. He calls the tune and I dance the fucking jig. One mistake, one little fuck-up, is a twenty-year stretch. Maybe more. But do I whine about that? No. I play ball anyway. I get the fucking job done. Every time. And now he wants to play these games with… with…" he gestures toward the other side of the house with the bloody washcloth. The he looks at me. "Why is she here?"

"Who?" I ask.

"Who. Fuck you, who. The hot lips in my bathroom screaming your name."

"Oh. She's just doing what she's told. Doing her job."

"Her job. Which is what? Take pictures? Set me up on some underage bullshit? Get me pinched for that? For *that*?"

I nod like all I can do is agree the world has gone crazy.

"And why the fuck are you here?"

"Me?" I shrug. "I'm here just in case things go wrong. Things went wrong, Garrett. You weren't supposed to figure things out so quickly. Now we have a situation."

"What situation?"

"Two girls locked up in your bathroom, for starters. But the real situation is the one you just laid out there on the phone a minute ago. You know enough to bury everybody. I think that's how you put it. How do you think that makes the man feel?"

"I don't care how Hell feels. He doesn't scare me."

"I'm not talking about Hell and you know it. I'm talking about the man, Garrett, the only guy that really matters in this game. Don't answer, I'll tell you how it makes him feel. It makes him feel insecure. Makes him want to be sure you still have some skin in the game. That puts me in a car with Hot Lips following Hell all the way out here just to get a little insurance. So, there you go."

"Insurance." Garrett shakes his head in disgust. I shrug.

"Nothing like evidence of rape to put the man at ease."

"Rape. She's an illegal Russian whore. They start young over there. All I did for him? Fuck him."

I want to end the charade. I want to step on Garrett Hoosier's face and break his nose into smaller pieces. I take a breath and let it out. It sounds like commiseration mixed with a little judgment.

"I'll be sure to pass that along," I say, waiting for his expression to reflect the gravity of those words. Now he's thinking he has no choice but to kill me. He swallows. He doesn't like the taste.

"But let me ask you something, Garrett. None of my business, but since we have worked for the same employer… he actually talked you into taking your retirement payment in free girls? Girls and a car?"

Garrett looks at me but says nothing. I take it as a confirmation and shake my head.

"No thanks," I say. "When my time comes? I'm not settling for that nonsense. Cash only. 'Course, what am I gonna do with hot girls?" I give him a self-deprecating laugh. "Look at me, I'm like a hundred. Viagra keeps my eyelids up. I'll take the cash. You, my friend, settled for payment that's only gonna get you locked away. You settled cheap and dumb. No offense, man."

"All I've done for him," he says again. "Sault Sainte Marie? Fuck. That job took more than steering an airboat the wrong way."

"I know," I say.

"That's high-stakes coordination. And the feds aren't fucking playing around. They're always changing things up, switching work schedules. New oversight every fucking month. They don't trust their own people."

"I know. That's some real stress. Working that way."

"No shit that's some stress. And fucking Stateville? The shit I pulled for him in that hell hole? Surveillance cameras every fucking place? Knowing which con you can trust for the price of a nickel-balloon of horse up someone's ass. Or a shiv in a bar of soap? I fucking delivered, man."

"I know."

"The man owes me," says Garrett like a sullen child. "Send Hell to my house? My house? With this bullshit? Fucker needs to show some gratitude."

"You let him off cheap, Garrett," I say. "A few girls and a car? Come on. Tell me there was more."

He nods, holding the cloth on his nose with both hands. "There was. It's gone."

"Well, you're getting the girls for free and there's no room left in the garage." I take an obvious look around. "And now I've seen the palace on Franklin Street. So that leaves drugs or gambling."

He's about to tell me where to stick my guesses but then another possibility occurs to me.

"Or a boat. You're a water guy. You bought yourself a great big boat, didn't you, Garrett? Too heavy for that trailer hitch on the pickup that's almost falling off. Sail or motor?"

Garrett stares up at me for a beat or two. Then he gives in.

"Sail. Thirty-five-foot."

I whistle. "That's a home away from home. A floating bachelor's pad. I get it. I have a version of that dream. I'm thinking maybe the Keys. Mexico. Someplace warm. Where's she docked?"

"She isn't." Garrett sighs and babies his nose. "Had to give her up. I was under water."

"Under water," I say with a smile. "Tell me it wasn't a bad loan, Garrett. Tell me the man did not give you a boatload of cash that you used to buy an actual boat you couldn't afford to keep. And then you lost the boat because you couldn't pay the juice on the loan that came from same shark-suit pocket that the retirement bonus came from in the first place. Tell me you're not that dumb."

Garrett pulls the cloth away and looks at it like the answer might be written in the stained impression of his own face. He doesn't say anything. I can't help but laugh.

"So, for all your brave and brilliant work, the man gave you a slap on the back and a bunch of dough. You bought yourself a car. Then that got old, and you went for the big dream you couldn't afford. It's a money-pit in the water. So, you went back to the man for some help. Let me guess; he was delighted to lend a hand to such a loyal soldier. Then you came up dry, once, twice, three strikes and you're out, and he took the boat."

"Fuck you, man," he says. "It's none of your business."

"So now the bank account is empty, the house is mortgaged up to the chimney, the boat's gone and the man has essentially cut you loose for the price of a car you can only drive in the summer. Sure, you get all the free sex you can handle, you get to feel like a real stud ten minutes at a time, but that doesn't really cost the man anything, now does it? Kind of makes *you* look like the free whore, doesn't it, Garrett? No wonder you're bitter."

"What's happening?" shouts Isis. "We're in the fucking bathroom! Get us out of here!"

Garrett picks the Glock up off his leg and points it.

"Time to go shithead," he says. "So much as itch for that piece and I'll put a hole in your head."

"Hardly fair, Mr. Hoosier," I say. "I could have done the same to you ten minutes ago."

"Fuck fair. In fact, why don't you just open your coat, ease the gun out with one finger, set it on the floor and slide it over with your foot."

I shake my head.

"That won't do," I say.

"No?"

"Nah. Think about all the work."

"Work. Sounds easy enough to me. Want me to start counting?"

"Garrett. Are you listening?"

"I'm listening."

"I'm not giving it up without a fight. Okay? We both know that. You'd do the same, which is why I never asked you for your Glock, there. Maybe you win the fight. You've got the draw, so let's say you win. A hole through my head, as you say. Now you've got a dead old man in your kitchen. Sure, self-defense, breaking and entering, all that. I get it. You can call the cops and make a go at that, but the two screaming women locked up in your bathroom are going to crumb that plan in a hurry. Which leaves trying to keep everything quiet and out of sight. How many of your neighbors heard that Stingray shrieking holy hell from your open garage? How many are looking at that beautiful car right now, wondering what's going on over at 4792 Franklin? How are you going to get rid of a dead old man and two screaming women? Guess you could kill them too. Shuts them up, true, but triples the weight you gotta heave up into the bed of that shitty pickup. Serial killing is a young-man's game, Garrett. And risky. You want to avoid the man sending you up the river for what's locked up in that bathroom of yours, but what do you think he's going to be able to do with a triple homicide?"

Garrett closes his eyes for a long blink. I keep at it.

"See, I'm thinking maybe the better way is for me to keep the gun, leave your stately manor, and take the girls with me. I'll deliver the man your message and then you can deal with whatever comes on your own. How does that sound for a plan?"

"Let us out! Are you even still here? If you can hear me, call the police! We're in the bathroom!"

"Zip your fucking coat up," says Garrett. "All the way."

"That works." I do as he says, zipping all the way to my neck, sealing Sig inside.

"Car keys," he says. "Now. Push that button again and it's all over. I promise."

I dig into my pants pocket and toss him the keys. "Closest I'll ever get to a car like that. I'll grab the girls and we'll all get out of your hair. Lead the way."

Garrett shakes his head with a silent laugh. He leaves the bloody cloth on the floor and stands. I can tell the new elevation is good for a fresh shot of pain in his head and maybe some wooziness.

"Right," he says, nudging his broken, bloody nose forward in the direction he wants me to walk. "Thanks, but I'll let you lead."

"Funny thing is, Garrett, it seems to me what you need most is money. Most natural thing in the world would be for you to ask the man for a little work. Get back in his good graces. But after today…" I grimace. "You said a lot of things to Hell that you can't take back. And to me."

"I'll take my chances," he says, standing up. "Let's move."

NINETY-SEVEN

He walks the hall with Garrett Hoosier one step behind. They pass the dining nook and then a dark, square room full of dark, square shapes worshipping an enormous television glinting in the corner. The curtains are thick, pulled over the windows from which Garrett might have been able to watch Ray lying on his back in the middle of the street counting clouds.

On a low table is an empty round plate missing its square brick of lasagna noodles and cheese. Next to that is a cellphone that knows how to make a sound in Hell's pocket.

"Nice place," says Ray. "Cheery."

"Shut up, asshole."

The hallway right-angles toward a bedroom. The open door is slicing an ugly yellow light into a pie-shaped offering that it leaves on the dusty hallway floor. The room immediately before the bedroom has its door closed, like maybe it's not interested in pie or anything else. Like maybe it's already full.

"This it?" asks Ray.

Garrett doesn't answer, instead reaching past Ray to turn the knob. He pushes it open with the hand that isn't holding a gun to Ray's ribcage.

"Daddy's home," says Garrett into the dark room. The response is Cleo's voice.

"You're not my fucking daddy," she shouts. Garrett clicks the light switch.

They are sitting together on the floor in front of the open vanity, faces up and blinking in the light, taking in new information, particularly the bloody mess that is Garrett Hoosier.

Cleo is fully dressed. The other one, Emily, is fully undressed except for a navy-blue towel she has managed to pull over her narrow shoulders and a vinyl shower curtain that, stretching across the bathroom, still clings stubbornly to the metal shower rod by one ring.

She is pale. The contrast between her raven-black hair and the Slavic-white face is arresting. Her lips came out of a tube.

She is young. This is not an adult. Ray's face goes hard. He's remembering Scooter's defensive confusion. *She said she was nineteen.* I can see Ray wants Scooter to die all over again.

Emily looks at Garrett, then at Ray and back again. They are the same to her. They are, together, whatever horrible thing comes next in her life. Her expression lacks a name; equal parts terror and rage, perfectly balanced on the knife's edge of uncertainty, ready to tip one way or the other.

"Mack!" says Cleo, Egyptian-eyes wide. "Thank god."

They sit cross-legged, facing each other. Emily's left wrist is connected to Cleo's right by a pair of silver handcuffs that pass behind a bend in the pipe under the sink. Cleo's brown lankiness next to Emily is disconcerting. They look like a misfit apprentice team working together to fix Garrett's plumbing.

"What the fuck did you do to my shower curtain?" Garrett whines. He steps in and tries to rip the curtain out of Emily's free hand, but she balls it up into her fist, curling her body into it so the curtain wraps around her shoulder. Garrett tries again, both hands this time, even the one with the gun. "Let it go," he shouts. The kid doesn't budge, bracing herself. Garrett lifts his foot to push against her head. Or maybe to kick it.

Ray steps in before Garrett can do whatever it is he has in mind, slipping one foot behind Garrett's other heel and aiming his fist for Garrett's face. A punch in the nose is usually enough to stop most people from doing whatever is it they're doing. It works twice as well with Garrett Hoosier whose nose has already learned a thing or two.

He teeters for half a second before reeling backward. One hand clings instinctively to the shower curtain, a lifeline for a man going backward over a cliff. The other instinctively covers the pulpy, gelatinous mess Garrett used to call a nose. All of which leaves the Glock one hand short, dangling from Garrett's trigger finger as he struggles against gravity and lasagna.

The last curtain ring holds. The rubber stoppers at each end of the shower rod do not. The rod rips free and crashes down into the tub after Garrett with a loud clanging. Garrett's head ricochets hard between the silver faucet and the porcelain as his wrist slams against the side of the tub, sending the Glock clattering across the tile to somewhere by the toilet.

Ray stretches one leg into the tub and steps firmly on Garrett's chest. Garrett howls in pain, both hands cupping his nose, looking up at Ray through the clearest patches in the dirty vinyl shower curtain. He flops and wriggles beneath Ray's foot.

"Calm down," says Ray. "Listen to me, Garrett. You'll live. Unfortunately. Stop it. Relax or I'll add some weight. Where are the keys to the cuffs?" Garrett continues to thrash. One hand leaves the nose for a go at Ray's ankle, but the shower curtain keeps getting in the way. Ray adds a few more pounds of pressure. "Focus, Garrett. Keys."

Something mysterious convinces Garrett that spitting blood up at Ray's face is a good idea. If he could see anything through the shower curtain before, he can't now.

"Mack, they're in his pocket." Cleo's voice is rapidly regaining its calm. "Front right pocket."

Ray bends his knee, increasing the weight on Garrett's chest.

"Keys," he says. "Front pocket. Let's go, Garrett. Sooner you help me out here, the sooner we're gone."

Somewhere beneath the red smear over his head, Garrett is weighing his options. Not fast enough.

"How hot does the water get in this place, Garrett? You like a hot bath after a long day? Not going to feel good on the nose."

Ray reaches in and cranks the knob, sending a vigorous stream of water over Garrett's head. Garrett seems to shrink in the tub, trying to keep his head beneath the shower curtain. It doesn't take long.

"Okay! Okay! Fuck you, motherfucker! Okay!"

"Keys," shouts Ray over the water. "Drop them in the tub."

Garrett fishes in his front pocket and yanks out two sets of keys, one set is tiny and silver. The other comes with a fancy fob and a panic button. Garrett tries to sort one from the other with one hand, but Ray reaches down and takes everything. The shouting and squirming starts all over again.

"Not the car! Not the car! That is my fucking car! I earned it!"

Ray pockets the car keys and passes the handcuff keys backward to Cleo. He turns off the water.

"Here's the deal, Garrett. Cooperate, and maybe I let you keep the car. Continue flopping around like a fish? Fish don't drive. Understand? Keep fighting me and I give the keys back to the man and you can try and collect it from him. That work for you?"

Garrett's body softens. He brings both hands back to cover his nose.

"Get the fuck out of my house."

Cleo is standing next to Ray, looking down at the thing in the tub.

"What are you going to do?" she asks.

"Hand me the cuffs," he says. "Where are her clothes?"

"This is pretty much how I found her."

Cleo hands him the cuffs and slips the keys into his front pocket. Ray slowly takes his foot off Garrett's chest. Garrett pushes the curtain off his face with his forearms and takes a deep, sopping breath.

"Her clothes are somewhere," Ray says to Cleo. She sticks her face over the tub.

"Where's my fucking phone, you pig?"

All Garrett can manage is to glower back at her.

"Try the bedroom," says Ray, easing her away. "Take her with you. Don't touch anything and keep her close. Wait." He hands her his own car keys. "I'm the Impala on the corner. Wait for me there."

"I thought you drove her out here," growls Garrett sullenly. "Who the fuck are you?"

The tub has a slow drain problem. Garrett pushes himself up to a seated position, still keeping one hand against his face. He looks like he might have a follow up question.

But then the scream stops everything. Every would-be word, every thought, every heartbeat, arrests itself and falls away in instant deference to this high, clear sound, packed with rage and pain.

The girl, Emily, is a suddenly naked, feral presence standing at the foot of the tub. Her young eyes are rimmed in a red, murderous savagery, as if they are the source of the shriek. She holds the Glock shakily with both hands, pointing it at Garrett's face. The words are just a kind of indecipherable keening.

"Nenavizhu tebya! Umri! Nenavizhu tebya! Nenavizhu tebya!"

Garrett shrieks, hands defensively out in front of him, and drops backward down into the bloody puddle in the tub. Emily squeezes the trigger with both forefingers. Again and again and again. The empty clicks are somehow louder than all of Garrett's terror.

Then there is quiet in the tiny room. Garrett opens his eyes in shock. He and Emily stare at each other, strangely united in confusion.

Ray leans down over the tub and ratches the cuffs around Garrett's wrist.

Garrett looks up at him. I can tell those eyes are playing back everything that has happened since he tripped over Ray's foot in the hallway. Ray smiles.

"I know, I know," Ray says, his tone oozing commiseration. "Hoosier daddy?"

NINETY-EIGHT

I'm almost back through the garage and headed for the driveway. The Stingray reminds me about the keys in my pocket. I go back inside and drop them in the cup of cold java with the bullets. That reminds me of Garrett's cellphone. I go to the living room and grab it out of the charger on the table, poking it in the screen with a finger. It glows to life with a screensaver of Garrett in the stern of a USCG icebreaker, dressed for the moon, boot up on the wench of a crane and pointing at the Toronto skyline.

The phone is smarter than I am. One look at my ugly mug and it makes me for a stranger up to no good. It asks for a code, then gives up and goes dark. That sends me back down the hall to the bathroom.

I open the door and turn on the lights. Funny what an angry Glock will do to a middle-aged sphincter. Nothing so funny about the smell. Garrett looks up at me with a messy expression, both hands still stretched beneath the sink.

"One more thing," I say, bending down. I tap the phone and hold it up to his face. "Do you recognize this guy?"

Garrett focuses on the screen. Even through all the blood, the phone recognizes him like an old friend, opening itself up for a hug.

My thumb keeps the phone active until I make it back to the car. Isis is riding shotgun and Emily is in the back, curled up on the seat, knees pulled up inside her yellow coat likes she's trying to disappear. I hand Isis the phone.

"You know how to keep this thing from relocking?" I ask.

"Easy," she says, taking it.

"Somehow I figured you'd know that." I twist myself over the back seat and look down at Emily. "How you doing back there, kid? My name is Ray. Maybe

Cleo told you that I'm a police officer with the Chandler Police Department. You're safe now. I know you're pretty angry and scared, but are you hurt?"

She doesn't look at me. She doesn't move.

"Good luck," says Isis, thumbs flying. "I haven't heard any English out of her yet. Here." She hands back Garrett's phone. "It'll stay on now. Least it's got a full charge. Better than I can say for Raj's phone."

"Yeah, you want to tell me what the hell happened?" I ask. I fire up the Impala and start rolling. I don't know where I'm going yet, but anyplace away from the corner of Grover and Franklin strikes me as a good bet. Isis tucks her long, dark hair behind her ear.

"We're sitting back there at the corner waiting for you and the big guy comes out to his truck. You know, like, without her. She's still inside. I called you twice, but you didn't pick up. Thanks, by the way."

"I was on the phone. I can't always tell when someone is calling."

"You need a new phone, Mack."

"Raincheck on the lecture, Isis. What the hell happened?"

"The big guy is pulling away and Raj decides to follow. We start rolling and the front door to the house opens and I can see her inside. She's got, like, nothing on and she's trying to get out into the yard. Like she's afraid of being left behind. Shithead in there catches her by the wrist and yanks her back in and slams the door. Raj is half a block past the house already, but I decide I can't just leave her, so I open the car door and force Raj to stop the car. I didn't tell him what I'd seen. There wasn't time. I told him to keep following the truck and that I would wait for you back at the corner. I thought about calling the police but then I figured *you* were the police and you'd be there any minute. I slammed the door and walked back up the street. Raj took off. He's probably pissed. There was no time to think it through. I just… she needed help. I couldn't leave. I didn't think there was any choice."

"You did good," I say. "Thinking things through was a luxury you didn't have. Your gut made that call."

I leave out the part about how her gut also left Raj alone without a working phone tailing a killer named Hell who now is all but certain to suspect he was followed to Garrett's house.

"How'd you end up inside working on the bathroom plumbing?"

"I was trying to see inside. I went around back and saw that shed back there and

I just…" Isis begins to cry. She buries her face in her hands as all the bottled-up stress and fear escapes. Nothing I can do but shut up and let it happen. Eventually, she comes up again laughing and wiping her eyes. "I started calling my cat."

"Your cat?"

"Yeah. Bootie. All black, one white paw. She died years ago. Which is like this whole horrible story…" she sniffs, cleaning herself up, "shit… anyway, I walked out to that shed shouting her name, like real loud."

My phone rings like maybe it's worried about the dead cat too. I put the story on hold and answer.

"Mack?"

"Raffi."

"Can you talk?"

"Since I was two."

"I got some information on this Garrett David Hoosier guy like you asked."

"Let me guess. Graduated from the Marine Corps in 2001. I'm betting two tours in Iraq and maybe a stint in Afghanistan. Then he gets his papers. Garrett has always liked boats, so he joins the Coast Guard just long enough to leave his boot print on the side of the cutter *Mackinaw*, flying the flag and busting up the ice in Lake Ontario. After that he comes ashore and hops the fence to work for US Customs and Border Patrol. Somewhere along the line CBP puts him in an airboat out at Sault Sainte Marie, working marine patrols and looking for illegals trying to tap the American dream through Lake Michigan. That gig lasts awhile, but then Garrett leaves. Maybe they gave him the boot or maybe he left on his own. Either way, he's not quite done with government payrolls. He applies for a job with the Illinois Department of Corrections. They snap him up and send him out to Stateville to keep an eye on convicts like Wayne Bishop. Make sure nothing bad happens."

Santiago sighs. "Jesus, Mack."

"Don't think so, Raffi. Jesus wouldn't be caught dead at Stateville."

"You saying Hoosier did Bishop?"

"No. But maybe. Not looking at crime is what Garrett does best. Part of the job description. But he didn't stay in Stateville long. Garrett finally retires after a life of government service. He ends up with a shitty house outside of Chicago mortgaged to the rafters to pay for a thirty-five-foot sailboat he no longer owns and a tricked-out Stingray convertible with an alarm that could shatter windows over in Seattle. He's got a pickup that could die at any time. He likes to hunt and fish. Single, no kids. He buys his sex off the rack, and he couldn't build a proper outdoor shed if his life depended on it." Silence on the line. "Raffi? Still with me?"

"Anything else?"

"He's got a thing for frozen lasagna and puts a lot of lead in his coffee. What'd you find out?"

"What's left?"

"Come on, got to be something."

"The part about Stateville," says Raffi. "He got himself fired. They didn't like his temper. Mack, if you already knew this stuff…"

"I didn't know anything. Look, I need you to do me a favor, Raffi."

"You don't say."

"Our friend Garrett Hoosier needs a police escort for some medical treatment."

"What kind of medical treatment?"

"Broken nose with complications of incontinence."

"You broke his nose?"

"No, he got in a fight with his own floor."

"And the incontinence?"

"What can I say, guns scare the shit out of him."

Isis snorts out a laugh. I toss her a pretend scowl.

"Where is he now?" Santiago asks.

"Handcuffed to the bathroom plumbing. There's an empty Glock taking a bloody bath in the tub, by the way."

"And you're at the scene?"

"Negative. This thing is getting hot, Raffi. I'm finally putting it all together."

"Yeah, okay, but you arrested him for something, right? You didn't just…"

"Arrested, I detained him. Let's call it that. Garrett needed some focus time."

"But you identified yourself as a police officer. Tell me you identified…"

"He might be under the impression I work for Big Man."

A long pause, wrapped in a sigh.

"Great. That's great, Mack. Plenty of people already think that. You actually trying to make that list longer?"

"Look, I know I'm cutting some corners…"

"Cutting corners? Mack…"

"I know. I can't afford to get sidelined. Not now." I can hear Santiago looking at the inside of his eyelids. Isis is looking at me. I roll my eyes. "I can't come in, Raffi. I can't come in and I can't cool my heels standing around Garrett's driveway with a bunch of cops playing twenty questions. Odds are that all of this gets me canned and I'm back walking the shopping mall beat, but I can't slow down now."

"Stretch Martin and Wexler are going to be disappointed. Twill too."

"Oh?"

"Yeah. Homicide wants a word. Everyone's asking where you are. Oh, including a couple of hard-ons from OAG."

"That was fast."

"Twill says they're looking for answers about that flash drive and your exchange with Judge Jolie this morning."

"Terrific. Thanks for the heads up. I'm gone."

"Hold on," he says. "I also ran the plates you gave me. Alpha Tango Bravo 773."

"What'd you get?"

"It's a company truck. Owned by an outfit called XXL Enterprises. I looked them up. XXL owns all kinds of companies that own all kinds of other companies."

"What kinds?" I ask.

"All kinds," says Raffi again. Some pauses are heavier than others. This one weighs a ton. "All kinds including a fish wholesaler out in Aurora and a certain drycleaners I now see in my sleep."

I grip the wheel so hard the car jags.

"Still with me, Mack?" asks Raffi. I can hear the smile over the phone.

"You enjoyed that, didn't you?"

"Immensely," he says.

"You're worth your weight in gold, Raffi."

"Then I'll try to start eating more. I'll get you as much space as I can with Twill and Stretch. And I'll call dispatch and send a car out to Hoosier's place. You're on your own with OAG; I'm staying away from those guys. What's the charge on Garrett?"

"No charge. Make it a welfare check. Someone called in a concern about a shrieking car alarm and a naked woman trying to get out of the house. Don't ask. Just get a car out there. The fewer details in your head the better."

"I hear that," says Raffi. "What are you doing?"

"I've got my nose to the ground chasing Hell around Illinois. Put out an APB on those plates. Black F-150. Location only, no contact."

"Got it."

"Thanks. Gotta go, pal."

I end the call and hit the gas, trying to manage the icy streets while navigating the lightning storm in my head. Isis has lots of questions. She wants to know what I know about everything worth knowing about anything. I ignore the questions and check on Emily in the rearview mirror. She's still in her dirty yellow cocoon. The only clue that there is someone inside are wisps of black hair and two legs from the knees down.

"Where are we going?" asks Isis and not for the first time.

"Still working on that," I say. "Finish your story. You were telling me about your bootie call."

"Funny," she says. "He was all black with one white paw. I loved that cat."

"What the hell happened, Isis?"

"So I'm calling and calling out by the shed and the asshole eventually comes out the back door and I tell him my cat is in his shed. I tell him he got in through the opening under the eaves and that he won't come out. He starts to work the lock on the door and I turned and just, like, fucking bolted for the back door of the house. I beat him by a mile and locked the door. Then I locked the front door. I figured we'd be safe until you got there. Guess I forgot about the garage. I didn't even think about it. I don't even have a garage. Anyway," Isis gestures toward the back seat, "I found her in the bathroom, cuffed to the sink. I think he locked her up just so he could come out and deal with me. I think she's Russian. He called her a Ruskie whore. Emily's not a Russian name, you know."

"Do you speak Russian?"

"Come on," she says like I'd asked he if she was telepathic.

"Worth a shot. Did he hurt you?"

"Lots of yelling and threatening at first. He wanted to know who I was. Who sent me. I didn't tell him anything. I tried to storm out and he got physical, yeah. Nothing too bad. He took my phone and wanted the code. I kept giving him the wrong numbers and it locked him out. That really pissed him off. I could have done some damage but then the gun came out and I pretty much did what he said after that. He chained me up to her and turned out the lights. Then he was on the phone yelling at someone. I couldn't make out the words."

"I got all of that," I say and give her a look. "You're not just a pretty face, are you? Who knew you had those kinds of guts inside, Isis?"

"My dad liked to go after my mom. He found out early."

"How'd you know I was in the house?"

"I didn't," she says. "I was getting scared. I figured shouting a name would freak him out."

I make the freeway and point the Impala east. My hip and my shoulder are more upset than ever about the fall on Franklin. My head is beating out a Buddy Rich hit parade. The wound in my face feels like it's trying to whistle through the bandage. My eyelids are sandpapering my corneas from lack of sleep. I need someplace I can be still and think things through. Somewhere dark and quiet where the pillow and the cat and the bottle all know their places. None of that is likely. I reach over to the glove box and fish out a pack of Camels. Isis confiscates them and puts them back, snapping the door closed.

"Don't think so," she says. "Not while I'm here."

"Raj smokes," I say, sounding about twelve.

"I'm working on that," she says. Then her regal, Egyptian face starts to worry. "You think he's in trouble? I mean, like, are you worried?"

I refocus on the road. Up ahead I can see the same taxi she does. Raj isn't in it, but we both imagine he is.

"Don't know," I say. "If he keeps his distance, he should be okay. But any amateur Dick Tracy heroics… This guy, Hell, he knows he's being followed. That means Raj is at a disadvantage and doesn't know it. And we can't reach him."

"He'll call," she says like she's trying to make herself believe. "He'll find a way to check in."

We all keep the chaos in our heads for a few miles. The place I want to be is the last place I should go. Turns out that doesn't matter as much when you're already up to your neck in killers and deputized civilians and the cops want to devour your day with questions. Not to mention the humps in Homicide and the suits in the Attorney General's office. Them too. They're all in line banging at my door.

The Impala can see the exit just like I can. It makes the turn.

"Where are we going?" asks Isis.

I let the question hang, dialing my phone. Three rings and I think I'm out of luck. But then it turns out there's still a little luck left in the bottle.

"Mack?"

"Hello, Doris."

NINETY-NINE

He got the place right. If he can't go home to bed, *Bucks* before opening is just the kind of warm, dark and quiet Ray needs. The cash on the ceiling flutters in the forced air like a make-shift palm and the traffic outside is just regular enough that a few stiff drinks would soften that sound into imaginary waves.

But *Bucks* is offering a kind of relaxation Ray can't afford. Look at him at the bar. He wants a drink. And after that he wants several more. Doris pours him a coffee and slides it across the bar, placing both of her hands over one of his. She follows his gaze to the line of beer bottles on the bottom shelf.

"I wonder how that one tastes," Ray says, pointing.

"You get coffee and only coffee, Mack," she says. "I'm not open and you're not drinking. Besides, you'd hate it. That one's a serious German beer for beer lovers and you hate beer generally." She nods at Cleo and Emily in their booth across the empty bar. Emily is curled up on the seat. Cleo is working her phone. "Two young ones. When I encouraged you to start dating, that's not what I meant."

Ray twists around for a look, then squares his shoulders to the bar again.

"I'll feel safer at the prom if I have one to administer CPR and another to call an ambulance."

"Has she spoken any English at all?"

"*Nyet.*"

"Shouldn't you just take her in?"

"Not until I know more about who she is and what's going on," says Ray. "Once I take her in, she's as good as gone and I lose my access. Those are shark infested waters, Doris. On a good day I only trust three people over there and one of them is me. I need to talk with her first."

"And so you're here to learn Russian?"

"No. I'm here to keep her off the radar. While you were brewing coffee, I made a call to someone who can bridge the language gap." Ray takes a sip and winces. "You might have liquored this up a little."

Doris smiles and shakes her head.

"No chance. Rough day?"

"My hip and shoulder teamed up and picked fight with planet Earth. They lost. Meantime, I've got this kid out there chasing Hell in a taxi. That's going to end badly unless I figure out a way to call him off."

"Maybe you can't save everybody, Ray." Doris' eyes offer a familiar kindness. She squeezes his hand. "Not everybody is your responsibility."

"Yeah, well, this guy is my responsibility, Doris. I'm the one who put him out there. He's doing this for me. Whatever happens…"

Ray reaches into his pocket and pulls out Garrett Hoosier's phone. He stares at it.

"What's that?" asks Doris.

"This is probably a bad idea is what it is," says Ray. "But I'm fresh out of good ones."

He raises a finger to put Doris on hold. Then he pokes the phone until it dials the last person Garrett Hoosier yelled at without a broken nose. It rings twice.

The voice on the other end is slow and deep.

"Call to say you're sorry?"

"No," says Ray. "If you want apologies you have to get at the back of the line. Wait time is a couple of years."

"Who is this and what have you done with Garrett? Something painful, I hope."

"No, no. That's not my style. I'm the kind who just wants everyone to get along."

"Detective Mackey." The voice broadens and lifts into the sound of a smile. "Should have known you were the one dogging me to Garrett's. How you doing, Ray?"

"I'm getting old, Hell. Everything hurts."

"Sorry to hear. Guess this means Garrett is in cuffs."

"You could say that. He's right here if you'd like to say hello. Oh, hang on. He's shaking his head. Garrett doesn't want to say hello. I think you scare him.

You know, Hell, you'd have more friends if you changed your name. Something softer. Hades, maybe. Purgatory."

"Why are we talking, Detective?"

"Because Garrett here suddenly has a lot to say about you. Lucky for him I speak canary. And your girl, here, is doing her best impression of a Russian clam. She hasn't said anything yet, but that'll change with a couple square meals and a kind word. Then we'll know everything we need to know. I thought maybe you could turn yourself in and save the taxpayers a bucket of money."

"Sorry," says Hell, the smile in his voice completely gone. "Little busy at the moment. Maybe you and I can catch up later. I'll drop by your place when I'm free."

"Need directions?"

"I could find it in my sleep. I'll let myself in."

"When can I expect you?"

"When you least expect me. And I'll be on time."

"Sounds fine. I'll have a drink ready. What's your favorite? Wait. Let me guess. I was in a bar recently thinking about you. They had all their choices out on display and I'm thinking to myself, Hell strikes me as a lager guy. Something strong and full-bodied. A beer that can pop the tops off all the other beers. You know, just like you popped the head off Scooter Pleasants' dirty little neck. So, I'm going with a beer called *Helles Bock*." Ray winks at Doris, who looks back at the line of bottles behind her. "It's got that whole Bavarian, Middle Ages feel to it. That's my guess. How'd I do?"

Ray listens, lifting his eyebrows at the silence in his ear.

"Hell? Still with me? What I can't figure out is whether you guys get to pick your own names or if Big Man picks them off a master-criminal happy-hour drink menu. How high-up in the pecking order do you have to be before you get a drink name? And where is beer in the hierarchy? Are mixed drinks higher or lower? If I ever join up, I'd like to be Dr. Forester."

Silence.

"Truth is, Hell, I don't work alone any more than you do. I'd like to take credit for following you to Garrett's but I have to give all of that to other officers. They do the tedious legwork and then I get the call to come out and have interesting conversations with shit-birds like Mr. Hoosier here. Meanwhile, the boys are still out there, running shifts, tag-teaming that F-150 of yours all over greater Chicago. I'll get another call as soon as you do something stupid and you're in cuffs too. Just like Garrett."

Silence.

"'Course, getting you in the back seat will be interesting. I've warned them about that. They don't make squad cars for people like you. They're going to need a van. Maybe a semi. But they'll figure it out. Between the three of them, not one knows the name Sarah Vaughan or Lena Horne, but they sure know how to take a man into custody. Even someone like you, Hell."

Silence.

"Hell?"

"See you soon, Ray," he says at last, the voice full of lead. "Got to catch a taxi."

ONE HUNDRED

The feeling in my gut keeps its muddy shoes on and makes itself at home.

It reminds me of a dream I used to have. I'm standing on the roof of the orphanage, plotting my escape. The penguins are inside shouting my name, looking for me under every bed. The roof across the street is too far away to make a jump for it, but I'm full of desperation and fresh out of good choices. The two-story orphanage is suddenly six stories and growing. Biggest problem is that the roofing under my shoes is rotting out from under me as I hop from one foot to the other, stepping around the crumbling holes. Through one of those holes, I can see the penguins down there looking up, shouting my name and holding up their crosses like slingshots. I'm ready to make the leap but, when I look up, there stands Droopy McCallister. Everything about him weighs too much for that decrepit roof; especially the smile, uncoiling like a fat snake beneath those dark, ball-bearing eyes. The sinking feeling starts in my gut. Then there's the cracking sound from all around me. That's when I wake up.

It's the same crumbling, sinking feeling in my gut now, except now there is nothing to wake up from. I'd give anything for a dream, even a bad one. I'd wanted Hell to believe he was under surveillance by law enforcement professionals, not some scrubby Pakistani cab driver working a favor in exchange for a junior G-man badge. I'd wanted to keep Hell on his best behavior. I'd wanted him to act like most people act when they think others are watching and taking notes.

Instead, I've poked him in the eye. I've made him angry and begged him to teach me a lesson.

Doris is sympathetic. She doesn't like to see me beat myself up. She's offering hope that everything will work out. But in my head the story ends differently. In my head I keep imagining Suri, pulling the trigger on a silver canon larger than her own head, again and again, swinging that thing at everyone in her path, fighting her way out of the Bloomington blood bath that I, with the best of intentions, had arranged for her. I worry that now I've done it again, this time offering up Raj as the innocent sacrifice. In my head I can see him curled up in the trunk of his own cab, parked on some corner of the city that no one will care about until the air around the cab starts to stink and someone makes a call to get the thing towed. Maybe that's not until the weather warms up. No one has a key to the trunk and that's a good thing.

Except me. My brain has a key. I've seen a lot of bodies. I know exactly what Raj looks like in there.

A knock at the door rattles every nerve in the room, yanking me out of my own head. Doris walks over and opens it.

Nadia King is in heels and a long, dark coat, hair perfectly tousled and cheeks freshly wind-scrubbed. Her smile makes it across the bar to the stool next to me before her shoes are over the threshold. She gives Doris a polite nod and sends me a nervous little wave.

I've known Doris long enough to read her mind. The combination to her brain is written on her forehead. She thinks I've been holding out. She thinks I've invited my secret girlfriend to keep me company in a time of crisis. I get off the stool and walk over to make the introductions. They shake hands and then both look to me for what's next. I jerk my head for the occupied booth. I'm a little surprised to see Emily pushing herself upright. She is alert, worried but attentive, her eyes fixated on Nadia like a couple of lost children.

Doris watches me slip Nadia's coat off her shoulders and lay it carefully in the neighboring booth. She gives me a quizzical look as Isis slips out to make room for the newcomer. I pretend I don't know what the look means, nodding my head back toward the bar. Doris and Isis take the hint and leave us to it.

I slide in next to Nadia so that we are both facing Emily. The girl looks at me nervously, then down at Sig, still nosed into his holster, then back to Nadia.

Nadia turns to look at me. The booth is small but not so small that she couldn't have more space if she wanted it. I can feel the bends in her hips and knees and ankles. The cold air is still tangled in her hair. She smells like a summer in Minsk.

"Tell her she's safe," I say. "Tell her I'm a police officer. I just need her to answer a few questions. Tell her I don't want her to be afraid."

Nadia nods and squares herself to Emily. The kid is breathing through her eyes.

"*Vnimatel'no slushayte to, chto ya vam govoryu. YA postarayus' pomoch'. On ne govorit na etom yazyke. On politseyskiy. My ne mozhem doveryat' politsii. Kivnite golovoy, chtoby pokazat', chto vy ponimayete.*"

Emily nods, looking at me and then away, back to Nadia.

"Good," I say. "Ask her what her name is."

"*On khochet znat' vashe imya. Skazhi-ka,*" says Nadia.

The kid swallows. I know she can scream, but her name comes out in a whisper.

"Mila," she says. Another swallow. "Mila Evgenia Kozlova."

I give her my best smile, patting myself on my chest.

"Mila, my name is Ray." I speak slowly, placing my hand on Nadia's shoulder. "And this is Nadia. We want to help you."

Nadia smiles and leans into the table a little.

"*On sobirayetsya zadat' vam voprosy. YA perevedu. Derzhite rot na zamke. Otkazyvaytes' otvechat'.*"

"How long have you lived in this country?" I ask.

Nadia translates. Mila shakes her head. I try again and get the same result.

"How did you come to this country?"

Another rejection.

"Where do you live, Mila?"

Her eyes widen and she shakes her head at Nadia with a little more vigor. Nadia tries again. Lots of different unintelligible sounds, same result.

"Sorry," says Nadia. "She's scared to death."

I keep my focus across the table, making my hands into the shape of the man who, as we sit here, may be ripping the door off the side of a taxi.

"Mila, I'd like to know about the very big man who drove you to that very ugly house. How do you know him? It is very important that I find this man."

Nadia waits until I am done. Then she looks at Mila.

"*On khochet, chtoby vy dali yemu imena. My ne mozhem nazvat' imena. YA khochu, chtoby ty otkazalsya. Pokazhi yemu, chto ty boish'sya. Poprobuy uyti. On ostanovit vas. Togda pozvol' mne pogovorit' s nim. Sdelay eto seychas.*"

The human face can translate horror into any language. Mila's eyes go wide and she tries to stand and slide out of the booth at the same time. I extend an arm to keep that from happening.

"Hold on, Mila," I say, looking to Nadia for help. "Hold on."

Nadia leans over and places her fingertips on Mila's shoulder.

"*Zhdat'. Zhdat'. Pozvol'te mne pogovorit' s nim.*"

Mila relaxes like someone has kicked her plug out of the wall, folding her hands neatly on the table. Nadia nudges me with her knee. We slide out of the booth and take two steps away.

"She's scared," says Nadia. "I think she doesn't trust the police."

"We've got that in common," I say.

"Well, she doesn't know that. You're a man with a gun. Let me just sit with her for a few minutes. I'll see what I can find out."

Nadia lays her palm on my chest and sells the idea with a smile that makes it all the way up to her eyes. I'm hesitant, but I don't have much to lose. I nod and saunter back over to the bar and wait. I can hear Doris in the back, giving Isis the grand tour, laughing and getting on like a couple of sorority sisters. I sit with my back against the bar, keeping my eye on Nadia and Mila.

Nadia does the talking; Mila does the nodding. Her lips never move.

From the front door comes the sound of a key working the deadbolt. Kyle Aubrey pushes his way in and stops short in surprise when he sees me. He looks exactly like Woody from that old show about the bar only with a completely different face and build. Voice is different too.

"Mack…"

"About time, Kyle," I say, looking at my watch. "I'm dying of thirst. The service here is terrible."

"What…"

"Boss is in the back," I say, jerking my head. "She's going to tell you not to serve me anything but coffee. I'm fine with that as long as you're willing to get fired and do what I say."

Kyle takes in the women in the booth as he slips out of his backpack and coat on the way to the bar. His eyebrows ask me the question.

"Less you know the better," I say.

"Okay." He keeps walking, sizing me up. "How's your face?"

"Still attached. They teaching you anything in that school of yours?"

"Sure." Kyle makes his finger into a hook for his coat and backpack. "Lots of stuff."

I try the coffee again. It's cold now and it still hasn't turned into bourbon. I put it back down and push it away.

"Dazzle me, kid."

Kyle pauses in the doorframe to the hallway that leads to the supply room and back office.

"Jack Kerouac never learned to drive. Vladimir Nabokov had to work a day job until he was sixty. Ernest Hemingway once stole a urinal from a Key West bar called *Sloppy Joe's*. He said he'd pissed away so much money in that place he deserved his own urinal."

I nod and point to the money overhead.

"By that logic, I think I'd like to take home this ceiling."

"You're not the only one," says Kyle. "How's your latest pot boiler coming?"

"Slow. I finally know all twenty-six letters I want to use. Hard part is knowing the right order."

"What's it called?"

Normally not information I divulge, but Kyle's sincerity is hard to resist.

"Working title is *Message in a Bullet*."

"Catchy," he says. "But it seems to me that maybe the message *is* the bullet. Food for thought, Mack."

Kyle disappears into the back and leaves me thinking about the book. Detective Jack McMannis is still stuck in Chinatown at three in the morning waiting for some help. The camera in his hand tells him he's being watched. He doesn't know the half of it yet.

Over in the booth it's still Nadia doing all the talking. Mila sits hunched in her yellow cocoon, hands stuffed deep into her pockets, nodding every so often. The hands make an appearance twice: first to wipe tears from her eyes, and second to hold her nose for a sneeze. She's one of those silent sneezers. Makes me wonder if at some point in her seventeen trips around the sun the difference between living and dying depended on whether someone could hear her sneeze. I might have other theories but the piece of paper that flutters to the floor when she yanks her hand out of her pocket makes me lose interest.

The silent sneezes keep coming. By the third one I'm starting to worry about brain damage.

I stand up and walk back over to the booth as casually as I can manage, swinging my car keys on a finger. I put my foot on the scrap of paper so no one can see it.

"How do you say bless you in Russian?" I ask.

"*Bud'te zdorovy*," says Nadia looking up at me.

"*Gesundheit.* How's it coming?" I drop my keys and stoop to pick them up off the floor, slipping the scrap of paper out from under my shoe. They both go in my pocket.

"I'm doing my best," she says apologetically. But that's not very good, I'm afraid. Trust takes time."

"Doesn't it though," I say.

I saunter back to the bar, fishing the scrap of paper out of my pocket as I go. It looks to be part of an envelope torn into the size of a small business card. I flatten it out against the polished wood. There's just enough room on the scrap for a phone number that I recognize. I pull Garrett's phone out of my pocket just to confirm. I'm guessing that Hell's phone number is almost too big for any space it's written on. He writes like a nine-year-old with a fat, black-grease pencil. Each number looks like it could twist the head off any letter in the alphabet. I can see through the paper that there's more on the back. I flip the scrap over.

Замок

Rarely have I been so electrified to see something that does not make any sense. My world-weary heart is excited enough to sound like a telephone. I pull out Garrett's phone again without thinking, then pat myself down for the phone that keeps ringing.

"Hey, Mack."

Not the voice I was expecting. This day got out of bed hating straight lines.

"Sandra? Thought you were back east with your mother."

"Never got on the plane," she says. "Mom likes her drama with two lumps of inconvenience. Turns out she'll be fine. They're keeping her for a couple of days. The drugs keep her sleeping as my sister sits a twenty-four-seven bedside-vigil. Trust me, there's no hospital room in this world big enough for the three of us. We'd all end up in traction. They'll call me if she takes a turn."

I've got a cross-examination all worked out for her, starting with what kind of flowers might go best with her sister's pneumonia, but I know now is not the time.

"Glad to hear she's improving," I say.

"Thanks. Meanwhile, what the hell, Mack? I'm gone one day and suddenly OAG is asking for files and setting up interviews? The only thing I can get out of

Raffi is that it's all about you and some list you dug up and a very angry judge."

"The less you know, the better, Sandra. I've got nothing to hide. Tell OAG everything you know. Tell them I said hello. That why you called?"

"Not entirely. Rafael just got pulled into a meeting with the boss. Twill's worked up and pacing his office about something. Rafael wanted me to call you and tell you that your APB-locate on a black F-150 popped up on the radar about five minutes ago."

"What?" I can tell by the way both Nadia and Mila suddenly look at me from across the bar that I've lost volume control. "Where?"

"Northbound on forty-five. He just cleared I-80. CPD has one unit keeping a distance. Officer Larson, Edward J."

"Ed Larson. You know him?"

"I lose track anymore. He's new. Newish."

"You have his number?"

She does. I'm up and behind the bar looking for a cocktail napkin and a pen. Doris comes through the back door thinking the worst, Isis and Kyle on her heels.

"Hey, now," says Doris. "I can't leave you unsupervised for…"

I hold up a hand to Doris and she cringes as she figures it out. I ask Sandra for the cop's number.

"Got it," I say. "Thanks, Sandra."

"Anything else I can do?"

"Sure, I'll bet there's lots of things. Juggling maybe. Magic tricks. Gotta go."

"Mack, when you're clear, let's put our heads together on this OAG investigation. I need to be more in the loop here. I'm worried about stepping on your toes. I don't want to… you know."

"Step on my toes all you want, Sandra. These days most people aim for my face. Gotta go."

I end the call and dial the cop trailing Hell on wheels. I introduce myself and Officer Larson updates me on his location.

"See any cabs around?" I ask. Ed Larson thinks that's funny.

"Cabs? You mean, like taxis?"

"Yeah. Yellow."

"You kidding? They're everywhere. You have a plate number?"

"No. Driver is Pakistani."

More laughter.

"Right," I say. "Keep your distance, we're coming to you."

I disconnect the call and reconnect with my surroundings. Doris, Isis and Kyle are each on a stool looking at me across the bar, three faces waiting for information.

I deal out three cocktail napkins from the stack in front of me.

"Had a dream like this once," I said. "What'll you have? It's on the house."

"What's happening?" asks Isis. Her face has freshened up its worry. "Did you find Raj?"

"Maybe," I say. "I gotta scram."

"I'm coming," she says, standing. I point at her.

"No way, Cleo. Not this time. You've had enough excitement for one day. I'll pay for a cab."

"Don't be silly," says Doris, turning to Isis. "I'll drop you wherever you need." She looks back my way, jerking her head toward the booth in the back. Mila and Nadia are in their own little world. Mila's talking up a storm. "What about her?"

Things are moving too fast. I just found her. I can't turn her loose. And I can't turn her in.

Doris reads my face like a book she's read before.

"I'll take her with me. I'll take her to my place. Your friend can come too. They can keep talking. Kyle's got the bar. I'll sit on her until you call."

I shake my head.

"It's not something I can ask, Doris."

"You didn't ask, Mack. You're *behind* the bar now. Let's see if you know how to take orders."

I brace myself against the bar like I'm trying to push it across the room, head down, thinking about Doris' offer. Nadia doesn't give me the chance. She slides out of the booth and grabs her coat. I leave the others and meet her at the door. She hands me her coat and turns around, slipping her arms down into the sleeves. I pull it up over her shoulders as she pulls her hair out over the collar in an aromatic waft. Nothing about any of this should be sensual, but all of it is anyway.

"All she tells me is that she's afraid," says Nadia, turning. "She says if she tells the police anything she'll be dead within a day." She starts counting on her fingers. "She won't tell me who she's afraid of. She won't tell me where she lives. She won't tell me what she does for these people. I mean, besides the obvious. She slipped once and let on that there are others like her, but I don't know who or where or how many. Whoever she works for has locked her up pretty tight."

"That much is clear," I mumble. I look at her directly, lowering my voice but taking a step closer to make up the difference. "What would you say to continuing the conversation with Mila over at Doris' place?"

Her eyes sadden, the delicate wrinkles at the corners arranging themselves into regret.

"Can't, Mack. I've got to pick up Danika. I'm already late. I'm so sorry. I tried."

"You did, Nadia. And I'm grateful. Will you do me a favor and just ask Mila if she minds hanging out with Doris for a while. Tell her I don't want to turn her over to the police and I'm trying to keep her safe."

Nadia nods and turns, walking back to the booth. A quick exchange, some pointing at Doris and then she's back in front of me, looking at her watch.

"She seems okay with it," she says. "Anything to stay out of the police station. I really have to go, Mack."

She keeps moving for the door, making a polite nod over my shoulder to Doris.

"One more thing," I say, putting my hand on her arm. I hold out the scrap of paper. "What does this mean?"

She takes it and looks at it.

"It's a phone number."

"Other side."

I watch her eyes. Maybe the easiest thing I've done all day.

"I don't have any idea," she says, her face beautifully baffled. "Someone thinks three A.M. is okay, I guess."

"Three A.M. is never okay, Nadia."

The smile is suddenly back with a vengeance. She lays the palm of her hand over my bandage.

"Maybe that depends on who you're with when the clock strikes three."

ONE HUNDRED ONE

It's a day for breaking traffic laws and wishing the Impala had its own flashing party hat. I'd like to arrest Old Man Winter and most of greater Chicago for obstruction.

Officer Larson calls twice with updates and Isis calls once from Doris' front seat to ask more about Raj. She instructs me to keep her informed. I can hear Doris in the background telling Mila she has to dig to find the seatbelt. I tell Isis I need to keep the line clear and shut down the call as I change lanes to get around a red pickup. The guy driving shows me his pet bird. Two of them. I give him a polite nod as I mash the buttons on my phone.

"Been looking for you," says Stretch. Absence has not made his heart grow any fonder.

"So I hear," I say. "How's the Scooter puzzle coming?"

"Hard puzzle to solve with you keeping half of the pieces in your goddamned pocket, Mack."

"Whatever do you mean?"

"Play it cute if you want. I'll get a warrant. Maybe a smaller room will change your mind about what it means to cooperate."

"Stop the routine, Stretch. That one barely works on the civilians. What do you want?"

"I want you to come in so we can have a serious conversation, just you and me, homicide detective and murder suspect."

"I'm flattered. But I'm also a little busy."

"I can take care of that in a hurry."

"I can pencil you in for some time when I have nothing better to do, or you can just tell me what it is that's got your panties in a bunch."

The red pickup is back in the next lane. The driver has a handlebar mustache that works like a set of parentheses around whatever filthy phrase he keeps shouting at me. I can hear Stretch sigh through the silence on the phone.

"Casey Randall Sweet," he says.

"Ugly, unfriendly guy. Big mouth. When he smiles, he's a dead ringer for a dead walleye. What about him?"

"We followed up with Billy Wise out in Aurora at the fish place. Doesn't know anybody named Hell. He remembers Scooter but had no idea he's dead. He says you showed up suggesting that Scooter was ratting on him and that you kept twisting his tail over this Casey Sweet guy. Now that he knows about Scooter, Billy's convinced you and Sweet are trying to frame him for the murder. We tried to talk him off that ledge but he wasn't having it, so we left him yelling and carrying on about getting a lawyer."

"Sounds about right. You should ask Billy about the fastest way to clog up a toilet. That really gets him worked up."

"I don't... are you done?"

"Yeah, yeah. Sorry. Go ahead."

"So, we track down Casey Sweet and he says you showed up one night demanding that his girlfriend hand over one of her collector dolls. Says you threatened him. Says he finally gave you the thing to get you to leave them alone. Next thing we hear OAG is up IAD's ass because you've got some secret list of muckety-mucks on the take. And I'm told it's no coincidence that the three homicide cases my department has pending before Judge Jolie are all being reassigned to God-knows-who. So, I'm in the middle of this goddamned thing about Scooter, knowing a whole lot less than when I started, and I can't help thinking that's exactly what you had in mind. So, I want to know what the fuck is going on, Mack. I want to know what put you on to Casey Sweet. I want to know everything about this... this... doll. I want to know how any of it ties in with this OAG investigation. And if you think I'm kidding, Mack, I'll just tell you right now that it's looking to me a lot like you were out stirring the pot, making people angry at Scooter and creating a list of suspects before you did the job yourself."

I can't help but laugh.

"Funny, is it?"

"You ever thought of writing fiction, Stretch?"

"No, that's your thing. I want some answers, Mack."

"What if I give you Scooter's killer instead?"

"What are you talking about?"

"The aforementioned Hell. I'm on my way to put him in handcuffs now. That sound like a good time to you?"

"You found him? Where is he?"

"Now he's headed east on 183rd with a CPD cruiser keeping its distance. I'm trying to catch up."

"It's not a crime to be big and strong, Mack. I don't have any evidence to hold him for murder. I have more evidence to arrest you for murder."

The driver in the pickup is close to multitasking his way into an accident. It takes a superhuman focus to manage a double-fisted gesticulating meltdown while operating a vehicle at seventy-five miles an hour. This guy can't handle his own mustache.

"I'm not arresting him for murder," I say.

"What's the charge?"

"Sex trafficking, for starters."

"Trafficking? You have a witness? Wait, is this the mute kid in yellow you told us about? Emily?"

"Gotta go, Stretch. I called to extend the invitation. Be there or not. I'll call when I have a location."

I drop the phone in the seat and fish the badge out of my pocket. I press it up against the window so the anger management candidate in the red pickup can get a good look. Funny what a little new information can do to calm a person down.

ONE HUNDRED TWO

I pull up window-to-window with Officer Larson's cruiser. He nods at the parking garage across the street. It's a stand-alone box, six stories high; entrance and exit right next to each other. Once upon a time the garage serviced a shopping mall one block to the south. The mall has been dead now for two years.

"No change," says Larson. He's young and buff with a crewcut. I can tell he's still full of himself for being a cop. I remember that person in the mirror like it was a million years ago. "He went in and hasn't come out." He points. "Staircase and elevator are right there. No foot traffic in or out since I've been here."

"What about other cars?"

"Maybe. I circled the block when I got here. Not since I parked. What do you want him for?"

"Depends on who you ask," I say, looking around for Raj's cab.

"Need me to hang around?"

"How much can you bench?"

"Two-fifty."

"Then yes."

"What's the play?"

"We're waiting for homicide and another unit."

"From Chandler? Not exactly our turf."

"I am aware. Sit tight. I'll pull around behind."

I circle the block just to get a sense of where we are. If I end up chasing this monster over the ice on foot, I want to know where he's going. The neighborhood has seen better days but that's nothing new. Mostly small, single-story buildings, each with some home-grown business hanging on by its fingernails, fighting for scraps of attention as the internet sucks up all the market share.

A life-sized cut out of Rick Blaine is leaning up against the window frame of *Vintage Video* like it's the doorway to the *Café Américain*. Humphrey's hat is crooked, but he doesn't seem to care. The only thing on Bogey's mind is printed in big red letters on the thought bubble someone has hung like a white cloud above his head: "Be Kind. Rewind."

I pull in behind Larson, kill the motor and wait. Enough time passes that I'm just about ready to go in without any backup. I even pull the door handle. That's when another black-and-white rounds the corner. Stretch and Donovan are one car behind. I get out and walk back to lean in their window.

"Okay," says Stretch. Donny Howe is eating something fried out of a greasy white bag. "So?"

"So, Officer Larson over here says our guy is inside. Twenty, thirty minutes now."

"This garage connect to anything?" asks Donovan. I shake my head. Stretch cranes his neck around, trying to see around me.

"Well, what the hell's he doing in there?" he asks.

"Pushups, maybe," I say. "Let's go find out after Donny finishes clogging his arteries."

"Fuck you, Mack," mumbles Donovan, brushing food from his coat. Donny was the guy on the squad who always seemed to forget his sense of humor at home. Stretch lets a laugh slip out as he opens his door. For a second it feels a little like old times.

ONE HUNDRED THREE

Six of them. Three uniforms and three plainclothes. Six guns. Six sets of cuffs. Then there's me, floating along behind, useless when it comes to stuffing Hell into a back seat, but I can bear witness to whatever happens next. I'm the only one who's not freezing.

Ray is out front, the lead goose as the others follow in a loose triangular wake, every head pivoting back and forth for a black F-150. The garage is only a quarter full, which makes disappointment easy to recognize. Plenty of pickups. Some of them black. But no cigar.

They walk each floor, ramping their way up to the top of the garage. Ray's line of sight is the first to clear the top deck. The wind surges over the north wall of the garage, closing his eyes and stealing his breath. He turns in a slow circle, taking in the empty rooftop.

Almost empty.

Ray gestures toward the southeast corner. Everyone stiffens and turns. There it is, tinted windows quietly taking in the view, idling as the wind plays with the exhaust.

Ray advances, stiff-arming the Sig Saur like a two-handed flashlight as the others fan out, moving forward behind him in a human parabola.

Ray shouts for Hell to turn off the engine, open the door slowly, hands in the air, all the things you're supposed to shout in these sorts of situations. Stretch slips into position along the passenger side with Donovan and Larson stopping at different positions about twenty feet behind Ray, both taking aim at the driver's door. Ray repeats himself, a little louder this time.

But Hell's not listening. Nothing changes. An icy gust broadsides the F-150, rocking it, maybe just to stop the shouting and move things along. Larson breaks his stance long enough to breathe on his hands, like he's afraid they might freeze to his gun.

I can see Ray is losing his patience. He looks back and gives the crew a nod. Then he steps up to the truck and yanks open the door.

ONE HUNDRED FOUR

I'd bet one of my pickled kidneys that Hell is not an easy-listening type. I'd bet that when he gets home from a long day of killing people and selling girls into sexual slavery, he pours himself a tall, cold *Helles Bock* beer and settles into the musical equivalent of napalm.

But it's "The Girl from Ipanema" that tumbles out into the wind when I open that door. Not the Stan Getz classic with Astrud and João Gilberto. No, this Ipaneman has been stripped of all shape and personality so some Chicago easy-listening station can squeeze her into elevators and bank lobbies without anyone noticing.

It's Hell's way of telling me he's not concerned. I'm sure he'd tell me himself, but he's not around. So, he's let a flautist and a string quartet deliver the message.

I give the cab of the truck a quick inspection, then I look around until I find the face that belongs to Officer Larson. I'm not usually one to dress down newbies in mixed company but I'm cold and every bone in my body wants a drink and Hell is someplace warm and laughing.

"Goddamnit!" I stuff Sig back in the holster.

Larson recoils.

"Listen," he says, holstering. "No one came down those stairs. I'm telling you. No one. And no one came out of that elevator."

"Then you explain it," I say.

"I don't know. He… maybe he was hiding behind some other car. He waited for us to pass and then he slipped out behind us."

We all stare at each other for a second. The kid can think on his feet, I'll give him that.

"That's possible," says Donovan. We all walk to the edge of the roof and look over the edge at our cars parked along the curb below. The wind tries to push us over the concrete half-wall, but we all hold our ground.

Stretch turns back around and leans against the ledge.

"What about other cars?" he asks. "Leaving."

"No," says Larson. "None. Just..."

He doesn't finish. We all look at him.

"You might want to finish that sentence," I say.

Larson points down at the street. We all track his finger west.

"There was plenty of traffic on this street," he says. "While I was waiting, this guy comes up and tells me his car is dead. No phone. He needs a tow. So, I call it in as he's standing there. He doesn't know his street names so I'm trying to tell dispatch where to send the..."

"Jesus, Larson," I say. "Get to the punchline before we all freeze to death."

"Then what's her name, Sandra Booth calls on my cell for an update, so I'm dealing with her and the dispatcher and this guy that needs help with his car all at the same time..."

"You weren't paying attention," I say. "That's the punchline. Damnit."

"I was trying to keep my eye on the exit, but... I might have missed something. I looked up once and there was this taxi. He was basically even with the exit ramp, headed that way. West."

"A taxi?" I don't mean to shout at him, but I also don't mean to knock him to the ground and bang his head against the roof of the parking garage, so I figure I'm half successful. I take a step forward. Larson's got his hands up in the air. The others are looking at me like I might be as crazy as the rumors suggest. Stretch stands up from against the roofline barrier, ready to intervene.

"What kind of taxi?" I ask.

He doesn't answer. He doesn't have to.

"Christ."

"I can't say it was coming from the garage. But," Larson sighs. "But it's possible."

"It's possible. Well, that's just great." I start to walk away but then my brain catches up with what he just said and pulls me back. "Sandra called?"

"Yeah. I kept her apprised. Just like you."

"Why?"

"Because she asked me to." Larson shrugs and looks at Donovan and then at the other two uniforms for support. Donovan is busy working his own confusion.

"I don't get it," Donovan says to me. "Are you saying this hump drove his truck into a parking garage and then called a taxi to come pick him up?"

"Something like that," I say.

"And just left the truck running?"

"He's done with it," I say. "Get it dusted. I'm guessing he wiped down the interior, so I'd make sure to check the gas cap. The tank is half-full, so that means he filled it before he knew he was about to abandon ship. I want to know this shithead's real name. I want to know where he takes the bolts out of his neck at the end of the day."

"Look at IAD playing detective," says Stretch. Donovan laughs.

My phone interrupts. I pull it out and look at the screen. Bad timing. I mash the button anyway.

"I'll call you back," I say, disconnecting before Doris can say anything. I turn and start walking for the exit ramp. Stretch has other ideas.

"Where are you going? We need to talk, Mack. I'm not fucking around. I've got a job to do here."

"Then do it, Stretch," I say, not looking back. "Find Hell. He's your guy."

At the top of the ramp something catches my eye. I stoop. All that glitters is not ice and snow. I usually love being right almost as much as I hate being sober. But this time it doesn't feel so good. I stand again and point down at the ground, yelling back at the group.

"Broken glass. He jacked the cab. Make sure you bag it."

I wait until I'm in the stairwell and two floors from the street to call her back.

"Sorry," I say. "I couldn't talk."

"She's gone, Mack," says Doris. Her voice is ragged. "I'm so sorry."

It's enough to make me stop in mid-step.

"What do you mean? Mila?"

"Yes. She seemed comfortable. She was on the couch with Barkley. She looked so... I went in the kitchen to pull the nachos out of the microwave and get her something to drink. I was in there maybe five minutes. I'm in the car now. I've covered the whole neighborhood. She couldn't have gotten far, but... She's just gone. She's just..."

ONE HUNDRED FIVE

Ten o'clock and Ray is one with his recliner.

He needs to be in bed. He *wants* to be in bed. Ask him and he'd say the recliner is more comfortable. He'd say he's too lazy to get up and climb the stairs.

He'll never admit the fear. Doesn't want to give it a foothold by acknowledging that it even exists. But there it is anyway. Fear.

Ray is old-school that way: don't admit to the things you don't want to be real. He's great friends with denial. It's why Marlo dying threw him for such a loop: he couldn't accept it. Same reason it took him so long to admit to me. I'm an inconvenient reality. Admit to me and then you have to admit that something inside you is broken. And that's no good. So he tried to explain me away as a temporary stress condition. After that I was supposedly a booze-induced figment of his imagination. He admitted to alcoholism just so he could avoid admitting to a dissociative disorder. The alcoholism became an ally in his effort to drown me in bourbon.

But eventually the ol' guy pulls his head out. Eventually he comes around. And at some point, he'll own up to the fact that he's afraid to go upstairs to bed and get the sleep he needs. Sleeping leads to dreaming. He can feel those dreams floating in the dark, hanging just outside that cigarette glow of consciousness, waiting for him to snuff out the light. Then it's feeding time.

Last time Ray went upstairs to bed he was forced to come downstairs again and scream goodbye to his legs. That's what is waiting for him up there if he lets himself sleep deeply enough to dream. He's afraid of that dream. He's afraid it will be Marlo holding the chainsaw. Or worse, she'll be the one with no legs and a hood over her head and he'll be the one with the saw.

But it's not just the dream. Reality has got him pretty shaken too. Why else keep Sig comfortably tucked away, nosed into the harness still nestled beneath Ray's armpit? He's afraid Hell is coming for him in the night. He doesn't want to be upstairs asleep for that. He doesn't want to surrender the ground floor again. Whatever is coming, it's going to use a window or a door. Ray wants to be there when it happens.

So, here he is, one with the recliner, Phil stretched out in his lap, purring warmly beneath his hand, working overtime to neutralize his worry. His other hand holds a full tumbler of Old Forester. The glass is cold and clinks more than it purrs, but it delivers comfort in other ways.

The music ran out an hour ago. He wants to get up and put on something smokey and slow; some dripping, Blue Note gem that he hasn't heard in ages. Carmen McCrae, maybe. "Last Night When We Were Young." Or "My Future Just Passed."

Marlo loved the early Carmen.

But rolling Carmen out of her carboard sleeve and putting her on the spindle would take getting out of the chair. Rousting his bruised bones. Displacing Phil. That's not happening.

So, he sits and stares.

He listens to the wind outside sweep the cold silence around him like a broom.

He worries.

A call to the taxi dispatch had eventually unearthed Raj Malik's plate number. The all-points was now three hours old. Every cop in greater Chicago was keeping an eye out. Ray's phone not ringing is the loudest thing in the room.

Every so often he changes the worry channel. Mila Evgenia Kozlova. *Emily.* Gone again. Hard to blame Doris for what he should have anticipated all along. The blame is all his.

He wonders if she is already back in the harness, proving her loyalty. Appeasing Hell.

Or is she in the wind, running for her life, just like Suri. Where is that dirty yellow coat?

The fire pops. His body jolts, sloshing the Old Forester over his wrist. Phil stretches and contains the spill with a dry, raspy tongue.

He strokes her tiny head, scratching the back of her ears.

Marlo's cat. A shelter rescue. Now Ray is the one abandoned. Phil is returning the favor.

There.

Ray stops scratching.

And again.

Another minute or two and he might have started to doze. Another minute or two and he wouldn't have heard the sound out in the wind.

Again.

He sure hears it now. Look at the attention in those eyes. Look at the muscles stiffen as he slowly brings the recliner upright, setting the drink on the table.

It's coming from the backyard. Something snapping. Or crunching. Something giving way.

Ray lifts Phil from his lap and lowers her toward the floor, moving so slowly that her paws stretch down for a landing that must feel to her like it may never come.

But it does come. Nothing like gunfire to speed everything up.

ONE HUNDRED SIX

Phil disappears in an instant, moving faster than should be possible for a cat her age. We have that in common whenever the shooting starts.

I'm out of the chair and down on the floor, Sig drawn and crabbing my way for the front door before I can think about what's happening.

A shotgun is what's happening, from the sound of it, somewhere behind my house. I get to the front door and stop moving. I reach up and kill the lights and the room implodes down into the dull orange glow of the fire. I keep Sig pointed toward the place where the living room meets the hallway. That's where they're going to show up first. I aim for the top of the door frame so I can catch Hell in the top of his head as he stoops.

I listen, focusing my hearing past the sound of my own heart and lungs. I listen for the little sounds, the ones to give me some clue of direction and number. But there are no little sounds, only more big ones. Another shotgun blast and then something heavy smashes against my back door.

It changes my mind about seeing the top of Hell's head. I'd rather see the back of him just so I can trade one surprise for another. I pull myself up and throw open the front door ready to unload on whoever might be waiting. The night wind is such a frigid and immediate presence my reflexes almost send a bullet through the air across my dark and empty street. There's no one here but me.

I move around the side of my house as quickly and quietly as I can. The cold is like something wild, devouring exposed flesh. I try to keep my focus, working the probabilities. I'm guessing it's just a single shooter. If there were two or more, someone would have been assigned to cover the front of the house as Mr. Shotgun and company kick in the back door.

On the other hand, he's probably not completely alone. He got here somehow and I'm guessing it wasn't on foot swinging a shotgun. Too cold for a late-night stroll. He could have driven himself, but I don't think so. I should have taken a closer look at the cars parked on the street. One of them has a person inside with coked-up eyes on my house waiting for Hell to come striding out my front door, chiseled smile on his face and a shotgun over his shoulder. If so, this was meant to be a quick job: in through the back door, paint the wall with my brain and then it's back in the car and away. Doesn't explain why the shooting started early. Or why he needs a gun at all, for that matter. Maybe so much the better if he scares me to death.

I can't solve that riddle just yet because now I'm worried that I've been spotted by some wheel man waiting at the curb. He'll be coming up behind me any second now, looking to ruin my surprise. Ahead of me I can hear the violence against my back door resume with a vengeance. I pause at the corner, Sig at the ready, but I can't stop anticipating the ambush.

I turn my head to look behind. The wind is throwing shadows against the house that seem solid enough to aim at. So I do. Bad move. The sound of running fills my head and I turn back.

Too late. Another shotgun blast rips open a hole in the night.

The shooter is around the corner and knocking me backwards to the hard ground like I'd stepped off a curb in front of a bus. I have time for a single thought; just one, as I fall and as my arms flail backwards. All I can think to tell myself is to tighten my grip on Sig. I'll never beat Hell hand-to-hand. It'll take a well-placed bullet to even those odds, maybe six. If I lose this gun, I'm dead.

The fall hurts. I knock my head pretty good. If I'm still alive tomorrow, I'll wish I wasn't.

But it's not as bad as I had expected. The bus on top of me is not so heavy after all. I still have air in my lungs and Hell has yet to land a punch or unscrew my head from my shoulders. Better yet, it turns out I get to keep the gun.

With my back to the ground, I swing Sig up front and center, holding it tightly with both hands and jabbing the muzzle straight into Hell's eyeball.

"Ow!" Raj clutches his face with one hand. "Fuck!"

I take my finger off the trigger, my brain scrambling to keep up. Wasn't a bus after all. It was a taxi.

Marlo, suddenly in my head, uncrossing her legs and pouring herself a drink.

We see what we expect to see, Ray, whether it's there or not. Too many guns in your line of work for that not to get someone killed eventually.

"Raj?" I ask, stupidly.

Another shotgun blast, this one with a blister of light. It's coming from the second floor of Judith Kravitz' house, just behind the far corner. Raj pushes himself off me and starts to run. His shoe snags my shoulder, and he wipes out into my garbage cans. Then he's back up and moving.

"Judith!" I shout up into the dark. "Judith! Don't shoot! Judith!"

I can hear Raj skid to a stop near the driveway. We're both listening now.

"Raymond?" Judith's voice is thin and far away, a flimsy reed of sound in the wind. I can see the tip of the shotgun barrel moving just beyond the corner of the house. "Is that you?"

ONE HUNDRED SEVEN

It's almost 10:30 when I make it back to my living room. Raj is looking more relaxed since the last time I saw him. The fresh log on the fire isn't so relaxed. It hisses and pops behind him on the hearth as he sits with Phil in his lap. He keeps my tumbler of booze from getting lonely by holding it up against his eye.

"So that's how you watch your drinking," I say. "I should try that. You sure did a number on my back door."

"Sorry." Raj rotates the glass. "I was trying not to die. Way to use your gun to scoop out my eyeball, by the way. Neat trick."

"That's why I never carry forks on the job. Safety first."

Raj smirks and hitches his chin toward my next-door neighbor. "How is she?"

"Defensive. Said she fired every shot into the air. Just trying to scare you off. Said she saw you coming over her back fence. She assumed you were coming for her."

"Right. Would she have assumed that if I was White?"

I point my finger and give him a look.

"Easy there, sport. You're the one creeping around in the dark. If I'd seen you out there, I wouldn't have aimed at the moon."

"Okay," he says. "Fair enough, I guess."

"Judith's not too keen on any of the races. She lives alone. She's got some friends but mostly it's her against everybody. If it wasn't for Phil, here, she'd have killed me a long time ago. That said, probably good you weren't carrying a prayer rug. Her late husband was regular Army. Two tours in the rice paddies. That's his gun. She keeps it close." I give my amputee couch a kick on the corner. "Recent events have keyed her up a little."

I head to the kitchen for a cloth full of ice and a glass of cubes to call my own.

"Surprised the cops haven't shown," he says so I can hear him. "My ears are still ringing."

I leave that hanging until I'm back in the room. I hand Raj the icepack.

"Does that no-alcohol rule of yours come with a near-death exception?"

Raj shakes his head and hands up the drink. I take it and pour the Old Forester into the new glass. The ice cracks and pops as I set the empty on the table and collapse back into the recliner. I try not to groan but trying just makes it louder. I can see Phil weighing her options from Raj's lap. She stays put. I don't blame her.

"I called it in," I say. "Sounds like the dispatch phones were lighting up. I told them it was a case of mistaken identity. They're not sending anyone now. Where the hell have you been, Raj? You're making me old."

"Yeah?" His tone tells me he's still keyed up. "You think I've been out having a good time? Don't blame me for making you old. That's like saying you're making me Pakistani. That's like…"

"Settle down, kid. I just want the story."

Raj closes his eyes and forces a long sigh.

"Sorry," he says. "Cleo. Is she okay?" I can tell from his face that, even with all the excitement, this is the most important question in the universe.

"Cleo's fine," I say. "She calls me every hour on the hour, worrying about you. Start talking."

Raj presses the ice against his eye. Then he lowers it again and looks at me. That look tells me everything but the details.

"Hell came out of that house," he says. "Got into his truck and took off. I started to follow. Cleo just, like, opens the door and starts to jump out. I slam on the brakes, but she keeps shouting at me not to lose him. I tried to argue with her, but she walked off. I mean… I don't have any idea what's…"

"I know this part," I say. "I'll fill you in later. Or she can. What happened?"

Raj keeps looking at me like he doesn't want to let it go.

"She's fine, Raj," I say. "I'll bring you up to speed. I promise. What happened?"

"He kept driving. All over the place. No rhyme or reason to it. Cleo had her phone with her and mine was dead, so I couldn't call. And just this morning I bought a stupid used dispatch radio from…"

"I know that part too. It's a lemon. You told me. Keep going."

"All I could do was follow him. Eventually he's doing circles in the Orland Park area, then he finally slips into this parking garage."

Raj falls silent and his face clouds over. He strokes Phil like a living talisman. I wait.

"I wasn't even thinking any more at that point. I was just following. Where he went, I went. I never should have gone into that garage. I parked on the ground level and waited for him. When he didn't come down…"

"You drove up."

"Yeah," he says, like he's confessing to a crime.

"And when you got to the roof that's when he punched your window open and asked for a lift."

Raj's face unclouds and astonishment takes over.

"How did you…"

"Later," I say. "Your window is in a little evidence baggie now if you want it back. Keep going."

"He smashed my window, like you said. He unlocked the doors and got in the back seat. He said the only way I'd live is if I did exactly what he told me to do. I believed him, Mack. I mean, this guy…"

"I know."

"Fuck."

"I know, Raj. Keep going."

"He told me to drive so I fucking drove. You know? I've never been so scared in my life."

"I've seen the man. I get it. Where'd you go?"

"Where *didn't* we go. Everywhere. I could tell he was focused on whether we were being followed. He liked that back window. It's, like, cold as a meat locker in the car, even with the heat blasting. I'm freezing my balls off, but he seems fine. Just… looking out that back window. He'd tell me to turn left or right on a dime. So I did. We zig-zagged all the way downtown. Then he told me to head for O'Hare. I get on the freeway. He pulls out a cellphone and makes a call."

"A call. Could you hear?"

"Yeah. He didn't say much. Just 'Airport. Terminal Three.' Then he said, 'Yellow Cab.' And then he leaned forward and, like, palmed my entire fucking head with his hand…"

Silence. I look at Raj and wait. His skin is getting paler with the memory.

"All I could think was that he can't kill me because we're flying down the freeway, but that if he wanted to... like..." He winces, looking at his own open hand in remembered amazement. "Just that one hand..."

"Yeah, I know about the hand, Raj. His other one is just like it. What else did he say?"

Raj looks at me, his expression sharp and full of fear.

"My name, Mack. He moved his mouth right up behind my ear and he said my name into the phone. I know he read it off the license card, but he said it like, like... Jesus, Mack. He said, 'His name is Rajnish Malik' and then he read my license number into the phone. Then he ended the call."

Raj shakes his head and reapplies the bag of ice.

"What else?" I ask. But he's not ready to move on.

"He knows who I am," says Raj in a whisper. "*They* know who I am. Who are... *they*, Mack?"

I push the ice around in the glass with a finger. Then I take a drink.

"That's a complicated question. Maybe we can get into that later." I rock the recliner forward and put my elbows on my knees, looking at him directly. "But right now, Raj... I need to know what happened."

He stares at me like maybe he's not in control of his own thoughts enough to continue. I wait.

"Sorry," he says at last, with another long sigh. "So, we get to the airport and sit in the drop-off zone for about fifteen minutes. And he's just sitting there waiting for something and looking out the window and just, like... I'm praying for him to just get the hell out. Then he does. He closes the back door and bends down outside my busted window and says 'tell Shirley Temple I'll see him soon. Tell him it's gonna hurt.' Then he just walked off."

Raj takes the icepack off his eye and tosses the cubes in the fire. He looks at me.

"That's you, isn't it?" he asks. "You're Shirley Temple."

"Well, I'm not Carmen Miranda, kid. Keep going."

"I watched him go in. All that time with him in my back seat and the only thing I wanted was to get him out of the car and then just hit the gas and put as much distance between us as possible. But then..." Raj laughs and shakes his head like he can't quite believe the words coming out of his own mouth. "I kept following him."

I give him a laugh of my own.

"You couldn't let go," I said, nodding.

"I couldn't let go."

"I know what that feels like. Not a healthy impulse. If you're lucky, it'll clear your cases. If not, it'll break your bones. Or worse. What happened?"

"I got out and headed for the terminal door. I guess I figured I was safe with so many people around and I wanted to see if he got in some line for a ticket. Figured you'd want to know the airline."

"You figured right."

"I never made it through the damned door. Before I know what's happening there's a guy on each side of me. I gave them a fight but in three seconds they stuff me into the back of this shitty little Plymouth. Smelled like body odor. I still can't get that stink out of my head. There was this guy at the airport guarding a pile of luggage who saw the whole thing. He tried to help and started shouting and banging his hand on the trunk. Lot of good that did. They took off."

"How many in the car?"

"Three of them. The driver looked Asian. Philippine maybe. The guy on my left was young, white, clean shaven. The guy on my right was black, older, bald. Three-day beard. I think he might have been in charge. He'd nod his head and the others would step to."

"What'd they say to you?"

"Not a single word. They just sat there. Each one had hold of an arm. I kept shouting and asking questions. No one said anything. Then I started to get scared. I figured this was the part where they take me to some dark parking lot and shoot me."

"Where did they take you?"

"A dark parking lot."

"Okay."

"About two miles from the terminal. Some equipment warehouse. And I thought, well, shit, you know, this is it. I started crying like a fucking baby. The driver pulls around to the back of the warehouse and the white guy drags me out of the back seat as I'm hanging on to the seatbelt for dear life. It took two of them. All of that and none of them says anything. Not one word."

"They obviously didn't shoot you, so…"

"No. They patted me down. They got back in the car. And then they drove off."

"What did you do?"

"What could I do? No fucking phone. I walked all the way back to the terminal. Two miles in the wind, six million degrees below zero. They probably wanted to save the bullet for someone else and freeze me to death. I get to the terminal and my cab is gone. I ask around and find out it's been towed. Took me three hours to get a ride to the impound lot and then bail my car out of jail. Then I drove straight here. But then I'm like totally freaked out that I'm being followed, and I don't want to lead anyone to your doorstep, so I parked three blocks away over at the church and walked, cutting through yards and looking over my shoulder. I thought your neighbor's backyard was yours. She corrected me."

"With both barrels," I laugh. Raj doesn't see the humor.

"I'm scared, Mack," he says. "Like, I am totally freaked out. These guys, whoever they are, know who I am. I thought I was dead tonight."

"You almost were dead tonight and I'm the one who almost killed you. If Hell or his crew had wanted to kill you, they know how to do that kind of thing. I think you served your purpose."

"Which was what, exactly?"

"Transportation. And to make me look like an idiot, something I can do for myself."

"I don't think I can go to my place. Can I crash here tonight? I can sleep on the…" Raj looks at the sloping couch and then thinks better of it, pointing at my recliner. "In the chair."

"Sure," I say. "But this is probably the least safe place in the city right now. You'd be safer sleeping on the interstate."

"Why?"

"These people want to come over and even out my furniture." I point to the backyard. "I thought you were them."

Raj stiffens and looks around uncertainly. Phil picks up on the sudden change in his pulse and lifts her head, ready to jump. Raj points to the floor.

"They're coming here?"

"Depends on whether Hell is one of those guys who keeps his promises. Not sure you'll want to be around for that."

"Then what… what… Jesus."

"Yeah, he's big on promises too but I stopped holding my breath a long time ago. Look, Raj…" My phone rings and I hold up a finger. "Bet I know who this is," I say, digging into my pocket. Turns out I'm wrong.

"Ray Mackey?"

"Speaking."

"This is Officer Willis, CPD. Have a minute?"

"Start talking and let's see. This about the shots fired?"

"Shots fired? No, I'm calling about a 10-14. We've responded and done what we can do, but I wanted to give you a call anyway."

"What's the situation?"

"Dispatch got a call from 1540 South Bremmer. Broken window and suspicion of someone in the backyard."

"Well, it's been a night for that kind of thing," I say, glancing at Raj. His face stretches into a question mark. He thinks it's Cleo. I shake my head. "What's it got to do with me?"

"We responded. Talked to the homeowner and conducted a perimeter search. We flushed out a Caucasian female. Five-eight, blue and brown. Married to the homeowner. Name is Nadia King. She says she knows you."

It's a one-two combination that gets Officer Willis my full attention. I'm not sure if it's the idea of Nadia being a prowler or being married that does the trick, but I haven't been this awake since Judith started pulling triggers.

"Yeah, we're acquainted," I tell him. "Who's the homeowner again?"

"Steven King."

"Come on."

"Steven with a V. Not the writer."

"Shame. I thought this was going to be interesting."

"It's interesting enough. Turns out they're married but separated for a couple of years. She used to live at the same address until things went south and they made separate living arrangements. Husband confirms. He says she's unstable, but she has never tried to break in before. We ran a check on the title and she's not on it. They have one daughter, age nine. She was inside asleep."

"Danika. Is this about her?"

"Depends on who you ask," he says. "Husband suspects that, but she denies it."

"What's she say?"

"Not much until we put her in the car to take her in. That's when she says that I should call you. Says she's working with you on a case. Says you can confirm that she's a not a criminal, good person, yada-yada. She wanted to call you, but I wouldn't let her at the time, so she gave me your phone number. I asked her about the case. She said she couldn't tell me. I asked her if this case of yours had anything to do with why she was hiding in the backyard and breaking her husband's windows. She said she couldn't tell me. She said I should tell you that he's the one who took the doll."

The news must light me up better than an electric fence. Raj's eyes widen in concern.

"What?" I ask. "Who? The husband? Steven with a V?"

"Yeah. You know something about that? The doll?"

"Maybe. What else?"

"I ask her what doll she's talking about and she clams up. I ask if she knows where the doll is or who her husband took it from. I get nothing. I ask if the doll belongs to their daughter. She shakes her head. I ask her to describe the thing. She wants to keep that to herself too, but then says the doll is small with black hair and a yellow coat."

It's enough to slosh the bourbon out of the glass.

"Holy…" My brain is on speaker. I choke on the rest in silence. Raj has a new question on his face. Officer Willis is curious too.

"What's wrong?" he asks.

"Nothing my drycleaner can't fix," I say. I'm out of the chair and looking around for my keys. Raj is more confused than ever. But Phil gets it. She's off Raj's lap and leaps up to lay claim to the lounger, circling once before finding a position that won't change until I come back, which we both know could be hours from now. "I'll meet you," I say to Willis. "Have you booked her yet?"

"Negative. I had the car in reverse and the husband comes out and says that he's not pressing charges. He doesn't want her arrested. Surprising, because he was running pretty hot when we plucked her out of his backyard. He was on the phone for a while so someone must have told him to take a breath. Now he's all about compassion for the mentally ill. Emotionally disturbed, he said."

"She seem emotionally disturbed to you?"

"Seemed upset, yeah. Something's not right in her world. Doesn't mean she's, you know, nuts or anything."

"So you let her go?"

"Yeah. So, we got her to promise she'd go home and leave the guy alone. Told her if we got another call, we'd come find her and take her in. She seemed to get it. She took us up the block to her car and we watched her drive off. Free as a bird, right? But get this. Before she goes, she rolls down the window and tells me to call you anyway. I asked her why I should do that. She closed the window and drove off. It's late so I was going to let it go until tomorrow, but then I thought maybe I should dial you in. You know, just in case there's something I'm not seeing here."

"Appreciate the courtesy."

"Is there?"

"Is there what?"

"Something I'm not seeing."

"Always. But that's just part of the job, isn't it?"

"You got that right. My partner bets that this gal's your CI. I say no. There's a whole beer riding on it. Care to comment?"

"One of you is right," I say. "The other one isn't."

"Thanks. Need us to follow up on anything?"

"No," I say, trying to work a shoulder-shrug into my tone. "I might check in with her in a couple days just to see what's going on. Not real interested in playing shrink or marriage counselor."

"You'd have to be pretty crazy yourself," says Willis.

I let that one go. No use telling him that I've got more than enough crazy to go around. I end the call and start mashing more buttons.

"We gotta go," I tell Raj. "Let's move."

"Where are we going?"

"To your traumatized taxi," I say. Isis answers before the phone makes it through the first ring. She doesn't say hello.

"Did you find him?" she asks. "Is he okay?"

"Take a breath, kid. He's been working on a story to tell the grandkids one day. Meantime, he's looking for a place to spend the night and charge his phone without people shooting at him."

"What? Are you serious?"

"Yeah, why? You have a suggestion?"

ONE HUNDRED EIGHT

Ray drops Raj at his car, leaving him with a shattered driver's window, Cleo's address, and a lot of questions Raj can't answer for himself.

Ray has plenty of his own questions, including whether Raj would have taken a raincheck on a sleepover with Cleo just to ride shotgun with Ray. Truth is, Ray would welcome that. I'm lousy company. I'm too nosey and I don't know how to keep my opinions to myself. I usually leave him feeling lonely, which is odd because I never leave him at all.

But lonely is not stupid. He feels lucky Raj is still drawing oxygen. He'll take lonely any day.

Ray separates two Camels from the herd. Raj lights up and then holds the flame out his window.

"Off to an interesting beginning," says Ray. "You and Isis. Lot of excitement for a first date. I suggest you slow it down. Take your time."

Raj laughs some smoke out into the cold and starts his car.

"Relationship advice? Really?"

"Why? Just because I'm older than you? That makes me more qualified, kid, not less. I'm no stranger to women."

"Oh yeah?"

"Yeah. They see me coming a mile off."

"Believe me," says Raj, "Last thing I want to do is hurt Cleo."

"Believe me," says Ray, "Cleo's not the one I'm worried about."

It's a two-Camel drive over to South Bremmer. Ray cracks the window and cranks the blower so the hot and cold can fight over the smoke. The plastic back window looks a dingy yellow in the following taillights. It pops and wheezes in and out like he's inside one of his own cancer-bait lungs. He thinks to himself that if he lived in the Bahamas, he wouldn't need a back window. If he lived in the Bahamas, his car would be a boat. His gun would be a fishing pole. The only ice to care about would be in his glass.

Traffic is light. The cars that are on the road are slow and keep to themselves. The moon rolls over, slipping a shoulder out from beneath the covers for a couple of miles. The streets of outer Chandler shiver in shades of alabaster until the moon disappears again. He hits the high beams and dials Nadia's number. Voicemail. He leaves a message asking for some attention but acting indifferent about whether he gets any. Act too eager and the fish never bite.

When he reaches South Bremmer Road he slows the Impala to a crawl, counting backwards to himself as he reads the house numbers. The homes here are big with lots of elbow room. Long driveways across spacious lots tucked into snow-capped hardwood groves. Unlike Garrett Hoosier's neighborhood, Steven King's tony habitat is missing the crap in the yard and the overflow street-side parking. The richer the neighborhood, the fewer the cars. He can count the number of cars he sees along the curb and in the driveways on one hand.

Of those cars, he can count the number he recognizes on one finger.

ONE HUNDRED NINE

I keep my speed steady, gliding past her like I don't recognize the car. If she wants to pretend that I haven't called, then who am I to spoil her fun.

The house I want is a hundred yards up the street, just as the road starts to meander off to the left. I pull up to the curb and cut the engine. I'm guessing the last time this neighborhood saw an Impala with a plastic window was sometime just before never.

I climb out into the wind and head for the door. I know Sig is where he's supposed to be, but I double-check anyway. From a football field away, I can feel Nadia's eyes all over me. I poke the big house in the ringer. The door itself must have cost a fortune. I wait and listen, wondering about the kind of man who shells out for such a wide and attractive door. After a heavy click at the knob, the big slab of wood swings soundlessly open and I get my thin and unattractive answer.

"Steven King?" I ask.

"Yes," he says with something like a smile. He has short, salt-and-pepper hair on his head and a drink at the end of one arm. He's younger than I am, just like most people, but his face is in a hurry to cross the finish line. His cheeks are sunken and saggy, and his teeth are too perfect not to be imposters. His eyes are small, yellowing stains on a wrinkled sheet. I show him my badge.

"Ray Mackey from the Chandler Police Department. I'm sorry it's so late. I'm here…"

"You're here because my wife called you with some lie about the safety of my daughter."

His expression is the same. The smile is about as real as the teeth.

"Something like that," I say. "Mind if I step inside so we can talk without freezing to death?"

"Can this wait until tomorrow?" he asks.

"I wish it could," I say. "I'll try to keep it short."

Steven shakes his head and lets it droop with a sigh. He steps back from the door and lets me in. Most of my living room would fit in the foyer. In the background is a staircase that wants to be in the movies. Steven-with-a-V lifts his glass.

"Drink?"

"No, thanks," I lie. "Better that I don't. You'll never get rid of me."

Steven walks away, talking as he goes. I follow.

"It was only a matter of time," he says. "I'm assuming you already know that she tried to break in?"

"I do. I spoke with the responding officers. I'm told she broke a window."

Steven turns just long enough to nod. He leads me to a small but well-appointed dining room connected to a long, stainless-steel kitchen. It gleams in the light through the arched doorway like a knife. Steven gestures to the table and I pull out a chair.

"Yes," he says, sitting across from me. "A window next to the back door. She used an ice pick I have out there. Put a hole through the window about the size of this glass. Not big enough to get her arm through and unlock the door. Then the motion lights scared her back into the trees. I don't think she'd thought about those lights. They're bright and they're on ten-minute timers."

"And why do you think she did this?"

"To steal Danika. I called…"

"And Danika is your biological daughter?"

"Yes. I called the police. They came out and shooed Nadia away. And so now we're on to the next game, which is for her to call and suggest that I'm some sort of danger to my own daughter." His eyes and his smile widen simultaneously to go with an incredulous laugh. "I'm not a danger to anyone, Officer Mackey. Especially my own daughter. Not even to Nadia, who is obviously doing her best to provoke me."

"Why do you think that is?" I ask.

"Don't know. She's not stable. She's never been completely stable." He gives me a look I'm supposed to understand but don't. "You know how it is; the young and gorgeous know how to turn unstable into just another flavor of sexy."

"If you say so. This instability of hers come with a diagnosis?"

"No, not that I'm aware of. She's had more than a few moments of crazy, but all basically just fits of irrational nonsense that last for a few days and then she's fine. But now." Steven shakes his head in consternation. "Something's changed. She's worse recently. Manic. You know?"

"Drugs?"

"I doubt that," he says, taking a drink. "Nadia's never been the drug type. But then I don't know what she's doing with herself these days. I'm the one who should be worried about Danni. Nadia has always been a good mother, but I don't know what accounts for the change in behavior."

"You could have pressed charges."

"Didn't have the heart. Not once I calmed down. I called my lawyer when the cops were here. He talked me out of the tree. I told them to just let her go. She needs help. Psychiatric help. What does arresting her do except make everything worse. She's my wife. Danni's mother. How can I have her arrested?"

He's got a pleading look on his face like he wants an answer. I don't give him one.

"I can't do that," he continues. "I can't. It's just a stupid broken window. But," his finger straightens like it's testing the wind, "it is time to get the lawyers involved in other ways. I know that much. I'd hoped to avoid that, but…"

"Is there some kind of custody order in place?"

"No, no. We'd agreed to manage the separation without courts and lawyers. And I was never in favor of the separation in the first place. She wanted out and eventually I… you know, what I'm I going to do? My hope was that she got whatever it was out of her system, and we could just pick up where we left off. We take turns with Danni roughly every two weeks."

"How has that gone?"

"Okay mostly. Past few months, though…"

Steven sighs and turns his glass in place on the table.

"What about them?"

"Nadia stopped bringing her back when she was supposed to. At first, I just let it go. I wanted to be accommodating. But then I started getting more insistent. She's my daughter too, you know."

He pauses to give me a shrug in search of understanding.

"Of course," I say.

"That led to some fights. Not physical or anything. But they were hurtful.

This is the first time she's actually tried to break in. And now we've obviously gotten to…" he breaks off and gestures toward me across the table. "We've gotten to this part. All of which is wasting everybody's time. Including yours."

"Don't worry about me," I say. "I get paid to waste time. What does Nadia do for a living?"

"She spends my money is what she does. She has a healthy allowance. I don't begrudge her a cent. I give her whatever she needs."

"No job then?" I ask.

"Not unless she's got something going that I'm not aware of. Which I guess is possible but I'm not sure why she'd be working for a wage given what I'm paying her. I'm leasing her house for her too, just so we can be separated in style. I always figured it would be temporary. Now I'm not so sure."

"And what do you do for a living?" I look around at the finery. He doesn't miss the point.

"I've done well for myself," he says with a nod. "I spent most of my adult life in finance. Started out with Roby and Harris Investments. Then I left and I ran my own private equity shop for a decade. It seriously under-performed. I had the common sense to pull the plug while I was still ahead. I haven't missed it. I have lots to read."

I can't help a small laugh.

"Read? Ever think of writing? A name like yours? You're one book and a sloppy signature away from a fortune."

"You're not the first to suggest it," he says.

"Tell you what," I say. "I'll ghost write for you and we'll split the royalties."

Steven-with-a-V isn't in a laughing mood. He drowns a polite smile in the scotch, then gives me his best wrap-up look.

"So, not to be rude or anything, Officer Mackey…"

He lets the unfinished sentence dangle above the table. I've been shown the door before, and this feels about the same as always. I figure it's as good a time as any for the slap. I lean in.

"Nadia says you're the one who stole the girl. That true, Steven?"

The change-up hits him square in the face, and much too fast for him to counterfeit up some confusion. What I get back instead is recognition, followed by the capillary dilation that normally comes with alarm. Steven may or may not have her, but he sure knows who I'm talking about. Which makes everything he has told me so far about as bankable as a three-dollar bill.

"I… who? Danika?"

"No. Not Danika. The other girl."

"What girl?"

"Russian kid. Teenager with a lot of grown-up friends. She wouldn't be here someplace, would she?"

"I honestly don't have any idea of who or what you're talking about," he says with a swallow. "Are you accusing me of something?"

"No," I say, leaning back in the chair and switching up the tone again. "But your wife sure is. I'm not doing my job unless I at least ask you the question."

"Okay. So?"

"So, now I've asked. I've asked and you don't have any idea what Nadia's talking about and that's that. I'll leave you alone." I push back my chair, then stop, lifting my eyebrows. "If you're sure about that answer, that is."

"I'm sure."

"Okay then. Thanks for the talk, Mr. King."

We look at each other across the table which is now buckling beneath the bullshit, his and mine. I thrust out a hand. He looks at it like the business end of a shotgun. Then he takes it anyway and gives it a shake. I don't let go as easily as he would like.

"I just need to check in on Danika," I say. "Make sure she's okay."

ONE HUNDRED TEN

Steven King leads, ascending the grand staircase with one hand on the white stone balustrade as it curves its way to the second floor. Ray follows, head on a swivel, taking in everything he can.

He is surprised to have gotten this far. We both are. I expected the guy to get his lawyer on speakerphone for a lecture about search warrants and probable cause. Instead, Steven has decided to go with the easy, *if-it-pleases-you* demeanor of a man with nothing to hide. That makes him either smart or stupid.

The stairs summit to a landing that opens to a wide, crème-carpeted hallway. Ray counts four rooms ahead of him. He wants to look for Mila in every one of them. Steven doesn't give him the chance.

"This is Danni's room here," he says in a whisper, stopping at the first door. "I suspect she's asleep."

He turns the knob and slowly nudges it open.

A pinkish glow pushes its way out into the hall. Danika King is sitting up in bed, face turned toward the opening door. Her left arm is thrown over the shoulder of a stuffed green dragon with smokey-red eyes. Her right hand holds an open book. The bedside lamp glows in the center of a cotton candy nimbus.

"Hey, Sweetie," says Steven. "You're awake."

"I'm reading a story to Vladimir," she says. "He can't sleep."

"I have someone here who wants to talk with you for a minute."

Steven steps back and lets Ray into the room. Danika sits up straight and releases Vladimir. The dragon pitches sideways into the wall.

"Hey, kiddo," says Ray. Danika's face inflates with recognition and hope.

"Hey! How come you're here? Is my mom here?"

Ray crosses the room and takes a seat on the foot of the bed.

"Nope. Just me. Mind if I come over and sit down?"

"Are you going to read us the story?"

"Well, no. I just wanted to come by and see how you're doing. That okay?"

The ringtone is a tinny concerto. Johann Sebastian wants out of Steven King's pocket. Ray and Danika both turn at the sound as Steven fumbles.

"Yeah," he says curtly into the phone. "No. Now? Hold on." He lowers the phone, looking at Ray and pushing the door open a little wider. His hand gestures: so *you've seen her; time to go.* Ray pretends not to understand, adjusting his position on the bed.

"I need to take this," says Steven, enlisting his eyebrows to help carry the message.

"Don't let me stop you," says Ray. "Come get me when you're done."

Steven's face hardens in irritation. He steps out into the hall and pulls the door closed behind him. Ray turns back to Danika. Her tousled blonde hair is pink in the lamplight.

"So," he says, hitching his chin at the door. "Staying with your dad tonight."

Danika nods. "Sometimes I sleep here."

"Do you take turns at this house and your mom's house?"

"They're both my houses."

"They are?" He waits for the nod. "Pretty lucky girl to have two houses. Which one do you like best, this one or the other one?"

"The other one," she says. "That's where I keep all of my clothes and all of my things. Except Vladimir." She turns and pulls the dragon upright. His mouth is open. A pointed red tongue hangs between soft white teeth. "He stays here for when I come back."

"All alone?"

She nods.

"Must get lonely."

"Dragons don't get lonely," she says. "They like being alone."

"Didn't know that," says Ray. "I thought everybody gets lonely. I get lonely sometimes. What about you?"

She has to think about it. She glances at Vlad, as if consulting. Then she nods.

"Sometimes I get lonely. When my mom brings me."

"Brings you where? Here?"

She nods.

"How often is that?"

Danika holds up three fingers.

"Five?" Ray asks. "Really?"

Danika looks at her fingers, then back again with an expression of disapproval. She thrusts her hand up to his face like maybe he can't see them.

"This is three," she says.

"You've only been here three times?"

"Three times since I can remember."

"Oh. Three times since you can remember. I see. Well, it seems like a pretty nice place. What kind of things do you do when you come here?"

Danika looks down at the book in her hand and shrugs.

"Do you do fun things with your dad?"

"He reads and talks on the phone and does his computer." She pokes her fingers at an imaginary keyboard, jogging her head back and forth in silly pantomime. "I watch TV in the TV room with Morris. And I can draw and do puzzles."

"Who's Morris?"

"A deer. He's in the TV room."

"A pet deer? Wow. Some guy, your dad."

Danika closes her eyes into a practiced face-palm, shaking her head. Then she looks at him.

"Not a pet deer. A deer on the wall. Morris used to be alive, but he isn't alive anymore because he was shot with a gun, except the bullet killed him where you can't see because only his head is on the wall. When I was little, I pretended he's a dragon with his head through the wall so he can watch TV too." She thrusts the book at him. "Will you read this story to Vladimir?"

"Is that how Vladimir gets sleepy?" Ray asks. "A good story?"

Danika nods. Ray takes the book. It's thin and wide. A purple cartoon dragon soars over a green mountain valley, dotted with curious goats. A boy and girl cling to the long, scaled neck. Everyone seems to be having a good time. The title is written in bold Cyrillic script, silver with hooks and swirls. Ray flips through the pages. The words are few, huddled in short, mysterious groups beneath each illustration.

"I don't know how to read these words," he says. "Maybe you can read the book to me."

"Will you fall asleep?" she asks.

"God, I hope so, kid."

Danika smiles and crawls out from under the covers on all fours. She sits next to Ray and takes the book from him, opening it across her lap and his, flipping the pages. She swings her legs next to his. Her small bare feet appear and disappear beneath the white flannel nightgown. She points to a purple dragon, eyes glowing red from deep within a cave.

"This is Tibor, and he lives alone in this mountain and that's why he's so lonely."

"Thought you said dragons don't get lonely."

"Only Tibor does, but he's not lonely anymore because of what happens. Don't interrupt or you won't fall asleep."

"Sorry."

She turns the page to a picture of the boy and girl lying on the floor, staring at the ceiling of a tiny, dark room. A television in the background sprays a sickly green light. Danika pokes at the page. "This is Wenzel and this is Aniya. She's not afraid of anything and Wenzel is afraid of everything, especially dragons. All they do is go to school and watch TV and they are so bored that they want to have some adventure."

"Some adventure. I see. Even whoosey-whatsit over here? Scaredy-pants?"

"His name is not whoosey-whatsit. It's Wenzel. He doesn't want adventure at first because he's afraid, but Aniya protects him."

Danika narrates the story from memory, turning pages and pointing to pictures. Ray pretends to follow along. He's convincing enough, but he keeps glancing up at that door. He's thinking about where Steven has gone. Maybe he's nearby, still within eyesight to make sure Ray doesn't wander up the hall. Then again, what if he isn't nearby? What if now is a perfect time for wandering?

Ray looks down again just as Danika is turning another page. He stops her suddenly, slapping the page back down with two fingers. Tibor the purple dragon is perched on a crumbling stone tower, blowing blue flame over a fat lake at sunset.

He remembers the dream. Marlo at the campsite, wind in her hair with her saddle shoes up on an antique desk; big blue dragon across the lake, talons gripping the battlements just so.

But amazing as that is, it's not what has caught Ray's eye. He points.

"What's that word?" he asks. "What does that mean?"

"That means where the princess lives because she is locked inside the tower." Danika points to a tiny stone window just below Tibor's claw. "She's inside here and Tibor…"

"So, wait, wait. This means tower?" he asks, keeping his finger on the word.

"No. This says castle." She pokes her little white finger at the front door of the big stone building, then launches into the plight of the imprisoned princess.

Ray's not listening to a thing she's says. He can't stop stroking the word on the page with his finger.

He never knew it was a word.

It's the shape of it he likes: замок.

It fits the hole in the story like a puzzle piece. Or a key.

ONE HUNDRED ELEVEN

My childhood was tragically short on books. There was only one bookcase at St. Evangeline's and only enough room for stories by the original Beatles: John, Luke, Mark and Mathew. The penguins made sure everything else hit the trash. I'd have killed for the gospel of Tibor the purple dragon. Had I told the penguins that I remember the picture on page fourteen from an especially vivid dream, right down to the black talon crumbling a stone battlement into powder above a blue lake, they'd have clutched their beads and started muttering to themselves about exorcisms.

I keep stroking the letters with my thumb. замок. замок. замок.

Exorcism is the wrong idea. Maybe wrong by exactly 180 degrees.

Just about the last thing I want to do is cut short story time. But I do anyway. My head is a tornado of old information with new meaning. Storytime is a luxury I don't have.

"Let me ask you something," I say. She looks up at me with a frown.

"If you keep interrupting you won't fall asleep from me reading."

"If I fall asleep from you reading, you'll need to feed me breakfast. Your dad wouldn't like that."

"He makes pancakes sometimes."

"Raincheck. Have you seen…"

"I have checked," she says. "It's wintertime. There is no rain."

My head may be a tornado, but somehow, she's managed to reach into the chaos and pluck out a laugh.

"Boy, can't get anything past you, can I?"

"Nope."

"Listen, have you seen another girl in this house today? A girl older than you? Black hair, yellow coat?"

Danika shakes her head.

"Has your dad had any visitors today?"

She nods.

"Who?"

"Police visitors. I heard them downstairs. I was sleeping and they talked so much I was awake."

"Did you see them?"

She shakes her head.

"How did you know they were police?"

"I heard them. They were talking about my mom. Vladimir wanted to eat them."

I pinch Vladimir's claw and pull him between us.

"Likes the taste of law enforcement, does he?"

"Pizza is best," she says. "I don't know what police taste like."

"I'm guessing a lot like chicken."

"I said he couldn't bite them because they were police, and he would go to jail."

"Good advice. What about before the police came over? Anyone come to visit?"

She shakes her head.

"Sure?"

Danika nods.

"Okay, kiddo," I say with a pat to the knee. I have to go now. Let's get you and Vlad tucked in."

"Vladimir," she corrects. "He doesn't like Vlad. Are you going to see my mom?"

I pull the covers up to her neck, careful to keep Vladimir's wingtip out of her eye.

"Yeah," I say. "Pretty good chance of that, I think. Want me to give her a message?"

She frowns in thought, then rolls away from me, pulling the dragon into her body.

"I hope she's not lonely."

I turn off the lamp and slip out through the door. I'm expecting to see the man with a name that sounds like a billion dollars holding an empty glass against the wall with his ear. But the hall is empty. I stand and listen to the house around me for a few seconds. Nothing. It's the kind of plush, upper-class silence that guys like me never get to hear. The silence in my neighborhood is louder.

I look both ways. The staircase and the United States Constitution are to the left. I head the other direction to see if there's a different girl behind door number two.

I turn the knob and push. The door opens into cold, stale darkness. The hallway light forms a fat sword on the carpet at my shoes, elongating across the floor and up the far wall, stabbing itself into a windowsill across the room. I step in and take a look around.

A large, bare mattress is sandwiched between a metal bedframe and three caseless pillows in a pile. The sheets have made it across the room to cover a chair and a dresser. The pillowcases have been pulled over the bedside lamps, giving them a hooded-hostage look.

There's a closed closet door along the far wall. I walk over and make sure the hinges work.

Plenty of hangers and clothes zipped up into hanging plastic bags. Exactly zero kidnapped Russian girls. I unzip one of the bags. Could be that Steven King is cross-dressing, but I'm guessing the blouses belong to Nadia. I zip up the bag and try another. Same story.

"You seem lost, Detective." I turn to find Steven in the doorway, still holding his cellphone.

"Always," I say, closing the closet door. "Only way to find what you're looking for."

"You think I keep stolen Russian girls in a closet?"

"Could be," I say. "I've seen stranger things. Bagged a guy once who liked to keep his corpses stuffed under the kitchen sink."

"Gruesome," he says perfunctorily. "Let me show you how to find the front door."

"What. No grand tour?"

Steven-with-a-V is not in the mood.

"Not tonight," he says. He steps backward into the hall, extending his cellphone in the direction of the staircase. "After you."

"Okay," I say with a nod, leaving the room. "Let's do the grand tour with a warrant and a lot of other cops."

"Probably for the best," he says.

I head up the hall for the stairs, thinking about who I should call to work the warrant as I sit outside in a car and keep an eye on the place. Steven closes the door to the bedroom and follows.

"Pretty great kid you've got on your hands," I say, starting the descent. Steven is not interested in bantering with the interloper. I keep at it anyway. "She invited me to stay for breakfast. Hope you don't mind. Says you make a mean pancake."

I reach the bottom of the stairs and leave the carpet for the beige travertine tile that gleams across the foyer. I turn back to tell Steven that he should expect another, much longer visit before the night is out. I can see from his face that he's left his confidence and easy-going charm upstairs. His expression is tense now. I can't tell if he's angry or afraid or something in between. I'm about to ask but then I see that the cellphone in his hand has turned into a Ruger .38.

"Okay, don't do this, Steven," I say, opening my palms. "That's a narrow road you're on. There's no turning around once you get started. So maybe just don't start. Think of Danika."

"Gun on the floor."

I pretend I'm hard of hearing.

"Just turn over the girl and let's work this out."

"I don't have any other girl," he says. "I told you that already, but you don't want to listen." He takes another step down and holds the Ruger so it's pointing at my brain through my left eyeball. "Gun. Out of the holster with one finger and then set it on the floor."

"Really? You're going to shoot a cop inside your own front door? How do think that's going to work out for you in the end, Steven? I think the sloppy signature book idea is much better for you."

"I'm not asking again."

He swallows and adjusts the grip on the Ruger. That finger of his tightens against the trigger. I don't think he's got the stones to do what he's threatening. His intention is not my concern. It's the involuntary twitch that's got me worried. The finger spasm connected to the startle reflex. The impulse trip wire connected to the heart muscle. For all the big talk, most cons doing time for pulling a trigger will tell you they were surprised to hear the gun go off. Most of them are telling the truth.

I hold my hands out from my sides and make a slow production of slipping Sig out of his holster with one finger. I set it on the tile at my feet.

"Kick it to the door," he says. His face is red and starting to glisten. I do as I'm told and send Sig spinning away across the foyer into the front door.

"This is a big mistake, Steven," I say.

"Show me your ankles," he says. "Lift your pant legs."

I do as he says.

"Take your coat off. Drop it on the floor."

"I know that phone call up there wasn't just a friendly stock tip," I say, unsleeving my arms. "You've got some scary people pulling your strings. They're not the kind of people you say no to. I get that. But you don't want to do this. They don't care about you. You will go down alone for all of it. Be smart."

I let the coat drop. He flicks the Ruger twice.

"That way."

I walk slowly through rooms I haven't yet seen. Every ten feet is something I could grab and swing blindly backwards, maybe catching him in the face or knocking the gun away enough to turn the tables. An extra-long golf club would be nice. A ceremonial spear. But everything I see is too short, which makes for long odds against a twitchy finger. Steven's entire nervous system is primed and waiting for me to drop or dodge or turn around. From the sound of things, he's keeping three steps behind, maybe four. He's no dummy. Neither am I. So I keep walking.

"Can I ask where we're going?"

He doesn't answer. We enter a suede-brown room with chairs squatting like mushrooms in the vicinity of a large television. The only one ready to watch anything is a ten-point buck with his head through the wall. I look up at Morris as I pass underneath. He's shy on good advice for not getting shot. His glassy black eyes tell me I'll be lucky to keep my head on.

"That door," says Steven from behind. "Open it."

The door is in the back of the room. I do as I'm told. The knob has a lock on it but twists freely. On the other side of the door is a wooden staircase down to a gray concrete floor barely illuminated from the light up here in the den. Whatever is down there is used to the dark. Just inside the door is a light switch that might answer some questions, but it's keeping its head down.

"All the way down," says Steven. I hesitate at the threshold. This strikes me as one of those no-turning-back moments. If someone puts a gun to your head and tells you to get in the trunk of a car, your chances of survival are better if you just start running and make the bastard take the shot. This basement feels like a trunk.

"Steven, listen," I say. "Let's talk this thing out."

"You'll get to talk all you want. Just not with me. Get moving."

"Well, if they want to talk, then…" I start to turn but the heel of Steven's shoe interrupts, ramming into the small of my back. I pitch forward, hands out, trying to break my fall without breaking my arms.

The world spins. Gravity does its thing. My head and face do their best to slow me down as the darkness swallows me like a snack tossed into the gullet of some beast.

Stillness. But the stillness is fleeting. Like a dream you don't want to slip away. The concrete is cool against my cheek. I hurt all over, but nothing as bad as my tongue, which feels like I've been licking a threshing machine. I slowly lift my head and spit out the blood. I listen for Steven, but all is quiet behind me. I groan, rolling over onto my back. Light flickers to life with a click.

Concrete walls and a ceiling to match the floor. Rows of gray metal shelving packed with bankers' boxes. A long strip of fluorescent lighting. I loll my head to the left. A boiler and two large water heaters are in the corner keeping company with a couple of brown rubber garbage cans and a white chest freezer. Behind me to the right is the staircase. I have to arch my back to bring the whole thing into view upside down.

Steven is sitting on the top step, forearms resting on his knees. The Ruger is on the step next to him, barrel poking out into space. We look at each other for a long second. Steven wipes the sweat from his face with both hands. He wipes his hands on his pants. He picks up the gun and points it down at me. Then he stands.

"Told you to shut up," he says, descending halfway.

"I was just about to. You didn't let me finish."

"Stand up."

I have to do it in stages. Sitting upright is no picnic and nothing close to dignified. I see stars as the blood in my head reacquaints itself with China. The trickling sensation down my left cheek tells me the staircase took a bite out of my face. I wipe the blood off with my hand and look at it. I can't tell if it's from a brand-new hole or if the fall just opened up the old one. I spit again, spraying the floor with blood. If I die in this place, I want to make sure Forensics has a field day.

"Up," says Steven, taking another step down. It takes a lot of grunting, but I do what he says and wait for further instructions. He jerks the Ruger. "Get in the freezer."

"The freezer?" I cast a doleful look toward the big white box in the corner. "Let me get this straight. Unless I help you to kill me by suffocation, you're going to kill me with a gun? You really haven't thought this one through, Steve."

"I don't want to kill you," he says. "I'm supposed to keep you on ice."

I'm as surprised to hear my own laugh as he is.

"That's just an expression, Steven. It doesn't literally mean…"

"You like your kneecap?" he shouts. His face is red again and the glisten on his skin is coming back. I'm worried all over again about being shot by accident. "Your hand? Your foot? Get in the goddamned freezer."

We do the staring thing again. Then I turn and walk over to the freezer and open it up. A cloud of coldness envelops my face. The inside of the lid is crusted over with ice. The belly of the thing is full of packaged meat, I'm guessing distant relatives of the ten-point buck upstairs waiting for Danika to turn on the television. I look back at Steven who is now all the way down the stairs.

"It's occupied," I say. "Let's try again later."

He points the Ruger at the garbage cans.

"Unload it," he says.

"Lot of spoiled meat," I say like that would be a shame.

"Stop talking and do it."

I do as he says, just not as fast as he wants it done. It comes out one package at a time, dropping like boulders into the cans. He shouts at me to pick up the pace, but I keep it slow and steady. The frozen meat is wrapped in butcher paper and dated with a black Sharpie. The packages on top are eighteen months old. I can see some closer to the bottom that go back three years.

"What is this? Venison? You're not eating it fast enough, Steve. You need to pick up the pace. You need to start eating deer for breakfast. Deer pancakes. Dear oat…"

"Shut! Your! Mouth!"

He points at me angrily with both hands, the one holding the Ruger and the other one, which I see is holding a pair of small brass keys. I'm guessing they fit the lock on the freezer door perfectly.

I know it's going to take two packages. I separate them from the rest. I dig deep.

Another package goes into the can. Another. Another. I can tell my concerns about suffocation were silly. I'll freeze to death long before the air runs out.

"Got any bourbon I can take with me to keep warm?"

He doesn't answer. I reach down and grab the two I've been saving.

"Jesus," I say, mostly from down inside. "This one is four years old, Steve. That's a crime right there."

I toss the left-hand package out of the freezer just like all the others, give or take a couple of inches. It glances off the rim of the rubber can and clatters across the concrete.

I don't waste any time. My right hand swings up and out of the freezer like a catapult. I unload the frozen brick of deer meat and send it rocketing for Steven King's head before the first brick has stopped spinning. Steven realizes his mistake even before he can return his full attention to the place it should never have left. The meat hits him square in the face.

It sounds exactly like a gunshot.

ONE HUNDRED TWELVE

Ray can move when he needs to. For a guy his age? Not too shabby.

Not faster than a bullet, of course. He's made a calculated bet that the first brick of venison will pull Steven's aim away from center, even just a little.

The first bullet blows a divot out of the concrete wall next to the water heater. It's the second bullet Ray needs to worry about.

Ray pushes off from the freezer hard, like a defensive tackle at the snap, breaking through the line of scrimmage and headed for the quarterback. Steven corrects his aim, swinging the Ruger on a trajectory to intersect with Ray's face, and then pulls the trigger again.

But Ray's face is not where it should be. Lunging has brought his head low, beneath the second bullet, which explodes into the wall above the freezer. Steven goes down hard with his arms flailing and Ray's head in his gut. The Ruger flies free, sliding sideways toward the shelving. Steven tries his best to wriggle away and lands two good shots to Ray's head. Ray manages to hang on and flip Steven onto his front, kneeling onto the small of his back. They're both breathing hard. Ray drags him backward far enough in one yank to be able to hook the Ruger with the toe of his shoe.

"Who's coming?" Ray pants, knocking the side of Steven's head with the barrel.

"Fuck you," says Steven.

Ray grabs him by the forehead and bangs his face once into the floor. Steven wails.

"You're going to break my fucking nose!"

"I'm getting good at that," he says, pulling Steven's face back off the floor. "Who's coming?"

"I don't know," he shouts, hands trying to cover up the concrete at the point of impact. "I don't know. I swear. I don't know. I got a call."

"A call from who?"

"I don't know. I told him you were here. He said to hold you. He said people were coming. That they wanted to talk to you. They're looking for the girl. That's all I know."

"Who called?"

"I don't…"

Ray pulls Steven's head back another six inches, bowing his neck.

"Ow! Stop! Stop! Stoli! That's the only name I know. I swear to God. Stoli." Steven starts to cry. Then he starts to sob. "I need protection. I need protection."

The brass keys are on the floor in front of them, eight inches away, glinting in the fluorescent light. Ray drops Steven's head and scoops the keys up off the floor. He stands, pulling Steven hard by the collar and jabbing the Ruger into his ribs.

"Get up. You want some protection? I'll keep you protected." Steven stands.

"You will?" He wipes his nose on his sleeve.

"Sure." Ray pats him down and takes his phone. Then he pushes him over to the open freezer chest. "Get in."

"What? No…"

"Yeah. It'll protect you from spoiling. All I need is a Sharpie. What's today's date?"

Steven resists. He flails and protests but a stiff knee to the gut takes all the wind out of the fight. Ray stuffs him inside with the rest of the deer. He slams the lid and locks it. Steven kicks from inside the box. Ray yanks the freezer plug out of the wall and knocks politely on the lid.

"You're just using up valuable oxygen, Steve. I figure you've got at least an hour. I'll be back to arrest you before then. So, relax. Chill, as the kids say. Breathe shallowly. Pray I don't die."

Look at him go. He's forgotten his age. He's forgotten how much he hurts. He takes the stairs two at a time, Ruger in one hand and Steven's phone in the other. He tries not to trip as he pokes frantically at the phone. Steven's phone doesn't talk to strangers. He tosses it aside and runs through the house, retracing his steps for the front door. *People are coming,* he thinks. *People are coming.*

The coat is still right where he dropped it, about a foot away from Sig, barrel still kissing the front door. There are two phones in that coat, his and Garrett Hoosier's. Either will do. He only needs one of them to call for help. And that's the only thing on his mind. *People are coming.* He needs…

"I heard a big noise," says Danika in a soft voice, full of fear.

Ray stumbles clumsily to a stop at the edge of the foyer. She is halfway down the staircase, blue eyes wide with alarm. The sight of her fills him with a momentary shock.

"Danika!"

It comes out too loud. Too harsh. Like she has done something wrong. Her face recoils as if he has tried to slap her. Her eyes start to fill.

"Christ," he says. He thinks she looks small and alone. Her dad is in a freezer. "I'm sorry, honey. I'm sorry. You just surprised me. You have to go upstairs to your room."

"I heard a big noise," she repeats in a way that is pleading and apologetic.

"Yes, I know you did. Everything is okay, but I need you to go back up to your room and close the door. Can you…"

Tears now.

"Where is Daddy? I want to be with my mom."

They're coming, Ray. People are coming. He ignores me and takes a slow breath anyway.

"We probably need to make sure Vladimir isn't scared," he says with a smile. "Don't you think?"

She looks up, blinking out tears. She nods.

"Okay, then," he says. He tucks the Ruger in his belt and turns toward the door, scooping up the coat and the Sig Saur. He climbs the stairs and scoops her up too, moving fast. "Let's go."

"You hurt your head," she says pointing. He wipes his wrist over his left cheekbone. It comes back bloody.

"Yes, I did."

"That's a gun," she says.

"Yes, it is." He noses Sig into the empty holster.

"Do you shoot people?"

"Not if I can help it."

In the bedroom he sets her on the floor and lowers himself to his knees, lifting the pink bed skirt and looking under the bed. He grabs Vladimir by the neck and hands him to her.

"I want you and Vladimir to stay under the bed."

"Why?"

"Because you need to keep Vladimir safe. You need to hide with him. Can you do that for me?"

Danika nods, dropping to her hands and knees. He holds her by the shoulders and looks into her face.

"I'm going to turn out the lights and close the door. No matter what you hear, no matter who calls your name, I want you to stay quiet and under the bed until I come and get you. Can you do that?"

"Even Daddy?"

"Even Daddy. Can you do that?"

She nods again, tears starting to gather anew.

"Promise?"

"I promise," she says.

"Does Vladimir promise?"

Danika looks her dragon in the red smolder of his eyes, then back up at Ray. "He promises."

She slides under the bed. Ray grabs a pillow and stuffs it in after her.

"Everything's going to be okay, kid," he says, wanting to believe his own lie. "See you soon."

He hooks his coat off the floor and bolts for the door, closing it behind him. He lurches down the stairs, taking two at a time, jamming his hand into the pockets of his coat for a phone.

People are coming, he thinks to himself.

But he's wrong. He is wrong, and now he knows it. *People aren't coming*, I tell him.

People are here.

ONE HUNDRED THIRTEEN

Leaving the door unlocked. Steven was thinking ahead. Why make your visitors ring the bell when you're busy putting someone in your freezer?

I'm three steps from the bottom of the stairs digging for a phone and the front door starts to swing. I drop the coat and keep moving, drawing both Sig and the Ruger as I go. I tuck up against the wall and let the door open over me.

There are two of them, salt and pepper, wearing thick boots, dark coats and matching knit skullcaps pulled low over long, cinder block heads. Big bags of muscle, these guys. Their favorite thing is counting to ten over and over in a room full of mirrors and weights. Second on the list is probably killing people. Shaving on a regular basis is somewhere near the bottom, right above reading and thinking.

It's the black guy who enters second, so it's his job to close the door and see me standing there with my hands full. He swats his partner in the arm. Now they're both paying attention.

"I've got one for each," I say. "My job gets a whole lot easier if half of you stops breathing. So, let's see who wants to die first. Hands behind your heads. Turn around and get down on your knees. Real slow."

They both stand and stare. Not a twitch. I straighten my right arm forward, like Sig is a dog eager to touch noses.

"Let's make it you," I say.

The black guy slowly puts his hands behind his head and turns around. The other one does the same.

"Down," I say. They don't like it much, but they do as they're told. "Here's the way this is going to work. I'm guessing you both know what a pushup is, so get in position. Let's go. Pretend you're in gym class. Arms stiff. Chest and knees above the floor."

I give a quick glance up the staircase to make sure Danika is not up there watching. The boys assume the position and I kick their legs apart. I belt the Ruger and keep Sig in close contact with one spine, then the other and back again as I pat them down and empty their pockets. I come away with two phones, two Glocks, two wallets, and a folding knife. I flip open one wallet, then the other. Leon Fipps and Harold Baur. Chicago addresses. I spot a bundle of black plastic strips sprouting from Harold's belt. I give the bundle a stiff yank.

"What have we here?"

I toss the phones, guns, wallets, and knife into the corner by the door; everything except the bundle of black zip ties. I'm guessing these boys aren't here for questions. They're strictly transportation. Tie me up and haul me off to someplace where someone else can ask the questions without worrying about the neighbors.

"You brought party favors," I say, wagging the zip ties in the space between Harold's face and the floor. "I was going to use your shoelaces. These are much better, Harold. Do the boys at the gym call you Harry or Hal?"

I'm mildly curious about how long they can keep themselves propped up like this. Leon shifts all his upper weight to his left arm, scratching his nose with his right. I use Sig's muzzle to tap him in the temple.

"Okay, showoff. Leon Fipps of Chicago. I want you to lay flat on your face, arms at your waist. Anything else is going to hurt like something awful. Do it now."

Leon lowers himself to the floor. I extract a zip tie from the bundle and hold it in my teeth. Then I pull the Ruger back out of my belt, careful that my right hand keeps Sig in contact with Leon's spine.

"Okay, Harry," I say. "You can sit up, facing me. Turn around slowly and look me right in the barrel. Don't think about it, you'll hurt yourself. Just do it."

I wait until Harold is in position and looking at me. His hands are flat against the floor at his sides, fingers like tree roots looking for good soil. His lips are large and fleshy with a scabbed-over split down the right side. His eyelids hang low like fleshy biceps. His beard is a matted, dirty ginger. Maybe it's a face Harry's mother could love, but there's no one else on that list. I open my mouth and drop the zip tie in his lap.

"Zip Leon's wrists behind his back," I tell him. "Nice and tight."

Harold picks up the plastic strip with his fingers and looks at me like I've asked him to eat it. Those half-dead eyes do not inspire confidence. I push the tip of the Ruger into the flesh of his leg, right above the knee.

"You'll never do another squat-thrust."

When he's done, I roll Harold over on his face, belt the Ruger again, and kneel on his back so I can zip his wrists together. His back muscles are hard and ropey. It's like kneeling on a bag of angry snakes.

The problem is clear now. I'm sure younger cops can work a zip tie with one hand. I'm going to need three hands: two to work the zip tie and one to hold a gun. That leaves me one hand short. I can feel Harold waiting for me to put the Sig down. We both know that will be his last best chance to turn the tables.

Too risky. I turn Harold back over and sit him up. I extract another tie with my teeth and drop it in his lap.

"Zip his ankles," I say. He gives me a look. "I know. Poor you. Do it anyway."

When he's done, I get Harold back around and down on his face. I belt the Ruger. Keeping Sig trained, I reach over and grab Leon by his newly zip-tied ankles, lifting his legs and rotating his body on the slick travertine until his beefy thighs are pressing heavily over Harry's shoulders and head, mashing his face against the tile.

"What the fuck!" shouts Harold. "Fucking pervert! Get him off me!"

He's angry, sure, but he can't move, or at least not easily and that's all I care about. I push against Leon's legs, using them as a lever to keep Harold's upper body flattened against the floor. Harold groans.

This will do. It'll have to.

I set the gun down on Harold's back between his shoulders and work quickly, pulling his tree-trunk arms behind him and zipping them tightly at the wrists. As I work, I try to keep things positive, telling them the news about *Miranda v. Arizona* and all the free things they can get. They've heard it before, I know, but I try to keep it fresh.

I reclaim Sig and spin Leon around so that he and Harold are once again pointed the same direction. I pull another tie from the pack and zip Harold's right ankle to Leon's left. Then I grab the knife from the pile of confiscated weapons and cut the tie that bound Leon's ankles together.

I've still got three ties left in the pack. I stuff those in my pocket and retrieve my coat from the stairs, rummaging for my phone.

I hold it in my palm, giving it a long, dubious look. Five minutes ago, this was the thing I had wanted most in the world. Five minutes ago, all I wanted was to talk to a police dispatcher. Now I'm not so sure. Now I've got places to be. Two hours of flashing lights and stupid questions in Steven King's foyer will be hard to take. Not because I don't know the answers, but because I can't get that image out of my head.

The image of a soundless word: замок.

It's like one of those bad songs with a meaningless rhyme that keeps playing on a loop in your brain until it drives you crazy. Maybe it helps to already be a little crazy, but now I think I know what that stupid rhyme means. I think it might actually make some sense.

Mila's not here. She never was.

I brush the dark screen of the phone with my thumb, wondering if I can secure the scene and get clear before I push any buttons.

I glance down at Harry and Leon, their faces turned toward each other, whispering with their eyeballs, trying to strategize a way out of their predicament. Which means we're all busy doing the same thing.

The reality is hard to ignore: this situation is more complicated than leaving Garrett Hoosier under the bathroom sink. This time I've got two muscle pigs in the foyer, a guy downstairs in the freezer and a girl upstairs under the bed. Too many moving parts to just leave. Plus, I'm getting a reputation for making a mess and leaving the clean-up to others. Not a winning strategy for a guy who wants fewer people to hate him.

I look back at the phone in my hand. I bring it to life and my thumb gets to work. I call in an *officer-needs-assistance* with the address to Steven King's house and a brief description of the situation. I'd like to keep the police from accidentally firing at little girls and dragons, but I'm not sure I want to clue in Tweedledee and Tweedledum here about the potential hostage opportunities that are upstairs under the bed. I tell dispatch that responding officers need to call me before entry so that I can advise further of special circumstances. I give the dispatcher my number.

I end the call and trade the phone for the Ruger. I stand them up. It takes them three tries, but they finally get there.

"Now," I say. "I've got to go get your boy, Steve, out of a big white box before he freezes or suffocates. Since I can't trust you lug-heads to stay here and behave, you're coming with me. I will accept slow, forward movement. Anything else is a great big problem with a loud, painful solution. Any questions?"

"Fuck you, shithead," says Harold.

"That's not a question. Not real bright, are you, Harry? Good try though." I stand aside and point with both guns. "That way."

Coordination is not their thing. It takes a while and it's anything but pretty. The house isn't designed for big men walking two abreast on three legs. There's a lot of pivoting and side-stepping that no one, including me, had counted on. They fall twice and Steven is now out a nice table clock made of crystal, but I get them to the den eventually. They pause at the place where the open door meets the staircase. They don't seem to like the basement idea any more than I did. For all the live entertainment, Morris up on the wall isn't missing the television.

"Down we go," I say from behind. Harold complains under his breath. Leon turns his head.

"Look, man," he says in an impressive baritone. "Let's cut us a deal. Here and now. Straight up, no bullshit. Let's get you on up in this game, man. Everyone got them an itch. Money. Girls. Little medicine. We hook you up good, brother."

Leon's hoping I'll be so surprised he can speak that I won't notice his left elbow softly bumping against Harry's right side.

"Hook me up?"

"Yeah, man. You know."

"For real?"

"No shit, man. Whatever you want."

"Whatever I want. Sounds interesting. What I want, Leon, is information. Let's talk about it downstairs."

Leon's elbow touches softly twice more and then jabs hard into Harold's obliques. Leon bends deeply at the knees with Harold only a second behind. They both leap in unison, turning as a single, three-legged monster to face me.

That, in any event, is obviously what they intend. Hard to do with Leon trying to turn right as Harry wrenches himself around to the left. Twenty extra pounds means Harry wins the physics contest, pulling Leon backward into him. Had Harry's hands been free, he might have been able to save them both, anchoring himself against the doorjamb.

All I can do is watch them go, wailing down into empty space.

At least the light is on.

ONE HUNDRED FOURTEEN

It's enough to make you feel sorry for the staircase.

They take out the railing, landing in a groaning heap at the bottom, face down, still joined at the ankles but with Leon's head and shoulders beneath Harold's torso. They're both moving and making noise. Ray tucks the Ruger back into his belt and heads down the stairs. He steps over them, then bends down and pulls the one off the other.

"Everybody okay?"

Leon tries to arch his back so he can look around. He groans and lays his face back down on the concrete.

"Tell me about it," says Ray. "Nobody is sticking that landing tonight. You do get some style points, though."

The white chest in the corner is thumping. Ray walks to the freezer, digging for the key in his pocket. He unlocks, then slowly lifts up the lid from the far end of the freezer, keeping Sig at the ready.

A white brick of meat sails out of the box and clatters across the concrete. Steven flings an arm over the side of the freezer, trying to hoist himself up and out in a single move. Ray brings the lid back down sharply, just once, against his head.

"You're pitching needs work," says Ray. He props open the lid, reaches in and grabs Steven by the belt, hauling him out onto the floor. "Told you I'd be back. How you doing?"

Steven lies in a ball, panting. He looks up only briefly, then away.

"The cold shoulder? Come on, Steve. The freezer was your idea."

"Fuck you," he says, shivering.

"Yeah, well, everyone says that. For a famous writer you're not so original. I brought your friends. My friends are on their way."

Funny, because Ray's got no friends. Even as he says these words, I can tell he's wondering now just how fast they're coming. For friends, you hurry. You even use lights and sirens. He'll be lucky if they show at all.

Steven lifts his head and looks over at the others. He sits up and slides backward, propping himself against the freezer. He hugs himself to get warm. Ray shakes his head.

"Sorry. No time to get comfortable. I want everyone together. On your feet, hands behind your back."

Steven stands and turns around. Ray holsters Sig and zip ties Steven's hands. Then he walks him across the room.

"Down," he says, tapping his shoe. "All in a row. Harry, Leon, this is Steven King. No autographs, he's not who you think. Steve, this is Harold Baur and Leon Fipps, Olympic synchronized stair divers from right here in Chicago."

Ray pulls a zip tie from his pocket.

"Steve, you have the right to remain silent. Anything you say... you boys know the words, chime in if it feels good... anything you say can and will be used against you."

By the time Ray has finished the recitation, Steven's left ankle is bound to Leon's right. Ray stands over them like three marlins on the deck of a boat.

"Who wants to talk to me about a missing Russian girl? First person to show me a little cooperation gets a recommendation for leniency from yours truly. And I'm true to my word. Ask anybody. But this offer is only for the first person to speak up, not the second. And it expires as soon as the cops show up."

Everyone is quiet. Harold and Leon pivot their heads on the concrete, one way, then the next. Steven keeps still.

"No takers? Steve? Leon? A good word from me and you're on the path to a deal. One of you gets to take that deal away from the others. Harry? That you? How'd you like to do half the time Leon here is going to do? Maybe a quarter. Leon, I don't make you for a chump. You gonna let Harry do that to you?"

He knows this is all pointless. He knows that Harold and Leon have not yet had an opportunity to do anything that might excite a prosecutor. Maybe the guns are stolen. Maybe they've got outstanding warrants. And he figures Steven is probably looking at a plea deal for first-time assault. Maybe attempted false imprisonment. Absent outstanding warrants and felony possession of a firearm, the three of them are in for some serious inconvenience. He knows it and they know it.

But he keeps at it anyway, talking the same schtick he's talked a million times before, nudging them in the hips and ankles with the side of his shoe, trying to get them to cough up something helpful. He'll take anything.

"Ain't done shit, man," says Leon. Harold jerks their shared leg as a warning. Leon turns his head. "This is some bullshit right here."

Ray squats so he can see Leon's face. Leon's nose is dribbling blood.

"Yeah? What's with the Glocks and the zip ties, Leon? Why are you two even here? Come to visit your buddy, Steve? I'm guessing you've never been here before and wouldn't know Steve from Adam. So who sent you? Don't answer that one. We've got your phones. We can figure that out easily enough. And I'm going to find the girl, too. You had better hope she's alive and well, Leon, because I'm going to make sure you share the pain. Understand what I'm saying?"

Leon doesn't answer. He's too busy thinking. Ray keeps up the pressure.

"I'd want to stay clear of that if I were you, Leon. Let Harry and Steve take the fall for that shit. Your mama may have raised a criminal, but she didn't raise a chump, did she? Tell me what I want to know and maybe I can tell the D.A. that you're the only one here who gave a damn about finding the girl before something bad happened to her."

Leon gives a hard blow through his nose, spraying the concrete.

"Don't know nothing about no fucking girl," he says.

"Okay. Say I buy that for now. Tell me who I should be talking to. I'll ask that guy these questions and give you the credit for what I find out."

Harold jerks his leg again. Leon jerks it back.

"Clock's ticking, Leon. You're about to take the fall for something a lot bigger than you realize."

"Fuck you," says Leon.

"You sure about…"

It's the bumping sounds from upstairs that stop him. His phone rings right on cue.

"Time's up." Ray stands, stepping over them for the stairs. "The boys in blue are here. I tried to help. Don't go anywhere."

He heads up the stairs, pulling out the phone to tell the uniforms where he is. He wants to warn them about the girl and the dragon under the bed. He wants everyone to be prepared. He looks at the screen.

Turns out it's Ray who's not prepared.

Unknown Caller. Number Blocked.

ONE HUNDRED FIFTEEN

Those four words. *Unknown Caller. Number Blocked.* Those four arrows to my chest.

I am frozen three steps below the open door. All the motors have seized, except the one that works my heart, which rabbits instantly up to double-time, inflating my eyes and pumping adrenaline into my veins.

My first instinct is to answer. To shout her name into the phone. To tell her I'm sorry.

But I know better. There's no one on the other end of this phone with a voice. The connection is not in answering the call. The connection is simply in the sound of it. The ringing itself. A ping, a pulse, shot like a mote of light from some distant galaxy in order to convey only one thing: *I am here.*

I am here.

It rings again, an old-time telephone, like the ones that rang back in the day when the world made sense, or at least something that passed for sense.

I can't stop staring. *Unknown Caller. Number Blocked.* Those four words.

I can feel the pressure building inside my head. Each new second slams into the pile of time that has stopped moving, registering in my temples like a fifty-car free-for-all on an icy freeway.

Above me, the light from the den suddenly goes dark.

Everything in me that has arrested now surges forward. I stop the phone from ringing and swat the light switch at my shoulder, plunging the stairway into darkness. I stuff the phone in my pocket and yank Sig out of bed. I hold my breath and listen to the silence above. My brain scrambles to catch up, grappling for scraps of relevant information.

Keys.

Where were the car keys?

Two wallets, two phones, two Glocks, and a folding knife. No car keys. Harry and Leon didn't walk to this job. Which means I either missed the keys in the pat-down or… *fuck*… or the keys stayed in the car. Harry and Leon brought a wheelman to keep the keys company. And the wheelman got tired of waiting.

Quiet movement from above. Slow. Careful. Heavy.

I rush up the remaining stairs, lunging the last foot over the threshold and up onto the floor of the den. I can see him before I land, a solid mass in motion through the dark room. It's a human shape with three arms. My gut tells me this is a time to shoot first and identify myself later. I don't get the chance for either.

The third arm lights up the room, sparking fire and throwing bullets ten at a time. Wood splinters above my head and a hole opens up on the floor three inches from my face. I push backward hard, emptying Sig into the room as my feet and legs follow the downward slope of the stairs. I catch a brief glimpse of the shadow diving behind the recliner that sits beneath the buck on the wall. Below me, Harry and Leon are shouting furiously for rescue. I flail upward for the doorknob and slam the door closed.

The blackness on the stairwell is complete. I feel around frantically for the light switch on the wall. When I find it, I keep it centered in my mind and smash it hard three times with the butt of the gun, shattering the plastic.

I want to take the steps three at a time, but I know better. Not in the dark. I've taken these stairs the fast way once already. I reach for the railing that is no longer there and nearly lose my balance over the edge. The boys are still shouting so I have a good sense of where that last step is. I pause long enough to return the empty Sig to the holster and draw the Ruger from my belt. It's no match for an AR-15 or whatever this guy is swinging, but I don't have many options. It's either the Ruger or throwing frozen bricks of venison.

The door above thumps. I whip my body sideways and aim, if you can call it that. I fire off two Hail Mary's up into the dark. The sound is loud enough to stop all the shouting. If I'm lucky, I punched a couple holes through the door in just the right spot. If I'm not lucky…

The door flies open and I leap from the stairs without thinking about anything except getting clear of what's coming. My foot catches and somebody's leg sends me sprawling. The shooting and the shouting start up again at the same time. They become part of the same awful sound. It's the sound that will either haunt me the rest of my life or send me into the next world.

I roll on my back to see the wheelman silhouetted in the doorway, working the automatic like a firehose. I squeeze off two more shots and roll away until I hit the freezer.

The noise stops. The room is choked with acrid propellant. Behind me I can hear the water heater is spurting.

The optimist in me wants to believe I clipped him. That he's up there dead or wounded.

The optimist in me has yet to win the lottery even once.

At the base of the stairs, the muscle pigs start up again. Even Steven joins in. My eyes have adjusted enough to see the three of them trying to inchworm away in different directions. I fire one more shot up toward the empty doorway for cover. Then I stand, drop inside the open freezer, and lower the lid.

The return fire is merciless. I have never been to war, but I have been in a small country house, huddled in a bathtub, as a tornado screams overhead. This is worse. I try to make myself small, pulling my knees into my chest and keeping as many of the remaining frozen blocks of deer between me and the freezer wall as I can.

It goes for an eternity of bursts. Short, long, short. The garbage cans full of frozen meat provide some decent cover, but the freezer takes a few for the team anyway. I can hear the metal-on-metal contact like ball-bearing hailstones on a metal roof. But the angle is all wrong. If the wheelman was firing at the box from ground level, I'd already be gone; up in the big dream buying St. Peter a drink and asking about a girl I know. But the wheelman is afraid of getting picked off with a single-shot Ruger or being hit in the head with a frozen brick. So, he's up there trying to get the job done at a hundred-fifteen-degree angle. So far, that's not working.

I figure the Ruger has only a couple of rounds left. Either I can pick this guy off as he comes down for a look, or I'm going to die in a mostly empty meat freezer. The gunfire keeps coming. But the bursts are shorter now, and the empty spaces between them are mercifully longer.

Then there is silence. I wait, listening.

Silence.

I un-ball myself, carefully, shifting my weight from my left hip to my knees. I slowly unfold, easing my back up against the freezer lid, slipping the barrel of the Ruger into the widening crack. The opening is not wide enough to see up the stairs. All I can make out are three long, dark lumps on the concrete, closer to me than they used to be. Nothing moves.

I wait for sounds of descent. I know the sound is coming, so I will either have the patience to wait for it and to choose the precise moment or…

And there it is. A step. Descent.

I push up just a little more. Three blocks of venison that are stacked up against the inside of the freezer wall lose their nerve. The sound is loud and horrifying, threatening to transform the freezer from a jack-in-the-box surprise into a coffin.

I listen. The sound of descent has stopped. Not good.

I grip the Ruger with both hands and heave myself upward for all I'm worth. I fire the first shot at the staircase before I'm fully set and have eyes on the wheelman. I'm counting on the second bullet, probably the last, to find its mark. Hit or miss, I'm ready to dive out and make a break for the shelving in the back of the room.

Quick movement on the stairs. Gunfire. Not a spray this time, just one syllable that skips off the floor to my left. I adjust my aim just as the freezer lid is falling back against my body. I knock it back open with an elbow and readjust, the Ruger pulling both hands forward like a dog on a tight leash. I squeeze the trigger twice and get two clicks: once for each bullet that isn't actually there.

I drop the gun and hurl myself out of the freezer and down into the small, hot lake pooling on the concrete floor from the punctured water heater. I slip, going down a second time and coming up wet before I can push off for the shelving in the back of the room. I can feel the nerves in my back and neck pricking hot beneath my skin, trying to guess the exact place the next bullet will enter my body.

Turns out it's not the shooter's bullet that stops me. It's her voice.

"Mack?"

ONE HUNDRED SIXTEEN

He adjusts course, carefully moving for the stairs. Stepping over bodies. Then he can see her.

Shock has taken full control. Her eyes are wide and her entire head wobbles in a constant tremor. Her arms keep the gun as far from her chest as possible, both hands clutching the thing like a slippery grenade.

Ray climbs the stairs slowly. He speaks softly, using his best toddler-in-a-mine-field cadence. He's got both hands outstretched; fingers splayed. His way of trying to keep the bullets inside the Glock.

"Nadia," he says again. Sirens rise in the distance like birds of grief and warning. "You're okay. Let's set the gun down. Can you do that? Just set it down."

He's up high enough now that he can see the boots of the wheelman just above the top step.

He tries to hold her eyes in his. He tries to connect. But Nadia can't see his eyes because her brain is in the way. Her mind can't see anything except the dead man on the floor behind her and the grotesque array of bodies tied together on the floor below. He's blocking her view now with every new step up the stairs, but that doesn't matter. She's already seen. There's no unseeing that. Not now or ever.

The right side of his body is soaked with water. His shoe squishes.

"Nadia."

It's too dark for her to make out the details below. The face of her husband. The steady, sticky exsanguination of three bodies emptying themselves across the concrete like overturned cans of paint, mixing with the hot water from the punctured heater that still gurgles and hisses in the dark. She hasn't seen any of that. Doesn't matter. Death has a smell. Violence has a smell. A terrible, gut-wrenching vibration that will repattern your DNA if you let it. If you get enough of it.

And Ray is bringing it all up the stairs with him. The smell. The vibration. It reaches her before he does, turning her stomach.

She vomits on the stairs. Ray closes the distance quickly, seizing the Glock with both hands and pulling it away. Another heave dissolves into sobbing. He places a hand on her back. Nadia looks up at him suddenly. Remembering. Wiping her mouth.

"Danika." The name comes out desperate and wet with fear.

"She's okay," says Ray. "I've got her hiding. She's fine. Take a breath. Danika is fine."

Outside, the sirens crescendo and then stop. Ray's phone rings.

ONE HUNDRED SEVENTEEN

We've been at it an hour or so when Twill finally shows. I'm holding Danika and Vladimir in my arms, looking out through the living room curtains as two uniforms cluster around Nadia on a nearby couch asking questions.

The closest Twill can park is two houses away. I watch him open his car door and unfold himself, blowing red and blue steam out into the cold air. Danika points.

"My boss," I say. She yawns and lays her head on my shoulder.

"He's tall."

"He eats his vegetables."

"And he doesn't have any hair."

"Hair won't grow at that altitude."

"I don't like vegetables. Except on pizza so I can pick them off. Do you have to do what he says because he's your boss?"

It should be impossible to make a guy laugh in these circumstances, but somehow she pulls that off.

"Yes," I say. Twill looks up at the top of the driveway. His eyes find mine through the window. "I do. I absolutely do."

I hand Danika off to Nadia so I can meet him in the foyer. Twill and I separate near the doorway so the EMT's can get a gurney through. The shape of the sheet on top is too big for Leon or Steven. The wheelman is already gone.

"Christ almighty," says Twill.

"Wrong shroud," I say, nodding down at the gurney. "This here is Harold. You're up early."

His eyes make the trip up the sopping right side of my attire to my face. The EMT's have replaced my bandage with something clean and visible to passing planes.

"Your cat must be loaning you some of her lives," he says.

"I should hope so. She eats better than I do."

"Let's have it. Try to skip the bullshit."

I pull him into an out-of-the-way corner where the dress code is latex and paper boot optional. He crosses his arms and listens to a mostly accurate, mostly complete version of events. The part about Mila gets his temperature up.

"So you found her and then you lost her," he says.

"More or less. Yeah."

"More or less? You used civilians to find her, you turned her over to a civilian to hold her, and then you lost her all over again. Then you come out here in the middle of the goddamned night because you think she might be here, which turns out to be not at all true. So now we've got four bodies and no Emily. Do I have that about right, Detective Mackey?"

"Almost," I say. "Her real name is Mila."

I can see his jaw grinding in anger. He jabs a finger in the direction of Nadia, still answering questions on the sofa with Danika's head in her lap.

"And her? Are you… involved?"

"No. But thanks for thinking that's possible."

"I'm beginning to think anything is possible with you. Why is she here?"

I tell him the same story Nadia is busy telling anyone who asks.

"She's married to the homeowner. Steven. They'll be wheeling him out in a minute. Separation is going on three years and the mutual custody is wearing thin. She stopped thinking Steven was a safe parenting option. So, she dropped by to claim the girl even after the cops told her to stay away. She lets herself in, hears shooting, grabs a Glock from the pile of guns on the floor and comes running. She ended up putting the wheelman down just before he gave me a new set of eyes in the side of my head.

"That makes her a brave woman and you a lucky ex-cop."

I look up at Twill.

"Yeah?" I ask. "Already?"

"I'm done, Mack," he says firmly. "This doesn't work."

He looks down at the palm of his hand and starts counting on his long fingers.

"You're a person of interest in the Pleasants homicide investigation. You've put yourself and IAD at the center of an investigation by the OAG. A once prosecution-friendly judge has now all but waged war against the Chandler Police

Department and we've lost our calendar on at least half a dozen pending cases. You've secretly deputized, apparently, most of the citizens of greater Chicago to either chase dangerous criminals or to safe-house victims against their will. That's called false imprisonment, by the way. And now…" He gestures loosely at the chaos around him. "And now you're ground-zero for an investigation into four brand new homicides. I've got a sinking feeling all of that is just the tip of the iceberg under my ass. My neck is a foot longer because of you, Mack, and everyone I report to knows how to swing an axe."

Twill shakes his head, staring into space. I know he's not done. I wait.

"I asked you to be patient. To keep your head down. Do solid IAD work. Give me a chance to ease you in. You pushed and I told you to stay in your lane. Above all, I told you to tell me everything. Keep me in the loop. Somehow, in all of that, you heard exactly the opposite."

I want to argue with him. Plead my case. I keep my bitten, throbbing tongue in my mouth.

"So, no, Mack. This isn't working for me. I can't do anything but suspend you until all these investigations have wrapped up. But you need to start polishing your resume." Both of his hands make large swirling circles in the air, indicating the entire house. "And I'd leave this part out if I were you."

Another ghost on a gurney makes its way through the house to the foyer. The guy walking backward opens the door. A blast of frozen air rushes in to engulf the body, like the EMT's are feeding meat to a beast they have chained up out in the yard.

A graveyard homicide hump, poor bastard, appears from around a corner flipping through a notepad. He looks up in time to avoid Twill's shoulder. He gives us both an eye roll. "What a shitshow," he mutters more to himself than to us. He keeps moving.

"Does a resignation work better?" I ask Twill.

"For you or for me?" Twill shakes his head, withdrawing the question. "We'll figure that out. Go home, Mack. Get some sleep. Be glad you're not dead. Come by tomorrow and sign off on your suspension-pending. We'll talk more then."

I nod in Nadia's direction.

"I want to see them get home. They've been through a lot tonight."

"We'll assign a unit, Mack. Go home."

I look up at him, hoping my no-drama acceptance of being out of a job will be good for one last indulgence.

"It needs to be me, LT."

Her car is still parked where it was a lifetime ago, back when I was younger and drier and fully employed. Danika is out like a light, bundled up in Nadia's arms. I've got Vladimir by the neck. He seems unphased by all the bloodshed. His tongue is still in one piece and enjoying the cold air, which is more than I can say for mine.

We walk in silence. All the houses are flashing. All the windows gawk in red and blue speculation. My sopping pant leg stiffens in the cold wind.

Nadia buckles Danika into the back seat and closes the door. She pulls the car keys from her pocket, then turns and kisses me on the mouth, laying the palm of her hand gently on my bandage.

"Brave thing you did," I say. "You saved my life tonight."

"It's not real," she says. Her eyes fill up again and she buries her face in my shoulder. She whispers, either because she doesn't want Danika to hear, or because she doesn't have enough energy to push sound out of her throat. Or both. "None of this can be real, Mack. I can't believe Steven… It's just so awful. I hated him for so long, but I never wanted him dead. I never wanted… And I shot at you. I could have killed you too. You could be dead right now. You could be down there with the rest of them."

I push her back for a good look, drying her face with my thumbs.

"You had one good shot in you. I'm glad it was only one and I'm glad you made it count."

She smiles a little and wipes her face. A gust from the north plays in her hair.

"Goodnight, Mack," she says.

"You mean goodbye, don't you?"

Confusion. Concern.

"I don't…"

"Oh, sure you do," I say. "This is the part where you and the kid and the dragon hightail it out of Dodge and leave the rest of us scratching our heads. You've been working for that all night long."

"Mack, I'm not understanding. I…"

"You've understood everything from the very beginning, Nadia. I'm the slow one here." I pluck the keys from her hand and walk around the front of the car. I unlock the passenger door and open it. "I'll drive."

We look at each other over the top of the car. I can see she's counting all her options. It doesn't take her long.

ONE HUNDRED EIGHTEEN

Ray stops by the Impala on the way out of the neighborhood. He gets out, opens the trunk, and digs around inside. Nadia watches him through the passenger window. Her face wants to know what he's doing. I know exactly what he's doing.

It's a kind of neurosis with him. Like his obsession with keeping the gas tank at least a quarter full. Or making sure there's at least one spare Old Forester on stand-by. An empty gun is no good. It's not about the odds of trouble. A gun only exits for one thing. That one thing is to blow a bullet out of the barrel. Ray has never been one for paperweights or doorstops, so he keeps it loaded. Even if there is next to no chance he'll need it. Even tucked away in the safe, he makes sure it's holding the full fifteen plus one in the chamber. You never really know.

He finds what he needs, draws Sig and ejects the empty magazine, substituting the full clip and dropping a spare clip in his pocket just for good measure. He noses the gun back into the holster and closes the trunk. Inside the home of the late Steven King, cops pass back and forth behind the shades like rats in a shadow box. He climbs back into Nadia's little blue Nissan and gives it some gas.

"Where are we going?" The question comes with plenty of attitude. "I just want to go home, Mack."

"Of course you do," he says. "You must be exhausted."

"I am. So…"

"So, we're not going home."

"Why? Where are you taking me?"

"Your choice. We'll either go to wherever you've stashed Mila, or we can go to the Chandler Police Department."

He makes a rolling stop at the end of the street, turns the wheel and heads west.

"What are you talking about?" she asks.

Ray looks at her, but only briefly.

"You know. Police department. Big building with lots of tiny rooms. You've seen it. Bunch of steps and flags out front. We can wake up a social worker for Danika and then get you booked."

"Booked?" He finds her eyes are no less beautiful for being wide and panicked. "Booked for what?"

"I'll think of something. We'll start with obstruction and go from there. Where'd you hide Mila?"

"Have you lost your mind?"

"Yeah. A while ago. I'm learning to live without it. Where's Mila?"

Nadia rotates away in her seat, offering her shoulder as she broods out the window. Ray nods to himself and keeps driving straight to nowhere in particular. He pats himself down for the Camel he doesn't have. The moon is an empty white socket hanging open over windblown streets made of cold, blue glass.

"Don't suppose you have a cigarette," he asks.

"I told you already," she sulks. "I don't smoke."

"Funny."

"Oh? And why is that?"

"Because your mother thinks you do. She thinks you're a Parliamentarian, just like the rest of your family. She's very proud of her brand."

"Well, then she's mistaken."

Ray nods.

"Could be, yeah. Ivah's mistaken about a lot of things. She thinks your daughter is a boy. I'm guessing the problem is that she doesn't have any pictures of her granddaughter around to remind her. Not a single one. I found that strange. Not very motherly. Then again, it's not especially daughterly of you to never visit your elderly mother locked up in that place."

"I do visit," she says, mustering umbrage on demand. "Every chance I can."

"Tell that to Frank."

"Frank? Who is Frank?"

"You wouldn't know him. Dour guy with a flask in his pocket and a nametag on his cardigan that says *Frank* in big capital letters. He sits at that big wooden desk in the Golden View lobby with the visitor log that doesn't have your name in it more than once. He's the one who had to point out the short way up to your mother's room."

"That Frank," she says.

"Yeah, him. And there's only the one picture of you up there, by the way. According to the backside, that photo was taken twenty years ago. Ivah and Dmitri were here in Chicago raising Joe and Alex. You were what, fifteen? Mugging for a camera outside a church in Novogrudok with your buddy Belka and ten other girls? How does that work?"

"None of your business. I was visiting."

"I don't think so. I think you were home. And I'm guessing Belka is just your friend's nickname. The back of that picture identifies a *Verochka*, age fifteen. And I don't think that's you."

"You don't know anything."

"Sure I do. I know all kinds of things. I know the Cubs aren't going to the World Series. I know that if the cards add up to eighteen and you say *hit me* then you deserve to be hit. I know booze and cigarettes can't kill you if you die of something else first."

"You don't know anything interesting."

"I know that if Ivah had named you after her grandmother, one of you would have said so when she pried open that doll and pulled out that little slip of paper. The photo on the shelf isn't about you at all. It's all about a girl named Verochka, aka Belka. How's that for interesting?"

"You seem to have some kind of point, Detective. Why don't you just make it and then take me home."

"A point? No. I don't have a point. Ask anybody. Everyone I know thinks I'm pointless, except maybe people who ask me for directions. My cat thinks I hung the moon, but that's less about having a point than knowing how to open a can of tuna. I'm just saying that you're too good a mother to be a bad daughter. So, I'm guessing you're not a daughter at all, or at least not Ivah's daughter. Verochka is Ivah's daughter. So I think maybe it's time you finally come clean about why you've been jerking me all over Chicago by the nostrils."

Exasperation. Frustration.

"I'm not… I haven't…"

"You are and you have." The words come out with some volume to go with the anger. Ray checks in on Danika in the rearview mirror. Her head is ninety-degrees sideways. Her mouth hangs open just like Vladimir's. The dragon is the only one back there who's awake. Ray lowers his voice but keeps the edge. "Stop with the nonsense, Nadia. Would it help if I called you Ginny Southside?"

She looks at him with an expression reserved for lunatics.

"Oh, come on," he says. "Stop the theatrics. So you take your mojitos with a double slug of gin and a side of organized crime. Nothing to be ashamed of. You going to tell me where you stashed Mila, or do I head downtown? You've got until this next exit, so I'd make it quick."

Her eyes start to fill like little blue buckets. She turns back toward the window.

"Okay," says Ray. He swats the turn signal. "You should have brought a toothbrush."

Nadia turns away from the window.

"Wait," she says.

"I'm listening."

"She's in a hotel."

"Still listening."

"Motel 6."

"Want to narrow that down a little?"

He has to wait for it, but she coughs it up eventually.

"Watseka," she says.

"Watseka?" Ray laughs. He exits the freeway just so he can get back on again and head the opposite direction. "Boy, you weren't taking any chances, were you? Watseka. Good choice. No one's looking for her in Watseka. Inconvenient as all hell, but…"

He breaks off and gives her a sideways look.

"Unless maybe it's not inconvenient at all. Not for you, anyway. Yeah, I get it now. Your plan was to swing by Watseka on your way out of town. Pick Mila up once you busted Danika and the dragon out of Steve's place, then head east. New York. Boston. Maybe Florida. Someplace you can disappear."

"Am I under arrest?" she asks.

"Would you like to be?"

"Maybe you've forgotten that I just saved your life back there."

"I haven't forgotten. Thanks for that. Maybe you've forgotten that you are the only reason I was there in the first place."

"I never asked you to…"

"Sure you did. You tried to snatch the kid on your own, and when that didn't work you got the cops to send me a message, one you knew would make me drop everything and come running. And I did, too. I was hoping I'd find Mila locked away in some closet. Silly me. You wanted me to yank Steven out of his comfort zone and haul him in for questioning. Somewhere in all of that you were planning to show up and take possession of Danika. You figured Steve would have his hands full pleading his innocence about a missing girl he's never laid eyes on. Then, while Steve and I are playing twenty questions, you and the kid are on the road to Watseka to pick up Mila and then it's off to who knows where. That was the whole point, wasn't it? To get lost forever. To bury yourself so deep that not even Big Man can find you. How am I doing?"

"Terrible."

"I doubt that. You were parked out there waiting for the right time to drop in, but then the muscle showed up. You weren't expecting that. All you could do was watch with a sinking feeling in your gut. A few minutes later you see the wheelman climb out of the car and go inside and you start to get worried. What's a woman to do? You get out of the car and walk to the house and put your ear to the door. You hear the shooting. Maternal instinct takes over. You step inside, panicked. Lucky for you there's a pile of guns on the floor so you grab one and come running to join the party. You're not looking to save me. I know better. You're just afraid maybe Danni's in middle of a room full of bullets. It's like all those stories you hear of a mom lifting up a car to get her kid out from under a tire. You were ready to walk right into Hell. Kill everyone in the room if you had to, me included. You may not be Ivah's daughter, but you're Danika's mother. No doubt about that."

"That's the first thing you've said that makes any sense."

"Good. I'm on a roll. What I want to know is what the kid was doing over there in the first place."

"He's her father," Nadia says, turning back to her window. "Was."

"Yeah, he was her father all right. I had a father like him once. Danika's got a better bond with the deer head in the den. She's only been there three times since you and Steven separated. Why tonight?"

Silence. She's still devoted to the window. Ray keeps at it.

"Best I can figure is that taking custody of Danni is how they're keeping you in line. Steven keeps her until you do whatever it is you're supposed to do. Probably deliver me on a silver platter. They think I've stashed Mila away for safekeeping because she never turned up in the system. They want her back because she's got some stories to tell. They think your eyes and lips and the rest of you can help solve the problem. But they've got no idea that you're the one who stashed her. Your problem was how to keep Mila hidden and still recover Danika. That's where I came in."

Ray gives her a look. Her shoulder shrugs him off like it has eyes of its own.

"Decent idea, I guess," he says, "but you should have parked a block further away from the house. Wrong kind of neighborhood for this kind of car. You'd have been less conspicuous wrapped in Christmas lights. I knew I was being played the second I turned onto South Bremmer."

"Oh, you're so smart," she says. No way he can see the eyeroll, but he knows it's there anyway.

"Not smart enough," he says. "I should have ignored your little message and stayed home. I don't need to drive across town to feel shot at. My neighbor already has that covered. But I came out anyway, didn't I? I played your little game. I guess things didn't play out like you expected. These kinds of games never do."

"I don't want to talk," she says. "Can we just ride?"

"Ride all you like, I don't mind. I'm guessing you didn't tell them the part about meeting with Mila at *Bucks* to play translator. And you didn't tell them about tailing Mila to Doris' place. All you had to do was wait at the curb until Mila got the chance to give Doris the slip and come running. That's why Doris couldn't find her. By the time Doris had any idea, Mila was long gone, curled up in that seat just like you are now. And why not? Mila trusts you. You speak her language. She knows you're on her side."

Nadia keeps quiet, but I can tell she's all ears. So can Ray.

"What I can't figure is whether you already knew Mila when you walked into the bar, or if you just identified with her situation. Maybe you've got something in common. Maybe you see Mila and it's like looking in a funhouse mirror. Watching you two, I should have realized that was an awful lot of Russian in a conversation that delivered no information. You were busy telling her all about the future, weren't you? That, and making a chump out of me."

"It wasn't difficult," she says.

"No, making me a chump was the easy part. The problem, Nadia, is that Mila may trust you, but Big Man doesn't. Big Man trusts you about as much as I do. He knows you're ready to run and so he grabs up Danni and hands her over to

Steven just to make sure you're trying your hardest to work me over for Mila's location. Your instructions were to do whatever it takes. Something much cozier than a slice of pizza, if necessary. You didn't like that idea much and I don't blame you. You already knew everything Big Man wanted to know, and I knew nothing. More pizza and some pillow talk is as pointless as it is cruel. Maybe you're corrupt to the core or maybe you're just a nice girl in the middle of a hard life, but I don't make you as cruel. So, you get it in your head to skip the charade with me, spring Danika on your own, beat it all the way out to Watseka, grab Mila, and make a run for it. Guess you get some points for guts."

He lets it sit for a minute as he navigates around two cruisers pulled up to a minivan on its side. He nods at the flashing lights as they pass.

"Winter claims another victim," he says.

Two officers are talking to an underdressed man trying to bury his fingers into his own armpits. Everyone looks miserable.

"I could take the winters just fine if it wasn't for the cold and the ice," he says. "I'm thinking of moving to the Florida Keys. Or maybe West Antigua. Buy a boat. Do some fishing. Antiguan law requires that all ice be contained to coolers or glasses. They've got the common sense to keep it off the roads. We love freedom just a little too much in this country. The ice gets to go everywhere it wants."

He's hoping for something like a laugh. But the switch-up gets him nothing.

"Anything you want to say to me, Nadia? Now's the time to help yourself. A little cooperation can go a long way. I'll take almost anything. Pick a question. How do you know Mila? Who put the flash drive in the doll? Who set all of this up? What's Big Man got on you? What's he got on Ivah? Must be something. The two of you should put in for an Oscar. I'm the runaway favorite for sap of the year, but it's an honor just to be nominated."

They ride in silence, Nadia's back to him as she weeps quietly against the window. He leaves her alone and lets Interstate 57 do the talking. The road mumbles and hums beneath him, telling stories he's heard a thousand times before. Most of them are about Marlo. He's used to hearing those stories alone. This time he's got a woman riding next to him and a kid sleeping in the back, magnets made of flesh and bone, pulling the memory out of him. It's the drive back from Columbus, Marlo's father ten days in the ground, that comes rumbling up through the tires.

Because I want a family, Ray.

Spend a few weeks walking around in my shoes, Marlo. That'll change your mind.

No. Don't make this about homicide. The world is a cruel and terrible place full of awful people and broken homes. I get it.

Do you? Working insurance fraud claims from the top of a glass tower got you that gritty perspective on humanity, did it? Chasing Victor Roby around the court system? When was the last time you pulled a kid out of an oven, medium-well?

Stop.

When was the last time you found a fifteen-year-old working the street for her old man's crank money, her arms so tracked up she looks like a human cribbage board?

Stop it. That's an excuse, Ray. This is all about your own childhood. You need to air out your past. Let in some light. We can make some of that light ourselves.

Sure, I'm all for trying to make the light, just as long as it never actually happens.

Does it sound like I'm joking to you?

You're my light, Marlo. You and I are enough.

No, Ray. We're not. We're not enough. My mother is a widow now. If one day you don't come home, I want something of you in the world. I want to look into your child's eyes and see you looking back. What if I don't come home one day? You okay with being alone like that?

Marlo... If ever you don't come home, Marlo...

"She's not like me," says Nadia. She wipes her eyes and sniffs and straightens herself in the seat. It takes him a second.

"What?"

"Mila's different."

"Different how?" he asks.

"I wanted to come here. This country. I was excited. We all were. Some were scared to leave home. I was not scared. I was just excited. I was sixteen. I couldn't wait to get out. I'd already basically left my parents. We hated each other. There was nothing for me there. Except Belka. I loved Belka. Ivah's niece."

"Verochka."

"Yes," she says, conceding. "Verochka. We were close. Belka's parents... her dad was in prison and her mom died so she didn't really have anyone except her Aunt Oksana, who was her legal guardian but treated her like a dog tied up in the yard, and an older brother. Anton. He was in a gang. Belka had nothing. She wanted out as much as I did. More than anything. We were going to live in

America with Belka's aunt Ivah and her uncle Dmitry. America. We dreamed of that day."

Nadia laughs in spite of herself, covering her mouth with her hand.

"Belka had Jovah's academy photo. She was always talking about how I was going to marry her cousin Jovah and she would marry one of his handsome policeman friends. She'd hold Jovah's photo in my face and tell me to kiss my husband. She liked to imagine these elaborate dinner parties. She talked about them like they had actually happened. All our children were around the table. She could describe every one of them. And the rich neighbors. Life in America."

"She never made the trip, I take it," says Ray. Nadia's smile melts away.

"She was supposed to come. She got arrested. Belka was always in trouble. I went on without her. They promised she would join me later. They told me I had to go, or I would miss my only chance. So I went. They promised Belka would be coming. They said they would go back for her as soon as she was out of jail. I know they must have tried because Ivah was connected."

"Connected how? That's a special word in some circles."

Nadia shrugs out a long sigh.

"I don't know. The people who brought me over knew who Ivah was. They said I was going to live with her and that she was making them go back for Belka. They always said it like… you know, like Ivah gets what she wants. And I know Ivah wanted it to happen."

"How's that?"

"After Ivah's sister died, she sent Belka all these letters. Belka kept them and we read them again and again. Ivah had sons. She wanted a daughter. She wanted Belka. She wrote about all the things they would do. She'd probably have gotten Belka over here eventually, but Belka ended up killing a police officer in Minsk."

"Sweet kid, this friend of yours."

Another non-laugh, this one dark and heavy.

"Belka wanted to marry a cop and she ended up killing one. She went to prison just like her dad. Then she died in a riot. Very sad. She was a good friend. But she liked trouble. I'm sure Ivah was crushed. She wanted Belka as much as Belka wanted her."

"And Ivah got you instead," says Ray.

"No. Ivah didn't want anything to do with me. I didn't meet Ivah until… well…" She doesn't finish. She doesn't have to.

"Oh," says Ray. "I get it. Stupid me. You didn't meet Ivah until Big Man cast you in a bad play called Ray the Rube and the Russian Doll."

Nadia nods without looking.

"So then you never even had a chance to meet the family."

"No," she says. "Just Ivah. She hates me. She thinks I should have helped Belka somehow. Like I took Belka's place on the boat. She spits on me. The woman can hold a grudge."

"Smoking Parliaments will do that to a person," says Ray. He looks at her with a wry smile, hoping to catch her glance. No chance of that. Nadia keeps her eyes in her lap. "Okay. So, you're sweet sixteen and ready for America. How'd they get you in?"

"It took a long time. Minsk, Berlin, London, then Quebec, then to this camp outside of Ottawa where some of the group stayed behind and we picked up others. Then to Sault Saint Marie. They put eight girls on a boat while the rest of us waited. The boat came back a week later. That boat took us to another boat. A fishing boat. They put each of us into these big, like, these rolling fish carts. There were dozens on board but only a few were used for people. There was ice on top but a door underneath and a space just big enough inside for a person to curl up."

"Not a very big person," says Ray. Nadia looks at him.

"Women and girls," she says. "It stunk terribly inside. They let us out one at a time and kept rotating the whole trip. I remember how good it felt to get out and breathe fresh air. Cold, but the sky was blue, and the water was so beautiful. I told myself it was all worth it to live in America. But I was never out of that crate long enough."

"Long enough to put on a pair of rubber boots and have your picture taken with a Lake Michigan walleye."

Nadia looks out at the road for the memory. Her eyes come back amazed.

"Yes," she says. "I do remember that. They wanted us laughing and smiling, holding up a dead fish. How did you know? Who told you?"

"No one told me. I've seen the catalogue. Even rubes like me get it right on our own every now and then."

"I don't know that word. Rube."

"It means sucker. Check the dictionary and you'll see my picture."

"Then I was the rube," she says. "I didn't know the truth. We were all told we'd have good jobs until they could match us with rich American men and then we could retire and raise our babies. It would be a better life than any of us had back in Novogrudok. Or Bialystok. Vilnius. We were from all over by the time we got on that boat. None of us knew what the work would be. They lied to all of us. One girl knew. She kept saying it was all about sex. We hated her. But she was right. We were fools to think they would train us. That we were getting a better life. There was no training. For anything. You don't need training to have sex and carry drugs. No one married a rich American and retired."

"Except you," says Ray.

Nadia closes her eyes and lays her head back against the seat, letting it loll sideways to the window.

"I was lucky," she says eventually. A wistful smile. "Steven saved me. I only spent a year and a half in the stable. That's what they called it. A stable. Like we were horses. I got the higher-end clients. Businessmen mostly. Men with money and hot water and soap. Most of the others in the stable…" She stops, avoiding the rest of that thought like a dark corner in West Garfield Park. "Well. I was lucky. They sent me to Steven's house a few times. He was always nice to me. I didn't have to do anything I didn't want to do. Sometimes we just talked. He wanted me for himself."

"I'll bet he did. And they just let you go?"

"Steven did work for them. I was a gift. They wanted to keep him happy."

"Work. What kind of work?"

"Investment accounting."

"You mean cleaning dead presidents."

"I don't know what that means."

"Money laundering."

"Then why don't you just say money laundering?" Her tone is sharp and irritated. "Must you always talk in… in riddles?"

"Beats lying and scheming and leading people into a tornado of bullets."

They look at each other over the dark seat, the accusation in the air between them, glinting in the on-coming headlights. Nadia breaks away first.

"I don't even…"

"It means feeding crime money into legal business investments so that the money you make appears legitimate."

"Then yes," she says. "It was definitely money laundering. He called it investment accounting. I didn't ask questions. I was barely eighteen by then and grateful to be living in a big house with a man who treated me like a person. Not like some animal in a stable. He did things for me. Nice clothes. Jewelry. Good food. My English was not so good, so he got me a tutor. I wanted to be a good American wife. I worked hard to speak without my accent. He took me places. It was like the life Belka and I had dreamed about. I was happy. Mostly. After a couple years I was bored and wanted a job. Steven helped me pass the real estate exam and found a firm that would take me. We faked a bunch of paperwork and I sold houses for a while. I didn't like the work so much, but I felt like a normal American woman."

"Okay, so you marry the guy, nature takes its course and along comes dragon girl back there."

"We did not marry. They forbid it. I wasn't legal. It would raise too many questions. Steven said marriage was not important to him. We didn't really talk about it. And then, yes. Danika." She looks at him. "Do you have any children?"

The deflection feels like a fishhook. Marlo is in his eyes.

"No," he says. "There should be a law against me being a parent."

"You don't think you'd make a good father?"

"I can barely manage myself. But I'm not interested in me right now."

"They change everything, Mack," she says. "Danika changed everything."

"Changed how?"

"Steven already had two kids from two previous marriages, and they all hate each other. He wasn't interested in doing it again. He demanded an abortion. I refused. We fought all through my pregnancy. He became difficult to live with. I did too, I suppose. We were always shouting. Finding fault. He felt rejected. My life stopped being about him. Danika was my only priority. Everything was about her. Steven resented her from the first day. He wanted to put her up for adoption. I refused."

She turns her body to look at the seat behind her. Ray uses the mirror. Vladimir has heard everything, but the kid is still asleep. Nadia faces forward again.

"On her fifth birthday we had this epic big fight. Awful. Just… Steven hit me. Like, really hard across the face. It was the first time he'd ever done anything like that. And that was…" She shakes her head, remembering. "That was it for me. I took Danika and we moved out. We stayed with a friend of mine until that became unworkable. I moved back home briefly. He was all nice and apologetic. He tried to show me that he had changed. But it was the beginning of the end. I wanted out. He didn't fight my decision to leave. He felt guilty. He bought me a small house for us to live in. He paid my expenses. This car. He supported me just enough. Nothing, like, super expensive or anything. He didn't want me getting too comfortable being away."

"Waiting for you to come to your senses."

"Yes. He expected it was only temporary. He expected me to forgive him and move back. He said he was ready to be a father. He might have been ready. I let him keep her for a night here or there."

"Three times she told me."

"It was more than three. But not many. I think Steven was lonely. He told me he wanted me to move back. I refused. That made him angry. He threatened to cut me off. Sell the house out from under me. I told him I would manage on my own; I'd stay with friends until I could figure things out. That's when he threatened to take full custody. He said I didn't stand a chance as an illegal. He said if I wanted to keep Danika, all I had to do was move back home." She glances fleetingly up at Ray, then away again. "That's when I went for help."

"What kind of help? From whom?"

Either the words are stuck in her throat, or she doesn't want to answer.

"From… From the people…"

"Big Man," says Ray. "Christ. You went to Big Man for help."

"That's just a name. A ghost story. It keeps everyone frightened."

"You think the organization runs itself?"

"I'm saying I only know the people that…" She falters again. "The people that…"

"The people that sold you," he says. He tries to choke down the bile and to not sound the way he feels. He tries. But Ray tries a lot of things that never work out. "You went to the people who sell other people. You went back to the goddamned slave traders."

Nadia's eyes turn sharp and hot.

"Oh, do I disgust you? Officer? You want to judge me like I'm a common whore? You think life in Belarus was any better for me? I was sixteen. I'd have been dead a long time ago, just like Belka."

"I wasn't…"

"I'd never have had Danika. She's everything. She's the only thing. I'd do it all again for her."

"Nadia, protecting these people is not…"

"I'm not protecting anyone but myself and my daughter."

"Who, Nadia?" He has to squeeze the shout down into a hoarse whisper. "Goddamnit. Who did you contact?"

She looks at him with an expression brimming with fear and anger. Her voice is pleading.

"They kill people for less, Mack. Much less."

"I can protect you."

"You can't. You know you can't."

"You were already on the run. You think giving me a name makes it any worse for you than it is already? Why don't you give me a chance to help?"

It's enough to make her think. He lets her look out the window in silence. He gives it two hundred yards, but then he can see it's not enough to change her mind. I've seen every hand of poker Ray Mackey has ever played. So I know a long-shot bluff when I see it.

"Stoli," he says. It's a gamble that the guy ringing Steven King's phone in the middle of the night is the same guy working the issue for Nadia. She looks up at him, surprised. Bingo. He makes the lucky guess look like he's two steps ahead. "Okay? Stoli. I'm tired of the goddamned street names. I want the man's real name."

"I don't know his real name. That was the first time I had ever talked to him. I said Danika and I needed to be free of Steven."

"How'd that go over?"

"He said it was none of his business. He told me to go home and be a good wife. I told him that I would fight and die to keep my daughter. I said I would defend myself. That if Steven went for custody, I'd tell the judge what I know about Steven's work."

"Which is what, exactly?"

"Nothing much. Only that it was work he did for… for *them*. That it was about money. I made it sound like I knew everything. I'm not going to be the only criminal in the courtroom. If I am illegal, then Steven is not legal either."

"Quite a bluff. You're lucky that didn't get you killed. It still could."

"I had no choice."

"What'd he say?"

"He said he would talk to Steven."

"And?"

"And it worked. I never heard another threat. For about a year, life went back to the way it was, except that Steven completely stopped contacting me. The direct deposits kept coming. I stayed in the house. I thought it was really over. I never let Danika go over to that house again and Steven never asked again. I thought it was over."

"Right. Then, out of the blue, someone needs a favor."

Nadia closes her eyes. She nods.

"Yes."

"That's how this always works, Nadia. It's never over until they tell you it's over. And you'll know when it's over because they'll use a gun or a knife or a rope to avoid any misunderstanding. Who tapped you on the shoulder? Stoli?"

"Yes."

"Let me guess; he wanted you to make Jimmy's acquaintance and then wrap him around your perfect little finger."

"He said they just needed Jack for a favor. He told me what to say. I didn't ask why. I didn't care. I just wanted out. He said it was simple and no one would be hurt."

"That makes you simple for believing him. Someone always gets hurt, Nadia. Sometimes lots of people."

"I wanted out."

"Yeah, you said that already. But you can't get out by going in deeper. That's like diving into the ocean to stay dry. But that's what you did. Now you're so in over your head that you have to look up to see down."

"I just told Jack the story they wanted me to pass along."

"Come on, Nadia. You played that story like you were on Broadway. You planted yourself out at the design store in Schaumburg where Jimmy spends his time, hiked up your skirt and waited for him to show up and take notice. You put your real estate chops to good use by showing him a good time in an empty house. You let him take you out on the town. You went to all the hot clubs like a couple of teenagers with new fake ID's. Stoli set you up with some fairy dust to carry around in your purse just to keep Jimmy loose and happy. And he sent Hell along disguised as a small building just to make sure you'd remember who you were working for."

Mentioning Hell is good for a little extra attention. Nadia's eyes widen. Ray can feel her alarm in his heart muscle.

"Yeah, that's right," he says. "I know all about Hell. We talk on the phone a lot."

"You're not serious," she says.

"I wish I wasn't. I figure it was Hell slipping you the coke at one of those clubs. He called you Ginny Southside like you were old pals. He thought he was being cute, giving you a name like you were a regular soldier for the cause. He thought it was catchy. And maybe it is. Ginny Southside. I admit it's got a certain ring. But Hell should have kept his canyon of a mouth shut, because Jimmy was all ears and memory that night. Jimmy didn't know what the name meant, but I sure did. I'm not done with this puzzle, maybe not by a longshot, but I've got all the corner pieces."

"He's a frightening man," she says, looking away. "I have nightmares about him."

"He is dreamy that way. And tall for a psychopath. He turns a lot of heads. He likes doing that."

Nadia places the tips of her fingers on Ray's shoulder. Her face is pinched in new concern.

"Is Jack… is Jimmy hurt? No one was supposed to be hurt. It was supposed to be easy."

"Jimmy's fine, unfortunately. And your pal Stoli was right: it was easy, maybe a little too easy. You and Jimmy leave the club scene and go to his place. You climb in the sack and start with the pillow talk. You tell him stories about a valuable heirloom lost in the criminal justice system, a Russian doll that no one remembers or cares about anymore. You make sure to dish on Ivah, your supposed mother, who you represent as a hateful, half-demented crank so far around the bend that she wouldn't know a Russian doll if it dropped out of the sky and started making Stroganov."

"I didn't say it like that."

"Maybe not, but that was the gist. Everyone figures you won't have any trouble getting Jimmy properly motivated. It's not much of a stretch to think he's going to reach out to me, his cop brother-in-law, and ask for a favor. He'd do it just to impress you. He'd do it to keep the kisses coming and to stay in your good graces so that maybe you'll cut him in when you unload the doll."

"Yes," she says softly, almost to herself. "That was… that's how it was supposed to be."

"Not half-bad as plans go. If there's one guy who knows how to put the rube in ruble, it's Jimmy Kline. Only it worked a little too good, didn't it? Jimmy had too many dollar signs in his eyes. He wouldn't shut up about it. Too many questions. Prying for details as he was lining up appraisers and fences. You kept Stoli informed, and Stoli could sense the double-cross coming a mile away. He knows Jimmy because he knows Jimmy's type. He realized Jimmy's going to get me to hand over the doll when I find it and then he's going to disappear, cash it in for a plane ticket and a pile of white sand someplace the natives don't speak much English. Pretty sure that was *not* the plan."

"No."

"So Stoli gives you a new assignment. He tells you to forget Jimmy Kline. Dump him like a useless pile of garbage under a swoosh of great hair. He gives you a new assignment, which is to drop by the squad room and work me over yourself. Sprinkle Jimmy's name into the conversation and give me a smile I can't resist. Turn yourself into the loving daughter of a sympathetic old widow who just needs to recover what's hers. Stoli thinks maybe that will be enough to get me in the harness. Turns out he was right, wasn't he?"

Ray gives her a look and she turns away like it burns.

"I'm sorry," she says. "I didn't have a choice. He told me Steven was suing for full custody. He showed me a court filing Steven's lawyer had prepared. Steven was…"

"Lawyer's name," says Ray.

"What?"

"Who was Steven's lawyer?"

"I… I don't know. It was just a… I didn't read the name."

"Doesn't matter. I know who it was. Go ahead."

"He was giving me thirty days to come back home. Stoli told me there was nothing he could do once the courts got involved. He said Steven would probably keep Danika. He said I would be deported. I was terrified I'd never see her again."

The memory pulls out the cork and the tears start up. Nadia buries her face in her hands. Her shoulders tremble. Ray sighs and pats his pockets all over again. Unlikely for him to have missed a cigarette the first time around, but it doesn't hurt to try. He lets her go until she can come up for air. Then he picks up where she left off.

"So Stoli hinted he could make everything better for the price of a favor."

Nadia takes a ragged breath and wipes her face with both hands. Then she nods.

"He said he could help before the courts got involved. He'd set me up someplace Steven would never find me. He promised I could take Danika and go. He said I would be free. I was a fool."

"Join the club. So Stoli gets Ivah on board and you two host a little doll-opening party just for me."

"Yes."

"Suppose I had just turned the thing over to you the night before, paid for the pizza and left?"

"I was supposed to open it. Show you the message inside. I didn't ask why."

"It was never about the message. It was about the flash drive. Who put it in there?"

"I don't know anything about that. I was as surprised as you were."

"Maybe, but Ivah wasn't so surprised, was she? She shook that littlest doll with some purpose. She knew it wasn't about the love note. She's in this thing deeper than you are. She knows things you don't. Which means they trust Ivah more than they trust you. Why do you think that is?"

"I don't have any idea. I did what he told me to do. I thought I was done. I thought I was free. But then…"

"Yeah, but then Mila turns up. I pluck her out of Garrett Hoosier's bathroom, and I don't put her into the system where they can find her. They don't know where she is, and they want her back. Stoli figures you're his best chance to learn where I'm hiding her, so he asks you for another favor."

"Yes. I told him no. I told him I had to be through with all of it."

"Nice try. I'm guessing he wasn't taking no for an answer. And he made sure you stayed focused."

"Steven picked Danika up at school. Then Stoli called. He said I could have her back as soon as I told him where to find Mila. I was so upset. I didn't know anything except that they were basically holding Danika hostage. Then twenty minutes later you called and asked me to come to the bar to translate. I couldn't believe my luck."

"You've got some funny ideas about luck."

"I showed up planning to learn where you were taking her. I was going to tell

Stoli, get Danika back and just… I wasn't going to pack or anything. I was just going to get her in the car and drive and not stop. Just keep driving."

"Not how it played out."

"No," she says. The sound is distant and forlorn. "I couldn't. Not once I started talking to her. I told you Mila was different."

"Different how?"

"I wanted to come to this country, Mack. I was desperate to come. But Mila…"

She breaks off, shaking her head like she's decided not to finish. Ray keeps his mouth shut.

"They didn't lie to Mila. They didn't entice her. They just took her. She's from Ukraine. Kyiv, I guess. She said they just yanked her out of bed in the middle of the night. They just took her. She thinks someone over there was getting even with her people. Someone paid money, like you pay someone to pick up your trash and take it away. I may have been a fool, but I made the trip because I wanted to. Mila was just… stolen."

"And then I stole her from them, and you stole her from me," says Ray.

"I'm trying to set her free. I could have told them. I could have just made a phone call. Your friend Doris would be dead. Mila would be back in the stable or worse. I couldn't do it. She's so innocent. You want to try to protect her, Mack, but you can't. You'll only end up putting her someplace they can find her. You'll put her in a cage where the fox can find the chicken. They'll pick her back up eventually. Then they'll either kill her or make her wish she was dead."

Nadia turns fully sideways in her seat, gripping Ray's arm with both hands. Tears slide over her cheeks, tremble on the soft ledge of her jaw and disappear into the darkness below.

"If you have any compassion in you, then you'll let me take her away. You'll let us all disappear."

"I can't do that," says Ray.

"Why not?"

"Because I have a responsibility, Nadia, and I have too many mirrors in my life. And because indulging your fantasy that you can just safely disappear is not on my to-do list. They'll find you. They always do. I've been playing this whole damn thing from the hip and now I'm out of a job. I should have refused to participate in your Easter egg hunt from the beginning. You make quite a first impression, and shame on you for using your kid's charisma to sell me on the favor. But now I'm in this game up to my eyeballs and I'm not about to just shrug my shoulders on my way back to the shopping mall and wait for you to wash up on some beach without a head."

"What do you mean you're out of a job?" she asks. "He fired you? The tall man fired you?"

He wants to tell her off. He wants to give her a lecture about actions and consequences. His coat pocket has other ideas.

He doesn't recognize the short, electronic burble. It's not a language his phone speaks. Ray stabs his hand into his coat and pulls out the phone that isn't his.

Garrett Hoosier stares at him from the deck of the USCGC *Mackinaw*, peering through columns of cell phone apps. The battery icon at the top of the screen is red. Nine percent. The top of Garrett's forehead is behind a long, green rectangle. Ray is decades behind when it comes to cellphone technology, but he knows a texting bubble when he sees one.

"Mack," says Nadia. "Mack. Mack!"

He glances up in time to yank the wheel and share the road with another pair of headlights. Then he looks back down at the phone and opens the texting stream.

There is only one bubble in that stream.

It's not the bubble itself that makes him hit the brakes.

It's the photo inside the bubble that does it.

ONE HUNDRED NINETEEN

Nadia is full of loud questions. Something about stopping in the middle of the road. The kid is awake now too and not so happy about it. I block out the noise and stare down at the phone in my hand. Doesn't feel like a phone. It feels like I'm holding the Russian doll all over again. Her enigmatic smile comes back to me like a bad dream. Secrets inside secrets. Surprises inside surprises.

"What's wrong? Mack, what is it?"

"Mommy, why are we stopped?"

I keep my focus. The only thing in my head is this phone. Inside the phone is a green text bubble. Inside the bubble is a photograph. Inside the photograph is an open car trunk. Inside the trunk is Jimmy Kline, curled up like a big fetus, his ankles and wrists bound, silver duct tape over his mouth and wrapped around the back of his head. His face above the strip of tape is bloody. His eyes are wide portals of pure terror. It's a look with no illusions about the future.

At the very center of everything –in the small, dark space bordered by Jimmy's knees, abdomen, elbows and the edge of the trunk –is Phil.

My wife's cat looks out at me through time and space. Her eyes each have an outer band of yellow. Inside the yellow is the pale, ocean-green that holds in its center a thin dark diamond, an elliptical black hole standing on edge. Somewhere inside the starless velvet at the center of those eyes is my wife. Marlo.

So Marlo may as well be in that trunk too.

"Christ," I whisper, more accusation than prayer.

"Mack!"

A long, fat horn of sound punches its way in through the back of my head. I look up to see light flooding the rearview mirror. The semi is in the passing lane, blowing by us with an angry, bending bellow that fades slowly into the distance.

The Nissan quivers like a leaf in the breeze.

"Mommy!" Danika takes her cue from Nadia, deciding we're all going to die. Human history makes those pretty good odds, but I'm reasonably sure we'll all make it off Interstate 57 before we join all the others.

"Mack! What the hell is wrong? What are you doing? You're going to get us all killed."

I drop Garrett's phone back in my pocket and give the car enough gas to jolt us all back against our seats. It's enough to shut everyone up, but that lasts maybe two or three seconds.

"What's happening? That's them, isn't it? That's Stoli."

"Mommy!"

"Everyone settle down," I say, and not too nicely. "Whatever you want to say, keep it to yourself for now. I need to think." I look around in the rearview mirror until I find Danika's fearful eyes. "Vladimir? Can you hear me back there, buddy? There's no reason to be afraid. Danika's going to keep you safe and quiet. This girl is the bravest kid I've ever met. You're in good hands."

Danika takes the cue and puts on a brave face. The dragon makes a sudden appearance in the mirror. He seems unfazed by all the drama. He'll be fine. Unless the kid smothers him to death.

They do their best to stay quiet. Mother and daughter talk in whispers every now and then. Turns out Vladimir thinks pizza or ice cream would help tamp down the hysteria.

I try to keep us on the road without losing myself inside the photo I now can't get out of my head. A dozen competing scenarios play out. By the time the Watseka *Motel 6* rolls into view, I have eliminated all of them but one: Jimmy went by the house to make another pitch for selling the doll and splitting the proceeds. He rehearsed the proposal out loud on his way over. Only I'm not home. I'm guessing that the guy who answered my door had an Adam's apple about the size of my head, but that doesn't do Jimmy much good. He wants to run, because Hell tends to bring that out in people. But Jimmy can't run because suddenly there are a couple of guys behind him, each holding a party favor. Hell invites everyone in for a little chat and a game of *what hurts more* while they wait for me to show up. I don't show up. I'm busy across town counting bodies and getting fired. Eventually, they get tired of waiting. Or maybe Judy Kravitz starts in again with the shotgun. They grab up Jimmy and stick him in a car. Hell decides to bring Phil along just to make things that much more personal. Just to be sure I play ball when the time comes.

We sit in the parking lot. I stare at the photo on Garrett's screen as mother and daughter and dragon fill the car with whispers about how late it is and how they just want to go home. The number at the top of the screen changes to eight percent. I turn to Nadia, holding up the phone.

"You and Garrett Hoosier-Daddy shop at the same phone store. Don't suppose you've got a car charger handy."

Nadia opens the glove box and pulls out a white cable. She plugs it into the dash and hands me the other end. I stick it where it belongs. Garrett's phone makes a sound and brightens. I put my index finger to work on a response.

What do you want?

The wait is less than a minute.

Stupid question. Get them ready. You can keep the kid.

I look out all windows for a tail. Nothing.

Sorry. I don't work for criminals.

Sure you do, Ray. Always have. It's the taxpayers you don't work for. Not anymore. Again.

That one makes my blood run cold. Only a handful of possibilities went into that text, all of them bad. Either Twill got orders to fire me from someone else, or Twill told someone he was going to fire me, or Twill told someone in the last thirty minutes that he had fired me. Or… Another bubble pops onto the screen.

Still with me, Ray?

I let it sit. I try to think my way through. I can't. I don't have enough information. Another bubble surfaces.

Tick-tock.

Not such an uncommon phrase. Last time I heard those words I was on the floor of my hallway with a hood over my head. The nightmare comes flooding back, wanting to replay the chainsaw bit. My thumbs carry on without me.

When and where?

Go get her. Stay tuned.

I stare at the screen, trying to think. I scroll back up to the photo. Phil's eyes pick up where they left off, boring into my brain. I've often wondered whether she's telepathic. She isn't. There are no answers in those eyes, only a demand that

I do something and do it quickly. She wants a plan. I don't have a plan.

I take another hard look. That's when I see it. The blob of fluorescent color eighteen inches above Phil's head. It's a long way from a plan. But it's a start.

I put Garrett's phone upside down on the dash and pull out my own phone.

"Don't touch that phone," I say. "Stay here."

"Where are you going?"

"Nowhere fast. Stay here."

I climb out into the cold and close the door. I poke in the numbers as I separate myself from the car. It rings in my ear until I get voicemail. I end the call and repeat. Second time does the trick.

"Mack?"

"Up and at 'em, Raffi. You're sleeping your life away."

The groaning is thick and muffled.

"It's… one-thirty-five in…"

"I know the time. What I don't know yet is the place, but that's coming soon enough."

"What are you…"

Santiago doesn't finish. I can hear him sit up in bed. I wait for him to clear the cobwebs. Nadia is watching me from the front seat.

"With me yet?" I ask.

"The fuck, man?"

I give him some basics. The story is like a smooth rock skipping across a lake. It sails over some of the best parts, including my pending unemployment and the whole idea of hostages, human or feline. Then I tell him what I need.

"Who are you meeting, Mack, and why?" he asks.

"Don't know just yet."

"The hell you don't."

"You catch on fast."

"Why can't it wait until tomorrow?"

"It is tomorrow."

"Later today. When the fucking sun is up, man."

"Because I've got a fish on the line right now. He won't wait, Raffi."

"You need back-up. You can't do this shit alone."

"I'm working on that."

"And why do I get the babysitting gig? I mean, why not just…"

"Because there are more unicorns in Chicago than people I trust. I can't keep a woman and two girls with me and do what I need to do."

"Which is what, exactly?"

"Meet a guy about a thing."

"Thanks."

"Point is, it's just too dicey. I can't have them anywhere nearby. And I can't turn them over to Chandler PD."

"Why not?"

"Because CPD is on the wrong side of this whole equation, Raffi. We work in a rats' nest. Turn them in and we lose control."

"You mean you lose control."

"Yeah. I lose control. They get processed into a system full of eyes and ears and long, pointy noses. Big Man is blind and deaf right now and that's the only edge I've got."

"Thought so. You're meeting with Big Man's crew."

"I didn't say that."

"This is fucked up, Mack."

"What isn't, Raffi?"

I can hear him sigh and rub his face with his hand.

"Jesus," he whispers to himself.

"Maybe. But he's always busy. I called you first."

"What the hell am I supposed to do with them?"

"I don't know. Drive them around long enough for me to take this meeting and get clear. Go get some breakfast someplace. It's on me. But use a drive-through. No one gets out of the car. Nadia and Mila can feel Big Man right around the corner and they don't trust cops or strangers. That means you've got two strikes before you even show up. Give them half a chance and they're gone. But the mother will never leave the daughter, so if you keep Danika close, you'll at least keep Nadia in check. Mila's harder to predict. She might bolt on her own, but I think she trusts Nadia. So if you keep the girl close, odds are you've got all of them. That makes the dragon the lynchpin to everything."

"The what?"

"The dragon. Can't miss him. Big tongue. Lots of teeth. Goes by Vladimir. Danika will have him by the neck. Keep Vlad in the car and you've got everybody. Easiest gig you've ever had, Raffi."

"Saying that just makes it worse, Mack. You're already in a hole halfway to China so stop digging. What about Twill?"

There it is. The question is like the party guest you hope never shows. Expected but never welcome.

"You must still be half-asleep," I tell him with a laugh. "I'm not calling LT at one-thirty in the morning."

"Well, you called *me*."

"Yeah, but *you* can't fire me, Raffi."

"I'd do it if I could, Mack."

"I have no doubt. Tell you what; if anything goes south, I'll save everybody the trouble. I'll take all the heat and turn in my badge first thing in the morning."

"Yeah. Sure you will. Damnit, Mack."

"You're a good egg, Raffi."

"Don't do this thing alone, man."

"I'm never alone."

ONE HUNDRED TWENTY

Reclaiming Mila means I have to take everyone into the *Motel 6* with me. I get mother and daughter and dragon out of the car and point them across the parking lot. I keep Nadia in the lead and Danika by the hand. The kid's got Vlad by the tail. He seems just as happy to be bobbing upside down and backwards.

"Are we going to sleep here?" Danika asks.

"No. Sleeping is for cars and desks and courtrooms."

"No. Sleeping is for beds, and this is a hotel."

"No. This is a motel, kid. No one sleeps in motels."

"They have beds." She points. "That sign says so."

"Not for sleeping."

"What are they for?"

"Lying down in the dark and listening to other people not sleeping."

"How come no one is sleeping?"

"Guilty conscience."

"What's a conscience?"

"Ask your mom."

"Hey, Mom?"

"That's enough," says Nadia. "Both of you."

We climb the metal stairs and walk to the end of the second floor, trailing three plumes of white steam. The cold squeezes my face like it's trying to pop a balloon. My tongue is so swollen it can't stay clear of my teeth which keep scraping the raw bite wound. I'm half inclined to follow Vladimir's example and just let the thing flop out in the cold air.

Nadia stops at the end of the building. The number on the door includes a two for each of us. I put Nadia in front of the peephole, and I linger off to the side. I give her a nod.

They've worked out a secret knock; three sets of two followed by a single. Makes me wonder who needs a knock when there's a peephole. Unless maybe a knock is supposed to mean trouble and Nadia is trying to get a warning through the door with a knuckle. We all keep our positions. I imagine Mila on the other side of the door, trying to read Nadia's face through the peephole. Danika breaks the silence.

"Vladimir is very tired, Mom."

Nadia looks down and strokes her head.

"I know, honey."

The door opens with a slow squeak, Mila's face filling the widening gap, until the brass chain has had enough. One look at me and Mila has second thoughts. I'm used to that reaction, so my right shoe is one step ahead, keeping the door from closing. Mila retreats into the room. I could spend fifteen minutes trying to negotiate my way past the chain, but I don't have the time, so I put my shoulder to the task.

Twenty years ago, busting through would have been easier than breaking into an envelope. Now, on the eve of my second pretend retirement, it takes me three tries, each more forceful than the last. Each time my body connects with the door, my bones remember the staircase in the home of the late Steven King, and the icy intersection outside the house of Garrett Hoosier. On the third and final lunge, as I feel the lock rip out of the wall, the pain in my body remembers the sharp knee digging into my back as a guy with giant boots fires up a chainsaw.

The door flies open and I catch Mila in mid-retreat to the narrow space between the bed and the window. She's in the same ratty jeans and blue spaghetti-strap tee that she was in when I lost her the first time. Her long black hair hangs damp behind her back. A wet bath towel is draped over a chair next to the yellow coat that started everything. I can see that a hot shower has stripped away all the rage that earlier had tried to put another hole into Garrett Hoosier's face with an empty gun. What remains is a wan, terrified, teenager in the middle of a never-ending nightmare.

I get everyone in the room and close the door behind us. I give Nadia my best *I really mean it* look.

"If she runs, Nadia," I say as privately as I can. "If she jumps out of the car at a stoplight. If she makes a break for it in the parking lot. If she tries to give me the slip on those stairs out there. Anything. I'm taking you to that place we talked about in the car. Understand? I don't make a lot of promises in my line of work, but I'll make that one. Your best chance of avoiding the place we talked about is to convince this girl to trust me."

"Tell me where we are going," Nadia says. Mila and Danika are both looking at her. Then at me.

"I'm trying to keep all of you safe. I can't do that if she runs. If she runs, then I give up. Okay? I'm about to be out of a job. Tonight is the last night I have any control. I'll have no choice but to turn you over to someone else. They'll put you in the system and you'll just have to take your chances. That makes me the last person who gives a damn, Nadia. If she runs, they'll find her again. And then, if she's not already dead, she's going in the system too. Got that? So, I need you to convince her to come with us and get in the car. She needs to trust me. Can you do that?"

She has to think about it. She looks at Mila and then down at Danika. Then she gives me a single sharp nod. I was hoping for something a little more emphatic, but it will have to do. Nadia looks past me to Mila.

Dela poshli ne tak, kak planirovalos'. YA ob"yasnyu pozzhe. Nam nuzhno poyti s nim. On pytayetsya nam pomoch'. Yesli my ne budem sotrudnichat', on otpravit nas v tyur'mu.

I don't know many Russian words, but I'm not half bad with Russian faces. Mila's face is an open book. I can read everything from fear to hope and back again. She gives Nadia a question that sounds like it's in three parts. Nadia makes change with a *nyet* and two exasperated shoulder shrugs.

"She wants to know where we're going," says Nadia. "So do I."

"You're going to someone who can keep you safe. You can trust him. He saved my life once. He'll save yours." I tip my head sideways to the others. "And theirs. But we need to hurry, Nadia. Time is running out."

"What about you? Where are you going?"

"Straight to Hell. Let's get moving."

I get everyone in the car, adults in back, children and dragons in the front. I get resistance from all concerned, but keeping mother and daughter separated is the only way I can be sure they don't make a run for it. I lean inside and check

Garrett's phone for an update. Nothing so far. I close the door and walk out in front of the hood, pulling out my cell.

I have a vague idea of where I'm going, but no idea of what I'm going to do when I get there. Whatever that is, Santiago is right about not doing it alone. Since he can't be in two places at one time, I call the only other person I can trust not to shoot me in the back. Sure, he hates my guts and wants to see me dead, but I'm not in a position to be picky.

"Mack." Stretch Martin sounds like someone has hit him over the head and stuffed him a sock drawer. "This better be good."

"Wakey-wakey, pal. You insisted on me keeping you in the loop. This is what that looks like."

"It's almost two in the goddamned morning."

"You think Big Man keeps office hours?" I change my tone into something soft and sarcastic. "Look. Sorry. My bad. Maybe you're too sleepy. We can handle it without you. Later, Stretch."

I can hear him moving.

"Fuck you, Mack. Hold on."

ONE HUNDRED TWENTY-ONE

I drive west as fast as the Nissan will carry us. Outside, the two o'clock hour is cold and savage and dark, mashing itself against our little blue bubble of heat.

It's a quiet ride. In the back seat Nadia and Mila keep to their respective windows. Up front, Danika's eyelids are losing the fight with gravity. Vladimir is all tongue and big-eyed questions about what in the hell I think I'm doing. I wish I had a good answer.

I'd settle for a bad answer.

Garrett Hoosier's phone glows at me from the dash. I keep it where I can see it, fighting with myself over whether I actually want any new information. I need time. Every minute that goes by without a when-and-where instruction from Hell is another minute that I have to try to beat him at his own game.

On the other hand, there are Hail Mary plans and then there's whatever it is I think I'm doing. If I'm headed in the wrong direction, it would be better to know that sooner than later.

"How can you ask me to trust a stranger? A man I've never met?"

I glance up into the rearview. Nadia has asked the question without looking, as if to someone standing on the freeway.

"I'm not asking you to trust a stranger," I say. "I'm asking you to trust me."

"And why should I trust you?"

"Because right now you could be in a cell with ink on your thumbs wondering where your kid is. Instead, you're here watching me bend myself into a pretzel trying to get you clear of the mess you've made for yourself."

"So, this is all my fault?"

"No, you had a lot of help. Question now is whether anyone gets another birthday."

"You could have just let us go."

"You're right. I could have. You can thank me later."

The *Aurora Chevron* is right where I left it. Everything is dark. I imagine the clerk at home, probably some half-broken doublewide, burrowed down into her bed under six or seven blankets, sleeping next to six or seven butts crumpled into a glass ashtray on the nightstand. Probably a cat nearby. Maybe six or seven of them. She strikes me as one of those older women who collect cats for company. They each have a personality and an opinion about what's on the tiny television in the corner. I remember the plastic hair clamp and the nicotine-stained forefinger bobbing up and down as it pointed the way to *Windy Wharf Seafoods*. She's nice enough, but she's alone at the bottom of a well and just barely this side of crazy. Which I guess makes us kindred spirits.

Makes me think of my own cat. Phil burns two holes through the blackness in my brain. She wants out of that trunk. It's not the small, dark space that's the problem so much as the cold. That and being cooped up with Jimmy Kline.

I kill the headlights and circle the lot, rolling to a stop along the backside of the store. I keep the car running and the heat blowing. In the rearview mirror Mila whispers a question. Nadia shrugs.

"It's not open," says Danika. I turn to see her awake and looking at me. She points a little finger. "Because the lights are off. That means it's not open. It's open when the lights are on."

"How'd you get to be so smart?" I ask. I nod at Vlad. "He teach you these things?"

"No. He only knows how to eat people."

"And pizza."

"And pizza. But mostly people. Bad people."

"Then he'll never go hungry," I say, looking out past the gas pumps to the access road. My face and my tongue are picking fights with the rest of me over who hurts the most. The only thing I want more than a Camel is three Camels, along with a cold drink, a hot bath, and a soft bed. I want them all too much to line them up. I want them all at once. I'm thinking about how to feather my bathtub with a mattress when I see a pair of headlights slowing.

"Everybody stay here."

I climb out into the cold and almost close the door. Ronald Reagan's advice about Russians comes to mind: trust but verify. Pretty sure he wasn't talking about non-apparatchik women and children, but I figure if I have to trust them to stay inside the car, then maybe I should at least verify they can't drive it away. I lean back inside and turn off the engine, pulling the keys out of the ignition. I give Nadia a heavy warning look. She rolls her face away, showing me her cheek like maybe I've never seen it before.

I've seen it plenty. I've stared at it up close.

Santiago kills the headlights before he reaches the final turn. The black Dodge Intrepid rolls to a slow stop ten feet away. Thirty seconds and I'm already cold enough to shatter. I pull the handle and climb inside, keeping an eye on the Nissan for any signs of impending escape. All is still.

"Good timing," I tell him, holding my hands up to the blower. "We just got here."

"How they doing?" he asks, looking past me for a glimpse.

"Tired and scared. You?"

"Me?" He rubs his face. "I'm too tired to be scared. This is fucked up, man. We should both be in bed."

"I don't roll that way, Raffi. But good for you for being brave enough to love who you love."

He laughs through his irritation. Then he squints.

"You look like shit, Mack."

"And you want to take me to bed," I say, shaking my head in pathetic disappointment. "Your seduction needs work."

"Is it just me or did that bandage get larger since the last time I saw you?"

I touch the bandage gently. It feels like a punch in the cheek.

"I put my best face forward down a long staircase. I've been icing it with venison."

"I don't want to know."

"You're smarter than you are sexy. You ready for this?"

"Let me call backup. At least have someone on alert."

"No, Raffi. And I mean that."

"I won't put the word out that it's you. I'll say it's me. I'll say…"

"No, Raffi. I want your word, or I get back in that Nissan and go with Plan B."

"Which is what?"

"I don't know that yet. It's the one before Plan C."

We look at each other for a few seconds. Santiago nods his head.

"Okay. Shit, Mack. Tell me you've got someone coming."

"I've got someone coming."

"Gee, thanks. Is that actually true?"

"Guess we'll see." I fish some cash out of my wallet and hand it over. "There's a 24-hour drive-thru diner about five miles west on Hinkley. Go get everyone some eggs. The dragon likes bad people over-easy with syrup. Maybe this thing is all over before you finish eating. I'll call you when I'm clear."

He sticks out his hand and I give it a shake.

"Good luck, man," he says.

"Thanks, Raffi. I promise you'll regret it."

"I already do."

I pull the latch and crack the door. Then I turn back.

"Don't suppose you've got a cigarette on you."

"I don't suppose you've accepted Jesus Christ as your personal savior," says Raffi.

"What kind of friend are you anyway?"

"The kind who won't give you cancer."

"It's not for me. It's for the kid."

"Yeah?"

"Yeah. She and the dragon smoke like a couple of chimneys."

ONE HUNDRED TWENTY-TWO

Ray packs everyone into the Dodge and thinks twice before he closes the door. He pulls out his phone and aims it at Nadia and Mila in the back seat.

"Put your hands behind your backs," he says. "Try to look miserable."

"We don't have to try," says Nadia, putting her hands behind her back.

"I know."

"And you're stealing my car."

"Borrowing." He aims the phone. "Nobody say cheese."

It's just us now, me and Ray, alone with each other again.

We watch them drive away like an old married couple seeing the kids off to college or closing out another Thanksgiving dinner. Nadia turns and looks at him through the back window. Next to her, Mila's coat glows dimly like a dirty yellow sun. Ray holds out a wave as the darkness swallows Santiago's car whole.

He climbs back into the Nissan and starts it up to blow the heat. He holds Garrett's phone in his palm. There are no new bubbles in the stream.

Go get her. Stay tuned.

Five minutes.

Ten.

Hell has gone quiet. He finds that unnerving. He worries that something has gone wrong. Somehow his plan to stay one step ahead has fallen two steps behind. He worries that he is being watched. That he has been followed from the beginning. That now, somewhere between the *Aurora Chevron* and a local 24-hour drive-thru, a black Dodge Intrepid is full of holes and on fire. He wonders about the possibility that someone has put a bug in Nadia's car; that he's been a flashing red blip on someone's phone from the beginning. Not impossible, he thinks. I give him all the reasons it is highly unlikely. Ray's not listening to me.

He climbs out and gives the Nissan undercarriage a three-hundred-sixty-degree inspection. He searches the trunk and the glovebox and jabs his arms around under the seats. Then he returns to where he started, sitting in the driver's seat staring at Garrett's phone.

Go get her. Stay tuned.

Something is wrong, he thinks. He wants to lay the seat back, feeling around for the lever. He finally finds it and pulls. The seat slams backward, rattling everything in his head that already hurts. He curses up at the ceiling of the Nissan and rolls his head to the side so he can keep watch out the window. But then he closes his eyes. So now he's watching exactly nothing.

He tells himself he's working the problem.

And he is. Lack of sleep is a terrible problem.

ONE HUNDRED TWENTY-THREE

My entire body jolts to the memory of a jangling phone. Garrett's plastic noisemaker is still in my hand. I stare at the screen like maybe the sound was heralding the arrival of a new message.

Go get her. Stay tuned.

Another old-timey clanging. I get the right phone involved this time and answer it.

"We're five minutes out," says Stretch.

"What do you mean, we?"

"Me and Donny. Who'd you think?"

"Just you, is what I thought."

"I don't ride without a partner. You know that. Where are you guys set up?"

I make an angry grimace at the phone like I want him to see it but glad he can't.

"Meet me on the access road north of the parking lot. I'm in a blue Nissan. Keep it slow and dark."

I end the call and pull Sig out of bed just long enough to make sure he's ready to go. I nose the gun back into the holster and put the car in gear, rolling past the pumps toward the road beyond. I look almost exactly like a guy who knows what he's doing.

I beat Stretch to the rendezvous by five minutes. In the distance, *Windy Wharf Seafoods* squats in the dark like a couple of cinderblocks. There are three cars in the front parking lot. None of them are a champagne-colored Chevy Malibu. I start to worry all over again that I'm wasting my time. Not that I expect to find Jimmy's car parked out front, but I'm always disappointed when things aren't a lot better than I expect.

In the rearview I can see Stretch and Donovan roll up slowly out of the darkness. The gray Monte Carlo stops behind me. My phone rings.

"Where is everybody?" asks Stretch.

"Let's talk in person," I say. "Just you."

The phone goes dead. I watch in the mirror as Stretch opens his door and unfolds himself from the front seat, climbing out into the cold. He opens the passenger door of the Nissan and gets in. His knees start a shoving match with the dashboard. The top of his head brushes against the roof.

"You look awful," he says.

"Thanks. Nice to see you too."

"You get beat up again? That bandage is bigger."

"No, my face is getting smaller. I'm blaming my shrink."

"Whose piece of shit car is this?" he asks, craning his head around toward the back seat.

"Friend of mine."

"Your friend is a sadist."

"Yeah, well, maybe you should have thought about that when you decided to be tall," I say. I get back a look that could puncture armor.

"Where the fuck is everybody, Mack?"

"Where they need to be," I say.

"And is that anywhere nearby?"

I pat my pockets.

"Don't suppose you've started smoking."

"Mack, where, the fuck…"

"It's just us, Stretch."

A moment of silence.

"Just us," Stretch repeats with some incredulity.

"Yeah. And Donovan, apparently, because something I said to you on the phone somehow convinced you that this was a plus-one invitation."

"He's my partner. Who knows we're out here?"

"Nobody."

The energy in the car changes a little when I say this, clicking him just a hair out of hostility toward apprehension. It's nothing Stretch says or does. It's an electric current that connects any two people within close range. Spend enough time in the company of loaded guns and itchy trigger fingers and you start to pay attention to that vibe.

"Nobody," he repeats. "You mean, like… actually nobody?"

I get the concern. He'll pretend like he's worried about the two of us… three of us… up against some small army of Big Man goons, but Stretch's real worry is me. I'm the guy rumored to be in Big Man's pocket. I'm the guy on a list of murder suspects in his investigation into Scooter's death. I'm the guy asking him to meet me alone in the middle of the night at the corner of Nowhere and Nothing. Sure he's worried. He's worried about me. That's why he yanked Donny out of bed in the first place. I watch him shake his head at me.

"Just… Well, that's fucking great, Mack. You said…"

"I know what I said. If I'd have told you the truth, you'd have either stayed in bed or showed up after calling it in. I can't have this on the wire, Stretch. Too many people listening."

"Why me?"

"You're among the few cops I trust."

He looks at me like I've just proposed.

"What part of *I hate you* do you not get?" he asks.

"I get all of it, Stretch. You hate me. You don't trust me. You're worried I'm going to solve your murder investigation with one bullet to the back of the head. I get it. But you hate me for all the right reasons. You're mistaken about those reasons, but your hateful heart is in the right place. That's not really good enough for me but I guess it has to be because I've got nothing else. Don't love that you brought Donny along, but…"

"What's wrong with Donny?"

I give him a look.

"What's wrong with Donny. I look like a doctor to you? I'm guessing his parents dropped him on his head a lot. Beyond that, maybe nothing is wrong with Donny. Maybe everything. Donny and I never clicked. But you and me?" I give him something like a smile. "We clicked once upon a time, Stretch. Hate me all you want. Your priorities are right. Always were."

"I'm touched. What the fuck are we doing here, Mack? Where is Hell?"

I hold up Garrett Hoosier's phone.

"Hell is on the other end of this short conversation. Or he was, anyway. He's been quiet for a while."

Stretch squints, scrolling the texting stream with his finger.

"Who's the poor guy in duct tape?"

"That's Jimmy. The ladies call him Jack."

"Who is Jimmy and what's he doing in a trunk?"

"Jimmy is Marlo's kid brother. He's in a trunk because he knows how to put the Jack in jackass like nobody's business."

"Is this a long story?"

"Yes."

Stretch exhales through his nose like it will never end. He points at the screen.

"And that's Marlo's cat, isn't it?" he asks. "You called me out here to save your fucking cat. Mack…"

Stretch fumbles for the door handle like he's ready to leave. It's all show, but I play along.

"Hold on, now. Hold on. It's cold out there. You'll freeze to death. I called you out here to put Hell in a bag for the murder of Daniel Scooter Pleasants. And, not for nothing, Stretch, but we also have him for spearheading Big Man's human smuggling and sex-trafficking operation."

"And?"

"And, yeah, to save my dead wife's brother and cat."

"Oh, don't drag Marlo into this just to help your case. You never deserved Marlo."

"At least we agree on something."

"That's your cat now. *Your* cat, Mack."

"Fine. My cat."

"No wonder you want to keep this quiet."

"You want to collar Hell, or don't you? You want to go back to bed? I'll handle it myself. Take your knees and get out." I flick at him with a couple of fingers. Now I'm the one who's all for show. "When I bring him in, I'll be sure to say you had the chance and chose not to get involved. A few laps around the rumor mill and that will start to sound like you had ulterior motives. People will start to wonder who's really buttering your bread. Then you'll know how I feel. You can sit in the homicide corner and watch my star rise for bringing down a king pin. I'll invite you to the medal ceremony."

Stretch tries to lean his head back against the seat. It only comes halfway up his neck. This is why giraffes don't fly coach.

"A king pin. Goddamnit, Mack."

I point a finger at the *Windy Wharf.*

"That's where they bring them. Women and girls from all over, stuffed inside rolling fish crates." I hold up Garrett's phone. "The guy who owns this phone used to work CBP up in Sault Sainte Marie. He was an expert at steering the boat the wrong direction when he needed to. I'm guessing they've got a dozen different joints between Green Bay and Saginaw. They've been using this place for a decade at least. Get them out of the crates, hose them down, warm them up, and then put them to work wrinkling sheets all over the Midwest. Welcome to America."

"Witnesses?"

"Yeah. A couple."

"Where?"

"Raffi Santiago is buying them breakfast as we speak."

Stretch nods slowly to himself.

"And Hell wants to trade," he says. "The women for Jimmy and the fucking cat."

I elbow Stretch in the bicep.

"Pretty dang smart for someone so tall."

Stretch points into the dark at the *Windy Wharf.*

"And the swap is happening there?"

"No. I seriously doubt that. They'll pick someplace they don't do business. Still waiting on Hell to give me the word."

"You don't know where the meet is? Why are we here, Mack?"

"Because we have a better chance at this game if we show up before we're invited. Maybe we can shut the fun down before it starts."

"What makes you think Jimmy's even here? He could be anywhere. In *any* trunk of *any* car in any parking lot within a hundred miles of Chicago."

I shake my head and point at the half-taillight in the photo, just beneath and to the left of Jimmy's anguished eyes.

"That's Jimmy's champagne Chevy Malibu. I have nightmares about that car."

"Why's that?"

"Because that car always means Jimmy is somewhere nearby with his hand stuck out and his mouth moving."

Stretch nods at the phone.

"Looks like they found a way to fix both of those problems."

"Yeah. Wish I'd thought of that."

"The car could be anywhere, Mack."

"Yeah. Could be. But it used to be here. Maybe it still is."

"How do you know?"

I move my finger a millimeter.

"That's dry, painted concrete. No ice, snow, water. It's inside a garage."

"Okay. So?"

I expand the picture. Jimmy's terrified eyes loom larger and larger. I point to the small blob of neon at the very top of the image, obscuring a narrow strip of the open trunk. It looks like a tiny day-glow orange half-moon.

"What is that?" asks Stretch.

"That's a fingertip inside an insulated rubber glove, just like the kind you use to keep your hands from freezing when you're digging around in the ice for a dead walleye. I'll bet those gloves are all over the place in there. Standard issue for fishmongers who want to keep their hands warm and their fingerprints private. Last time I saw gloves like these they were on a guy who made the dead walleyes look pretty. We were playing twenty questions behind that warehouse."

Stretch pulls the phone closer and squints at the day-glow orange fingertip in the image.

"Jesus."

"I'm thinking more like Billy Wise or one of the dozen or so Russians that work here. I figure there's a chance they'll keep Jimmy in there until they're ready to bait the trap. Maybe Hell invites me out to some landfill and Jimmy stays right where he is, nice and cozy and dry in his own trunk, until they're sure they don't need him anymore. Then they'll take Jimmy to the landfill to keep me company."

"Or maybe *this* is the trap," says Stretch, pointing through the windshield. "Ever think of that, Einstein? Maybe they're inside waiting for you."

"Not without Nadia and Mila. Big Man wants his witnesses."

"Why the hell aren't they in protective custody?"

"Because…"

"Because you don't trust anyone but yourself," he says.

"Because the last woman I entrusted to police custody had to shoot her way out just to stay alive."

"Bloomington," he says with an unconscious nod. "Your snitch… what's her name… Suri."

"Yeah," I look up at him briefly. "Suri in bloody Bloomington. I'm tired of making things easy for him."

"Him."

"Big Man. José fucking Beggemon. King of the turds. He's all over Chandler PD like a bad smell. Chicago PD too."

Stretch pinches his eyes. I let him think things over as we both stare out at the *Windy Wharf Seafood* buildings frozen in a dirty puddle of light. Nothing moves over there.

"Last time we raced out to meet you, you gave us a tour of an empty parking garage. We going to do that again?"

I have a sick feeling in my gut that I'm all wrong. I start to worry that maybe Stretch is right. Hell has been one step ahead of me from the beginning.

"Odds are pretty good. Yeah."

"Okay," he says. "Here's the deal, Mack. I'm not doing shit without Donovan. Okay? He comes or I'm out. I promised he'd stay involved in this case and I keep my promises. We need more out here than just the two of us anyway."

"Well, he's already here," I say. "I can live with Donny if he stays off the radio. No one calls this in except me. Unless I'm dead, then you can call whoever you want. If that doesn't work for you, then I'll carry on alone."

"I'm not going to lie for you, Mack. When they ask me why I came out here, I'm playing it straight. I was under the impression this was a sanctioned op."

"Yeah, yeah."

"This will get you fired. You know that, right?"

"I'm not worried about getting fired."

"And if we do bag Hell, then he's mine. I don't want to fight with you about investigative jurisdiction. He's all homicide first."

I look at him as I mull it over. I pretend it hurts. I guess it does a little. "Yeah. Fine. You can have him."

Stretch takes another long look at the warehouse in the distance. Then he looks back at me. For the flicker of an instant, I can see the Stretch Martin I knew in the old squad. Back in the day.

"Okay," he says. "It's your show, Mack. Where do you want us?"

ONE HUNDRED TWENTY-FOUR

We roll forward with the lights off. I take the south side. Stretch and Donovan disappear around the north end of the warehouse.

I see three parked cars, all on my side of the building but each in a different part of the lot. I ease up slowly alongside each one of them, just close enough to have a look inside. They're all empty.

Empty is the wrong word. They're full of everything but humans. Trash mostly. Bottles and bags. Half-eaten food escaping half-open packaging. Dirty rags that might be clothes. Whoever drives the white Honda with the jerry-rigged passenger mirror is addicted to *Costco* cheeseballs. He's also got enough Sudafed on the floor of the back seat to decongest every horse in the next Kentucky Derby. Somewhere in south Chicago there's a garage sharing space with a meth lab covered in cheese-dust fingerprints.

I park Nadia's Nissan up against the building and climb out into the cold. In the distance I can hear a siren on the freeway. In the other direction something hard is banging against something harder. These are the only sounds tall enough to keep their heads up above the wind; everything else drowns in silence beneath the frigid hiss. I pull my collar up against the cold and yank Sig out of bed for some company.

The front doors are locked. The retail face of *Windy Wharf Seafoods* is dark and dead inside, like a stiff on a slab, only the eyes on this face are black and glassy. There's a guy in the reflection I used to know. He thinks it's Halloween. He needs a friend to buy him a drink and put him to bed for a week.

I could be that friend if I had the time. But time is my new fiction. I've got more friends and money than I have time. The poor sap in the window is on his own.

I keep moving, working the perimeter counterclockwise, trying to keep the building between me and the wind. There are two doors framed into the long stretch of brick that leads to the back loading bays. I try them both and get what I expect. When I reach the southeast corner of the warehouse, I lower myself to the size of an eight-year-old and take a peek around back. There's a dumpster in the way. The only thing I can see is the smell. I stand up and roll back around the corner. I pull out my phone.

"Anything?" I ask.

"Tight as a drum," whispers Stretch. "You?"

"No. But someone is here or coming back soon."

"Who?"

"The white Honda belongs to a Sudafed rep."

"Meth-head."

"I'm guessing."

"What about the other two cars?"

"Harder to say. But Mr. Meth isn't out here meeting with himself. My money is on at least three people on the premises. What's your twenty?"

"Northwest corner," says Stretch. "I've got three company vans backed up in front of the loading bays. No signs of life as far as I can tell. Where are you?"

"Behind the dumpster. You can save the comment."

"Okay. So, what now?"

I take a cautious step over a grimy cinder block and out past the cover of the dumpster. Three white refrigerated cube vans come into view, each sporting the *Windy Wharf* logo. The wind gives me a stiff shove in the face, and I step back behind the building. I jab a hand in my pocket and pull Garrett Hoosier's phone out just to see if I've missed anything.

Go get her. Stay tuned.

"We need to get inside this fish factory. If Jimmy's car is anywhere, it's in there."

"And if it's not?" Stretch asks.

"Then maybe there's someone or something inside that will tell us where it is. I'm thinking Mr. Meth and his pals are in there and will know something."

"I'm not breaking into a business for you, Mack. Not without a warrant." I can hear Donovan say something in the background about a duck or a truck. "Donovan's not up for that either."

"Settle down," I tell him. "I'm not asking."

The cinder block at my feet is full of crazy ideas about windows. I kick at it, spinning it on its plate of ice. I look behind me toward the front of the building. Question is whether I'll have the strength to throw a block of concrete once I've carried it to where it wants to go. I push the phone a little tighter against my ear, hoping for some warmth.

"You two try the back doors," I say. "Let me know what you find."

"Hold on." Stretch's whisper has taken on a new suspicious urgency. "What are you going to do, Mack?"

"Pretty sure that's not something you want to know in advance. Check Donny's diaper for some plausible deniability and then see if any of those bay doors are unlocked. I'm going to check the front door again. Keep the phone line open."

"Goddamnit, Mack."

Stretch has more to say but the words disappear in the wind as I drop the phone in my pocket and bend down, hoisting the cinder block with both hands. The thing is as cold as it is heavy. I set it down and try again by gripping it with the sleeves of my coat. Back in the day I could have carried two of these things, one in each hand, swinging them in the breeze like a couple of pompoms. Now I'm lucky if both hands can manage a single. Odds are I'll throw my back out before I can throw the cinder block in.

I know you're supposed to lift with your knees, but my body is big on democracy. My knees outnumber my back two-to-one and they're not interested. So I put my back into it, lifting the block off the ice with one slow and steady pull.

That's when I hear the sound.

It's a sound without pain. I hear it in my ears, not my back. It's a soft boom. Metal. I lower the block back to the ground and reclaim my phone. Stretch is already talking.

"…that?"

"I'm here, Stretch. What was that sound? Did you hear it?"

"I said it came from one of the vans."

"Move in," I say. "Nice and slow. Meet in the middle. Stay close to the building. Tell Donny to hang back so he can cover from behind. I don't like to be surprised when I'm surprising someone."

I clear the dumpster and tack back toward the building, trying to stay away from the ice. I can see Stretch coming around the north end of the warehouse, stepping cautiously. He's got the same giraffe-escaping-the-zoo quality that I remember from so many stakeouts past.

Stretch reaches the first van before I reach anything. We both pause as he leans in close and listens.

Twenty seconds. Thirty. Steam leaves his body in long moonlit streams, ravaged into tatters by the wind. Stretch looks my way and shakes his head.

In the background I can see Donovan bouncing in place at the corner, trying to stay warm. We keep moving.

Stretch reaches the second van and we repeat the drill. He waits for a few, then shrugs his shoulders. I signal for him to stay where he is as I close the distance to van number three. He nods and I move forward.

I come to a stop behind the back left tire. I can't hear anything but the wind.

We're wasting our time.

I start thinking again about windows and cinderblocks. Makes me wonder if Nadia's car has a jack in it that will do the job just as well without all the heavy lifting.

Fifty feet away, Stretch spreads his arms into a silent question. I put my ear up against the wall of the cube.

Nothing. Then a cough. A voice. Two voices. A third.

I look up at Stretch and nod.

Stretch looks back to the corner and jerks his head in my direction. Donny comes running.

Donovan Howe is good in a fight. He knows how to knock heads and quiet a room down in a hurry. He's a guy you like to have standing behind you in those first moments when everybody is still deciding what should happen next.

But running is not Donovan's thing. Never was. He's too thick around the middle. And his limbs don't know how to work together as a team. His is the kind of body that, once it really gets to moving, seems to bring out gravity's mean streak.

Donny makes it all the way to the first van before he catches a slick tongue of ice and goes down hard on his back. Mother Earth evicts the air from his lungs out into the cold. The sound is easily loud enough for me to hear. Stretch and I look at each other. We're both wondering if it was loud enough to punch through the insulated metal walls of a refrigerated cube van.

We don't have to wonder long.

ONE HUNDRED TWENTY-FIVE

The door to the van makes a rattle and starts to roll upward. Ray trains Sig on the opening. Around him, he can sense movement. Donny getting to his feet. Stretch loping forward. But he tries to block all of it out, focusing instead on the game of inches unfolding directly in front of his face.

The space at the bottom of the door makes a gap, growing slowly until Ray is looking at the toes of old hiking boots threaded with dirty-white electrical wire. The boots grow with the gap. Five inches. Six. Ray is about ready to introduce himself when the door sticks.

A hand hanging from a thin wrist appears next to the hiking boot, just long enough to set down a .38 Special with blue duct tape wrapped around the grip. Whoever's doing the pulling on the other side needs both hands for the door. The guy could probably put some muscle into it and yank the thing free with one hand, but he's trying to keep things quiet. Slow and steady. He's like the magician's pea trying to peek out from underneath the shell.

Ray is a lot of things he shouldn't be. Indecisive in brief moments of opportunity is never on that list. He stoops and rams both hands into the dark opening beneath the door, using Sig to swat the .38 out of the truck and seizing the rising wrist with his left. Ray pulls hard and sharp against the arm, like he's Quasimodo waking up Paris.

Something of the man on the other side, probably his head, connects violently with the door as the van erupts into a fury of shouts and scuffling. Ray gives the wrist a twist and another hard yank and gets an entire forearm out into the cold. He slams the door down, pinning the disembodied appendage in place against the bed of the truck. It flails like a snake in a snare, trying to withdraw through the coat sleeve. Ray applies more force. From the sound of things, the arm doesn't like being separated from the filthy mouth on the other side of the door.

"Mack!"

Ray looks. Stretch is behind him now, about as low as a tall man can get, down on one knee, positioned safely right of center, Glock at the ready. Donny is just arriving.

"Get clear," says Stretch. "Let's go."

Ray lets go of the door handle, releases the wrist and pivots to the side of the van, stepping on the .38 and then kicking it away. As the arm disappears inside, Ray cups the bottom of the door with his left hand and pulls up. It sticks again at six inches. So he yanks at it again, harder this time. The door rolls up and away.

A battery-powered lantern reveals three men, two back toward the cab playing tug-of-war with an open canvas gym bag and a third closer to the open door, clutching his own arm.

Stretch and Donny start shouting introductions.

Ray doesn't join in. He's too focused on Billy Wise, who has stopped yanking at the bag but can't bring himself to let it go.

Ray shakes his head pathetically, raising his left hand and connecting the tips of his thumb and forefinger. He holds the circle of fingers up and forward for Billy to see.

Anyone else would think it odd to be flashing the OK symbol at such a time.

Not Billy. He's been around the block. He knows the diameter of a toilet drain when he sees it.

ONE HUNDRED TWENTY-SIX

Billy and I lose the connection when Donovan charges into the van. He spins Billy around, ripping the bag out of his grip and mashes his face against the side of the truck. Billy's head gets a hard knock, which turns out to be the on-switch for his mouth. Donny gets an earful and takes it as a request for more abuse, so he reintroduces Billy's head to the metal wall of the van. Billy takes exception, wanting to get Donny's mother involved. There's no end in sight.

"That's enough," I shout as I climb in after the guy with the wire-laced hiking boots and the sore arm.

Stretch has the third guy flat on his face and is patting him down. He looks up briefly and gives Donovan's leash a stiff yank.

"Donny, knock it off! Get him outside."

Donovan does as he's told, giving Billy the rag-doll treatment on the way out. Billy cuts me a look as he passes. His mug is just as lopsided and ugly as I remember, but the fear adds a new dimension. Here's a guy who can see the future. None of it's as good as the worst day in his short, ugly life on Earth so far.

The owner of the hiking boots has scooched up against the wall of the van, massaging his arm. He tries his best not to look at me. Ratty, black beard. Lean, sallow face with a partial set of gray teeth. He has a cut on his forehead from where he rammed it against the door trying to get his arm back. The blood seeps out in a thin, straight line, navigating the eyebrows without much problem. That's because there's only one of them. The right eyebrow has been shaved clean and replaced with a tattoo of a hawk with its wings spread, its talons disappearing into the folds of the man's large, oyster-sized eyelid. The blood makes it all the way to the tip of his nose before running out of real estate.

"You good?" I ask Stretch over my shoulder.

"Yep. Search that one. This guy was double-strapped. Ankle and hip." Stretch grabs some hair and pulls. "On your feet, asshole."

I give the guy at the end of Stretch's arm the once-over. He's young. Maybe late twenties. Long, weedy-blond hair escaping a black skull cap. I'm guessing a year or two ago he could have passed as just a regular kid, short hair, nice smile, working after class bussing tables, saving up for spring break at Daytona Beach where he can put his charm through the paces. Now he's the after-picture on a don't-do-meth ad campaign. His body still has its youthful frame, but everything above the shoulders belongs on a ghoul pushing seventy-five. The guy tries to catch Hawkeye's attention as Stretch marches him out of the truck. Hawkeye isn't looking.

I get Hawkeye on the floor into a spread-eagle and pat him down. He comes up clean, but only because his .38 is outside on the ice. I shout out to Stretch to collect the gun as I sit him back up against the wall of the van. I point at the bird of prey above his eye.

"What's that? A sparrow? A finch? Canary?"

He turns his head, not talking. I squat down in front of him and swat him on the shoulder.

"Just kidding around," I say. "You Fenimore Cooper groupies are hard to miss."

Nothing.

"Alan Alda, then."

Nothing. I start to wonder if I should be speaking Russian. An apple-green butane lighter is on the floor by the lantern. I stretch for it and pull it closer.

"Yours?" Hawkeye doesn't answer.

I give it a flick. The flame appears like a genie. I send out a silent wish for a Camel and a warm place to watch it get shorter. A floating bar in Bimini maybe. Or bending a couple of palms on some West Antiguan hammock. The genie shimmies itself in apology.

I drop the lighter and reach behind me for the canvas bag. Inside that bag is another bag, this one is clear plastic. Inside are two bricks. Not the kind of brick you throw through a window or stack into buildings, but the smaller kind made of heroin bundles. Five bundles to a brick which makes this an expensive canvas bag. I also see a couple of syringes, a bottle of water, a tinpot cooker and a scattering of urine test strips. I look back at Hawkeye.

A bright, red drop hangs, elongating, quivering on the tip of the man's nose like it has nothing to live for. It makes the leap down into the dirty beard and another one lines up to take its place. I grab the man's hand and press his palm up against his forehead to stop the bleeding.

"You're a mess," I say.

"Fuck you."

His breath is swinging day-old roadkill by the tail.

"Ah," I say with a nod, "he speaks. And he's upset. I get that. We interrupted. You boys are trying to play amateur chemist and we're getting in the way."

I grab a test strip out of the bundle behind me and wave it under his nose.

"You know you don't have to pee on these things to detect fentanyl, right? You'd be surprised how many people don't know that."

I get nothing for insulting his intelligence. Hawkeye is playing hard to get. He picks at his pant leg with his free hand.

"I busted some guys once. Bunch of punks playing gangster out in West Loop. Everybody had their peckers out and I thought I'd walked into a jerk-off contest. Turned out they were pissing on these test strips. They'd already shot up, see. Then someone fell over dead and the others got good and scared. One of them knew a guy who knew a guy and they scored some of these test strips and all three of them start to do what comes naturally. That's when I walked in. I don't know about the fentanyl, but they all tested positive for wet hands. And stupidity. I'm guessing that killed all three of them eventually."

Hawkeye leans his head back against the van. He tries his best to look bored.

"Fuck," he says, holding me in suspense. "You."

"Me? Yeah, you said that already. Tell me something, Hawkeye, while it's just you and me in here. I can tell already my partners out there are all wrapped around the axle about these drugs. And I get that; don't get me wrong. Lot of skag in this bag. I'm guessing ten, fifteen years a piece for you boys."

I get a look of mightily suppressed alarm, so I keep at it.

"What, your first dive on a heroin bust? You're in for a rough ride. Prosecutors love the heroin cases these days. Anymore, you can't even get the time of day for seizing a moderate amount of coke. And the meth cases are just, well, come on, no offense, Hawkeye, but they're depressing. Pathetic. Dime-a-dozen, bottom of the barrel work for any ambitious prosecutor with an ounce of self-esteem. But the heroin…" I cast a lingering glance back toward the open bag. The plastic lantern is on its side in the corner bleeding a dull, orange light. "Still sexy. In the right amount, heroin is a prosecutor aphrodisiac. Big heroin busts still grab those headlines. Maybe that's why you and your homies out there decided to diversify; leave the meth and the *Costco* cheeseballs in the garage and go out and get up on the horse. Go get you some real attention for a change. Well, congratulations. Now you've got some."

Hawkeye pulls his palm off his forehead and looks at the blood. He wipes it on his pants. He looks back at me with a slow, weary blink. He wants to look like he has better things to do. But I can see the stress start to change the shape of his forehead. Like the hawk is starting to squeeze that left eyeball just a little too hard.

"So I get it, Hawkeye. I do. But the truth is I'm not a drug cop. I don't care about drugs. Leave me the bourbon and the nicotine and you can keep the rest. Maybe you were buying some heroin tonight, maybe not. Maybe you, personally, were just along for security. You know? Maybe your job was just to answer the door. You were the look-out, am I right?"

Hawkeye looks at me, wheels turning behind those big ugly oyster eyes.

"In my experience, the look-out guy is always the low man on the totem pole. If there's anyone who stands a chance of getting off with a slap on the wrist, it's the look-out guy. What's a guy get for minding the door and listening for trouble if that's really all he was doing? I don't know. Couple of years? Three? Not good, of course, but maybe not a hard-core felony. Good thing you set that gun down when you did. Smart." I tap my temple with a finger. Then I point. "You got another jumper there on your nose."

Hawkeye wipes his nose with the back of his hand. He looks at the smear like he's reading.

"Problem for the look-out guy is always that everybody else is trying to pin the whole thing on *him*. Suddenly the lowly look-out guy becomes the criminal mastermind who should take the fall for everyone else. The system is not going to let anyone off easy without a human sacrifice. And the look-out guy is usually the dumbest and the most loyal in the group. He's the one most likely to keep his mouth shut and take the hit." I look at him with some dubious encouragement. "That you, Hawkeye?"

He doesn't answer. But he swallows.

"Look, like I said, I don't care. I'm not a drug guy. I'm a people person. A *dead*-people person. And right now, Hawkeye, I'm all about keeping people from turning up dead. You help me do that and maybe this little drug problem goes away for you. Maybe you're back in the garage by tomorrow night, eating cheeseballs and cooking up another batch of meth just like always. I can't promise, but maybe I can help."

He's not buying a word of what I'm selling. But he wants to. I get my index finger involved.

"But if you don't help, Hawkeye, and if I end up with another body, and if it turns out you really did know something, then I can promise I'm coming to you as an accessory to murder. Understand what I'm saying? The drug problems will seem cute."

We play the staring game for a few seconds. I start to stand.

"Okay," I say. "That's fine. I only need one of you. I'll go talk to the others. Billy's always good for a deal. I'll give it to him."

Hawkeye looks up, popping like a dry cork.

"What the fuck do you want from me, man?"

His voice is reedy and cracking. He knows better than to have any hope, but it sounds like he has some anyway. I lower myself again.

"I'm looking for a champagne-colored Chevy Malibu. No passenger-side mirror. In the trunk is a white cat…"

"A cat? Like, you mean like a fuckin'…"

"Yeah. A white cat. Also a bunch of silver duct tape wrapped around a lousy excuse for a person. I'm all ears for anything you might be able to tell me about any of that."

Stretch is suddenly in a cloud of steam at the back of the van. We both look. He's holding Hawkeye's .38 by the trigger guard."

"Need a hand in here?" he asks.

"Two seconds," I say. Stretch points to the canvas bag.

"Slide me the bag."

I give him a look.

"Two. Seconds."

Stretch and I spend at least that much time looking at each other. He sighs out some more steam and steps out of view. I look back at the human wreckage in front of me.

"Now's your chance, Hawkeye."

His eyes narrow. His neck juts his face my direction.

"I was just here to keep an eye out. Like you said."

"Sure, sure. Of course. Did I tell you? I can always tell."

He gestures around the inside of the van.

"I don't even know what any of this was all about."

"You're pushing your luck, shit-bird. Tell me what I want to know."

"I don't fucking know, man." He sounds exasperated. Like we've been at this for days. "Zero and me were supposed to hook up with Billy like three hours go. Billy…"

"Zero? His name is Zero?"

"X.E.R.O. Like Hero with an X."

"That's a name?"

"It is in New Zealand, man."

"Okay. So you're supposed to meet Billy."

"He kept calling and putting it off. I didn't want to meet at all, man. None of this was my idea. I mean…"

"Yeah, I got the part about you being innocent. Skip it."

"We figured Billy was jerking us around. Like he couldn't deliver. I wanted to bail, man. I was like…"

"What was Billy's excuse?"

"He said there were people here. He needed them to clear out before we came. We waited, like, fucking forever."

"People. What people?"

"How the fuck should I know? People. Not fuckin' cats, man."

"Funny. I really like meth-head burnouts who can keep a sense of humor on their way to prison. Gives me some hope. Have you seen the car I'm looking for or not?"

"No."

"You see anyone else around this place when you got here?"

"Na, man. Just Billy."

"Where's the money?"

"Don't know anything about money. I'm the look-out."

I point behind me at the bag.

"Billy brought a bag of bricks. He's giving away free smack?"

Hawkeye screws up his face and takes his hand off his forehead to look at his palm. He wipes the blood on his pantleg.

"Do I look stupid?"

"You really want an answer to that?" I ask. "Who's holding the cash?"

Hawkeye looks at me a little too long. He's starting to think on his own. It's all too much too fast. This game only works with slow steady pressure in a warm room and cold coffee. This guy knows he's gone too far. I can feel him shutting down. I keep pushing anyway.

"Look. Helping me trade you up for someone bigger is your best ticket out of the shithole, Hawkeye. It takes a lot of cheeseballs to buy one brick of heroin and I see two. I'm guessing you haven't seen that much money in your entire miserable life. That means you've got an investor. A moneyman. And right now, that investor has someone he trusts a whole lot more than he trusts you, sitting in a warm car someplace waiting for one of you to call him and tell him the load is pure and fentanyl free. That's his signal to deliver Billy a bag full of cash. Am I right? Let's call him. What's his number?"

I can tell before I'm done asking the question that he's not going to answer. I pretend to interrupt something that was never coming in the first place.

"Don't answer that. Answer this instead: why do you think he chose you boys for the job, Hawkeye? This isn't your thing. Look at you. You don't even have real shoelaces. I'm sure you've got a favorite corner or two out in West Garfield. Or Washington Park. Or Lawndale. You're good for a few hundred a day slinging the worst cheese-flavored homecooked meth this side of the moon. But a bag full of heroin? Come on. You're way out of your league and you know it. You boys got the job because you're expendable."

The hawk pulls up the eyelid for half a look. I'll take it.

"Your investor doesn't trust your supplier. A three-time loser like Billy Wise slinging a bag full of horse? That sound like a good bet to you? That sounds like a disaster to me. Your investor is sending you and Captain Xero out into the minefield to see if anything blows up."

He keeps his mouth shut, but his eyes are open and talking up a storm.

"You don't need me to tell you this, Hawkeye. You've had this sick feeling in your gut from the beginning, haven't you? And now it's already been too long. The guy in the car with all the money is driving away by now. He's headed home, Hawkeye. He's pouring himself a drink. And here you sit in the minefield. All blown up."

Hawkeye wipes his nose again.

"And?"

"Tell me who's pulling your strings and maybe we can put you back together again."

"Bullshit."

"Yeah? Bullshit? This seem fair to you, Hawkeye? What was your cut going to be on the resale? Ten percent? Five? You take all the risk? Then you boys go down for the deed and he doesn't? He's free as a bird and you're counting the minutes in public housing for the next decade? You going to let him play you like that?"

Hawkeye shrugs and looks away.

"You're a chump, you know that? You're too stupid to be on the street, doing what you do. Next time you're out, let's say ten, fifteen years older, looking to get back in the game, everybody who's anybody will know that you're the guy who'll do literally anything and take the hit for it. You want that sign on your forehead?"

His face pivots back my way. An unconvincing smile has hitched a ride under his nose.

"Sick of hearing you talk," he says. "Let's do this."

I've lost him. All I can do is nod.

"Your call," I say. "But I just gave you the best shot you're ever going to get. On your feet. Hands behind your head."

It takes a lot of grunting and groaning, some from each of us, but we both make it upright. I slap him between the shoulders.

"Better hope your money-man rewards loyalty, Hawkeye. He owes you a bottle or two when you get out. Hell, maybe a whole case, keeping his secrets like this."

"Anything but that vermouth shit, man. That's some nasty-ass juice."

I yank him by the arm so I can see his eyes again. They seem extra wide and intense, but I'm guessing that's just my own reflection.

"Vermouth?" I ask, trying to pretend casual interest.

"Yeah. So?"

"Sweet or dry?"

"Sweet. But it don't matter, man. It's all nasty."

"It's not for me either," I say. "I'm strictly a bourbon guy. Next time he pours you a vermouth ask for the dry."

"Why is that?"

"Pairs better with cheeseballs."

I call out for Stretch so I can hand Hawkeye over. Stretch shows up and turns him around, muttering about remaining silent and hiring attorneys as he zip-ties Hawkeye's hands behind his back.

"He needs a bandage," I say when he's done.

"A bandage?"

"Yeah. For his forehead."

"Good to know, Mack," says Stretch. "I'll be sure to go to the store and get him a bandage. What about a sandwich? Something to drink? You thirsty?"

Hawkeye brightens.

"Yeah, man. I could use something. Maybe a…"

"Shut the hole in your face. Let's go. What the hell is on your eye?"

I watch Hawkeye step down out of the van, navigating the ice below. He gives me one last look.

I try to keep the smile off my face. I try to keep the revelation from my eyes.

ONE HUNDRED TWENTY-SEVEN

Ray stands in the back of the van, staring down at his own shoes. Stretch wants to know what happens next and keeps the questions coming. But Ray's not home. He's off wandering the labyrinth of his own head. Putting things together. I've seen this before, plenty of times. Bombs could be going off. Ray is in the maze.

Question is whether he'll ever find his way out.

Stretch gives up and marches Hawkeye over to the others. Donovan has Billy and Xero sitting on the back bumper of the second van, hands zipped behind their backs. Everybody is hunched over against the cold, trying to pull their heads down into their shoulders. Hawkeye takes his place on the bumper next to Billy. Stretch and Donny confer by the wall, hands on their hips, shaking their heads and blowing enough white steam to keep the wind occupied. A minute or two of that and Stretch makes the trip back down to the open van. He looks in at Ray, still staring down at his shoes.

"What's with you, Mack? Is there a fucking on-switch someplace? Never thought I'd actually want to start you talking again."

Ray blinks and looks. With the help of the van, he and Stretch almost see eye-to-eye.

"What's the play Ray? We need someone to take custody. We have to call this in."

Ray starts to look down behind him at the canvas bag. He's already seen it, so he doesn't finish turning.

"We will," he says. "Eventually."

"Eventually?"

"Yes."

"And in the meantime?"

"In the meantime," Ray points to a brown metal door in the wall of the warehouse. A silver keypad is picking up the moon. "I want the code to that door."

Stretch turns and looks.

"Yeah, well we all want a lot of things, Mack. But no one is talking. Everyone is freezing and no one has the fucking power of speech. I'll bet no one knows the code anyway."

"Losing bet," says Ray. "Billy knows."

"Well Billy's not talking. We can call in for a warrant."

"No one is calling anyone. That was the deal." Ray jerks a thumb over his shoulder as he steps down out of the van. "Document the scene."

"Document the… And where the hell are you going?"

Ray doesn't answer. He heads Donovan's direction, leaving Stretch to take pictures and catalog the contents of the bag. I float along behind just to keep Ray company and remind him that he's getting too old for this kind of thing. I ask him to ballpark the odds that Jimmy and Phil will still be breathing after all of this is over. He's not interested in the odds and shakes me loose, but not before I get a number less than twenty-five percent.

I've seen the man bet everything on lower odds. I've seen him win.

I suggest that maybe it's time he check Garrett's phone.

Ray pats his pockets as he walks. He finds the phone and pulls it out into the cold. He stops. I read over his shoulder like always.

Westbound I-88. Under the Bliss Road overpass. Hood up. Hazards on. Girls in the back. One hour.

Nothing like a surge of adrenaline to warm the blood. Ray drops Garrett's phone back in his pocket and checks his watch. Thirty feet away, Donovan is holding up the warehouse with his back, waiting to see what Ray is going to do next. We both are.

"What's with you?" asks Donovan as Ray approaches, nodding to the coat pocket with the phone inside. "You finally get a text?"

"Turns out I can save thirty percent on my car insurance." Ray leans against the building, eyeing the three stooges sitting on the bumper. "How about you?"

"Freezing my nuts off," says Donovan.

"Should have left them home in bed, Donny. Anybody talking?"

"Bupkis."

"What about Billy?"

Donovan looks at Ray like he's seven.

"You know what bupkis means, Mack? I tried already, and I wasn't nice about it. He's not talking. What about your guy?"

"Hawkeye? Oh, sure. We're besties now." Ray looks at the sorry line-up sitting on the van bumper in front of them. "I'm guessing Xero had a burner on him."

"Who?"

Ray points.

"That guy."

Donny nods and digs around in his own coat pocket.

"Zero?" he asks. "What kind of perfect fucking name…"

"With an X," says Ray.

"Zerox? Why would you name…"

"Xerox has two X's, idiot. His name is Xero. One X, no Z."

Ray watches Donovan's face wrinkle into something suggesting mental constipation. In his hand is a Nokia flip phone. Ray takes it and opens it up, looking for recent numbers. There aren't any.

"What are we doing, Mack?" asks Donovan. "Let's just call it in and…"

"Nobody's calling anybody," says Ray.

"Then what the fuck are we supposed to do with these shit-birds?"

Ray lets the question hang, pushing off for a walk up to the van. He points his chin at Billy Wise.

"Let's go for a walk," he says.

Billy's little finch-eyes don't like being trapped in his wreckage of a face, darting all directions for cover. His mouth is a lopsided smear of something you step around on a sidewalk just to be safe.

"I'm not saying one fuckin' word to you," says Billy. The other two look from Ray to Billy and back again.

"You just said seven or eight words I didn't even ask for. Why stop there?"

If Billy could cross his arms in defiance he would. All he can do is shut his mouth and stick out his lip.

"Good," says Ray. "That's good, Billy, because you really need to concentrate on how you're going to live through the night. Meanwhile," Ray holds up the Nokia burner, "I thought I'd tell you a few things you just might want to factor in."

Ray turns and shambles away along the side of the building. When he stops for a look back, Billy is still sitting and staring, wrestling indecision. It takes him another minute. But then he finally stands up from the bumper, looking to Donovan for permission.

Donny rolls his eyes and shrugs.

Billy makes his way across the skin of ice to Ray, who leans one shoulder against the building and waits. Billy stops and listens, hands behind his back, stubby fingers flexing and balling up against the cold, while Ray explains the world as he knows it, holding up the Nokia burner every so often to make his point. Everyone else watches from a distance, not hearing, blowing steam, trying to read the body language of the old guy and the ugly guy, looking for some clue to the future.

They don't have to wait long. Three minutes pushing into four. Billy turns on his heels and heads back toward the group with Ray close behind. Doesn't take much to see that Billy is a different man than he was four minutes ago. The fear is entirely out of the bottle now, adding a new dimension of ugly to a face that doesn't need any extra. Billy Wise seems just a little wiser. He moves like a man with purpose. He passes between Donovan and the others and keeps walking.

"What's happening?" asks Donovan as Ray passes. "What did you tell him?"

Ray doesn't answer. He follows Billy to the brown metal door in the wall. All of us watch.

Billy speaks. Ray's index finger pokes. Ray twists the knob and yanks open the door.

ONE HUNDRED TWENTY-EIGHT

The *Windy Wharf* warehouse is packed with alliteration and plenty of stink. It hits me like a fish to the face, but the warm air keeps me moving forward. Billy hits a light switch with his shoulder and a cold, bluish light falls from fluorescent tubes like water. I take a good look around.

Several rows of long tables. Rolling tubs. Boxes full of knives and other tools for hacking and cutting and sawing. Fat, red hoses coiled on the floor and a smaller, dark-green variety of hose dangling from central overhead pipes like snakes from a branch. Against the side wall are dozens of tall, black rolling carts, neatly and precisely arrayed like legions of rectangular soldiers waiting for battle. The carts are the kind Billy was unloading on the day we first met, each one the perfect size for a couple hundred pounds of ice and walleye with the occasional smuggled human.

The concrete walls and floor are painted a slick battleship gray. I keep turning in a slow circle. The place has got just about everything you'd expect for a fish monger's warehouse except an ugly car with a trunk full of hostages.

A large, empty rectangle stretches out in front of the middle bay door. I walk a few steps for closer look. Turns out the rectangle isn't so empty after all. Three or four drops of motor oil have been working on a bad silhouette of Abraham Lincoln. Makes me think the rectangle would fit Jimmy's Chevy like a glove. Outside I can hear Stretch yelling at Donny to stay where he is.

"Satisfied?" asks Billy.

"Almost never," I say with a brief look. Billy's face is losing definition in the new warmth. "Where is the car that used to be parked in this spot?"

"What car?"

"Okay. Let's pretend you don't know. I'll show you what car."

I walk up next to him and pull out Garrett's phone. I scroll up to the photo and show it to him just as Stretch is stepping through the door.

"The car with a trunk full of prison time and your day-glow orange thumb on the lid."

Billy squints and leans in.

"That's not my thumb," he says. "That could be anybody's." He gestures. There is at least one pair of those gloves on every table.

"Yeah," I say. "Anybody's thumb including yours. Maybe a jury sees it your way, maybe not."

"It's not me."

"You were here when it went down, weren't you, Billy?"

"Mack," says Stretch from somewhere behind. A quarter turn finds him holding the canvas bag. I ignore him, turning back.

"You were part of this."

"No. I swear to God, man. This…"

"God is tired of taking your calls, Billy."

"No, no. This was not my thing. I mean I was here, but I wasn't inside. I was parked outside, waiting for everyone to leave."

"Right. You were outside hanging around so you could sling a little stolen heroin to Hawkeye and Captain Xero. I'm guessing you hid the stash on site. Maybe the load passed through this very room, covered in fish guts, and you managed to pull a couple of bricks for yourself when no one was looking. Couldn't resist. Old habits die hard, don't they, Billy?"

He doesn't answer.

"Right. So you set up a buy for when you figured no one would be here. Turns out you were wrong. Three in the morning and the place is crawling with criminals. So you have to wait. Don't want to risk giving your employer the right idea about you."

"My employer?" The question comes out as a laugh. "*Windy Wharf* is…"

"I'm talking about Big Man and you know it. Stop jerking me around."

Billy looks down at his shoes like a kid caught soaping windows.

"Let's be crystal clear, Billy-boy. Big Man knows you've been skimming. Okay? That's a fact. Randy Sweet set you up but good."

A flash of rage hits Billy's face like heat lightning. Then he overcompensates by widening his eyes to look innocent. He misses by a mile and takes to sputtering.

"I don't… I don't…"

"Oh, sure you do. Randy made a truckload of promises to the dynamic duo out there for the specific purpose of catching you in the act of selling Big Man's stolen product. I'm guessing you've pinched his product before. Well, someone on the other end knows how to count, Billy. Things didn't add up. Randy sent you the meth-heads as buyers with a pocket full of cash and you bit the hook."

Billy keeps shaking his head with his mouth open, but someone has turned off the sound. I take a half-step closer.

"Randy Sweet's the only guy I've seen who has a fighting chance against you in an ugly contest, Billy, but you've got him beat six ways from Sunday in the stupid department. I always figured people called him Mouth because Randy's pie hole looks like it belongs on a grouper. But that's not it at all, is it? Randy's got himself a legit nickname. He's got himself a drink. That makes him a soldier for the cause. Mouth's got Big Man's ear and a case of sweet vermouth in the kitchen cabinet. And that makes you a horse thief with a rope around your neck. How'm I doing?"

Billy lowers his head. He looks like he might be sick.

"Don't answer, Billy. I'm hitting homers over here and you know it. The floodlights are shattering over the scoreboard and it's raining glass. The sky is falling, pal. You still want to stand here and play games? Or do you want to live? You want to keep all those limbs of yours attached? Maybe we can work on getting you some protection."

That gets his attention.

"What kind of protection?"

"A pair of shin guards unless you tell me what I need to know."

"I got you in here, didn't I?"

"Good start. I want to know where that car is."

"I don't know. I… I wasn't…"

I can feel Stretch behind me, looming in silence. Whatever he had on his mind when he stepped into the warehouse is long gone. He's soaking all of this in like a sponge.

"I've got a clock ticking in my ear, Billy. If I don't get the help I need, and I mean right this instant, then you've got a serious problem. And I'm not talking about doing time for slinging horse. I'm not talking about you going down for whatever kind of death comes out of the trunk of the car I'm looking for. Sure,

I'll make sure you pay for all of that, but that's not something you should worry much about, Billy. Because you'll never make it that far. Big Man's going to snuff you out like a human candle. Where did they take the car?"

Billy Wise has a sudden case of the shakes. His face is pleading.

"I can't go to Cook County lock-up. I can't do gen-pop anywhere, man. Send me to another state. Michigan. Ohio."

"Ohio?"

"And I want a new identity."

"Yeah? A new identity? Jimmy Hoffa's available. You like Jimmy Hoffa? You want that one? How about Shirley Temple? Stop bargaining and start talking."

"You have to promise, man."

"I promise I'm walking away in three seconds."

Two and a half seconds are a memory before he makes another sound.

"*Deke's*. I think they took the car to *Deke's*. I don't know for sure. But maybe *Deke's*. Maybe."

"*Deke's*. What the hell is *Deke's*?"

"*Deke's Auto*. Out on North Picking."

"Okay. And how do you know this?"

"I don't know anything, man."

"Truer words have never been spoken, Billy. How is it you suspect they took the car to *Deke's*?"

"I might have… I was tired of waiting. I might've put my ear the cargo door. Someone kept saying *Deke's*."

"Someone. Someone who?"

I can see the blood rising again in Billy's face like a red tide. Naming names in this business is the kiss of death so he presses his lips together like he's trying to hold back the ocean. But Billy's already been kissed, and he knows he's going to remember it forever. So now the instinct not to rat on others tastes rancid. What he really wants to do is spit the name out onto my shoes. I wait patiently for hate and revenge to work their magic. When the name finally comes, it's got enough angry force to make a hole in Billy's face.

"Mouth," he says. "Fucking Mouth."

ONE HUNDRED TWENTY-NINE

He's found that higher gear. Getting him there is tougher by the year. But when he finally finds it, Ray is a force of nature. A couple of lucky breaks in a race against time and he becomes unstoppable. Doesn't mean he'll win. Doesn't even mean he knows what he's going to do next. It just means he's finally moving with enough momentum that people tend to either get out of his way and let him pass or get flattened.

Stretch and Donovan learn the lesson all over again. There are at least a dozen reasons to call in the drug bust and put three suspects into immediate custody. All twelve die an ugly, unprincipled death on the warehouse floor. Stretch finally concedes, deferring as he promised. Donny keeps shaking his head like a screw has come loose somewhere in the back of his neck.

"I'm not going down for this, Mack," he whispers, casting a glance at the three mopes now sitting out of earshot against the wall, relieved to be inside out of the cold. "You've got to call this in."

"I will," says Ray.

"Then do it."

"I'm tired of saying it, Donny. There's no time. I've got a meeting."

"This is just more of your bullshit paranoia, Mack. What the fuck are you afraid of?"

"Oh, nothing. Just missing out on a chance to save some lives and bring down a psychopath wanted for murder and for running what I'm guessing is the largest human trafficking operation we've seen in a while."

"Save some lives? How many of those lives are humans? This is fucking nuts." Donovan says, this last bit under his breath with a glance up at Stretch, hoping for support. "And he's with IAD. He's supposed to be all about the rules. Why do we want this shit in our jacket, Stretch? Wexler's not going to cut us any slack for listening to crazy."

"Look," says Ray. "Donny. Take a breath. I get it. I do. I get it. You're worried about yourself. But we're flat out of time. Clock is ticking. How about this: you stay here and call it in by the book. Wait for Aurora PD to show up and make sure they get all of the details right. Stretch and I will head out and take care of business."

He says it like he means it; like it's the answer to everything. I know otherwise. It's a big bluff intended to end the jabbering and get on the road. The man has a thousand and one tells, all of them too small for anyone else to see but me. He's gambling that Donovan cares more about being left behind than crossing T's and dotting I's on a drug bust.

"Fuck you, Mack."

"Then let them go. I'm not here to cuff slingers anyway. Aurora PD can pick them up later."

"Not letting them go. Christ, Mack. This is a decent-sized heroin bust. We're not letting anybody go. I just want to be clear that when the shit hits the fan this was not my idea."

Somewhere inside his roiling impatience, Ray finds a relaxed smile and slips it on. He gives Donovan a knock on the shoulder with a sideways fist.

"Come on, Donny. Who's going to believe you've been having ideas?" He doesn't let the insult land. "This is all on me. I'll take the hit. You were both dead-set opposed. Or you can both hang back and I can do this next bit alone."

Stretch and Donovan look at each other in silence. Stretch shakes his head.

"Fine," says Donovan. "And the drugs?"

Ray holds out a hand toward Stretch and the canvas bag.

"If I end up having to bargain with Hell, then I want all the bargaining power I can get my hands on."

Donovan laughs in disbelief.

Stretch ignores the vote of no confidence and hands Ray the bag.

"Your show, Mack."

Hawkeye and Xero each end up locked in their own fish cart, rolling to opposite ends of the long wall, surrounded by empties. It's cramped and it stinks but the alternative is a cold cube van. They each take a pass on the hypothermia and squeeze inside without complaining.

"You can make all the noise you want," Ray whispers into the cart as he rolls Hawkeye into the shadows. "But I'd try to be quiet if I were you."

"What? Why?"

"Because the people who own this fish joint also own the stolen horse you were trying to buy. They already know who you are. Better that they not know you're here."

Ray rolls the cart into place and turns, making a bee line for Billy Wise. He's alone, sitting against the wall. His face says he wishes he was a different person.

"Make yourself tall again," says Ray, grabbing him under the arm. "Let's go."

Billy plays heavy.

"Where? Where are we going?"

"Car ride. Up."

He struggles to his feet, not looking so much taller after all.

"*Deke's*? Are you going to *Deke's*? I can't be seen with you, man."

"Thanks, Billy. I'm used to that."

ONE HUNDRED THIRTY

Billy makes the ride out to *Deke's* on the floor of the back seat, babbling about unfairness. I could tell him a story or two of my own.

Droopy McCallister and the boys once complained to Mother Penguin that I'd peed all over the statue of Saint Anthony of Padua. Anthony was missing an arm and had been set in a corner of a supply room on the second floor of the orphanage. The wet trails in the dust were easy enough to spot. They weren't mine, but that didn't matter much. All pee trails looked the same to Mother Penguin.

Important thing was that she knew how to count. Droopy had three witnesses, including a half-Mexican from Riverdale named Brewster Sanchez. I had no one on my side except the wet, one-armed patron saint of lost things, and he wasn't in the talking mood. So, I ended up taking a ruler to the knuckles and then I did hard time, scrubbing every inch of Saint Anthony's plaster robe and the rest of that storage room, and the entire upstairs hallway, with cold, soapy water and a broken brush.

The hell of it was that Brewster was the only kid in the place I had considered to be a friend. We used to cover for each other, one standing guard as the other pissed out of the second-floor window trying to hit the courtyard fountain below. Who needed to defile Saint Anthony for a good time? Word eventually got back to me that Brewster had made the whole thing up for more friends. Turned out Droopy had opened his inner circle and I was the price of admission.

Not fair, no. Not by a long shot. But I learned a valuable lesson.

"You never really know who your friends are until you know who *their* friends are," I say up into the mirror. "You're too trusting, Billy. Should have seen Mouth coming a mile away."

Billy leaves off on the babbling and takes to shouting.

"It was Mouth's idea to steal the shit in the first place! He came to me! I said no fucking way, man! No way!"

"Until you said yes. Until you assured Mouth that you were just the chump he was looking for and told him to sign you up. That about right, Billy?"

That shuts him up, which is more than fine by me.

Stretch's headlights aren't helping my headache. I tap the brakes a couple of times and he seems to take the hint, backing way off.

Two phones are on the dashboard. I pick up the one that belongs to Garrett Hoosier just to see if Hell has anything new to say for himself. No change.

Westbound I-88. Under the Bliss Road overpass. Hood up. Hazards on. Girls in the back. One hour.

I figure it's time for an encouraging response just to keep him on the hook. I try to keep the car on the road as I peck out six letters.

Coming

Billy lifts his head for a quick view around.

"Not this way, man," he says. "Take Hill Road."

I look in the rearview mirror at the empty back seat. I can just see the top of his head.

"You said North Picking Road."

"Yeah, but that'll take you right past the front gate. If they're there, they'll stop you. If they stop you, they'll see me. Take Hill Road. Next right. Trust me."

I weigh the odds that Billy is trying to even the score with me for all those cracks about toilet drains and being too trusting.

"Trust you? You've got an odd since of humor, Billy."

"Please," he adds.

It really is a magic word. I hit the turn signal. The phone that is still on the dashboard takes immediate notice. I set down Garrett's phone and pick up mine.

"What are you doing?" asks Donovan. "He said North Picking."

"He's having second thoughts. Seems to think a frontal approach on North Picking is a bad idea."

"You trust him?"

"Who, Billy? As much as anyone."

I can hear words in the background.

"Stretch wants to know if we should follow you or stay the course?"

"Stay together," I tell him. "Until we know what we're dealing with."

I wait while Donovan and Stretch trade words. One of those words is *crazy*. Another is *trust*. I can hear just enough to tell that Stretch is backing my call and that Donny isn't so happy about it.

"This is not smart police work, Mack," says Donovan finally. "I guess I'm just speaking for me, but this whole thing stinks. None of this feels right. I'm not down with any of it. One way or the other, this is your last night on the fucking job."

I've got half a dozen responses cued up, none of them flattering to Donny. I keep them all to myself and end the call.

Because when you're right you're right. And Donny's right on all counts.

Nothing like a well-named road. The elevation is gentle, but Hill Road climbs enough for a partial view of the buildings that line the Fox River. The cold and the wind have whipped the moonlight into a thin, luminous frosting. Everything is a ghostly blue. The lights of Naperville glow in the distance like chips of phosphorescent ice. A couple of smokestacks further east get me to patting my empty shirt pocket.

"Lights, man! Turn off your fucking lights."

Billy is sitting up in the back seat just like a normal person only twice as ugly and with no arms.

I do as I'm told and kill the lights.

"Pull over up here," he says. "We should be almost right above it. You might have to walk down a little, but you should have a pretty good view."

I turn my head.

"Is this the part where I get out for a look around while you run away?"

"No," he says with a lack of conviction.

Stretch is just coming over the rise. His headlights go dark, and the Monte Carlo angles slowly in behind Nadia's Nissan. I open the door into the wind.

"Let's go, Billy."

The four of us traverse the crest of broken, frozen bush scrub, through holly and hackberry and pine, sounding like a herd of elephant in a peanut factory. Billy is in the lead, complaining about the branches in his face because his wrists are bound. I keep one hand on his shoulder just to keep him from getting any ideas. Stretch and Donovan bring up the rear. Billy adjusts course a couple of times, but we don't have to walk long before he stops at a large sycamore and juts his chin forward.

"Down there," he says. "Through those trees."

Deke's Auto Scrap and Salvage is all by itself except for a sheet metal fabricator two lots to the west with access by a different road. I can see the southern half of the salvage yard, which includes the gated entrance area sandwiched between a wall of tires to the west and a wall of compacted cars to the east. The rest of the yard is obscured by a stand of evergreen halfway down the slope between where the four of us are freezing in our shoes and North Picking Road.

We all crane our necks for a better view. There isn't one.

The deepest I can see into the lot is the dirty white façade of a double-wide trailer that I'm guessing smells like grease and dead cigarettes and that comes complete with a crooked bulletin board, a rickety black metal filing cabinet, a broken desk and an out-of-date pin-up calendar that no one has the heart to throw away. I can make out Deke's name on the big red and white sign above the door.

The windows to the office are dark. A single flood lamp on a metal pole casts a dull-orange glow over the yard. The front gate is closed and presumably locked. Nothing down there moves except whatever the wind chooses to move. Which is almost everything.

Another stiff gust and the sycamore at my shoulder creaks. My ears burn with cold. My collar doesn't reach but I pull at it anyway. Deeper inside, my gut is warm but no more comfortable. It flips over uneasily, begging for attention. It always knows when something is wrong. Dead-on accurate, every time.

Problem is, accurate is not the same as articulate. *Something* is wrong, but I don't know what. Could be I'm hungry. Or, could be I'm not as alone as I think I am. Last time my gut wanted attention, two men were in my house waiting for me to come downstairs to help shorten my couch with a chainsaw. The time before that, a hotdog with relish on the corner of West Chicago and Oakley fixed the problem completely.

The wind gives the sycamore another push. It creaks and nudges me in the shoulder. A chill shoots up my spine and I turn reflexively for a good look around.

"What?" asks Stretch.

"Nothing," I say, half-believing.

In a normal person, a sense of being watched might help clarify gut feelings.

But the Triple-D of my broken-down psyche means I always feel watched. Nothing new there. Even now, I see myself from above the tree, turning and looking back in the direction of Hill Road for someone watching me. There is someone watching me. Me. Always.

As for the chill up my spine, the rest of me is near frozen; why should the spine be any different?

The best I can deduce is that my gut knows a waste of time better than the rest of me. It's worried that precious minutes are slipping away as I'm out here looking to die of hypothermia.

"Well?" asks Stretch next to me.

"Waste of time," I tell him. I don't try to hide my disappointment. "If Jimmy's car is down there, then it's just another brick in that wall. And if that's really true, then I don't want to see whatever is still in the trunk. So let's hope it's not true."

"We could go down and search," he says.

"Brought along some bolt cutters, did you?"

"No. But maybe we could climb the fence. Chain link. We could clear that."

I shake my head, secretly appreciating the effort he's making to keep me from being completely wrong about everything. Something in him knows tonight is the end of my road. Or he knows the odds for Jimmy and Phil are something south of terrible. He wants to give me every chance.

"You could probably step over it," I say. "I'd fall and break my ass in two. We're out of time, Stretch."

"So?"

"I'm just going to have to show up and take the meeting. See how it plays. I thought if I could find Jimmy's car…" I don't finish. Instead, I take another look down through the tangle of branches at *Deke's*. Nothing. "Damn it."

Donovan reaches between us and knocks Billy on the shoulder.

"I want to know how pencil-dick here knows about this little spot," he says.

It's a good question. We all look at Billy.

He takes a second to choose his words.

"My buddy and me used to come up here and drink sometimes. And other things."

"What other things?" asks Stretch. "Drug things?"

Billy's face darkens like an ugly toddler staring down a spoon full of peas. He looks at me for permission to keep his mouth shut.

"In for a penny," I say with a shrug. "You're in the cooperation business now, Billy."

"Maybe it was a sex thing," offers Donovan. "It was, wasn't it? Coupl'a sword swallowers playing tonsil hockey in the back seat."

"Let him talk," I say.

Billy grits his teeth and shakes in the cold. He's not dressed for a winter hike. The words come out in frozen chips of sound, which makes it harder to know which ones are true and which one will stink of rot once they thaw.

"Deke runs a chop shop out of that yard," he says. "Used to anyway. Don't know about now. This was back in the day. My buddy gave him a car once and got stiffed for the parts. He had this whole blackmail thing worked out. He stole this big ass camera he didn't know how to work. We'd come up here and drink and take pictures of Deke cuttin' deals. 'Til Itchy broke his arm and the camera got smashed up. The whole plan fizzled. I had nothing to do with any of it, man. It was totally Itchy's thing."

"Itchy?" asks Donovan, irritated at the sound of the word. Or the feel of it.

"Yeah, man. Had himself a condition."

"I don't want to know," I say, turning back for the car. "Time to go to work."

They all watch me go. I can feel each of them wondering what the plan is now.

That makes four of us.

ONE HUNDRED THIRTY-ONE

Ray is bent into the trunk of the Nissan, using the lid as a shield against the wind, doing what he needs to do to prepare. Behind him, the others sit thawing in the idling Monte Carlo.

What does a man think at a time like this, right before that first domino starts to tip? What goes through his head?

I don't know about other men. But I know about Ray. He's thinking about the book half-written. The unresolved arc of character. He's wondering what will happen to Detective Jack McMannis if he, Ray Mackey, never comes home again to finish what he started.

Someone, surely, will burrow through Ray's personal effects. Probably before Doris has written his obit. Someone will come to his home and open every drawer and cupboard, looking for love letters from José Beggemon, or a canonization approval from the Pope, anything to either absolve him or incriminate him definitively, for the sake of history if nothing else. Because, to the rest of the world, Raymond Mackey is an unresolved character and people hate not knowing what to really think of him. They'll want to know the final answer to the riddle of this man. And whoever it is, some cop, or some desk jockey with a badge tucked into his suit pocket, will pull Ray's laptop out of a banker's box full of belongings and scour it for clues.

Which means he or she will almost certainly find the file that contains the half-written book.

Message in a Bullet. Who wouldn't double-click a title like that?

Whoever it is will read the thing; will follow the footsteps of Detective McMannis from the first page to the last, finally catching up with him in a dark parking lot outside a Chinatown Target, bent into the front seat of a dead man's

Pontiac with a camera in his hand. That's where Jack McMannis' trail will abruptly end. Arc unfinished.

Ray pulls Sig out of the shoulder harness. He ejects the clip, gives it a once over and then reinserts. He wants to nose Sig back into the holster. I suggest that he clear the chamber first; that he leave it empty. It's against every instinct in the man's head. It's a terrible idea. But I suggest it just the same.

I can't tell you why.

Maybe because there's a voice in my head just like I'm the voice in Ray's head. Maybe my voice is just an echo of whoever is in my head and it keeps going all the way back to some unfathomable point of origin; like the listening version of looking through the wrong end of a telescope. I don't know who suggested it first. Maybe no one. Maybe I'm as crazy as Ray is.

Clear the chamber. That's the voice in my head. I pass it along.

Ray slides back the action and catches the bullet before it hits the trunk. He puts the bullet in his pocket and then puts Sig to bed. He fishes through the canvas bag confiscated from the *Windy Wharf* cube van and tucks Hawkeye's .38 Special with the blue grip into his belt. He extracts the heroin, re-zips the bag and then closes the trunk of the Nissan. The wind lunges for his face like something hungry released from a cage, looking to get under that bandage.

What happens to all the unfinished characters? How do they find their way?

And who will be there to greet them?

That's what he's thinking.

ONE HUNDRED THIRTY-TWO

I'm the one following now. I keep my speed down. I catch a red light on purpose, letting the taillights of Stretch's Monte Carlo disappear into the gloom. Before I reach the Bliss Road overpass, Stretch is calling from the next offramp.

"We're at Exit 109. I've got a decent view of the exit and the freeway," he says. "Either way we should spot you and we can follow. But listen, that's not going to help you much if things get ugly under that overpass. We're a good mile downstream."

"Hell is big," I say, "but he's no dummy. He didn't pick a place where a clown car full of cops can idle around the corner. He'll have someone on the overpass with a long, clear view. And if you think he's rolling up with a trunk full of hostages then I've got a bridge to sell you. We're going for a ride. Question is where."

"What if they put you in a different car? I can only follow what I recognize."

"I'll express a strong preference for staying in this car. They'll want me to think I can drive away once we've made the trade. Taking me hostage doesn't get them what they want. They'll need me to make a phone call."

"Yeah, unless they can get you to make the call by breaking your fingers."

"Come on. How do you dial a phone with no fingers?"

"I'd worry about your legs."

"Yeah. That's a risk. These guys always pick on the legs."

"You're really hanging out there, Mack," says Stretch. "I don't like it."

"I'm not wild about it myself. But I figure he wants Nadia and Mila. Turning them over gets me a quick bullet to the head and then everybody disappears. But I don't have Nadia and Mila. Maybe an empty back seat keeps me alive for a while. If he believes I'm willing to trade."

"You said yourself he's no dummy. How could this guy think you're going to turn over anyone? I don't care who he's got in a trunk, he's got to know this is a fantasy play. Cops don't turn over hostages."

"Bad cops might. Cops on their way out without any future. Cops who may as well do what they can to save their own."

"Yeah? That you, Mack?"

"Guess we'll see."

"Maybe an empty back seat just pisses him off and you get a bullet hole without any questions. Maybe that's the whole point. Maybe that's why Hell was waiting at your house in the first place."

"Could be."

"Well?"

"Well, I didn't deal these cards, Stretch. I'd ask for a fresh drink and a new hand if I thought it would make a difference, but this game doesn't work that way. I'm guessing Hell expects me to be alone in the car with an ace up my sleeve. He'll be looking for that ace. That's you, by the way, so stay sharp out there. He knows I'm not going to lay anything down without eyes on living hostages. That's the only way to find Jimmy and Phil."

"I keep forgetting about the cat. Jesus. What the fuck are we doing, Mack? Let's get real here. Can I do that with you for a second?"

"Shoot." I hear Stretch take a breath and let it out.

"Marlo's gone," he says. "You don't owe her this. And she'd never ask. The fate of the brother and the cat is… is… it is whatever it is. Marlo would kill you herself for trying any of this. She's not in that trunk, Ray. She's not around to be saved. You can't bring her back."

An eighteen-wheeler passes on my left, followed closely by two cars with drivers who give me looks they must keep handy for slowpokes. They both change lanes and speed away past the semi. I can see the Bliss Road overpass rising in the distance.

"Well, as long as we're getting real, Stretch…"

"Okay."

"Remember the bottle we shared in the breakroom after Marlo died?"

"Yeah," he says wearily. "I remember."

"You were trying to put me back together. I asked how you and Connie survived losing little Joe?" Silence on the phone. I can feel his viscera tearing, separating around the old wound. I keep on. "You told me that you hadn't survived. Nothing saved you. Jesus was a big no show. Your faith sunk like the *Titanic* and never resurfaced. You said you were still only part of a person. You said I would always only be part of a person."

"Yeah." Stretch empties his lungs again. "Yeah, I remember, Ray."

"Turns out you were right about that. And the part of me that's left doesn't give a shit how much it's going to hurt. Or how long I'm going to last. It doesn't count cards or play the odds or read any warning labels. The part of me that's left only really cares about the parts of *her* that are left. Two of those parts are freezing in a fucking trunk, Stretch. And for the record, I *do* owe her this. This and a whole lot more."

Silence on the phone as I angle the Nissan off the road and into the envelope of darkness beneath the Bliss Road overpass. Interstate 88 stretches out away from me in the moonlight like a dead gray vein.

"Okay," says Stretch. "I get it. I don't like it. But I get it."

"I'm under the overpass. Time to go. Listen, if this goes bad…"

"Yeah," he says. "I know. Nadia and Mila."

"The system is Big Man's tuning fork. It's a goddamned spider's web. He'll find them."

"I understand, Mack. I'll figure something out. Try not to die."

ONE HUNDRED THIRTY-THREE

Hell on Earth makes me wait. I sit idling under the Bliss Road overpass, hood up, hazards on, just like I was told. I send out a text, pretending not to know that he's probably waiting directly above me.

I'm here. Where are you?

I don't expect an answer, so I don't wait for one. I use the time for a conversation with the Duty Sergeant working the graveyard for the Aurora Police Department. I tell him a story about a heroin bust and a couple of meth heads locked up in a fish warehouse. I leave everybody's name out of it for now and give him the code to the back door. He wants to know the charge.

"Stupidity," I say.

"That's not a crime."

"Well, it should be. Try possession with intent and lots of both. Start with that. We've got the third suspect in custody, and we've bagged the evidence. We can get you officer statements. You'll see three cars in the lot. Impound all of them."

"Pretty bossy for someone who doesn't work here. Why are we cleaning up your mess?"

"It's not our mess. We found the mess in Aurora and swept it up into a nice pile before we had to tend to other business."

"Why can't I have names? There's paperwork."

"You want names? Hawkeye and Xero with an X. Those are some names."

"Cute. Which one are you?"

"Call Lieutenant Twill at Chandler IAD when the sun comes up. He'll act surprised, but don't fall for that. Drop the name Ray into the conversation and watch everything clear up in a hurry. There, now you're swimming in names."

"Thanks a whole lot. Were the suspects Mirandized?"

"Yes. Then we read them both a bedtime story and turned out the lights. They're secure for now but they need to be out of that warehouse before someone shows up for work and turns on the lights."

I can feel him scratching his head.

"Well, my LT is a stickler for warrants. And he may not let us hold them under these circumstances. Not without evidence and officer statements actually in hand."

Headlights have been coming and going in the rearview mirror. But now a new pair shows up that isn't in such a rush. The car pulls off the road fifty feet behind me and hits the high beams. Then the red and blue disco lights start.

"So don't hold them," I say to the Duty Sergeant. "Unlock them and send them home. It's your town, Sergeant. I never wanted them in the first place. My date is here. I gotta go."

I stare into the blazing mirror and start thinking my way through the license and registration conversation that's coming. I'll also need to explain my roadside predicament and why, exactly, I don't need the police to lend me any assistance. Flashing my shield for the last time in my career might make that conversation an easy one. Then again, the last time I thought my badge might make things easier I agreed to help a beautiful woman find her mother's Russian doll.

The lights are too bright for me to tell if there is one cop or two. The driver door opens. The man who steps out looks like a standard issue hump in uniform. The posture and gate are also standard: slow and steady, one hand on his firearm as he makes his way in the wind for the Nissan. When he reaches my left taillight, he crosses behind the car to the passenger side, stepping into the narrow space between the car and the concrete wall of the overpass. Suddenly he's not so standard. I switch to the passenger mirror and mark his progress. He stoops and cups his hand against the glass.

This guy doesn't want my license and registration. He wants a good look into the back seat. He's looking for passengers.

He turns and moves back behind the car, knuckling the trunk twice. I take the hint and pull what I think is the trunk release lever. It turns out to be the seat recline lever. I rocket backwards, all but falling into the back seat. The cop knuckles the trunk again, a little harder this time. I return the seat to where it belongs and find the right lever this time. The trunk lid opens, dowsing the headlights in the rearview mirror and putting me back in the dark.

I adjust the mirror. I can see his arms moving in the strip of light below the open lid.

It takes him all of four seconds. The trunk closes and his headlights blow through the back of the Nissan all over again. I watch him walk back to the flashing cruiser, Billy's canvas bag in his left hand, swinging in the wind.

The cruiser swallows him up. We sit and idle together in our separate cars like we're waiting for a tow truck. That, surely, is what the few people who blow past us must think.

All I can do is wait for what comes next. My nerves get me to patting my coat pockets for something to smoke to help pass the time. My fingers come up empty, but the heel of my shoe can feel that brick of skag under the front seat. Guess I'm all horse and no camel tonight. I figure the cop is back there on the phone bringing Hell up to speed about everyone and everything that came up missing in his search of the Nissan.

In my head Billy's canvas bag is still swinging in the wind. It takes me a second, but then my spine lights up.

The bag.

Excluding me, only five people could know that bag was in my possession. Last I checked, three of those people are zip-tied and don't have use of their hands or access to a phone. The other two are sitting in the front seat of Stretch Martin's Monte Carlo, waiting to make a difference in the rest of my life.

And only one of those two people suggested that I try not to die tonight.

Clarity usually brings me some measure of calm. Understanding is usually a balm. Not this time. This time clarity and understanding have teamed up to punch a hole in the boat. A cold panic starts to trickle into my chest.

The halogens blazing in from behind make me self-conscious. I keep my upper body still, fishing my cellphone out of my pocket. I try to think of something clever. Something that will work. I come up blank and make the call anyway. I keep the thing in my lap and put it on speaker.

"Mack," says Stretch. "What's happening?"

In the background I can hear Donovan putting a question to Billy. I can't tell if I'm on speaker. I do my best to sound idle.

"Still waiting on Hell. My guess is he's going to make me sit a while. In the meantime, I thought of something else I need you to do for me in case, well, you know."

"What's that?"

"Nadia has kid. A daughter named Danika."

"Okay."

"Danika lost her father tonight. He's full of holes now, zipped up in a bag."

"Sorry to hear. What the hell does that have to do with me?"

"Danika's trying to figure out what it all means. She's getting bulldozed by all the big questions, like why and how daddy died."

"Okay. So."

"So if I get out of this tonight, I plan to help answer those questions. And if I don't..."

"What, me? You want me to..."

"She's just about the age of your Little Joe, Stretch."

I can feel those words find the old wound. At least I've got his attention.

"Imagine if you didn't come home from your shift one night when Little Joe was that age. You'd want someone who gave a damn to sit down with him and help explain all the how's and the why's." I'm not trying to irritate him, but I keep pushing enough to do it anyway. "I mean, seriously, Stretch, wouldn't you?"

"Jesus, Mack. I don't... I don't know the how's and why's for this kid. And we don't have time for..."

"It'll all be in a report. You can read it. The how's and why's are pretty simple, Stretch. When I wasn't paying attention, Danika's dad made a phone call he shouldn't have made. He invited some guys over that he shouldn't have invited. He was in a dicey situation with me poking around his house, asking questions and breathing down his neck. He knew things were about to go bad and he wanted some company. You know, someone to have his back. I get that. When your gut gets a queasy feeling that things are about to head south, you may as well have someone you really trust sitting right next to you, don't you think?"

He doesn't answer. I figure I'm on the speaker and the three of them are thinking I'm over here with a gun to my head trying to babble out some kind of SOS. I guess that would make them about half-right.

"So these two bruisers came through the door first. I dealt with them easily enough. But it was the third guy still out in the car I never counted on. He waited, see. He let things unspool with me and the goons inside until the time was right to show up and turn everyone into Swiss cheese, including Danika's dad. I'd have been next, but then Nadia put him down."

"*Nadia* put him down?"

"Yeah. Long story. Point is, I never considered a third guy out in the car, Stretch. Just like the guy in the car never considered a mom with a gun. He was out there on his phone keeping everyone in Thugville dialed in without any idea that mom was in a car half a block away watching from the shadows. That's a lot of people sitting in cars that no one really stopped to think about. This game is full of surprises, isn't it?"

"For fuck's sake, Mack. Get to the goddamned point. What do you want from me?"

"Danika's a sensitive, kid, Stretch. Smart but tender. Understand? You can't give her all the gory details. You'll have to frame this all as a lesson about judgment and trust. You know, the big issues. Her dad trusted the wrong people. Danika did too. She trusted me. I was supposed to make everything be okay. I actually said those words to her before the shooting started. *Everything's going to be okay, kid.* Well, everything's not okay, Stretch. Understand me? It's all the opposite of okay. Daddy's full of holes. He's in the bag now. Once a guy is in the bag, he's never coming out. Danika's too young to understand that, Stretch. But you do. You understand. You should, anyway. I feel like I let this kid down. I've created another person in the world who should never trust the police."

"You're losing it, man. You need some sleep. Let's abort this thing and go home. We'll finish things up back at the fish place, put out an APB for the car and go home. I'll buy you a drink. How about it?"

"No, no. Look, Stretch, I'm just trying to help this kid. Her world is upside down. She needs someone she can count on. It's like how you were telling me after Little Joe passed that the only thing that saved you was knowing you had Christ in your corner. You always had someone sitting right beside you that you could count on. Never take that for granted, Stretch."

Silence.

"Danika needs that now. I don't know what's going to happen to Nadia and there's a decent chance I won't be around. So, I'm thinking it might all depend on you. Understand? If I'm not around, you need to be ready to step up."

I can't read the dead air in my ear. Behind me, the red and blue disco goes suddenly dark.

It's Donovan's voice I hear next. It's under his breath, not meant for me.

"I'm telling you, man, he's… the guy is fucking cra…"

"Listen, Mack," says Stretch. "You need to pull it together. All that shit can wait. The kid's new best friend is about to be some psychologist working for Child Protective Services. They'll cover all those issues and more. Okay? So, either shut the fuck up and focus or let's call it a night. What's it gonna be?"

No telling whether he has taken the hint. Nothing else I can do.

"Showtime, Stretch. I've got a cop behind me."

"A cop? Whose cop?"

"Isn't that always the question? I'm guessing he's the advance team. I don't know who signs his paycheck, but I've got an idea or two about who he works for."

"Watch yourself, Mack."

"Always do."

I end the call just as the headlights behind me swerve out of the mirror. The cruiser angles back onto the road and speeds past me. I try to get a glimpse of the guy's face but the most I can tell is that he was riding solo. The car roars away up I-88, leaving me alone again under the overpass.

Thirty seconds. Four headlights approach and then slow. One pair pulls up behind, right about where the cruiser had been. The other pair belongs to a black pickup. It pulls up in front of me, half disappearing on the other side of the Nissan's engine hood which is still shaking in the wind like a paper sail. I check the side mirror. The car behind is a low-riding, snail-gray Ford Granada, complete with a cracked windshield, a missing a license plate, and four sets of shoulders inside.

Movement comes from the truck in front. The driver's door opens and the truck spits out a wad of humanity that belongs stuck to the underside of a bleacher. He's not much for skipping meals, this guy. Timberlands below and a black knit ski mask on top. In between the boots and the mask is a body that stays away from rice cakes and revolving doors. The only thing I really care about is the Uzi on a shoulder strap pushing open the right half of his coat. For a fat guy, he knows how to move. He covers the distance to my door like he's trying to beat the line to a food truck.

He clicks the muzzle against the window as he takes a good, long look at the empty back seat. I open my window a little, making a point of taking my time.

"I don't see any women," he says into the crack. He sounds genuinely surprised, which I find genuinely surprising.

"I'm not surprised," I say. "Jenny Craig's a woman; how about trying a date with her? Maybe it's time you break things off with Jimmy Dean."

"Fuck you." Again with the barrel to the glass. "Where are they?"

His accent is from some puddle of sweat south of the corn belt. It's as doughy as the rest of him, almost too big to fit through the crack. His vowels are too slow to keep up, dragging across his tongue like wet bags of sour mash in the dirt.

"Nearby," I tell him. "A phone call away, handcuffed in the back of a car waiting for instructions."

I hold up my phone to the glass and show him the picture of Nadia and Mila in the back of Raffi's Dodge. *Try to look miserable*, I'd told them.

"You must think we're stupid," he drawls, squinting at the phone. All kinds of words want out of my mouth. I'd bite my tongue, but I did that already tonight.

"Course not. But I'm not stupid either. My associate is ready to drop the women wherever you say. A freeway, just like this. Or out in the middle of nowhere so you can pick them up. I don't really care. But nothing is happening until I get a good look at what I came for."

I'm still holding the phone against the glass and he's still squinting.

"You were s'posed to bring 'em," he says. "You were s'posed to have 'em in the back seat."

"And trade them for what?" I ask. "Where's your end of this bargain?"

He straitens, pointing the Uzi directly at my face. I take the phone off the window. My Triple-D kicks in. I can see myself through the roof of the Nissan looking out of the window into the barrel of a submachine gun. I look old. Defenseless. Frightened. I abstract myself backwards in space. Ten feet. Twenty. Thirty. I'm way up in the wind now, looking down through the overpass. It's like I'm trying to stay clear of the coming spatter. I can't help but wonder how long after my body dies my brain will continue to receive the video feed from above.

I change the channel and wonder whether Stretch is still alive. If these guys know about Billy's bag in the trunk, then they know about the cops waiting a mile up the road. Maybe they've sent a car full of masks to take care of that problem. Maybe Donovan has already solved it for them.

"Guess we got us a 'lil problem," he says through the black hole in his mask. "I can think of one solution."

"Yeah? What's that?"

"Have them girls delivered right here, right now, or I take your fuckin' head off."

"So you guys come away with nothing but the body of an old cop? You think that solution is gonna satisfy anyone on your end? This Nissan is worth more than a dead version of me. My guess is your head ends up in the bag with mine. I've got a better idea."

"Which is?"

"Go to Hell. Which car is he in? Or maybe he's someplace sitting by the phone. Tell him I don't do business with lackeys. I want to see him in person. And while you're at it, tell him I don't fork over *my* hostages without laying my eyes on *his* hostages. He's no dummy, your boss. He knows all of this already. He knew my back seat would be empty. Go tell him anyway so we can get on to the next step. And they'd both better be alive and well, by the way, or I drive away from this whole thing and Hell gets bupkis."

He's staring at me through the window, a fat raccoon with an Uzi, chugging steam through the hole in his mask and contemplating the future. I give him another poke of fake bravado, trying to keep the quaver out of my voice and my pants clean. I put the window down all the way, move the Uzi out of my face with a finger, and look up at the three holes in his mask.

"Hello? Anybody in there? You know what bupkis means? It's not a kind of sausage."

"Hand over the gun."

"That's never happening. Stop fucking around and let's get this thing done. I've got places to be."

The steam coming out of his blowhole makes the shape of a laugh. Something in what I said turned out to be funny. I'm guessing it was the part about me driving away.

"Don't go nowhere," he says. He lowers the Uzi, then turns and waddle-walks back to the truck. I get a bad case of the shakes. I put the window up like maybe the cold and the wind are to blame. I know better.

He's gone three minutes going on four, just long enough to get an earful of instructions. When he returns, he stands at the window. I open it a crack. He gestures at the car behind.

In the mirror I can see the back door of the Granada open. One set of shoulders gets out of the car and heads our way, high off the ground and hunched into the wind. I can tell they all shop at the same mask store. He keeps one hand in his coat pocket. The other hand stays out in the cold, but I'm guessing that's because the .357 won't fit. The fat raccoon wants my attention.

"Follow this truck," he says pointing at the idling pickup. Then he swings the Uzi sideways toward his friend. "He's ridin' with you just to make sure you don't get lost."

The newcomer tries the back door, but no one says please so he stays where he is. I get another Uzi-knock on the window.

"Open up."

"I'll follow," I say. "You think I'm out here for the fun of it? I showed up and took the meeting, didn't I? I'm here. Why would I drive away now?"

"Open. The. Fuckin'. Door."

"You know, I'm starting to worry the mask is cutting the oxygen to your brain. When was the last time you ate? Maybe you're peckish. I'm telling you a chaperone's not necessary."

He leans forward. I'm nose-to-barrel with the Uzi again. The mask hole elongates a little. It ranks right up there with the creepiest smiles I've ever seen in my entire life, clowns included.

"It is necessary," he says slowly. "It's necessary if you want to get who you came for. It's necessary, Detective wise-ass, if you don't want to die under this overpass. So you think about it. I'll give you a second or two. Go ahead. But understand this as you're thinkin' about things: we don't gotta make another phone call."

ONE HUNDRED THIRTY-FOUR

We don't gotta make another phone call.

It's not the grammar that bothers me so much as the plural pronoun. *We.* The fat raccoon didn't say *he.* He said *we. We don't gotta make another phone call.*

That tells me whoever is riding shotgun in that pickup is the one making phone calls. He's in charge of this crew: the raccoon with the Uzi and the lug in the seat behind me with a magnum pointed at my back, and probably the other three goons back there in the Granada. It's his crew. But he's answerable to the guy on the other end of the phone and I'm guessing that's Hell.

Hell's not with them. He's waiting someplace out of the wind. He's comfortable. In phone contact.

Raccoon slams my hood down, climbs up into the truck and puts it in gear.

I venture a glance in the rearview as I turn off the hazards and follow the pickup out onto the road. The Granada rides my bumper. The ox in the back seat nuzzles the magnum up against the left side of my head. Everyone's nervous about me making a move on the way to wherever it is we're all going. I'm nervous that one bump on the road to Hell will cost me an ear.

A mile passes like ten. The freeway signs are excited about the nearness of Exit 109, or maybe that's just me. I have to force myself not to show any particular interest as we approach. The pickup in front blows by the exit ramp. I slot my eyes sideways in their sockets, looking for Stretch's Monte Carlo as we pass. My peripheral night vision isn't what it used to be. I don't see much of anything.

I try to keep my eyes out of the rearview mirror, so I don't risk giving away the game. I let the exit come and go like it's of no interest. I wait until the last possible second. Turns out that was too long. I can see a pair of headlights, but I can't tell if they came from Exit 109 or if they were already on the road.

I catch the eyes of the man in the back. He hasn't uttered a single word in all the time I've known him. Makes me wonder if he knows any words I might understand.

"You like the cold?" I ask.

I don't get a response. Big surprise. He keeps the gun in his lap and his face pointed at the side window.

"I don't know anybody who actually likes cold weather. I know people who tolerate it. They're used to it. You know, they accept it. But that's not the same as liking it. Everyone I've ever known hates the cold. What about you? Seems to me you might actually enjoy this temperature. That makes you a rare breed, my friend. Russian, maybe. Slavic anyway. It's in the eyes. I'm guessing your answer to winter is a big bowl of borscht. Am I right?"

Nothing.

"Me, I'm thinking of getting out. Going someplace warm. Hawaiian houseboat maybe. Or some little shack on a beach where I can count the number of people on one finger. Hey, I don't suppose you're a smoker, are you? You non-English-speaking Russian killer-criminal types are over-represented in the smoking demographic. I figure the odds are pretty good you're packing a lighter and something to set on fire. Feel free to say *nyet*."

He leans forward and knocks me in the patch on my cheekbone with the gun.

"Shut the fuck up and drive, man. I'll set *you* on fire. You want that? 'Cause I sure as hell do. Say another fucking word, and the thing I light up is you."

For a non-English-speaking Russian, he does a great impression of a thug born and raised on the streets of Chicago. I keep that observation to myself and drive.

The pickup passes the next exit. I take a look in the rearview and find that pair of headlights behind the Granada. The headlights slow. Then they exit the freeway.

It's just me out here.

Another mile and the pickup brake lights pulse for Exit 111. He even uses a blinker. I think about letting the fat raccoon and his boss commit to the exit while I keep sailing up I-88. The English-speaking, non-Russian charmer in the back seat is thinking the same thing. He knocks the barrel of the .357 against the side of my face again. I hit the blinker and follow.

The pickup exits, summits the ramp, crosses above the freeway, and then takes the on-ramp in the opposite direction, sending us right back the way we came.

Smart. Raccoon is looking for tails other than his own. As we pass Exit 111 headed the other direction, I look for signs of company. Signs of hope. I don't see any.

"Oh, well this is fun," I say. "How long are we going to play this game?"

It gets me another knock in the face with the gun. Then the guy leans back in the seat and sighs, which tells me he's wondering the same thing.

Three miles later, the pickup flashes a blinker at the Bliss Road exit, right where we started. We roll south on Bliss until we cross I-47. That's where Bliss turns into Wheeler and we're suddenly moving west. The pickup starts blinking again when Wheeler Road meets up with North Picking Road.

North Picking. Turns out Billy Wise had been right all along.

ONE HUNDRED THIRTY-FIVE

We all pull to a stop at the chain-link gate. Raccoon climbs out of the pickup, Uzi still around his neck banging against the doorframe. He walks around the front of the truck, crossing into the headlights and stands with his back to us, adopting a classic ATM posture, head bent, hands in front, trying to work the lock in the cold. The light inside the fence is a dirty yellow dog, pulling against its pole in the wind, clawing at the edges of shadow and lunging for the gate it can't quite reach. The wind billows raccoon's coat out away from his fat little body, forcing him to try to hold the thing closed with one hand and poke at the lock with the other. I glance up in the mirror at the ox behind me.

"See, the trick is to put the coat on first, then the gun. That way you can zip up and stay warm when your boss lets you out of the truck so you can pee through a fence. Your boy's gonna get his hands wet."

Ox makes a laughing sound. Then he adjusts his mask and leans forward and gives me another knock in the cheekbone just so I don't get the wrong idea.

Raccoon finally gets the numbers right and pushes open the right side of the gate. He returns to the truck and eases forward until the pickup is through the gate and nosed in the direction of the door to the dirty, double-wide trailer, right below the sign that reads *Deke's Auto Scrap & Salvage*. I nudge the Nissan along until Ox knocks me again in the bandage.

"Right here," he says.

I take the hint. I put the Nissan in park and have a quick look around as the Granada pulls up behind off to the right. A hundred feet or so to our left is a wall of tires. The same distance beyond the passenger window is a wall of flattened cars. Forward and to the right, past the edge of the office trailer, is an opening to another, much larger, unlit part of the yard. I can see the shapes of other cars, pre-flattened, piled up in several tight rows in a way that reminds me of the Dan Ryan Expressway, right where the I-90 and the I-94 shake hands every Friday afternoon.

On the nearside of that pile-up is the wide, orange belly of a crane. In the background is a big square shadow that I figure must be a garage. I'm betting somewhere inside is the chop shop Billy mentioned. If I were an ugly Malibu with a trunk full of tear-stained duct tape, that's exactly where I'd be.

The feeling tightening inside my heart is the realization that I should have busted into the yard just like Stretch suggested. I could have skipped the meet-and-greet and the scenic tour of Aurora. My instincts were right. It was a good plan. It was a good plan until I decided it wasn't a good plan. There's nothing quite like being wrong about being wrong when it's too damned late to change your mind.

In my rearview I can see the driver of the Granada get out of the car and walk back to the gate. Maybe I know the guy, maybe I don't. Masked men all look the same to me. He is on the big and lanky side for a wheelman. Makes me wonder about the other two still inside the car. It occurs to me for the first time that maybe Hell has been behind me the whole time, riding shotgun in the Granada. Raccoon doesn't want to give that part away, so he's been making phone calls from the pickup truck in front, over my head to Hell who's sitting in the car behind.

The wheelman closes the gate and returns to the idling Granada, taking a moment to look my way with one hand draped over the top of the open door. I know he can't see me looking at him, but it feels like it anyway and I fight the urge to avert my eyes. Eventually he slips back behind the wheel and closes the door.

The flare of taillights in front of me yanks my attention forward. The pickup is in reverse, rolling slowly backwards until it's even with me and the Nissan. I take a good, long look, but the passenger window is too tinted for me to see inside. No more than twelve inches separate us. I couldn't open my door to get out of this car if my life depended on it. Which it probably does.

Behind me, Ox leans forward in his seat. I get another sharp barrel kiss to the check bone.

"Cut the engine. Hand back the keys."

"No," I tell him. "But I'll meet you halfway." I turn off the engine and find his big dumb eyes in the mirror. The mask makes him look like a thumb with a black coat on.

"Motherfucker want to die, I guess," he says. I can tell it's not a new line for him. It's an old favorite. His baritone fills those words like a big hand in an old glove. I ease my own hand inside my coat for Sig, palming the grip but keeping him in bed for now.

"Guess you can kill me for a set of car keys if you want," I say, "but that'd make all this a sorry waste of time. You boys go through all of this for a dead cop and a shitty Nissan? I'm guessing someone higher up your food chain wants to come away with something more valuable for the trouble. But hey, you go on ahead and make the decisions for everybody. I'm sure they won't mind."

I watch him lean slowly back in his seat. His eyes look at me through their holes. The menace is palpable. His life has left him mean and angry and he's looking for any opportunity to express himself. But he's a dog on a chain and we both know it.

"Also," I say as much with my eyes as my mouth, "hit me with that thing again and I'm going to start thinking maybe you're not so smart."

I can tell he's about to debate the issue, but he doesn't get the chance. The pickup window next to us starts sliding, disappearing down into the door. The passenger has a mask on just like the others. All the holes are the same.

It's the holes inside the holes that are different.

He leans a sawed-off shotgun casually against the open window. Then he points at me, moving a long finger in a slow circle. I let go of Sig and reach for the key in the ignition. I turn it just one click so I can lower my window and let in the wind. I smile at the mask.

"Hey, Mouth," I say. "What's doin'?"

ONE HUNDRED THIRTY-SIX

It takes him a few seconds. Must be unnerving when you realize the mask hasn't done its job.

Eventually Casey Randall Sweet pulls off the wool. He's made sure to have a smile ready. If you can call it that.

Now it's Ray's turn to be unnerved. Anonymity is a beautiful thing among people who don't have to kill you. Of all his options upon recognizing Mouth, not playing dumb was easily the dumbest. The odds of Ray driving out of this meeting just pancaked.

"Detective Mackey," he says.

"What I wouldn't give about now for a hot bowl of your girlfriend's soup."

"Ex-girlfriend."

"Sorry to hear. I'm guessing she couldn't take the doll fetish."

"Here's the way this works, fuck-o." His lips are raw and chapped from the cold and sweaty from the hot mask. He wipes his mouth with the back of his hand then uses the wadded-up mask on his face like a towel. "I want your gun. I want the women. And I want to know where you put the smack." He makes a nod toward the back seat. "Twitch and my boy there is going to put a bullet or two in your spine."

"Thanks for the wish list," says Ray. "You want mine?"

"Not really."

"I want Hell. Get him out here with the rest of us. He's too big to be such a chicken shit."

"You're not worth his time," says Mouth. "You deal with me. So. The women. Where are they?"

"On stand-by. I'll drop them wherever you tell me, but only when I get Jimmy and Phil alive and well."

Mouth laughs. Mirth on that mug is horrific. Like the sun rising over a landfill.

"Jimmy and Phil," he sneers. "Right. Which one is the fucking cat?"

"The one with a tail, moron. Once your people have the women then you watch us drive away."

"Just like that."

"Yeah. Just like that."

"And we don't kill you all because…"

"Because that gets messy."

"Who gives a shit about messy? Not me. Messy is good."

"Maybe you care more about staying alive."

Mouth opens the chasm in his face for a soundless laugh.

"Oh, yeah?"

"Sure. Think about it, Mouth. You need those drugs back. You want the credit for the recovery so maybe Hell and Big Man don't get wise to the fact that you were the one who arranged for Billy Wise to nick two bricks of horse in the first place."

The laugh has died on Casey Sweet's face. It hangs for a lingering second before sloughing off in the wind. What remains is rage and worry.

"Fuck you," he says.

"Yeah? Fuck me? Well, maybe. I'm not in such a great position here. I get that. But you're not sitting so pretty yourself."

Mouth snorts.

"How you figure that?"

"Billy Wise is singing quite a song. Half the lyrics are missing, but there's enough of a rhyme for me to figure it out. Bottom line is you need those horses back in the stable and I'm the only one who knows where to find them."

Food for thought. Mouth gives him a couple of slow, considered blinks, like his eyes need to chew the idea into smaller bites.

"So, you're here to help me out, are you?" he says, finally.

"Figured we might help each other."

"What makes you think I need the help?"

"Anyone stupid enough to use Billy Wise to steal from Big Man needs all the help he can get."

Mouth huffs out something like a laugh and shakes his head.

"You're missing something, Detective."

"I'm missing lots of things, Randy. Muscle mass. Youthful optimism. I'd settle for a cigarette."

"Not talking about cigarettes."

"I misplaced my faith in humanity a while back. You seen that lying around someplace?"

"You're missing information."

"Yeah? What kind?"

"You think you can bargain. You think your friends are coming. You think they're out there waiting for a phone call. Sweet. And a little sad, you thinking we'd just let something like that slide." He lets me look at him in silence for a second or two, just so he can see my face change. "Staking out the freeway exit? Come on. We took care of it, okay? You don't have any friends now. Important you know that." Mouth pivots a little and pushes his face out the window into the wind. "No one is coming. Understand? Everyone is gone. And you've already lost your job. Again. You're playing for your life now, Detective."

Mouth retracts himself back into the pickup and says something to the fat raccoon that Ray might have been able to hear if he were paying closer attention. If he was paying attention, he might be able to yank the sawed-off by the barrel right out of Mouth's hands.

But he's not paying attention. He's inside himself now, his attention falling away from the moment, back down into the well of empty space where there is no clawing wind, only the howling stillness of inevitability. *No one is coming.*

Desolation wraps him, looking for a way in.

Everyone is gone. No one is coming.

Stretch never even made it on to the freeway. Ray's phone call had given Donny a bad feeling. He'd watched Stretch's eyes soak in the truth and had known the game was up. Donny had decided to take Stretch out right then, before the car was rolling and everything got complicated. Then he took care of Billy in the back seat. Now Donny's in the wind, two bullets lighter and working on the story about how he never left his bedroom.

And it was Ray's phone call that had started the music; he'd put everything into motion. Maybe Stretch had taken the hint and maybe he hadn't, but Donny sure had.

Which makes it all Ray's fault. All of it is on him. That's what he's thinking.

Everyone is gone. No one is coming.

The interior of the pickup flares as the fat raccoon opens the door and steps out, slamming it closed again. He walks around the front of the truck and squeezes himself as much as he can between the two cars so that he can press the tip of the Uzi against the front windshield of the Nissan. The guy in the back seat leans forward and smacks the barrel of the .357 against the side of Ray's face. Once. Twice. Right in the bandage. Ray winces. Ox laughs and sits back again.

Stretch is dead. You got him up in the middle of the night and killed him with a goddamned cellphone. Everyone is gone. No one is coming.

He wants to scream. He wants to set everyone on fire with his own rage and then rip Sig out of bed and start shooting. I do my best to counsel otherwise. I give him a clear back seat perspective, from his own head and shoulders rising above the seat, down to the .357 Magnum aimed through the seat at his spine, and then out through the front windshield to the business end of a submachine gun scraping the glass. I give him the whole picture. He doesn't stand a chance. He'll be dead a dozen times over before he can get his hand to the shoulder harness.

Ray's not convinced. But it's much worse than that. He doesn't care. He's tired. Defeated. He's ready to call it a night. He's ready to call it a life.

The only card I have left to play has Hell's face on it. So I lay it down for Ray to think about.

If you're going to cannonball into the next life, shouldn't Hell at least be in the splash zone? Hell gets a pass because you're too angry and full of hate for yourself to wait? Hell gets to put you down without ever getting out of the car? Way to hand him the game, Ray. Quitter. Loser. What would Marlo say? You already know what she'd say because you've heard her say it too many times to forget.

Give me a bad man over a good quitter any day.

Ray takes a breath. It's longer and deeper than he needs. He tosses his eyes up into the rearview mirror and nods his head once at the Uzi.

"When fatso out there starts shooting, how many bullets you think you're gonna catch? Thirty rounds per second gets you at least fifteen or twenty, don't you think? If I twitch wrong, you die too. That okay with you?"

It gets him a third whack in the face with the Magnum. The barrel misses the bandage and hits him in the side of his left eye. Ray jerks sideways, just like anyone would. But the fat raccoon outside doesn't see it that way. He's anticipating a lunge, so he tenses, pushing his body against the Uzi and the Uzi against the glass, moving as Ray moves. In the back seat, Ox falls sideways, covering his own head like it might do some good against a shitstorm of metal.

"Christ!" shouts Ray. "Take it easy! Take it easy!"

"This shit is as easy as you make it," says Mouth calmly.

The raccoon relaxes. Ray and Ox slowly sit back up in their seats.

Mouth points. "I want whatever you're strapping, nice and slow. Two fingers; drop it out the window. Then you're gonna come sit in here with me while the boys search your ugly-ass car. Then you're going to make a phone call to get the wheels turning on the women. While we wait, we're going to talk about the other thing."

"Drugs or dolls?"

"Cute. You're not acting like a man who wants to see the sun rise."

"Sunrises usually give me a headache."

"The headache is coming first this time."

"When do I get what I came for?"

"When I'm satisfied."

"How do I know they're not dead? How do I know you won't off me as soon as I make the call?"

"You don't."

"Don't like those rules much, Mouth."

"Tough shit. Let's have the metal. Real slow."

"I'm not here to give you guns. You've got too many of those already and they're all pointed at me. Look." Ray holds up both hands like he wants to play pattycake. "If you see a gun in my hand, you can shoot me. How's that? We're here to trade, so let's trade already and then go home. Somewhere out there is a bottle of sweet vermouth calling your name. I want what I came for. Where are they?"

Mouth rotates his shoulders just enough to make eye contact with Ox.

All it takes is a nod. Ray never sees it coming.

ONE HUNDRED THIRTY-SEVEN

He's fast for a beast of burden.

While I'm worrying about the Uzi in front of me, Ox turns his left arm into a crowbar and pulls my neck back against the headrest, cutting off the air. I stop caring so much about the Uzi and get both hands involved to keep my face from turning blue. Turns out that's exactly what Ox wants. Before I have time to think, his right meat hook is inside my coat yanking Sig out of the holster. He keeps the pressure on my airway as he reaches around to pat down my abdomen and both hips. He's got more leverage that I've got strength in my fingers. Not much I can do but suffocate.

I give up trying to loosen his arm and flail my hands backward for his eyes. I miss those but find an ear and give it a hard twist. It hurts him enough to turn the air back on. It also makes him mad. He shoves my gasping face hard against the steering wheel. The Nissan horn bleats out a long objection as both of his hands take a quick tour of my back waistline for other weapons.

I stop resisting and start coughing. Ox keeps my face mashed against the wheel, handing Sig through the open window to the raccoon who hands it through the pickup window to Mouth. Ox removes the pressure and resumes his place in the back seat long enough to reclaim the .357 and come forward again, slamming the barrel into the side of my head like he's trying to pound a nail into a fence post. He gets in five good hits before I'm almost able to grab the gun.

I'm so close.

Ox pulls away. He's starting to appreciate the risk of acting out of anger over a sore ear. Maybe he can see the fat raccoon ready to blow out the windshield. He'd put us both down just to keep me from getting a gun I can use.

Ox gives me a final shove into the steering wheel and collapses into the back seat.

I'm at risk of blacking out. I focus on the pain to stay conscious. My hand goes to the brand-new throbbing hole in my head and comes back slick and red. Outside in the wind, fatso is laughing like he's stumbled into the funniest show in town.

"You could have just given it up like I asked," says Mouth through the window.

I turn and look at him. He waggles Sig in the air like a toy. I try to speak, but the words come out as a spasm of coughs. My throat feels like an old shoe on the freeway. It hurts to breathe.

"Didn't catch that," says Mouth.

"I want. To talk. To Hell. Tell him. I have. A deal."

"A deal. You have a deal, do you? What deal is that?"

Another spasm seizes my throat. I keep my hand pressed against my head to try to stop the bleeding. My stomach has seen this movie and wants out. Getting sick all over myself is a real possibility.

"A prize for the mantel," I say eventually. "Something… It's something he wants more than anything."

"What's that?"

"Access."

"Oooooo," Mouth mocks. "Sounds important. Access to what?"

"I make the offer to Hell. In person. You learn when he learns. That is, if he wants you to learn."

I can see Mouth thinking it through, trying to weigh risk and reward. Trying to guess what in the hell it is I'm talking about. If he figures it out, I'll be impressed. Because I have no idea.

"Fuck you," he says.

"Why not let him decide? Call him up. Get him out here."

"Enough of this shit," he says, looking at Ox. "Get him out, search him and turn the car inside out."

I can feel the bag of muscle shift toward me from the back seat. Outside, raccoon repositions himself against the car and the muzzle against the windshield. I brace for pain, looking for places to grab hold.

Garrett's phone dings and glows to life on the dashboard.

"Speak of the Devil," I croak. "Your boss has something to say."

I keep both hands in the air, leaning forward in the seat so I can read. The green bubbles are coming in rapid succession, like gas escaping the muck at the bottom of a cesspool.

Thanks for the help Ray
Couldn't have done any of this without you
The girls are fine
We made sure they finished breakfast
Your cop friend lost his appetite. Sorry
Give Marlo my best
And tell Mouth I prefer Churchill martinis

All I can do is stare at the thing. The car smells like blood. My mind reaches out for Raffi Santiago and brings back a picture of what he must look like now. Stretch and Raffi dead in one night. Because of me. I did that. My stomach flips over and an acid slug of bile climbs my throat looking for the exit. Mouth is shouting.

"I said give me the fucking phone!"

Ox knocks me in the head with his elbow and stretches an arm into the front seat, snatching Garrett's phone off the dash and tossing it through both open windows to Mouth. Mouth fumbles it and disappears under the dash to pick it up. I watch his big ugly fish hole move as he reads. His expression corkscrews into confusion. He scrolls up to read the whole thread. I let him finish. It's almost all I can do to keep from vomiting. I start talking instead.

"It means we've both been fucked," I say. Mouth looks up.

"You, maybe."

"Me? Oh, I'm definitely fucked. But that's not news." I point at the phone in his hand. "The news is that you're fucked too, Mouth. Probably your whole crew. Hell's got the women. Why does he need either of us now? He doesn't. I'm guessing you wouldn't know a Churchill Martini if someone dumped one over your head."

I can tell he has no idea. I can tell that this is the question he didn't know how to ask me. I give him a second or two to answer, then I educate the ignorant.

"No vermouth," I say. It hurts to smile. I give him one anyway.

Mouth's face is slack as the gears inside grind slowly. I keep pushing.

"He's done with you, Mouth. He knows you and Billy have been skimming Big Man's product. He just texted your pink slip."

Confusion bleeds away into fear. It's like someone pulled a plug inside his throat and all the blood wants out of his face.

"Looking a little pale, pal. You need a chance to lie down for a while. I think maybe that chance is coming sooner than later. Big Man's got a pillow just for you."

Anger spikes some fresh color into Mouth's cheeks. His too-small eyes harden beneath a glaze of fear-fueled hate and his over-sized teeth emerge from beneath his lips like tombstones in a crowded cemetery. He stiff-arms my gun out into the cold so that I'm staring Sig straight in the eye. *Nothing personal,* says Sig.

"This is going to feel good," says Mouth. "Splitting open that face."

"How about we just split the drugs, instead? We could both stick it to Hell for a change. A brick for each and we don't look back. It'd buy you the plane tickets you're gonna need and some spending money on the other side. It gets me a retirement that sucks just a little bit less. That might feel just as good as putting me down and getting nothing in return. Maybe better."

A hitch in his breath, then he makes up for it with a soft laugh.

"You're pathetic," he says. "You'll say anything."

"True. Guess I'd have to show you for you to believe me."

"Guess so."

"I can do that. But I want some assurance, Mouth. We each get half, you give me what I came for, and I get to see another sunrise or two. Can we agree on that much?"

"Not going on a fucking goose chase with you, man."

"Don't have to. I can show it to you right now." Mouth's little eyes get a little bigger. "Do we have a deal?"

I look at him looking at me, trying to find the catch. I notice that Sig is getting a lazy eye, drifting sideways. I keep pushing.

"Jesus Christ, Mouth. How hard can it be? Help me help us. Can we split the smack or not?"

Mouth pulls Sig back inside the truck.

"Okay," he says. "Sure. Let's see what you've got?"

"Tell me where they are first."

"What, the cat and the crybaby?"

"Yeah."

"In the trunk of a car."

"I know that much. Where's the car?"

Mouth points Sig through the windshield beyond the trailer to the darker depths of *Deke's Auto Scrap & Salvage.*

"Car's right back in there. Now. Your turn."

"I need to know if they're alive."

"Looked pretty fuckin' alive to me. Last time I saw them. I've been on your ass ever since. But, you know. It's a dangerous world."

"I need to see them."

"Fork over the shit. You can see them all you want."

"How do I know that's true?"

"Because you put us here on the honor system with this deal. That shit works both ways. Let's get to it or we pick up where I left off."

I start to lean sideways, but Mouth has a problem with that. He makes the sound you make for a toddler reaching for a vase or a dog squatting on the carpet.

"I'm not stupid. Just tell me where it is."

"Glove box," I say with a nod.

Mouth jerks his head at Ox who leans forward, stretching a hand over the passenger seat to the glove box. It opens. He grabs the bag with the brick inside and hands it behind me through the window. Mouth stretches out into the wind to grab it.

Time slows and stretches, elongating into the future.

In this new, evolving moment, Mouth is exposed. Vulnerable. Sig is still in the picture, but temporarily aimless as Mouth reaches. The wind blows just a little harder. It occurs to me that this might be my only chance to do some damage.

Marlo is in my head, reclined, eyes half open, tubes snaking out of her arm. I'd moistened her lips with a wet paper towel. I'd told her she deserved better. I wasn't talking about her pancreas. She knew what I meant. I just didn't know she knew.

You deserve a second chance, Marlo.

People who think they deserve a second chance have usually wasted their first, Ray. We deserve what we settle for. You see what you want in life, and you go after it. You grab what you can while it's in front of you and you leave the regrets behind. I lived the hell out of my life. I regret nothing. You've still got some time on the meter. I suggest you use it.

My right-hand fingers are sticky with blood. I separate them, ready to make a lunge for Sig.

Mouth stretches. He gets his fingers on the brick. The moment lingers in the wind. Then it blows away. Sig and the brick retract into the pickup. I don't have to wait long for the inevitable.

"Good," says Mouth. "Now where's the other one."

"We had a deal."

"So sue me. Give it up –no lies, no games –and I'll let you go get your fucking cat. Okay? There's your deal."

"We were going to split…"

"I'm gonna split your face, okay?" Sig is back out in the cold, pointing at my face. "That's what we're splitting tonight if you don't cough it up. Is it in the car?"

"Yes."

"Where?"

"Goddamnit!" I hit the steering wheel like it's to blame for everything.

"Where?" he says again with a laugh.

"Taped to the engine block."

Mouth juts his head out toward the raccoon. "Engine block. Check it out."

He gets a quick nod in return. Raccoon lets the Uzi hang to his side and gives two sharp knocks on the hood.

"We had a deal," I say again. My head is still bleeding. I push my hand against the wound. "I need the money. I'm out of a job."

"You're about to be out of a life. Pop the fucking hood."

I lean forward and pull the hood release. Raccoon stuffs his ten stubby fingers in the crack and finds the latch. Then he pushes the hood up into the wind like he's hoisting a sail. And disappears behind.

You, me and my pancreas are out of second chances, Ray. You're only going to get one. Don't wait around for another.

ONE HUNDRED THIRTY-EIGHT

He's already in a better place. Everything has stopped hurting. Pain is a luxury reserved for the living. It's for people who think they'll have to endure it. You have to care about pain to feel it. The more certain a man is he's about to die, the less the pain matters.

So Ray's not feeling a thing.

He lets go of the hood release and leans slow and easy back into the driver's seat. Easy enough to do. Harder to make it look like your hands aren't busy. His left drops beside the driver's seat for the recline lever. His right hand finds the blue duct tape grip of Hawkeye's .38 Special under the seat.

His eyes close in a long blink and he takes a last full breath. For anyone else, this is where the prayer goes.

Left hand and right hand, working together in one, fluid movement. Important to grab with the right before pulling with the left. Once you pull, there's no going back.

Ray grips the .38 and yanks the recline lever. The driver's seat rockets backward onto Ox's knees, putting Ray's head in the vicinity of the man's lap. Ox doesn't think. He reacts. Pure reflex. He doesn't extract his arms from beneath the seatback now mashing against his legs. He simply fires the magnum in blind surprise, blowing a hole in the floor of the Nissan.

Upside down to Ox, Ray jams Hawkeye's Special up into the soft spot that sits right behind the chin. He twitches a sticky red finger and sends a .38 caliber bullet up through Ox's soft pallet and into whatever he's got for a brain, dropping him sideways onto the back seat.

From the pickup, Mouth shouts in alarm, wrenching his torso sideways in his seat, angling Sig out the window and behind him at the back seat of the Nissan.

Ray needs to be lower, below the window line, but the seat is propped up on the knees of a dead man. That makes him a reclining duck. He swings the .38 toward the pickup, but not nearly fast enough. Mouth has the shot and Ray knows it.

What Mouth doesn't have is a bullet in Sig's chamber.

Mouth squeezes the trigger like he means it, but the Sig Saur is a step behind, quietly feeding a first round from the magazine up into the empty chamber. Another squeeze of the trigger would do the trick, but Mouth has already lost his aim, falling sideways onto the driver's seat as he tries to avoid a duct-taped .38 Special targeting his head. Both guns fire at once, missing wildly. Mouth reaches behind his head, fumbling for the doorlatch with one hand and firing with the other. He opens the driver's door and tries to one-arm backstroke his way outside, firing Sig with every kick.

Ray tries to find an angle on Mouth that's not already full of flying lead. What he finds instead is the Granada in the rearview mirror, all doors opening, guns emerging first. The back window of the Nissan atomizes in a spray of glass. Ray yanks at the door lever, pushing hard. The door swings less than a foot before smacking against the pickup. In front of him, a fat raccoon moves out from behind the hood of the Nissan, trying to manage his adrenaline and the Uzi swinging from its strap. The man's eyes are as wild and as wide as the rest of him. Ray rams the .38 forward through the open window and sends a bullet into Raccoon's chest. He goes down hard with his finger on the trigger.

The Uzi lets fly like a sprinkler in June.

ONE HUNDRED THIRTY-NINE

I do my best to curl up in a ball and use the car around me as a flimsy shield against Armageddon. The wind has turned ear-splittingly loud and full of metal. From all the shouting behind me, I'm guessing the Granada is full of people again. The Nissan windshield gives up the ghost and the pickup windshield does the same, turning the air to glass.

Another long burst and the Uzi goes quiet. Just the cold air now, rushing to get out of Dodge.

I lift my head up and steal a glance out the window. Raccoon is toes up. I peek into the cab of the pickup. Empty except for the abandoned sawed-off shotgun Mouth traded for Sig.

I look in every direction. I figure I've got fewer seconds than fingers before Mouth pops up in one of the Nissan windows and takes my head off.

I hear new, careful sounds from the Granada. They don't know if I'm dead or playing dead. I can feel the hand signals flying in the wind between Mouth and his crew. They'll come at me from different directions. Distract me from the left and kill me from the right. Make a small sound in front and a great big sound behind. I've seen this movie more than once. I'm missing the feedbag full of popcorn and a flask of Forester.

I figure playing dead just brings everybody in and gets me killed all the sooner, so I throw myself onto the safety glass in the passenger seat and push open the door with my fingers. The wind closes it right back in my face, but I make sure to get Hawkeye's gun wedged in the crack. I fire a round at the Granada just to let them know I'm still a threat. The wheelman is climbing out, mask still on. He holds his ground and fires back twice. He's two for two in the strike zone, one slug punching through the door about an inch from my face and the other shattering the passenger window, covering me with more glass.

I do my best to survey the window frames around me for Mouth. The single light on its pole outside the office trailer sways like the mast of a sailboat in high seas, turning absolutely everything into a weaving shadow of someone who wants to pull my plug and send me up into the big dream.

I'm not getting any advance warning. I'll see him when I see him. Or I won't see him at all.

Another peek back at the Granada. Both front doors are wide open. Left to themselves, they'd slam closed in the wind. They don't, which means there's one guy on each side of the car keeping them open. Both back doors are closed. Makes me think Hell is inside playing it safe, waiting for all the noise to stop before he troubles himself to climb out and plant a flag in my chest. Awfully chicken shit for a goliath psychopath. I plan on telling that to his face right before I put a hole in it.

But no one is moving or shooting. Best guess is that Mouth is out there squatting in the line of fire. Wouldn't want to accidentally shoot the crew boss. If I'm right, that puts Mouth crouching somewhere near the Nissan's right taillight, on his way up the passenger side to give me a taste of my own gun. If I'm wrong…

I don't wait to find out. I sit up quickly and spin in place, swinging the .38 over the back of the passenger seat. I can see the hump of Mouth's back, creeping around third base and headed for home just as I suspected.

The sudden crunch of safety glass in the seat gives me up. I can see him start to flatten against the right rear tire to take away my angle. But lowering his back only raises the top of his head above the window line. A warning shout from the Granada. The wheelman starts to unfold from behind the open door, bringing his gun hand into position.

Below me I can see Mouth's body react. I've got the shot for maybe another half-second. So I take it.

Click.

Who goes to a high-stakes heroin deal with only four bullets in the gun? Maybe someone with a cheeseball addiction and an eyelid tattoo and a blue duct-tape grip. It's a good lesson I'll never have to learn.

Mouth drops out of sight and the Granada boys put me into something like the shooting gallery at the Illinois State Fair. I twist away and dive blindly for the back seat but it's already full. I end up wedged between the front seats looking out the shattered back window. On the back seat, Ox lay thoroughly perforated and bleeding beneath a glittery blanket of windshield. Without any bullets, I'm left to throwing handfuls of safety glass at anyone who tries to shoot me.

My cheekbone and the seeping hole in my head recognize the .357 Magnum that Ox is still holding in his hand. I wrench it free and put two rounds across the yard. Both Granada boys take the hint and duck away. The next shot is for Mouth, still flat on the ground and trying to inchworm backward out of the crossfire. It's a low-percentage shot. I'm too far back and he's too low. If I could reach the back door latch and open the thing just a crack, then I could improve those odds considerably. Problem is, my left hand can't reach the latch, which makes opening the door and holding a gun both right-hand jobs. I've only got one of those.

My head is still a leaky faucet. Gravity wants to divert the blood into my right eye. I use my left hand to smear it all another direction before taking possession of the Magnum. I aim for where I expect Mouth to be once the door is open. My right hand stretches for the latch, ready to pull the lever and then push with my fingertips in a single motion. I'll be lucky not to shoot my own hand off.

I never get the chance.

ONE HUNDRED FORTY

Turns out the chain link around *Deke's Auto Scrap and Salvage* is no match for a 1978 Monte Carlo with tinted windows, a reasonably new engine and a meticulously restored interior, moving at something in the neighborhood of thirty miles an hour at the point of contact. The gate explodes into the yard, the right side coming off its hinges and spinning sideways through the air like the ace of spades headed for the hat, smashing the Granada's back window.

I can't see who's behind the wheel, but I don't have to. I recognize the long arm sticking out of the driver's window, working that Glock like a New Year's Eve party favor. Stretch is punching holes in the wind and not much else, but he's making enough noise to ruin some underwear and send everyone scrambling. All three Granada boys are out of the car and running for cover, turning and shooting as they go. The chicken from the back seat is big. But he's not that big.

Where the hell is Hell?

Mouth must figure it's now or never. He rises like a phoenix from beneath the window frame, rotating my way. He's aiming for the front seat, where all the noisy glass is. It takes him a second to see that I'm not there anymore. I grip the Magnum with both hands and fire through the glass.

Now he's a phoenix with one wing, headed back for the ashes. Mouth jolts, stiff-armed and spinning, clutching at the new hole in his right shoulder. He packs six or seven bad words into one unintelligible scream and then gives it all up for gravity. His gun-hand knocks hard against the open window frame on the way down. Turns out that was the last straw for five fingers on an arm already having a bad day. Sig drops, hitting me in the face on the way to the back seat. I'm so used to guns hitting me in the face I don't even flinch.

Sig and I stare at each other for a half-second reunion. That's more than enough time because I'm only half-believing. Part of me expects to wake up in a recliner under an empty bottle and a thirsty cat. Could be the head wound talking. It's the gunfire outside that sharpens me up again.

I grab Sig, pull the door latch, and wriggle the rest of me into the back seat. I make my way over Ox and out the door, dropping down on top of Mouth's legs. He's on his face and half-crawling, still coming to terms with the new wind tunnel in his scapula. He's not expecting company and starts kicking.

"Mack!"

I look across the yard to see Stretch taking cover behind the open door of the Monte Carlo. For an instant I see Billy Wise in the back seat, diving for the floor. Donovan is on the other side of the car exchanging bullets with one of Mouth's crew who has squeezed himself into a good position underneath the Granada. It's a tight fit, but he could have done worse for himself: there is no easy way to hit him from the Monte Carlo without lying flat on the ground and taking the semi-automatic spray head-on.

The other two Granada boys have made it all the way back to the office trailer, taking positions in darkness. I can see they've taken out the front windshield of the Monte Carlo. Stretch is crouching, shooting and shouting at the same time.

"Mack!"

I've already got my hands too full to pay him any attention.

Mouth keeps kicking and tries to flip himself over. My balance goes sideways, but I right myself and get enough leverage to ram an elbow down into his open shoulder. The elbow is too big for the bullet hole, but it settles him down anyway. Mouth flattens out on the cold ground and cries like a baby in need of attention. So I give him some. I shove one gun behind each of his ears: Sig on the right, Magnum on the left. I lean in so he doesn't miss anything important.

"Cry all you like, Randy. Keep still and maybe we both get to see that sunrise. Move once and I'll see it without you. Got that?"

"Fuck!"

I take it as a yes. The guy under the Granada lays down another carpet of metal. Stretch is still working the crouching giraffe routine. He yells again.

"Mack!"

He points at the Granada in front of him. He wants me to take out the threat. He thinks I've got a shot. He's wrong about that. Sitting on Mouth, I'm too high and the guy with all the bullets is too far under the passenger side of the car. I'd have to climb off Mouth and lie flat on the ground. Might work if I was alone, but I'm not alone. Mouth will make sure I get a third eyeball. Best I can do is lay down some cover so Stretch and Donny can get out from behind their doors.

Gunfire suddenly from the back of the yard. One of the Granada boys has climbed up onto the roof of the trailer. He's got the high ground and he's going to make the most of it. He targets the Monte Carlo. Stretch and Donny make themselves even smaller than before. I'm sure I'd get the same treatment, but the hood of the Nissan is still up and blocking the view. The guy underneath the Granada starts up again. Now Stretch and Donny are getting it high and low. I can feel the momentum in this fight start to shift back to where it started.

I keep the Magnum up against Mouth's left ear. Then I put Sig to work on the Granada, one bullet for each tire. First shot misses, but then I'm two for three. The driver's side of the car collapses down to the rims, leaving no room for a person except maybe on the far edge of the passenger side. Stretch takes the lesson and blows out the right rear tire, knocking the Granada down another couple of inches in the back.

The man underneath starts screaming. The words are foreign, Russian maybe, but I don't need a translator. I know bone-crushing pain in every language. The guy is now inside a Detroit-iron waffle press, and he doesn't like it. But his finger still works. The semi-auto belches in undisciplined bursts from under the car. Now it's the Monte Carlo's turn to lose some tires. Stretch and Donovan are quickly back in the car, trying to keep their shoes from bleeding. A fresh round of incoming fire from the roof of the trailer reminds them to keep their heads below the dashboard. Billy's ugly mug pops up once in the back seat and then disappears again.

The bursts from under the Granada get shorter and less frequent. I can't see the shooter anymore, but I can see the tip of that gun. He keeps trying to swing it my direction, but he can't move. He's too hemmed in. Then the bullets stop entirely. Turns out the guy's packed more dirty Russian words than ammo, so he keeps those coming. That and the screaming in pain.

Stretch is unfolding his legs from the front seat to resume his crouch behind the door. One of the Granada boys plants a slug into the hood and everybody ducks. Donovan returns fire.

"You okay?" I shout.

"Oh, I'm great, Mack. I'm terrific. Hey, you think maybe we can call this in now? I mean if it's *fucking* okay with you?"

The Russian under the car seems to think we're talking to him. Donny and the Granadas keep shooting the breeze.

"Knock yourself out," I say. "I'm all out of secrets. I gave my last one to you."

We look at each other across the yard. He knows what I mean. Stretch shakes his head.

"You're wrong," he shouts into the wind. Mouth wails and wriggles beneath me. I push the Magnum in a little tighter behind his ear and shout back.

"You sure about that?"

"You're crazy, Mack."

"That's what everybody says."

Stretch nods and reaches in for the radio. He has to straighten his spine a little to do that.

Sometimes a man forgets his own height.

ONE HUNDRED FORTY-ONE

Half of Stretch's left cheek seems to tear away and disappear in the wind. He's falling sideways away from the car before the sound of the shot even registers as something of consequence.

Now the yard is as cold and quiet as death. Nothing but the wind. I can't hear him hit the ground. But I can feel it in my chest. He lies there like a long lump of dirt.

I feel a surge of rage again, building in my heart, pumping extra blood into each trigger finger. I want nothing more than to make Casey Randall Sweet pay the ultimate price for my misjudgment. They all line up in my head for a turn. Everyone I have ever failed. Stretch and Raffi Santiago. Nadia. Mila. Danika. Suri. Marlo too. Always Marlo. Why does Mouth get to keep drawing oxygen? I push the guns in hard on either side of his neck like I'm trying to make the barrels touch.

Mouth doesn't respond. He's limp. He doesn't move at all.

Stretch, suddenly, screaming and holding his face with both hands.

I'm up and running without thinking. I aim both guns in the general direction of the trailer and lay down some disincentive, diving behind the driver's door of the Monte Carlo. Incoming fire pocks the hood. I catch Donny's eyes across the front seats, wide with alarm.

"Goddamnit, Mack!"

"He already has," I say. I pull Stretch back behind the door and point to the radio. "Call it in."

It takes him a second, but then Donovan lunges for the radio as I turn my attention to assess Stretch, first throwing a glance toward Mouth who hasn't moved a muscle. I can't help but wonder if he's still among the living. Then I don't care.

Stretch bellows up at me, his cheek hanging open and gushing. I open his coat and his shirt and rip at his undershirt until enough of it pulls free that I can use it to wrap his face. I tie it off hard and then pull at the scarf around his neck like I'm trying to start a lawnmower. I wrap his face up as best I can. It covers most of the mouth, but I give him a hole for the nose and one for his left eye. Then I zip him back up. I grab Stretch's hand and hold it against the wound.

"Push hard," I say. "Keep pushing. Help is coming."

Stretch screams in pain. Behind me, Donny is barking into the mic. Officer down. Our location. Multiple active shooters. Immediate back-up and ambulance requested. The works. I try to keep Stretch's spirits up.

"The bullet cut your face open, but it didn't stick around to do anything worse. It's all about the bleeding. Keep the pressure on and you're coming out of this with a new nickname."

Something is wrong. I feel it more than I know it. Out of everything that is terribly wrong in my life, something is worse than I expect. The feeling comes with another wave of dizziness, and I fall back against the open door. The yard is swimmy and the urge to vomit is rising. I have to focus to beat the wave back down. The guy on the roof of the trailer sends over another bullet, blowing apart the sideview mirror above my head. The guy under the Granada keeps screaming Russian gibberish. Donny keeps barking into the radio. Stretch keeps vocalizing his agony. All of that is the same.

Something is wrong.

A new motion in the periphery. For a guy with a face like a fish, Mouth knows how to play possum. He's suddenly up and loping toward the trailer. I grapple for the guns I dropped so I could play nurse. I fling my arm around the open door and send a bullet Mouth's way, but the man keeps moving.

The possum stops at the dead raccoon. His one good arm reaches for the Uzi. The Granada boys can see what's happening and get busy giving him some cover. The Monte Carlo may as well be a tin can on a fence post. Donny crouches lower in the seat and puts some more muscle into his voice.

"Officer down! Multiple active shooters! Request immediate assistance!"

Mouth yanks the Uzi free. Hiding behind the door gives me no clear shot. If I want the shot, I lose my head. Best I can do is fire blind and hope for the best. I give him both barrels from under the door.

I wait and listen for the Uzi.

Nothing.

Stretch moaning. The Russian cursing his fate. Donny shouting into the radio.

No Uzi.

Something is wrong. I venture a peek.

Mouth is flat on his face, Uzi at his side. He's not gripping the hole in his shoulder. A bullet from the trailer hits six inches away from my leg, opening a hole in the icy dirt.

"Repeat! Request immediate assistance!"

Stretch moans. I look over at Donny curled up in the front seat gripping the radio, his eyes unfocused.

"Repeat! Multiple active shooters! Officer down!"

Mother Penguin used to tell us that the Kingdom of God belongs not to the right, but to the righteous. Maybe so. But when it comes to Donovan Howe, I'll put the right in righteous six days a week and twice on Sunday. Nothing feels quite like being right, not even salvation.

ONE HUNDRED FORTY-TWO

Look at him. Even with a leaky head and a squishy gut, Ray's in the game. He's got more strength now than he's had all night.

He sets the Sig Saur carefully on Stretch's leg for safe keeping, rotates his body up and into the front seat of the Monte Carlo, keeping his head below the dash and the Magnum in his left hand at the ready. He grabs Donovan's gun by the barrel and pulls it like he's working a slot machine until it wrenches free. Donny never sees it coming. He reacts in confusion, thrusting the radio mic forward into Ray's face like it might spray something toxic.

"Wha... what the fuck, man?"

"Funny thing about radios, Donny." Ray grabs the mic and gives it a stiff yank, sending it tumbling down into the foot well. "You have to push the little button for anyone to hear what you're saying."

"I was pushing the goddamned button."

"No, you're pushing *my* button, not *the* button. If you'd been pushing *the* button, I'd've been hearing a response from Dispatch. Only voice I hear is yours. How long have you been on the take?"

"What? I..."

"Cellphone."

"What?"

"You need to learn some new words, Donny. I've watched a lot of people die today and I don't mind you being next. Give me your cellphone."

"This is your career, Mack," he says, twisting his face in ruddy rage. "This is fucking prison time. Understand me? I will make it my mission..."

Ray pivots the Magnum a degree and blows out the passenger window, obliterating the sideview mirror. Donny jolts in place and finishes his mission statement in a sharp, yelping scream. The guy on the roof of the trailer hears the shot and instinctively returns fire. Donny digs furiously in his pocket for his phone.

"Drop it in the seat," says Ray, blindly giving Stretch a soft kick in the shin. "Still with me Stretch?" Stretch groans a response. "Good. Keep the pressure on. Donny, I'm not asking again."

Donny drops the phone in the driver's seat.

"I will not rest," he growls, "until…"

"You're going to get us all fucking killed, man!"

"That you, Billy?" asks Ray, pocketing the phone. "Thought maybe you were asleep back there."

"Fuck you. I never should have fucking helped you. This is bullshit, man. We're all gonna die."

"Figured that out, did you? Glad you're paying attention, Billy. You're just in time for a lesson on how to work a police radio. But first…"

Ray levels Donovan's Glock, sets down the Magnum, and hooks a finger through the pair of handcuffs Stretch keeps in the side of the door. He holds one silver ring out across the seat.

"Left wrist. I'm asking nicely, Donny. You think I'm all wrong, I get it. The feeling's mutual. We'll let the suits sort it out."

"Your fuck-buddies at IAD, you mean."

"I don't work there anymore. You're right about me being done. You're my last arrest. You can Mirandize yourself; you know the words. And until the cavalry shows up, you are one with this car, just like the rest of us. I'll give you the whole front seat. If you…"

Two more rounds from the rooftop. They both have a full-body clench and one of the headlights explodes.

"If you want to wait for backup with a shattered kneecap, we can do it that way too. I'll even let you get a tourniquet ready. But make your decision so we can all get back not getting shot in the head by the Granada boys."

"I'm gonna be there, Mack," says Donovan without moving his lips. "When they…"

"Yeah. I've heard this story before, Donny." Ray points the Glock in the general direction of his left knee. "Let's go."

Donovan slowly holds out his left wrist. Ray brings the cuff down sharply with a practiced snap, yanking the other end toward the steering wheel. Donovan resists, pulling away. Ray gives another sharp yank on the cuffs toward the driver's side of the car.

But he feels the yank in his own leg. Outside, Stretch is clutching and pulling. Hard to understand a man whose face is so tightly wrapped, but Ray recognizes his own name.

"Mack!"

He tries to keep a solid grip on the cuffs and hold his own in the tug of war as he looks down at Stretch. The man's hand is slick with blood, like he'd found a wet red glove to press against his face.

His eyes are wide and panicked.

He's fumbling for Sig, still perched on his leg.

Donovan pulls hard at the cuffs. Ray's left grip isn't what it used to be. He can feel the metal ring leaving his grasp. He doesn't look. He lets it go. Donovan doesn't matter. Not anymore.

Funny. But in a sad way. A man now with so many guns within reach and no time to use any of them.

ONE HUNDRED FORTY-THREE

It's the Granada wheelman. No mask now. Broad, handsome features beneath a wool skullcap. Tall and black as space, wide shoulders hung with long, branch-like arms. He's standing maybe ten feet behind the Nissan. In his left hand, Mouth's sawed-off shotgun hangs at his side. In his right, he aims a silver cannon; some fifty-caliber monstrosity that belongs in a Dirty Harry movie. The wind wants his open coat. A disbelieving laugh gets stuck in my throat.

His is the confidence that comes from a clear, unobstructed shot with rooftop cover.

Mine is the resignation that belongs to fish in a barrel.

In the time it will take me to swing Donny's Glock toward the Nissan, I will have a new hole in my face. I have two cards in a shit-for-luck hand, both of them deuces. One is the hope that the wheelman is terrible with guns. The other is the hope that he's out of bullets and doesn't know it.

There's nothing for me to do but start the ending.

As I shift my weight, I can feel Stretch moving beneath me, reaching for Sig on his leg. I can sense the wheelman move too, straightening that arm to keep it level, lifting the big, shiny thing just a little higher in the wind. I wrench my right arm up and sideways in a back-handed Hail Mary, pulling the trigger much too early, less out of any sense that I can hit this guy and more because pulling a trigger is the last thing I can do in this life. I may as well do it before the lights go out.

Two shots, almost simultaneous.

The wheelman drops where he stands.

I look. Stretch is cringing, curled up against the car, nothing in his hand but his own bloody face.

Sig is on the ground. I pick it up. Cold as ice.

Two more shots from the roof puts me back behind the door, confused and not breathing, looking at the dark and windy world behind Stretch Martin's Monte Carlo.

Through the busted gate, across the street, a black Dodge Intrepid is smoking a tailpipe. Rafael Santiago stands up slowly from behind the hood.

I have things to say. Things to think. Things to understand.

Donny has other plans. I can sense him moving and I do my best to dive back inside the car for the handcuff leash. I miss it by a mile. Donny is out the passenger door and running for the back of the yard. I crawl through the front seat, a gun in each hand, and dump myself out onto the ground on the other side. By the time I'm upright, he's almost to the trailer. A shot from the roof sends him off to the right, deeper into the salvage yard.

I send a bullet from each gun up to the trailer just to buy me some space and I go after him. He's a shadow now and getting fainter with every step. Everything in me hurts again. Oxygen is playing hard to get. The sensation of wind cooling hot blood on the side of my face makes my stomach flip over. I only make it a hundred feet before I get tunnel vision and a wave of fresh nausea takes me to my knees.

I can't even catch my breath, let alone Donny. I raise Sig and try to aim. Not thinking, only wanting. I watch him go, now just a shadow slipping into darkness as it rounds a tower of used-to-be cars.

But then the running shadow drops. Drops hard, as if the darkness had become a wall and refused to take him. As if my wanting Donovan to stop was all that was ever necessary.

But how? Why?

It takes me a second. Then I get it.

Raffi, I think, amazed, looking back toward the black Dodge I can no longer see. Raffi at a hundred yards through the wind and the dark. He must have sold his soul to shoot like that.

A sound from above. Hot alarm floods my brain, pricking up the hairs on my neck. I am an easy target for the shooter on the roof. I drop and roll, then scramble up and half crawl, half crab my way back to the Nissan, cringing in anticipation of the shot that is only a finger-twitch away. It never comes.

I jackknife myself between Nadia's Nissan and Mouth's pickup. I try to stop from panting so I can listen.

Nothing.

The lone light pole in front of the *Deke's Auto Scrap and Salvage* office keeps all the shadows dancing. The roof is dark and still.

I scoot backward to the front windows of the Nissan and the pickup where, a lifetime ago, Mouth and I played our little games. Looking through the Nissan I can see Stretch on the ground, rolling back and forth and holding his face. I want to shout that I'm still in the game, just to keep his spirits up. Just to keep him fighting. I even open my mouth a little.

But then Billy's body steals my thunder.

He's stretched out behind the Monte Carlo, both hands still in their cuffs, reaching for the road beyond.

Most of that story writes itself. I go chasing after Donny into the dark and, suddenly alone, Billy does what comes naturally to a man of his experience. He throws himself in the front seat, wriggles out the open passenger door and makes a run for it, hoping the Granada boy on the roof has his hands full.

It's the ending I can't figure. Easy enough to chalk up another kill for Raffi. Except that I never heard the shot. Come to think of it…

The answer hits me like a clown with an extra pie. My whole body stiffens. I want to start shouting.

"Mack!"

Raffi's voice, in a harsh whisper. I turn and squint for the Dodge. The car is still there, but no longer idling. I don't see Raffi.

"Mack!"

Another quarter turn and I make him on my side of the road, in the trees up against the newly gateless fence. I hold up a hand to keep him where he is, then I go back the way I came, slipping myself from between the Nissan and the pickup. I crawl beneath the front bumper of the pickup and then make a dash into the darkness along the far-left side of the yard until I hit the chain-link. I stay as close to the fence as possible, detouring around piles of scrap, until I'm face-to-face with Rafael Santiago.

"You saving my life is becoming a bad habit," I tell him between pants.

"You're welcome. I've been following since the gas station."

"Thought you were dead. You never went to the diner?"

Raffi shakes his head.

"Breakfast didn't seem right. I was planning to keep my distance like you said.

I've been parked up the road, backed into a little ATV trail. I couldn't see shit, but I could hear all the noise. When you called, I figured…"

The words are little electric needles.

"I called? Me? *I* called?"

"What? Yeah."

"What the hell did I say?"

"Nothing. It was your number, man. I figured you needed help." Raffi jerks his head at the carnage in the yard behind me. "I think I figured right."

"I called you?"

"You saying you didn't?" Raffi cocks his head. His eyes change focus. "Mack, you're in bad shape, man. You need a hospital."

"Stretch is worse. We need to call this in."

"Already did that," he says with a chew of gum.

"What? When?"

"Just before I dropped him." He nods to the heap on the ground that used to be the Granada wheelman. "They're dispatching medical and police from Aurora. Chicago too. Won't take long. I know you said not to, but… well, fuck that, man."

My adrenals still have some gas in the tank and this news kicks them into high gear. I look over his shoulder for the Dodge and then back to him. I forget to whisper.

"Nadia, Mila," I bark. "Danika."

"In the car," he says. "Scared to death. They're not going anywhere. I took the key and gave Nadia my nine-millimeter just in case. You've got other worries, Mack. We've still got a shooter on top of that trailer to deal with. After that, you're about to get a lot of questions about why you just shot a cop in the back. Running away without a weapon, as far as I could tell."

"Two minutes ago, I was going to ask the same of you."

The faint wail of sirens swells up against the wind like a lone gull over the sound of the surf.

"Me?" Rafael is incredulous. Defensive. "I'm not threatening you, man. I'm just saying… I saw what I saw."

"I'm guessing the boys in ballistics will show otherwise."

"What…"

"No time, Raffi. Stretch needs help and I need your keys."

I nose Sig into his holster and hold out an expectant hand.

"My keys? Where are you going?"

"Straight to Hell. I think. I'll explain later. Keys. Hurry, I'm getting older over here." Raffi pulls out his keys and hands them through the fence. I trade Donny's phone. It won't fit through the hole, so I have to toss it over. Raffi plucks it out of the air with one hand.

"What's this?"

"The goods on Donovan Howe, just in case I don't come back."

"And why would that be, exactly?"

"Maybe I get a better offer, Raffi. Maybe there's more to life than springing leaks in each other and pretending it all makes sense. Go help Stretch keep the blood inside his face."

"What about the guy on the trailer?"

"Stay low and move fast, just in case. But I'm betting he's dead." I point. "Come in this way. Hug the fence line until you're even with the pickup. Then cut in that way. Get Stretch in the back seat and keep your head down. Keep an eye on the trailer if you need to but I'd worry about the opposite direction if I were you."

I don't point. You never know who's looking. No need to give away the game if you don't have to. Raffi doesn't need the finger-point anyway. He turns slowly to look directly behind him, through the trees at the hill rising above North Picking Road.

He's got a lot more questions when he turns around.

But I'm already gone.

ONE HUNDRED FORTY-FOUR

He's an easy target from behind. If he's wrong about the Granada boy on top of the trailer, it will be the last time he's ever wrong about anything.

But, right or wrong, Ray's lost all concern for who's watching from behind, me included. He only cares now about what's in front of him: the black Dodge Intrepid across the road and the hill beyond, rising up into the wind-whipped night like the stubbled hump of some beast thought to be long-extinct but that now, suddenly, seems ominously alive.

He circles around the back of the car and yanks open the driver's door. He gets three screams and a gun in his face.

"Nadia! Stop! It's me! Put it down. Everybody take a breath."

The front seat is empty. They've got Danika on the floor in the back, the two adults each folded sideways on top of her. Danika is bawling as if from beneath a pile of laundry. Nadia is the only one now upright. She's choking the grip of Raffi's Beretta with both hands and her elbows have disappeared up into her arms. The gun quivers like she's trying to squeeze the bullets out of the barrel.

"Nadia! Breathe!"

The words are a slap. She blinks. She takes in a sharp breath.

"Mack!" His name comes out locked inside a sob. "What's…"

"Hold on to something," he says.

Ray climbs in and slams the door. He starts the engine, cranks the wheel and throws the Dodge in gear, spinning the car so that it's pointed the other way. Then he gives the car as much gas as North Picking Road will tolerate.

"Mack, you're bleeding, you're… Are you…"

Ray glances in the rearview, angling it his way.

"Jesus," he breathes at the undead thing looking back. "I'd shoot me too."

"What happened?"

Ray readjusts the mirror so he can see them. Mila is upright now, pulling Danika up onto the seat. Their faces are ashen and streaked with tears.

"Still working on that," says Ray.

"Where are we going? Where are you taking us?"

"Off of this road before rush hour."

"Why?"

Ray ignores the question and tosses one of his own into the back seat.

"Where's Vladimir?"

Danika wipes her runny nose and disappears for a second beneath the seat. Then she holds up the dragon so he can see.

"There you are," says Ray. "You weren't scared, were you, pal?"

Danika sniffs.

"He wasn't scared," she says.

"That's his hungry face, then?"

She looks at the floppy red tongue. Then she nods.

"Hungry. Got it. Well, we're fresh out of bad guys, Vlad, so maybe some pizza. Will that work?"

More tears. Then a smile.

"Okay then," he says. "Pizza it is. First let me get us off this road."

The fork that splits North Picking from Hill Road is on them in an instant. Ray slows enough to make the turn, then kills the headlights and guns the engine, fishtailing up Hill Road. After a minute, he stops and turns the car around, pointing back down the way they came. He puts it in park.

Mila is suddenly uncorked. Her mother's tongue is angry and afraid, venting to anyone who will listen. Ray doesn't understand a word. He doesn't have to.

"Hang in there, kid," he says, detaching Rafael's key ring from the key in the ignition. "Tomorrow's coming."

"What are you doing?" asks Nadia. "I thought..."

Ray slips the various keys to Rafael's life in his pocket. Then he opens the door and steps outside.

The wind is alive and wailing with sirens. He feels light-headed. He wobbles in place and braces himself against the open door. Beneath him, somewhere down on North Picking, waves of sirens approach and recede. In the distance there are more. Packs of wolves on the hunt.

Ray leans back into the car and motions for Nadia. She opens the back and walks around to join him in the crook of the open door. She still has Raffi's Beretta. Her other hand hovers around his face, looking for a place to land. There isn't one. She tries to hand him the gun.

"Keep it for now," he says. "You're still in this."

"Mack, you need a hospital. What are we doing?"

"I don't have any time, Nadia. You don't either. I want you to listen to me."

Her eyes are touring his bloody head. The bandage on his cheek soaked through and peeling.

"Nadia. Listen."

"Yes. I'm listening."

"Take this car. Drive slowly. Use your blinkers. Stop at every light. Don't get pulled for something stupid. I want you to get out of Aurora. Take I-90. Head for Rockford. There's a bus station on Walton Street. Leave the car in the lot. Put the gun and the key under the seat. Lock all the doors. Do you have money?"

"Yes."

"Buy three tickets to Minneapolis. Don't wait at the bus station. Don't wait anywhere within walking distance of the bus station. Get a cab to take you to a hotel. Sleep if you can. Get everyone some food. I just committed you to pizza, so don't make me a liar. When it's time, call a different cab company to take you back to the bus station. When you get to Minneapolis, buy three tickets to the east coast." He puts one hand on each of her shoulders. "Pick a city, Nadia. Pick a life. Don't tell me what you have in mind. What I don't know I can't give up."

"Mack," she says. "What will they do? The police, I mean."

"Nothing they haven't done before. I'm looking forward to a quieter life. That's what you need to do. Get a quiet job and live a quiet life, Nadia. Stay off the news. Don't get arrested. Chicago is old and dead to you. Understand? Don't look back. Don't call anyone. You don't have any friends now. Make new ones who know you by different names. Because he'll be looking, Nadia. He has a thousand eyes and he'll be looking. He won't stop looking. Understand?"

Nadia nods once, then again, wiping her face with the back of her hand.

"Okay. Get going. Time's wasting."

Ray moves out of the way so she can have the driver's seat. She hesitates; slips her hand against the side of his neck.

"I'm sorry," she says.

"Save that for someone who deserves it. I should have let you go from the very beginning. I should have told you I'm not in the doll-finding business and shown you the door. But you had to get those eyes of yours involved. Your eyes and the rest of you along with the adorable kid and the pet dragon. I bit that hook but good. You and Big Man went sucker fishing in Lake Lonely and reeled up a whopper."

He's not expecting the kiss. It's too fast. It's there and gone, already a memory. If she had wanted to kill him, it would have been easy.

"You're a good man, Mack. A good catch. For any woman. Including me. Maybe if…" She lets it go. "You didn't deserve any of this."

"I deserved all of it and more. Maybe I'm not yet the oldest guy in the world, but I fell for the oldest trick in the book. The only ones who get to have a clean conscience in this mess are that girl in the back seat and her dragon. Be grateful you've got them to look after you."

"I am grateful. What about you?"

"What about me?"

"Who's going to watch after you?"

"I've got that covered. Get going, Nadia."

He turns and leaves her at the door. The girl is sitting at the back window, watching him doe-eyed on Mila's lap, Vladimir's tongue pressing happily against the glass.

He stops himself, just for a moment.

Then he keeps moving, pushing into the wind.

ONE HUNDRED FORTY-FIVE

I wait until Raffi's Dodge is rolling back down Hill Road. Danika waves. I raise my hand. Then I turn, yank Sig out of bed and start walking.

It's another quarter mile at least. All up hill and into the wind. I should have used the car a little longer. Another couple thousand feet. I was thinking of them: Nadia and the others. Maybe I wasn't thinking at all. Maybe a pistol whipping is not the way to kick-start an uphill hike. My lungs are nostalgic, remembering every last Camel. They want me to sit down. Maybe it's a concussion and hypothermia that finally takes me up into the big dream. A little brain swelling, a short nap on the side of the road…

Give Marlo my best, Hell had texted.

The thought fills my head. Marlo in blue flannel. Brown tendrils in the breeze. Autumn riots in the periphery and the lake behind her is burning orange and gold. The indulgence is leaving her eyes. She wants me to take the picture already. I linger in the view finder. I can't stop looking at her. Who knew the lens was a time machine? A portal. A tunnel through which my future self might crawl to be with her again in that ever-elongating moment. I'm still there, holding that lens in the breeze. Looking at her look back at me. The eyes. The mouth.

Could she see me then? My future self, beaten and bleeding, half-dead from loneliness, a man I could never have fathomed, looking at her, wanting only that the moment never end; that the sun never slip into the lake, extinguishing itself into smoldering darkness. Marlo knew everything. She saw everything that I never could. So could she see that too, as I lingered in the view finder? Could she see me back then, looking at her from here?

A hard, painful lump beneath my leg.

I remember seeing the log, half-submerged in old snow and dead scrub. I do not remember sitting down on it. Reclining would feel better. Just on the other side, where the frozen ground falls away enough to provide a little shelter from the wind. I close my eyes for another look through the view finder. Marlo is gone. All is dark. So much the better.

The wind. Relentless. It blows the tangled deadness of weeds back and forth over my fingers.

Again. Again.

It feels like the dry rasp of a tongue.

Phil.

I open my eyes.

Phil goddamnit. I push myself up off the log. It's not pretty. I put one foot in front of the other.

The big sycamore is right where we left it, a hundred feet or so down the slope, surrounded by dirty snow and dead scrub. I stop and brace myself against the trunk, waiting for my breath to catch up. Down the hill glows a carnival of pulsing red and blue light. Bursts of radio static work their way up through the trees like a flock of restless, infernal birds trying to roost.

I can see three Chicago black-and-whites jammed into the place that *Deke's* chain-link gate used to be, disco-lights spinning. One and a half Aurora cruisers are next to part of an ambulance. The stand of evergreens further down the slope keeps me from seeing much more. I can't see the Monte Carlo. I can't see the Nissan. I can see only part of the trailer. Nothing to write home about.

Hell is taller than I am. A lot taller. But he's not that tall. He's not tall enough to get the angle on Mouth. Or Donny. Or Billy. Or the rooftop Granada boy. So, then, how?

How?

Why is no slouch of a question either. It keeps yanking at my sleeve for an answer. I'm too wrapped up in *How* to give *Why* the time of day.

How? He'd have to clear those evergreens. I remember Billy's story about his pal, Itchy, taking pictures to blackmail Deke for running a chop shop. Billy said the plan went bust along with Itchy's arm and his stolen camera.

The wind gusts from behind, pulling an aching creak out of the sycamore.

The answer shows up out of nowhere, like it has always been part of the scenery. Itchy broke his arm *and* the camera. That's no coincidence. He fell on his arm *while* he was taking pictures.

I remember the squishy, something-is-wrong, you-are-not-alone feeling in my gut the last time I stood on this hill looking down at *Deke's*.

Or maybe I feel it all over again.

I spin to face uphill, pointing Sig as straight up the trunk of the tree as I can manage.

Spinning and tipping my head backward on sloping ground is about as good a recipe for vertigo as I can come up with on short notice. Up becomes down. My hands flail outward, trying to control the spin. I hit the ground shoulder first and roll, losing Sig in the process. I come to a stop soon enough but figure it's only going to take him a second or two to get me in his sight and flex his finger. I feel around for Donny's Glock in my belt. But now that too is gone.

I'm face down in the scrub, my heart beating fresh blood out of the hole in my scalp. The thing in front of me in the dirty snow is not of this place. Not a rock or a twig or a leaf.

It's an M-1 shell casing.

I roll over on my back, hoping I can look Hell in the eyes. I want to know if giants roost in giant trees. I want to be right about the world one last time before I go.

The sycamore branches are thick and tapering, forking endlessly up into the dark.

They look like roots.

ONE HUNDRED FORTY-SIX

It's a dramatic emergence from the trees at the bottom of the hill. He steps out onto the road, both guns hanging from his left forefinger. He identifies himself. Tries to. Nobody listens. They're all over him like he's trying to deliver a football to an endzone. It takes Santiago using his outside voice and both elbows to free him.

The ambulance has already left with Stretch. Awake, they say. Asking for him.

They want him to sit in a cruiser. He doesn't want to sit in a cruiser. He wants to search the yard for Jimmy's car. No one will let him. Something about falling down.

He's made his pitch for nicotine. Twice. No one's having it.

The steps to *Deke's* trailer provide the next best windbreak. They've got his head bandaged now. He looks like a revolutionary fife player in a reenactment production, cooling his heels off-set, waiting for the shooting to resume.

"I need to look," he says. "I need to find that car."

Raphael shakes his head as he pulls out a new pack of gum.

"They're searching," he says, looking down at Ray on the step. "You need to stay where you are."

"They need to check the garage back there. If it's anywhere it's in the chop shop."

"Could all be bullshit, Mack. Car could be anywhere in the state."

"Yeah." Anger now, or something like it. "Or it could be in that goddamned garage."

"Mack. Stop. They're looking. We're doing everything we can."

He recognizes the tone. He's used it himself to calm the hysterical. *We're doing everything we can.* Only it's toward no good end. Because they're usually dead in the end, whoever they're looking for. Everyone knows it. We just don't need the wailing and screaming. So, have a seat, ma'am. Have a seat, little Timmy. Try not to worry. We're doing everything we can.

A hump working for Aurora PD brings the bottle of water Raffi requested. Raffi opens it and hands it down. Then he sits on the step next to Ray.

"That guy on the roof," Raffi says, jutting his thumb up and behind. He pulls out a stick of gum longways with his teeth, like he's eating a cigarette. "Right through the top of the head."

Ray digs into his pocket and produces the M1 shell casing. Raffi takes it.

"You ever get tired of being right?" he asks.

Ray adjusts the bandage around his head and shrugs.

"You ever get tired of hitting the bullseye at the last possible second?"

Raffi turns the shell end over end in his fingers.

"M-1."

"Yeah. With a scope and a suppressor, just to keep things quiet. I'm guessing Hell gathered up the other three shells and gave up looking for this one when the sirens started to hurt his ears."

"Aurora Special Crimes is running the show," says Raffi. "Little runty guy. Bivens. Or Bevins. His boys say he's brand new on the job. Out of Wisconsin. Memorized all the rules while his mom packed him a lunch. It's a good bet he's going to take you back up the hill before they're done down here. Maybe they'll find the other shells."

"Maybe." Ray looks him in the face. They stare at each other. "He was there the whole time, Raffi. Up in that goddamned tree as Stretch and Donny and I were scoping the yard and listening to Billy yammer on about Itchy."

"Itchy?"

"Forget it. Point is, Hell could have ended things right then and there."

"But he didn't."

"No."

"Why not?"

Ray looks away at the forensics team squatting around the Granada wheelman, taking pictures and bagging Dirty Harry's gun as the wind rips the steam out of their mouths.

"I'm still working on that part," he says. "He waits up in the goddamned tree, Raffi. In the bitter cold. He lets us all go on our merry way. He lets it all play out. The meeting under the Bliss Road overpass. The showdown here in the yard. All of it. Texting me just enough to keep the game going the way he wants it to go. All the way through the fireworks." Ray takes a long pull on the water and points. "Then he takes down Mouth. The guy on the roof. Then Donny. Then Billy Wise. Man, what a short, miserable little life that was. He could have killed Billy up on the hill. He didn't. He waited."

Ray looks at Rafael.

"What," says Raffi.

"Nothing." He looks away again. Drinks his water. The act of swallowing turns into a slow nod. "Starting to make sense."

"Yeah?" Raffi snorts. "To you, maybe."

"This… this whole thing was all about Hell hitting Mouth and his crew. Bad blood of some sort. Trust issues. Competition for Big Man's affections. Something. Hell uses me to get all the fish into one barrel. He made me think it was about reclaiming Nadia and Mila."

"It wasn't?"

"Maybe. Maybe they were part of it. Maybe Hell walked off with only half a loaf tonight. But I'm guessing Nadia and Mila were a pretext to bring Mouth and his crew to the party. Just like Jimmy and Phil were for me. Prisoner swap, plain and simple. Mouth thought he was here scoring some big points. Hell tells him to bag the women and put an end to me and maybe he rises in the ranks. Hell's gonna put in a good word with Big Man once the dust settles. But Hell had other plans. Maybe I deliver Nadia and Mila, or maybe I deliver a bunch of cops. Hell doesn't care. Maybe Jimmy and Phil are alive, or maybe they've been dead since he opened the trunk and took their picture. Doesn't matter. Hell doesn't care. He doesn't need to deliver anything to me. I'm a dead man one way or the other. It's the meeting itself he wants."

Raffi nods.

"Get everybody together. Wait for someone to start shooting. See what happens."

"Right. Get the cops to kill the crew and the crew to kill the cops. Sit back and see who's still standing. Hopefully nobody. That makes for a clean forensics story. But if someone is still walking around when the shooting stops, or if it looks like someone is making a break for it and might see tomorrow, then Hell takes out the survivors." Ray starts pointing again. "One. Two. Three. Four."

"Right."

"Climbs down out of the damned tree and goes home for a cold Helles Bock." Rafael looks.

"A what?"

"It's what giants drink after a day of twisting the heads off the little people."

"Whatever, man. I'm worried your headwound is doing all the talking. Sure you don't want to sit in a warm squad car?"

"I'm sure. The cold is the only thing keeping me awake. No offense. And I'm tired of sitting in cars. I want to sit in a boat for a change. A boat floating around Bermuda. Maybe West Antigua." Ray puts an elbow to Rafael's ribs. "What say, Raffi? You and me. Let's go fishing for hangovers in Bermuda."

"I don't drink or fish." Raffi looks. "And speaking of cars…"

"What, you want me to tell you the whole story again?"

"No. I heard the story the first time, Mack. I just don't believe you."

Ray digs the key ring out of his pocket and hands it over.

"You left her a gun, Raffi. You think she wasn't going to use it?"

"Not on you."

"*Especially* on me. I'm lucky I'm sitting here without a nine-millimeter bullet for a nose."

Raffi looks at the keys in his hand.

"And I guess I'm lucky that, somehow, in the middle of being kicked out of my car at gunpoint, you had the presence of mind to grab my house keys. This is one miraculous fucking night, Mack."

Ray nods.

"Miracles abound, my friend. No reason she wanted you locked out of your house." Ray looks. Raffi's not buying a word. Ray nods. "Lot of questions coming, Raffi. Lots of questions from lots of people. When all the dust settles, I'll buy you a drink someplace quiet and tell you a story or two."

"I don't drink."

"They can leave out the booze and give it to me. I'll buy you a stick of gum. Meantime, don't sweat the car. I'm sure Nadia will dump it someplace. She's no dummy."

"And you have no idea where I might find it. Like, no idea."

Ray shrugs. "Could be anywhere."

"Yeah, well maybe an ABP is a good idea."

Ray pats Raffi on the knee.

"Maybe give it a day. It'll turn up. You get a look at Donny's phone?"

Raffi's head slips into a slow shake. He doesn't want to let Ray change the subject. He does anyway.

"I turned it in. It was locked. What's it gonna show?"

Ray looks. Shrugs.

"How should I know? The eggheads will open in up. Then we'll know."

Raffi laughs to himself.

"Fuck you, man," he says. "Am I not out here in the middle of the night freezing my balls off babysitting your ass?"

Ray gives him a lopsided smile.

"Yeah, but that's only because you need a ride home."

Raffi stops chewing.

"You're making me want to unshoot the fuckin' wheelman, Mack. What's in Donny's phone?"

"What's in Donny's phone. Well, I'm guessing there's a text to some number we don't know with a tip that you took Nadia, Mila and Danika to a nearby diner for breakfast. And another text that Stretch and Donny were staking out the on-ramp at Exit 109, waiting for someone to follow. And another text that I had possession of the heroin Billy stole from Big Man at Mouth's behest. I'm guessing Donny's thumbs were working double time as Stretch was ten feet away writing his name in the snow. Donny's information made its way to Hell, who then spoon-fed it to Mouth. Doesn't take long before I take the hint that you're dead at the diner, Stretch is dead on the freeway and Nadia and Mila and Danika are sharing the trunk of a car. Game over. Nothing for me to do but start shooting. Just to make things fun, Hell sends me a text that he only drinks Churchill martinis."

"I don't get it."

"Neither did Mouth until I explained it."

"What's it mean?"

"It means fuck you, Mouth. It means I caught your hand in Big Man's heroin jar and daddy's pissed. It means you're a dead man. So, suddenly, Mouth's got about as much reason to hang onto his bullets as I do. It was Hell's way of lighting the fuse."

A small man wearing an Aurora PD hat and a shield swinging from his neck steps out of the crime scene trailer and heads their direction.

"Bivens?" asks Ray.

Raffi nods. "Bevins. I think." A pause. "There's something else, Mack," he says. Ray nods.

"You called LT."

"Yeah. I called LT. I had to get out in front of this. You said to call it in. I figured…"

"Relax. You didn't get this far by being stupid, Raffi. Woke him up, did you?"

"He was up. Some big shootout among the well-to-do's out on South Bremmer. I didn't ask."

"What'd he say?"

"Nothing good. Said he already fired you."

"He did already fire me. Funny how liberating that was."

Bevins slows, but he doesn't stop.

"Gentlemen." His voice is a lot taller than he is.

He keeps walking past the trailer for the scrap yard beyond.

"I'm told they found your missing car."

ONE HUNDRED FORTY-SEVEN

Following Bevins is like walking a small dog through deep snow. His little legs are moving but we're making slow progress. I want to knock him out of the way and put on some speed for the garage squatting in the gloom ahead of us. There are a few hundred cars stacked like long, ugly bricks on either side of the yard. I don't even need to look. Because I know the Malibu is not among them. It's in the garage. It's in the chop shop. Raphael walks half a step behind me, just in case I start to tilt sideways.

Bevins isn't aiming for the garage. He veers left toward a knot of cops looking up at the stars.

I'm slow and careful about it. Looking up hurts my entire body and sets my head in a slow spin. But I do it anyway.

I'll be damned.

"How's it feel to be wrong for a change?" asks Raffi.

Every boy has his own idea of a flying car. Mine was never a champagne-colored Chevy Malibu. George Jetson wouldn't be caught dead in that thing. I don't see the crane or the excavator on which it sits. I don't even see the big orange magnet attached to the roof. Well. I see them, but they don't register in my battered brain. All I really see is Jimmy's Malibu, up there swinging in the wind against a storm of starlight.

The stars start to spin. I must be tilting because I feel Raphael seize my elbow.

"Easy, Mack," he says. "Let's go have a seat."

I lower my gaze to uncrimp my neck.

"I'm good," I lie, pulling my elbow free. "I just can't tip my head back."

"Get it down," says Bevins to the others. "Get someone out here who knows how to work this thing. Call dispatch for a heavy equipment operator."

One of the cops takes off at a run.

Another cop predicts it will be hours before dispatch can find, roust and deliver a certified crane operator at four-thirty in the morning.

"Let's shake the owner," says another. "Deke. What's his last name? Get his operator out here. Probably lives ten minutes away."

"I want a department-approved contractor," says Bevins. "A certified crane operator. The regs are clear on this. We wait."

I'm ready to forget my place in the scheme of things. I'm ready to tell him that anyone still alive up there in the trunk of that car will die of hypothermia or bleed out or suffocate while we're down here waiting to cross the t's and dot the i's. I try to keep my tone respectful.

"You don't have time," I say. Everyone turns and looks; cold, wind-red faces all around. "You've got a life and death situation up in that trunk. If we're lucky."

"Got a license to operate a Class D commercial vehicle, do you?" asks Bevins.

"No."

"Neither do I." Bevins points without looking. "Neither do they. You ever see a situation go from bad to worse?"

"Not in the last twenty minutes."

"I'm not violating Department policy, Detective."

"I'm not asking you to. Not yet. I wouldn't touch that rig with a ten-foot pole. These are bad people we're dealing with."

"Thanks for that. You need to sit down before you fall down."

"Okay, but maybe hear me out."

"I'm not here to negotiate with you. Go sit down."

"Okay. It's too bad though."

"What's too bad?"

"Too bad Aurora doesn't have a fire department."

Bevins' expression changes like someone's just pulled out the pin that keeps all his face muscles tight. A couple of cops on his team look down at their shoes.

"I don't know how they do things in Wisconsin, but I'm guessing AFD can get a boom truck out here in just a few minutes. Back it in and send someone up in the basket to see if we have a life to save. Meantime I'll bet the guy who works the boom on a Class A twenty-five-ton firetruck is a qualified operator for this little Class D crane."

Bevins looks around at his team. He gets a few shrugs and a couple of nods.

"We can try that," Bevins says, nodding like he's always game to try something new. He reaches for his radio to put in the order, but the mic squawks like it doesn't like being touched. The voice at the other end says Aurora dispatch wants to know the make and model of the magnetic crane.

"Stand by," says Bevins with extra authority. He knocks the nearest uniform in the shoulder. The cop inside the uniform trots around the front of the excavator, climbs up onto the track pad, and opens the door to the cab.

Funny how sometimes you can't hear something until it stops making sound. Electric current is like that for me. Power goes out in my house and suddenly I can't believe how loud electricity is.

The Malibu drops, plummeting through thirty feet of wind and pancaking over a stack of already flattened iron, ten cars high. Then the Malibu teeters off the wall, down onto its own roof, like a one-eared, Champaign-tinted fat man rolling out of bed, four tires to the night sky.

All of us stand and stare, unable to move, like whatever cut power to the magnet also flicked some switch in our brains, killing everything but the power of speech.

"Oh… Holy…"

"Fuck!"

"All I did was open the door!"

I'm the first one moving, but I can feel Raffi close behind. I make it to the driver's door of the Malibu and kneel. The fall has taken care of the window. I reach up inside for the trunk release. I give it a hard yank. It takes three pulls before I hear it unlatch. Even as I'm letting go and starting to rise, I'm listening for the sound of a body falling out of the upside-down trunk. I don't hear anything but the sound of a crowbar hitting the ground. Then I hear Raffi.

"Empty," he says. "Nothing."

Maybe Raffi doesn't know a white cat and a duct-taped man when sees them. I want to walk back and have a look for myself. But I don't make it that far. I'm frozen in mid-squat.

The trunk may be empty, but the back seat isn't. Guess this is my night for being wrong. Raffi is standing beside me.

"Christ," he breathes.

"Not by a long shot, Raffi. They call this one Hell."

He's been folded in half. If he were alive, he could bite his own shoe with any straining. This is a man I used to look up to. His face seems even bigger for not being on top of a four-story building. It's the size of a suitcase. His mouth is open. His eyes are black and empty.

"Why in God's name…"

"God had nothing to do with it, Raffi."

"Then…"

"Because a man this big won't fit in the trunk. And because there's always a bigger man."

ONE HUNDRED FORTY-EIGHT

Bevins wants a look at the tree on Hill Road just like Raffi predicted. Six of us make the trip in two cars. Raffi sticks by me like a rescue dog without the barrel of whiskey around his neck. The heat feels like a warm bath I pretend not to love. It makes the ride much too short. We round the hairpin from North Picking up onto Hill Road just as the sound of an ambulance passes beneath us.

"That one's for you," says Raffi.

The car is too warm. I don't realize my eyes are closed until his elbow pokes me in the ribs.

"Doing okay, Mack?" he asks. "Let's stay awake maybe, yeah?"

The cold air sharpens me up again. I do a lot of pointing from the top of the slope. Bevins tells Raffi to take a cruiser and drive me back down the hill. He promises to be in touch and leaves us at the cars, taking two guys slowly down to the sycamore. Camera lightning flashes every half-step. Another cop walks Hill Road both directions with a flashlight, head bent, like he's looking for a lost wallet.

"Okay," says Raffi. "Let's find you an ambulance." He turns for the nearest cruiser.

"I never made Hell for a tree-climber," I say, staying put. "And he wasn't a marksman. Not a precision type of guy. His idea of a good time was breaking things in half. Bridges. Buildings."

"So," Raffi sighs. "Then who?"

"Ain't that the question of the hour. Someone we don't know. Some guy who grew up with a BB gun for a third arm. Probably progressing from squirrels to dogs to people before he was done growing pimples." I point off toward *Deke's* down the hill. "Those are hard shots. Up in a tree? Freezing cold? Strong wind?

Tough for someone without a lot of training. Military, I'm guessing. Maybe American. Better bet is Russian. Maybe a private contractor. Or maybe he's on the regular payroll. He's headed for a private airport right about now. Time for a vacation."

"If you're Big Man, why kill a soldier like Hell?"

I give him a look.

"If I'm Big Man?"

"Just saying."

"If I'm Big Man, I'm not so happy about that soldier leaving giant, bloody boot prints on my white carpet. We had the goods on Hell for sex trafficking. Garrett Hoosier will sing. We had custody of Nadia. And Mila. And there's my cab driver friend, Raj, who led the cops all over Chicago in a car chase with Hell in the back seat. Raj can connect Hell and Hoosier. That's a lot right there, not to mention being a person of interest for twisting Scooter Pleasants' head off. So, if I'm Big Man, maybe I figure it's only a matter of time before the State of Illinois builds Hell a special cage. Maybe I don't like the idea of Hell making new friends with big promises."

"Maybe Hell was stepping out, looking to set up his own lemonade stand."

"Yeah. Could be Hell's head was getting too big. Which, you know," I look at Raffi. "Obviously."

"So then this was all Big Man. He's the one who wanted all the fish in the barrel."

"Best guess? Yeah. Hell was too busy playing me and Mouth to realize he was the one being played. Hell started the text conversation and Big Man finished it. Funny thing about texting: you never know whose finger is doing all the letter-poking. I'm guessing Hell set everything up. He baited the trap with Jimmy and Phil. He got me to keep Nadia close and to pull Mila out of hiding. He motivated Mouth and his crew into action. And then, just when Hell thinks everything is going smoothly, he gets his ticket punched. Big Man takes over. His people break Hell in half, stuff him in the back seat, and get the car up in the air."

"Why? Why the crane?"

"Go figure, Raffi. Good way to keep Mouth and his crew from spoiling the surprise. Maybe just his twisted idea of fun."

"Fun with you?"

I laugh at the oxymoron.

"No. Not me. I served my purpose for Big Man. I'm all out of fun. Besides, he had to figure I'd be full of holes before I ever had a chance to find the Malibu Crackerjack box and the giant prize inside."

"Then who's he playing with?"

"Everyone who's still left. You. Twill." I nod down the Hill. "Bevins. Everyone under the delusion they have some control over the social order."

"All of this, for that? Lot of trouble," he says.

I pat myself for a Camel before I remember my own life. The dried blood all over my hand helps with that part.

"Come on, Raffi. People go through endless amounts of money and trouble for that little dopamine hit. Ever play a round of golf? Ever been to a casino?"

"Dating," he says with a laugh.

"Dating. There you go. I'll take your word for it. Plus, Big Man's protecting himself."

"How?"

"Think about it. Hell was feeling the heat. We probably only know the half of it. He was going down sooner or later. Big Man just made it sooner. That sound you hear is a dozen different casefiles slapping closed and entire police departments moving on. Some earnest sleuth with a badge will spend some late nights and weekends trying to figure out who slayed the giant, but the forensics will take him nowhere. Big Man knows what he's doing. Eventually the suits upstairs will think resources can be better spent. They'll decide the murderer of a murderer is no one to lose sleep over."

The cop with the flashlight passes us, headed the other way. He glances up as he goes.

"Fat-tire mountain bike," he says with backwards point. "Tracks go that way."

"Smart," I say to Raffi. "Stretch and I would have checked out a parked car. That would have given away the whole game. He parked someplace safe. Rode a bike most of the rest of the way. Ditched the bike someplace dark and walked down to the tree. That means the M-1 is collapsible. He's got it in a bag slung around his back or shoulder. And it means you're looking for an SUV or a van; something big enough to handle a mountain bike without a lot of trouble. Probably stolen. You're gonna find it in some field or a ditch, burned down to the lug nuts."

"Not my investigation, man," Raffi says. He doesn't say that it's not my investigation either. But he wants to.

"More yours than mine, Raffi. If I'm out, then you need to know what I know. Or think I know."

He nods to himself. We listen to Bevins and the others down the hill. I'm not hearing any eurekas.

"Someone could have dropped him off with the bike," says Raffi. "Then picked him up."

I shake my head.

"No. This cat's an assassin. He works alone. Trust gets him an orange wardrobe and a pair of plastic slippers. Maybe he's already learned that the hard way. He keeps to himself. He climbs trees and takes care of business and then he disappears."

We listen to the wind. Down below Bevins says something I can't make out.

Raffi looks around uncomfortably. Then at me. I can feel the question he doesn't want to ask before he asks it.

"Jimmy," he says.

I shake my head and kick a little at the ground.

"Jimmy's in the fish-feeding business. He and Hoffa are comparing first names."

"You sure?"

"Sure enough. Why keep him around? The hostage exchange was all bullshit staging for Mouth and I to come together and do our thing. The open-trunk photo of Jimmy and Phil was all he needed to plug me into the game. After that…"

I don't finish the thought. I shake my head instead. *I'm sorry, Marlo. I keep failing you.*

"Could have just left Jimmy's body in the trunk," he says.

All the headshaking is starting to hurt. The pain wakes up the dizziness.

"Too tidy. Why leave those puzzle pieces connected?"

"And Phil?"

The nausea I've been fighting all night decides there's no time like the present. I double over away from Raffi. He grabs me by the shoulders to keep me from faceplanting into Hill Road. Good thing, because dropping my head so fast has revealed the universe for the roulette wheel I always suspected. Raphael waits until I'm done. Then he gets stern.

"Okay, Mack. Enough bullshit. Get in the fucking car."

ONE HUNDRED FORTY-NINE

He's stubborn to the end. Getting sick has helped his energy. Medics follow him around *Deke's* yard aiming pen lights into his eyes. They want him in the ambulance. He'd rather make the trip on his own.

"You can't drive, Detective."

He's not listening. He keeps walking. He finds the cop who accidentally returned the Malibu to Mother Earth. Turns out the door to the crane was attached to piece of wire wrapped around a console switch that disengages a battery powering the magnet. Simple.

"What's the point of that?"

"Stop looking for points, Raffi. You'll hurt yourself. Arsonists like to see things burn. Big Man likes taking a seat in the back of your head. He likes being there, even when you think he isn't. You do something ordinary like open up a door and the sky falls. Pretty soon, he's everywhere, whether he is or not."

"Detective…" The EMT crosses his arms and juts out a hip.

"I heard you. I'll get there."

"You can't drive in your condition."

"Yeah, well, then Raffi here will take me."

"I don't have a car anymore, Mack. Remember?"

"We'll take the Nissan," he says, pointing. "We don't need windows. A little fresh air…"

It's not that he doesn't want to leave the yard. Seems like it, but that's not it. He doesn't want to leave the job. He knows this is it for him, again. As soon as he's in that ambulance, he stops being a cop and starts being a patient; an old bag of flesh and bone, looking for a way to make the pain stop. They'll discharge him to an empty house with a crooked couch and an endless parade of investigators with bags full of sharp questions to stab into his ears. His wounds will heal soon enough. The meds will run their course. And then he'll still be an old bag of flesh and bone, looking for a way to make the pain stop.

And it won't. Not ever. There isn't enough Old Forester in the world. That leaves all the old hurt inside and me up above telling him how he looks from the rafters. Before too long he'll do anything to shut me up. But that's never happening. Not as long as he's got a brain and a functioning memory. I'm as mortal as he is. He knows that's the only way to shut me up. Guess we'll see just how deep the well really is.

All of that starts with the ambulance ride.

"The Nissan's a crime scene, Mack. Just get in the damn ambulance."

"Yeah, yeah." He shoots Raphael a dirty look. "Alright. One second. One more look at Hell before I go."

"Mack…"

He trudges past the Granada and the Nissan with its hood still up and the wind whistling Dixie through a couple dozen bullet holes. Raffi trails behind as the medics hang back and shake their heads. When he reaches the Malibu, he navigates around to the passenger side and squats.

He knows better than to touch anything. He looks at the broken, upside-down giant in the broken upside-down car. He sees the wound for the first time. They shot him before they broke him. The bullet went in the left ear. No exit wound. It's still inside.

"Hell's head is too big. The bullet got lost and tired. It gave up trying to get out."

"Mack. Let's go, man."

"Does Hell look like a yoga-type to you?"

"Mack."

"Me neither. So how do you fold a man like Hell in half?"

Fingers to the shoulder.

"Mack, you really…"

"Wait." He points. "Look at the neck. That's a hell of a scrape. All the way… it's halfway up the back of his head. See?"

Raffi leans in. Ray keeps pointing.

"You don't shave a man's neck with a cheese grater and then shoot him in the ear."

"Maybe you do."

"Okay, maybe you do. Or maybe you sit him down behind a car for a little chat. Maybe he's not listening, so you shoot him in the ear. Then you back over him with the car. No." Ray looks down at Hell and then back up to Raffi. He stands, using Raffi for support. He's mumbling now, more than talking. "Not a car. A truck."

"Mack."

"Something that catches a big guy like Hell about mid-shoulder. Anything lower just pushes him over. It's gotta be something…"

"Let's go, man."

Ray leaves the Malibu and makes his way for the two cops dusting the cab of the crane.

"Flashlight?"

The two exchange a look. They're not interested in giving a flashlight to a man with bloody hands.

"Then give it to him," says Ray, nodding at Raffi. "Just for a minute."

Ray circles the excavator. Raphael follows, shining a light wherever Ray points. He squats again. They both do. He points at the platform between the trackpads.

"There."

"Where?"

"Here. Make sure they sample this. And the crossbeam underneath."

"Why, again?"

"Because that's Hell's neck razor. They killed him right here, Raffi. I think Hell was on site, preparing for the big party. He got some company he wasn't expecting. More likely he was working with some guys who had orders from on high. They sat him down, cleaned out his ear wax with a small caliber bullet, and then they backed over him with this crane. Stuffed him in the Malibu. Then they lifted him as close to Heaven as Hell can ever get."

Raffi stands, slowly rising above Ray, leaving him in his squat.

"Got a theory of my own," Raffi says. Ray looks up.

"Yeah?"

"The Malibu trunk was full, Mack. They brought Jimmy here. They unloaded Jimmy here."

"What?"

Ray struggles to stand, pulling against Raphael's arm. Raphael's other arm is pointing the flashlight beyond the crane to the top of a wall of old tires.

It's not the pure white body that gives her away so much as her green eyes, flashing in the beam of light. Ray feels those eyes in his chest.

"Jesus Christ," he whispers.

It's Santiago's turn to shake his head.

"No. Looks like Phil to me, Mack. But you might thank him just the same."

ONE HUNDRED FIFTY

Something about hospitals. You aren't who you think you are. You aren't who you want to be. Instead, you're this.

Not pretty. The opposite. But it's honest.

He looks at me like he can see me. Like we're in a staring contest. He doesn't like me up here. Three minutes conscious and he's already tired of the company.

Like it's a picnic for me.

They've cleaned off the blood. That took away his only color except for the bruising on the right side of his face and across his neck like a mottled purple scarf. They've improved on the revolutionary fife-player motif. The bandages are white again. One on his cheek and another on the side of his head, each covering its own seam of cat-gut needlepoint. He's a science experiment now. Or a player in some avant-garde theater of the macabre. Both maybe. The human-eggplant hybrid in a production of Frankenstein.

"You're awake," she says, checking his tubes.

He rolls his head so that he can't help but see her. Flowered scrubs. Hair in a tight blonde bun. Somebody's granddaughter. He swallows twice before the words can climb their way out into the beeping, windowless room.

"Boy," he croaks. "You medical-science types know everything."

"Funny. Nice nap?"

"I dreamt I was trying to sleep. People kept poking me with questions."

"Next time don't show up with brain swelling." She produces a muscular index finger and points it to the ceiling. "Follow my finger."

"Follow it where? I don't even know you."

"Molly." The smile is efficient. "I'm your shift nurse. And you are Officer Raymond Mackey."

"Good to know. Have we met?"

"Just now. I have the power to make your life miserable or tolerable. So, follow my finger."

He watches it move. Left to right and back again. Like she's scolding him for being injured.

"Very good."

"Thanks. I've looked at things before."

She pokes at a computer screen on a rolling stand.

"Understand you had a rough night."

"The night was fine. Morning was hell."

She looks up at him briefly, then back to her screen.

"I'll say. Severe concussion. Severe dehydration. Blood loss. Facial lacerations. Cranial contusions. Cerebral edema. Don't suppose you suffered any boredom."

"No. But I'm working on that."

"Come on now. You just woke up."

"Seems like an eternity. What time is it?"

She looks at her watch, drifting back toward the bed.

"We're right at eight o'clock." She reads his confusion like a pro. "And by that, I mean eight o'clock at night. They'll release you tomorrow if everything checks out and you behave yourself. Doctor Soome wants…"

"Sue me?"

"S…o…o…m…e."

"Hope he's got a sense of humor."

"None. He's attending. He wants you here another night to make sure the edema's not an issue."

It's coming back to him. He's heard all of this before.

"Meantime, you just try to relax. We'll be checking on you more than you like." The finger he once followed dangles a big red button on a small gray cord. "And you know what this is."

"Sure. That's how I order my bourbon. I take it over two cubes in a cloud of smoke."

"Keep it up. I'll make sure they hold you another week. I can get you some information on recovery programs if you'd like."

"I'm not so good with steps," he says.

"Which ones?"

"Only the first twelve. I trip over having to trust in a higher power."

"You're alive and talking to me, aren't you?"

Molly gives him a look, then hangs the button over a spare hook on the IV stand and turns to leave.

"Oh," she says turning back. "You had two visitors while you were asleep. "A man named Raphael brought you some clothes and one stick of gum. I don't ask questions. Those are in a bag in that chair over there. I'm supposed to tell you that Stretch pulled through and Phil is fine. And," she pats her apron and extracts an envelope. "Last shift a woman dropped this off for you."

He takes the envelope. "What woman?"

She shrugs. "Don't think she left a name."

"What'd she look like?"

"Last shift, Detective." Molly turns and heads for the door. "I wasn't here. Let me know if you need anything."

"Drink."

"Nope."

He opens the envelope. Inside is a slip of paper with the logo for the Rush Copley Medical Center in Aurora, Illinois. *Doctors with a Passion for People*. He flips it over. On the back is a phone number in blue pen.

He stares at the number because there's nothing else.

He doesn't need anything else.

ONE HUNDRED FIFTY-ONE

We roll by Stretch's room on the way out. The lights are off and the door is closed. The nurse at the station says early evening would be better. Twill thanks her and turns me around. We roll back the way we came.

A befouled coat sits folded on my lap. I take it on faith that it's mine. It's not something I want to recognize. Beneath the coat is a plastic bag of clothes that smell like blood and the late Steven King's water heater. Under the bag are my discharge papers and a sheaf of prescriptions.

"Pretty smooth ride, LT," I say. "I could get used to this."

"Don't," he says from above and behind. "It stops at the curb."

"If I'm cleared to drive, I figure I can walk myself out of the ER."

"Rules are rules, Mack. I know that's an alien concept to you."

Nurse Molly appears from around a corner, purse on her shoulder, scrubs flashing under an open coat, just showing up for her shift. Her face is pink with cold. She tosses me something like a smile and squeezes my forearm as she passes, not slowing down.

"Watch yourself, Detective," she says.

The wind acts like it's glad to see me. The cold and the late-morning light compare blades. Everything hurts, but nothing quite like my head. I've got a pill or two in me, but they need some friends.

Twill makes me put my clothes in the back on top of the recycling. Even the coat. He doesn't like the smell and he doesn't want my DNA rubbing off on the upholstery. I'm not offended. I am grateful to ride up front like a human. He blasts the heat and points the Navigator east, toward Chandler and the rest of my life.

"You didn't have to make the trip, LT," I say.

"Every time you're unsupervised my phone rings with a new apocalypse. I don't have the time for another one."

"I appreciate it just the same."

"I told you I'd personally drive you back to the mall. I keep my promises."

"Look. I know you're sore about…"

"Sore?" His face whips my direction with a look that hurts my head. I turn and look out the window at the people of Aurora, living their lives.

"Save it, Raymond. We're way past sore. Sore is a fond fucking memory."

"I understand."

"No," he says. "Trust me. You don't understand. You have no appreciation for the magnitude of the shit-tsunami in your wake. The Chief is so far up my ass I can taste shoe leather. The OAG wants to ransack Chandler IAD for information about that goddamned spreadsheet. Judge Jolie and more than a few others on the bench want to gavel the entire department back into the stone age. I had breakfast this morning with the DA who told me it's going to be awhile before any of his prosecutors will be able to get so much as a bathroom pass from the trial courts." Twill's got so much to say his fingers get involved. "I'm talking about routine continuances. Suppression of evidence motions. Warrants. Subpoenas. I'm talking basic benefit of the doubt, Mack. That takes a long time to earn and half a second to destroy."

A memory shoulders its way through the pain in my head. I'm sitting in Judge Jolie's chambers, explaining my own unpopularity. I'd told her that when the stink of corruption is on you, the benefit of the doubt is just too expensive, too difficult for most people to reach. That was before she threw me out of her office. Now she and her buddies on the bench are going to teach my lesson to the entire police force.

"Look, I brought forward information that…"

"You brought forward a toxic lie that impugned the integrity of the single most liked and influential criminal trial judge on the bench, who now believes that we either cooked the information and passed it on to the press, or conveniently looked the other way as this… this *poison* works its way through the bloodstream. She feels knifed in the back and so now everybody over there feels knifed in the back."

I know he wants me to sit here and take it quietly. We all want a lot of things.

"One, unless the poison was cooked and then spread onto the blade of a knife, you're really mixing your metaphors, LT. Two, I didn't cook or pass on anything to the press. I…"

"Doesn't matter whether you actually did it, or not, Mack. Perception is everything, particularly for the courts and OAG. Now Chandler PD is right back to being the thing rotten in Denmark. And the stink is coming from IAD. From *my* office."

"You mean from me."

"The whole office. Me included. But yes, you, Mack. All your baggage stinks to high heaven."

"Let's be clear, Lieutenant. I brought the information to you. Only you. You made the call to send it up the food chain, not me. What else was I supposed to do with it? Ignore it? Toss the flash drive in the dump?"

"That would have been better, yeah. Because trash belongs in the dump."

I snort and shake my head. That doesn't help things. Twill ratchets up the anger another notch.

"You want to be clear? Okay, then let's be crystal fucking clear, Mack. You kept me in the dark until the last possible second. Until the moment of your big fucking reveal. You left me no room to maneuver. No opportunity for me to selectively read in someone from upstairs on this thing. Soften the ground."

"Cover our asses, you mean."

"Yeah, that's exactly what I mean. And you can uncurl your lip about it. That's the world we live in, and you know it. And you're goddamned right I sent it up the food chain. What other choice did I have? All of this was going upstairs sooner or later, and you chose later. *You* did that. *You* kept it all to yourself. So that *you* could keep control. So that *you* could maneuver around me."

I've got half a dozen churlish responses, uncharitable potshots at an over-sensitive, holier-than-thou judiciary and the politics of law enforcement. But I beat them all back. My gut turns gutless and is suddenly on Twill's side of things. My Triple-D kicks in. I look like I'm sitting in the passenger seat of big daddy's car after having been picked up from the principal's office. Truancy. Vandalism. Something. The unvarnished message from my other self is that Twill is right, and I know it.

So the accusation is coming from me now. It's the worst kind of betrayal not to be on my own side. I feel stabbed in the head with a poison knife.

I watch Aurora slide by us in its cold, windblown silence and let him fume. Two minutes. Five.

Two guys blowing steam as they push up the door of a dirty blue delivery truck.

A banner at a car dealership has ripped free, waving for help.

A man at a bus stop is eating out of an orange cellophane bag. Probably not cheeseballs, but it makes me think of Hawkeye anyway. Not so much the man himself as his blue-duct-taped .38.

Right where I needed it to be, the moment I needed it.

Why under the seat? Dumb place to store a back-up piece. Too hard to reach; easily kicked around. Why there? The place in my memory where I thought that one through is all mush. Like trying to understand why you do things in a dream. Why?

The question goes double for Sig's empty chamber. I never leave that chamber empty.

I'd be dead. But for Hawkeye's .38. But for Sig's empty chamber. Dead. I'd no longer exist. No more looking down on myself. Perching on my own shoulder. I'd know all the answers to all the questions I'd ever cared to ask. Makes me wonder if I'd still care.

I can feel my brain rolling up its sleeves over the other question that has no comprehensible answer: if I didn't call Raffi for help, who did?

I turn to Twill.

"So then the spreadsheet…"

He looks back, like maybe he's irritated to hear my voice. His dark wool cap gives me some idea of what Twill looked like as a younger man underneath a full head of hair. We all used to be younger.

"The spreadsheet is bullshit," he says. "Jolie volunteered her bank records, which show no such deposits. She's beyond livid."

"Yeah, I got that part. What about His Honor?"

"Chief said he hasn't heard from the mayor directly. Royce's office is avoiding the whole thing until such time as there is an official investigation that he is forced to acknowledge. His people have a back-channel open with OAG and they insist the spreadsheet deposits are bullshit."

"Big surprise. You think they're gonna admit…"

"They provided bank records, Mack. OAG has confirmed. The spreadsheet is a fiction."

I can feel my blood pressure rising, inflating a balloon inside my head.

"Tony Riggs is on that sheet, LT. We know he was taking payments. And others. Quentin. Smitty. Deno. Pete Phelps. They were all on the sheet. Did they check out?"

The question gets me a rueful laugh.

"No idea, Mack. You see, we need a court to authorize the subpoenas. And like I said, those wheels are grinding a little slowly at the moment."

"Shit. They're real, LT. They've got to be."

"Maybe. But why do I care about Tony Riggs? I already know he was dirty. Smitty and Pete and most of the others too. Old news. But a sitting judge and the goddamned mayor of Chicago? Come on. It's bullshit and we just smeared it all over two branches of government."

"There's good reason to be concerned that Mayor Royce…"

"No." I get the face again. It hurts just as much as the last time he whipped it across the car. "I'm not listening, Mack. If you say the word drycleaners, I will stop the car and you can walk. We're done with that. Understand? That plug is pulled. I gave your… your… Whatever you want to call it…"

"Evidence."

"Evidence my ass. Royce's name on a drycleaning ticket? It was a hunch based on your interpretation of an account from a hooker CI you never registered and who nobody has ever seen and who may or may not still exist. No corroboration whatsoever to back up this flyer of yours."

"Suri wasn't just making it up, LT. She…"

"Enough. Just stop. I gave your hunch all the oxygen I could. It's all going in a box, Mack. When OAG audits my ongoing investigation files, how am I supposed to explain parking Raphael in a car outside the mayor's drycleaner for a couple dozen hours?"

"What Raffi does on his vacation…"

"No. It's done. It's all going in a box. And it's none of your concern now anyway." He points. "Because you're just as done. Be grateful *you* aren't going in a box."

"What do you call working security at a shopping mall? If they'll take me back."

He moves his head like he's watching a slow game of tennis.

"No. Don't stick your lip out at me, Mack. You don't get to play the sympathy card. I gave you every chance. You blew it. You knew how this was going to end. You made your choice."

I nod and look out the window. Hard to argue with that.

"And I was referring to a pine box, by the way. You should be dead right now. If it weren't for Santiago."

"Again," I say.

"Again."

"The man can shoot."

Twill settles back in his seat and closes his eyes for a long blink.

"The paperwork on this thing is going to be…" He decides to let the rest of whatever he was about to say come out as a sigh. "You were right about one thing."

"That seems unlikely."

"Arty Dunn dumped a can of worms on that witness stand. Chief wants me to open a new IAD file and dig in."

"Let me guess. He wants to know if Arty was in the protection racket business with Tony Rickens."

He shakes his head. "Broader. The entire relationship with Rickens. Plus, whatever squeeze Arty was putting on Scooter Pleasants, which puts Scooter's murder in the mix. Plus, the 2005 *Tap Root Kegs* fire. Soup to nuts, Mack. Everything. Wants me to work with Property Crimes for Arty's case files and coordinate with Wexler in Homicide on all the dead-people issues. The DA's office is going to open its own investigation, so they're going to want everything IAD develops in our investigation, which blows a hole in IAD's confidentiality mandate, something the Chief has never seemed to understand. So that's going to be a big fight. It's a cluster headache before I even get a label on the file."

"You realize that looking into the entire relationship between Arty Dunn and Tony Rickens means going back…"

"Yeah. I know. Back to Arty working security for *Kings Flush Casino*. The murder of Nathaniel Marciewicz. All of it. Thanks for that, Mack. None of that would be on my plate if it weren't for you. I don't have enough to do, so I may as well study ancient criminal history. I didn't sign up with IAD to work cold homicide cases."

"You wanted to work bad cops, LT. Arty more than fits the description. Let me know if you need some help."

I mean it for a laugh. It comes close enough. Twill reins it in and looks at me sideways.

"Goddamnit, Mack." It comes out as a whisper.

"I know, LT. Everything I touch. Believe me."

"I believe you."

"Any word on the Curtis Root murder case?"

"What case," he mutters. "There is no case. Not against Wrigley Menard, anyway. Chief told me the DA flushed the whole thing two hours after Jolie declared a mistrial."

I nod.

"Judge Jolie predicted as much. You can bet Mickey Shaw was promising to use the press as a club to beat our dirty laundry in the town square."

"Chief said the DA told him the trial team was still reeling and demoralized from Arty's testimony. The case was like dancing with a corpse. No one was really looking forward to another song."

"Never seemed like a tight case from the beginning," I say.

"There'll be a lot of talk about continuing the investigation. Bringing Root's killer to justice. All that bullshit. Then we'll never hear another word about it. Menard was bait. Prosecution bit the hook and got their ass dragged up onto the beach."

I look at him.

"That's a lot of fishing and beaches. I think maybe someone wants a vacation."

Twill looks back at me and away again at the road in front of him. I can see the exhaustion and the stress. I'm guessing that between the two of us I've had more sleep than he has in the past twenty-four hours. I don't get a response for another couple hundred yards.

"This is a young man's game," he says, hitting his turn signal.

"Name one that isn't, LT," I say. Then I point. "Keep going. My car is outside Steven King's place."

He nods. I make a sound to myself. It catches Twill's attention.

"What."

"Steven King," I say. "Seems like a couple years ago."

"Lot of bullets in that man."

"It was that angry little 'v' in his name that killed him. His Ph was low. His parents should have thought that one through. Things might have turned out better."

The Impala is right at the curb where I left it. No one has bothered to replace the plastic back window with glass. Disappointing but not unexpected. It hasn't been stripped for parts. Still has four full tires. I'm guessing this is not that kind of neighborhood. Or maybe the two cruisers in the driveway and the yellow crime scene tape across the door has deterred the scavengers.

Twill pulls up alongside. I open up and climb down onto the road. My legs and back complain. Gravity hurts everything. There's a square of red paper under the wiper of the Impala, flapping in the wind. I yank it out and give it a read.

"Just in time," I say. "Homeowners Association is counting backwards from forty-eight. They like a clean curb."

Twill pushes a button. The backside of the Navigator opens like the upside-down belly of a C-130. I take the hint and grab my clothes. I rummage through my blood-stained coat for the thing I need to give him. He takes the badge through the open window as the rear door hisses closed. Twill extends a hand.

"Knew there was a chance this was going to be a short ride," he says. "Never thought it would be this short."

"You're a good egg, LT." I give his hand a shake. "That's not just a bald joke. No one else would have ever tried."

He winces a little.

"I'd play sick for a while if I were you. Get your feet back under you. What's coming…"

"I know."

"It's going to make a colonoscopy seem fun."

"I've been on that carnival ride before."

"Your suspended-pending status will last a while. There's a lot to sort out. Eggshells all over the damn place. It will move slowly."

"So, in the meantime you want me to behave myself."

Twill shakes his head.

"I know better."

"Want me to resign?"

"Yes. But I'd talk to your IFOP rep before you do anything rash. Hard to say how all of this will play out. Resigning may not be in your best interests. You might want to force a termination. Go to the press. Make a stink. All that bullshit. That's up to you and the jackals. I can't advise you on that part."

I almost pat the Navigator like it's a horse and walk away. I almost don't ask the one question I haven't wanted to ask. Once you crack an egg, there's no putting it back together. Just ask Humpty.

"Who did you tell?"

An empty beat in the wind. I get a furrowed brow.

"About what?"

"About giving me the boot."

"Nobody. Santiago. When he called from *Deke's*. I… I expressed myself."

"Yeah. Aside from Raffi."

"Nobody."

"Nobody?"

"What did I just say, Mack? Nobody. Not a soul. Why?"

"Because me losing my badge has been all over bad-guy radio."

His eyes sharpen.

"What are you implying?"

"Maybe just a bad memory. Or maybe a guilty conscience."

"Or maybe you're wrong."

"They got it from somewhere, LT."

"They made it up maybe."

"Hell of a lucky guess. Luck like that? They should put away the guns. Play the stock market."

He faces forward for a second or two. A detective in blue paper booties opens the front door to the home of the late Steven King, author of nothing except fictional accounting. He gives us a once over, then closes the door again.

"You're reckless, insubordinate and too impulsive," says Twill. "You don't play nice with others and, as long as I'm being honest, you've got a drinking problem that makes you a liability."

"Thanks, LT."

"But you're a good detective, Mack. I don't believe you're in the pocket. Never have. And you're a long way from crazy. Try to keep your head up."

He gives it more gas than necessary. The Navigator jolts like a horse under a spur.

I watch him go, patting my pockets for what's still not there.

ONE HUNDRED FIFTY-TWO

It's a wait at the pharmacy. It hurts too much to stand. My back wants to think about Steven King's staircase and my head wants to be closer to the floor. So, I sit in a chair where everybody can get a good look at me and my bloody coat and worry about the transit bus that hit me.

I nod at a short-haired woman in a long wool coat the color of cinder. There's a young, towheaded boy attached to her arm, but I figure she knows that already. She looks away. He doesn't. I can see myself in his eyes. I'm the business end of a bad dream only I'm sitting under the drugstore fluorescents between the multivitamins and the denture crème and something about that seems wrong to him. A visage like mine should dissipate upon waking with a hug and a cool glass of water in the glow of a nightlight.

I want to tell him about all the roads that lead to this chair. I want to tell him what not to do in the world. Who to stay away from. What not to take for granted. I want to button him up inside his mother's coat.

I glance at my wrist to break the spell. My watch is busy running in circles, like it's chasing something that doesn't want to be caught. I do the math on the mileage, factoring in the traffic. I figure I've still got plenty of time.

But then I always think that. We all do.

Sonny's is too bright and busy. My head prefers a small, dark coat closet, preferably locked, but I can't think of one of those nearby that serves a decent breakfast.

I let the door swing closed behind me and blow on my hands as I give the place a once over. Cleopatra is unloading a tray onto a four-top by the window. I give her a nod and cut through a party of six, headed for a booth in the back. I haven't sat down since I parked my car, about two minutes ago. It feels wonderful.

Cleo's horror-stricken face makes it to the table before she does. She can't control her arms, which move in slow, loose circles in front of me, hands like birds looking for someplace to land that isn't covered with dried blood or gauze. They give up and land on her own face, one flat against each cheek.

"Oh… my… God. Mack…"

"Good morning, Isis."

"It's afternoon. And what the hell is so good about it? What the fuck happened to you? Did the Hell-guy do this? Are you okay? Are you… are you…"

"I'm fine. Stop worrying. Nothing a wheelbarrow full of Percocet won't fix. Hey, I don't suppose…" I put two fingers to my lips and let her figure out the rest.

"No smoking. You know that. Jesus. You and Raj with the cigarettes. I'm making him quit."

"Good for you. Start confiscating and save them for me."

She's not listening. Or she doesn't care. She can't stop shaking her head. The gold hoops on her lobes flash in and out of the sleek, black waterfall she uses for hair. She looks both ways and then slips down into the booth.

"Mack… you look… you look…"

"Fabulous is the word you're looking for, Isis. Give it a try."

"Tell me what happened."

"Long story. You're going to lose some friends in the kitchen and your tips are going to suffer."

She takes another quick look around.

"What are you doing here?"

"Ordering breakfast and taking a meeting."

"Meeting who, the coroner?"

"Funny. No, he's a little busy this morning."

She looks at me like I'm an empty glass.

"Afternoon."

"Right. What's your special today?"

"I'm not playing this game, Mack," she says, standing again. "It was on the sign out front. You never order the special."

"The sign lost all its vowels in the wind and, anyway, it's a new day for me, Cleo. I'm taking stock. Turning over a new leaf. This is day one. What's the chef recommending?"

She sticks out a hip and pokes at the inside of her cheek with her tongue.

"The special today is the prosciutto, parm and rosemary omelet with a side of breakfast potatoes."

I give her an appreciative nod.

"Sounds delicious," I say. "Special, even."

"Yeah?" she says, knowing better. "One of those, then."

"No. Not today. Thanks though. Let's try a black coffee, two over-easies with bacon, and…"

"And a buckwheat pancake on the side."

"I was going to say cigarette, but if you say so. Glad to hear you and Raj are still doing whatever it is you two haven't stopped doing."

"What he hasn't stopped doing is talking about you. I think he's in love."

"I know he's in love, and it's not with me."

"He'd want me to call and tell him you're here."

"No need," I say. "I called him myself. He's outside."

Cleo turns for the windows and back again.

"Outside? Doing what?"

"Watching. It's what he does best next to driving taxis and offering me Camels. You could learn a lot from him, kid."

"I don't want to know," she says, leaning in, one hand on the table. The next part comes in a whisper. "And, not for nothing, that's not what he does best."

I watch Cleo glide through the diner and disappear into the kitchen. I pass the time by keeping an eye out for people who might want to kill me. She's back in record time with the coffee and food. I pop a couple of pills and try to enjoy myself before the show starts. Turns out I don't have long to wait.

ONE HUNDRED FIFTY-THREE

"Mack," she says, slipping sideways into the booth.

My face can feel the cold wafting out of her hair, sloughing off her black wool shoulders and onto the table. Her glasses are half-steamed. Behind the glasses, her eyes are still watering from the wind. She smells like winter through an open front door.

"Sandra Booth," I say. "Pull up a last name. Take a load off. What brings you to the cheap side of town?"

"You do," she says, pulling off her gloves finger by finger. The steam on her glasses thins and disappears. "You picked the place. I just follow instructions."

"I figured that out about you. You do as you're told like a pro. Question is, who besides me is giving you the instructions?" I hold up a finger. "Don't answer that yet. Let me buy you lunch while we both still have an appetite."

She combs her fingers through her hair, cleaning up after the wind.

"Strange looking lunch," she says with a nod to my half-empty plate.

"I got a late start. I'll get to lunch around dinner time."

She gives my face and neck a once over.

"Fall out of bed?"

"It only looks that way. I haven't seen my bed in days."

Isis shows up with a question on her face.

"Just some coffee," says Sandra, looking up. "I'm not staying but a minute."

"A minute?" I ask as Isis leaves. "How am I supposed to fit all of my questions inside a minute?"

"That's easy," says Sandra. "I'm not here to answer your questions. I'm here to deliver a message."

Isis shows up with the coffee. We pause until she leaves again. I slide a couple thimbles of crème across the table.

"A message. You could've delivered a message on the phone. Or written it down. That was a lonely phone number you left at the hospital."

"It's not a message that fits on a slip of paper. It's an in-person kind of message."

"Ah. The in-person kind. My favorite. You going to shoot me under the table?"

"Why would I shoot you under the table?"

"Because the place is full of people. I figure you're shy about that sort of thing."

"Why would I shoot you at all?"

"Not sure yet. Maybe John-Wilkes is climbing around in your family tree. All my messages these days seem to come in bullets."

"You've obviously been through a lot. But you need to relax a little. You've got me all wrong, Mack."

"Do I?"

"Yes."

"Good to know. What's the message?"

"There's someone who wants to meet with you. Not to shoot you. To talk to you."

"Talk about what?"

"I don't know."

"What's his name?"

"I don't know."

"You don't know. Then how do you know he doesn't want to shoot me?"

"I guess I don't."

"You know, you're not so good at this messengering gig, Sandra. Don't quit your day job."

"I don't have a day job anymore, Mack. Guess, that gives us something in common."

She just doubled my attention. I push my plate aside to make room.

"How long have you known I'm done?" I ask.

"Does it matter?"

"No. What matters is who you learned it from and who you shared it with."

"That's not why I'm here."

"Why are you here?"

"I told you already. To take you to a meeting."

"Right, a meeting with you-don't-know-who about you-don't-know-what."

"That's about right," she says. "That's how they do."

"Who?"

"I don't know."

"What kind of meeting?"

"I don't know."

"Did Twill put you up to this? Is this his idea of an intervention? I'm not interested in AA until they swap out the coffee for bourbon."

"I don't work for Twill anymore. He has no idea I'm here. This isn't about AA."

"Could be, Sandra. You don't seem to have a clue what this is or isn't about."

"Trust me."

"I'm trying to. Tell me why you're leaving IAD."

Her eyes take another tour of my horror-show face. They're sensitive to violence, cringing behind her glasses. She is not so composed as she would have me believe.

"Change of scenery, I guess," she says. "I need to do something different."

"Conflicts of interest are exhausting, aren't they?"

Her look goes on for a while before she gets a smile big enough to dunk in her cup.

"Yes. Conflicts of interest are exhausting."

"Connecticut?"

She shrugs.

"Maybe." She takes another sip and sets aside the cup. She grabs up her gloves. "Settle up, Mack. Let's get going."

"To this meeting of yours?"

"It's not my meeting. It's your meeting."

"Then why are *you* here?"

"Because I'm someone you trust."

"Do I?"

"Sure you do, Mack. We work together."

"Not anymore."

"But we used to. You weren't with IAD long, but we always got on okay. I always liked you. We helped each other out, didn't we?"

"Yeah. Sure we did, Sandra. You come here alone?"

"Yes."

"And you expect me to just come along for the ride?"

"No."

"Good."

"We're not riding anywhere. We're walking. It's important that you go. I don't want to keep anyone waiting."

"Who's waiting?"

"I don't know."

Isis appears with two small plates, one with three strips of bacon and the other with two small blueberry muffins. She sets them where the other food used to be.

"Comes with the special," she says, not leaving. I give my best dismissive nod.

"Thanks, Cleo. Any time with the check."

"Muffin?" I ask when we're alone again.

"No."

"How's your mom?"

"My mom?"

"Yeah, you know, the eighty-one-year-old in a Connecticut ICU with a bad case of this-could-be-it pneumonia."

Sandra reclaims her mug and sips.

"She's fine. Better."

"Glad to hear. I was worried."

"Sweet."

"Yeah, well, that's me. According to your mom, your sister has pneumonia without any flowers to cheer her up. That's too much pneumonia in one family and too many telephones in an ICU."

Her eyes keep their composure, waiting for more. So I give her some.

"Taking a break from the office to have some face time with your ailing mother made sense. But then you were back like you'd never left. The miracle of modern medicine, I guess."

Sonny's coffee is not good enough to justify all the attention she's giving that cup.

"Someone's been busy leaping to conclusions," she says finally.

"I do a lot of leaping, Sandra. The only conclusion I've landed is that you got sloppy with your cover story."

"And why would I need a cover story, exactly?"

"Exactly? Couldn't tell you. But whoever's pulling your string got concerned you'd be discovered, or worse. He didn't want to lose his mole in the Chandler IAD, so he gave the string a big yank right about the time Arty Dunn disappeared. He wanted you out fast, too fast for you to come up with a good reason. I'm sure he was busy making mayhem and hiding bodies, but he shouldn't have left the excuse part up to you. You went with Mom-and-pneumonia, probably because your sick sister was on your mind. How am I doing?"

"Depends. Are you trying to confuse me?"

"So then, poof, you're gone. I'm guessing a hotel room someplace, about as close to a Connecticut ICU as you are right now. But then two things happen at about the same time: Arty shows up on the witness stand and I find a certain flash drive inside a wooden doll. All hell breaks loose. Gavels start pounding. Investigation files start to open. The Office of Attorney General wants information for breakfast. Your dark master decides he wants you back in the field, taking notes and passing them along. Mom makes a miraculous recovery."

Sandra lets out a small laugh.

"So, I'm a mole, is that it?" she asks.

"You tell me, Sandra. Are you?"

"You think I'm a mole because my mom wasn't sick? She was sick. She's still sick. The pneumonia was mild. The dementia is bad and getting worse. My sister did not have pneumonia. Instead, she had a co-dependent gene and a plane ticket to Hartford. She covered the health crisis. I took a day of leave and then came back to work."

She sips, lifting her eyebrows.

"What else you got?" she asks. I don't much like the surge in confidence, but I keep that to myself.

"Your memory is too good."

"My memory is too good?"

"Yeah. How many open cases did Chandler IAD have when you started?"

She considers the coffee. Looks at the ceiling to add things up.

"Forty-five or so."

"How many of those were Phase 1, under ninety days old?"

She has to think. I nibble on a strip of bacon.

"Fifteen," she says. "Not including the weapons discharges for Juarez and Baker. They were Phase 1, but those two were re-files, so…" She ends the sentence with a shrug.

"Sandra, I can't remember my own birthday half the time. If you can remember things like that, then how is it you don't remember Tony Rickens yelling in your ear about the *Kings Flush Casino* burning up a dead Nathaniel Marciewicz?"

I can tell the question scores a point or two.

"Long time ago," she says.

"Elvis was a long time ago too. You remember him, don't you?"

"Come on."

"*Kings Flush* was a big case, Sandra. Your first as a liaison, making sure Chicago Fire and Chicago Homicide played nice and shared the sandbox. You remembered Michael Perry as the Fire Chief easily enough. But not Tony Rickens? Come on. Tony was not the kind of guy who slips the mind. Seems natural to expect that you'd clue me in to something like that when I asked for the report. But you didn't. You did the opposite. You said you couldn't remember who was working the homicide end of things. I wasn't buying that for a second. So I figure you wanted to kick a little dust over the past; make sure Tony stayed good and buried. His signature on the report was as fat and ugly as he was, but I made it out anyway."

She looks tired now. Not sleepy. Weary. Her eyes are starting to sag behind her glasses, buckling under the weight of the florescent light and her make-believe moxie. She looks like someone who isn't up to listening. I keep feeding her ears anyway.

"The real surprise was finding out that Arty Dunn was working casino security. I know you remember Arty. We've got a case file with his name on it. Turns out he and Tony Rickens were quite the pair back in the day. Tony taught Arty everything he knew before taking a big bite out of a little landfill in Dekalb. Question is why you chose to keep the past to yourself. I'm thinking maybe because Big Man didn't want me to know."

"Big Man?" She laughs.

"Yeah. And I'm not talking about Elvis this time."

"You think I work for José Beggemon?"

"Well, it ain't the taxpayers of Chandler, Illinois, honey."

"Creative."

"Far-fetched?"

"Even for you. Big Man's a ghost in the budget, Mack. Good for a police task force, not much else."

"If you say so."

"You think I'm in the pocket. Brilliant. You're way out of your depth here, Mack. You're lost."

"Nothing new there, Sandra. Being lost is the best way to find out where you are. The name Ed Larson ring a bell, or has he slipped your memory too?"

"Who?"

"Officer Larson. He's the cop who picked up the APB on a black F-150. He followed a great big guy in a great big pickup to a parking garage out in Orland Park. You picked up the thread from Santiago when he got pulled into a meeting. You decided that this was something you really needed to follow. So you called me about the APB hit like Raffi asked you to, and then you called Officer Larson on his phone and told him he needed to keep you informed. He did. Roll the clock forward and the big pickup turns into a small taxi with a broken window and a terrified driver. A friend of mine, by the way. They end up at the airport where the great big guy disappears, and the terrified taxi-driver gets squeezed into a car full of muscle."

"Why do I care, Mack?"

"Exactly, Sandra. Why *do* you care? Why do you care enough to follow that chase? Only reason I can figure is that you knew someone who was vitally interested in the police response. Like, how many units? Coming from which directions? That sort of thing. Helpful information if you're being chased and looking to avoid the net."

"Big Man," she says, shaking her head like she still hasn't gotten past that part. It's a good act.

"His people," I correct. "I guess you could try me on not knowing who those people were working for, but that's a tough sell. You're way too smart not to know a cesspool when you smell one. I'm guessing they're the same people who, thanks to you, got an advance peek at the Scooter Pleasants case summary."

"I have no idea what…"

"Come on, Sandy. Sure you do. That was the summary that said someone had set Scooter's truck on fire along with his smut shop. That turned out to be wrong. The shop got singed, but not the truck. I caught the mistake and made the correction before we issued the summary. Somehow, Arty's union rep got the memo before it was corrected. He went on and on about a burned-up truck."

"You're saying I leaked case information to the IFOP?"

"I'm saying someone leaked it and it wasn't me."

"I think you're saying a lot more than that."

"You're right, Sandra. I am. Your real boss sent the wrong messenger. I don't trust you like he thinks I do. Next time you want someone to follow you to a meeting, try not to lie to their face."

Her eyes register the slap.

"I haven't lied, Mack. I…"

"You said you came alone."

"I am alone. What make you think I'm not?"

"Three pieces of bacon and two muffins."

She looks like I switched languages.

"What?"

I nudge the two new plates of food her direction.

"See, once a strip of bacon comes inside out of the cold it turns into a blueberry muffin. So, I'm pretty sure your two muffins are sitting at that window table over there." I nod and she looks. "They showed up right after you did. No food. Just coffee that they aren't drinking. They haven't taken their coats off because they don't expect to stay. That leaves piece of bacon number three, here, sitting in a car someplace drumming ten fat fingers against the wheel waiting for me to show up with a muffin under each arm and a .45 caliber blueberry stuck in my ribs."

She closes her eyes and takes in a lung full.

"You've got someone watching the diner. Jesus."

"No, he was busy washing feet."

"You're crazy, Mack."

"Yeah. I heard that about me. I think that's why I'm still alive. You're going to have to take this meeting alone, Sandra. Good luck in your retirement. It's not all it's cracked up to be."

"I told them you'd be stubborn," she says, almost to herself.

"Who, Sandra? You told who?"

"I don't know. How many times do I have to tell you? I'm supposed to show you this."

She digs into a coat pocket beneath the table. My heart can feel Sig in his harness, ready to go. I pull my hand off the table to my lap.

Next time I see her hand it's holding a sheet of paper folded into quarters. I take it and open it up, expecting a threat I'm supposed to read. Turns out to be an atom bomb dressed up like a photograph. Her eyes are waiting for mine.

"Who gave you this?" I demand.

"I don't know." She says it with a smile that begs for a slap. "Would you like to find out?"

Cleo returns with the ticket. She waits for me and Sandra to stop staring at each other. I fold up the paper and trade it for my wallet. I fish out Andrew Jackson and hand him up.

"Thanks, Isis," I say.

"You want to take those muffins with you?" she asks, pointing. I can feel her eyes on the side of my head. I don't look. I give my answer to Sandra instead.

"No, but I think they're coming anyway."

"Want me to call you a taxi?"

Bless her half-Egyptian heart. She's trying.

"I've got a ride."

Cleo digs into her apron. She produces a single Camel and Raj's butane lighter.

"Blindfold?" I ask, taking the contraband.

"Fresh out," she says, nodding at Sandra. "Ask her. Watch yourself, Mack."

ONE HUNDRED FIFTY-FOUR

It's an odd foursome. They push through the front door of *Sonny's* and hunch their shoulders into the wind, moving along the cold, gray street like they don't like each other much. Sandra Booth is in the lead, Ray a step behind, and two men, one white, the other Asian, both with lumps in their coats. No one is talking.

Ray has his own lumpy coat. Either no one has noticed, or no one cares. He passes Raj smoking in his front seat without so much as a wink. He's not thinking about Raj. He's thinking about that photograph. That and the Camel.

At the corner they wait for the light, then cross the street to a green Plymouth Breeze with tinted windows and a saggy tailpipe smoking at the curb. The antenna is bent ten degrees and the right front fender has a sob story of some sort. The rear passenger window slides down, revealing an older black woman in the back seat. She turns and wrinkles her nose at the wind, looking up at Sandra.

"That's it," says Sandra. "I'm done. This is over."

The woman gives a slow nod. "*Merci. Bonne chance.*"

Sandra nods.

"He's got an extra pair of eyes somewhere."

The woman looks up at Ray with old eyes that are amused and disappointed at the same time, moats of bloody milk around islands of chocolate brown. She's got a couple of eyebrows large enough to have their own opinion about things and a head of coiffed, mahogany-brown hair that stops just above her earrings. Her lips are a matronly red, like she's on her way to church to kiss the grandkids.

She jerks her head a little, leans back and slides the window back up. Ray sees a man in the rising reflection he doesn't recognize. He's covered in bandages with a bruise over his throat. I'm fifteen feet behind and five feet above. He can't see me, but he can see what I see: a man who's too old for the abuse. A man not up for whatever fight is coming.

"Next life, Mack," Sandra says. She points a key fob at the black Sentra two spaces away. The car flashes and beeps. She hands the Asian man the keys and climbs in the passenger seat.

"Next life, Sandra."

One quick illegal U-turn in the street and they're gone. The man next to Ray walks around the back of the Plymouth and opens the opposite back door. He holds it open like a valet at the *Ritz*.

Ray stands in the street, not moving, wondering how many cats will die before curiosity finally gets around to him. The back window lowers again, erasing Ray's reflection from the top down.

"*Allons-y,*" she says, moving her hand impatiently. "*Allons-y.*"

It's not the imperial attitude that finally convinces him to walk around and climb in.

It's the cigarette in her hand.

ONE HUNDRED FIFTY-FIVE

I'm ready for the spread-eagle and the pat down. The lug holding the door doesn't seem interested. He's clear-eyed and well-fed, this one. He likes a clean shave and a woody cologne after he's done showering off at the gym.

I give him a careful nod and he shuts me inside the Plymouth next to the smoking French woman. I reach into my pocket and pull out the only three things that are on my mind. One of those things I use to set fire to another. The third one I open up and lay on the seat between us.

I blow out a blue stream as Frenchie picks up the photo with a small, self-congratulatory smile that she doesn't want me to miss. My battered brain luxuriates in its cloud. She bobs her own cigarette with a nod as she looks at the paper.

"You know how to get a man's attention," I say.

I put my head back and take another drag. I hold in the smoke for a blink that starts to feel like a nap, then I open my eyes. We're moving, angling off from the curb out into traffic.

"Where are you taking me?" I use the question as cover to look around for Raj. I catch him across the street with his blinker on. No one answers. "Anybody got a French dictionary?"

"That won't be necessary," says Frenchie without a look or so much as a hint of an accent. "I speak many languages."

"Common sense is my favorite. You speak that one?"

"I do."

"Where are we going?"

"In circles," she says. "Just like you. But slow enough for Mr. Malik to keep up without breaking any traffic laws. Let's not encourage lawlessness."

I smoke and give her a good look. Long dark coat over something thin and pink. Winter over summer. Her shoes are on the wrong side of town, slick pink leather with a beaded buckle and a short heel. I'm guessing they've got a big closet full of friends. Her lobes have been dipped in mother-of-pearl. She's not dressed for a killing.

I try to sort out which of the ten thousand questions wedged into the doorway of my larynx should make it out first. I point to the photo. She hands it back to me and looks idly out her window like she knows nothing else can happen until we get past this part.

I soak it in all over again. A circular banquet table dressed in white. At the far side of the table, martini glass in his hand, looking up at the camera, is a young Sam Royce, chiseled chin, jet-black hair just so, laughing green eyes, long before he had any right to be called Mr. Mayor. Just behind his right ear is a goatee attached to the face of Anthony Rickens, bent at the waist, stress-testing the seams of a tuxedo.

There are a lot of other people at and around the table, most I don't recognize. They all shop at the same campaign button store. The idea of Royce working in the Illinois House of Representatives has made everyone thirsty. He's just getting started in politics and everyone wants to be along for the ride. It's a well-dressed mob brandishing crystal and skewered olives. But I can pick out a couple of faces.

Al Nosek. Nutsack to anyone who asks me. CPD Lieutenant for too many years. He retired about the time Twill got the keys to the Chandler IAD. Nutsack's last official act was showing me the door for mob connections I never had. His last unofficial act was colluding with the department shrink to leak my psychiatric file.

On the other side of the table, two chairs away from the man of the hour, is Alexi Novak. Alex to this group. I recognize his mug and the tux from the photo in his mother's living room. He's got both eyes on Royce.

Long time are friends, Ivah had said. *Jovah is hating.*

On the nearside of the table, closer to the camera, I make out the profile of someone who looks like Victor Roby. Has to be him. His hair is already on its way out and his complexion is not yet in its candlewax years, but it's him. Long head with flaps for ears and a nose that belongs on the back of a Great White. I can make out half a smile on the half a face in the photo. He's enjoying himself. Victor obviously can't see the future. A few years later he'll have to pay a small fortune for trying to collect insurance on some burned-up warehouses that stood too close to Victor's lighter. He'll write the check and feel lucky to stay out of state housing.

To Victor's left is Steven-with-a-V, gesturing some hilarity across the table. Here's a man who's loving life. And why not? Drink in his hand. A bullet-free body. Back home he's got a ten-point buck on the wall, an imported trophy wife in the bed, and a basement freezer full of venison, wrapped and dated.

Victor's right hand is stretched out over the white tablecloth. Two fingers are resting on the wrist of a woman with her back to the camera, face rotated toward him ever-so-slightly. A younger, attractive woman on the arm of an older man as rich as he is ugly. That makes her either a cliché or a working girl. Whatever she is, the two fingers on her wrist make her Victor's for the night. The arm of the cliché disappears up into the sleeve of a black, tailored silk blouse with a scoop-back obscured beneath a tumble of long brown hair. Next to her is an empty chair in front of an empty glass and a dirty plate. I'm guessing the napkin in the seat belongs to a photog with an itchy finger.

"Who took this photo?" I ask.

"Someone with a camera," says Frenchie. "Bad start, Detective. Try again."

"Okay. Who am I talking to?"

She shrugs.

"I've always liked Marie. Good name."

"Is it yours?"

"Of course not."

"It beats Frenchie. Who do you work for, Marie?"

"Best guess," she says with a pull on her cigarette. Her eyes really know how to look at people.

"Government," I say. "The Bureau."

It gets me an amused look from beneath a cocked eyebrow.

"Do I look like someone the FBI invites to the Christmas party?"

"Maybe that makes you perfect."

"Maybe that makes you delusional."

"Maybe. That's familiar territory for me. But your boys have that regulation stick up the ass. They know how to keep their mouths shut and they don't feel the need to flash any metal to make me a believer." I pat the seat between us. "The ride is nicely banged up. Love the crooked antennae. Problem is that real bangers take a certain pride in their transportation. This thing is an embarrassment to any self-respecting lowlife. I'm guessing this is the same car that snatched up Raj at the airport and spit him out in an empty parking lot, far enough away for some exercise but close enough to the terminal to keep from freezing to death."

I wait to see if her face is handing out reactions. Nothing.

"Raj has a couple of good eyes and a memory, but somehow he gets to live to tell me the whole ugly story anyway. That makes your boys something other than a pack of criminals wanting to stay out of jail. So, yeah, Marie, I'm guessing undercover law enforcement. How'm I doing?"

Marie decides to smoke rather than answer. I keep at it.

"What I can't figure is who Hell was to you. How is it that a guy like that can just make a phone call from the back of a cold taxi and get your boys to run interference at the airport? Hostage in the front seat. Bunch of cops scratching their heads at an empty F-150 idling at an empty parking garage in Orland Park. Hell wants to get himself out of Dodge. So he tells Raj to head for the airport and makes a phone call. Gives up Raj's name and cab number, just so your boys know who to detain as Hell slips away. He could have snapped Raj's neck like a toothpick. No one would have been the wiser until he was long gone and airport security came by to move things along. Instead, Hell calls you. Or someone who works for you."

I take another hit, looking at her without seeing. It's just the puzzle in front of me now. I'm picking up pieces off the floor of my swollen brain and snapping them into place.

"Probably not a surprise request, was it?" I ask. "Sandra was keeping you informed, but she lost the trail at the parking garage. So, I'm guessing you were waiting for Hell to reach out. But why is that a phone call you take, Marie? Who was Hell to you? When he calls, what language do you speak? I'm putting all my chips on German."

I let her exhale. She takes her time.

"*Richtig*," she says. "*Deutsch*."

"What's his real name? No one names their kid *Helles Bock*."

Frenchie Marie cracks a window to let out some smoke so we can see each other. We exit I-57 for I-80. We are, in fact, driving in circles. I check the back window for Raj. I can't see him, but I know he's back there someplace. Kid's learning how to tail a car.

"Burkhart Lang," she says when her lungs are empty. "Your colleagues – former colleagues, I should say –matched him up this morning. You're a bit out of the loop, I'm afraid."

"Always happens when I'm unconscious. Former colleagues. You must read the same newspaper everybody else does. How do I get a subscription so I can keep up on my own life?"

"I've got a reception to attend, Detective. Is that how you want to spend your time?"

"No. Who was Herr Lang to you?"

Marie shrugs.

"You tell me."

We share a long look.

"Alright," I say. "I will. He was an opportunity."

"An opportunity."

"Yeah. He was a big man walking around with a pocket full of dirt on a bigger man. You were making a deal with a minion hoping to bag up the Devil."

"Interesting."

"Isn't it, though. Meantime, you didn't care who Hell killed. Whose head he unscrewed. What child he sold or gave away to human garbage like Scooter Pleasants and Garrett Hoosier. You and whoever signs your paycheck had larger concerns. You were happy for him to keep working as you watched from the bushes. All the better to help you hang his boss. That's who Hell was to you. That makes you as evil as he was. And twice as stupid."

"Evil and stupid to boot," says Marie through another drag. "My, my."

"Sorry to say, but if dunce cap fits… You people stopped checking your blind spot. Hell was playing footsies with two masters at the same time, telling you and the boss what you each wanted to hear while he kept his own plans to himself."

"And what plans were those?"

"We'll never know. But I'm guessing a guy like Hell doesn't get his ambition off the rack. He was an extra-large man with extra-large dreams. That right there makes him a liability on any team effort. Then you come along dangling the keys to the kingdom: an opportunity for Hell to flip on the boss and clean house. You figure you'll take him out of commission for a decade, maybe less, on some bullshit reduced charge. Something small with a few years attached. Easy-peasy. A single pushup for a guy like that. That's what you told him, anyway. Maybe you had plans of stabbing him in the back and sending him away for good. Or maybe you told yourself you'd worry about putting Hell in the crosshairs whenever he made parole. Doesn't matter. Hell wasn't playing your game. He was playing his own game. He told his boss all about you and whatever deal you were selling. I'm guessing they knocked steins and had a good laugh or two. Hell thought he was building loyalty points. Problem was Hell had his own blind spot. His boss can smell a slab of meat when it's starting to spoil. That's what got Herr Lang a bullet in the ear, a broken spine, and a skyride in the back seat of a Champagne Malibu."

I point my Camel at her through the smoke.

"That happened because of you, Marie. You got that guy snapped like a wishbone at a church picnic. Didn't see that one coming, did you? Now you've got a broken giant and nothing to show for it except the nightmares for what you let him do."

She snorts out a soft laugh.

"I sleep fine, Detective. You've got a flair for the simplistic, you know that?"

"People are complicated, Marie. The games they play are complicated. But the truth inside is usually pretty goddamned simple. So, tell me why I'm here or let me out at the next corner."

I'm so full of it I have to fight to keep from falling sideways. I want to be out of this car and back into the cold where nobody knows anything about as much as I want to cut my Camel short. Marie gives me an appraising look and a slow nod.

"You seem to like lectures about blind spots," she says. "So, let's talk about blind spots."

She holds the cigarette in her lips so her hands can pull a black leather purse up off the floor and dig around. She has to move aside a smaller bag of cosmetics and a nine-millimeter Baretta to extract what she wants. It's another folded piece of paper, just like the one I'm already holding. She hands it over with two fingers and I open it up. Turns out the inside is completely different.

I recognize the drycleaner. Dirty little building squatting under a large, pink crabapple. The tree is in full bloom, which puts the photo sometime in late spring or early summer. Sometime long before Raffi started collecting license plates. I'm guessing Marie doesn't care so much about the building or the tree. She's all about the guy in the Cubs cap stepping through the front door. It's like putting a hat on a light bulb.

"Twill."

I can't tell if I actually make the sound of his name or if the very thought of him in my head is enough to escape my skull and knock around some smokey air molecules. I look up at Marie. She lets me work it through.

"You've been on Orland," I say. It comes out dreamily slow and hypnotic. "Sandra was your eyes and ears inside IAD. Because of Twill? You've been watching him?" I shake the paper at her. "Him?"

"Question is why haven't you?"

I stare at the photo. All that time. Raffi sitting outside the drycleaner, taking pictures. Not a word from Twill that he knows the place.

My brain plays back every conversation Twill and I have ever had. Every facial expression. Every scolding. The leak of Scooter's complaint about Arty. My termination. Everything old is suddenly new. I've been putting together a puzzle with pieces from the wrong box.

More. By-the-book Twill lets me moonlight for Nadia King, strictly against policy. That gets me a flash drive and a spreadsheet. I bring it all to him. He passes it up the food chain. *Look at what one of my guys just found.* Boom. Any investigation against the mayor suddenly verboten from on high.

Suri. Bloomington. The thought hits me sideways and I jolt in my seat. Twill had assigned Quinten Young to tail Suri and Carl. Quentin shoots his partner in the back, paints the walls with Carl, and goes gunning for Suri. Just like he was supposed to do. I've been tiptoeing around Twill's shock, shame and remorse when all this time...

Marie is watching my face like I'm the best show in town.

"Why?" I whisper. "He was the one who brought me on board. And he had to fight for that."

"Maybe he knew you'd get things done. Or maybe he's a good soldier. Does what he's told. We all work for someone."

"Sandra was all about Twill," I say to no one in particular.

Marie slips me a sideways look, then back out the window. The cold air sucks out some smoke.

"Then something happens. She gets spooked. She cooks up a bad excuse and tries to leave. You put her back in play, but she's not happy about it. She starts drawing lines. Making ultimatums. So you can't use her. You've lost an inside asset. You want another. You *need* another. Because now the shit is really starting to fly. The judiciary. The Chief. The Mayor's office. OAG is going to turn everybody upside down for pocket change. You need someone on the inside. So, you give Sandra one last assignment. Get ol' Ray Mackey to take a meeting. You figure I'm going nowhere at light speed. You figure I'll jump at the chance."

I stare at the photo in silence.

Twill, I think to myself. Christ. *Twill.*

"Well, you're wrong about that, Marie." I hear the words as if they came from someone else.

She swings her face my direction, takes a final pull, then crushes the butt into the back of the passenger headrest, letting it drop to the floor.

"Am I?" she asks.

"Yes."

"Because you've got better things to do? Security at the mall? Collecting bottles?"

"No. Because I'm not the mole everyone thinks I am. Because I don't work for you."

"Like I said, Ray, we all work for someone. Who, exactly, do you think you've been working for all this time?" Her face wrinkles into comic disbelief. "The taxpayers? You *have,* in fact, been the mole everyone thinks you are. You just never realized it. Maybe this is your chance to right the ship."

"Funny word, maybe. And if I don't?"

She shrugs again in the way I have come to hate in the space of a car ride.

"Free country," she says. "Kind of."

"Yeah?" I'm angry now. Capsizing. Grappling for leverage. "And what country are you from, Marie?" I point at the butt on the floor. "Your cigarettes aren't from around here."

"International problems require international solutions. There's a bigger picture." She gestures at the photo in my hands. "Not a picture that fits on a sheet of paper. In fact, it's not a picture at all. It's an odor. Corrosion. Decomposition. Decay. It's in the walls, Ray. The rafters. The plumbing. The vents. The circuits. The foundation. Different countries are simply different rooms in the same house."

"Why me?"

"Because you've got a good nose. You can smell it too. You haven't yet explained it all away as something else. Like most people have. You might act like you're ready to move on. Just let it all rot. But it's only an act. You're not okay with the smell."

"I can smell bullshit like the best of them. So, I'll ask again, Marie. Whoever you are. Why me?"

"Because you're obsessed with him," she says. "And because I think he's obsessed with you."

I don't have to ask. I know the answer. I ask anyway.

"Who?"

Marie gives me a sad smile and then freshens up her lipstick.

"You're like a new kitten to him," she says. "All he needs is a strand of yarn. A toy bird on a stick. And look at you go. This way. That way. Wherever he wants. Hours of entertainment. Except you're not just a kitten. Are you, Ray?"

All I can do is stare at her. My ears are ringing like distant air raid sirens.

"You're his best man in the field. You make it all happen."

"Bullshit."

"Think so? How is it you rode out of *Deke's Auto Scrap* without a sheet over your head? You think his assassin couldn't pick you off if he wanted? If those were his instructions?"

I watch the cars in the lane next to us, jockeying for position on the way to nowhere. A man driving a white pickup makes me remember Mouth. I catch the guy in mid-yawn. He looks like he's screaming.

"Assassin," I say, finally looking back. "I'd have said sniper. Shooter."

"He doesn't miss," she says. "Kyiv. London. Istanbul. Vienna. Prague. Houston. Seattle. Cologne. He's going for a world record."

"So, then you know who he is."

"Well." She tosses those eyebrows. "There's knowing and there's knowing. Our list keeps getting shorter. We keep narrowing. We came closer this time. Closer than ever."

"What happened?"

The sad smile again. Like she's explaining death to a child.

"What happened? Ray. You helped set him free, is what happened. You and that blind spot of yours."

The car exits the freeway on a long, sloping curve. It feels like we're spiraling into a chasm. My pulse pounds away in my head. I'm woozy all over again.

"No." It's the only syllable I can manage. I'm too busy seeing his face at counsel table, sitting next to Mickey Shaw. Marie leans sideways a little.

"What you want to bet he celebrated his release up in a tree?"

"That's not… That's not…"

"Really? Is it his name that's in the way? Guess I should have called myself *Wembly Stadium*. Or *Doublemint*. *Bazooka Joe*. You might have believed those names more than Marie." She lets it sit a beat or two. "Names. Backgrounds. Prior convictions for dealing grass. They're easy, Ray." She gestures at the pages I hold. "Pieces of paper. Blips on a screen."

We ride in silence as my brain spirals; errant, disconnected thoughts like streaks of light drawn into a black hole. Marie pats me on the knee.

"Or maybe I'm wrong. If I recall, I'm twice as stupid as I am evil. I'll defer to your greater knowledge on that. Do you want the job, or should we drop you at the curb?"

I look at her and swallow, hauling myself out of the muck of my own head.

"Pass," I say. She looks at me with the vaguest hint of surprise. "You're right about my nose. I lie down with you, and I'll never get the stink off."

Marie nods. She taps her boy on the shoulder muscle.

"Up here at the corner."

He hits the blinker.

"Besides," I say. "You people missed the boat. I'm out of IAD. Out of policing. For good this time. That bridge is on fire."

The car glides to a stop outside a sad, gray strip mall. Shoes. Fingernails. Mufflers. Not a bar in sight.

"If you say so," she says. "But I think you seriously underestimate our resources, Detective. Nothing is on fire that needn't be on fire." She extends a wrinkled black hand. I almost shake it. "Photos please."

I hand her the two sheets of paper. She takes the one of Twill, refolds it and slips it into her purse.

"Why don't you hang on to this one," she says, handing back the other page. "A memento."

I take it as I'm opening the door. The wind takes my ash. The car floods with winter.

She doesn't let go of the paper.

I look. Her polished red thumbnail is pressed firmly into the back of the woman sitting next to Victor Roby.

"Smart," she says. "And lovely. It's not that we *can't* see what's in our blind spots. It's that we don't want to see."

She sounds like she's a million miles away. I feel too heavy and weak to move.

"She went much too soon, Ray. I'm sorry for that. I really am." I try to look at her. I can't. "Now get out of the car."

I step out, dropping the Camel to the ground. I hold the creased sheet with both hands and close the door with a hip. Frenchie Marie disappears into the wind.

I lose track of time. Standing and staring are my only options, so that's what I do. I'm still at it when Raj skids to a stop twenty feet away.

"Mack."

I thought she was an arm-candy cliché. Rentable even.

"Mack."

A third option shows up. The feeling surges through me like water from a broken dam. I stand and I stare, and I drown myself in the ache.

Marlo.

ONE HUNDRED FIFTY-SIX

Hard to say, really, which is the greatest disappointment.

The recliner, with which Ray has been one for hours now.

The fire, which has provided welcome heat and the only light in a room now burnt orange and swaying with shadow.

The three Camels, curled up in their dish.

Phil, who has refused to leave the rise and fall of his chest.

The bottle of Old Forester, tall and dark caramel brown, the posture of a loyal soldier by his side to the end. Within easy reach. No judgment.

Or Nina Simone, whose *I Get Along Without You Very Well (Except Sometimes)* now wafts the smoke like she is stirring warm bathwater with a finger.

You'd think any of them might do the trick. Certainly in combination. But no.

I, at least, am not a disappointment. I am as he ever expects. Reliably judgmental. Discomfiting to the end. The unscratchable, out-of-reach itch.

He drops his arm over the side of the chair, sets the tumbler on the floor and pours. He doesn't need to look. He looks instead at his two-legged couch, slouching toward the fire like an old leather avalanche.

He sets down the bottle and dips a finger in the glass. Phil lifts her head, knowing. Expecting. She takes the drop with a rasp of tongue. She shakes her head in a rapid twitch, then resettles into the crook of his left arm and closes her eyes.

"Wish you could tell me who opened up that trunk," he says. He leaves the glass on the floor and strokes her head with his thumb, feeling her precise, delicate skull beneath her softness. "I should sit you down with a sketch artist." He glances at her downy, seemingly oblivious form. "Right? Get you on the witness stand.

Point your little paw. That man, there, Your Honor. He's the one."

He lifts his glass from the floor.

At least you were able to leap, he thinks. You saw your chance and took it. Jimmy, not so much.

He drinks to Jimmy, wondering where they took him. How it ended.

Then he loops back around to the same ugly slideshow playing on the walls of his bruised and soggy brain. Orland Twill in a Cubs cap, stepping out into sunlight. Wrigley Menard up in a tree. Danika King, little hand pressed up against the back seat window of Raffi's car. Sam Royce at the table, Tony Rickens' goatee tickling his ear. Frenchie Marie shrugging, her red thumbnail in the back of Victor Roby's date.

Marlo.

Marlo.

Marlo.

I get along without you very well, Nina lies.

Another drink to sink them. To drown them all. Hasn't worked so far. But he keeps trying.

It is not wholly unproductive time. To the contrary, nothing like soaking a concussion in bourbon to help a guy loosen up; unbolt what he thinks he knows and start over. Question everything. He's torn apart the puzzle in his head and put it back together. It's all making more sense now.

In some universe, things making sense might have lent more comfort than a cat and a Camel by a warm fire. It doesn't. Not in this universe.

Ray leans forward with a groan, careful to keep Phil where she is and his bourbon where it belongs. His fingers pull his phone from the coffee table.

Two rings gets him the voice he wants. Sleepy. Irritated. But there.

"Yeah."

"How's black beauty?" he asks. It takes a second or two.

"One piece. No scratches. Gun and key under the seat."

"Where?"

"Bus station. Rockford. Three tickets to Minneapolis. They're headed west. We're putting the word out. Making some calls. How's Phil?"

"Glad to be home. Thanks for that."

"No prob. How are you?"

"Like a bug on a windshield. Glad the wipers have finally stopped."

"Tell me you're taking those pills with water, Mack."

"Yeah. The ice in the glass melted a long time ago. That was water."

"Mack."

"About tomorrow," he says.

Raffi knows better than to mother him. Nothing he can do. He lets it go.

"Yeah. What."

"Come an hour earlier."

"Earlier? You're three sheets, man. I can hear it in your voice. How about some rest?"

"Work to do, Raffi."

"What kind of work?"

"Police work. Bring a set of bracelets."

"What? One, I always have a set and, two, why?"

"One, I don't have a set and, two, I'm not police anymore. See you in the morning."

He pushes the button. Just him now. Again. Phil stretches. Him and Phil. And me.

He trades the phone for the tumbler and the memory of Marlo's back. Her hair. The edge of her face.

Nina bows out just before the next record drops. Carmen McRae wraps her arms around the room for a slow spin. She breathes the question on everybody's mind. *How long has this been going on?*

Phil yawns and lifts her head. She looks around like she's trying to make sense of the room after a dream. She shakes her head again like what she sees doesn't fit the way it's supposed to.

"I know the feeling," he says, stroking the length of her body.

He does, too. Like waking up inside of a dream, that feeling; recognizing everything just enough to know it's all wrong, but not enough to know how it's wrong. There are puzzles within the puzzles. Secrets within the secrets. At the bottom of the well is another well. And another one below that.

When he gets like this, he starts to imagine that I'm her. Up here, looking down. Who's to say I'm not? Who's to say our brains aren't for rent to the highest bidder, or the most interested? They bring all their ideas and crazy notions. They unpack, decorate the place with their memories and judgments and ride around for a while. Who's to say I'm not her, floating in the basket of a hot air balloon tied to his beltloop so she can have easy access to his ear?

It's the entire room, now, that turns around the spindle of Carmen's voice.

How long has this been going on?

She comes to him through the smoke. He closes his eyes to see her better.

It's the smile he sees first, so secret it almost isn't there, the burn of a cigarette through dense fog. Knowing, but not sharing. Then the big blue eyes. Then there's the rest of her, small and round and old as dirt beneath a lacquer smooth finish.

I hold you in the deepest part of me. That's what the little slip of parchment had said. Meknikov's missive now coming up on two hundred birthdays.

I hold you… YOU… in the deepest part of ME.

It puts the reader, the holder of the note, at the center of it all. *You.*

Him. Ray.

The doll is gone. It's Marlo now. Through the viewfinder. Hair suspended in the breeze. The lake behind her, blazing in autumn. Those enigmatic lips, implacable in what they never say.

You, Ray, are the center. *You* are what is on the inside, waiting to be discovered. From the very beginning. You. Take the damned picture.

He opens his eyes. Blinks at the room. He wants to shake his head like Phil.

The more things make sense, the less sense they make.

ONE HUNDRED FIFTY-SEVEN

He doesn't trust me to drive hungover and concussed. So, we take his car. Raffi keeps the Dodge clean and tidy. The dashboard gleams. It's even got a back window, real glass too, not a plastic sheet, so you can see where you've been. And maybe who's following you, which is the best way I know of to see your future.

Riding shotgun is fine by me. I watch the buildings drift by, chunks of cold, gray stone bolting down the tarp of cloud in the wind. They get shorter as we go, and fewer, as the gravitational pull of Chicago weakens with distance. Raffi drives in silence, for miles now. He's trying to make sense of it all. I stay out of his way until he needs me.

I also try to stay out of the mirror. I'm tired of the shock. I look worse than I feel, which always makes me feel worse, setting off a race to the bottom that might never stop. I have a new compassion for rotting fruit dropped on the side of the road.

"And you got all of that from who?" he asks. I'm still thinking about my face. I almost give him a laundry list of concussors. I turn. He's talking about the story.

"I got a lot of it from Wayne Bishop's old cell mate," I say. "August Thelonious Pepper, aka Monk. He did his stretch in Stateville and came out the other end with a thing against lying. He's staying clean turning a transit wrench for CTA. He seems straight up now. I'll get you his number so you can follow up. Remind me because I've already forgotten."

"So, Wayne Bishop steals a van. The van is full of frozen fish. The fish are full of smack. Did he know?"

"Bishop? About the drugs? Doubt it."

"So he just stumbles onto a van full of heroin. That's one lucky score, man."

"Was it?" I ask. "That lucky score got Wayne killed."

"True. Okay, so he lives high on the hog for a while and decides to go back for more. But they're waiting for him. They bait the trap and they're ready. They give him a choice."

"Play the patsy or eat a bullet," I say. "Wayne decides he doesn't like the taste of bullets. He goes for playing patsy."

"For the murder of Officer Joe Novak, of all people."

"The same."

"And the guy running the game, according to Monk, according to Bishop, is some dude in boots that everyone calls Captain."

"You're batting a thousand, kid."

I lean back and look out the window, letting him tell me the story that I just told him. Raffi's as good at the remembering game as he is at using a bullet to find a far-away face in the dark. Hearing it all from someone else helps me comb through the details again. It's all still conjecture. A theory of the case. It's relationship to reality is roughly equivalent to what police sketch artists do every day. And I'll take that. It's a start. A place to start asking questions. Just enough to set the table for confessions.

"And you think laying all of this out on the table as I swing a pair of handcuffs gets us a confession?" Raffi sounds like a mind-reader, but not yet a believer. "Because I gotta say, man, what you've told me isn't enough to keep anyone locked up overnight. And we're not talking about just anyone, Mack. You'll need an extra tight case anyway and from what I've heard so far, this thing won't fly for any longer than it takes a lawyer to show up. Maybe less."

Turning my neck to look at him hurts too much. I do it anyway.

"You have anything better to do today?"

"Me?" Raffi laughs. "No, man. LT yanked me off drycleaner duty. That case is done. Guess that leaves me with nothing but a shit-ton of regular IAD work and feeling my hide drying up on LT's wall next to yours."

I grind my teeth about the mayor's drycleaner. It's bad enough the mayor gets a pass. It's infinitely worse that I made it happen. I don't know the face of Big Man, but I can feel his smile.

"Don't flatter yourself, brother," I say. "Your hide is never making it up on that wall next to mine."

"Twill's by the book," he says. "Don't take it personally. He's in a shitstorm. I wouldn't trade places with Twill right now for anything. My question is how you want to play this thing because, you know, at the end of the day, I'm gonna have to account."

A moving truck full of things I want to know about Orland Twill is beeping in my head, backing over everything I once thought I knew. In that truck is the photo of Twill walking out of the drycleaner that Raffi has been staking out on Twill's orders. I'd like to know what Raffi thinks. My queasiness wants some company.

"Okay then," I say instead. "We walk in, lay it all out like it's all airtight, see if that loosens the jar. You and your shiny badge can go in first. I'll play the heavy. I'll tell the story. You stand back and nod your head a lot. On the debrief, tell Twill you knew I was off-leash and you decided it would be a good idea if I had some adult supervision. All true, by the way. Don't own any part of this that feels wrong. Are we good?"

I let him think it through.

"I can do that," he says eventually. "But here's something I don't get."

"Shoot."

"Why wash her hands? Why scrub Bishop's DNA out from under Ivah's fingernails? You'd think they'd want to keep that."

"I'm sure they did. I'm guessing that was the whole point of clawing him in the face. But then at the last minute someone realizes that those fingernails of hers are too dirty not to clean."

Raffi shakes his head at the road.

"You lost me."

"Jovah comes over to Ivah's place after his shift, just like always. Only this time he's got more on his mind than tucking her in and having a quiet Parliament in the study. Time for a heart-to-heart with mom."

"About?"

"The past and the future. My guess is that baby brother Alexi had finally gone too far; further than Jovah's oath to serve and protect could stomach."

"Drugs?"

"Maybe. Better bet is women. Girls. Helping Big Man bring them over by the fishing boat load. There's a calendar on the wall of *Windy Wharf Seafoods* you should see. What started as an effort to smuggle Belka over, became a career path for Alexi. Jovah just couldn't look the other way."

"Belka is who again?"

"Ivah's niece. Her dead sister's kid stuck in a hole halfway between Novogrudok and Minsk. The daughter she never had."

"She seems to have a lot of those."

"Doesn't she though? She collects them to throw tea parties for unsuspecting schmucks like me."

I shake my head at having been so thoroughly rooked. Raffi swats me in the arm.

"Could have happened to anyone, Mack. Nadia was something."

"It literally could have happened only to me, Raffi. And, yeah," I give him a look, "Nadia was something. But thanks for trying. Point is, Belka may as well be Ivah's daughter. Alexi's job is to get her here. It's all a matter of money. Ivah and Alexi scrape it together and get it to the right people, being careful to keep brother Jovah out of the loop. I'm guessing that's how Alexi's association with Big Man got started."

"And?"

"Swing and a miss. They picked up Nadia, but Belka got herself arrested instead. No one knows it at the time, but Belka's on a direct path to killing a cop in Minsk and dying in a prison riot. That's years off. Meantime Ivah wants Alexi to keep trying. He's a good son. He keeps trying. But that's an expensive hobby."

"He has to work it off," says Raffi. "He goes in deeper."

"Right. He works enough to pay for the delivery service and then some. Crime pays, apparently. They dirty his pockets, and he starts to thrive. Problem is..."

"Problem is Jovah."

"Problem is Jovah. He's no dummy. He hears things. Sees things maybe. Alexi is headed south in a hurry and big brother just can't get himself to not see what he sees. I'll bet a Camel or two that Joe tried making a direct appeal to brotherly love and got turned away. So, that left nothing for him to do except drop a dime on his own flesh and blood. That means a tough talk with mom."

"And Ivah didn't like it."

"'Course not. What's to like? Alexi's her baby boy. Alexi's the one who promised he's gonna bring Belka across the ocean for some apple pie and Fourth of July fireworks. Alexi's the one who always seems to have extra cash to share, probably because guilt always pays about as well as crime. He hasn't been so successful in bringing Belka over like he's supposed to so I'm betting his status reports to Ivah came in fat envelopes. What's not to like about a doting son with a pocketful of the American dream?"

"Jovah, meanwhile…"

"Jovah, meanwhile, is a finger-wagging scold in a uniform. Ivah told me all Jovah cared about was the police. The police were his only family, she said. She tried to downplay it, but I know betrayal when I hear it."

"Okay. So Jovah comes over."

"They argue. Jovah does all the talking; Ivah does all the not-listening. When he's done laying down the law, he puts her to bed. He goes into the den to smoke and decompress and think about sending Alexi to prison."

"But you're thinking Ivah's not in bed."

"Not for long. She's in the hall closet looking for that gun."

Raffi whistles and shakes his head. His eyes cut sideways, full of doubt.

"Pretty stone cold, Mack. For a mom?"

"Hard to know how that played out. She's scared. Angry. Lots of emotion. No power. Maybe she wanted some help making her side of the argument. Or to tell Jovah that she'd kill him, or maybe she'd kill herself, if he went through with it. Or maybe she is stone cold, Raffi. Maybe she's always been stone cold. You think Lizzie Borden warmed up in old age?"

"Lizzie Borden was acquitted."

"Come on, cub scout. So was O.J. Doesn't matter. Whatever thoughts took Ivah to the hall closet, she gets herself there. She gets the gun and heads for the den. And there he is, standing in the dark at the window, smoking a Parliament. The guy who's about to piss on everything. The embodiment of all her problems and fears. Belka will be gone forever. Alexi will be in prison. The money will dry up. But maybe none of that has to happen."

"She has to think she's going to die in lock up. So why…"

"Her fear was doing all the thinking that night, that's why. And her trigger finger took care of things. Irony is, according to Ivah, Jovah was the one who gave her the gun and taught her trigger finger what to do. Hell, maybe it was an accident. She points but doesn't mean to shoot. Just trying the idea on for size. Happens every day with a loaded gun."

Raffi is quiet, squinting his eyes like he's trying to see something in the distance that won't come into focus. I keep trying to sharpen things up.

"So then she's all over him. *Jovah, Jovah, my boy. What have I done? I didn't mean it.* It reads like a Dostoyevsky bedtime story."

"She gets his blood on her hands," says Raffi.

"Right. First call she makes is to Alexi. The call logs show she reached out after eleven o'clock. She doesn't have a good explanation for a call way past her bedtime to someone who normally had the dayshift when it came to checking in on her. Jovah had the nightshift. Ordinarily maybe she'd call Jovah, but he was busy bleeding out in the den. So she calls Alexi. She tells him everything. Alexi takes over. Gets on bended knee with people closer to the dark lord than he is. Explains that his mom just killed his hero-cop brother in order to protect him, Alexi. Doesn't want mom to go to prison. Explains that if mom gets sent up for murder, the hunt for a motive will be intense. Everything Alexi has been doing for Big Man will see daylight. That means Alexi has some real skin in the game. And so does Hell, who was running the trafficking operation."

"And if Hell has skin in the game, so does Big Man."

"Right. So, someone comes up with a better plan."

"Isn't the easiest plan to kill Ivah?"

"Sure. But they've got Alexi to worry about. He's not going to like the kill-mom plan. Could have pulled Alexi's plug too but maybe they want to keep Alexi around a while. Maybe they've got plans for him."

"What kind of plans?"

I venture the neck pain for another look across the Dodge.

"Long time friend of Sam Royce? You tell me, Raffi."

"Jesus," he whispers with a head shake. "Grooming him?"

"Like a prized poodle headed for Westminster. That's my guess. They've got Alexi hooked on easy money and that warm family feeling. And they've got more than enough goods to keep him from stepping out of line. Point is, they want to do right by Alexi. Built some loyalty. They need a plan to keep Ivah's ass out of prison and protect the organization. So, they decide to make her a victim. Find a new shooter with a ready-made motive."

"Bishop."

"A little on the hairy side, but conveniently short and crazy. He likes to steal things and has a long record to prove it. Just so happens, Bishop's in a van full of frozen fish and a gun barrel in every orifice. All his new friends are waiting for the order on what to do with him. The order is to hold him. Someone is coming to offer him an acting job."

"The Captain."

"Stands to reason," I say. "Turns out Bishop is game; highly motivated to help. They bag him and throw him in the trunk and haul him out to Ivah's place. They stage the scene like it's a Broadway set. They wipe Ivah's bloody fingerprints off the phone and everything else she has touched. Change her nightie. Get her in a clean robe. That's when someone stops to think about those fingernails. What if Jovah is under those fingernails? How does that happen if the police find Ivah tied up in the kitchen? Probably also started to think about how powder burns don't come off with a light rinse. So, they scrub her hands until they hurt. She remembers that part almost more than anything else. She kept saying *they.* *They* washed my hands. *They* tied me up. Too many years have passed. She doesn't have the same control over the script. Bishop wasn't out there by himself, Raffi. He had company."

"The scratches on both sides of his face," says Raffi.

"Right. They had her do it again with clean hands. Poor schmuck."

"So they tie her to the chair in the kitchen. Drop a bag over her head. Turn Bishop loose. Call the cops for shots fired. They're lucky someone hadn't done that already."

"Couldn't have picked a better murder scene if they'd tried. Deep lot. Surrounded by tall trees and bad neighborhoods."

"Gunshots were normal," says Raffi.

"Like birdsong in June. So, they let Bishop run. Ivah picks him out of a photo line-up like a pro. Chicago PD picks him up a week later."

"And the story is…" Raffi pauses to think it through. Then he starts again. "The story is Bishop was robbing the place. Gets interrupted by Ivah. She scratches him in the face. He's not interested in killing anyone. He neutralizes her by tying her to a chair in the kitchen and putting a trash bag over her head. Then he's interrupted by Jovah coming to check on his mom, per the norm. He hides in the den. He's got the gun from the closet. Boom."

"Boom. That's the story."

"And it stuck."

"Yeah. It stuck. They framed up Bishop but good. House full of fingerprints; a scratched-up face; his DNA under Ivah's nails. They made him put a second slug in Jovah so he'd be the one with the powder burns."

"Plus Ivah's things in his apartment," says Raffi.

"Including Ivah's Ruger all cuddled up with Bishop's fingerprints. Then there's the ponytailed lawyer on the take; and a signed, arguably coerced confession. Plus, an elderly, highly sympathetic, bereft victim with enough information to convict and enough infirmity to help gloss over any inconsistencies in her story."

"And the Russian doll under his bed?"

"Planted by someone in Big Man's pocket. May as well have been a grenade. The apartment photos had already been taken, so it looks for all the world like fabrication of evidence by some over-zealous cop looking to improve the odds of a conviction. You know how we get over cop killers, Raffi. When Joe Novak caught that bullet, the whole force lost its shit."

"So, the planted doll and the coerced confession gets Bishop reasonable doubt and a plea deal. Why? Why do that? Why not let him be convicted for murdering Joe Novak and let him take the needle?"

"Long wait for that cocktail, Raffi. In our system? Years. That was one reason they eventually killed the death penalty. Too much time and money for all the risk of getting it wrong. For Big Man, that meant a lot of time for Bishop to sober up and get loud. Everybody around him is full of free advice. They're all experts on ineffective assistance of counsel. New lawyer gets involved. Some frisky public defender looking to prove a point. Once Mickey Shaw is out of the picture, Big Man starts to lose control. Why risk that? Why wait and see? I'm guessing the Captain told Bishop that if he played ball, they'd forget all about the stolen van full of drugs and let him go with a short sentence in Stateville. Why not keep that bargain? Let Bishop take his showers with every other two-bit convict killing time and counting backwards to daylight. Death row lock-up is a small population and a lot harder to reach. Big Man made sure Bishop stayed where they could hand him the soap."

Raffi nods.

"In the meantime, the planted doll gives CPD a big black eye."

"Right. Nothing wrong with that. That never gets old."

"And why doesn't Bishop just... you know... tell the truth?"

"I'm guessing Wayne Bishop was promised a short stint. In and out for burglary. A lot better than the do-it-yourself justice he was looking at for stealing a van full of stuffed grouper. He was ready to give peace a chance."

"Yeah, but..."

"Besides, Raffi, who's he gonna tell the truth to? His lawyer? To Mickey Shaw? Try again."

"To anyone who will listen, man."

"Yeah? Well, Monk listened. You think he believed what he heard?" I point. "You're listening, Raffi. Doesn't sound like I've got you in the bag yet. Hell, I'm not even sure I'm in the bag yet. Who believes a story like this from a hairy nut-job like Bishop, looking to wriggle out from beneath a murder rap? Don't answer, I'll tell you. The only one who's likely to believe that story is some guy with a ten-year beard, a tinfoil hat and a picture of Sasquatch on his wall."

"Christ," says Raffi, shaking his head. We both stare out the window like there's something to see.

"Yeah," I say. "I'm guessing his picture is up there too."

"Or you could be wrong about all of this," he says with a shrug. "Just sayin', Mack. Lot of guesswork here."

"Yeah. Or I could be wrong."

The Golden View Senior Community hasn't changed a bit. Alice waves her pennant at us through the front windows as we approach.

"Morning, Alice," I say as we push through the doubles. Her big orange socks look like ski boots poking out from beneath her robe. "Next season the Bears are going all the way," I tell her. "I can feel it, Alice. It's coming."

She turns her chair in silence, face slack, mouth open, tracking us as we pass. I'm not sure if she can't figure out who I am and how it is I know her name, or why a man who looks like he belongs in an emergency room is coming to a retirement home.

The green cardigan is at the front desk with Frank inside, filling up both sleeves just like always. On the big screen behind him an old woman in a tiara is holding a sparkler. She fades away into a man and a woman putting together a jigsaw puzzle.

Frank puts down his pen, straightening himself as we cross the lobby. He adjusts the flask inside the cardigan like I don't have eyes. He can't help himself. His tells are two-by-fours to the head.

"What's doin', Frank?" I ask. He's too busy sizing me up to respond. "I know. I look amazing. This is Officer Santiago. We're here to pay Ivah Novak a visit."

Raffi's got his badge out. He holds it up against the glass partition so Frank can see.

Frank doesn't care about the badge. He can't stop looking at me.

"Frank…"

"I'm sorry," he says with a swallow.

And that's all he says.

But those saggy, sallow, bloodshot, alcoholic eyes keep on talking. They tell me that Ivah Novak is dead.

They tell me that I'm right.

ONE HUNDRED FIFTY-EIGHT

We try for a low-down from the Golden View medical director, Clifton J. Milk, Jr. He's likeable enough for a pale, bespectacled, pencil-thin ginger with no chin and extra teeth. He gives all his answers to Raffi because he doesn't want to get caught staring at me. The feeling's mutual. I give him both eyes anyway. He's the first guy to make me feel handsome in a long time.

Turns out the time of death was yesterday afternoon, just about the time Twill was rolling me through the front doors of the hospital.

"Cause?" asks Raffi. He gets a shrug.

"Hard to say. No autopsy yet. Probably nothing out of the ordinary for someone Ivah's age and stage. Probably the heart."

"Heart attack?" asks Raffi.

"I didn't say that."

"No, you didn't. Did Ivah have any particular medical condition that was putting her at immediate risk?"

Milk's face starts to curdle. He recites chapter and verse from the Golden View medical information policy. Seems we need a court order, which will require an open investigation, which will require evidence we don't have. It's easier to wait for the autopsy. Milk's face seems to know that already.

We excuse ourselves back to the lobby. I give Frank a look to suggest that maybe the flask in his pocket knows where he can find the key to Ivah's apartment. No dummy, Frank.

Everything is still here, except her. Ivah Novak left the world with an empty water glass on the coffee table next to six Parliaments still in the pack.

"So this is it," says Raffi. I look around to see him standing at the étagère in front of the wooden doll.

"Careful," I say, joining him. "She's quiet enough, but full of surprises."

He reaches, then stops himself.

"I'll get her dusted," he says. "Just to see."

I take him on a tour of Ivah's photos, both sides, front and back, pointing out Nadia and Belka in the line of girls standing in front of the white stone church. I pull the frame off the shelf and the photo out of the frame and flip it over.

Verochka (15) 1995. St. Nicholas, Novogrudok.

"That's Belka's real name," I say.

"Verochka."

"Named after Ivah's babushka, Belka's great-grandmother. Same woman who enthralled the maker of that doll." I point at the doll up on the shelf, telling Raffi about the note inside and how to find it. The doll looks down at me, the eyes, the lips, like maybe she enjoys being talked about. Raffi cocks his head with a smile.

"There's a love story at the center of this whole ugly mess?" he asks. "Who'd have guessed?"

I want to tell him the truth. I want to tell him that there's a love story at the center of everything. Inside the doll and the doll and the doll, there it is, love, the center of all gravity. When some dreamy-eyed sap says it's love that makes the world go 'round, he isn't kidding. Love is the axis. Love is the spindle. The vinyl whirls and the music plays, and we all hang on for dear life. As long as we can. Because there is nothing else but that music.

I let it go. Raffi's too young. He still thinks he gets to pick the song.

"I'm guessing a little research will confirm the modern-day Verochka died in a Minsk prison riot. She and Aunt Ivah shared a gene for killing cops. How's that for romance?"

"Mack, if you think anyone is reopening Joe Novak's murder, you're dreaming. It'll never happen, even if you can show Ivah was murdered. And she probably died of a heart attack, just like the man said."

"That's not what he said, remember?"

"Implied."

I pinch a couple of air molecules so he can see.

"A little investigating. Never know where it might lead."

"This is not my case, Mack. I work for IAD. And in that capacity, I'm out here babysitting you. I'm not investigating anything."

"Yeah, but somebody is, Raffi. Or should be. If Ivah's autopsy turns up hinky? Should be some kind of investigation, don't you think? And with me walking a beat between *Macy's* and *Best Buy*, somebody's got to make sure that investigation gets it right."

I put the photo back in the frame and pick up its neighbor. I angle it towards Raffi and point.

"Nadia said this handsome couple were her great-grandparents. A lie, but not far from the truth. I'm guessing those are Ivah's grandparents. Great grandparents to Jovah and Alexi."

"And Belka." Raffi taps on the hard, impatient woman sitting in the back of the buckboard. "Which makes this beauty the original Verochka?"

I look at the photo, connecting with those frozen black eyes. They pull at me, across space and time. Who'd have guessed what's behind those eyes? Who'd have guessed what's inside the secret chambers of that woman's heart.

My flower. I hold you in the deepest part of me.

The frozen impatience of those eyes. They remind me of Marlo at the lake. *Take the damn picture.*

"Right." I pat Raffi on the shoulder. "You're going to be an expert in Belarusian genealogy before you're done."

Raffi's laugh is missing out on the humor. I point to the photo of a young Jovah and Alexi shooting at each other around the Christmas tree. Jovah's rifle is a shiny brown plastic. Alexi is aiming back through the branches at his brother with a wild, unrestrained joy on his face.

"This one is the key, Raffi." I flick the frame with a finger. "See if you can figure it out."

I leave him at the étagère, holding the photo of the boys up to his face as I take a quick look around. The place doesn't exactly scream filicidal cop killer. It looks suspiciously like an old lady's apartment. It smells like she wasn't allowed to smoke and that she did it anyway. There's no vending machine in the lobby and Ivah's shopping days were long gone, so someone was smuggling them in, just like prison. She was getting paid in cigarettes. I wonder how many packs of Parliaments it costs to pretend that Nadia King is your daughter.

I poke around the place, trying to find some middle ground between respectful and nosey. I miss the mark by a mile. Raffi finds me in the bedroom closet up to my elbows in a cardboard box.

"What are you looking for?" he asks.

"Memory lane."

"You know, there are a few rules for cops about this sort of thing."

"I'm not a cop anymore, Raffi. Avert your eyes."

I pull out the white photo album and flip through the thick plastic pages. Most of it is dedicated to Jovah in his dress blues, graduating from the police academy. Right off a recruitment poster.

"He sure had the look," says Raffi, squatting next to me. "Where can I get a jaw like that?"

"Try Amazon."

I close the album and set it on top of the first one, which was full of Ivah and Dmitri in New York, the happy couple fresh off the boat. Her body is taller, thinner than she ended up. Her face is softer. Happy. Everything is in front of her. The future loves to lie that way.

I pull out the last album.

The boys when they were young. It's what I was hoping to find. The first set is from the same Christmas that made it up onto the étagère. Raffi points.

"Same photo," he says, tapping the Christmas tree. "Almost. So what's the key? I don't get it."

"What kind of rifle is Joe using?" I ask.

"Mmm. Looks like a plastic Winchester."

"That's my guess. And what kind of rifle is Alexi using?"

Raffi squints. He reaches. Pulls the album closer to his face.

"It's not a rifle. What is that?"

I take the album back and flip the page.

The family –Ivah, Jovah and Alexi –sprawled on the floor around the tree, I'm guessing it's daddy Dmitri behind the camera. The thing that's not a rifle is at Alexi's side, half-buried under wrapping paper. I tap the photo. Raffi answers his own question.

"It's a crutch," he says.

"Yeah. And judging from that brace, on that leg, little Alexi had a tough time making friends on the playground."

I keep flipping pages, five of them before I find what I expected. Roughly the same ages, only summer. Alexi has his arms up under a basketball hoop, Jovah just behind going for the three-pointer. There are three white, high-top tennis shoes in the picture. And one black boot. I give it three slow taps.

Raffi sits fully on the floor, leaning back against Ivah's bed. He looks at me looking at him.

"What are you saying?" he asks.

"I'm saying Jovah Novak was murdered in the middle of July. Who wears boots to an abduction and frame-up in the middle of a Chicago summer?"

"Boots… You mean… You're saying Alexi Novak was the Captain?"

"Yeah. Why not?"

"Mack, Wayne Bishop could have been talking about cowboy boots, contractor boots…"

"Yeah. Could have. But when you're being pulled out of a cube van by the hair on your face and told that you have one chance not to die, why do you care about the cowboy boots or contractor boots of the guy offering you the choice? Why does that stick in your memory a year later when you're blabbing away to August T. Pepper in the top bunk after lockdown?"

"Mack, I don't…"

"You're right, Raffi. You don't. You don't care about the boots. You care about how the guy walks. What sticks in your head is that he walks differently than most people. That's something you remember. It's the *walking* that makes you care about the boots. And then you realize that there's something strange about the boots too. All Monk remembers, a billion years later, is that Bishop was saying something about boots. But Monk wasn't there, was he? If Monk had been in Bishop's shoes, he'd have remembered how this Captain guy walked around as he offered him his life back."

Raffi stares at me like I've turned into a goat. He shakes his head in disbelief.

"Jesus."

I shake my head.

"Sandals. Totally different."

He's not in the joking mood.

"You're way out there, Mack," he says. "I mean…"

"Am I? Let me tell you a story, Raffi. Few days ago, I get yanked out of a bad dream by a noise in my living room. I get my drunk ass out of bed and go down to check it out. When I make it to the hall at the bottom of the stairs all I get for my trouble is a bag over my head and a tree trunk across my neck. Looking back, I'm smart enough to realize that the tree trunk was attached to Hell's right shoulder. I've been tossed around before, but never like a cork in a hurricane."

"Hell," he blurts. "I forgot to tell you. They've got his name."

"Burkhart Lang," I say. "Yeah, got that."

"How…"

"Doesn't matter. Let me finish. So, there I am, face down in my living room. Hell is doing his impression of George Washington sailing into Valley Forge, using my head like it's the prow of that rowboat. His job is to keep me still. He leaves all the talking to his partner, who makes it clear that if I don't tell him where to find that Russian doll, something bad is going to happen. Well now I'm curious, because things already seemed pretty bad to me. So I tell him I don't play with dolls and the talking guy decides it's time to make good on his promise. He heads outside to get the surprise, which turns out to be a chainsaw to cut off my legs. And you know what I don't think I will ever forget as a long as I live?"

"The chainsaw?"

"Well. Besides that."

"What?"

"The sound of his boots moving across my floor. Like he was carrying something really heavy on one side of his body. Something heavier than a chainsaw. It's not the boots I remember, Raffi. I had a bag over my head. I never saw the boots. What I remember is the sound of his limp. The Captain's limp. Alexi's limp. That and the smell of the cigarettes on his breath."

ONE HUNDRED FIFTY-NINE

Raphael is doing more thinking than talking. He looks like he's focused on the road in front of us, but he's a million miles inside his own head. I can almost hear the gears grinding.

I watch the traffic and sympathize. It's like any puzzle: once you snap a piece into place, it's hard to stop obsessing over the next piece. In the shower. While you're eating. Reading the paper. It's an itch too deep to reach. I'm guessing today's revelations will cut Raffi's forty winks down to twenty. Maybe fifteen. Mission accomplished. If I'm out, then somebody needs to be on the inside, putting things together. Losing sleep.

Then there's Orland Twill. I want to walk Raffi into the new universe of concern I have about his Lieutenant. But that's still a pitch-black room full of furniture. Too early to send him in there to bang up his shins.

Besides, those kinds of questions will take him down to zero winks. I've already got that part covered.

"Quite a family," Raffi says, coming out of his fugue. I answer without looking, like I'm talking to the big brown woman in the little white Honda one lane over, singing to herself.

Singing. Like we're a different species.

"Ivah kills Jovah to protect Alexi. Fast forward a whole bunch of years and Alexi ends up doing the same to her. Norman Rockwell it ain't."

"Wait." Raffi looks. "You think Alexi was in on it?"

I shrug.

"I'm sure Big Man got a nurse to make Ivah's coffee, but I'm guessing Alexi knew it was coming. His job was to keep cashing the checks and to let it happen. He's trying to sleep with the idea that it was going to happen in the next few years anyway."

Raphael shakes his head with a whistle. We drive another five miles before he comes up again for more air.

"So… So, they never actually wanted the doll."

"No. They wanted me to think that keeping the doll out of my hands was important enough to kill for. They wanted me to find it. They wanted me good and curious. Once I found it…"

"You open it up. Find the flash drive. Print out that spreadsheet. Turn it in."

"Right. Better than rolling a Trojan horse up to the police department and knocking on the door. But, the same basic idea. Makes me wonder if José Beggemon likes the classics."

"The more you thought someone was trying to kill you for the information, the harder you'd sell it to Twill as authentic. And then he'd do the same with the Chief and on up the food chain."

"Like bringing a bowl of spoiled potato salad to the church picnic. Now the whole justice system is doubled over with the shits."

He rides a while on that one, shaking his head every now and then in quiet amazement. Then he looks at me.

"You know, Mack, that whole scheme only works on a good cop. The lazy cops don't follow up. The bad cops sell the doll and go on vacation. Someone out there believes in you, man. Trusts you to be you."

"I'll be sure to put Big Man down as a character reference in my next job interview. But thanks for that. You're going places, Raffi."

"Speaking of which," he says. "Where am I dropping you, man? Your place?"

"One more errand," I say. "Probably useless at this point. But it needs to be done and since I don't have a day job anymore, you're the one who needs to do it."

I get a suspicious look.

"Where are we headed?" he asks. I point to the on-ramp for northbound Interstate 55.

"Straight to the bottom of the barrel."

The sun has been bound and bagged and rolled up in a carpet of gray cloud so the winter wind can take it someplace where no one will hear. My head still feels like the tin can in the gutter everyone likes to kick on their way to someplace better. The pill in my stomach is doing about as much good as the pills in my pocket. In the middle of all the pain is Ivah Novak, standing in the middle of her den doorway. I look at her looking at Jovah in the back. She turns and looks at me, behind and up, like I'm on the ceiling looking down. Like she knows I'm there. Then she turns back around so that crooked, nicotine-stained finger of hers can take care of business. Boom. The thought of the sound sends a ripple through the pain in my head.

The jolt makes me younger. I drop into the black leather chair across from Mother Penguin's desk.

If it wasn't you, Raymond, then who? she asks.

I have my suspicions, but I shrug my shoulders anyway. I was no rat, even then.

But Jesus sure was. He was either in Droopy McAllister's pocket along with everyone else, or the supply room was too dark for him to see that it was little Brewster Sanchez giving St. Anthony a golden shower. Mother Penguin's eyes didn't much care. They were busy looking for the ruler. Her bloodless lips kept moving.

Lying is a mortal sin, Raymond. You have a deceitful soul. You will have a hard life and you will live it alone. Good people will learn quickly not to trust you. They will want nothing to do with you. The Devil, I suspect, will gladly claim you as his own.

Raffi glides the Dodge to a brief stop at a traffic light on the outskirts of Aurora. Across the street a group of men are trying to slide their business shoes across an icy parking lot to the front door of a *Pizza Hut*. One of them has made it safely. He props open the door with a foot, holding out a helping hand like he's at one end of a rickety rope bridge. Like they've all risked their lives for a cheesy slice of heartburn.

Makes me remember Nadia and Danika at *Pizza Maria*, diving into a Chef's Mistake as I dove deeper into a mistake of my own. Turns out I'm not the only one remembering.

"I forgot," says Raffi.

He reaches inside his coat and pulls out a slip of paper.

"Found this beneath the driver's seat, under the gun and the car keys. I think it's for you. That or she wants to be reimbursed."

I hold it up to the light and give it a good look. It's a receipt from a place called *Mafia Mike Pizza* in Rockford. Three sodas. One large pizza, half Hawaiian, half pepperoni. All for $27.73. She tipped something average and paid in cash. No dummy, that one.

It's the thought of Vladimir's tongue that makes me smile.

"And on the back," says Raffi.

I flip it over. It looks exactly like the back of a receipt with six words written in thin, loopy script.

It's not a place for sleeping.

I flip the receipt back over. Nadia has made some faint underlines beneath four letters and a number: **M**afia. Mi**k**e. H**a**waiian. Pepper**o**ni. $27.7**3**. It seems inexplicable and random until I do some mental rearranging.

Замок.

I nod and fold up the receipt and hand it back. Raffi gives me a look that goes arm-in-arm with a disbelieving laugh.

"Come on, man," he says.

"What."

"You're telling me you actually know what that means? No place for sleeping?"

"Yeah," I say. "That's easy. She wants me to go to a motel."

"A motel?"

"Yeah. You ever been in a motel that seemed like it was for sleeping? The thin walls. The prison cot mattress. The chatty radiator. Lots of people aren't looking to actually sleep in the first place. Those who are, can't. I mentioned that to Danika when we scooped up Mila from the *Motel 6* in Watseka. Nadia must have been paying attention. She keeps impressing me."

"Yeah, I'll bet. And now she wants to meet you at a motel?"

It's my turn to do the looking.

"One, get the surprise out of your voice. I'm not that old and I clean up okay when I'm not bleeding from the face. Two, get your mind out of the gutter, Raffi. Nadia's long gone."

"What motel," he asks.

I point through the windshield at the dingy, brick shoebox coming up on the left.

"That motel."

ONE HUNDRED SIXTY

The Castle Motel. I remember the clerk at the *Aurora Chevron* when I was first trying to find *Windy Wharf Seafoods.*

If you pass the castle, you've gone too far.

She had no idea how right she was.

It sits on the corner curb like two loaves of bread that fell out of someone's grocery bag sixty years ago. One dirty, plaster loaf points north, the other east. Single story. Each building sports seven double windows facing the street, brown curtains pulled. On the other side is an icy parking lot that nuzzles into the corner of the motel, like it's trying to get out of the wind. There are seven red doors on the east wing. The north wing has six red doors and one black door on the end. Every door has one small brass eye. The black door is the only one with a name tag.

There's an ugly iron pole in the center of the lot. I'm guessing that once upon a time the pole held up a sign that read the same as the one still clutching the edge of the roof. The font is made to look like fat chunks of stone, stacked into letters. The 'M' has been artistically fortified with battlements. It's missing the dragon, but I imagine it there anyway.

Raffi is still hung up on all the questions that start with *how.* I have to get a pen involved and write it out for him on the back of the receipt.

3amok.

"First time I saw it was in a message on Nadia's phone," I say. "I thought it was all about appreciating the early morning hours. It took a nine-year-old and a picture book about dragons to help me put it together." I point to the number. "Turns out that's not a three. And those two have nothing to do with the sunrise. And these two here don't mean that everything is okay." I give him back the receipt so he can stare at it as I take in the place that's not for sleeping. "Because it isn't, Raffi. Nothing about this place is okay."

Raffi puts a thumb under the Russian word.

"And it means motel?" he asks.

He squints at me, confused, like maybe I've broken something inside. I'm ready to suggest that he stick to shooting people in the nick of time and leave the thinking to someone else. Then he shows me his teeth. He elbows me in the ribs and heads for the black door with a nametag that says *Office*.

Raffi gives it a few stiff knocks and we stand shoulder-to-shoulder in the cold, waiting for signs of life. I stare at the black rectangle, feeling oddly like I've been here before.

"We should figure out who owns this dump," he says.

"You already know enough to place a winning bet."

Raffi looks at me.

"XXL Enterprises," he says. I nod.

"Dissolving as we speak."

Raffi's ready to try again, but I turn away and look at the empty parking lot behind us.

"They're all gone," I say. "They cleaned house while I was busy making friends at *Deke's Autobody*."

"Who, exactly?" he asks.

I pat my pockets until I find what I'm looking for. I use my teeth to pull a Camel out by the nose. It feels cold so I warm it up. Then I turn south, pointing over the laundromat across the street, roughly in the direction of *Windy Wharf Seafoods*.

"They show up at the *Windy Wharf* in rolling crates, freezing and stinking of fish. They get unloaded. Hosed down. Dried off. Packed into a refrigerated cube van and brought here. Hot shower. Soft bed. Best sleep they've had in weeks. Welcome to America. Only problem is they can't leave the castle. Not without permission and a ride. That takes a paying client, selected and arranged in advance. No telling who you might get. Maybe he's shy. Maybe he beats you as part of the fun. Most of them have been putting up with that and worse from wherever they came from so they stick it out for the brass ring. Like they have any choice. They all think they're getting a husband out of the deal. That's what most of them thought they were signing up for. A movie-star-businessman-professional-jock-husband with lots of teeth and money looking to start a family."

I pause for a long pull and a blow into the wind.

"But that never happens, Raffi. Almost never. Nadia got lucky. If you can call it that. Nadia got lucky a couple of times."

"And Mila?"

"Yeah, well, Mila got snatched out of her bed with a bag over her head. Mila was a stolen piece of meat in a yellow coat."

I leave him standing there and start trying doors. I knock and twist. There's no one around to hear the knocks so I just start twisting knobs. I've already racked up three strikes when I hear my name. I turn back to see Raffi stepping into the office.

"Guess there's no need to lock an empty room," he says when I step in.

And it is empty. It's even clean. I smell ammonia. The carpet is brown, better to hide all of the grime and dirt that will never come out in a million years. But they vacuumed it anyway. Raffi steps out of the bathroom and crosses in front of me to the bedroom.

A bedroom. Hell of an office. I'm guessing whoever pulled desk duty got to play round robin with the tenants.

"They cleaned," says Raffi.

"Someone knew we were coming. We're more likely to find a zebra than a partial fingerprint."

The main room stretches from the parking lot side of the building to the street. A countertop juts out about halfway along so it can pretend to be two rooms: a living room and a kitchenette. The kitchenette is a sickly green color and about as empty as my stomach. All the cabinets are wide open, just to prove the point. The living room belongs to a broken fawn-colored recliner in front of an empty television stand. In the corner, a cheap folding table is holding up a glass ashtray that sparkles in the dim light like it's new.

Raffi bangs around in the bedroom. I turn in a slow circle so the Camel can have a look before it gets any shorter. Then I step into the kitchenette and do what comes naturally.

The bulb in the refrigerator is as burned out as I am. A white coffee mug on the top shelf is cozied up to an empty six pack carton and a couple of soft apples. If the mug could wink, it would. It settles for cursive and exclamation points.

Chicago! Bean there, Done that!

"Bedroom's clean," says Raffi, reemerging.

I'm getting used to seeing things people want me to find. I pull out the mug and set it on the counter. Raffi points.

"What's that?"

I look inside, poking my finger around. They're all the same except for the numbers. I pull one out into the light and let it dangle.

"Just a mug full of room keys."

"In the fridge?"

"Someone's having a little too much fun," I say. "Let's go."

We take them in sequence, one by one, red door by red door. The rooms are all basically the same. Filthy and foul. Dark and dank. The ones that aren't freezing are roasting. The mattresses are old and thin, stained and sagging toward the floor. In some, the stench is hard to take. I'm guessing the last person to clean any of these rooms went home at the end of the day to catch up on the Watergate hearings.

In each room I recognize the backside of the thick, brown curtains I saw from the street. The curtains are the kind that don't open, hanging on the other side of the black iron bars that brace each window. All the doors have been retrofitted to lock from the outside.

It's the same in every unit. The closets are empty, the refrigerators are half-full, and all the faucets complain. Nothing new to learn. The roaches under the pillows aren't talking. I'm expecting the same results in the next one as I leave Raffi in Room 6A and key open the last door of the north wing.

Turns out I'm wrong.

The wind from the parking lot rushes in ahead of me, fluttering a paper on the counter.

Not a newspaper. It's the kind that gets spit out of a printer. It's clean and white and folded neatly in quarters. I step inside and grab the sheet as the outside air pushes it toward the far edge of the counter.

I open it up, carefully, like it's a credit card statement or a jury summons.

There's only one photo. Grainy. But good enough. The fold creases are like channels for my attention, just so I don't miss what I'm supposed to see. I don't need the help. Seeing isn't the problem.

I'm starting to learn. This is how she argues. This is how Frenchie Marie likes to punch you in the face with a thousand words at once. I can't decide whether it's a promise or a threat but, then again, I'm pretty sure that's how Frenchie likes it.

Worry and relief wrestle each other to the epicenter of my headache. It feels like they're wearing golf shoes. I fold up the paper and stick it in my coat pocket.

"Anything?" Raffi asks, stepping in. A fresh gust comes in with him, searching the room around me in an angry, cold swirl that sets my face to aching.

My triple-D kicks in. I see us from behind, two guys standing shoulder-to-shoulder in a dark, ugly room. The one on the left shakes his head. He used to be a cop. That's me.

"A day late and a dollar short, Raffi. Nothing here but ghosts."

ONE HUNDRED SIXTY-ONE

"'Department sources confirm multiple open and ongoing investigations.'"

Only part of him is listening. He's paying attention in other ways.

She looks too nice for *Bucks*. The hair. The nails. The lips. The dress. The shoes. She's not here to stay. She's going places. Uptown places. Romantic places. Places that can do without forced-air ventilation to keep the cash on the ceiling warm. Places where the walking dead don't saunter in, pull up a booth and start drinking.

"Where are you going," he interrupts. Doris looks up from her phone.

"What?"

"Tonight," he says. "Where is he taking you?"

"I don't know, Ray. Dinner. Someplace nice."

"You trust him, this guy? Mr. Second Date? Is he the one?"

"Is he the one?"

"Yeah. You're moving pretty fast here, seems to me."

He watches her face catch the words.

"Seems to you? Well. It may seem that way to you, Ray. But it seems to me like my second date in fifteen years. Can I finish?"

"Just sayin' it seems like maybe…"

"Can I finish, or do you want to keep on pretending to be my father?"

Doris leans back in the booth like she wants him to have plenty of room to think about it. They get a mildly interested look from one among the smattering of regulars. Above, Miles keeps blowing his horn. Sarah keeps singing *Goodnight, My Love*. Over at the bar, Kyle Aubrey is cleaning glasses and holding court with somebody's daughter.

The man of mild interest turns back around. Ray gives the tumbler another turn on the table. He takes a sip and sets it down again.

"Yeah, yeah," he says. "Sorry. Keep going. Department sources confirm."

Doris eyes him for another second or two, then lifts her phone to read.

"'Department sources confirm multiple open and ongoing investigations, including by the Office of the Attorney General, into the allegations against Judge Jolie and the origins of those allegations. The same Department sources have declined to elaborate on the nature of the allegations other than to note that, if confirmed, the allegations would suggest, at the very least, a strong conflict of interest with her judicial oath.

"'Beth Markel, spokesperson for the Will County Court System, has confirmed that Judge Jolie has recused herself from all criminal cases, which have been reassigned pending formal resolution of the concerns. "The business of the court system continues on unaffected," assured Markel.

"'She declined, however, to comment on any particular case, including that of State v. Menard in which Judge Jolie recently declared a mistrial. State prosecutors subsequently declined to retry the defendant for the murder of Curtis Root, founder of the popular *Tap Root Kegs* restaurant chain. The District Attorney's office has declined comment, citing the pending investigations.

"'Michael Shaw, defense counsel representing Jake Menard, says the mistrial was appropriate. "My client and I are obviously pleased with the result. The charges should never have been brought in the first place. The State's case never made any sense. I've promised not to comment more fully on the evidence or testimony, and I will hold to that promise. Mr. Menard is enjoying his return to freedom, and I wish him well."'"

"Question," says Ray. Doris looks over her phone.

"What."

"Do you go Dutch on theses dates, or does he pay for everything?"

"'Chandler Police Department sources confirm multiple open and active investigations into trial testimony given by Property Crimes Detective Arthur Dunn who, under questioning by Mr. Shaw, admitted to giving perjured testimony. Dunn also admitted to an association with Anthony Rickens, a seasoned detective working for the Chicago Police Department recently shot to death in a Dekalb landfill. The testimony elicited at trial strongly suggested, but did not substantiate, that Detectives Dunn and Rickens were involved in the arson of the original *TRK* restaurant and that they were in league to intimidate protection money out of business owners, including Curtis Root. Defense Counsel Shaw encouraged patience.

""""We all need to let state investigators do their job and sort this mess out," he said. "There are a lot of questions to ask. But I'll go on record to predict that Judge Jolie will come through it all just fine. She's a credit to our judiciary," Shaw emphasized. "You'd have to look long and hard to find a judge with more integrity. I cannot, sadly, say the same for the Chandler Police Department which needs to get its house in order.""""

"That's enough, Doris," he says. He holds up the glass like a shield. "I can't take anymore."

She lowers the phone to the table.

"Well, I thought it was interesting," she says. "So far, *The Hawk* is the only paper with a story."

"There's a reason for that."

"Which is?"

"*The Hawk* is not a newspaper. There's no paper involved and even less news."

"I thought maybe you'd want the scoop."

"Teddy Myerson doesn't use a scoop, honey. He's strictly a shovel guy."

"Myerson." Doris lifts her phone and scrolls. "Is he…"

"Yeah. He is."

"You know him?"

"Teddy? Oh sure. We go all the way back to Monday. He followed me to a pizza place once for a quote. I gave him several to choose from. Don't read me anything Teddy writes unless it's a suicide note."

"Well, that's awfully harsh," she says.

"You think I'm terrible."

"I think you're out of sorts because you're in pain," she says. "I think you need more sleep and less booze."

"You act like those things aren't connected." He lifts his glass of amber. "You act like this isn't iced tea pretending to be bourbon."

"That was your choice, Ray. Remember? And a good one too."

"Goddamned pills," he says to the glass. "Someone needs to make a pain pill that's not for teetotalers."

"Maybe use the pills as an opportunity for you to step away from the booze for a while," she says.

Ray scowls at the idea, but Doris keeps coming.

"Oh, don't give me the look, Ray. I'm not saying twelve-steps away. Just one step. Try that for starters. Iced tea in a tumbler. *Looks* like bourbon."

Ray's face is offended.

"Looks like… Keep talking like that and you'll go broke before sunrise. You'll be on a stepladder pulling your mortgage payment off the ceiling."

"I'll do fine," she says. She pulls the glass from his hands and puts some lipstick on the rim.

"Yeah," he says, taking her in all over again with a sigh. "I suppose you will be fine, won't you? You know we're starting to sound like an old married couple?"

"We know each other too well."

"Unlike you and Mr. Second Date." She looks. He tries to correct. "I'm happy for you, Doris."

"Are you?" She gives him back the tumbler, clinking the ice. "Happy doesn't seem to be the right word."

"Yeah? Well what word do you have in mind?"

"Rhymes with jealous," she says without a smile.

"I think you've forgotten how to spell brotherly. He's no good for you, Doris."

"You don't even know him."

"I know his type."

"Which is?"

"Human male."

"You want me to date lesbians?"

"Let me think about that for a while. I'm going to need a dark room and some privacy. Meantime, he's no good."

"Yeah? Then who is good for me, Ray? That you?"

It's a self-inflicted wound and he knows it. Doesn't make it hurt any less. He stares down into his glass of tea and shakes his head.

"No," he says, quietly.

"Didn't think so. Maybe worry about yourself for a change, because I got to tell you, Ray," she gestures at the mess across the table, "this is getting to be more than I can handle by myself. You could be dead. You look…" They've already been through this part, but Doris looks ready to start crying again anyway. There's more than enough horror here for a second round of *you could be dead.*

She reaches out as if to touch some part of his battered face, then gives up. "You could be… Jesus, Ray."

"I could never be Jesus. I think we both know that. It's all about the wine with that guy. Turn some water into bourbon and I'm your man."

"Joke. Have fun." Her eyes were already watery blue, now they're threatening to spill. "I'm serious, Ray. You have to stop this. You're not thirty-five anymore. One of these days your luck is going to run out."

She's not telling him anything he doesn't already know. So he's not listening. He's falling backwards into old photographs. He lifts the glass and remembers what's not inside. He sets it down again.

"Let me ask you something, Doris. You ever worry that you didn't really know Buck?"

She looks at him wearily, blinking back the tears. She looks at her phone for a time-check, then back again, anger at the edges.

"What?"

"Like the years you were with him weren't enough to show you everything about him. Like inside the person you married was another person, and maybe another person inside that person, a person you never really knew."

"Ray, what on earth…"

"And what if that… that *inside* person… the person you never got a chance to open up and meet, was someone you wouldn't have liked so much. Maybe someone you hated."

She looks at him through a softening silence of disquiet, venturing nothing, like maybe he's not quite done. He isn't.

"What if we never really knew them, Doris?" he asks. "What if we never bothered to look deep enough inside because we loved what they showed us on the outside?"

Doris sets the phone down and reaches across the table. He hands her the glass. She sets it aside and takes his hand in hers.

"I knew him, Ray. Every last atom. Buck was good and he was bad and he was strange and funny and cheating and brilliant and ridiculous and pathetic and wonderful and I knew the man through and through. He was my big, black, beautiful Buck and I knew him like I know myself. And you knew Marlo, Ray. Every last atom. And she knew you. There was no hiding from either of you."

Ray nods with a lack of conviction. He takes another sip of disappointment.

"You're tired. You're in pain. Hell, you're probably in withdrawal. And you feel kicked to the curb. Again. I know that hurts, honey. I do. I know you hate not being a cop. You can tell me all day long that you're glad it's done, but I know it hurts. You don't have to hide it from me."

He makes a sound and moves his head in his cantankerous way, trying to shake her off. She doesn't let go.

"No, listen. Listen to me. Maybe it really is a good thing you've been turned out. Maybe you'll live a little longer. Pick up with the writing again, Ray. Go get yourself an agent and a movie deal. That'll show 'em."

He looks up at her, his eyes lingering around her face before any sound makes it out over the table. The wrinkles at the corners of her eyes show up whenever she gets earnest.

"A movie deal," he says.

"Sure. Go be the next Stephen King."

"Did you say that with a *ph* or a *v?*"

"What do you think?"

"I think I'll have a double of whatever you've been drinking."

"That's all this is, Ray," she says. The wrinkles are getting deep. "You'll shake it off. It'll pass."

"You're right," he says.

"Yeah?" Her eyes shine with encouragement.

"Yeah. It does rhyme with jealous. You look beautiful. You could thaw this whole frozen city and wake up all the flowers."

She smiles a little. Her watery blues start up again, but her phone wants some attention. She flips it over and looks at the screen.

"He's here," she says, wiping her eyes. "Not sure how you're always able to make me cry right before I go out on a date."

"It's a talent. I can make a woman cry like nobody's business. You're welcome."

"I've got to go."

"You know, a real man comes in to get you," he says. "He even gives you his arm, so you don't slip on the ice."

Doris slides herself out of the booth, stands, and smooths the dress against her body. She pulls her coat and purse off the bench.

"Finish your tea," she says. "Go home. Go to bed. Curl up with Phil rather than the Forester. Let's talk tomorrow. Take me someplace nice for lunch."

She kisses him on the forehead, then lifts his chin with her finger. She smells like a memory you never forget.

"I've told Kyle not to give you a single drop," she says. "He's a good kid, Ray. Don't make me fire him."

He watches her pull on her coat as she walks across the bar, liberating the blonde tresses to spill out over her collar. A wave to Kyle and she's through the door in a gust of wind. All the dead presidents wave goodbye and think exactly what he's thinking. Everybody's remembering what it was like to be alive.

Ray stares into the tumbler. It was empty when he started and it's twice as empty now. He looks up at me in the corner. As if he can see me looking back. As if I'm the one who can get him a real glass of juice and make all the pain go away.

He knows better. We both do.

He grabs the blood-stained coat next to him, thinking about the frozen Impala with a plastic window waiting for him up the street. Thinking about the book still half-written, *Message in a Bullet*. Thinking about Phil. Thinking about how unfair it would be to deprive Phil of her drop of ambrosia just because his brain got a little big for his skull and his body hurts enough for a pizza-sized Percocet. He stands, ready to fight that injustice. But his phone has a different idea.

He looks at the number. Sits again. Pushes the button.

"What, you miss me already?"

"Hardly," says Twill. "Got a minute?"

"I've got lots of minutes, LT. I'm drinking iced tea and getting drunk on minutes over here. Let me guess, Raphael briefed you on our trip out to the *Castle Motel*. You want to fit me with an ankle monitor and read me the definition of suspension."

"Yes. But you get some points for avoiding a third bloodbath in forty-eight hours."

"You're welcome. It's only because there was nobody there."

"I have no doubt."

"We missed them by a day, LT. Looked to me like every room was recently occupied. That's a lot of stolen women and girls all moving into new housing someplace. Maybe an opportunity for some honest cop paying attention."

"I've alerted Major Crimes. Special Victims. The Task Force too. The word is out, so we'll see what turns up. I'm not optimistic."

"Me neither. Want me to write something up?"

"That's not why I'm calling."

"I know. You're calling because Sandra took a powder without giving you two weeks' notice. That leaves you with a stack of case files too heavy for you to lift. I'd love to help, LT, but I've been pondering the definition of suspension…"

"How did you know about Sandra?"

"A little bird told me," says Ray.

"This bird have a name?"

"Yeah. I call it Sandra. We got together for some bacon and blueberry muffins at a goodbye lunch."

"Could have told me, Mack."

"You're right. I could have. It wasn't my news to share, LT."

Twill sighs into the phone like he's trying to blow a paper sailboat across a bathtub.

"I didn't call you to talk about Sandra, Mack. Or her caseload."

"Let me guess…"

"No. Stop. You're already zero for two on the guesses. How about listening for a change?"

"Sorry. Probably the caffeine. I'm not used to this tea thing. I'm all ears."

"I just finished talking to the Chief."

"He's working late."

"Everybody over here is working late. Thanks to you. The Chief is big on venting after sundown."

"Well, the man has a lot on his mind."

"Too much. Two days ago he wanted your head on a spike outside in the parking lot. Dead wasn't good enough. I talked him down to my way of thinking, which was a suspension pending your eventual but certain dismissal. It took some doing, but after a long conversation I thought he'd be satisfied with that as long as he could be assured that you'd eventually be out. For good this time."

"And here I thought it was you who wanted me out."

"I did. I do. That hasn't changed."

"But something has changed. Hasn't it?"

"Yes. The Chief has instructed me to downgrade the suspension to short-term, disciplinary. Failing to properly advise. Failing to call for back-up."

Ray stares into empty space, listening to that last part again in his head.

"Excuse me?"

"I wanted to add insubordination. He put me off. You're his new best friend, Mack. Called you a hero. He's put you on the list for a commendation. Acting above and beyond the call."

Ray holds the phone to his ear, not speaking. Two men, three tables over are laughing. Ray Charles is singing about the outskirts of town. The presidents gossip in the hot breeze.

"Mack?"

He has to blink to come unstuck.

"Quite an about-face, LT. Why?"

"He said new information was coming to light about what went down in Aurora. Chief's pretty close to Stretch Martin, who just happens to be up and mumbling now. I suspect Stretch has been putting in a good word or two."

Ray stares out across the bar, not seeing. His mind's eye has Stretch's bleeding face up on the big screen. Turns out to be the wrong slide. He trades it for Frenchie Marie smoking a cigarette.

I think you seriously underestimate our resources, Detective. Nothing is on fire that needn't be on fire.

"Mack?"

"Still here. What are you telling me, Orland?"

"I'm telling you that the terms of your suspension have changed. I'm short-handed and have a workload problem. That means *your* hands are full and now *you've* got a workload problem. Take two weeks without pay then get over here and stick your oar in the water. The OAG investigators get you first. The homicide investigators get you next. I get everything of your carcass that's left over. The Chief said he'd set the commendation ceremony for when you get back."

"You don't sound happy about this, LT."

"I'm not. I tried to find you another department. Figured you'd appreciate being back in Chandler Homicide. That way Wexler can get the 3:00 AM phone calls for a change, so he can get his ass out of bed and go count up all the bodies."

"No dice?"

"Wexler won't have you and the Chief wasn't having it anyway. He wants you in IAD. So, no offense, but no, I'm not happy, Mack. The Chief isn't happy either. Maybe he was just tired, but this seemed to give him no pleasure. And that's what I can't figure out."

He all but mumbles that last bit. Ray waxes poetic.

"Ours is not to reason why. Ours is but to do and die."

"Butchering Lord Tennyson doesn't make it any better. And IAD is hardly the Light Brigade. Tell me all of this at least makes you happy, Mack."

"Will that make a difference, LT?"

"No. Not in the least."

"Then let's leave my feelings out of it. See you in a couple of weeks."

Ray pushes the button and opens up a pocket to receive the phone. Then he stops himself. He opens the *recent calls* list and scrolls. No mystery here. Not to me. He's looking for her footprints.

Unknown Caller. Number Blocked.

Last time she called he was headed up Steven King's basement stairs to shake hands with the wrong end of a semi-automatic. Nothing since. That silence feels like a cold shoulder. Like she's gone for good, leaving him alone to wonder who she was in the first place.

Unknown Caller. Number Blocked.

He redials and puts the phone to his ear.

Nothing. He listens to outer space for a good fifteen seconds, then he lets that stretch into thirty. He ends the call to nowhere. Drops the phone in his pocket.

He puts on his coat and heads for a stool at the end of the bar. Kyle Aubrey is still mixing martinis for the woman who has been keeping him occupied all night. A little eavesdropping gets him the names of Alexandre Dumas and Victor Hugo, so he figures they're either classmates or this is some highbrow flirting.

He takes a seat and stares at the line-up of bottles against the back mirror as Aretha pours herself out of the speakers and into the opening verse of *Drinking Again*. Kyle doesn't leave him alone for long.

"How do you feel, Mack?" he asks.

"With the tips of my fingers. How do you feel?"

"With my heart," says Kyle without missing a beat. Ray gives him something like a smile.

"You win that one, kid. You're sharp tonight." He points. "Hand me that bottle, will you?"

Kyle winces like he's been stung.

"I've got some pretty strict orders, Mack. I'm…"

"Settle down. I just want to see the bottle. You can keep me company while I look."

Kyle turns. He grabs the bottle off the shelf.

"This isn't you," he says, handing it over.

"No. It isn't. It's somebody else."

"Yeah? Who is it?"

Ray moves his thumb back and forth across the label like he's brushing away decades of dust.

"Captain Morgan," he says. "It's got his name right on the bottle. Friends just called him Captain. You can tell it's him because of the boots. You could hear this guy coming for you, Kyle. It's the boots you remember."

"Guess you two go back aways then," he says. Ray shakes his head.

"No. Never been much of a rum guy. But he came over a few nights ago and helped redecorate my living room. He's still got the boots, but I'm guessing no one has called him Captain since his promotion."

"What do they call him now?"

"Now?" Ray holds the bottle of rum by the base and uses it to point. Two shelves up, third from the left. "Now everyone calls him Stoli."

"Also not you," says Kyle. "I'd keep him out of your living room too if I were you."

"If you were me?" He hands Kyle the bottle and stands. "Buddy, if you were me, you'd be in the market for a new couch."

The wrong idea gets him a look of muted disgust.

"Maybe," says Kyle. "But I think I'd start with a new coat."

Ray looks at himself in the mirror, bandages, bruises, bloodstained coat and all. He nods.

"Good idea," he says and heads for the door.

"Watch yourself, Mack," says Kyle.

"'Til my eyes bleed, kid. 'Til my eyes bleed."

The door to Bucks closes behind him with a thud. Ray stops to zip up against the dark, cold wind. He pats himself down, wakes up a Camel and puts it to work. The folded piece of paper from Room 7A comes out with the lighter. He opens it up for another look as he takes the first hit.

She doesn't realize that she's looking into a camera.

To her credit, she's inside the restaurant and the camera in question is all the way across the street inside a car parked in the lot of a certain drycleaner. Ray can tell because the *McDonald's* that owns the table at which she is sitting has the same graffiti-tagged sign he has seen the dozen or so times he has driven past the drycleaner to see if Raffi was at his post.

But Raffi didn't pull this trigger. Someone that answers to Frenchie Marie took this shot. Which means Frenchie has been watching Raffi watch the drycleaner the whole time. That's a Pandora's box inside a Pandora's box. He sweeps all those questions aside so he can focus on just the one that won't go away: *What's Suri doing in Chicago, eating a Big Mac across from the mayor's drycleaner?*

It had been enough just that Suri was still alive. He'd figured he could dine out on that news for a week or two. He was wrong. It lasted fifteen minutes before the question showed up. *What in the hell is she doing?*

Turns out he's not the only one with a question.

"Got another one of those?"

It comes from the tall, soft tower of dark rags in the corner of the entry. Ray folds up the piece of paper and tucks Suri away for later. He blows out some smoke and puts his answer to the small rectangle of whitishness near the top of the tower of rags.

"These things'll kill you," he says.

"Lots of things'll kill you." The voice belongs in a bucket of wet gravel. The man blinks his pink, wind-boiled eyes. The black rags lift a little, like somewhere inside was a shrug. "Not enough love will kill a man. So will too much."

Ray digs out the pack of Camels and shakes another one loose.

"You worried about too much love?" Ray asks.

"Yes, sir," he says. "Once upon a time I had more love than I could handle." The man takes the cigarette and places it carefully at the hole in his beard. He leans down toward the flame. He takes a long pull and blows it out again. "Been dying ever since."

Ray trades the lighter for his wallet. He fishes out a twenty and hands it over.

"Thank you, brother," says the man.

Ray nods and steps out onto the sidewalk, pulling his bloody collar up against the wind. He turns his back to *Bucks* and to the neon snakes flickering above *Wicked Squid Tattoos* next door, and to the heavy metal screeching out of *The Bar* two doors down like a wounded animal, and to the relentless club music bumping-and-grinding its way through the door of *Prancers* and out onto the corner of Seventy-Fourth and Warner to molest the traffic.

He heads the other direction, toward *The Bodega*, dark and quiet behind its black bars, and *Sandwich Heaven*, with a picture of a Philly Cheesesteak on the window that doesn't resemble the thing they drop onto a plate. He's aiming for the small parking lot with four cars in it. He knows which one is his because it's missing a window and the key in his pocket fits like a glove.

He sticks the key in the ignition, then remembers. He reaches down under the seat and feels around until he finds Scooter's .38. He pulls it out into the weak light.

Wouldn't have done Scooter any good, he thinks, weighing the thing in his hand. Hell would have tied the barrel in a knot. He'd have opened the thing up and emptied the bullets into his maw and chewed them up like candy. Then he'd have gotten back down to the business of twisting Scooter's head off his shoulders.

Ray opens the glove compartment. The empty space where the doll used to be gives him pause. Just long enough for him to feel her smile from across town, up on the shelf.

She gets the prize, he thinks. She's the only one who's happy. She and her man.

He tosses in the gun and slaps the door closed. He fires up the Impala and aims for home.

I ride in the back, watching him through the smoke.

Hard guy to figure, Ray. Beat down for being so beaten up. Lonely. In pain six ways from Sunday. The more he learns, the less he knows. His best years are so far behind him he needs a telescope just to remember. And here he is headed home to pamper Phil and moon over Marlo. He'll hit the bottle and pay the price like he always does, but this time with interest because of the Percocet.

And yet. And yet.

Ray's going to get up in the morning. He'll take a long shower and change his bandages and pop a pill and pull something off a hanger in the closet. And then he's going to get back down to business. He'll call Doris to pass on lunch and then he'll get back in the car and go see a guy about a thing. Maybe the guy will be a windshield specialist, but I doubt it. I'm guessing the guy works at *McDonald's*. Or maybe he'll know a thing or two about the security cameras out at the *Golden View Community*.

Look at him work that Camel. He's already thinking. Putting things together. He can't help himself. A two-week stay-at-home suspension gets him a two-week head start without anyone looking over his shoulder.

Except me. I'll always be looking over the man's shoulder. We're the same, him and me. We both feel the eyes at our backs. He knows it's me. I know it's her. And then there's whoever else is out there in the bushes.

And we're not self-conscious about it either. Being watched. Not anymore.

We still are who we are. We still do what we do.

Ray holds the Camel between his lips and turns on the radio. He tunes in Chicago Oldies. It's a title that refers to the audience as much as the playlist, but he likes it anyway. Billie Holiday is halfway through *The Very Thought of You*. He turns it up. He feels like she's sitting right up there next to him.

Not Billie. Marlo.

We are who we are. We do what we do.

Whoever may be watching.

For Your Consideration

Independent writers and publishers, deprived of the reach and resources of their gold-plated, establishment relations (by a difference that requires astronomical telescopes and laser technology to calculate), live and die by the reviews of their readers, or the lack of such reviews. The same astronomical tools and laser technology is necessary to measure the depth of gratitude the author feels for those who, having now finished this novel, are willing to leave a review on Amazon to either encourage other readers or warn them away. It takes just a moment, and you will have made a tremendous, even if incremental, difference in the lives of those who read independently published books and those who write them. Also, Heaven. You'll go to Heaven. Eventually. Thank you.

Reviews at: https://amzn.to/3CKOP88

Visit Owen Thomas at his author website for information on upcoming books, photos, videos, excerpts, interviews, purchase links and to register for updates: www.OwenThomasLiterary.com.

ABOUT THE AUTHOR

Owen Thomas is a life-long Alaskan living on Maui because life is too short for long winters. He has written six books: *The Lion Trees* (which has garnered over sixteen international book awards, including the American Writing Awards, the Amazon Kindle Book Award, the Eric Hoffer Book Award, the Book and Author Book of the Year, the Beverly Hills International Book Award and, most recently, a finalist in the Book Excellence Awards); *Mother Blues*, (a novel of music and mystery set in post-Hurricane Harvey Texas, Finalist for the American Writing Awards and the Book Excellence Fiction Award, and collecting a Bronze in the Readers Views Reviewers' Choice Awards); *Message in a Bullet: A Raymond Mackey Mystery*, (the first in a series of detective novels, shortlisted for the Best Mystery Book of the Year by Forward INDIES Book of the Year Awards and collecting a Silver from the eLit Book Awards); *The Russian Doll: A Raymond Mackey Mystery* (the second book in that series); *Signs of Passing* (a book of interconnected short stories and novellas, and winner of fourteen book awards, including the 2014 Pacific Book Awards for Short Fiction, the Indie Reader Discovery Award, the Great Southwest Book Festival, has garnered placements at the Paris, London and Los Angeles Book Festivals and was also named one of the 100 Most Notable Books of 2015 by Shelf Unbound Magazine); and *This is the Dream* (a collection of stories and novellas that explore that perplexing liminal distance between who we are and what we want; Finalist for the American Writing Awards and the International Book Award in short fiction, and collecting a Bronze in the Readers Views Reviewers' Choice Awards). Owen maintains an active fiction and photography blog on Facebook, Tumblr and on his author website at www.owenthomasliterary.com.